THE BIG
AIIIEEEEE!

THE BIG AIIIEEEEE!

An Anthology of Chinese American and Japanese American Literature

Edited by Jeffery Paul Chan, Frank Chin, Lawson Fusao Inada, and Shawn Wong

A MERIDIAN BOOK

MERIDIAN
Published by the Penguin Group. Penguin Books USA Inc., 375 Hudson Street,
New York, New York 10014, U.S.A.
Penguin Books Ltd, 27 Wrights Lane, London W8 5TZ, England
Penguin Books Australia Ltd, Ringwood, Victoria, Australia
Penguin Books Canada Ltd, 2801 John Street, Markham, Ontario, Canada L3R 1B4
Penguin Books (N.Z.) Ltd, 182-190 Wairau Road, Auckland 10, New Zealand
Penguin Books Ltd, Registered Offices: Harmondsworth, Middlesex, England

First published by Meridian, an imprint of New American Library,
a division of Penguin Books USA Inc.

First Printing, July, 1991
10 9 8 7 6 5 4 3 2 1

REGISTERED TRADEMARK—MARCA REGISTRADA
ISBN 0-452-01076-4
LC Number: 91-12040

Printed in the United States of America

PUBLISHER'S NOTE
This book contains some fiction selections. In these selections, names, characters,
places, and incidents either are the products of the author's imagination or, if real,
are used fictitiously.

PERMISSIONS
"Come All Ye Asian American Writers of the Real and the Fake" by Frank Chin.
Copyright © 1990 by Frank Chin. Reprinted by permission of the author.
"Lin Chong's Revenge: A Story from the Chinese Classic Novel, *Water Margin*,"
by Shi Nai'an and Luo Guanzhong (trans. by Stephen Kow, retold by Frank Chin).
Copyright © 1989 by Water Margin Press, Ltd. Reprinted by permission of Water
Margin Press, Ltd.

(The following pages are an extension of this copyright page.)

PERMISSIONS

To the memory of Toshio Mori, Kazuo Miyamoto, and Kai-yu Hsu

To all our children, Betsy and Jack, and Sam
Miles and Lowell, Jennifer and Aaron Bear

CONTENTS

INTRODUCTION

In 1974, we published *Aiiieeeee! An Anthology of Asian American Writers* (Howard University Press), and at that time we said, "Chinese and Japanese Americans, American-born and -raised, who got their China and Japan from the radio, off the silver screen, from television, out of comic books, from the pushers of white American culture that pictured the yellow man as something that when wounded, sad, or angry, or swearing, or wondering, whined, shouted, or screamed, 'Aiiieeeee!' Asian America, so long ignored and forcibly excluded from creative participation in American culture, is wounded, sad, angry, swearing, and wondering, and this is his AIIIEEEEE!!! It is more than a whine, shout, or scream. It is fifty years of our whole voice."

We had looked forward to including in *The Big Aiiieeeee!* solid poetry with a little introductory wordplay flashing on the glitter and riches in the works we presented. Then we read all the works we had accumulated, old and new, between the first *Aiiieeeee!* and this—the fiction, the poetry, the social science, the histories, the cookbooks. We read them all. If they were by, about, from, or to yellows, we read them a little more seriously than before. We read big newsstand magazines and the arty little magazines. We watched TV. We read first-generation works in translations we had to work to get, and we read the latest student writing put between covers and sold as poetry. Patterns we hadn't expected emerged.

The American-born, exclusively English-speaking Asian Americans were dominated by the Christian vision of China as a country without a history and a philosophy without substance. The social Darwinist philosophers and fictioners of the turn of the century taught history we now accept as both fact and stereotype, feeling there is no other history to know.

We begin another year angry! Another decade, and another Chinese American ventriloquizing the same old white Christian fantasy of little Chinese victims of "the original sin of being born to a brutish, sadomasochistic culture of cruelty and victimization" fleeing to America in search of freedom from everything Chinese and seeking white acceptance, and of being victimized by stupid white racists and then being reborn in acculturation and honorary whiteness. Every Chinese American book ever published in the United States of America by a major publisher has been a Christian autobiography or autobiographical novel. Yung Wing's *My Life in China and America* (1909: Henry Holt); Leong Gor Yun's *Chinatown Inside Out* (1936: Barrows Mussey); Pardee Lowe's *Father and Glorious Descendent* (1943: Little, Brown); Jade Snow Wong's *Fifth Chinese Daughter* (1950: Little, Brown); Virginia Lee's *The House That Tai-Ming Built* (1963: Macmillan); Chuang Hua's *Crossing* (1968: Dial Press); Betty Lee Sung's autobiographical expressionist pseudo-sociological *Mountain of Gold* (1972: Macmillan); Maxine Hong Kingston's *The Woman Warrior* (1976: Alfred A. Knopf), *China Men* (1980: Knopf), and *Tripmaster Monkey* (1989: Knopf); and Amy Tan's *The Joy Luck Club* (1989: G. P. Putnam) all tell the story that Will Irwin, the Christian social Darwinist practitioner of white racist love, wanted told in *Pictures of Old Chinatown* (1908) about how the "Chinese transformed themselves from our race adversaries to our dear subject people. . . ." The China and Chinese America portrayed in these works are the products of white racist imagination, not fact, not Chinese culture, and not Chinese or Chinese American literature.

If the woman warrior Fa Mulan; Monkey, of the childhood classic *Journey to the West*; China's language, culture, and history; the heroes, ducks, and swans of the Chinese fairy tale are all fake, as depicted in the Christian works, then what is real? No one questions the fact that, before the 1960s, the majority of Chinese Americans were non-Christian bachelor Chinamen. Only four works by Chinese American authors do not suck off the white Christian fantasy of the Chinese as a Shangri-La people. Two were novels published by major publishing houses—Diana Chang's *Frontiers of Love* (1956: Random House) and Louis Chu's *Eat a Bowl of Tea* (1961: Lyle Stuart). Shawn Wong's novel, *Homebase* (1979: I. Reed Books), and Frank Chin's collection of short stories, *The Chinaman Pacific & Frisco R.R. Co.* (1988: Coffee House Press), were published by small presses. However, these works alone do not prove the Christian works to be either fake or white racist. To do that, we have to turn to the history of the Asian Chinese and Japanese in white Christianity and in Western historiography, philosophy, social science, and literature.

For the truth of the Chinese culture and history that has been carried and developed into Chinese American institutions by the first Chinese Americans, we have to confront the real Fa Mulan, the real Monkey, the real Chinese first-person pronoun, the real Chinese words for "woman" and "slave" as they exist in the culture and texts of Chinese childhood literature, the ethics that the fairy tales and heroic traditions teach, and the sensibility that they express.

The Christian social Darwinist bias of twentieth-century white American culture combined with the Christian mission, the racist acts of Congress, and the statutes and city ordinances to emphasize the fake Chinese American dream over the Chinese American reality, the belief over the fact, and the fake over the real, until the stereotype has completely displaced history in the white sensibility. It is an article of white liberal American faith today that Chinese men, at their best, are effeminate closet queens like Charlie Chan and, at their worst, are homosexual menaces like Fu Manchu. No wonder David Henry Hwang's derivative *M. Butterfly* won the Tony for best new play of 1988. The good Chinese man, at his best, is the fulfillment of white male homosexual fantasy, literally kissing white ass. Now Hwang and the stereotype are inextricably one.

To destroy Japanese American history and culture as effectively as they destroyed Chinese America's, and to create that generation of Japanese Americans who could tell the story of how they "transformed themselves from our race adversaries into our dear subject people," the white racists had to intern the Japanese Americans—120,213 of them—in concentration camps during World War II. And they had to subject them to massive behavior modification and an indoctrination program to make them "Better Americans for a Greater America."

Before World War II and the camps, Japanese American writers had approached the problems of being English-speaking yellows, writing in an antiyellow America, as professional and technical problems. Those who were not writing on specifically Japanese or Japanese American subjects simply adopted white-sounding pseudonyms and published a variety of genre fiction. Others, encouraged by the Nisei editors of the English-language, Issei-owned newspapers, published poetry, fiction, articles, and essays that explored Nisei experiences and historical visions—Christian, secular, Marxist, and Buddhist—without an echo of the Christian self-contempt that is the substance and drama of all the Chinese American works.

The first Japanese American autobiography did not appear until after the camps. Monica Sone's *Nisei Daughter* (1953: Little, Brown) is meant to be a Japanese American *Fifth Chinese Daughter*. It is autobiographical, perhaps even Christian, but *Nisei Daughter* does not yield to being understood in terms of the Christian Chinese

American autobiography. The books that rewrite Japanese American Nikkei history and culture to conform to the Christian social Darwinist stereotype are books of sociology and history by Japanese Americans of the Japanese American Citizens League (JACL). The JACL betrayed Japanese America into the camps by fabricating an army "contingency plan" to use tanks and bayonets to round up all the Nikkei, within a twenty-four- or forty-eight-hour period, by force. The JACL pointed to a speech by Major Karl K. Bendetsen as its single proof. Bendetsen's speech before the San Francisco Commonwealth Club, in August 1942, described a plan to "commence" the evacuation of the Nikkei within twenty-four hours of an "emergency" such as a Japanese invasion of the West Coast. Given the size of the army at the time, the lack of tanks and sufficient weapons for basic marksmanship training, the lack of a published contingency plan to round up more than a hundred thousand people in cities, farms, and wilderness areas in Washington, Oregon, and California, and what Bendetsen actually said, one concludes that the army had no plan or even the capability to round up "all persons of Japanese ancestry" within a twenty-four-, a forty-eight-, or even a seventy-two-hour period.

The JACL histories of Japanese America, by Bill Hosokawa and Budd Fukei, apply the stereotype to Japanese American history with vicious and devastatingly specific effect. Because of an overdose of Japanese culture, the Nisei, victims of their parents' victim culture, were intimidated and overwhelmed by the gush of white racist rage and were short of the guts to resist the violation of their constitutional rights in the courts.

The camps were so successful in indoctrinating Japanese America into displacing the real with the fake that the Sansei, the third-generation Nikkei who despised the JACL, believed the history they were told. In *American in Disguise* (1971: Weatherhill), a Sansei sociologist, Daniel Okimoto, wrote the first Japanese American autobiography that exactly duplicated the form and content of the Christian Chinese American autobiography. He despised his parents' generation, the Nisei, for being too passive, too Japanese to massively challenge the constitutionality of the camps in court. He despised Japanese culture for creating pathological victims and patsies. The Japanese American autobiography as a low-maintenance, self-cleaning, self-destructive engine of white supremacy reached a certain peak with Mike M. Masaoka's autobiography, *They Call Me Moses Masaoka* (1987: William Morrow). Masaoka was the JACL leader who masterminded the betrayal and behavior modification of his people.

* * *

Non-Christian Chinese Americans and non-JACL Japanese Americans are now, and were then, the majority of Chinese and Japanese America. In the best-known Chinese American and Japanese American literature, the non-Christian, the non-JACL, and Nisei camp resistance simply do not exist. In Asian American writing and in American letters, the Chinese and Japanese American writers who write from the real, instead of ventriloquizing the stereotype, are pariahs and their writings are virtually underground, writings that are under siege by literary Gunga Dins and their white Park Rangers.

Here, we offer a literary history of Chinese American and Japanese American writing concerning the real and the fake. We describe the real, from its sources in the Asian fairy tale and the Confucian heroic tradition, to make the work of these Asian American writers understandable in its own terms. We describe the fake—from its sources in Christian dogma and in Western philosophy, history, and literature—to make it clear why the more popularly known writers such as Jade Snow Wong, Maxine Hong Kingston, David Henry Hwang, Amy Tan, and Lin Yutang are not represented here. Their work is not hard to find.

The writers of the real are very hard to find, and needlessly hard to understand. Here, we do the work of Monkey in *Journey to the West*. Life is war. Every human is born a soldier. All behavior is tactics and strategy. Deception is the basis of all warfare, the strategist Sun Tzu, "the Grandson," says. For the soldier, the essential skill in winning the war to maintain personal integrity is in the telling of the difference between the real and the fake. We tell it. You have more of the real of Asian American history and literature in your hands now than any of the fakes have ever held.

Gathering the essential works of the universal Chinese and Japanese childhood, the background and contents of the real, would have been easier had we paid attention to the Cantonese operas and Kabuki we were taught, as youngsters, to exclude from our serious perception and memory. It would have been easier had we not erased the stories the old folks, the busboys, and the immigrants told to describe the shrines, the posters, and the knickknack porcelain and clay figures of animals, babies, and warriors found on the shelves and walls of Chinatown and Li'l Tokyo shops and restaurants. Way past our childhoods, we had to gather "the stuff of the real" the hard way. We had to ask, inspect, corroborate, challenge, and prove the factual, textural reality of the stuff and its place in Asian universal knowledge. As we suspected, contrary to the stereotype, Chinese and Japanese immigrants were a literate people from literate civilizations whose presses, theaters, opera houses, and artistic enterprises rose as quickly as their social and political institutions. They are not few. They are not gone. They are not stupid. They were only waiting to be asked.

We wish to thank the many we asked, and the many who offered the benefit of their knowledge and talent without being asked: Frank Abe, the Academy of Motion Picture Arts and Sciences Library, Willa Baum at the Bancroft Library, Kay Boyle, Dwight Chuman, the East/West Players, Jack Herzig, William Hohri, David Ishii, Barbara Lowenstein, Dorothy Ritsuko MacDonald, Renee Mayfield at Howard University Press, Dale Minami, Henry Miyatake, the Modern Language Association, James Omura, Michelle Ota, James Paulaskas at the National Archives, Robert Sims, S. E. Solberg, Dana Spradling, Steve Sumida, Benjamin R. Tong, Jack Tono, Hope Wenk, the American Ethnic Studies Department at the University of Washington, and the University of Washington Library.

Jeffery Paul Chan
Frank Chin
Lawson Fusao Inada
Shawn Wong

Los Angeles, San Francisco,
Ashland, Seattle, 1989

Come All Ye Asian American Writers of the Real and the Fake

Frank Chin

San Francisco. Chinatown–North Beach. Night. About half past dead. Nineteen sixty. Temperature's in the sixties too, three days and three nights into a strange summer inversion over town. Hot night for Frisco. On a roof, listen . . . a Chinaman is playing flamenco guitar.

The Chinaman looks twelve years old trying to look older. Thousands of tuned cats screech before they die in three-quarter and six-eight time, crash on the walls of two-story Chinatown buildings across the street and fade. "I know I don't look Spanish gypsy," the Chinaman says. "I've been sick."

He gets a laugh.

Has all this been an elaborate racial joke? Does the authenticity of the music the Chinaman plays make a difference in judging this a racist joke? What if I say this is no joke, but my personal experience? What if I tell you a story about me living with gypsies that rings true? What if the story is true and the flamenco guitar is fake?

In the fifties our Chinaman knows Charlie Chan Fu Manchu banging Bijou on his brain is making the Chinese uglier and uglier to him by the second.

On the ground level, under the apartments full of Chinese, are flamenco nightclubs and restaurants. Carmen Amaya brings her troupe to the Sinaloa on Stockton. The guitarist Mariano Cordoba owns the Patio Andaluz on the corner of Stockton and Vallejo. Juan Serrano plays at Barnaby Conrad's El Matador, on Broadway. Down Broadway on the corner of Kearny is the Casa Madrid, where Cruz Luna and Rosa Montoya dance and Carlos Ramos plays the guitar. On Green near Grant, at the Old Spaghetti Factory, is a flamenco club called Los Flamencos de las Cuevas.

The Chinn brothers, Connie Hwang, born in rooms over Orangeland in Chinatown, Chester Chan, Chester Yuen, and a number of Chinatown and suburban yellows were attracted to the music and hung out with the Spaniards. Everyone who played flamenco knew the history and affected the part of a player saving the soul of flamenco from showbiz extinction, of making the difference between the real and the fake in dangerous times.

Why were Chinatown kids attracted to flamenco? It was the music of a pariah people, like the Chinese before Charlie Chan, like the Japanese Americans during World War II. Yet flamenco was not about the white racism of Spain. Not racist hate, not racist love, neither the nightmare of oppression nor the dream of being assimilated by the host defines their songs. The gypsies didn't need white Spaniards to be gypsies.

If all the white Spaniards were to disappear off the face of Spain right now, the gypsies and flamenco would not lose anything that holds them together. The gypsies would still be gypsy, and the flamenco would be flamenco. The only difference would be that they would have more room to grow.

Asian Americans born here between 1882 and at least 1966 cannot say the same.

What if all the whites were to vanish from the American hemisphere, right now? No more whites to push us around, or to be afraid of, or to try to impress, or to prove ourselves to. What do we Asian Americans, Chinese Americans, Japanese Americans, Indo-Chinese, and Korean Americans have to hold us together? What is "Asian America," "Chinese America," and "Japanese America"? For, no matter how white we dress, speak, and behave, we will never be white. No matter how well we speak Spanish, or sing, dance, and play flamenco, we will never be Spanish gypsies.

What seems to hold Asian American literature together is the popularity among whites of Maxine Hong Kingston's *Woman Warrior* (450,000 copies sold since 1976); David Henry Hwang's *F.O.B.* (Obie, best off-Broadway play) and *M. Butterfly* (Tony, best Broadway play); and Amy Tan's *The Joy Luck Club*. These works are held up before us as icons of our pride, symbols of our freedom from the icky-gooey evil of a Chinese culture where the written word for "woman" and "slave" are the same word (Kingston) and Chinese brutally tattoo messages on the backs of women (Kingston and Hwang).

Amy Tan opens her *Joy Luck Club* with a fake Chinese fairy tale about a duck that wants to be a swan and a mother who dreams of her daughter being born in America, where she'll grow up speaking perfect English and no one will laugh at her and where a "woman's worth is [not] measured by the loudness of her husband's belch." The fairy tale is not Chinese but white racist. It is not informed by any Chinese intelligence. This is Confucian culture as seen through the interchangeable Chinese/Japanese/Korean/Vietnamese mix (depending on which is the yellow enemy of the moment) of Hollywood. "They sell their daughters at thirteen years old into marriage or worse. . . . They know nothing of the love we have for our women," says Cary Grant in *Destination Tokyo*.

Ducks in the barnyard are not the subject of Chinese fairy tales, except as food. Swans are not the symbols of physical female beauty, vanity, and promiscuity that they are in the West. Chinese admire the fact that swans mate for life; they represent romantic love and familial bliss. There is nothing in Chinese fairy tales to justify characterizing the Chinese as measuring a woman's worth by the loudness of her husband's belch.

In *The Woman Warrior*, Kingston takes a childhood chant, "The Ballad of Mulan," which is as popular today as "London Bridge Is Falling Down," and rewrites the heroine, Fa Mulan, to the specs of the stereotype of the Chinese woman as a pathological white supremacist victimized and trapped in a hideous Chinese civilization. The tattoos Kingston gives Fa Mulan, to dramatize cruelty to women, actually belong to the hero Yue Fei, a man whose tomb is now a tourist attraction at West Lake, in Hanzhou city. Fake work breeds fake work. David Henry Hwang repeats Kingston's revision of Fa Mulan and Yue Fei, and goes on to impoverish and slaughter Fa Mulan's family to further dramatize the cruelty of the Chinese.

Kingston, Hwang, and Tan are the first writers of any race, and certainly the first writers of Asian ancestry, to so boldly fake the best-known works from the most universally known body of Asian literature and lore in history. And, to legitimize their faking, they have to fake all of Asian American history and literature, and argue that the immigrants who settled and established Chinese America lost touch with Chinese culture, and that a faulty memory combined with new experience produced new versions of these traditional stories. This version of history is their contribution to the stereotype.

The lie of their version of history is easily proven by one simple fact: Chinese America was never illiterate. Losing touch with China did not result in Chinese Americans losing touch with "The Ballad of Mulan." It was and is still chanted by children in Chinatowns around the Western hemisphere. Losing touch with England did not result in English whites losing touch with the texts of the Magna Carta or Shakespeare.

Their elaboration of this version of history, in both autobiography and autobiographical fiction, is simply a device for destroying history and literature. They describe it as a natural process. However, the shape, content, and moral values preached in the Holy Bible have not gone through this natural process between the languages and nations of Europe. Whites, settled in America for hundreds of years, have not lost track of the plots, the characters, or the authors of the most cherished fairy tales and adventures told in Western childhood. The values of Chinese fairy tales, the form and ethics of the classics of the heroic tradition, the names of the heroes, and the works themselves are written into the bylaws of the tongs and associations that run Chinatowns to this day. The characters of the fairy tale and the heroic tradition are found in figurines, statues, and calendar art. Their stories are told through toys, on flash cards, and in comic and coloring books throughout the country, in Chinese American homes and in Chinatowns—in the restaurants, on the walls, in the windows . . . At no time in Chinese American history was the real Fa Mulan obscure or inaccessible to a Chinese American girl or boy.

The real Fa Mulan is a chant that describes the oldest daughter of an aged father too decrepit to answer the Khan's call for him to mount and lead his estate's army into a great war, the perfect Confucian individual: a self-sufficient soldier. We are not here to offer an opinion of Fa Mulan, derived from our personal experience, but to answer the opinion of Kingston and Hwang. Here, we offer the best proof, the corroborative fact of the ballad itself, in Chinese, and in English translation:

木蘭詩二首　　　無名氏

唧唧復唧唧，木蘭當戶織。不聞機杼聲，唯聞女嘆息。問女何所思？問女何所憶？女亦無所思，女亦無所憶：「昨夜見軍帖，可汗大點兵；軍書十二卷，卷卷有爺名。阿爺無大兒，木蘭無長兄；願為市鞍馬，從此替爺征。」東市買駿馬，西市買鞍韉；南市買轡頭，北市買長鞭。朝辭爺孃去，暮宿黃河邊；不聞爺孃喚女聲，但聞黃河流水鳴濺濺。旦辭黃河去，暮至黑山頭；不聞爺孃喚女聲，但聞燕山胡騎聲啾啾。萬里赴戎機，關山度若飛；朔氣傳金柝，寒光照鐵衣。將軍百戰死，壯士十年歸。

歸來見天子，天子坐明堂；策勳十二轉，賞賜百千彊。可汗問所欲－－木蘭不用尚書郎；願馳千里足，送兒還故鄉。爺孃聞女來，出郭相扶將；阿姊聞妹來，當戶理紅妝；小弟聞姊來，磨刀霍霍向豬羊。開我東閣門，坐我西間床；脫我戰時袍，著我舊時裳；當窗理雲鬢，對鏡帖花黃。出門看火伴，火伴始驚惶。同行十二年，不知木蘭是女郎！雄兔腳撲朔，雌兔眼迷離；兩兔傍地走，安能辨我是雄雌？

The Ballad of Mulan
Anonymous

Sniffle sniffle, sigh sniffle sniffle.
Fa Mulan sniffles like her loom.
Do not ask how the shuttle shifts.
Do ask why a girl cries herself sick.
Ask her: does she pine.
Ask her: does she yearn.
No, this girl does not pine.
No, this girl does not yearn.
Last night I saw the battle rolls
For the Khan's great army.
The Roll Book runs twelve rolls.
Roll after roll lists my father's name.
Father has no grown sons.
Mulan has no older brother.
So, I'll buy a horse and saddle
And ride for the family in father's place.
East Market: buy a good horse.
West Market: buy a saddle and blanket.
South Market: buy bridles and reins.
North Market: buy a long whip.

Dawn: So long Dad and Mom.
Sundown: Camp by the Yellow River.
Don't ask this girl to hear Dad and Mom calling her name.
Do ask her to hear the coursing Yellow River gush and tinkle.
Dawn: Leave the Yellow River.
Sunset: The peaks of the Black Mountains.
Don't ask her to hear her parents wailing her name.
Do ask her to hear the Tartar horses whinny
On Swallow Mountain and blow chuff chuff.
Thousands of miles of war; battles all the way.
Over borders and mountains like birds we fly.
Tight northern air drums the watch.
The gaze of winter dawn flashes on chain mail.
My generals of a hundred battles: dead.
My soldiers, after ten years of war, hit the road home.
On the road home: An audience with the Emperor.
The Son of Heaven sits in his Hall of Light.
"Your valor fills twelve books.
Your reward amounts to a hundred thousand cash.
Now what does the girl want for herself?"
"Muklan has no use for any high court post.

Loan me the famous Thousand Li Camel to carry me home."
Dad and Mom hear I'm coming.
They meet me outside the walls and escort me onto our estate.
Big Sister hears I'm coming.
By the door, she rouges her face.
Big Little Brother hears I'm home.
He grinds his knife sharp sharp to go for a pig and a sheep.
Open my east chamber door.
Sit on my west chamber bed.
Off with the battledress of recent times.
On with the gowns of old times.
By the window fix my hair in "cloudy tresses."
Gaze in the mirror and fix the combs.
Outside there's my ally in battle.*
My ally is agog.
Shoulder to shoulder through twelve years of war . . .
He never knew I was a girl.
The he rabbit tucks his feet under to sit.
The she rabbit dims her shiny eyes.
Two rabbits running side by side.
Who can see which is the he and which the she?

This chant is the source of all subsequent novels and storybook versions of Fa Mulan. In none is there any instance of ethical male domination or misogynistic cruelty being inflicted on Mulan. She is not tattooed. She returns home to her realm and family and a banquet, not to some wicked Hwangian warlord who can't stand the idea of a woman general.

The poem ends with the Confucian ideal of marriage. In Confucianism, all of us—men and women—are born soldiers. The soldier is the universal individual. No matter what you do for a living—doctor, lawyer, fisherman, thief—you are a fighter. Life is war. The war is to maintain personal integrity in a world that demands betrayal and corruption. All behavior is strategy and tactics. All relationships are martial. Marriages are military alliances. Fa Mulan and her captains were allies, fighting shoulder to shoulder in war for

---

*Ally, *faw boon*, is both singular and plural. Novelizations of "The Ballad of Mulan" name two officers who partnered with her in twelve years of war and who, with confusion and excitement, see that she's a woman. To better approximate the flow of the chant into the closing image of Confucian romantic love, we have translated *faw boon* in the singular. Those who can hear the plural get a giggle wondering which of the brothers in the fire is the he rabbit, and anticipate both Muklan's sexual awakening and the romantic drama found between the lines.

twelve years. (One full cycle around the lunar zodiac—a lifetime in microcosm.) There is no sexual dominance in this childhood peek at romance.

If any Chinese fairy tale taught male dominance and the inferiority of women as a moral universal, it would be, as in the Bible, the marriage story. The symbol of the marriage vows throughout Asia is the Chinese fairy tale "Bright Pearl," or "The Dragon and the Phoenix." Every large Chinese restaurant in America seems to have the dragon and the phoenix flying on a back wall, with the word for "marriage" between them, usually rendered round like a ball. The ball is the bright pearl of the title.

Jade Dragon and Golden Phoenix are supreme in their respective heavenly realms of the River of the Milky Way to the west and Magic Mountain to the east. For hundreds of years, they pass each other every day, as they patrol their territories. One day, they both happen to stop at Fairy Island and meet for the first time. They fly around the island together and blurp! a huge crystal such as never has been seen before in heaven or earth pokes up through the island and flashes in their eyes. To keep it from being taken from them, they decide to put their signature on it by carving this crystal into a perfect sphere: a "bright pearl." Both the dragon and the phoenix bloody their beaks and claws working on the crystal. Hundreds of years of carving. Hundreds of years of polishing and finishing.

Finally, the pearl is finished. They turn human. The dragon becomes a handsome young man. The phoenix, a lovely young maid. They live on the island, love each other, and love their pearl. Then it's stolen by the keeper of the celestial jewels, the Queen Mother of the Western Paradise.

The Queen Mother hides it away in a gold box locked inside of nine rooms, behind nine doors, to which she has the only set of nine keys. But she can't resist showing off the pearl at a gathering of the gods come to celebrate her birthday, and the light from the pearl reaches the lovers. They fly up to the highest heaven, crash the party of the gods, and, in the struggle for the pearl, the gleaming gem rolls and falls off highest heaven toward earth. Dragon says he cannot live without the pearl and dives after it, transforming back into Jade Dragon as he flies. Phoenix says she cannot live without their pearl and dives after it, returning to her bird form. Between them, they cushion the pearl's fall, but fall it does, crash, into China, and with it the dragon and the phoenix. The pearl becomes West Lake; the dragon becomes Dragon Mountain to the east; and the phoenix becomes Phoenix Mountain to the west of the lake. The telling of the story closes with a folk song still sung around West Lake, in Hanshou city:

A bright pearl falls from heaven
And become West Lake.
Dragon and Phoenix love their pearl,
And now they are mountains by West Lake's waters.

There is no natural or imposed male domination of women in this fairy tale. Jade Dragon is supreme in his domain of the Milky Way, as is Golden Phoenix in hers of Magic Mountain. Man and woman become allies. Love emerges out of the labor of making the pearl and maintaining the alliance, though the forces of heaven and earth are arrayed against them and their pearl. There is no delimiting of male or female behavior, work, or morality here.

2

The works of Kingston, Hwang, and Tan are not consistent with Chinese fairy tales and childhood literature. But how do we account for their consistency with each other and with that of the other Chinese American publishing sensations of the past, from the first book ever published in English, in America, by a Chinese American— *My Life in China and America* by Yung Wing, 1909—to Jade Snow Wong's *Fifth Chinese Daughter*, which was the immediate predecessor of Kingston's work and influenced it? That's easy: (1) all the authors are Christian, (2) the only form of literature written by Chinese Americans that major publishers will publish (other than the cookbook) is autobiography, an exclusively Christian form; and (3) they all write to the specifications of the Christian stereotype of Asia being as opposite morally from the West as it is geographically. The social Darwinists of the turn of the century regowned this stereotype in social scientific jargon, and white writers—from Jack London to Robert Heinlein—made art of the stereotype. The stereotype, and its corroboration in science and art, sharpened the racist laws against Chinese and Japanese, from Congress to city hall. The stereotype—as moral, scientific, artistic, entertaining, and legal fact— taught, inspired, and haunted the first American-born, English-speaking generations of Chinese Americans and Japanese Americans who would become the first authors of Asian American works in English.

The stereotype they were taught in school and church clashed with the reality of their Chinatown and Li'l Tokyo experiences. Those who were to be published simply blanked out all experience that didn't gibe with the stereotype.

The American-born generations and the colonial middle-class immigrants—likewise indoctrinated in white supremacy, in Singapore, Hong Kong, and Christian Taiwan—talk of their art as being above the history and people it portrays. They speak of recasting the Christian social Darwinist heroines of Chinese culture as both victims and destroyers of that culture, as being morally superior to the real works and the culture they characterize. We expect Asian American writers, portraying Asia and Asians, to have a knowledge of the difference between the real and the fake. This is a knowledge they have admitted they not only do not possess but also have no interest in ever possessing. They are, thus, reflexive creatures of the stereotype. They talk about the agony of the stereotype but, when pressed, have no idea how to describe it.

This is the stereotype of Asia, Asians, and Asian Americans:

The first yellows came to America with no intention of settling. They were sojourners. They intended to stay in America just long enough to make a fortune, then return to China or Japan to live high on the hog.

Chinese and Japanese culture are so misogynistic they don't deserve to survive. The men are intelligent, brilliant and perverse—either pervertedly good, like Charlie Chan the good Christian convert, or pervertedly evil, like Fu Manchu, whose strange idea of torturing white men is to send them to bed with his beautiful nympho daughter. Even the bad yellows are, thus, subcutaneous white supremacists.

Asian culture is anti-individualistic, mystic, passive, collective, and morally and ethically opposite to Western culture.

All of that is false. The yellows were not sojourners. The proof: tongs. Chinese and Japanese culture are not more misogynistic than Western culture. The proof: Chinese and Japanese childhood literature, and history. Asian culture is more, not less, individualistic than Western culture. The proof: Asian childhood literature and history. If Asian childhood literature and history and Asian American institutions established by the immigrants belie the stereotype, why does it endure, and where did this monster come from? It came, as it still comes, from pure white racist fantasy and wishful thinking born of white racial self-contempt. We can follow the grain through white writing, back into white history to Marco Polo and the pope in Rome.

Marco Polo has just dropped by the Vatican to pay his respects after getting back from Cathay loaded down with gold, precious silks, and an amazing concoction called gunpowder, an inventory of teas, spices, and all manner of precious finished products. The pope is moved to compliment young Marco on his plunder. This stuff is not booty, not won by conquest or superior craft. This whole caravan and astounding technology and wealth are free samples. China wants to do business. Marco is to be the Chinese Fuller Brush man.

All this stuff is the Chinese version of the little free bottle of perfume. The pope doesn't want to hear this and throws Marco Polo in jail to get China out of his system. The pope suddenly has a big problem. There is, according to the current interpretation of scripture, no civilization other than Christendom, the only civilization made with Godliness. So, by definition, any civilization east of God would be non-Godly, and founded on false and opposite morality. This moral oppositeness white writers express in queer behavior they call Chinese, and in the sexually repugnant, comically effeminate yellow men and yellow women who will become, in the words of the Baptist missionary Charles Shepherd, "choice souls" ripe for salvation.

The highest and lowest minds of the nineteenth and early twentieth century described Asian culture as being stagnant, morally inferior, irrelevant, or nonexistent. "In the East," writes Georg Wilhelm Friedrich Hegel, ". . . conscience does not exist, nor does individual morality. Everything is simply in a state of nature, which allows the noblest to exist as it does the worst. The conclusion to be derived from this is that no philosophic knowledge can be found here." For Hegel, a darling of the Marxists, "The fear of the Lord is the beginning of wisdom." The trouble with the yellow people of the East is, as the pope said in the thirteenth century, the Asians are not Christian.

"The Eastern form must therefore be excluded from the history of philosophy. . . . Philosophy proper commences in the West." So says Hegel, in *The Philosophy of History*. And the much revered nineteenth-century historian Houston Stewart Chamberlain, writing philosophically in his *Foundations of the Nineteenth Century* (1910), states the stereotype as truth, as fact:

The peoples that have not yet adopted Christianity—the Chinese, the Indians, the Turks and others—have all so far no true history; all they have is, on the one hand, a chronicle of ruling dynasties, butcheries and the like; on the other, the uneventful humble existence of countless millions living a life of bestial happiness, who disappear in the night of ages leaving no traces beyond . . . their culture, their art, their religion, in short their condition may interest us, achievements of their intellect, of their industry may even have become valuable parts of their own life, as is exemplified by Indian thought, Babylonian science and Chinese methods; their history, however, purely as such, lacks moral greatness, in other words, that force which rouses the individual man to consciousness of his individuality in contrast to the surrounding world and then—like the ebb and flow of the tide—makes him employ the world, which he has discovered in his own breast, to shape that which is without it. . . .

No more has . . . the Chinaman—the unique representative of Positivism and Collectivism; what our historical works record as his "history" is nothing more than an enumeration of the various robber bands, by which the patient, shrewd and soulless people, without sacrificing an iota of its individuality, has allowed itself to be ruled: such enumerations are simply "criminal statistics," not history, at least not for us: we cannot really judge actions which awaken no echo in our breast.

The stereotype was passed to American-born yellows as an article of faith by missionaries and laws that allowed only Christian Chinese to marry and only 105 Chinese to enter the United States per year.

A traditional tool of Christian conversion, the autobiography became the sole Chinese American form of writing, with Yung Wing's mission-schoolboy-makes-good Gunga Din licking up white fantasy in the first Chinese American autobiography, *My Life in China and America*. Every Chinese American autobiography and work of autobiographical fiction since Yung Wing, from Leong Gor Yun and Jade Snow Wong to Maxine Hong Kingston and Amy Tan, has been written by Christian Chinese perpetuating and advancing the stereotype of a Chinese culture so foul, so cruel to women, so perverse, that good Chinese are driven by the moral imperative to kill it. Christian salvation demands the destruction of all Chinese history: that's the Second Commandment, children.

The autobiography is not a Chinese form. Dr. Sun Yat Sen's revolutionaries of 1911 wanted more than an end to the Manchu Empire, more than an end to dynastic imperial government. They wanted to Europeanize China. The literary leaders wanted even more than that. They wanted to Christianize China through new Chinese writing. Hu Shih wrote that the Chinese had to develop biography and autobiography for their inspirational moral effect. In his own *Autobiography of a Man at Thirty*, Hu Shih stated, "Writing my autobiography makes me feel very Christian." It should: autobiography is a Christian form, descended from confession and, Hu Shih believed, from testimony. St. Augustine's *The Confessions* is generally acknowledged as the first autobiography; Hu Shih said the Gospels of the New Testament—the books of Matthew, Luke, and John—were the first autobiographies. To the Chinese, the autobiography is definitely a Christian form.

To this day, among the Chinese, only Christians write autobiographies. All authenticate the stereotype through the author's yellow voice and experience. From 1909 to the present, only the work of three Christian (perhaps two Christian and one semilapsed Christian) writers is Christian, autobiographical, and not white racist in form or content. The main differences between their writing and that of most Christian Chinese are literary, historical, and sexual. Unlike the pack of Chinese Americans, Sui Sin Far (Edith Eaton), Diana Chang, and Dr. Han Suyin write knowledgeably and authentically of Chinese fairy tales, heroic tradition, and history. Their greatest departure from all the Chinese American autobiographies and autobiographical fictions is in their description of Chinese men. Read them, and this fact jumps out of their books: the only Chinese men who are not emasculated and sexually repellent in Chinese American writing are found in the books and essays of Sui Sin Far, Diana Chang, and Dr. Han Suyin. These three women are unique unto themselves, for they are Eurasians. Diana Chang and Dr. Han are the daughters of Chinese men. Sui Sin Far was the daughter of a Chinese mother and British father. Diana Chang and Dr. Han both spent a significant part of their childhoods and youth in China.

Sui Sin Far was born in England and grew up on the road and at sea, moving around the world, with her father, painting. At the turn of the century Edith Eaton, using the pen name Sui Sin Far, which translates from the Cantonese as "Water Lily," was sickly and physically small. A lone champion of the Chinese American real, she fought the rampant stereotype and antiyellow racism that were encouraging the passage of exclusion laws. Literary critic S. E. Solberg reminds us of the fact that Sui Sin Far's short fiction and autobiographical essays are the only knowing and sympathetic writing on Chinese America of the time, and the only contemporary portraits of Chinatowns from Toronto to Seattle by a single sensibility. In her own time, the Chinese considered Edith Eaton a heroine, a champion of Chinese integrity in America. She knew the stereotype and in "Leaves from the Mental Portfolio of an Eurasian" movingly confronted its effect on people's perception of her and on her own perception of the Chinese.

Diana Chang's autobiographical 1956 novel, *The Frontiers of Love*, criticizes Chinese culture and history knowledgeably. The real is real in her work, and the women are as real as the men. No straw-man China. No stereotype.

These three Christian Chinese Eurasians were not born and raised in America, where the stereotype came out of the laws, out of the schools, out of the white literary lights of the time, out of the science, out of the comics, movies, and radio night and day toward World War II.

The Christian Chinese Americans coined the term *Chinese American* to distinguish themselves from heathen Chinamen. The autobiographics of the pseudonymous Leong Gor Yun (1936), of Pardee Lowe (1943), Calvin Lee (1965), and Jade Snow Wong (1950) plead with whites to make the distinction between the Chinese American and the Chinaman of the Fu Manchu stereotype. Chinese Americans were Christian, accepted the scientific white racism of social Darwinists, and developed the form of their autobiographies as an argument against the social Darwinist nightmare of a morally inferior, despicable yellow race conquering the white race and driving it to extinction in America. Chinese or Japanese, it made no difference. They were perverse in their behavior, no matter how much it resembled white Christian behavior. Their ability to mimic exactly was itself threatening. Such was the social science of America before World War II, former U.S. Senator from California S. I. Hayakawa contended before the Bernstein Commission on Wartime Relocation and Internment of Civilians in 1981. White racism did not have the stigma (of being either unsavory or immoral) that it has today. Hayakawa specifically mentioned two books that were influential: Madison Grant's *Passing of the Great Race, or Racial Basis of European History* (1916) and Lothrop Stoddard's *The Rising Tide of Color* (1920). The Stoddard book opens with the nightmare:

In the preface to an historical monograph . . . written shortly before the Great War, I stated: "The world-wide struggle between the primary races of mankind—the 'conflict of color,' as it has been happily termed—bids fair to be the fundamental problem of the twentieth century. . . ."

Before the war I had hoped that the readjustments rendered inevitable by the renascence of the brown and yellow peoples of Asia would be gradual, and in the main a pacific process, kept within evolutionary bounds by the white world's inherent strength and fundamental solidarity. The frightful weakening of the white world during the war opened up revolutionary, even cataclysmic, possibilities.

In saying this I do not refer solely to military "perils." The subjugation of white lands by colored armies may, of course, occur, especially if the white world continues to rend itself with internecine wars. However, such colored triumphs of arms are less to be dreaded than more enduring conquests like migrations which would swamp whole populations and turn countries now white into colored man's lands irretrievably lost to the white world. Of course, these ominous possibilities existed even before 1914, but the war has rendered them much more probable.

In Parabellum's 1908 novel, *Banzai!*, the ominous colored race is Japanese:

So it was after the terrible night of Port Arthur and so it was now.

It was of course as yet impossible to figure out in detail how the Japanese had managed to take possession of the Pacific States within twenty-four hours.

. . . A hundred thousand Japanese had established the line of an eastern advance-guard long before the Pacific States had any idea of what was up. During Sunday after the capture of San Francisco, the occupation of Seattle, San Diego and the other fortified towns on the coast, the landing of the second detachment of the Japanese army began, and by Monday evening the Pacific States were in the grip of no less than one hundred and seventy thousand men.

In P. W. Dooner's *The Last Days of the Republic* (1880), the invading army is Chinese:

The very name of the United States of America was thus blotted from the record of nations and peoples, as unworthy the poor boon of existence. Where once the proud domain of forty States, besides the millions of miles of unorganized territory, cultivated the arts of peace and gave to the world its brightest gems of literature, art and scientific discovery, the Temple of Liberty had crumbled; and above its ruins was reared the colossal fabric of barbaric splendor known as the Western Empire of his August Majesty the Emperor of China and Ruler of all lands. . . .

In Jack London's "Unparalleled Invasion" (1914), the loathsome invading and conquering race is Chinese, and it is quick reproduction and overpopulation that conquers the whites. To some, the end of America as a white man's land would come from the loins, not the muzzles, of the yellow peril.

The Chinese American "identity crisis," the Japanese American "dual personality," the yellow/white either/or that distinguishes Christian Chinese American autobiography from the work of the Chinese American writers included in this volume is the product of the Christian missionaries who dominated Chinatown history before the war, and their self-serving imaginative biographies, autobiographies, and novels.

In the autobiography and fiction of Baptist missionary Charles Shepherd, we at last find the Chinatown of the Chinese American autobiographies. And in his novel *The Ways of Ah-Sin* (1923), we find the prototype of the heroines of Jade Snow Wong, Maxine Hong Kingston, and Amy Tan—a girl named Ah Mae, a kind of Cantonese Cinderella in Chinatown: "as soon her tiny hands and body were able to perform service, she had become the family drudge. . . .

> But hers was one of those rare spirits, one of those hearts undaunted, which rise serenely above environment, as the beautiful lotus lily stands erect and with queenly dignity above the muddy waters beneath in which it has its roots and from which it has drained its life. Her little body, frail and often stooped by reason of much toil, had about it a grace that was indefinable. Her face wore ever the suggestion of a smile needing but slight incentive to awaken it to full radiance. Her deep brown—almost black—eyes, even when filled with tears provoked by ill-temperament, shone with a luster which convinced one that somewhere back of them was the dwelling place of a choice soul.
>
> It is not often that one discovers such a personality in the midst of such ignorance and oppression. But there are such; and at times God permits us to discover such a one. . . ."

The Chinese who refused to convert, the Chinese men, to Charles Shepherd's Christianity are all kin to Bret Harte's wily Chinese gambler, Ah-Sin, the "Heathen Chinee" of the poem "Plain Language from Truthful James" (1870); thus the title of Shepherd's novel: *The Ways of Ah-Sin*. Ah-Sin is the tongs, Ah-Sin is the non-Christians, the unsaved:

> The wily Ah-Sin does not represent the children of the Middle Kingdom at their best, the intelligent, industrious, high-minded group which are a credit to their native land and an asset to the land of their adoption. He represents rather, what might be called the unregenerate Chinese—we use the term advisedly. He and his tribe still exist. They have increased in number. They have waxed fat, prosperous and powerful; and in addition to their own native wiles and cunning, have adopted many of the ideas and vices of the lower strata of American society. They constitute today the greatest single menace to peace, prosperity, and social progress in every Chinese community in the United States; and perhaps Bret Harte did not after all so greatly err speaking of them as "heathen" and as perpetrators of "ways that are dark and tricks that are vain."

The missionary casts himself as the hero of a melodrama and the champion of the good but cowardly Christian Chinese who cannot fight for themselves:

> If this story should fall into the hands of my many Chinese friends, as more than likely it will, they will understand why I have written these things; for they have suffered much and long at the hands of Ah-Sin. They would like to say to my readers what I have said in the following pages; but as they value their lives, they dare not. This being the case I have undertaken to speak for them, as well as for my American friends and colleagues.
>
> If, on the other hand, this story should be brought to the attention of any of the tribes of Ah-Sin, I shall have no apology to make to them for setting forth this narrative of things as they are.

Shepherd dedicated his novel to another missionary, Donaldina Cameron, celebrated in Christian Chinatown history as "Chinatown's Avenging Angel." Cameron had a house for Chinese girls she "saved" from prostitution. She was, however, very picky. She only picked on prostitutes and whorehouses serving Chinese men. Whorehouses full of Chinese women serving a white-only clientele, like the one next door to her Cameron House, were blessed. The aim of this Presbyterian missionary was to brainwash the Chinese girls against sexual relations with Chinese men and to send them back to China to spread the Gospel and discourage Chinese migration to America. The bars on the windows of Cameron House's girls' dormitories were not to keep Chinese men out, but to keep the Chinese women from escaping.

The history of Chinatown, San Francisco, is told in the myth of the good missionaries, Donaldina Cameron of Cameron House and Charles Shepherd of the Chung Mei Baptist Home for Chinese Boys. Only now is their contribution to the creation and perpetuation of the dark side of the stereotype of the Chinese male as moral, behavioral, and sexual pervert coming to light. Cameron House was a factory for turning Chinese boys into the fulfillment of white homosexual fantasy. The *San Francisco Chronicle* of April 22, 1989, gingerly reported what Chinatown had been talking about for as long as Cameron House had existed:

> A Presbyterian minister resigned his ordination after being accused of molesting several teenagers while he was director of youth programs for a large Chinatown religious association, presbytery officials say.

Dick Wichman was accused of molesting at least 19 male teenagers under his charge in incidents that allegedly occurred 20 ycars ago at Cameron House, one of the oldest and best known religious organizations in Chinatown.

But Wichman cannot be prosecuted because the statute of limitations covering the alleged incidents has expired, presbytery officials say.

Oh, yes. And the good Christian Americanized Chinese American of white fantasy is Charlie Chan, an acceptable pervert, as opposed to Fu Manchu, the unacceptable pervert.

Charles Shepherd wanted to be just like Donaldina Cameron. In 1923 he founded the Chung Mei Baptist Home for Chinese Boys, across the Bay from San Francisco. In the autobiographical *The Story of Chung Mei* (1938), Shepherd, as in *The Ways of Ah-Sin*, time and again reinvents, retreads, retools the stereotype, huffing and puffing to give it some literary depth, some critical dramatic urgency and inspirational heartbeat to make themselves, their moral superiority, and their personality the reality of Chinese American history:

All who have read Charles Dickens's immortal novel *Oliver Twist* are familiar with the so-called "merry old gentleman" of London Town, one Fagin, whose practice it was to encourage small boys to steal and to bring to him the fruits of their depravations. In San Francisco's Chinatown, in 1923, there was actually such a man who was responsible for the delinquency of numerous small boys whom he encouraged to rob cigar stores and bring back to him quantities of cigars and cigarettes. For their plunder he paid these boys a small fraction of the real selling-price. Caught red-handed one night, five such boys were arrested and turned over to the Juvenile Probation Officer. Three of the group had already gone so far along the pathway of crime that there seemed but one course to be followed: they were sent to a reform school. The other two, however, were exceedingly young and had been more or less dragged into the affair by their older associates. They were not really delinquent, but were the victims of bad company. Surely they did not belong in a reform school. Yet, had there been no such places as Chung Mei Home, the Probation Officer would have had to choose between sending them away with the others or turning them loose to become the victims of other potential Fagins who might be lurking in the community. Chung Mei offered them a chance. . . .

I was born in the forties; I was old enough to have been one of the last of what Chinatown called "Chung Mei boys." My Uncle Paul was one of the first Chung Mei boys and like most was American-born, a United States citizen. In Shepherd's world, Uncle Paul was something else:

> Oh, yes we know where they come from, when and where they were born, who their fathers and mothers are or were—in fact, we know their past history quite completely; yet we don't really know who they are. . . . You see, while today they are just a bunch of Chinese boys—some of them very small boys—tomorrow they may be something quite different. For all we know, when we stand before them in an assembly we may be looking into the faces of, and giving advice to, big business men, social and religious leaders, educators and statesmen of the future. It would, then, be a serious matter if we should give the wrong kind of advice. . . . The boy who wants to build something may some day become a famous inventor. The one who repeatedly asks if we have found him a Saturday job will not unlikely become a prominent figure in China's industrial world. The boy to whom we assign extra work in the garden become a monarch in business—if we can get him to overcome a life of ease. And then, of course, the one whom we so reluctantly punish for a misdemeanor may some day become the president of China.

Charles Shepherd and the missionaries and the missionary groupie writers are the answer to Will Irwin's 1908 "hope that some one will arise, before this generation is passed, to record that conquest of affection by which the California Chinese transformed themselves from our race adversaries to our dear subject people."

3

Christian conversion is cultural extinction and behavior modification. The social scientists call it "acculturation." Acculturation is not a natural process. Charles Shepherd, the novelist, the missionary, the director of Chung Mei Home strutting before his corps of Chinese boys in a military uniform complete with leather Sam Browne belt, shows us how unnatural and humiliating a process it is, as he describes the creation of the first Chinese American English-language theater, established out of a need to raise money for the home:

"There are two things we must do," I went on to explain. "We must pray. We must ask God to put it into the hearts of folks who have money to give some of it to us. Then we must go to work and do everything we can to raise some money ourselves. God helps those who are willing to do their part. Anyhow, we would feel much better about asking others to help us if we had first done everything we could to help ourselves." Twenty-five pairs of expectant, mystified eyes looked into mine. They seemed to say, "What can we do to earn any money?" And then I unloaded on them the idea that led to the formation of the first Chinese black-faced minstrel troupe in the history of civilization. Most of them had never before heard of such a thing as black-faced minstrels; and none of them had any experience in entertaining the public; but from the moment I finished explaining they were all for it.

My Uncle Paul was a Chung Mei Minstrel. His picture is in Shepherd's book, in costume and blackface, between pages 124 and 125. I can't bring myself to look for Uncle Paul's face. On the photo facing 125, a Chinese boy in blackface, big white lips, a tooth blacked out, wears a wig and a dress, and sits back-to-back with a blond girl about eleven years old, with no apparent makeup on. Under the kinky spindly pigtails tied in little bows, through the blackface, the eyes could be . . . and Uncle Paul, seventy-five this year, won't look.

4

In the early twenties, all the ingredients of the stereotype were in place—in mainstream white philosophy, history, social science, literature, and religion. The young Chinese American Christians bought into the stereotype when they held their first Lake Tahoe conference, in the summer of 1925, and pondered the burning question "Does my future lie in China or America?" They asked the same question again and again, right up until World War II without once confronting the white supremacist phoniness of the question. The question was, of course, a phrasing of the either/or Chinese American dual personality identity crisis. It took Charlie Chan—the venerable detective sensation introduced by Earl Derr Biggers in 1925—to reshape the exclusion of Chinese from history, from philosophy, from literature, and from morality into the perfect image of the Chinese American as a self-destructive Ping-Pong game the Christian Chinese American autobiographers would embody as the "identity crisis." In *The Chinese Parrot* (1926), Chan has an unpleasant meeting with a Chinese tong man working a menial job in Reno, Nevada:

"It overwhelms me with sadness to admit it," Charlie answered, "for he is of my own origin, my own race, as you know. But when I look into his eyes, I discover that a gulf like the heaving Pacific lies between us. Why? Because he, though among Caucasians many more years than I, still remains Chinese. As Chinese today as in the first moon of his existence. While—I bear the brand, the label, Americanized." Chan bowed his head. "I traveled with the current," he said softly. "I was ambitious. I sought success. For what I have won, I paid the price. Am I then an American? No. Am I, then, a Chinese? Not in the eyes of Ah-Sing." He paused for a moment, then continued: "But I have chosen my path, and I must follow it."

The fact that this encounter with Ah-Sing is actually a schizoid internal dialogue is made obvious by Jon L. Breen in his writing about Charlie Chan's attraction to mystery fans:

It is the conflict of Eastern and Western values that makes Charlie Chan an interesting character. He criticizes ambition, the curiosity, the lack of tranquility of the Caucasian, but he sees more and more of these unworthy attributes in himself and is worried by it. Proud of his own vocabulary and command of the English language, he is upset by his offspring's use of slang. Listening to the pidgin English of a Chinese servant, he is torn between shame at the indignity of the man's condition and the feeling that somehow he has retained a basic Chinese identity that Chan has lost . . . proud that his children are American citizens, he is ambivalent about his own nationality.

Chinese Americans and Japanese Americans read portrayals of each other in white social science and fiction, out of self-defense, as white manuals on how good yellows and bad yellows behave. The two most influential and effective Nisei (American-born Japanese) thinkers in prewar Japanese American writing were the reporters/editors/publishers Lawrence Tanyoshi Tajiri and James Matsumoto Omura. They nurtured the Nisei writers. In America, the Nisei were the first generation of Nikkei, people of Japanese ancestry, to achieve fluency in the English language. Tajiri and Omura published the Nisei in Japanese American English-language newspapers and magazines, and love it or hate it, the Nisei wrote of and from the real world, not the stereotype. With the war, Tajiri and Omura became bitter enemies. Tajiri labeled Omura seditious and a traitor. Omura accused Tajiri of betrayal and worse. Both were for racial assimilation. Before the war, both thought of assimilation as a natural and inevitable sociological process. Both wrote about the portrayal of the Chinese and Japanese in the movies and popular novels. Two novels both wrote about as soon as they read them— and continued to mention during and even after the war—were Gene Stratton Porter's *Her Father's Daughter* (1921) and Peter B. Kyne's *The Pride of Palomar* (1921). Tajiri and Omura were morbidly disturbed by this genre of the novel's artfully presented intent to effect the writing of racist immigration, education, tax, and land laws.

The white novels that both the Chinese and Japanese Americans read for prescriptive and proscribed behavior were uniformly level-headed and romantic in their contempt for the Japanese. The all-American behavior and the excelling in school that might have won praise for a Chinese American, or so the autobiographies hoped, were cause for only more white contempt of Japanese Americans in Porter's *Her Father's Daughter*:

"If every home in Lilac Valley had at least six sturdy boys and girls growing up in it with the proper love of country and the proper realization of the white man's right to supremacy, and if the world now occupied by white men could make an equal record, where would be the talk of the yellow peril? There wouldn't be any yellow peril. You see what I mean?"

Linda lifted her frank eyes to Peter Morrison.

"Yes, you woman," said Peter gravely, "I see what you mean, but this is the first time I ever heard a high school kid propound such ideas. Where did you get them?"

"Got them in Multiflores Canyon from my father to start with," said Linda, "but recently I have been thinking, because there is a boy in High School who is making a great fight for a better scholarship record than a Jap in his class. I brood over it every spare minute, day or night, and when I say my prayers I implore high Heaven to send him an idea or to send me one that can pass on to him, that will help him to beat that Jap."

And in Peter B. Kyne's *The Pride of Palomar*, what might be seen as behavior giving the lie to the Chinese as sojourners and offering proof of their commercial adjustment and settling is, when applied to Japanese Americans, the Nikkei, cause for whites to redouble their contempt:

"Thousands of patriotic Californians have sold their farms to Japanese without knowing it. The law provides that a Japanese cannot lease land longer than three years, so when their leases expire they conform to our foolish law by merely shifting the tenants from one farm to another. Eventually so many Japs settled in the valley that the white farmers, unable to secure white labor, unable to trust Japanese labor, unable to endure Japanese neighbors or to enter into Japanese social life, weary of paying taxes to support schools for the education of Japanese children, weary of daily contact with irritable, unreliable and unassimilable aliens, sold or leased their farms in order to escape into a white neighborhood. . . ."

For all the hostility leveled at them in the bookstores, magazine racks, and public libraries of their West Coast hometowns, the older Nisei writer Toshio Mori wrote a collection of short stories modeled on Sherwood Anderson's *Winesburg, Ohio*. He was Buddhist, not Christian. His stories can be read as autobiographical, but his intentions are clearly more ambitious. And none of his characters in *Yokohama, California*, written before the war, suffer the schizoid agony of being torn apart by the conflicting parties of the dual personality or identity crisis.

The white racists hated everything Japanese because of Japan, the nation. Japan had defeated a white nation in a modern war, was embarked on imperialist adventures on the Asian continent, and demanded space in the same international compounds as did the European colonial compounds. The Nisei were optimistic, fired up with the responsibility of being the first American-born generation, certain that they would eventually distinguish themselves and their American integrity from the Japanese of Japan, and confident that Americans would recognize them as fellow Americans.

The first Nisei writers did something the Chinese did not do. They adopted writers and works to emulate. Toshio Mori emulated William Saroyan and Sherwood Anderson. Toyo Suyemoto modeled her poetry on that of Katherine Mansfield. Writing with Saroyan, Anderson, or Mansfield in mind as a mentor did not hinder these writers' efforts to portray Japanese, non-Christian characters, including men, with accuracy, insight, delight, and not a hint of stereotype or identity crisis.

The white racists hated everything Chinese because of what they and the Christian missionaries perceived as a more immediate threat to white supremacy than China: tongs. Sax Rohmer's arch-Chinese villain, Fu Manchu, slinks out of the twenties from novel to novel, king of the tongs and bent on a genocidal revenge on the white race for the Opium War. Bret Harte's Ah-Sin is a tong. Ah-Sing, the unredeemed Chinese in Charlie Chan's Chinese American identity crisis, is a tong. To the generations of American-born, the tongs have become the symbol of all Chinese heathen evil. These same Chinese Americans believe in the stereotype of the Chinese immigrant as a sojourner who came with no intention of settling. They do not know that the evil the tongs represented to the law, the Christians, and the white racists was permanence. The tongs were permanent institutions. And they had built permanent institutions, including two opera houses, by 1883, when Tavenier and Frenzany wrote, drew scenes, and made notes of their visit to San Francisco's Chinatown for *Harper's Weekly*.

For the Chinese Americans, the tongs were something to avoid, reject, denounce, and fear in order to prove their Americanness. The novels of Charles Shepherd showed them how. Shepherd's "tribe of Ah-Sin" is the tongs.

Leong Gor Yun's *Chinatown Inside Out* (1936) hypes the new generation of Chinese Americans' efforts to wipe out the "Fu Manchu face" and describes the self-destructive Chinese American internal war of identities as a hopeless war of young Chinese American Christians against the tongs.

> For the first time in history a good many innovations are taking place in the lives of the Chinese in America. The industrialization of China is calling home all but the young for the same reasons that their coolie ancestors came here to help conquer the West. Statistics show in the last five years more Chinese have left this country than have come. The proportion is about one arrival to two departures. This combined with the severe immigration restrictions (which will be even more strict a decade hence) and the economic instability, means one thing: a rapid depopulation of Chinatown. The Golden Mountain has turned to lead; it is time to go home—even to till the rice-fields. If one is going to be poor, it is better to be poor at home.
>
> But besides depopulation an active force is at work tearing up the roots of Chinatown. It is not too soon to predict that the younger generation, though it may live unto itself in or outside a Chinatown, will not live under the might of the Benevolent Charitable Association and its supporting cast— the Tongs, family and territorial organizations. The young have been gaining voice in civic affairs; they have already defied the mighty with the Laundry Alliance, and there is every reason to believe that they will go on. Spiritually

and mentally they are as far from Americans. But the circle will never be complete: they will be Americanized, never American.

Pardee Lowe's autobiography, *Father and Glorious Descendent* (1943), is the story of a young Chinese American Christian who despises the tongs and the Japanese who had invaded China; he badgers his tongman father into converting to Christianity, and the story closes with his acceptance by whites in the form of his marriage to a white woman. Jade Snow Wong seeks refuge from Chinatown in the Chinatown YWCA in her autobiography, *Fifth Chinese Daughter* (1953), and she sharpens the misogynistic edge of the Christian stereotype by closing her book with a recollection of her father, an ordained Christian minister and sewing contractor, apologizing to her for all the Chinese ill treatment and humiliation of women:

> Then one afternoon, driving home, he sat beside her, lost in reverie. When they were parked in front of their house, he told her a story: "I told you once that your grandfather would have been glad to see that you have learned a handicraft. I can add now that he would have been happier to see that you have established your own business alone, even though you must begin modestly for lack of capital."

The narrative, unusual in nature and length, continued:

> When I first came to America, my cousin wrote me from China and asked me to return. That was before I can even tell you where you were. But I still have the carbon copy of the letter I wrote him in reply. I said, "You do not realize the shameful and degraded position into which the Chinese culture has pushed its women. Here in America, the Christian concept allows women their freedom and individuality. I wish my daughters to have this Christian opportunity. I am hoping someday I may be able to claim that by my stand I have washed away the former disgraces suffered by the women of our family."

Jade Snow Wong lovingly paints her father as an ordained minister of white supremacy, fulfilling white fantasies. Rampant Chinese misogyny is a bum rap, a product of white Christian imagination, not history. What is interesting about this passage is that it takes the form of the Christian Chinese autobiography, reduces it to a paragraph, and stylizes the essential clichés of the Charlie Chan good

Chinese American honorary white into a portrait of an emasculated, impotent, morally grotesque father. He's Gunga Din carrying the white man's rifle and leading the white charge against his own people and history.

Leong Gor Yun says the old heathens of the tongs, of the Fu Manchu face, will die, leaving the Christian, the progressive, the Americanized forever short of assimilation, as long as they survive as a race. Pardee Lowe kills the bad Chinaman and serves Christianity by converting his father; and, named after a California governor, a good Christian son of a Christian, enemy of the Japanese enemies of America, he's as honorary a white as he can be and marries white into white acceptance. Pardee Lowe, the Christian sociologist, condemns Chinatown for speaking a language that is neither the Chinese of China nor correct English. Rather than identify it as a language that is neither correct Chinese nor correct English, he declares it a perversion of language, no language at all, and one more indication of the imminent dying off of the tongs (old-time, non-Christian Chinese whose repulsiveness has tainted the white perception of the eager-to-be-accepted American-born, English-speaking, educated, and ambitious Chinese Americans coming of age. Even William Hoy, writing a history of the tongs for publication by the tong of tongs, the Chung Wah Wooey Goon, listed in the phone book as the Chinese Consolidated Benevolent Association, better known as the Chinese Six Companies, promises the extinction of the tongs, the takeover of Chinatown by the American-born Christian Chinese Americans, the extinction of Chinatown, racial extinction and assimilation. The conflict between the heathen and Christian, the Chinaman and the honorary white, the despicable pariah and the acceptable pariah, the either/or dual personality and identity crisis feeds and flashes on the self-hatred of the mutually repugnant halves of the self in a kind of perpetual motion.

All the Christian Chinese American autobiographies, like all Chinese and Japanese American social sciences, promise and demand Asian racial extinction. Jade Snow Wong is the first to stylistically accomplish it by rewriting Charles Shepherd's novel, *The Ways of Ah-Sin*, as the autobiography of his "choice soul" ripe for salvation, Ah Mae. All the men in *Fifth Chinese Daughter* are louts, like Harte's Ah-Sin and Charlie Chan's alter ego Ah-Sing—especially her father; even though he's an ordained minister and a friend of Donaldina Cameron's, he's unredeemably Chinese. Repentance only makes him pitiful and impotent. As Pop sinks, she soars, and vice versa. The Chinese culture in the book is a mix of Chinatown detail and Christian boogey-man fantasy. It's a rigged universe in Wong's Christian autobiography. Yellow men don't stand a chance. The all-evil, all-powerful tongs are replaced by all of Chinese manhood. Misogyny is the only unifying moral imperative in this Christian vision of Chinese civilization. All women are victims. America and Christianity represent freedom from Chinese civilization. In the Christian yin/yang of the dual personality/identity crisis, Chinese evil and perversity is male. And the Americanized honorary white Chinese American is female.

With Kingston's autobiographical *Woman Warrior*, we have given up even the pretense of reporting from the real world. Chinese culture is so cruel and she is so helpless against its overwhelming cruelty that she lives entirely in her imagination. It is an imagination informed only by the stereotype communicated to her through the Christian Chinese American autobiography. "Jade Snow Wong gave me strength," she has said many times.

The missionary novels, autobiographies, and biographies are forgotten. The social Darwinist works of science and fiction are forgotten. All that is left is the sensibility they produced, the racist mind from which comes the voice of Maxine Hong Kingston.

Helping her along, giving her a strong scientific, and entertaining, foundation are Chinese and Japanese sociology and Hollywood. By the 1970s, the racist stereotype—of despicable Chinese men propelling a sadistically misogynistic culture that had no moral right to survive, and of victimized Chinese women seeking rescue and moral superiority in American and Western values—had so completely displaced history that it didn't need to be argued; it didn't even need to be asserted. In Betty Lee Sung's 1972 rendering of the stereotype through scientific rhetoric, *Mountain of Gold*, the morality of the extinction of the yellow race in America is a foregone conclusion. The only Chinese are the Charlie Chan Americanized Chinese, and no one expects them to be offended by the contempt for the Chinese or the racial self-contempt blatantly displayed in passages such as:

> Much to their credit, the Chinese view prejudice with a very healthy attitude. They were never overly bitter. They have gone into occupations which command respect and which lessen conflict from competition. The Chinese are not concentrated entirely in one section of the country. More dispersion away from the vortexes of San Francisco and New York should be encouraged. This ought to be a long range goal of the Chinese because distribution reduces the degree of visibility.

Where Jade Snow Wong and Betty Lee Sung authenticate their Chinese-ness with recipes for the perfect Chinese rice and Chinese long beans, Kingston, with a stroke of white racist genius, attacks Chinese civilization, Confucianism itself, and where its life begins: the fairy tale. She, the victim of Chinese misogyny, says that "The Ballad of Mulan," the children's game chant, a fairy tale playing on the sounds of weaving, is the source of the misogynistic emphasis of Chinese ethics. She takes Fa Mulan, turns her into a champion of Chinese feminism and an inspiration to Chinese American girls to dump the Chinese race and make for white universality.

American publishers went crazy for Chinese women dumping on Chinese men. In the October 1978 issue of *Cosmopolitan*, Lily Chang wrote, in "What It's Like to Be a Chinese American Girl":

Once we have broken away from the restaurants of Chinatown, we prefer lovers distinguished by a freer, more emotionally flamboyant style. In short, Caucasians.

Joyce Howe oozed white fantasy onto the pages of the *Village Voice* in a little autobiographical essay, "A Nice Lo Fang Boy," in 1983:

Lisa, who's just joined a business association for Asian American professionals, in order to meet more Chinese men, is still confounded by them. She says, "I don't know how they see me, or what they really want. Do they want me to be an independent American woman? Or, do they want what their fathers wanted? Chinese American men haven't yet dealt with their own conflicts." When she confesses to not having found many Asian men sexually attractive, others nod.

Chinese American women are not going to deal with Chinese American men until the men resolve their own conflicts? This is an extreme expression of the identity crisis. See how it incapacitates the race. The women and men of this sensibility are not—and, by their reckoning, never were—a people.

The Association of Asian American/Pacific Performing Artists (AAPPA) was founded by Christian Chinese American activist, sociologist, and actress Beulah Quo, the movie Charlie Chan's Number One Son, Keye Luke, and Charlie Chan's Number Three Son of the black-and-white TV series, James Hong. The Hollywood yellows are the closest Asian American approximation of celebrities that Asian America has. But Asian America did not produce either the roles they played or the works they performed. The Hollywood yellows have become well known doing white work with a white message. The reality of the yellows is of no import, for as Keye Luke said, "This is white man's theater, not Oriental theater, and we have to cater to that." They look on themselves as the symbols, the measure of the kind and degree of white acceptance, absorption, and assimilation. They wooed Maxine Kingston and were instrumental in the failed attempts to bring *Woman Warrior* to the stage.

After flexing her ancient and spurious master's thesis in sociology, Beulah Quo served as historical consultant in the making of the two-part "China Doll" episode of ABC-TV's *How the West Was Won* (1979). She and other AAPPA members—among them Robert Ito, Keye Luke, James Hong, and Rosalind Chao—filled the large and small roles of Chinese characters.

Quo and the AAPPA encouraged producer John Mantley to exploit the stereotype of despicable men and victim women found in Kingston's *Woman Warrior* and Hwang's *FOB*," and to create a brand-new vicious stereotype for the Chinese to live down. Three times "Chinese" say—and three times "China Doll" shows—Chinese men selling Chinese women, naked and in chains, in the streets of San Francisco's Chinatown. Chinese men never sold Chinese women, either naked in the streets or in chains. Never. The most rabid and imaginative race-baiting whites out in the streets of the time never saw it; not even in their nightmare fiction of foul heathens wiping out the white race with all manner of moral perversions did they dream of Chinese men selling women chained up and naked in the streets. No. If, no, even then, they were dreaming of the coming of Chinese women like Ah Mae, the choice soul ripe for salvation: a Jade Snow Wong and a Maxine Hong Kingston to renounce Chinese men and Chinese civilization, and to sing the praises of white supremacy and the one God; a Beulah Quo to declare "China Doll" "the most accurate portrayal of Chinese American history in American film."

Actor Robert Ito—a "guest star" in "China Doll" and, because of his role in the NBC-TV series *Quincy*, one of the better known members of AAPPA—was not at all disturbed by the reviews. In fact, he invented a new stereotype; he defended the departure from fact as being necessary to depict the "fact" that "there were abuses of women." He unabashedly referred to a racial stereotype to defend racial stereotyping, and nobody in the audience of Asian Americans flinched. Portraying Chinese culture as despicable, bashing the men, pitying and freeing the women, have become ends in themselves. To white America, we are nothing more than actors playing the parts of Chinese in a Charlie Chan movie. That's how far the Christian Chinese American autobiography and the stereotype have brought us from the real.

5

Maxine Hong Kingston has defended her revision of Chinese history, culture, and childhood literature and myth by restating the white racist stereotype. In a 1989 radio interview with Frank Abe on Seattle all-news station KIRO, she characterized the first Chinese Americans as being incredibly stupid and forgetful:

> They forgot a lot of the myths. Many changed myths because they had new adventures. Many changed myths to explain their new situations they were having.

Myths are, by nature, immutable and unchanging because they are deeply ingrained in the cultural memory, or they are not myths. New experience breeds new history, new art, and new fiction. The new experience of the Anglo-Saxon in America did not result in forgetting and confusing Homer with Joan of Arc but in new stories, informed by ethics symbolized by heroes and actions of Homer's epics and Greek, Roman, Judaic, and Christian myth. Her assertion—that the Chinese who settled and established Chinese America were any less literate; had an ethical intelligence any less informed by any less effective myths, any less explored, challenged, and deepened into any less of a living language by any less of a literature, theater, poetry, painting, from the folk up to on high—is corroborated only by belief in the Christian social Darwinist stereotype.

From Yung Wing's and Leong Gor Yun's in 1909 and 1936 to Pardee Lowe's in the forties, the Christian autobiographies are, uncomfortably, forced to make some acknowledgment to the real world of Chinese America, Chinatown, and tongs. Beginning with the work of Jade Snow Wong and Maxine Hong Kingston, we are free of the real world and are in pure white dreamland, where the real has no existence, no presence. The destruction of Chinese history, culture, and literature in a single stroke is more true than the real. The achievement of that truth in literature is, by Kingston's estimation, her invention, as she told Frank Abe:

> And I think to write true biography means you have to tell people's dreams. You have to tell what they imagine. You have to tell their vision. And, in that sense, I think I have developed a new way of telling a life story.

Since the tongs, the catch-all portmanteau boogah-boogahs of the Chinatown missionary autobiographers and social Darwinist fictioners, were permanent institutions, they gave the lie to the stereotype of

Chinese sojourners. Their corporate bylaws, filed with the California state attorney-general, appear in a document of a permanent institution. A reading of these bylaws proves that the Chinese settlers did not forget the myths Kingston has said they forgot.

One of the powerful Chinatown groups loosely called "tongs" is the Lung Kong Tin Yee Association. The Lung Kong is an alliance of four families: the Lau, the Kwan, the Chang, and the Chew families joined as one for fun and fighting. Article 1 of the bylaws reads like bylaws but, in form and content, it is pure heroic tradition, right out of Lo Kuan Chung's *The Romance of the Three Kingdoms*:

LUNG KONG TIN YEE ASSOCIATION OF U.S.A.
BYLAWS
ARTICLE 1. PURPOSE

Section 1. The name of this association shall be Lung Kong Tin Yee Association of U.S.A. (hereinafter abbreviated to be called The Association).

Section 2. The Association abides by the tradition of the "Confraternity at The Peach Garden" and the "Old City Meeting" of the four famous ancestors of Lew, Quan, Chang and Chew; and abides by Emperor Lew Pei's "Rule of Conduct." The objects and purpose being that the heritage of loyalty, righteousness, fraternity and solidarity of the Four Family Names shall enhance the spirit of cooperation of the families and promote general welfare.

Section 3. The Association is organized in accordance with the laws of the country, and is registered as a nonprofit organization.

Section 4. The principal office of The Association is located at 924 Grant Avenue, San Francisco, California, U.S.A.

Section 5. The flag of The Association is rectangular in shape, white in color with red edges and the Chinese characters of "Lung Kong Tin Yee Association of U.S.A." in black.

The Lung Kong Tin Yee Association, like all tongs, appeared in China only after it had been established in America. Tongs themselves are examples of the new art born of new experiences and informed by the ethics of the heroic tradition in Asian childhood literature and myth. The four families that make up the Lung Kong, imaginary descendants of the three heroes from three different walks of life, become blood brothers by swearing an oath in Chang

Fay's peach garden. The oath in the peach garden is the most famous scene in the most popular novel in Chinese history, *The Romance of the Three Kingdoms.*

To identify themselves with the most common and universal ethical values that every Chinese used to meet and to translate new experience into action, the tongs modeled themselves on the brotherhood of the peach garden oath and the heroic tradition. The Lung Kong, appealing for new members, used to woo them into their ranks with a little booklet titled *A Concise History of Lung Kong and the Genealogical Origin of the Four Families.* The opening paragraphs are clear and luridly appealing to readers who thrill to the heroes and histories of the best-known book of childhood:

A Concise History of Lung Kong and the Genealogical Origin of the Four Families

One of the most stirring periods of the Chinese people—a time of brave men, brutal warfare and court intrigue, woven in the tapestry of Chinese history as the era of the Three Kingdoms—is preserved for posterity by the Lung Kong Association.

Lung Kong is a confraternity of the members of the Four Families of the surnames of Lew, Quan, Chang and Chew. Among the Chinese people this tale, told countless thousands upon thousands of times, is a series of historic facts of four men whose spirit, sense of sacrifice for the people and their bravery made them bigger than life, and therefore legendary.

The legend began nearly two thousand years ago, in the era of the Three Kingdoms (220–280 A.D.). The reign of Emperor Sien, the Eastern Han dynasty, was in chaos. Disobedience, lawlessness and cunning plots of myriad warlords made for sufferings by the common people. Three patriots, namely Lew Pei (Yuen Tek), an uncle of the Emperor, Quan Yu (Yuen Cheung) and Chang Fei (Yee Tak) met at the latter's mansion, in the peach garden. They made a vow to be adopted, or blood brothers. To dedicate their lives together to achieve their goals. To help the country and the people.

Symbolically to the Chinese peach blossoms signify longevity. Their vows are carved in the longevity of history as "The confraternity at the Peach Garden."

Later the trio joined with Chew Yuen (Tse Lung) at Kucheng, the Old City, and finalized the fraternity and origins of the famous Four Families of Lew, Quan, Chang and Chew.

Lung Kong Temple

Throughout the seventeen centuries following their rites as blood brothers, the fame and good deeds of the Four Families heroes became a part of Chinese historic legend.

In the early period of the Ching Dynasty (1644–1911 A.D.) the principles of the Four Families were challenged again in an incident which resulted in the now official designation of the Lung Kong Associations. A Lew family at the village called Chiao Boh, Dan Shui Mountain area of Hoi Ping, province of Kwangtung owned a piece of land shaped in the contours of a dragon. A hill rose in the middle of this area. It resembled the head of a dragon pointed toward heaven. This phenomenon was interpreted as being caused by a supernatural force, and therefore, suspicious. Naturally, the hill was called Lung Kong, or the Dragon Hill.

At that time, the Lew family was weak, and its powerful neighbors coveted the area of the auspicious Dragon Hill. The Lew family solicited the help of the members of the Four Families to build a temple on the top of the Hill. Here statues of the four legendary heroes Lew Pei (Emperor Chew Lit), Quan Yu (Marquis Han Shou Ting), Chang Fei (Marquis Woon), Chew Yuen (Marquis Shun Ping) and of Kung Ming were consecrated and worshipped.

This event took place in the year 1661, the first year of Emperor Kang Hsi's reign. The sacred edifice was called Lung Kong Old Temple. This concerted Four Families action saved Dragon Hill from the greedy powerful neighbors.

The Lung Kong is obviously making its pitch to new members by using what is unforgettable to anyone who was a Chinese child, the stuff of pop cults, comic books, and personal honor.

A Beginning in America

From China, one of the oldest of civilizations, beginning in 1848 there came to young America an outpouring of Chinese who sought to better their personal fortunes, as men everywhere seek to do. Their first port of entry was San Francisco, which eventually became the capital City of Chinese in America. The Gold Rush and then the building of the transcontinental railroad swelled the Chinese population. By 1851, with a Chinese population of 12,000 in the city, a need was felt for some type of social organization for mutual help and protection, and thus was born the first formal Chinese association.

A few years later, the elders of the Four Families erected a Lung Kong Temple at Brooklyn Alley, off Sacramento Street, traditionally known by the Chincse themselves as The Street of the Men of Tang. This was the year 1876 during the reign of Emperor Kwong Shui. Spiritually it duplicated the original Dragon Hill temple, for here too were consecrated statues of the Four Ancestors of the Four Families.

While serving the ritual and spiritual needs of the members of the Four Families, the Lung Kong Temple in the United States functioned also as a fraternal organization. As did the others already created by other groups, Lung Kong fulfilled the social welfare needs of its people. From this period through World War II, the Chinese in America were subject to highly unreasonable legal restrictions, social pressures, an absence of civil rights and unequal employment opportunities. In the oppressive atmosphere of those times they had to turn to themselves. They had to care for themselves. These conditions fostered the social structures of the family associations. The district associations. These associations, like the Four Families, cared for their own sick, fed and housed their own unfortunate, buried their own dead.

They banded to fight discriminatory legislation against the Chinese. They arbitrated in legal questions. All of these organizations, in spirit and practice, were akin to the pattern of the Four Families' blood brothers in helping each other and the Chinese people.

Kingston asserts her technique and her biased Christian autobiographer's intelligence informed only by autobiography, dreaming up the imaginings and visions of the immigrants, and duplicating immigrants' mental processes. She speaks the language of the Chinese subconscious: no.

Freud found the keys to the subconscious and the dreams of Western man in Greek myth. For the literary critics of the world, he identified certain forms and certain themes, described their translation into other literature, poetry, and language of dreams, and traced them to their origins. The flow of the Western subconscious, from myth through literature, contributes to the place of books in the Western canon of literature.

The Chinese do not need a Freud to find the books and myths containing the keys to the most deeply rooted, most fully grown Chinese subconscious. The Chinese people—in the Chinese marketplaces, toys, comic books, popular household curio shop and restaurant art and design—have already set the canon, kept it, taught it, and used it. While every dynasty since the Ming—along with the Cultural Revolution and the theocracy of Indonesia—banned it and drove it underground, the Chinese people, no matter how dangerous it was to tell these stories, made sure their children heard the three classics of the heroic tradition: Lo Kuan Chung's *Romance of the Three Kingdoms*; Shi Na'an's *The Water Margin* (*Outlaws of the Marsh*); and Wu Cheng En's *Journey to the West* (*Monkey*).

In the autobiographies of Han Suyin and Sui Sin Far (Edith Eaton), and in the fiction of Diana Chang, Louis Chu, and Timothy Mo, the Chinese of China and Hong Kong, the Chinese immigrants in America and England, would think it strange for a Chinese from any part of the world not to know the heroic tradition (i.e., Ssu-ma Ch'ien; the strategy of Sun Tzu and Wu Chi; that life is war and all behavior is tactics and strategy).

Likewise, the Issei—Japanese first-generation settlers (immigrants)—whom Kafu Nagai (a rich playboy sojourner, writing in admiration of and influenced by Zola) portrays in his Seattle and Tacoma stories, *Amerika Monogatari*, and the Issei in Kazuo Miyamoto's *Hawaii: End of the Rainbow* and John Okada's *No-No Boy* would think it strange to find a Japanese not familiar with *Three Kingdoms, Water Margin*, and *Monkey*, as well as their own evolution of the forms of the heroic tradition, *Momotaro* (Peach Boy) and *Chushingura* (The Loyal Forty-seven Ronin), and the works of strategy by Sun Tzu and Wu Chi, in which all life is war and all behavior is tactics and strategy. The lessons of fairy tales like "Fox and the Tiger" and *Three Kingdoms* are perhaps easier for Western readers to swallow when they recognize that the lesson of the Brer Rabbit stories, such as "The Tar Baby," which America learned from the Gullah people of the Carolina Sea Islands, is that life is war and all behavior is strategy and tactics.

But before understanding these books, or before understanding the fairy tales of a Chinese childhood, we need to understand that obvious and disturbing difference between Judeo-Christendom and Confucianism that the pope had to explain when Marco Polo showed up with proof that there was some kind of advanced civilization way out there.

The differences between Western and Asian civilization are real, sharply defined, profound, and easily stated: Western civilization is founded on religion. Asian civilization—Confuciandom—is founded on history. Confucius was not a prophet. He was not religious. He was a historian, a strategist, a warrior. His basic thought was packed into two ideas that still speak from the heart of all Asian law, art, literature, and psychology. Asian children absorb these ideas early in the language, in lullaby and fairy tale. The first is the Confucian ethic of private revenge. The second is the ethic of popular revenge against the corrupt state, or the Confucian mandate of heaven.

Ssu-ma Ch'ien, the grand historian of the Han, gave the ethic of private revenge and the mandate of heaven literary form. He so completely absorbed the mandate of heaven in his writing that every sentence he wrote contains the kingdoms rising and falling, the nations coming and going of the mandate. He writes of his father, Ssu-ma T'an, the grand historian, passing the responsibility on to his son, from his deathbed. In one of many inevitably interconnected passages, Ssu-ma Ch'ien, rolling the syntax of the mandate of heaven, defines filial piety, personal achievement, art, literature, and Confucius all in the shape of the mandate of heaven:

> Now filial piety begins with the serving of your parents; next you must serve your sovereign; and finally you must make something of yourself, that your name may go down through the ages to the glory of your father and mother. This is the most important part of filial piety. . . . After the reigns of Yu and Li the way of the ancient kings fell into disuse and rites and music declined. Confucius revived the old ways and restored what had been abandoned, expounding the *Odes* and *History* and making *Spring and Autumn Annals*. From that time until today men of learning have taken these as their models.

The Book of Spring and Autumn Annals is a work of impressionistic Chinese prehistory and the fifth book of the Confucian five classics. The first four Confucian classics are *The Book of History; The Book of Rites; the Book of Changes*; and *The Book of Odes*. These are all books of history and what today would be called anthropology. The five classics are not books of dogma. The sum and ultimate art of Confucius' knowledge and wisdom, *The Analects*, is not a book of dogma or formula for moral improvement and founding a perpetual state. And, though it is Confucius' most personal and creative work, it is not an essay, not a novel, and not an autobiography. It is a "set."

As a form, the set expresses the civilization founded in history, the ethic of life that is war, and the belief that all men and women are born soldiers. We are born to fight to maintain our personal integrity. All art is martial art. Writing is fighting. In Western civilization, which is founded on religion, the individual trains himself to better express faith, belief, and submission to a higher moral authority, to overcome reality with dreams, and to defy the effects of knowledge with belief. The individual in the Asian moral universe trains to fight. Living is fighting. Life is war. The Western

believer sums up his life in the form that expresses the religious
content of the civilization, the autobiography, a combination of
confession and testimony that follows the rise, fall, and redemption
of the heroes of religious literature and its literary form, tragedy.

The fighter expresses his wisdom and essence in a set. One learns
tai chi, kung fu, and martial arts by memorizing a set of poses,
stances, and movement in a specific order and rhythm. Then one
recites the moves of the set. In the advanced stages of recital, one
begins to free-associate with the moves and poses of the set. One's
life and knowledge are in conversation with the set and even inform
the set. One then discovers how to use this move and that pose to
disarm an attacker in a fight. When the discoveries come during
every recital and with every move, one has moved from recital to
internalization. One is no longer reciting the set from memory; the
set is now an animal in one's instinct. When the situation arises, the
move will be there, without one's thought.

The way Chinese learn martial arts is the way Chinese learn
everything: memorization, recitation, and internalization. It's called
"the internal process." The master of a martial arts school has his
own sets to teach, besides the classics. His own style was probably
developed as a counter to the classics. Thus, to merely understand
and to be properly awestruck by the big picture of Confucius'
wisdom and art in *The Analects*, the Chinese say, one has to memorize *The Analects* in childhood and to recite them every day. The
discoveries of meaning are so profound and so precisely phrased
that they can be made only at certain stages in one's life, only after
one has experienced so much life, and, sometimes, not before one
has experienced so much life. Every day throughout your adult life,
a verse of Confucius will light up your mind and make sense of
everything that's happened since the day you were born. They say
that if one lives to a ripe old age, say forty-eight and beyond, *The
Analects* really turn on.

But the days when every Chinese learned to read *The Analects*
and the five Confucian classics are gone. Those who did memorize
The Analects as children, and then forgot them, find themselves
attracted to Confucius in their fifties. Most Chinese have made brief
passes at the five books, gone tossing with *The Book of Changes*,
read the first chapters of *The Book of History* in school, read a few
poems out of *The Book of Odes*, and left *The Book of Rites* to the
family's chief of protocol.

Confucius' main line into the depths of young Asian brains is the
fairy tale and the heroic tradition of *The Romance of Three Kingdoms*, *Water Margin*, and *Journey to the West*. The heroic tradition
extends to Japan and includes *Chushingura*. *Three Kingdoms, Water*

Margin, Monkey, and *Chushingura* all cite, quote, and dramatize verses from Sun Tzu's *The Art of War*, and Wu Chi's *The Art of War*. Sun Tzu and Wu Chi's books are two different scts designed to train one's instinct to live life as war and to not sell out.

Lo Kuan Chung's *The Romance of the Three Kingdoms* explores the nature of the ethic of private revenge on a grand "mandate of heaven" scale: The later Han Dynasty has run out of virtue and is falling into chaos. The corrupt and brilliant minister T'sao T'sao has gathered the power of the empire for himself and is well on his way to declaring an end to the Han and to making himself emperor of the Wei. The novel opens with the weakling emperor of the Han calling for fighters to band together and save China. Lu Bei (Liu Pei) (Lau or Lowe, in Cantonese) is a sandal maker and an heir to the throne of the Han. He sighs upon reading the emperor's call to arms. Lu has skin as fine and white as porcelain. His color is imperial yellow. Chang Fay (Fei), a dark-skinned, bristly-bearded, and pop-eyed landowner with the means to stock, arm, and maintain a small army, if he can find the right leader, hears Lu's sigh. They retire to a tavern for warm wine and talk of saving China. The light shining through the tavern door is blocked out by an eight-foot-tall red-faced, bearded man with fierce eyes, wearing green. This is Kuan Yu. He is a fugitive, wanted for murdering a county official. A farmer's daughter had begged Kuan to save her from the corrupt official who was forcing himself on her. He killed the official and, in crossing the mountains, changed his appearance and his name (to Kuan) to get past the border guards on the lookout for him. Inside the tavern he booms out, "Innkeeper! Bring wine and be quick about it! I have to get to town, join the army, and save China!"

The dark and bristly Chang Fay invites Lu and Kuan to his estate, where they might sit in his peach garden and enjoy the peach trees in bloom. In Chang's peach garden the three men from three different walks of life, and three different parts of China, swear an oath of brotherhood:

> We three, Liu Pai, Kuan Yu, and Chang Fei, though of different families, swear brotherhood, and promise mutual help to one end. We will rescue each other from difficulty and aid each other in danger. We swear to serve the state and save the people. We were not born on the same day, but we hope to die on the same day. May all seeing heaven and the abundant earth read our hearts, and if one of us turn away from righteousness or forget this oath, may heaven and earth and man strike him down.

The Chinese first-person pronouns that the three brothers speak and write—the Chinese *I*, *me*, and *we*—are all made of two crossed battle-axes. The ancient form of that character looks like a coat of arms. Like every coat of arms, the Chinese *I* means "I am the law." This is the first-person pronoun of the language of "life is war, and we are all born soldiers." Unlike the personal pronoun *I* in the languages of the West, the Chinese *I*, *me*, and *we* do not descend from the mysterious syllables *Yahweh* and do not mean "praise God." The Chinese *I* is not an act of submission to a higher authority but an assertion of the Confucian ethic of private revenge.

The brotherhood of the peach garden is a martial alliance of individual fighters. What counts in the oath is their promise to each other, to right any wrong done to a brother and to avenge a brother's death. In the course of the novel, they are joined by a genius of military strategy and statecraft, Kungming; later, Chu Geelung (the Chu of the Four Families—Lau, Kwan, Chang, and Chu) becomes like a brother to Lu Bei, the heir to the throne of the Han. The genius of Kungming's strategy regains the capital city for Lu Bei and the three brothers seem to have saved China. Kuan Yu, the red-faced and fierce-eyed, is killed in an ambush in the south. By the oath in the peach garden, Lu Bei is bound to avenge his brother's death. Kungming pleads with Lu Bei to stay in the capital, for to leave now would be to surrender it to T'sao T'sao and his forces, and would mean a continuation, rather than an end, of the war. Chang Fay appears with his armies ready to march to avenge Kuan Yu's death. Lu Bei must honor the oath of the peach garden. He leaves the capital, loses China, and, because the war goes on so long, neither Lu nor Chang lives to see its end. But the brothers of the oath of the peach garden kept their word to each other and, the Chinese say, that's what makes the Chinese great.

The brotherhood of the oath of the peach garden became the model for every subsequent brotherhood, club, and fighting and police force above ground, and for criminal gangs and Triad societies underground. And, as we have seen, the brotherhood of the oath of the peach garden is the model for the alliances of individuals in Chinese American tongs.

Kuan Yu is the most popular character from *Three Kingdoms*, even though he is not the main character. Popular culture quickly made the popular character in history, opera, and literature the god of war, plunder, and literature. He is the protector of high executioners, gamblers, and all entrepreneurs. He is the embodiment of impeccable, incorruptible personal integrity, and revenge. To the Buddhists, he is the Buddha Who Defends the Realm. To the Taoists, he is the Equal of the Eastern Peak and the Guardian of all borders. All clubs, groups, and fraternities of all kinds, from the Hong Kong Criminal Investigations Division to kung fu clubs and Chinatown gangs, claim and display Kuan Yu, more familiarly known as Kwan Kung (Old Man Kwan, or Grandfather Kwan) as their protector.

Kwan Kung, like the fairy-tale hero Nezha, the Lotus Boy, was an abused child who, betrayed by his parents, ran away from home without a farewell, never giving them another thought. Still, he is the exemplar of the universal man, a physically and morally self-sufficient soldier who is a pure ethic of private revenge. The most popular way of expressing the ethic of private revenge is a quote, reputedly from Confucius: "My father's enemy shall not live under the same sky with me." In *Three Kingdoms*, Kwan Kung's story heroically displays all the virtues of the talented total warrior; and it also shows the limits of individual talent.

Shi Na'am's *Water Margin* is popularly known as the sequel to *Three Kingdoms*. It explores the collective form of the ethic of private revenge, "the mandate of heaven." As *Three Kingdoms* follows the progress of an alliance of individuals into gangs, *Water Margin* follows the formation of an alliance of 108 outlaw gang chiefs and their gangs inside an impenetrable marsh and swampland about three hundred miles in circumference. This is the Water Margin, properly known as Liangshan Marsh.

Three Kingdoms explores the ethic of private revenge, the individual-as-soldier's constant battle to maintain personal integrity. All warfare is based on deception, Sun Tzu teaches, and in *Three Kingdoms* the three brothers of the oath of the peach garden learn, as Monkey learns in the childhood Havoc in Heaven chapters of *Journey to the West*, that the first skill to be mastered, the essential skill, is bullshit detection, the recognition of the difference between the real and the fake. As an adult, Monkey, on his mission, like the brothers of the oath in the peach garden, makes the difference between the real and the fake the difference between giving and taking life and death. As a mischievous adolescent, Monkey exposes the pomp and emptiness of all dogmas, all beliefs, all bureaucracies, all governments, before taking on the universe, as the "Equal of the Emperor of Heaven." Monkey is, in spirit and kind, not a parody or satire of the 108 outlaws of *Water Margin*, but an extension and expression of them.

Water Margin explores the idea of the mandate of heaven, or the Confucian idea of the oppressed people rebelling and forming a huge alliance to avenge themselves against the corrupt state. Thus another state, another dynasty comes into being to be corrupted by the power of ruling, and the mandate of heaven is cranked up for another unwinding of kingdom's rise and fall. Nations come and go. A harsh tale. One hundred and eight good men are outlawed by corrupt officials and led by Song Jiang (Soong Gong, in Cantonese) nicknamed "Timely Rain" (as in the kind of rain that breaks the drought and saves the crops), the outlaws combine their individual skills to turn a self-sufficient state maintained by the popular will of the five hundred thousand people inside the stronghold city walls and the countless people outside the marsh.

At first blush, heroes embodying character traits born of life is war and private revenge, and fairy tales that teach all behavior is tactics and strategy, all relationships are martial, might strike the exclusively Western mind as abhorrent and amoral. Newton's natural laws of motion challenged the Christian notion that faith is the basis of all morality. There had to be natural laws of morality, as objectively observable as Newton's natural laws of motion. The moral sense school thinkers John Locke, Francis Hutcheson, and David Hume informs Thomas Jefferson's paraphrasing of the Confucian mandate of heaven in the *Declaration of Independence of the United States of America:*

> We hold these truths to be self-evident, that all men are created equal, that they are endowed by their creator with certain unalienable rights, that among these are life, liberty, and the pursuit of happiness—that to secure these rights, governments are instituted among men, deriving their just powers from the consent of the governed; that whenever any form of government becomes destructive of these ends, it is the right of the people to alter or to abolish it, and to institute new government, laying its foundation on such principles, and organizing its powers in such form, as to them shall seem most likely to effect their safety and happiness.

Three Kingdoms, Water Margin, and *Monkey* are the staples of Asian childhoods from Korea to Japan, to China, Vietnam, Laos, Thailand, and Cambodia. Three military academies teach *Three Kingdoms* as a manual of military strategy. And they call *Water Margin* the sequel because it can be seen as a study in military administration and statecraft:

It is Song Dynasty, China. Every agency and bureaucracy in government has turned corrupt. The emperor is in thrall with corrupt eunuchs. The good and honest fighters are, one by one, falsely condemned for crimes they didn't commit and driven to turn outlaw. Of the 108 heroes of *Water Margin*, Sagacious Lu, the drunken major in the Northern Guards who beat a corrupt butcher-official, the Lord of the West, to death and turned Buddhist monk to establish an alibi; Tiger Killer Wu Song; Li Kooey, the Black Whirlwind; and the extraordinarily ordinary and middle-class Lin Chong, the Panther Head, have been childhood favorites for centuries now. They are the stuff of calendar and ceramic art, comic books, dolls, hand toys, and trading cards.

The time and situation in the story of the 108 outlaws of the *Water Margin* remind the Western reader of Robin Hood. The usurper, Prince John, is turning good men into outlaws who rally around Robin Hood and hide out in Sherwood Forest. All of the 108 outlaws have some extraordinary talent with a particular weapon. Tiger Killer, Wu Song, kills a tiger with three punches and three kicks, while feeling weak with a bad cold. His signature weapon is a singing dagger. The Black Whirlwind carries a thirty-pound battle-ax in each hand and, even to his fellow outlaws of the gallant fraternity, he is as low as you can go as a human being. He is stupid, brutal, impulsive, and bungling; but he is absolutely loyal to the good guys, and insanely protective of the leader of the outlaws, Song Jiang.

Song Jiang is not that great with any weapon. He can teach the fundamentals of the staff and spear, the bow and arrow, and the sword, but is no whiz at any of them. Before he turned outlaw, he was a lowly clerk in the county clerk's office. What is his signature fighting skill? What made Song Jiang the unanimous choice for leader? Administration. He recognized talent without jealousy and knew how best to use it strategically.

The 108 have all the professional, administrative, and technical skills necessary to feed, clothe, house, transport, and service a self-sufficient state. Each of the outlaws experiences a moment of "a hero recognizing a hero, a good man knowing a good man," at the instant of meeting, whereupon each individually swears an oath of brotherhood to the other, quoting the oath in the peach garden. Then comes the day inside the stronghold; Song Jiang calls the 108 chiefs together, in Fraternity Hall, to swear an oath of brotherhood. When the wars between criminal tongs threatened to bring Chinatown, San Francisco, under control of the state militia or police, a group of powerful establishment tongs and district and family associations formed an alliance to crush the criminal tongs and to maintain Chinatown as a stronghold of the culture of the heroic tradition. As the tongs are modeled on the brotherhood of the oath in the peach garden, in *Three Kingdoms*, the alliance of alliances—the Chung Wah Wooey Goon Chinese Consolidated Benevolent Association in San Francisco—was modeled on the oath of brotherhood of the 108 outlaw chiefs in *Water Margin*.

That the tongs and the Chung Wah remain powerful, vibrant, and popular, in spite of a century of Christians promising their extinction, is an indication that the Chinese immigrants and American-born generations did not reject or forget Chinese myth in the face of new experience and in the process of making new history and language.

Chinese American writing, in Chinese and in English, is another indication that the Chinese were as humanly intelligent and proud as any other cultured people in their ability to comprehend their new experience in terms of the myth and literature they had brought with them. The nineteenth-century Chinese who left corrupt, oppressive Manchu Dynasty China for America were blood and spiritual kin to the brothers of the oath in the peach garden, and to the 108 good and talented men, wrongfully outlawed and exiled by foreigners on the throne who were trying to destroy the Chinese with imperial law. That story was told 108 times in *Water Margin*. And that was what they found in America.

To cope with the myriad hidden and overt anti-Chinese laws, Christian prejudices, and American social customs, and a cast of American character types that might confound their progress, Wong Sam and Assistants summed up the wisdom of their experience in *An English-Chinese Phrase Book*, together with the *Vocabulary of Trade, Law, Etc.* and *A Complete List of Wells, Fargo & Co's. Offices in California, Nevada, Etc.* The "compilers," Wong Sam and Assistants, said this was a phrase book, a book of sets. It is also in the same literary form as Confucius' *The Analects*.

Wong Sam's sets are to be memorized, one by one. Each has its own intelligence, its own style and purpose, like a Monkey set and a White Crane set in kung fu; each set contains a unique animal. Recite the set, free-associate with the set, internalize the set, and Wong Sam's seemingly randomly selected phrases become a part of your instinct; then, say, suddenly, you're in a situation: Your Christian-convert boss is telling the cops why he's not paying you the wages he owes you. Instantly, without a thought, without a flash, phrases from this part of the set pop out of your mouth in English or, if you are a white, clerking in a Chinese-owned store (a definite possibility in certain towns), in Cantonese; and you hear, or you say:

I keep back a week's wages in order to secure his stay.

Please give me, now, that portion of my wages which you have withheld from me.

Christ is our mediator.

I am taller than he.

There is not a store which has not an interpreter—one who can speak the English language.

I asked them if they ever knew a Chinese store in San Francisco without one or more who could speak English.

I asked them if they knew of a store without one or more who *could* speak English.

Mr. Jones can do better than he.

Wong Sam glistens and sings with the gestures and re-creations of the heroic tradition. One translation of *Wong Sam* is "Yellow Robe." Lu Bei, the sandal maker who would be emperor, the first brother of the brotherhood of the oath in the peach garden, wears the yellow robe. Second brother Kwan Kung and third brother Chang Fay are assistants to Lu's bid for the throne. However, one need not translate the compiler's name to appreciate the art Wong Sam has made of the heroic tradition. The title itself is pure strategy and tactics, recalling the greatest strategist, Sun Tzu, "the Grandson," and Song Jiang, the clerk who would become leader of the 108 allied gangs.

He was the leader because he was not jealous of talent; he recognized talent, appreciated it, and knew how to use it with other talents to run the stronghold and wage war. His opinion of talent was respected because he knew the stories of each of the gallant fraternity and was familiar with the whole territory. He knew every stronghold and hideout, every gang and fighter and their vital statistics and reputation. His knowing where all the outlaw gangs were, in relation to each other on the map, made it easy for him to call them to the alliance in the Water Margin when the time came to ally against the imperial armies and navies of the Song. By the titles of his compilations, Wong Sam was telling the Chinese that these sets would train their instinct to deal with English and with "Trade" and "Law, Etc." The *Complete List of Wells, Fargo & Co.'s Offices* told the Chinese where every Chinatown west of the Mississippi was, and how to get there, for wherever there was a Wells, Fargo office, there was a Chinatown. The Chinese traveled from Chinatown to Chinatown via Wells, Fargo, and gave the company considerable business. Wells, Fargo was happy to publish and distribute Wong Sam to white and Chinese businessmen free.

Wong Sam's canny awareness of the laws affecting the Chinese is apparent in the series of phrases cited above that play the changes on the fact that English-speaking clerks translate in every Chinese store. In another sequence of phrases, Wong Sam plays with the ethics of the heroic tradition, and U.S. immigration law and *history*; in a very stylish way, he shows he knows more about the United States than the U.S. citizens know about the Chinese settling among them.

Wong Sam's 1875 *Phrase Book* was not obscure or inaccessible to the Chinese who passed through any one of the 382 Chinatowns listed. Chinese stores offered it, as did the contemporary equivalent of the magazine rack at the local bus station. The *Phrase Book* was revised and enlarged in 1878 and again in the 1880s.

The heroic tradition, and particularly *Water Margin*, informed the Chinese perception of being detained and interrogated with undisguised hostility on Angel Island, in sight of San Francisco. The poetry and graffiti they carved on the walls of the detention center recall the ordinary man of ordinary middle-class ambitions, wrongfully condemned to death by his corrupt commandant and hiding out at an inn on the edge of the Water Margin, where he hoped to meet gallant outlaws, like himself, and be invited to join them in their stronghold. On the wall, he has written a poem, the likes of which are on the walls of Angel Island. Even in a comic-book rendering of the scene, Angel Island Immigration Center's likeness to the inn on the edge of the marsh, in sight of the Golden Shores, and the outlaw stronghold's likeness to Chinatown, San Francisco, is not only obvious but exuberant:

Lin Chong's Revenge

The wine warms and depresses him. "When I was Master of Arms in the Eastern Capital I drank in every inn and tavern and had a few laughs. Who would have thought that *chok* Gao Qui would have brought me to this. The golden imprint on my face. Exile. I can't go home. No place is safe for me. I'm alone," he says to himself.

"Alone." He calls for brush-pen and ink. He's drunk and down and so acts like a down drunk and spills his emotions in poetry on the whitewashed wall.*

A tall man in fur hat, sable-lined jacket and deerskin boots turns from watching the snow to watch Lin Chong ink his brush and address the blank absorbent wall. The man in the hat has

---

*The raw expression of pure emotion in poetry is not a literary art in old Confuciandom. It's graffiti and a game of tactics and strategy that plays the shape and meaning of the intended poem against wet black ink and a whitewashed wall that absorbs ink and water like a paper towel. Every night the wall of poetry is whitewashed for the next day's weepy drunks.

cheekbones like clenched fists and wears a moustache and goatee.

Lin's hand is fast and sure. The strokes flow. The words stand. He throws the pen down and drinks. The words say:

> *Justice is his love; loyalty his glory,*
> *Everyone knows his fame;*
> *Everywhere they tell Lin Chong's story,*
> *The man of deeds: Lin Chong.*
>
> *Now he drifts like a reed on a boiling sea,*
> *Swirling from suffering to suffering,*
> *But when this hero takes the lead*
> *Even Mount Tai will bow at his name.*

The tall man in the sable-lined robe grabs Lin Chong by his belt and jerks him back off his stool before he can reach his spear. "You've got the wrong man!" Lin Chong says. "My name is Zhang."

The man laughs. "Ah bunk! You wrote your name on the wall, Lin Chong. You've got the golden imprint on your face. I know who you are!"

"So you're going to turn me in and collect!"

"Ha ha ha. Why should I turn you in? I admire your guts!" The tall man asks Lin to join him in a room open to a view of the lake and trees. "You bloody up and burn down half of Cangzhou, get three thousand strings of cash on your head and walk in here and write your name on the wall! Brave! Very brave, Panther Head. But I hear you're looking for a boat to take you to Liangshan Marsh. Don't you know that's a place of robbers and thieves who make their living plundering the people?"

"Where else can I go? The whole honest world officially made an outlaw of me. I have a letter of introduction to the leaders, and hope to join the gang in their stronghold."

"Perhaps the letter is by the Little Whirlwind Chai Jin . . ." the tall man says.

"How did you know? Ah, you're one of them! Of course! I have eyes but do not see Mount Tai!" Lin Chong says and covers his fighting hand in salute and bows. "Please tell me your name."

The tall man salutes respectfully and says, "This humble person is the lookout for Chieftain Wang. I am Zhu Gui, originally from Yishui County in Yizhou Prefecture. Among the fraternity I am known as the Dry-Land Crocodile. From my shop here I look over the travelers and passing merchants and

tell the stronghold who has what. I might have killed you, salted your meat and boiled your fat down for oil to burn in my lamps had I not seen you write your name. Men from the Eastern Capital speak of the great hero Lin Chong. I never thought we'd meet."

The Dry-Land Crocodile feasts Lin with fish and meat and wine in an open room on the lakeside of the inn. Half the night is gone when Zhu Gui says, "Please, don't worry about a boat. Get a little sleep first. I'll wake you when it's time."

Zhu Gui wakes Lin at the fifth watch, before daybreak. They wash and rinse their mouths and fortify themselves with five jars of wine and some meat. Just before first light, Zhu Gui takes up his bow, fits an arrow to the string, draws back and lets fly. The arrow whistles as it flies.

"What's that?"

"That's a signal to the mountain stronghold. A boat will come now."

A boat appears out of the reeds and moves quickly across the water to the inn. Zhu Gui accompanies Lin Chong across to the Golden Shore. No snow falls. The air is clear. Lin Chong sees huge trees growing out of the water and spongy marsh. Their trunks look impossibly big around. Fallen snow is clumped in the branches. Ice in the twigs.

These are cold hard times for Lin Chong. He looks for honor among wanton robbers and killers who pillage and plunder the people. But who says the gallant thieves want one more wanted

man? Will Marshal Gao force Lin Chong's wife into marriage with Young Master Gao? Will Lin Chong's revenge ever be done?

The Chinese Exclusion Act of 1882, the Christian China missions in Chinatowns, social Darwinist jargon becoming state and local law, the quota limiting to 105 the number of people of the Chinese race allowed into the United States from all parts of the world, and World War II combined to isolate the American-born Chinese in a world where they were the only Chinese, and the only English-language sources of information about them were Hollywood and Christians. The Christian autobiographers were the only Chinese Americans published by big commercial houses then, as they are now. The Christian Chinese American autobiographies fulfilled white fantasy in form and content. They praised Christian moral supremacy. They lived white supremacy in their hearts. They told of turning on the power of belief to stamp out first the tongs, then the real world, until, with Jade Snow Wong and Maxine Hong Kingston, the autobiography completely escaped the real China and Chinese America into pure white fantasy where nothing is Chinese, nothing is real, everything is born of pure imagination. In answer to the charge that she violates the heroes of two Chinese myths when she puts the tattoos of Yue Fei on Fa Mulan's back,

Kingston snaps with white supremacist arrogance, reaching for mystic rhetoric:

> I'm not even saying that those are Chinese myths anymore. I'm saying I've written down American myths. Fa Mulan and the writing on her back is an American myth. And I made it that way.

She's right. Until her first nonfiction autobiography there was no other Fa Mulan but the real Fa Mulan of "the Ballad of Mulan." Seven decades of nothing but one Christian autobiography after another had painlessly brought Chinese America to a self-contempt so deep that we were deaf, dumb, and blind to the absence of anything real in the writing of Kingston and her literary spawn, David Henry Hwang and Amy Tan. No offense was taken at characterizing Chinese fairy tales and children's literature of the heroic tradition as teaching both contempt for women and wife beating. Without batting an eye, the average Chinese American born here in the 1970s, or before, will applaud the notion that Chinese history and literature are irrelevant to the understanding of Chinese American history and writing. Clearly, Chinese American writing by Christian autobiographers has had the effect of displacing history with the stereotype. An attitude of racist prejudice about illiterate Chinese with bad memories and no self-respect, and that no good drives their belief that their belief and their dreams zapped all fact, all the real.

Then, as now, the Christian autobiographers are blind to the presence of the heroic tradition in every shop in every Chinatown, in the tongs, in the Cantonese opera they bring to local theaters and feature at their New Year's banquets, and in the huge gold dragons and phoenixes clawing the walls of Chinese restaurants everywhere. If Louis Chu were alive today, he would be surprised to see that we have to fight to have his *Eat a Bowl of Tea* understood as *Three Kingdoms* and *Water Margin*, Sun Tzu and Confucius fermented into a language of pure Chinese psychology, and writing in English as if it were a dialect of Cantonese. Chu tells a Chinese American story of exile, warlike loneliness, promises made and promises broken, marriage and betrayal, a hero running away from home to the original stronghold and to a new promise and new life—a story that runs from New York to San Francisco and is forever told in a prose atmosphere of singing symbols and symbols in chords, in flashing signs, and by following plot lines from the heroic tradition. In the New York City of Louis Chu's time, just before and right after World War II, the Chinese would have said it was crazy to think that in the 1970s people's minds would be wiped clean of *Three Kingdoms, Water Margin,* and the whole heroic tradition. Back in the fifties and early sixties, chatter about the tongs still lingered after the appearance of Jade Snow Wong's *Fifth Chinese Daughter.* As chumpy as the chatter was, it was some nod toward the real. Everybody knew that no less than former President Harry S Truman had called the president of the Chinese Six Companies the "Mayor of Chinatown."

That Wong Sam and Assistants and their *Phrase Book* are forgotten would have surprised a number of old-time yellow and white Californians who are, fortunately for their memories, all dead now. The *Phrase Book* swept the West in waves of thousands. Perhaps hundreds of copies of the three editions have survived in the hands of collectors, used book stores, libraries, and museums. For the Chinese Americans, the stereotype has completely, factually, and morally replaced everything real about the Chinese immigrants and the history and culture of Chinatowns and children's stories. And it happened so quietly, with such apparent painlessness. For Chinese America, there was never a period when white Christian missionaries and their Number One children were not the only examples of Chinese American history, culture, and writing.

The white racist stereotype of the perpetual dual-personality and identity-crisis, Ping-Pong didn't take over the intelligence of Japanese Americans writing in English until World War II and the massive internment of 120,213 persons of Japanese ancestry, the Nikkei, in concentration camps erected in California, Arizona, Arkansas, Wyoming, and Idaho. The first of what would become a wave of Japanese American autobiographies, which are like the Christian Chinese American autobiographies, was by a young man who had been a child in camp. In *American in Disguise* (1971), the third-generation Nikkei Daniel Okimoto wails against the burden of the dual identity and sees everything Japanese with a stomach-churning mix of nostalgia and the righteous moral contempt of Pardee Lowe, Jade Snow Wong, and Maxine Hong Kingston. Okimoto is not only a third-generation Japanese American, a Sansei, he is a sociologist and deserves credit for writing the first Japanese American sociological autobiography and for being the first Asian American to use the term *dual personality* to denote what had always been called the "identity crisis." Okimoto's autobiography is, also, not very subtle proof that the American concentration camps were behavior modification programs that worked. For the Sansei, the stereotype and the dual personality, take the form of an ugly, nagging, personal question: Why did their parents—the American-born Nisei, the second-generation Nikkei—accept and endure the obvious constitutional wrongs of the evacuation and internment without protest or resistance? Okimoto's painful answer is: Too much passive Japanese culture. Japanese culture is the culture of the pathological victim, born in camp to parents whose entire generation was too chicken to stand up for their rights in court. The Sansei have had a lot to live down. The bluesy Sansei angst, not the false history that produced it, not the science or facts that buzzed it, but the Sansei's *feelings*—that is the content of Okimoto's autobiography.

6

The three-and-a-half-year internment of Japanese Americans was a behavior modification program that worked. It worked because the Japanese American Citizens League (JACL), led by Mike Masaru Masaoka, betrayed Japanese America into the camps and assumed the leadership of Japanese America with government help. Had not the JACL asked the government to use the camps to "eliminate Li'l Tokyos," "the Japanese language," "Japanese accents," and "all the differences in behavior and mannerism" that distinguished the Japanese American Nisei from their "fellow Americans," the camps might have borne a greater resemblance to the protected free hotels the government said they were. Had Mike Masaoka not written a loyalty oath, pushed it on Nisei as a quasi-official certification of loyalty, and pitched it to the government in 1941—not long before carrier-based fighter bombers of the Imperial Japanese Navy attacked Pearl Harbor—the troubling questions 27 and 28 regarding one's allegiance to America and willingness to volunteer for the draft, the so-called loyalty-oath questions in the Application for Leave Clearance registration form of 1943, might never have been.

One effect of the JACL's betrayal and its power in camp was a massive change in Japanese American writing. Japanese American writers "abandoned" Japanese American history, turned rabidly against the Issei and Japanese culture, and fantasized about joyous acculturation, righteous white acceptance; first the women, then the men marry Japanese America white out of existence. Assimilation at last!

Before the war Japanese American writers of fiction, drama, poetry, and ideas were encouraged by publication in the English-language section of the Issei-owned, predominantly Japanese-language, J'Town newspapers. A Nisei, James Matsumoto Omura, had worked on several Japanese American newspapers in Seattle, San Francisco, and Los Angeles. In 1939, Omura began publishing and editing an all-English-language Nisei magazine of ideas and arts. He was the first to publish Toshio Mori's stories later collected in the Nikkei classic *Yokohama, California.*

When the government announced the evacuation and "relocation," Omura wrote all the Nisei writers he knew—and he knew them all—appealing for nickels and dimes to raise the money to retain a Washington law firm to sue the government for constitutional grievances and take the camps to court. Omura went before a congressional committee to oppose the evacuation and internment and denounce the JACL as being self-serving rather than representative of the Nisei. By this time, the JACL's finking—and its favor with the FBI, the office of Naval Intelligence (ONI), and the War Relocation Authority (WRA), the agency running the camps—made Japanese America, both behind barbed wire and loose in the West, outside of the "military zones," a JACL police state. The JACL was opposed to test cases and made pariahs of the Nisei who supported test cases. Not one Japanese American writer of fiction, poetry, drama, or ideas joined Omura's effort. Not one so much as answered his letter.

When restoration of the drafting of Nisei, without restoration of their civil rights, led to the large organized draft resistance at the Heart Mountain Relocation Center in Wyoming, Omura was the only Japanese American writer chronicling the resistance as it arose in virtually every camp and the only Japanese American writer to editorialize in favor of testing the constitutionality of the camps in court. A petition for redress of constitutional grievance in American and Anglo-Saxon law always begins with an act of civil disobedience, a resisting of an obnoxious law.

The only Japanese American nonjournalistic writer to deal with the Nisei resistance was John Okada. His *No-No Boy* (1957) focuses on Nisei, Ichiro, meaning "Firstborn," who refused to appear for his Selective Service pre-induction physical when he received his draft notice in camp. *No-No Boy* stunned us when we found it. *No-No Boy* was so great that we pooled our money, formed the Combined Asian American Resources Project (CARP), reissued *No-No Boy*, and sold it by mail order. Asian America rediscovered John Okada's novel twenty years after the JACL had denounced it and condemned it to lie boxed up in a warehouse. Now the University of Washington Press has taken over the CARP edition of *No-No Boy*, and our appreciation of Okada's accomplishment grows the more we learn about its relation to, and place in, Japanese American history.

John Okada based his novel not on his own life as a Nisei from Seattle who was interned at Minidoka, a camp in Idaho, and was an early volunteer who served in army intelligence, translating Japanese radio transmissions and dropping propaganda leaflets in the South Pacific; rather, he based it on the life of Hajiime (another word meaning "Firstborn") Jim Akutsu. Akutsu read of the organized resistance at Heart Mountain in articles written by James Omura in the *Rocky Shimpo*, a Japanese American newspaper published in Denver. He wrote to the Heart Mountain Fair Play Committee, in care of Omura at the paper. Omura, already being harassed by the JACL and the FBI for his reporting of the resistance around camp, did not forward Akutsu's letter, because he feared being hit with a federal conspiracy charge. Finally, in 1944, Omura was arrested and tried in Federal District Court in Cheyenne, Wyoming, as one of the leaders of the Heart Mountain resistance.

Once again, James Omura appealed to the writers he had nurtured and to the journalists he had worked with. Omura says, "They all abandoned me." He was acquitted but because the JACL and Mike Masaoka now controlled the writing of Japanese American news, Japanese American history, Japanese American fiction, and Japanese American poetry, no Nikkei dared acknowledge Omura's existence, and no one dared write of the JACL's betrayal or the resistance faded into the oral tradition of those Nisei and Issei the JACL-dominated Japanese Americans called "vengeful and vindictive." What was "nothing they dared tell" became nothing at all. tive." What was "nothing they dared tell" became nothing at all. Instead of seriously exploring what and where Japanese America suffers and hurts, most Japanese American writers, since camp, have opted to make art of the JACL myth of Masaoka's enlightened and inspired leadership of the Japanese Americans through World War II to white acceptance and assimilation. And what began as Shotaro Frank Miyamoto's JACL sociologist's prescription for racial extinction, *Social Solidarity Among the Japanese in Seattle* (1939), became *They Call Me Moses* (1987), Mike Masaoka's decidedly Christian autobiography, in which he offers his own dual-personality, Ping-Pong and Japanese American angst with undisguised, messianic pomp and pretense run amok. Just remember, Masaoka and his co-author, Bill Hosokawa, seriously believe Masaoka's scripture, and much of Japanese America still lives under its spell. After quoting Deuteronomy 34, from the *Living Bible*, chapter 1 begins:

My name is Mike Masaru Masaoka. Mike, not Michael. If that's an odd collection of names, it reflects both my American citizenship and upbringing and the Japanese part of my heritage.

Some of my friends, and some who are not my friends, also call me Moses. Moses Masaoka. They say that, like the Biblical prophet, I have led my people on a long journey through the wilderness of discrimination and travail. They say that I have led them within sight of the promised land of justice for all and social and economic equality in our native America, but that we will not reach it within my lifetime.

The JACL version of history has been the only version, by Japanese American authors, to reach print since 1942. The most influential JACL histories in the teaching and writing of Japanese American history and news are Hosokawa's *NISEI: The Quiet Americans* (1969); *East to America*, by Robert O. Wilson and Bill Hosokawa (1980); *JACL: In Quest of Justice* (1982). According to the JACL version of history, Mike Masaoka led Japanese Americans to accept the injustices of the evacuation and internment as their contribution to the war effort and prove their loyalty. Accepting and enduring camp, without protest or resistance, the all-volunteer, all-Nisei 442nd Regimental Combat Team proved Japanese American loyalty in blood and in lives given up on the battlefields of World War II, and won white acceptance. Thus the camps had the unexpected beneficial effect of accelerating the assimilation of the Nikkei.

The flight of Japanese American writers away from camp, the JACL, the resistance and postwar social ostracism of the resisters, and forty years of indoctrination in JACL revisionist history into dreamy personal experience and preciosity and into belief in their individual selves to transcend the truth are becoming embarrassing. Less pretentious writers, Japanese American women from showbiz for example, have written and researched the real and introduced a pile of freshly declassified documents from the National Archives that prove the JACL offered themselves as finks to the FBI and naval intelligence long before the war, and urged the government to run the camps as indoctrination centers in order to make "Better Americans in a Greater America."

To fill the gap of knowledge left by Japanese American fiction and poetry, we offer to the store of Nikkei common knowledge three documents written by Mike Masaoka as leader of the JACL. There are so many more, but three will do. In the first, a long-winded eighteen-page letter to Milton Eisenhower, the new director of the WRA, Mike Masaoka superciliously demands that the camps be run as indoctrination centers and describes the behavior that he wants modified and the method to be used. The second is the *JACL Bulletin #142:*

RE: Test Cases—April 6, 1942

The national JACL stands unalterably opposed to test cases to determine the constitutionality of the military orders. . . .

Masaoka is against test cases because good publicity is more important than good law. He calls the JACL's own Minoru Yasui "a self-styled martyr out to gain headlines" and reasons that Nisei who make test cases make bad publicity that results in white hostility toward the Nisei in wartime, which makes the Nisei maker of bad publicity un-American, seditious, and disloyal. Minoru Yasui, the first son of an Issei family of apple growers in Oregon, and the first Nisei to graduate from University of Oregon Law School, violated the army's curfew order against people of the Japanese race being on the streets after 8:00 P.M., and riding sidecar *ex parte* with Gordon Hirabayashi's test of the curfew order in Seattle, was on his way to the U.S. Supreme Court. Yasui answered Masaoka's *Bulletin #142* with a bulletin of his own; he also managed to have it mimeographed and distributed in Minidoka. After each paragraph of Masaoka's bulletin, he inserts his own response. He argues that good law is more important than good publicity. Yasui creates a debate between two of the JACL's most respected oratorical stylists. Because they are historically two of the more important Japanese Americans affecting the minds and writing of all Japanese Americans, their debate of the essential issue of the JACL's strategy— good publicity v. good law—is dramatic in its own right, and we offer it, whole, later in this anthology.

The third document, written by Mike Masaoka on WRA letterhead, is a WRA internal memo to the WRA director on "The Definition of Kibei" and is signed by Masaoka and two other JACL officers.

On April 6, 1942, the potential for the cultural and racial extinction of the Nikkei inspired Masaoka to tell WRA's Milton Eisenhower that the JACL wanted the Nisei put in camps without hearings, that the organization wanted the Nisei to be treated better than the Issei, that it wanted the "elimination" of the Japanese language and the elimination of Japanese accents. It was, all in all, an indoctrination program to create, out of the loyal Nisei, "Better Americans in a Greater America."

Masaoka's letter offered recommendations for the rules and regulations that would govern and administer the internees, the programs and privileges that would occupy and manipulate them, and the purposes and goals to impose on them, inside the ten enclosed communities of ten thousand each. He arranged his suggestions, recommendations, and bursts of sudden sermonette under sixteen categories. The sixteen categories of interests and activities made the difference between what Masaoka called "resettlement projects" and what was seen by all others to be concentration camps.

Masaoka categorized his recommendations as follows: Draftee Status, Public Relations, Education, Religion, Sports and Recreation, Publications and Radios, Health and Medical Facilities, Japanese Professionals and Specially Trained People, Business and Industry, Agriculture, Labor and Wages, Citizenship Recognition, Organization (Self-government), Private Projects, Induction or Assembly Centers, Semipermanent and Permanent Resettlement Projects.

Masaoka was proud of his letter. He felt it was influential and that it was successful in establishing the JACL as an administrative arm of the government in partnership with the WRA. In his final report of 1944, he wrote of delivering the letter to Eisenhower, in San Francisco, by hand:

Immediately upon his appointment, Mr. [Milton] Eisenhower flew out to San Francisco and conferred with the National President and Secretary regarding the problems incident to his post. At that time, the JACL submitted a long memorandum of recommendations and suggestions which, I am certain, influenced major WRA policy thereafter.

By Masaoka's reckoning, the JACL and the WRA were to be partners in running the camps as a controlled indoctrination program:

General Policies:
We believe that all projects should be directed (1) to create "Better Americans in [sic] a Greater America, (2) to maintain a high and healthy morale among the evacuees, (3) to train them to cope with the difficult problems of adjustment and rehabilitation after war, (4) to permit them to actually and actively participate in the war effort of our nation, and (5) to develop [sic] a community spirit of cooperative action and service to others before self.

Masaoka did not look on the Nisei in the "resettlement projects" as being imprisoned, under arrest, or confined against their will in concentration camps. Because they were not prisons, but "resettlement projects," no constitutional rights had been violated. The projects, by including all Nisei, indiscriminately, within their fences, were treating all equally and, therefore, were preserving and practicing American fair play and the American concept of innocence until proven guilty. Using this logic, Masaoka argued for denying the Nisei a hearing before putting them away in "resettlement projects":

Paradoxical as this may seem, we are opposed to Hearing or Determining Boards or Commissions which might attempt to determine the loyalty of those in these resettlement projects. We believe that the regular agencies of the government, such as the FBI, should investigate and intern or jail all disloyal or questionable persons, be they citizen or otherwise.

As if all Issei and Nisei were not already interned or jailed. Meanwhile, back home in the relocation center, no hearings for the Nisei:

Should a person be adjudged disloyal at this time because of something which he might have said or done years ago, he would be branded for life and would prove useless after the war.

We believe that the American concepts of justice—that one is innocent until proved guilty—should be applicable to all citizens, including ourselves. Until definite facts of overt actions of disloyalty can be shown, we believe that all persons should be accepted at their face value, as loyal and devoted citizens of the United States.

Thus, Masaoka joined the JACL and the WRA in the fiction that the concentration camps were real homes and not places of forced confinement. A part of the indoctrination in Americanism was the institutionalization of contempt for the Issei:

Because of the unusual and unprecedented requests made upon American citizens of Japanese ancestry, special provisions should be made to compensate them for the temporary loss of some of their privileges and rights. This might be in the form of "certificates" of citizenship of appreciation, or some other token which will help them retain their self-respect in their own eyes and in the eyes of their fellow citizens.

Americanism, to Mike Masaoka, was white supremacy. "We suggest that as much intercourse with 'white' Americans be permitted as possible," he wrote Eisenhower.

We do not relish the thought of "Little Tokyos" springing up in these resettlement projects, for by so doing we are only perpetuating the very things which we hope to eliminate: those mannerisms and thoughts which mark us apart, aside from our physical characteristics. We hope for a one hundred percent American community.

. . . One thing is certain: there should be no Japanese language schools.

Special stress should be laid on the enunciation and pronunciation of words so that awkward and "Oriental" sounds will be eliminated.

Masaoka, straight-faced, patriotic, and macabre, assured Eisenhower twice that 50 percent of the Issei would die as a result of the conditions of their old age, compounded by the evacuation and violent adjustment to the extremes of desert summers and winters; their deaths would make it easier to eliminate the Oriental sounds, thoughts, and mannerisms in the remaining Nisei.

Masaoka's tone became chummy and conspiratorial as he told Eisenhower what should be kept from the "evacuees":

The projects should be in full operation within a day or two of the arrival of the evacuees. Conditions and other considerations should be as normal and non-camplike as possible. No intimation or hint should be given that they are in concentration camps or in protective custody, or that the government does not have full faith and confidence in them as a group and as individuals.

In their pursuit of the elimination of everything Japanese in the Japanese American, the JACL dropped all pretense of being a civil rights organization and wrote WRA policy on WRA letterhead, a policy to "segregate" the Kibei in a separate camp for disloyals, and included a plan for breaking up Nikkei families by age and suspected loyalty or disloyalty.

WAR RELOCATION AUTHORITY

June 6, 1942

For: Mr. Eisenhower

Definition of Kibei: an American citizen of Japanese ancestry who has studied in Japan for a period of five or more years, all or part of which was after the year 1930, and all or part of which was after attaining the age of 12 or more.

In the case of families, if the husband is Kibei and the wife Nisei, the family should be considered Kibei; and if the husband is Nisei and the wife Kibei, the family should be considered Nisei.

Inasmuch as the parents sent the child to Japan in most cases, the parents should be held suspect, regardless of the number of other children which they may not have sent to Japan for study. In all cases, they may appeal their status.

If the child under question is 16 years of age or more, he is entitled to elect whether he chooses to be placed in the same classification as his parents or not, provided that his parents are declared suspect. If the child is under 16, he assumes the status of his parents, but on becoming of age may have the privilege of election.

Any person declared suspect may appeal to a special board of investigation, which might be composed of representatives of the military forces, the WRA and the Department of Justice. The applicant may submit the names of five persons, none of whom may be members of his immediate family or close relatives, to vouch for him or offer information regarding him. The board may call any or all of the persons so named and question them, if they so desire, or request them to make a recommendation concerning the party in question. All such persons must present their information under oath, so that all information of a false nature makes them liable for criminal punishment for perjury. The board may also call additional persons to present testimony, if they so desire, under whatever terms they may deem necessary and proper. It should be understood that all such testimony is purely advisory and is not binding per se on the investigating board.

Incidentally, we are in unanimous agreement as to the principle of segregation.

> Respectfully submitted,
> Mike Masaoka
> Ken Matsumoto
> George Inagaki

7

Masaoka was just the Nisei for John J. McCloy, the assistant secretary of war in charge of the "military necessity" that justified keeping the Nikkei off the West Coast and in camps. No less than sociologist S. Frank Miyamoto found a copy of Assistant Secretary of War McCloy's letter to Alexander Meikeljohn of the ACLU, dated September 30, 1942, which sang in harmony with Masaoka's vision of the camps as indoctrination centers for "Better Americans in a Greater America" and gave sociologists like Miyamoto a purpose. McCloy wrote Meikeljohn:

We would be missing a very big opportunity if we fail to study the Japanese in these camps at some length before they are dispersed. We have not done a very good job thus far in solving the Japanese problem in this country. I believe we have a great opportunity to give the thing intelligent thought now and reach solid conclusions for the future.

These people gathered as they now are in these communities, afford a means of sampling their customs and habits in a way we have never before had possible. We could find out what they are thinking about and we might very well influence their thinking in the right direction before they are again distributed into communities.

I am aware that such a suggestion may provoke a charge that we have no right to treat these people as "guinea pigs," but I would rather treat them as guinea pigs and learn something useful than merely to treat them, or have them treated, as they have been in the past with such unsuccessful results.

For the sake of the Japanese themselves, I would therefore wish that Dillon Myer [WRA director who succeeded Milton Eisenhower] would take some very long thoughts before committing himself to a principle of immediate and extensive release.

The anthropologists of the Community Analysis Section (CAS) of the War Relocation Authority and the social scientists of Dorothy Swaine Thomas's University of California Japanese Evacuation Relocation Study moved into the camps to study and change the Japanese Americans.

Nisei anthropologist Peter Suzuki, who was ten years old when he was evacuated from Seattle and interned at Minidoka, is currently studying the anthropologists who made their reputations in the camps—the grandfathers of today's American anthropology establishment. Suzuki has found their work "one or a combination of the following: self-serving, disingenuous, superficial, distorted, pseudo-scientific, bizarre, surrealistic, or ethnocentric."

In keeping with their belief that the Nisei could only prove their loyalty to America by being racially absorbed and assimilated out of existence, the JACL filled up the cracks of their weekly paper with stories reporting favorably, titillatingly, and encouragingly about the superiority of Nisei who married out white. In the *Pacific Citizen*, February 19, 1944:

NISEI INTERMARRIAGE RATE
SHOWN IN HAWAIIAN FIGURES

by John E. Reinecke

Honolulu, T.H.

"The[y] will not mingle their blood with that of other races . . ."—a typical charge leveled against Americans of Japanese ancestry—is not true in Hawaii. Not only has the war failed to check their normal rate of outmarriage, but, as the war has continued, the outmarriage of Japanese women has increased rapidly. During the past statistical year, 1942–43, according to the statistics of the Hawaii Board of Health, one out of every seven women who married, chose a husband outside her own race.

More than half of these outmarriages—7.44% out of 13.9%—were contracted with Caucasians. . . . The rise in outmarriage, from the fairly normal rate of 10.1% in 1940–41 to 13.96% after a year of war with Japan, is the direct result of the great influx of American men from the continent who have found Hawaiian AJA (Americans of Japanese ancestry) girls equally attractive with those of other descents.

The JACL president, Saburo Kido, urged assimilation and subtly warned Nisei to resist the temptation to congregate and re-create Little Tokyos:

EVACUEES EXPRESS HOPE OF INTEGRATION

During our travels, we have been impressed with the fact that a large number of Nisei who have gone to the Middle West or the Atlantic seaboard have the genuine desire to lose themselves in a new community and be forgotten.

What Mike Masaoka sugarcoated and decorated, Kido said plainly.

We admired them for this outlook because it indicated a sincere wish for complete integration and eventual assimilation.

Assimilation meant to Yokohama, California, no Little Tokyo, no ghetto:

We also heard the fear expressed about Nisei organizing their own group and thus falling into the same type of groove they had prior to the evacuation on the Pacific Coast.

Nisei acceptance of being drafted out of camp was central to the JACL's insistence that Japanese America wanted to be accepted and assimilated, and Saburo Kido said so, trying to keep the Nisei in the camps from protesting or resisting. He wrote in his column, "Timely Topics," dated February 26, 1944:

NISEI REACTION TO DRAFT BEING WATCHED

The action of the Nisei in connection with the draft is being watched closely by the people of this country. It seems inevitable that there are going to be some who are still embittered because of evacuation and therefore refuse to serve. We sincerely hope there will be few in the nine relocation centers who will take such a stand. . . .

At this time, it is ill-advised and most unfortunate for the future of all Nisei to take the stand against induction. . . . We have come a long way by having the draft reinstated. Through the conduct and record from now on, our road back to the return of all our rights will become a certainty.

It will be a tragic mistake if the Nisei in the relocation centers are misguided at the crucial moment. We sincerely hope that the leadership will be such as to influence the young ones to discharge their duties and obligations, and to maintain their faith in the government.

The JACL's *Pacific Citizen* came out on Saturdays. The *Rocky Shimpo* published on Mondays. On February 28, the Monday after JACL president Saburo Kido warned the Nisei against resisting the draft, James Omura, editorialist for the *Rocky Shimpo*, also had words on Nisei draft resistance. He linked the resistance to the Nisei right to redress of grievances raised by the camps:

We are in full sympathy with the general context of the petitions forwarded to Washington by the Amache Community Council and the Topaz Citizens Committee. We do not necessarily agree on all the points raised, however.

Insofar as the movement itself is concerned, the Nisei are well within their rights to petition the government for a redress of grievances. Beyond that, it would be treading on unsure footing. We must not forget that we are at war. This department does not encourage resistance to the draft.

He did not encourage resistance to the draft for its own sake. "Those who are resisting the draft are too few, too unorganized, and basically unsound in their viewpoints," he wrote, and expanded on the point. "Unorganized draft resistance is not the proper method to pursue our grievances." In a paragraph that would bring the FBI and JACL out looking for a crime to pin on him and names to call him, he offered support for draft resistance organized to accomplish redress of the violations of Nisei citizen rights:

> We agree that the constitution gives us certain inalienable civil rights. We do not dispute the fact that such rights have been largely stripped and taken from us. We further agree that the government should restore a large part of those rights before asking us to contribute our lives to the welfare of the nation—to sacrifice our lives on the field of battle.

James Omura's support of using the draft to take the government to court, namely his tactic of demanding what he called "a clarification of Nisei citizenship status" before Nisei acceptance of the draft, had been brewing for weeks in his *Rocky Shimpo* editorials. The *Pacific Citizen* and the JACL did their best to discredit him in the camps but failed, notably at Heart Mountain, where, with the promise of Omura's support for an organized effort to use the draft to sue the government, Kiyoshi Okamoto led his Fair Play Committee to stand against the draft. Aseal T. Hansen, community analyst at Heart Mountain, reported in February to the project director:

> THURSDAY, 24th. The Fair Play Committee distributed a mimeographed circular in English and Japanese throughout the community. This was the first written evidence of the existence of the Committee.
> It needled the Community Council for its inaction and called attention to Topaz and Rohwer where the Councils are "genuinely interested in clarifying the draft issue"; it suggested that such action the Community Council Committee contemplated was just to "save face"; it asserted that JACL and "many Nisei writers" would like the Fair Play Committee to shut up, accused them of "employing moral intimidation via propaganda, the FBI, etc., and claimed the right to freedom of expression. . . .

The JACL attacked the Fair Play Committee of Heart Mountain as un-American, disloyal, fomenting sedition, and jeopardizing Japanese American acceptance by whites. Within sixty days of Hansen's discovery of the only organized resistance to the camps and opposition to the JACL, the Fair Play Committee was stripped of its

leaders and destroyed as an organization by the JACL, the WRA
top hats at Heart Mountain, the community analyst, the FBI, and
the courts.

"Sedition" was the nature of the FBI case against Kiyoshi Okamoto,
Paul Takeo Nakadate, Ben Wakaye, Ken Yamagi, Frank Emi,
Minoru Tamesa, and Sam Horino. They were the leaders and visible
spokesmen of the Fair Play Committee inside Heart Mountain Relocation Center.

The FBI agent in action writes with nothing but teeth. You know
who the G-men are from the special agent's first line, when you hit
the name banged out in caps:

> Subject organization originated by KIYOSHI OKAMOTO, lat-
> ter part of 1943, at Heart Mountain Relocation Center, Heart
> Mountain, Wyoming, apparent purpose being championship
> of nisei rights in general. Upon announcement in January,
> 1944, that nisei would be accepted by US Army, the organi-
> zation, with subject NAKADATE assisting OKAMOTO, took
> up alleged discriminatory act of drafting nisei under present
> conditions contending that prior to taking nisei into army
> there should be a clarification of the citizenship status of such
> evacuees.

The FBI acknowledged:

> Portions of a report prepared by Mr. A. T. HANSEN, Com-
> munity Analyst at the Center, for Mr. DILLON S. MYER,
> Director of WRA at Washington, D.C., are being quoted here-
> inafter. Mr. HANSEN customarily writes a weekly report cov-
> ering various phases of the community life of the Center giving
> an analytical survey of causes and effects. The summary report
> for Mr. MYER is a digest of such weekly analyses, which, for
> the above period, were almost entirely concerned with the
> reaction of Selective Service on the nisei of the Center as the
> draft was the dominant topic of the community life. The follow-
> ing documentary material was obtained by the writer and Spe-
> cial Agent ROBERT G. LAWRENCE.

In this material, the work of Aseal T. Hansen, we have what the
anthropologist Suzuki called biased, self-serving, prejudiced, un-
scientific reporting and unethical collusion with intelligence agencies.
The community analyst wrote of himself in the scientific third-
person objective voice, offering a strange confession. He was new.
He was scared for his life among the Japanese Americans:

The Community Analyst was new on the job and he hesitated to show an active interest in the subject.

Where were the passive, obedient, collectively submissive Japanese of myth and sociology? Not in Heart Mountain when Hansen arrived.

The response of the residents was so intense and included enough hostile reactions that he felt his future usefulness might be impaired if it were known he was investigating selective service. The following report is what he was able to observe unobtrusively and will give some idea of what has been happening at Heart Mountain.

The opening of the draft to the Nisei, in January 1944, was a JACL dream come true. Hansen wrote that the JACL's satisfaction and joy over Nisei being drafted out of camps was not shared by the Japanese Americans inside Heart Mountain.

A very few persons adopted what may be termed the "official" viewpoint. That is, that the opening of selective service, even with the discriminatory features, was an important desirable step in the right direction; that it should be accepted without protest or objection; and that the problem of removing the discriminations should be left for the future.

The JACL program in a nutshell. From Nisei assistants acting as informants and from tattletales kissing up for a college education courtesy of Uncle Sam, "Hansen the hesitant" constructed a biased account of the Fair Play Committee.

Opposition to the draft became stronger and more widespread. The most tangible and purposeful expression of this was an organization, the Fair Play Committee. It had existed, at least in name, for some time before, to champion the rights of evacuees, but it had little importance and few members. Its chief leader stood in low esteem among the residents generally. (Agent's note: Reference is made to KIYOSHI OKAMOTO) In more tranquil times, they considered him overradical, unreasonable, irresponsible, and verbose. Now the Committee took up the draft and this leader soon had a following. . . . The Committee sought members actively at a fee of two dollars each in order to build up a fund. The position assumed was that *nisei* should refuse to be drafted until discriminatory and special treatment were eliminated. The idea at first (the strategy appears to have been changed later) was to get a test case by having someone not report when called and to fight the case through the courts for the purpose of establishing the illegality of evacuation and all that has gone with it. The only indication that analyst has of the kind of exhortations heard by those who attended the meetings are a few approximately verbatim fragments reported from the speech of the leader mentioned above in a block meeting: "The committee does not want to do anything contrary to the law. But we are guaranteed freedom of speech by the Constitution and we want to present all sides of the question." And later on, "Any *nisei* who reports for physical examination or induction is worse than Benedict Arnold; he is a traitor to the *nisei* cause." He had another angle in which he compared the relocation camp with prison, in which the prison was presented as preferable. When one gets leave from a relocation camp, he receives his railway fee and $25; a prison gives a person all of this and a suit of clothes to boot.

The Fair Play Committee's mimeographed English flyer of February 23, 1944, was titled "FAIR PLAY COMMITTEE/ 'One for all—All for one' "; by way of introduction, the committee said of itself:

The Fair Play Committee was organized for the purpose of opposing all unfair practices that violate the Constitutional rights of the people as guaranteed and set forth in our United States Constitution regardless if such practices occur within our present concentration camp, the state, territory or Union. It ha[s] come out strongly in recent weeks in regard to the discriminatory features of the new selective service program as it applied to the Japanese American nationals despite the loud and idealistic claims of nisei editors.

The Fair Play Committee scolded the Community Council, the internee self-government organization controlled by the camp administration, for failing to represent the internees' feelings on the drafting of Nisei from out of camp. What appears to be veiled criticism of the JACL became unveiled in the flyer's last paragraph.

The Fair Play is out to give you that side which the Assistant Project Director and the JACL have not presented. The Fair Play does not agree with many nisei writers, however, believes that they have the freedom and right to express their opinion. The Fair Play will fight for them for that right and privilege of expression despite the fact that some of the writers would want some people to shut up. In unfair practices of anti-groups they would like the Fair Players to shut up by employing moral intimidations via propaganda, the FBI, etc. Those methods do not obstruct the ideals of this group. In this instance, we take Confucius' saying: do not do unto others as you would not want others to do unto you.

On March 1, 1944, the Fair Play Committee appealed for money in the form of a series of questions and answers about itself:

Q. What's this Fair Play Committee about?
A. The Fair Play Committee (FPC) is organized to inject justice in all the problems pertinent to our evacuation, concentration, detention, and pauperization without hearing or due process of law, and oppose all unfair practices within our center, State, or Union.
Q. How do you think it can do just that?
A. By educational process, the use of the press, thru the courts or, if the FPC cannot do it itself, it will work jointly with or thru outside organizations.

The Fair Play Committee was not different from the JACL in every way, however. As in the JACL, the Issei were excluded from membership.

Q. Who can join this organization?
A. Citizens only.

The "citizens only" (meaning Nisei) made sense; only Nisei were being drafted, and only Nisei could resist the draft. Still, Nisei contempt for the Issei was not fully reciprocal. The Issei, who had trusted the Nisei enough to buy land in their children's names, still planned to keep their promises though the Nisei seemed to have betrayed them. The Issei encouraged the Nisei to clarify their citizenship in the courts; if the Nisei were citizens, the Issei's legacy to them—all the land bought and deeded to the Nisei—was safe. If the Nisei were not citizens, everything that the Issei had worked for was lost. To Issei like Uhachi Tamesa, who had lots of land and houses all over south Seattle, it was worth spending a few dollars for a lawyer to find out if his son, Minoru, was a citizen.

It was the Issei who subscribed to James Omura's *Rocky Shimpo* and passed it on to the Nisei, who, discovering Omura's editorials, columns, and reportage on the reinstitution of the draft of the resistance around the various camps, sent away to Denver for their own subscriptions.

Hansen reported on March 23, 1943, that "the circulation of the *Rocky Shimpo* has increased from about 1,000 to 1,200 during the past three weeks, a growth of twenty percent."

An Issei, Guntaro Kubota, offered to translate Fair Play Committee handouts into Japanese for distribution to the Issei. The Fair Play Committee leaders told Kubota thanks but no thanks, the risk was too great for an Issei. Helping the draft resistance might be considered sabotage by the government and mean rough treatment and deportation for Kubota. Kubota felt what the Nisei were doing was a great and noble thing and that, win or lose, helping them fight for their constitutional birthright would be the closest thing to a noble cause he would meet in his lifetime.

Guntaro Kubota was a Zen man. After years of wandering the continental United States, squandering the small fortune he had inherited, Kubota settled in San Jose, California, to teach the Japanese language to school-age Nisei children of Issei farmers, in a wood-frame, peak-roofed community center. He married one of his former students and farmed strawberries. Guntaro and Gloria Kubota were evacuated to Heart Mountain, Wyoming, with their three-year-old daughter, Grace. A son was born in camp. Guntaro insisted on naming him Gordon, after Gordon Hirabayashi, the sociology student who had violated the curfew in Seattle and challenged the constitutionality of the military orders.

Kubota wrote appeals to the Issei for money to support a test case, appeals that even in English translation seem more eloquent and sleek than the overbuilt patriotic rhetoric of the Fair Play Committee's straight English written by Nisei, who knew the lingo. Kubota took on the voice of a Nisei in his appeals to the Issei. It is a voice no Nisei, save perhaps novelist Kazuo Miyamoto of *Hawaii: End of the Rainbow* (1964), has come close to fulfilling. In one voice, in one breath, he makes the Japanese sense of honor, the samurai sense of nobility (*makoto*), and Japanese spirit one with the noble cause of defending Nisei honor with the high and noble principles of the United States Constitution.

Appeal to Issei
Hope of Your Cooperation for the Benefit of
The Japanese Race

Liberty or Death! Of one of these we have a choice. In the present hour situation we do not hesitate to take death, but after acquiring the liberty we will die. That is the spirit of the Japanese race. Guarantee of freedom is the privilege which is given to us, but do we the Nisei enjoy the same privileges and freedom as the other American citizens have? No, in the hour at hand we are denied these privileges. Should we then, on the other hand, fulfill those obligations that are asked of us?

Q: Where and by what plan are we the Japanese Nisei assigned to the Army?

A: We should be assigned according to the instruction of the Army, but after training none of us Nisei are assigned other than to the 100th battalion or the 442nd battalion.

Q: Can we the Nisei serve in the Navy, the Marines, the air forces or the armored forces?

A: We are assigned only to the army, but we are drafted as other Americans, we should be allowed to serve in any of the branches of the Army.

The newspaper report of Sergeant Kuroki, who made a brilliant and meritous [sic] account on the battle front of Europe, is full of insults and damaging statements. Even in an emergency like this, the anti-Japanese movements, like the land problems in the state of Colorado, take place. We cannot enjoy any of the privileges guaranteed by the law.

Stand up nisei. Fight for the claim of the true right. Our future is remote. We have to march on as free American citizens but we haven't much power intellectually or economically. We hope the issei will help us.

By March 3, "twelve men, out of a total of sixty-four, failed to report for their pre-induction physical examinations—two on Monday, three on Tuesday, seven on Wednesday." Hansen, the community analyst, said, "The increase is a significant index of what was happening to the community."

Nisei protest and civil disobedience was in the air. In a specially highlighted letter to the editor, in the Saturday (March 4, 1944) edition of the *Pacific Citizen*, the JACL showed off a new, reformed Minoru Yasui, who had once been a dashing, eloquent example of civil disobedience but now was writing against civil disobedience and Nisei protest of the "hardships and injustices" of the camps.

In public statements and in petitions to our federal government, we must emphasize our willingness to serve our country under the selective service, or else we, as the Nisei, shall have not only failed in meeting this challenge to demonstrate our loyalty as Americans but, further, we shall have jeopardized our entire future in America.

Yasui applies his superior intellect and his way with words to beat Masaoka at his own rhetoric. He raised the issue of redress, acknowledged the injustices, and, with word magic, made them disappear and made the Nisei who began the sentence sound trivial, disloyal, and guilty unless they dropped their challenge and submitted to the draft.

It is this writer's firm belief that in this particular situation we Nisei must demonstrate our willingness to assume fully and patriotically the obligations of citizenship before we are in any position to petition for a redress of grievances.

This is not the same Minoru Yasui who submitted himself to arrest in Portland in 1942. Before, Yasui had argued that wronged and violated is the position to be in to petition for a redress of grievances. Now he argued as eloquently for the JACL party line as he had against it:

If it is clearly demonstrated that we are eager to assume all the obligations of citizenship, the rights cannot be denied us. On the other hand, a recital of the hardships and injustices which we may have suffered are not of great concern to the family which has already lost a son or a brother on the atolls of the Pacific or on the European front; but if we can show that we are vitally interested in participating more fully in the war effort by becoming fighting comrades-in-arms, no-one can, and no-one will want to deny equal citizenship rights to equal Americans. . . . It seems clear that the Army authorities have extended the privilege of active service to us upon the basic principles of a democracy, for a mere matter of an additional 5,000 nisei soldiers among an army of 10 or 12 million men is of small military importance.

Yasui argued that the resisters were dupes, too young to know what they were doing or to have a mature thought of their own. He turned on his doubletalk to urge the government to isolate the resisters from one another in solitary confinement:

Those who might want to change their minds, convinced of the error of their ways, would probably not be tolerated. For these

separate and individual cells would allow considerable intro-
spection and self-analysis. It would supplant individual decision
for group pressure.

That same Saturday, March 4, 1944, the Fair Play Committee at
Heart Mountain attacked the JACL head in a mimeographed
broadside:

We, the Nisei, have been complacent and too inarticulate to the
unconstitutional acts that we were subjected to. If ever there
was a time or cause for decisive action, IT IS NOW! We, the
members of the FPC, are not afraid to go to war—we are not
afraid to risk our lives for our country. We would gladly sacrifice our lives to protect and uphold the principles and ideals of
our country as set forth in the Constitution and the Bill of
Rights, for on its inviolability depends the freedom, liberty,
justice, and protection of all people including Japanese Americans and all other minority groups. But, have we been given
such freedom, such liberty, such justice, such protection? No!!
Without any hearings, without due process of law as guaranteed
by the Constitution and Bill of Rights, without any charges filed
against us, without any evidence of wrong doing on our part,
one hundred and ten thousand innocent people were kicked out
of their homes, literally uprooted from where they have lived
for the greater part of their life, and herded like dangerous
criminals into concentration camps with barbed wire fence and
military police guarding it, AND THEN, WITHOUT RECTIFICATION
OF THE INJUSTICES COMMITTED AGAINST US AND WITHOUT RESTO-
RATION OF OUR RIGHTS AS GUARANTEED BY THE CONSTITUTION,
WE ARE ORDERED TO JOIN THE ARMY THRU DISCRIMINATORY PRO-
CEDURES INTO A SEGREGATED COMBAT UNIT! Is that the American Way? NO!
     The FPC believes that unless such actions are exposed NOW
and steps taken to remedy such injustices and discriminations
IMMEDIATELY, the future of all minorities and the future of
this democratic nation is in danger.
     Thus, the members of the FPC unanimously decided at their
last open meeting that until we are restored all our rights, all
discriminatory features of the Selective Service abolished, and
measures are taken to remedy the past injustices thru judicial
pronouncement or Congressional act, we feel that the present
program of drafting us from this concentration camp is unjust,

unconstitutional, and against all principles of civilized usage, and therefore, WE MEMBERS OF THE FAIR PLAY COMMITTEE HEREBY REFUSE TO GO TO THE PHYSICAL EXAMINATION OR TO THE INDUCTION IF OR WHEN WE ARE CALLED IN ORDER TO CONTEST THE ISSUE.

We are not being disloyal. We are not evading the draft. We are all loyal Americans fighting for JUSTICE AND DEMOCRACY RIGHT HERE AT HOME.

So, restore our rights as such, rectify the injustices of evacuation, of the concentration, of the detention, and of the pauperization as such. In short, treat us in accordance with the principles of the constitution.

. . . We hope that all persons whose ideals and interests are with us will do all that they can to help us. We may have to engage in court actions, but as such actions require large sums of money, we do not need financial support and when the time comes, we hope that you will back us up to the limit.

Again, the Fair Play Committee published a message to the Issei in Japanese, which accompanied their English-language handout to the Nisei. In the English-language version of the handout of Saturday, March 4, 1944, the Fair Play Committee said, "We may have to engage in court actions." To the Issei, in Japanese, there was no maybe about it. They had a lawyer. They were going to mount a test case.

The position of this organization is for justice and fairness. We are dissatisfied with the policy of the Army regarding the selective service draft. If we are to be asked to fulfill a duty to the draft, give the nisei the same equal privilege and right as you give to the other Americans.

This is our attitude, and we called an attorney in Denver, Mr. Samuel Menin, and asked his advice as to how to make a test case regarding we the Nisei who have no rights or guarantee of liberty, and we wished to know if a test case could clarify the nisei status. And this test case must be a great one. So we appeal to you for your cooperation and help, economically and intellectually, and in a few weeks we will send a man to your residence and ask for help.

The *Pacific Citizen* of April 1, 1944, sensed the end of the Fair Play Committee and the conviction of all the draft resisters and lay responsibility for their humiliation at the feet of James Omura and his editorials in the *Rocky Shimpo*. Editorials by Larry Tajiri, Saburo

Kido, and Minoru Yasui defended the camps and tried to use the conviction of the draft resisters to vindicate the JACL's betrayal. Yasui, himself a practitioner of civil disobedience, pooh-poohed civil disobedience. Tajiri attacked Omura in typical JACL fashion. He didn't dare use Omura's name, as if attacking Omura namelessly made Tajiri's argument logical.

> The editorial function of a newspaper should remain the province of its editor, but when the irresponsible carrying-out of this function approaches the thin edge of sedition and menaces the welfare of all Americans of Japanese ancestry, then it becomes the concern of all. It is difficult to believe that the present editorial policy of the *Rocky Shimpo* is based on any naive belief that it will enhance the welfare of the Japanese American group. Already the adverse has been the effect. The *Rocky Shimpo* appears to be deliberately engaged in attempts to undo the positive services which Japanese Americans at war and producing for victory at home have contributed.

Once more, the JACL justifies the constitutional violations, and endorses the concentration camps, and forecloses redress with self-serving patriotic rhetoric and pure contempt. The *Pacific Citizen* of April 1, 1944, was not meant as an April Fool's Day joke.

Meantime, back at the concentration camp, the dismantling of the Fair Play Committee continued in a little room where, on April 3, 1944, Heart Mountain Project Director Guy Robertson and Assistant Project Director M. O. Anderson "interviewed" Ben Wakaye, the treasurer of the Fair Play Committee, who had left question 27 unanswered and had answered yes to question 28. Robertson's interrogation reads like the script of a World War II spy movie. He feigned misunderstanding, he cajoled, he threatened, and he unrelentingly pushed Wakaye's panic button while pressing into the stuff of which FBI cases are made:

ROBERTSON: I understand you are a member of the Fair Play Committee.

WAKAYE: Yes.

ROBERTSON: You are treasurer at the present time?

WAKAYE: Only in name. All the money is gone; I don't hold anything.

ROBERTSON: Don't you have any money?

WAKAYE: Only $5.13.

ROBERTSON: Where is the money?

WAKAYE: It is all gone.

ROBERTSON: How do you pay the money out? Who gave you the authority to spend it?

WAKAYE: We haven't a checking account or anything like that.

ROBERTSON: Who tells you to pay the money out?

WAKAYE: Well . . . there are different ones . . .

ROBERTSON: Could you tell the group?

WAKAYE: That is like being a rat, isn't it?

ROBERTSON: I don't know. It isn't an underground organization, is it?

WAKAYE: I don't think some would like to have their names mentioned.

ROBERTSON: If that is the case, why would they be on this committee?

WAKAYE: It is a loose organization like . . . every block has someone representing them. They can vote on it.

ROBERTSON: Isn't it necessary that you have someone to tell you what to do with the money?

WAKAYE: What do you mean?

ROBERTSON: Yes you do, Ben. I know you're smart. They wouldn't let you act as treasurer and let you spend the money as you pleased.

WAKAYE: Well, it is the Steering Committee.

ROBERTSON: Who are they?

WAKAYE: I guess you know some of them since they tried to go out the gate the other day.

ROBERTSON: I would like for you to tell me.

WAKAYE: Those two and Okamoto. He is the chairman. Nakadate, he is the vice-chairman. Quite a number.

ROBERTSON: How about Frank Emi?

WAKAYE: That is the one I mean went through the gate. Emi and Tamesa.

ROBERTSON: Who are some more? How about Horino?

WAKAYE: Yes.

ROBERTSON: Okamoto.

WAKAYE: Yes.

ROBERTSON: Nakadate?

WAKAYE: Yes.

Robertson had broken Wakaye open, made him give names. He pushed harder. He worried on Wakaye's handling of the Fair Play Committee's treasury of two hundred dollars and searched for the author of the committee's bulletins.

Wakaye wilted fast under Robertson and Anderson's questioning and badgering until he said, "I am sure up a creek." Robertson's interrogation of Wakaye ended with Robertson trying to lead Wakaye into denouncing articles and editorials written in the *Rocky Shimpo* by James Omura:

ROBERTSON: They [the newspaper articles] say the camp is on the verge of a big strike and blow-up . . .

WAKAYE: That was false . . .

ROBERTSON: I think those false things should be corrected, don't you?

WAKAYE: I think the individual should come out and not put too much blame on the Fair Play Committee. Those articles that were written weren't from the Fair Play Committee . . .

ROBERTSON: I would make them retract it then.

WAKAYE: You mean the newspaper?

ROBERTSON: I mean the 'Rocky Shimpo' newspaper.

WAKAYE: Am I the only one who will have a hearing like this?

ROBERTSON: I am going to talk to you boys who are the leaders. Thank you for coming in, Ben.

The next day, April 4, Project Director Robertson and Relocation Officer W. J. Carroll interviewed Frank Emi. Okamoto was the brains, Paul Nakadate was the orator, and the soft-spoken Frank Seishi Emi from San Fernando, California—a grocer and seventh-degree black belt in judo—was the moral center of the Fair Play Committee. Frank Emi was a most ordinary and extraordinary Nisei. In an earlier "hearing," Emi had been interrogated by six camp staff officers, including Robertson, the chief of internal security, and Lieutenant John E. Kellog of the military police. Now, to put Emi in his place, Nobu Kawai of the JACL and Heart Mountain *Sentinel* camp newspaper staff, was also present as an adviser to the interrogators. At the end of his interrogation, Emi had the presence of mind to add, "There is one last request I would like to make. Could I have a copy of this hearing?"

Frank Emi is the kind of Nisei JACL history says never was, and the kind the Sansei wish there had been as they suffer unique emotional problems because not one of their mother and father's Nisei generation had the guts to stand their ground and fight for their constitutional rights.

The Issei say it is to the shame of the Nisei that they did not produce a "martyr" who went down fighting rather than yield to a white racism that then became corrupt government policy. The Sansei would have been satisfied with less than a Nisei martyr. In Nisei and Sansei autobiography, fiction, and drama, there are many

Sansei children yelling and crying and wringing their hearts out at their Nisei parents for being so good at being pathological victims and wimps. But one cause for their lingering self-contempt might never have existed had they grown up knowing the Heart Mountain Fair Play Committee and Frank Emi as well as they knew Mike Masaoka, the JACL, and the 442nd Regimental Combat Team.

The Nisei and Sansei have imagined many times the give and take of a WRA interrogation of a heroic Nisei. The Nisei hero of Sansei imagination cops out by enacting the stereotyped victim of a passive culture with poetry and poetic emotion. Not in any of our wildest dreams, recorded in print or on stage, have the WRA officials been perceived as canny, clever, and comical, nor have the Nisei under interrogation been perceived as cool, unsentimental, ordinary, and tough, as they are in the transcripts of Robertson and Carroll's second interrogation of Frank Emi.

Here we offer the "pertinent portions" of the interrogation, used by the government as evidence in Emi's conspiracy trial, to provide a taste of a leader of the only organized resistance movement inside the camps, and to show the qualities that attracted the trust and respect of the eighty-five Heart Mountain Nisei arrested for resisting the draft. Emi's attitude—his strength, his canniness, and his level-headed, even-toned cool—toward the Heart Mountain resisters was the stuff of the Nisei as hero. Had John Okada known of Frank Emi when he was writing *No-No Boy,* he would have given him serious consideration and, perhaps, a place in his novel. As fine and as accurate as Okada's imagination is, in his portrayal of organized resistance in camp, there are no leaders. Someone like Frank Emi is missing.

HEARING BOARD FOR LEAVE CLEARANCE

Rehearing
April 4, 1944

MEMBERS OF THE BOARD: Guy Robertson, Project Director
W. J. Carroll, Relocation Officer

INTERVIEWEE: Frank Emi
9-21-A [9-21-B]
Heart Mountain, Wyoming

USES 18559

... ROBERTSON: In the Fair Play Committee you boys have come out with the statement that you hereby resolve not to appear for pre-induction physical or for induction if

called. There is a law in our statute which says
that every citizen unless excused for some special
reason is subject to the call when he is needed in
the army, either in time of peace or in time of
war. Now that is a law on the books.

EMI: Yes.

ROBERTSON: Don't you think you should obey that law implicitly?

EMI: We are not saying that we will not go into the army
or anything, Mr. Robertson. Like myself, I would
go any time if I was out in California or if I was
given the rights of any other American citizen, and I
still say that I am not saying I won't go as soon as I
am treated as an American citizen should be treated.
I would be glad to go.

ROBERTSON: I think that is right; I think also you are making
a mistake in that you are trying to bargain with
the government of the United States on a law that
is on the statute books, and that just can't be
done. Now if you want to have that law repealed
you shouldn't disobey a law in order to bring it
up for repeal. There are plenty of ways to bring
the case up without deliberately breaking the law
of the United States. Don't you think it would be
better for you to obey all laws of the United States
and at the same time to work diligently to obtain
that clarification of citizenship, or whatever you
call it?

EMI: That is the best way, yes. At the same time, up to
now we have been suppressed in our rights and
privileges of American citizenship because the government said so, and we have more or less complied
with that order; but, that order, I believe, is unconstitutional. Of course, that is before the Supreme
Court now. I believe that order to comply with the
Presidential Proclamation and all was unconstitutional because the Constitution of the United States
states that citizens shall not be deprived of life,
liberty or property without due process of law. In
my position, I do not know just what my status is as
a citizen. I do not know whether I am a full-fledged
citizen; they say I am, but actual factors are a little
bit different. And, I don't know whether I am in the
same status as the Indians, aren't they wards of the
government, Mr. Carroll?

ROBERTSON: . . . Do you think the activities of the Fair Play Committee have been subversive?

EMI: I don't think so, Mr. Robertson.

ROBERTSON: Do you think you have influenced other people to not answer the Selective Service call?

EMI: No, I don't think so because at some of the meetings I have attended, they have always come out and stated that if the person wants to get into the Fair Play Committee just to evade the draft, we don't want them. They also stated many times at the meeting those people who had intention of joining the committee just to evade the draft were not welcome. As you know, it is up to the individual.

ROBERTSON: Let me ask you, Frank, what do you think you can do by refusing to appear before Selective Service to clarify your situation. What, in other words, have you in mind, what is your aim?

EMI: I just wonder if it won't bring more attention to the fact that we, as American citizens in here and subject to the army, as such, that it would call the public's attention to the fact that we haven't the rights of citizens and they would try to remedy that. Of course, they will have to see both sides of the question, if they only see that we are violating the Selective Service Act naturally there isn't anyone that would be in sympathy with us, but in a court that is where I think a person has the right to present both sides of the picture.

CARROLL: What are the requirements to be a member of the Fair Play Committee?

EMI: I don't know of any specific requirements. You have to be a citizen and consider yourself a loyal citizen to be a member.

CARROLL: Does their interpretation of loyal American citizen mean that they should not answer their draft call?

EMI: No. I think every loyal American citizen should protect and uphold the Constitution and the Bill of Rights.

CARROLL: Are you a member of the Fair Play Committee?

EMI: Yes.

CARROLL: And, following that, you think you are a loyal citizen?

EMI: I don't know. Many things can happen between now and tomorrow. I may think one thing today and one thing tomorrow.

CARROLL:	What if I handed you your draft notice right now?
EMI:	Right now I think you know the way I have been thinking.
CARROLL:	Would you go or wouldn't you go?
EMI:	I would go just as soon as my status and right are clarified.
CARROLL:	How can you declare you are a loyal American citizen, then?
EMI:	Taking the stand that I just told you, I believe that by doing that I am helping toward the rectification of the unconstitutional acts the government has committed.
CARROLL:	You already have a test case in court now. How can you further help it?
EMI:	That is my individual feeling. I don't feel that it should be left to someone else.

On May 20, 1944, Larry Tajiri, in the JACL weekly *Pacific Citizen*, stalked the sixty-three Heart Mountain draft resisters awaiting trial, in county jails in Casper, Laramie, and Cheyenne. His editorial defended the camps and the drafting of Nisei internees as just, and threatened with social ostracism those who opposed the JACL.

There is no greater tragedy than that of lives and futures placed in needless jeopardy by foolhardy action under the motivation of misguided zeal. Yet, this is the situation precipitated by the action of 63 young men from the Heart Mountain relocation center who have refused to report for induction into the army of the United States. These draft resisters have already been arraigned and are now in jail at Cheyenne awaiting trial.

. . . A final effort should be made to deter this group from proceeding with an action which can result only in permanently stigmatizing them as draft dodgers. The road they are taking leads only to final ostracism from American society. It is for their parents, relatives and friends at Heart Mountain and elsewhere to prevail upon them to accept induction into the army.

. . . Japanese American soldiers . . . have already proven their loyalty and devotion to America on the beaches of Salerno, the banks of Volturno, in the hell of Cassino and wherever American troops are fighting. Any act at home which would detract from that proud record, whatever the motivations for that act, is a disservice to those Japanese Americans who have already contributed in blood.

Japanese American soldiers fighting and dying in Europe were irrelevant to the constitutional questions raised by the camps. But the threat of stigmatizing and ostracism from the Japanese American community was genuine and, although Okada's *No-No Boy* fictionalized the life of Hajiime Akutsu, postwar Japanese America was a JACL police state, No-No Boys and draft resisters were the pariahs, and the Nisei vets were the JACL police.

The trial of the sixty-three draft resisters from Heart Mountain was scheduled for May. It took place in June. They were tried in U.S. District Court as No. 2973, *USA* v. *Shigeru Fujii*. They were convicted on June 27, 1944, and sentenced to three years' confinement in a federal prison. The married men did their time at Leavenworth, Kansas. The single men went to McNeil Island, in Washington State. In August 1944, another group of twenty-two draft resisters from Heart Mountain were convicted as part of *USA* v. *Fujii* and sent to either Leavenworth or McNeil Island to serve three years. At McNeil Island, they met Gordon Hirabayashi, whose curfew violation had become the first test case. He was a hero, an example to them. Hirabayashi also resisted the draft. And they mingled with the "Forty-four Ronin" who had individually resisted the draft from Camp Minidoka. Hajiime Akutsu was one of the Minidoka 44. For months, Akutsu had been reading James Omura's articles and editorials about the organized resistance that had been going on at Heart Mountain. Nisei men, from both Heart Mountain and Minidoka, were in prison for taking the same stand for the same cause of the Nisei and the Constitution; these men who had heard about each other, and had admired each other, met on the farm outside the McNeil Island federal pen. It's almost too much to be true—like a saying from the heroic tradition come to life: "A hero recognizes a hero, a good man knows a good man" by instinct, on sight. But it is true.

Given "good time" time off for good behavior, all the Heart Mountain boys sent to McNeil Island served two years of their three-year sentences. Jack "Jackson" Tono, from San Jose, California, the high-spirited practical joker and morale booster of the first group of sixty-three, burned up his "good time" and spent an extra twenty-six days in prison.

The conviction of the Heart Mountain boys for violation of the Selective Service Act gave the prosecuting U.S. attorney, Carl Sackett, the backing he needed to go after the leaders of the Fair Play Committee for conspiracy to cause violations of that act. The trial of Kiyoshi Okamoto, Paul Takeo Nakadate, Tsutomu Wakaye, Frank Seishi Emi, Minoru Tamesa, Isamu Horino, Guntaro Kubota, and James Matsumoto Omura finally started in October. The jury acquitted Omura. The newspaper editor from Denver was not a member of the Fair Play Committee and had never set foot inside Heart Mountain. But the trial and its aftermath financially ruined him, and the JACL dictated his ostracism from Nikkei society.

Okamoto, Nakadate, Wakaye, Emi, Tamesa, Horino, and the Issei Zen man, Guntaro Kubota, were sentenced to four years at Leavenworth. Their conviction was overturned on appeal in 1946.

On Christmas Eve, 1947, Harry S Truman, president of the United States, issued Proclamation 2762, which granted pardon to all the Nisei convicted of violating the Selective Service Act. The President's Amnesty Board, headed by Owen J. Roberts, a former associate justice of the Supreme Court, said in their report:

> Closely analogous to conscientious objectors and yet not within the fair interpretation of the phrase, were a smaller, though not inconsequential number of American citizens of Japanese ancestry, who were removed in the early stages of the war from their homes in defense coastal areas and placed in war relocation centers.

The board's reason for recommending that they be pardoned reads like a paraphrase of the Fair Play Committee's first bulletin:

> Prior to their removal from their homes they had been law-abiding and loyal citizens. They deeply resent classification as undesirables. Most of them remained loyal to the United States and indicated a desire to remain in this country and to fight in its defense, provided their rights of citizenship were recognized. For these, we have recommended pardons, in the belief that they will justify our confidence in their loyalty.

After the trials of the Heart Mountain draft resisters and the Fair Play Committee leaders, the JACL paper and its editor, Larry Tajiri, returned to the task of encouraging the assimilation of the Nisei by heaping praise on Nisei women who married out white, for their daring to be morally and sociologically superior. In his column, "Nisei USA," he pondered the question of "Evacuation and Intermarriage."

> The brave new world of the post war future may take a more enlightened view toward miscegenation. . . .
> This matter of intermarriage is especially timely at the moment because of an interesting by-product of the military orders on the evacuation and exclusion of persons of Japanese ancestry

on the west coast. This is the tacit recognition by the government and the military of the validity of intermarriage. . . . Although all persons of Japanese ancestry on the west coast were forced to evacuate under the orders issued by General DeWitt in 1942, some families were allowed to return to their homes soon after. These were what the army termed "mixed marriage" cases. Since then, evacuation of some 500 persons, mostly women and children, of the original 112,000 evacuated, have been permitted to return to the coast. Almost without exception, the women in these cases were married to husbands not of Japanese ancestry.

At first, it appeared that only Japanese American women married to Caucasians could return, but it now appears that most mixed marriage couples are so favored.

The women marrying out would have the effect of a siphon on the rest of the race. Once the women were proven acceptable, the Nisei men would follow, Tajiri wrote. He cleverly argued that not to marry out white proved the white racists correct, the suggestion being that Japanese American girls who married Japanese American boys were serving the white racist cause:

The argument is too often advanced by the Native Sons and other white supremacist groups that Orientals generally, and persons of Japanese ancestry, in particular, are non-assimilable. One of the arguments being used, even today, against the return of the evacuated Japanese Americans to California is that they cannot be "assimilated," and it is pointed out that Japanese Americans in California rarely married outside of their group.

Tajiri continued, pointing out the unfairness of the charge, given the California state law against white-yellow miscegenation; but even given the deterrent of the law,

the evacuation and the family registration undertaken by the Wartime Civil Control Administration disclosed that there were many more cases of intermarriage than had been popularly supposed.

Thus Tajiri proved the JACL truth that, historically, all Japanese America really wanted was racial extinction through the joys of assimilation.

The resignation and surrender of the spirit is called *shikataganai*,

and the Nisei say it is the word that describes the Japanese culture
in them and that suggests their inexplicably passive acceptance of
the evacuation and incarceration. *Shikataganai* is used to explain
why there were no Joe Kuriharas, no James Omuras, no Fair Play
Committee. *Shikataganai* also posits a people individually isolated
from history, with no functional sense of honor and decorum. Betrayal, not *shikataganai,* explains the Japanese American spiritless-
ness that came out of camp.

The Nisei came out of the camps manufactured, trained, and
indoctrinated in the loathsome stereotypes of Asia, Japan, and
yellow immigrants. They came out of the desert to outwhite the
whites and fulfill white racist fantasies. The Issei-Nisei compact was
no more. Those Nisei who kept the compact were exceptions who
proved the rule. They numbered two out of thousands. Only two.
Kazuo Miyamoto, the old Nisei doctor from Hawaii, would be
driven to race scholars and social scientists to write his people's
history after sensing the extent and value of what the camps had
forced the Nisei to forget. Toshio Mori, upon the announcement of
settlement and impersonal programs bringing the camps to a close,
honored the Issei-Nisei compact with an epitaph marking the end of
camp, and the end of a people:

We will leave individually, one-by-one, to some other locality
and some to the unknown beyond. . . . Our world will be gone,
and there will be no more little Tokyos. Yes, we shall see no
more the lantern parades and the kimonos of the past. Our days
of hightop boots, jeans, and the uniform mackinaws will be gone.
The "Tojo" hats will become useless with wear and tear, and
grotesque in new surroundings. We shall move on, willingly, into
the melting world of our land, forever to lose our racial identity,
however impossible, and assuredly certain to drop our differences
when we shall pass away from the earth of our mutual interest.

Hisaye Yamamoto writes on the nature of the Nisei:

For a writer proceeds from a compulsion to communicate a
vision and he cannot afford to bother with what people in
general think of him. We Nisei, discreet, circumspect, care very
much what others think of us, and there has been more than
one who has fallen by the wayside in the effort to reconcile his
inner vision with outer appearances.

Masaoka's visionary language has crept into Nisei art, and the
making of the difference between the real and the fake has become

the failure of the inner vision to reconcile with outer appearances: the clash of Western belief and Asian history.

The camp anthropologists, likewise, thought the Issei used writing to escape reality:

> The authority and the Analyst both feel that they have discovered something important about the cultural revivalism seen in the *Senryu Kai*. This cultural activity provides escape from the drab realities of center existence. It also recaptures Japanese cultural values of an apolitical sort.

The Nisei who assume the Issei author of "Duck" is merely sentimental, nostalgic, and longing for home are wrong. Shumpa Kiuchi's poem is a conscious echo of an old poem in an old heroic tale.

DUCK

April 1945

On the fishpond in front of a barrack
a duck is floating.
It is said that Mr. "A" caught it on his way home
from a fishing trip.
Caught in somebody's trap
and perhaps, when it freed itself,
one webfoot . . .
On top of that, the previous wing
is so badly hurt it cannot fly.

So deep is its sorrow
a piece of bread is thrown unnoticed.
It surely must have a parent-duck
and brother-drakes as well;
disconsolate, alone, the duck
is meditating in the shadow of a small rock.
Although its bluish-purplish plumes
glisten, resplendent in the morning sun . . .

Although the pond looks peaceful enough
you, thoroughly deprived of your freedom
can't resign yourself to Fate or to Destiny
O Duck, unable to fly!
From the bottom of my heart I sympathize
with you, who love Nature and Freedom
with an aching heart, a leg and one wing.

I don't want to predict your future;
I am reflecting
Your Fate and my present Fate
in the mirror of my heart. O Duck!

"Duck" echoes a poem in *Water Margin* where Song Jiang, leader of the 108 outlaws, writes in full retreat to geese.

The 108 outlaws have been amnestied and the emperor meets all of Song Jiang's terms with the proviso that he lead his army on an imperial mission. Before setting out on the mission, Song Jiang violates the rule of Sun Tzu, the philosopher of war, that forbids all religious practices when waging war, and consults a seer. The seer tells Song Jiang:

When the shadows of the wild geese pass, in the east there is no unity . . . Cocking an eye he scores his mark, at Double Woods full prosperity.

At Double Woods Crossing, one of the 108 heroes practices his archery by shooting geese out of the sky. The falling geese distress Song. The archer says:

I needed practice and saw them flying overhead. I didn't expect every arrow to score a hit. I must have brought down more than a dozen.

Song Jiang tells the archer:

A military man ought to practice his archery, and you're an expert at it. I was just thinking—these geese leave the Tianshan Range in autumn and fly south across the Yangzi with reeds in their beaks to where it's warm and they can find food, and don't return till the following spring. They're the most virtuous of birds. They travel in flocks of up to half a hundred, flying in orderly ranks with the leader at the head and the inferiors behind. They never leave the flock, and post sentinels when they rest at night. If a gander loses his goose, or a goose her gander, they never mate again. These fowl possess all five attributes—virtue, righteousness, propriety, knowledge, and faith.

If a goose dies in flight, all utter cries of mourning, and none will ever harass a bereaved bird. This is virtue. When a fowl loses its mate, it never pairs again. This is righteousness. They fly in a definite order, each automatically taking its place. This is propriety. They avoid hawks and eagles, silently crossing the passes with reed sticks in their beaks. This is knowledge. They fly south in autumn and north in the spring, every year without fail. This is faith.

How could you have the heart to harm such admirable creatures? Those geese passing in the sky, all helping one another, are very much like our band of brothers. Yet you shoot them down. How would you feel if it were some of your brothers we had lost? You must never hurt these virtuous birds again!

Yan Qing listened in penitent silence. Full of emotion, Song Jiang composed and recited a poem:

Jagged peaks draped in mist,
Three lines of geese across the sky.
Suddenly in flight a mate is lost—
Cold moon, chill breeze, a mournful cry.

He felt extremely depressed. That night, the army camped at Double Woods Crossing. Song Jiang brooded in his tent. He called for paper and writing brush and composed these lines:

Far from the startled scattered flock
in the vast clear firmament
a wild goose flies.
A lone shadow seeking a sheltering pond
Finding naught but dry grass, sandy wastes,
Open water, endless skies.

No poet,
I can only set down these few thoughts.
Dusk in an empty ravine.
Campfire smoke in an ancient fort,
I'm more dejected than I can say!

Though we've cleared the reeds
We've no place to spend the night,
When, oh when, will we see once more
The Yumen Gate to our homeland!

Drearily, I sob and sigh,
Longing to depart this hateful river.
Would that spring come soon again,
With swallows nesting in the beams.

Song Jiang showed what he had written to Wu Yong and Gongshun Sheng. His sadness and loneliness were quite apparent. He was very unhappy.

Song Jiang, pondering the fate of his brothers amnestied by the sovereign, could be Shumpa Kiuchi, an Issei writing from camp; the Issei writing from camp knows and dives into the heroic tradition, not to escape the camps but to confront and command them.

The camps are closing, the Nikkei are being encouraged to lose themselves into the world, just as the bandits of Liangshan were amnestied and freed to fight in the service of the emperor and his corrupt government. For the Issei and the heroes of yesteryear, the moment is the same. Corrupt officials, without the sovereign's knowledge, ultimately betray the 108 heroes and poison the leader, Song, with doctored imperial wine. The Issei, the outcasts of the outcasts, step out of their exile into the same laws and government that had betrayed them, girding themselves for more betrayal and extinction, at the hands of their children, out to win white favor. In Shusei Matsui's "From a Corner of an Arsenal," the rhetoric of the Nisei JACL is bitterly satirized—"discharged soldiers, cripples, morons"—in an assertion of Issei "individuality."

From a Corner of an Arsenal

June 1945

Again, this morning, it's that same bossy, ugly
face!
Young errand boys boisterously jumping about
Like frogs inside a well.

Silently, forcing a smile within my heart
I overlook everything with transcendental philosophy
For this is but an inescapable concomitant of war,
And since the Japanese are a special people.

Within the arsenal
Conglomerate races under the appellation "Caucasian"
Vie to make a porter out of me, just me.
It makes me sick to my stomach.

Within the arsenal are discharged soldiers,
cripples, morons:
I can't fathom why they're so haughty
Behind their facade "IT'S WARTIME!"
I wonder—can it be a sense of superiority
Of a so-called "New Order"?

Fortunately, I cannot wither
No matter how hard I'm trampled upon:
For I possess a living individuality and pride.

I'm satisfied—
This individuality that makes us what we are . . .

O repulsive face! Possessor
of an enigmatic character!
Even though I'm dying
I'm breathing spiritedly!

The Issei that emerges out of the mass of Issei camp writing stands contrary to all the stereotypes produced by the social scientists, the WRA, the JACL, and the Nisei writing in camp. The culturally myopic or, perhaps, patriotic social scientists never got beyond the number of syllables in a line, rhyme and scheme and thematic rules governing specific forms in their understanding of Japanese literature and culture. Had they known the works every Japanese child has known for centuries, they would have discovered exactly how the Issei used the past and the heroic tradition in literature to define the strategic problems of the present, in terms of an ongoing war against individual honor and integrity.

The classics of the Chinese heroic tradition—*Three Kingdoms, Water Margin,* and *Journey to the West*—inform the most universally known heroic tale of Japan, *Chushingura.* Like all the Chinese works, *Chushingura* makes reference to Sun Tzu and his thirteen chapters of verse on the art of war. Sun Tzu is the key to the popular Confucianist thought of the average Asian. Sun Tzu is certainly the key to form and dramatic logic in all these works. They all quote him and render him dramatic in the real world.

All the works of the heroic tradition—including the fairy tales and *Three Kingdoms, Water Margin, Journey to the West,* and "The Ballad of Mulan"—were banned in China during the Cultural Revolution. Culture and literature move from the bottom to the top, from the folk to the court, not vice versa as in the West, and the Chinese, as they had under the Tartars and Mongols, maintained the real underground, just as Song Jiang's 108 outlaws had maintained their integrity and Chinese culture in their marshland stronghold.

All Chinese culture, even the language itself, is banned in Indonesia today. The Chinese maintain and teach the language and culture underground, using the works of the heroic tradition. Chinese children in Indonesia meet secretly in a teacher's room. The teacher recites and writes a page from the heroic tradition on a chalkboard. The children copy, memorize, recite, and internalize each lesson as a set. At the end of the lesson, the students burn their papers (shades of Ray Bradbury's *Fahrenheit 451*!).

The heroic tradition ordinary Chinese families risk arrest, exile, and deportation to maintain, under anti-Chinese racist oppression, is the same heroic tradition Maxine Hong Kingston, David Henry Hwang, Amy Tan, and the Christian Chinese Americans fake and force into the stereotype.

Japanese American poet Mitsuye Yamada, known for her writing on the Nikkei concentration camp experience, said, "It doesn't matter . . ." when presented with a pile of Chinese children's books, lesson books, and comic books full of the woman warrior, Fa Mulan, as the Chinese know, cherish, and teach her. It does not matter that Kingston and Hwang have grotesquely altered Mulan's appearance, mutilated her body beyond recognition, and cast her as an enemy of the culture and values she championed and embodied. The falsification of all Chinese history and culture does not matter in the reading of Kingston and Hwang, according to Yamada. "What matters is perspective," she said. It's what they believe, not what they know that counts. It was just such an ecstatic mythical triumph of belief, of patriotic perspective over the fact of Nisei United States citizenship, that put Yamada and the Japanese Americans out of their homes and into concentration camps.

The case for redress was not a matter of perspective but a matter of fact, lots of facts dug up by Japanese Americans who were inspired to make the difference between the real and the fake by a Nisei woman with the fragility of the newborn, the beauty of an angel, the stomach of a goat, the *makoto* of Yuranosuke Oishi, and the voice of an angry, knowledgeable Nisei: Michi Weglyn. Until Weglyn's *Years of Infamy: The Untold Story of America's Concentration Camps* (1976) appeared, all the Nisei writing on the camps was for not being bitter. It was heavy on the sentimentality, the self-pity, and the overwhelming disorientation of the completely devastated victim. Weglyn's book effectively ended the sob stories for sob stories' sake, pointed fingers, named names, and hit the bad guys with the facts. The line of research she opened with *Years of Infamy*, and the former Amache inmate's personal example, inspired the Nisei to free their unspeakable anger and bitterness about the camps, and to use their anger to drive a new wave of research, exploration, and expression on the camps, to make the difference between the real and the fake.

Michi Weglyn's *Years of Infamy* was the first and is the only Asian American work to actually effect a change in Japanese American character and history. *Years of Infamy* brought Michi Weglyn, Aiko Yoshinaga Herzig, and Jack Herzig together and, continuing along Weglyn's line of research, the Herzigs uncovered the facts that the government had kept hidden and the lies that the government had told the Supreme Court in order to sell the camps as necessary and just. The new pile of declassified documents (signed by the authors of hard times for the Nikkei themselves) and Michi Weglyn's book led to the Bernstein Commission on Wartime Relocation and Internment of Civilians, which recommended that redress be made. The documents and Weglyn's book also formed the evidentiary bedrock of Peter Irons's *Justice at War* (1983), which led to the reopening of cases against curfew and evacuation violators Hirabayashi, Yasui, and Korematsu on a writ of *coram nobis*; supported William Hohri's National Council for Japanese American Redress (NCJAR) class-action suit (which the Supreme Court finally refused to hear), and contributed to the work of Richard Drinnon's *Dillon Myer: Keeper of Concentration Camps* (1987), to Peter Suzuki's anthropology on the camp anthropologists, and to this book.

Michi Weglyn's *Years of Infamy* got Japanese America up for proving and chasing redress by recovering what was lost and restoring what was abandoned. No book, no work of science, literature, or art has had such an immediate and palpable effect on Japanese American behavior and history since, truth to tell, Mike Masaoka's "JACL: A Japanese American Creed" and the WRA's loyalty oath. The difference is, Mike Masaoka and the JACL were imposed on the Japanese Americans to imprison them, and the same Japanese Americans were inspired by Michi Weglyn's book and example to individually break out of the fake. Not surprisingly, Weglyn's history of what lay behind the decision to pack Japanese America into concentration camps and their corrupt administration is a tale of betrayal, all kinds of betrayal. The revenge, demanded by these betrayals, she makes clear, is that her book, that exposé of white racist illogic in the highest and some of the strangest of places, being written by one who was despised, *is* the revenge.

Japanese American artists love Michi Weglyn and her book, but their art has not touched the facts and approached the challenge to the stereotype her work, and the work she has inspired, raises. Something happened. It is up to Japanese American art to express exactly what. All *The Big Aiiieeeee!* can say is that it matters that the Nisei were United States citizens. It matters that the JACL betrayed Japanese America. It matters that James Omura wrote to make the difference between the real and the fake in hard times. It matters that Michi Weglyn remembered his name. It matters that Shumpa Kiuchi's "Duck" evokes the heroic tradition and is much more than melancholy slop. It matters that John Okada fuels his novelistic imagination with the intelligence of a real No-No Boy and draft resister, not the inspiration of a righteous perspective. It matters that twenty-two thousand Nikkei were fingered and counted by the JACL and the government as resisters. It matters that the number was more than ten times the entire wartime JACL membership of eighteen hundred. It matters that Fa Mulan was not tattooed. It matters that the Chinese and Japanese immigrants came as settlers and established the tongs and tanemoshi, Chung Wah Wooey Goon and Nikkei Jinkai, as permanent institutions. It matters that Spaniards and Basques really mingled with the Chinese in San Francisco. It matters that all the Chinese and Japanese American writers in this book, no matter what they believe or what literary form they favor, make the difference between the real and the fake. It matters that the Asian American writers here are not—with one exception—yellow engineers of the stereotype. The pleasures of these works do not depend on the reader's ignorance of the real. It matters.

San Francisco. Chinatown–North Beach. Tonight. What holds the Asian Americas together, right now, at about half past dead? Aiiieeeee!

Wong Sam and Assistants

Who was Wong Sam? Who were his assistants? We don't know. We don't know how they convinced Wells, Fargo to print and distribute the bilingual *An English-Chinese Phrase Book* in its 130 offices throughout the West in towns where Chinamen lived and worked. We do know that whoever he was, Wong Sam revised the 1875 edition two years later, and Wells, Fargo published and distributed this larger version of the *Phrase Book* in more than two hundred towns with Chinese American populations.

This is not the kind of phrase book used alphabetically by subject. The Chinese learn writing, painting, philosophy, martial arts through a process of memorization, recitation, and internalization of specific "sets." In the *Phrase Book,* the sets contain strategy and tactics for business and criminal law, and for dealing with white people in general. These sets are "fast," unlike those of *The Analects* of Confucius, which take years—a lifetime—to internalize. No, these sets are meant to be memorized quickly, fun to recite, and internalized by the time a Chinaman has his first experience with a white man.

Try these phrases out loud with a different voice for every other line, and it will be instantly apparent that Wong Sam and Assistants' tactics and strategy for dealing with the white man's application of the law do not include submission, acculturation, and assimilation. The Christian prayers found at the back of the *Phrase Book* are themselves a strategy for raising money to publish the book.

Eighteen seventy-five.

Rye Patch, Nevada. Salem, Oregon. Sierra City, California. You have to do business. Get from one place to another, buy clothes, secure licenses. Have an answer for the cops when they ask why your friend is dead on your doorstep. Read these sets. Memorize them. Recite them. Free-associate with them, riff with them and discover how they work. Internalize them until all the phrases are instinct. Wong Sam and his assistants compiled a book of phrases that prepared the Chinese for any situation, anywhere in the American West. The *Phrase Book* is that set. Free! At any Wells, Fargo office.

———

An English-Chinese Phrase Book

你有乜貨物出賣
What goods have you for sale?

樣樣都有
I have all kinds.

我想買條好褲
I want to get a pair of your best pants.

你愛點樣價銀
What do you ask for them?

你舱減少些
Can you take less for them?

先生　不舱
I cannot, sir.

汝還有好過汝樣麼
Have you any other kind better than these?

汝肯賣賒款麼
Will you sell on credit?

我賣現銀　先生
No sir, I sell for cash.

倘汝俾好貨過我　我時
時與汝交易
I will come to deal with you always if you give me the best kinds (quality).

為何咁貴
How is it that it is so dear?

煩汝與我交易
Please give me your custom.

好貨稅餉太重　另值我
本銀十元
Well, sir, it costs us $10, and besides we have to pay very heavy duty on our best goods.

好生意
Is business good?

甚好　多謝
Very well, I thank you.

買客甚少
The buyers are very few.

生意焉舱興旺
How can the business be prosperous!

有人缺本
Some men lose capital.

有人賺銀
Some men get profits.

價銀太高
The price is too high.

我唔舱俾得咁多
I am not able to pay.

我賣甚公平
I sell very justly.

孩子我都不騙
I don't cheat, even a boy.

自然係眞
Certainly, it is true.

賣客甚多
The sellers are too many.

價錢憑貨物
The price depends on the goods.

佢應當對面講
He ought to speak face to face.

倘若我愛物我再回來
If I want anything I will call on you again.

吩咐攔阻
In order to prevent.

貨物頂好
The goods are first-class.

乜價錢嗎
What is the price?

價錢係真
And the price is fixed.

四元銀一叫順
Four dollars per dozen.

先驗明貨正買
Examine the goods before you buy.

我必先說汝知
I must tell you before.

我有時買來平
Sometimes I bought them cheap.

有時我平賣
Sometimes I sold them cheap.

我如今照市價賣
Now I sell them at market prices.

自然係真實
Certainly, it is true.

因謂稅餉太重
Because the duty is too heavy.

買賣甚艱難
To buy and sell is very difficult.

有時我買淂貴
Sometimes I buy them dear.

因此我賣亦貴
Of course I must sell them dear.

我一樣價錢賣
I sell them at one price.

中意咁多就買咁多
Buy as many as you like.

你要價錢高
You ask too high a price.

唔係價高　先生
It is not dear, sir.

不防我騙汝
Don't fear I am cheating you.

我有鞋帽衣服
I also have clothes, shoes and caps.

你肯俾我看麼
Can you let me see them?

倘你如意看就看　此物不
是好淂
If you like to see, you might see, they are not very good.

你肯賣平些
Can you sell it cheaper?

你愛幾多
How much do you want?

我如今無
I have none now.

俾貨我看過
Show me some goods.

汝愛幾多銀
What do you charge for it?

乜誰命汝來
Who sent you here for it?

我唔相信汝
I cannot trust you.

我下禮拜俾汝
I shall pay you next week.

我望汝相信我
I hope you will trust me.

我防汝走去
I fear you will run away.

為何汝唔買
Why don't you buy them?

我明日來取
I will come for them to-morrow.

信道理捱欺
Christians bear great trials.

佢強搶我物
He took it from me by violence.

我無意打佢
I struck him accidentally.

我認唔該佢還想來打我
I have made an apology, but still he wants to strike me.

佢無事打我
He assaulted me without provocation.

我賃汝樓要汝包水
I will rent the house if you include the water.

你肯去我包汝回
I Guarantee to bring him back, if he will go.

此人欲搽工銀
The men are striking for wages.

我身分足用
I am content with my situation.

你同佢闘款
You contend with him about the account.

裝滿箱蘋果
The box contains apples.

佢詐病
He feigned to be sick.

女人暈倒在會堂
The lady fainted in church.

佢誓了願
He ended what he said with an oath.

此樓無意燒了
The house was burned by accident.

此樓有意燒了
The house was set on fire by an incendiary.

佢想白認我行李
He tried to obtain my baggage by false pretenses.

佢強搶我泥口
He claimed my mine.

佢強霸我地
He squatted on my lot.

倘佢唔走我定然逐佢出去
I will expel him if he don't leave the place.

幾時滿期
When will the lease expire?

你幾時滿號
When is the expiration of you lease?

我下禮拜四滿號
Next Thursday my month will have expired.

昨日我工滿號一月
Yesterday was the expiration of one month of labor.

我下禮拜四滿號
My month will have expired on Thursday next.

佢簽名于紙上
He indorsed the note.

佢做我認頭
He went my security.

你肯誓願麼
Can you swear to that.

佢誓了願
He has sworn already.

佢誓願幾次
He swore several times.

我保佢前後
I guarantee him back and fore.

我包個樓係好個
I warranted the house to be a good one.

佢在審事堂誓假願
He perjured himself in Court.

佢在衙門誓願官府廳
He gave his oath to the judge in Court.

佢誓假願
He was fined for perjury.

佢託名捉拿
He was arrested for forgery.

倘有材料我可做工之于沒
If you find the materials I will furnish laborers.

倘沒唔賠我定劫沒家物
I will attach his furniture if you idemnify me.

倘若滿號沒無俾我定然封沒鋪之契
I will close the mortgage on your store if you don't pay me when the time has expired.

我定封沒鋪之契若滿號無俾
I will close the mortgage on your store if you don't pay me when the time has expired.

佢逼勒我可銀
He tries to extort money from me.

沒去假託逼勒佢照（招）
They are going to extort a confession from him by false pretensions.

逼佢招出
The confession was extorted from him by force.

唬怕勒逼佢招認罪
The confessions were extorted from them by threats

我保佢出監
I bailed him out of jail.

我掭水上船
I bailed the water out of the boat.

佢一仟五佰銀保單
He gave bonds for $1,500.

佢案情昨日十點鐘開審
His case was tried yesterday at 10 A. M.

官府定然定罪于過
The judge will certainly convict him.

佢受大頭人定佢罪
He was convicted by the jury.

佢如今定罪
He is now a convict.

佢取人來見証係真
He brought a man to prove the fact.

人曰我講所見之事
The man said: "I will testify what I saw."

佢口供已經信了
His testimony was believed.

佢搾治沒工艮
He will retain your wages.

佢騙了我之工艮
He cheated me out of my wages.

佢詿騙東家
He swindled his employer.

佢騙了我斯文銀
He defrauded me out of my salary.

案情昨日罷了
The case was ended yesterday.

後回審定了罪
He was found guilty, by the last trial.

決命佢去做十年苦工
He will be sent to the penitentiary for
10 years.

佢已經命去省監
He has been sent to the State Prison.

佢誣告我偷鏢
He falsely accused me of stealing his watch.

汝犯了國法
You have violated the Constitution of this State.

他眠埋伏之地
They were lying in ambush.

佢被誤殺
He came to his death by homicide.

佢被夜盜謀殺
He was murdered by a thief.

佢犯罪自儘
He committed suicide.

佢受賊人用繩索索死
He was choked to death with a lasso, by a
robber.

佢受人縊死
He was strangled to death by a man.

佢飢死在監
He was starved to death in prison.

佢在霜冷死
He was frozen to death in the snow.

佢在灣投水死
He was going to drown himself in the bay.

後尋數日捉治兇手
After searching for several days they caught the
murderer.

汝明淂係眞實
Did they find anything in his possession.

也有
They did.

佢受人陰殺
He was killed by an assassin.

佢想陰害我
He tried to assassinate me.

佢想陰殺我
He tried to kill me by assassination.

佢係功打之人
He is an assaulter.

佢在房淹死
He was smothered in his room.

佢捫死在房裡
He was suffocated in his room.

佢受仇人用炮打死
He was shot dead by his enemy.

佢受朋友用藥道死
He was poisoned to death by his friend.

佢想用藥道死
He tries to kill him by poisoning.

佢加刑死在監
He tries to inflict death by poison.

立意攻擊禍害肉身
Assault with the intention to do bodily injury.

佢手拈規例
He took the law in his own hand.

佢想奪去我位
He tried to deprive me of my situation.

佢不義搶去我工銀
He wrongfully deprived me of my wages.

我夜間回家
I go home at night.

我也回家
I have gone home.

我去歸
I went home.

我在家住
I abide at home.

我在大埠住
I abode at San Francisco.

我也曾在屋崙住
I have lived in Oakland.

我日出起身
I arise at sunrise.

我今早四點鐘起身
I arose this morning at 4 o'clock.

我有時上晝三點起身
I have arisen at 3 A. M. some mornings.

我四點鐘醒
I awake at 4 o'clock.

我今早五點鐘醒
I awoke this morning at 5 o'clock.

我有時七點鐘醒
I awaken at 7 A. M. sometimes.

我七點鐘開工
I begin work at 7 A. M.

我上晝八點鐘開工
You began work at 8 A. M.

我六點鐘開工
We have begun work at 6 A. M.

我綁起此麥
We bind the wheat up.

我綁洽個瘡
We bound up the wound.

我用鐵鍊綁洽個孩子
We have bound that boy with a chain.

汝毀了窗門
You break windows.

我毀了刀
I broke my knife.

他毀了國法
They have broken the laws of the State.

丟佢下水
Cast him into the water.

我捉個人入監今日
We cast a man into p[rison to-day.

人他放出去
They have cast the man out.

斬柴過個人
You cut wood for the man.

佢無意斬了隻手
He cut a man's hand off by an accident.

我斬倒此樹
We have cut the tree down.

乃日汝淂順便到來
What day is the most convenient for you to come?

汝幾時順便到此處
What day is the most convenient for you to be here?

汝乃日便到位
What day is the most convenient for you to be present?

乜日汝到來
What day can you come?

乃日汝如意來拜見
What day is the best time for you to call?

幾時汝有好機會到此
What day is the best chance for you to get here?

汝定乜日到來
What certain day can you arrive?

乃日汝可敢起程
On what day is it possible for you to depart?

乃日沒著便起程
What will be the most suitable day for you to start?

乃日沒可骰放落工夫
At what day can you leave the work?

乃日沒可骰離開事業
At what day can you get away from your avocation?

乃日沒骰得去
What day can you get away?

我唔估到沒來此處
I did not think that you would come here.

我唔曾望沒到此
I did not expect that you would be here.

我唔估沒肯來
I did not suppose that you would come.

我唔知沒顧來
I did not know that you would come.

我唔估沒想來
I never thought that you would come.

我唔估沒到來
I have not been expecting you.

我唔估係沒
I could not think it were you.

你驚揚於我
You have taken me by surprise.

我並無等候見沒
Well! I never expected to see you.

沒可骰來得
Is it possible that you have come?

順便來見
Call in when convenient.

不過係順便來拜見
I call in because it is convenient.

我因為得閒到來
I came because I had an opportunity.

我因為順便到來
I came because it was convenient.

一有便處我就到來
I came at the first opportunity.

我因方便到來
My convenience caused me to come.

我中意來
It suits me to come.

因合宜我來
There is an appropriateness in my coming.

我合宜到來
There is a fitness in my coming.

我因朋友唔來我就來
I came because my friend did not come.

我咁樣做因為我中意
I do so because I love to.

我來因我有個好機會
I came for I had a splendid chance.

我來因我有好機會
I came for I had a good chance.

我估我過時就入來
Well! I thought I would drop in while passing.

我估我行過之時順便入來見
Well! I thought I would make a visit while passing.

我估庭昔過此地
Well! I thought I would step in while passing by here.

我估我會庭一時之久
Well! I thought I would step in for a moment.

我來因我有得閒
Oh! I came because my time was not occupied.

我來因我在家無工夫做
Oh! I came because I had nothing to do at home.

我方便因此我來
The commodiousness of the cars enabled me to come conveniently.

你要乜野呀先生
Well, sir! what will you have?

好呀先生我幫汝做乜野
Well, sir! what can I do for you?

你想愛乜野先生
Well, sir! what do you wish?

尊駕汝要乜呀
Well, sir! what do you want?

你想買乜野先生
Well, sir! what do you want to buy?

一擔貨過崙屋每日來回

汝要幾多艮一個月
What will be the charges per month for a vegetable dealer and his two baskets to Oakland and return, daily?

我買汝貨我要汝送到我

處
I buy goods from you, I want you to deliver them to my place.

連箱借與我明日送回汝
Lend to me, with the box too, I will return it to you to-morrow.

我要汝包我出入費用
I want you to pay all my fare of coming and going.

你嫌我貨價錢貴因此汝

唔買
You dislike my goods because it is so dear, and you don't buy.

等幾日然後講汝知
Wait for a few days, then I will tell you.

汝幾時齊備
When will you be ready?

汝肯相信我
Will you trust me?

佢係拐帶之人
He is a kidnapper.

佢係我書館學生頭
He is a monitor in our school.

放牛乳油入碗櫃
Put the butter in the cupboard.

倒白糖出來牛乳盤
Empty the sugar into the milk-pan.

汝愛我幫汝
You want me to help you?

佢內外病症
He is sick in mind and body.

佢心算度即如他手做工

咁辛苦
He is performing hard mental as well as physical labor.

留住他一禮拜工艮等佢

在此長做
I keep back a week's wages in order to secure his stay.

多煩汝俾回我汝所留住

之工艮
Please give me now that portion of my wages which you have withheld from me.

耶穌係我中保
Christ is our mediator.

我高過佢
I am taller than he.

每間店鋪有一個出番之
人能說英話
There is not a store which has not an interpreter -- one who can speak the English language.

我問他知到乃一間唐舖
方一兩個皷說英話

I asked them if they ever knew a Chinese store in San Francisco without one or more who could speak English.

我問他知到乃一間舖方
一兩個皷講英話

I asked them if they knew of a store without one or more who could speak English.

中市人做得好過佢

Mr. Jones can do better than he.

佢欲强逼我

He wants to force me (compel).

我唔估到咁樣的

I didn't think it would cause such trouble.

或者佢做了

He might have cone it.

我們有長久審問

We will have a long investigation.

未曾伴段

It is not decided yet.

你自捉治佢或是沒查出
佢

Did you catch him yourself, or find out by inquiry?

沒有乜憑據足意來定
佢罪

Did you find any proof sufficient to convict him.

佢們尋出些物件在佢家
業之中

They searched and found something in his possession.

我唔知定是否

I did not know if it were certain or not.

我唔明白此件事情

I don't understand the whole affair.

若有乜撞板或偶然之事
我必來沒處

In case of failure or any accident I will come to you.

你可皷擔帶此案情

Can you be responsible for the case?

沒方受別人話

You don't accept others' information.

沒唔怕公義

Do you not care for justice?

你做事無好緣故

You do things without a just cause.

與我打合紅

Make a contract with me.

但沒記得通知我自然唔
遲

When you think of it inform me, so I will not be late.

准延遲些

Allow me a little longer time.

此人貪心

This person is covetous.

佢係唔自在

He is indisposed.

佢連累我

He implicates me.

佢禁監整路做苦工

He was imprisoned, with hard labor on the road.

佢在街上被鞭打了兩次

He was flogged publicly twice in the streets.

佢想走脫刑罰

He tries to escape from his punishment.

沒貴叫乜姓

What is your honorable surname?

我小妜黃
My humble surname is Wong.

我先聽唔見
I cannot hear you first.

汝觥等遲幾日
Can you wait a few days longer?

汝要我俾汝定銀嗎
Do you want me to pay you in advance?

若然汝敢就做
Do, if you dare.

我唔怕汝
I don't fear you.

你估汝可觥壓得住我
You think you can get the best of me?

佢暗算來佔人之工
He strives to underwork one's situation.

我一生唔曾做過咁事
I never did so in my life.

我即係汝使我咁做
I will do just as you tell me.

佢好小心人
He minds very well.

若佢依從咁樣做佢中意
在此幾奈都得
If he does as I want him to he can stay here as
long as he likes.

佢觥做起我工夫我必加
些工臽
I will increase his wages when he is able to do
all my work.

煩汝體固至緊
Please look out for him by all means.

我與佢買來
I bought it of him.

佢後來反口又要取多些添
He afterward backed down from his promise
and asked more for it.

望汝下畫相饒我待我拈
信去信館
I want you to excuse me this afternoon, so I
can carry my letter to
the post-office.

我上畫有些緊要事望汝
相饒我
I would like to have you excuse me this
forenoon, for I have some very
important business to do for myself.

我包汝無事
I guarantee that you will have no trouble.

此乃係佢無容和疑
I have no doubt that it was he (not him).

不勞其力
I won't trouble him.

我係寨主
Me as one of the stockholders.

我係伴人
Me as a partner.

此正埠係興盛埠
San Francisco is a prosperous city.

華哩河是個興旺邑
Vallejo was a flourishing town.

還回此款尾
Pay the balance of the account.

永不改事業
Permanent employment.

佢有恆久身分
He has a permanent situation

我暫時做住　任
I have a temporary situation.

我去勸開他們相打
I went and separated them while fighting.

我勸開之後佢被捉入衙
門
Both of them were arrested after I had separated them.

他們照例罰
They were fined according to the law.

放工
Dismissed from work.

煩賜我平安
Please have a regard for my welfare.

佢係假認高才之人
He is a pedantic man.

佢係多事之人
He is an officious person.

人叫佢做假認高才者
People call him a pedant.

滿城人知他是假認高才
者
He is known by the whole city as a pedant.

無和疑佢係假冒者
There is no need to doubt that he is the forger.

他們打爛窗門被捉
They were arrested for breaking the window.

此個係假冒之人
One of them was a forger.

汝未滿期切不可去
You must never go off without leave.

我滿號定然辭別
I will leave you when my month is up.

火船明日開身
The steamer will leave to-morrow.

由得他至下個禮拜
Leave it until next week.

我憎趕火車唔到
I hate to miss the train.

我防不色書
I fear to miss my lesson.

我唔失得至回家去
I did not miss it until got home.

馬利遲到
Miss Mary was late.

我用石打他但打不中
I tried to hit it with a stone, but missed it.

幾時放學呀
What time will the school be dismissed?

我想早來但我朋友來因
此轉回
I would have come very soon, but my friend came and kept me back.

因此我唔能來得早
On that account I did not come until now.

我見汝意思如此
I see that your opinion is so.

佢好羞恥
He was much disgraced.

汝務要早日報知
You must notify me sooner.

為何汝唔中意佢
Why did you dislike him?

乜汝唔中意佢
What did you dislike in him?

我自己定奪
I will form my own conclusion.

我自己判斷
I will decide for myself.

我務要体過佢做成否
I must see if it can't be done successfully.

我唔該
I beg your pardon.

煩汝相饒我
Please excuse me.

我無意做出
I did it accidentally.

佢推我過你處
He pushed me againtst you.

我冇難為佢
I did not tease him (plague).

佢先得罪我
He insulted me first.

此乃刻薄人
It was ill treatment.

倘若我唔告訴汝汝實係唔知
If I did not inform you, you would not know.

汝估此係真實
You thought it was true (actually so).

汝無路可報仇
Have you no way to take revenge?

案情
The case.

佢欠我銀唔肯還
He refused to pay the money which he owes me.

我今無工做煩汝有工舉薦我
I am now out of employment, and if you hear of a place, please recommend me.

汝打合紅請我倘汝唔中意就辭莫打
You have made an agreement to hire me, but if you find that I am not suitable you can discharge me, only you must not strike me.

倘若我買汝物我要汝送到我處
If I buy of you, you must send the articles to me.

我會做汝有乜工夫俾我拈回做
I understand how to work. Have you any work for me to take home to do?

兵人保護他營寨
The soldier will keep guard over our camp.

佢若無保護唔敢回家
He won't dare to go home without a guard.

花旗國內有許多人別國來做工
The United States contain a great many immigrants.

近日有二千別國做工之人離別大埠
About two thousand emigrants left San Francisco lately.

自從相殺過之今有許多人來北邊花旗做工
The immigration from Europe to New England has been very large since the war was over.

別國來做工之人不久冇來了
The immigration will soon be stopped.

加重刑罰于佢倘若佢唔實說

- They were going to inflict a severe punishment upon him if he had not
told the truth.

星之光反照在日頭來

The stars reflect the rays of the sun.

我甚煩悶時時回想我之事

I feel sorry whenever I reflect upon that matter.

聲音引動我甚

The tonic affects me very much.

佢愛情顯現甚好

He affects to appear well.

我辭此人因為佢吾顧自己行為

I dismissed the boy because he did not behave himself.

我工做唔起待至到六點鐘正做

My work will not be finished until 6 o'clock.

佢係錯了

He is mistaken.

汝係錯了

You are mistaken.

理應前者我有錯倘若吾係汝

I would have made a mistake some time ago if not for you.

我錯了

I am mistaken.

汝要拘治時候

You must restrict the time.

汝必然限定時候

You must limit the time.

汝限定時候

You must fix the time.

汝務要話定屆期

You must appoint the time.

點樣限定期

What is the limitation?

限定幾奈

How long is the limitation?

限款幾時完滿

When will the limitation expire?

冇人相伴佢不敢去

He dare not go without an escort.

我陪伴佢回家

I will escort him to his home.

佢講許多謊言想我有罪

He was intending to afflict me by telling many fibs.

返回坐落講正此語

Inflect that word rightly or go to your seat.

我是同姓兄弟

We are brothers by surname.

佢係我仝姓兄弟

He is my brother by surname.

佢醜因佢錯之事

He was mortified at his mistake.

佢傷口落藥然後正纏

His wound was mortified before they dressed it.

先生改正句書

The teacher modified the sentence.

凹與凸相對

Concave is the opposite of convex.

佢俾他地方契

He gave him a deed for the land.

佢見羞恥佢自己之惡行為

He was ashamed of his wicked deed.

佢有一萬艮本

He had $10,000 capital.

波市頓係馬市周失市個
京都
Boston is the capital of Massachusetts.

極大公議堂造在華臣頓地
The capitol building at Washington is very large.

枝鎗体見甚光
The spear looks very bright.

寫此字之人有高有瘦
The man who wrote this note was tall and thin.

多煩汝借張橙過我
Will you be so kind as to spare me one of your chairs?

汝餀背出此句話
Can you spell that word?

我想去收款
I shall go to collect my debts.

我今早去收了款
I made a collection this morning.

我体此款餀收得
I think they can be collected.

我收銀見他知佢們有仁
德之心
We can judge by the collection that the people are benevolent.

一大隊兵上大埠
A large company of soldiers landed in San Francisco.

講到實處佢不過係幾個
Collectively speaking, they were few.

佢係收款人
He is a collector.

正埠有收餀會所
San Francisco has a collectorship.

我想去城買些書
I wish to go to town and buy some stationery.

佢前日係賣書之人
He was once a stationer.

我來舉起此物
I shall raise this thing higher.

唐人起兵去保守自己地方
The Chinese Government are going to raise soldiers, in order to defend their country.

我來近時他起頭相望
They did raise their heads at the time when we approached to them.

我必然與他埋艮咁多淂
咁多
I shall make an effort to raise as much money as possible.

我今年養畜多過舊年
I shall raise more cattle this year than the last.

耕種人今年種許多麥
The farmers will raise much wheat this year.

我大中去体跑馬
We are going to the race.

人乃各國苗裔
The people of different races.

此症乃是內外症麼
Is it a physical or mental sickness?

此症內症嗎外症啞
Is it bodily sickness or mental sickness?

此板甚是粗魯
The board is rough

我住在咖欄呵叄唔（又
曰客寓）
I board at the Grand Hotel.

我就用板填 此吼
I will board up the hole soon.

搭在船上
On board the vessel.

一齊在船上
All on board.

一齊在船
All aboard.

佢在船跌落
He fell overboard.

吏部之所
Board of Civil Office.

刑部之所
Board of Punishments.

禮部之所
Board of Rites.

兵部之所
Board of War.

工部
Board of Works.

煩汝說我知此個是乜車頭
Will you please tell me what station is this?

煩汝好心話我知此個係乜車頭
Will you be kind enough to tell me what station this is?

佢有好大身分
He has a very high station.

元帥立佢兵將埋伏
The general will station his soldiers in ambush.

若他們賣完一處我餀做了
I would have done so if they were stationary in one place.

我甚忙速寫此字煩汝相饒我
Please to excuse this writing, as I am in a great hurry.

煩汝恕我信內所有寫錯之字
Please to excuse all the mistakes in this letter.

煩汝恕我信內之錯字
Please to excuse all the grammatical errors in this letter.

同上句
Please to excuse all the ungrammatical expressions in this letter.

汝有乜貨出賣
What goods have you for sale?

原告推遲此案等到禮拜一
Plaintiff postponed the case until next Monday.

但那被告之人要今日審此案
But the defendant wanted his case to be tried to-day.

佢有乜口供所講
What kind of testimony did they give?

佢証人有乜好口供
Did his witness give a good evidence?

被告之人定罪做兩年苦工
The defendant's sentence was two years in State Prison.

佢在衙門審出有罪
He had been convicted in Court.

我保佢出監
I bailed him out of jail.

我講我体見之事
I testify what I show.

佢信佢口供
He believed his testimony.

我不餀等汝
I cannot wait for you.

佢係我仇人
He is my enemy.

佢做錯事
He has done wrong.

此事合得汝意
Is this agreeable to you?

佢有好命運
He has a good fortune.

佢甚不遂願
He is very much disappointed.

汝朋友就來見汝了
Your friend is coming to see you.

汝幾時到此
When did you come here?

我前日見過佢
I have seen him before.

我甚歡喜見佢
I am very glad to see him.

佢無眞語
He does not tell the truth.

佢係收稅人
He is a tax-collector.

佢係收銀款人
He is a money-collector.

我收款
I collect the bills.

居在此使我甚大
It is very expensive to live in here.

因此我唔帶家眷到此
Therefore I did not bring my family here.

自然係眞
Certainly, it is true.

請了我今要回家去
Good-bye; I must go home now.

汝家眷在此麼
Is your family here?

我家眷在家，先生
My family is at home, sir.

我理自己生意
I only mind my own business.

多俾些我
Give me some more.

在此等候我回
You stay here till I come back.

汝去邊處來
Where have you been?

汝應該莫咁做
You ought not to do so.

汝知眞實
Are you sure of it?

夜盜昨晚被捉
A burglar was caught last night.

大賊昨晚被捉
A robber was caught last night.

佢定然俾官府查開
He will be examined by the judge.

無疑官府定佢罪
No doubt the judge will convict him.

佢定然坐長久了
He will be imprisoned for a long time.

佢朋友欲保佢出了
His friend tries to bail him out.

但係官府不肯俾佢保
But the judge refused to have him bailed.

因爲佢罪極大
Because his crime was so great.

佢要請極好狀師保護佢身
He has to hire a very good lawyer to defend himself.

佢 張 案 情 幾 時 開 審
When will his case be tried?

張 案 情 下 禮 拜 四 開 審
The case will be tried on Thursday next.

在 邊 個 衙 門
In what court?

佢 有 乜 證 人
Has he any withnesses?

我 貨 物 淡 唐 山 載 來
All our goods were imported from China.

我 貨 到 埠 值 幾 多 餉 銀 啞
My goods have arrived; how much is their duty?

我 貨 淡 此 船 來 在 邊 處 車
頭
My goods have come on a ship; at what wharf.
does she lie?

煩 汝 說 我 知 屋 主 叫 乜 名 字
Please tell me what is the name of my landlord?

幾 時 我 舖 滿 期 通 知
Tell me when the lease of my store is expired.

我 請 汝 車 要 汝 包 車 到 我 處
I hire your wagon and you must guarantee to
deliver the goods to the person to whom they
are directed.

汝 要 幾 多 價 銀 包 到
How much will you charge to guarantee that
there?

我 貧 汝 舖 要 汝 俾 張 樓 款
待 我 勿 俾 滿 期 了
I want to rent a store from you, but I want you
to give me a lease of
it that I may be sure the rent will not be raised.

倘 若 汝 知 得 誰 人 有 樓 出
貧 通 知 我
Please tell me if you know of any one who has a
store to let.

好 呀 先 生 汝 愛 乜 野 呀
Well, sir! what goods will you have to-day?

汝 今 晚 中 意 乜 野 呀 ， 先 生
Well, sir! what will you like this evening?

我 來 因 爲 我 在 寫 字 房 應 承
Oh! I came because I had no engagement at my
office.

我 來 因 爲 我 無 工 夫 阻 我
Oh! I came because I had no avocation to occupy
my time.

煩 汝 拈 此 信 去 書 信 館
Please carry this letter to the post-office for me.

多 煩 汝 與 我 傳 此 信
Please post this letter for me.

煩 汝 與 我 付 此 信
Please send this letter for me.

煩 汝 與 我 傳 此 信
Please forward this letter for me.

多 煩 汝 與 我 放 此 信 落 信 箱
Please drop this letter into the box for me.

Sui Sin Far

(1867–1914)

Edith Maud Eaton was a Eurasian born of a Chinese mother and an English father. She looked white but chose to live and write as a Chinese American. She traveled back and forth across the continent, from Seattle to San Francisco to Montreal, searching for a healthier climate. Wherever she lighted, she found the Chinese Americans.

Under the name Sui Sin Far, "Water Lily" in Cantonese, Edith Eaton produced a series of stories that give us the only contemporary Chinese American portraits and impressions of Chinese American life in San Francisco, Seattle, New York, and Montreal. The Chinese and Chinamen of her stories, like herself, do not fit the Christian missionary and social Darwinist stereotypes: the intelligent and sexually repugnant sissy Chinese man and the abused, pathologically white male supremacist Chinese woman. Amid the Christian missionary cant and social Darwinist scientific rhetoric, the racist science fiction, and the low racist humor that molded the image of the Chinese and Chinamen was one writer, writing from reality instead of prejudice: Sui Sin Far.

Leaves from the Mental Portfolio
of an Eurasian

When I look back over the years I see myself, a little child of scarcely four years of age, walking in front of my nurse, in a green English lane, and listening to her tell another of her kind that my mother is Chinese. "Oh, Lord!" exclaims the informed. She turns me around and scans me curiously from head to foot. Then the two women whisper together. Tho the word *Chinese* conveys very little meaning to my mind, I feel that they are talking about my father and mother and my heart swells with indignation. When we reach home I rush to my mother and try to tell her what I have heard. I am a young child. I fail to make myself intelligible. My mother does not understand, and when the nurse declares to her, "Little Miss Sui is a storyteller," my mother slaps me.

Many a long year has passed over my head since that day—the day on which I first learned that I was something different and apart from other children, but tho my mother has forgotten it, I have not.

I see myself again, a few years older. I am playing with another child in a garden. A girl passes by outside the gate. "Mamie," she cries to my companion. "I wouldn't speak to Sui if I were you. Her mamma is Chinese."

"I don't care," answers the little one beside me. And then to me, "Even if your mamma is Chinese, I like you better than I like Annie."

"But I don't like you," I answer, turning my back on her. It is my first conscious lie.

I am at a children's party, given by the wife of an Indian officer whose children were schoolfellows of mine. I am only six years of age, but have attended a private school for over a year, and have already learned that China is a heathen country, being civilized by England. However, for the time being, I am a merry romping child. There are quite a number of grown people present. One, a white-haired old man, has his attention called to me by the hostess. He adjusts his eyeglasses and surveys me critically. "Ah, indeed!" he exclaims. "Who would have thought it at first glance. Yet now I see the difference between her and other children. What a peculiar coloring! Her mother's eyes and hair and her father's features, I presume. Very interesting little creature!"

I was called from my play for the purpose of inspection. I do not return to it. For the rest of the evening I hide myself behind a hall door and refuse to show myself until it is time to go home.

My parents have come to America. We are in Hudson City, N.Y., and we are very poor. I am out with my brother, who is ten months older than myself. We pass a Chinese store, the door of which is open. "Look!" says Charlie. "Those men in there are Chinese!" Eagerly I gaze into the long low room. With the exception of my mother, who is English-bred with English ways and manner of dress, I have never seen a Chinese person. The two men within the store are uncouth specimens of their race, drest in working blouses and pantaloons with queues hanging down their backs. I recoil with a sense of shock.

"Oh, Charlie," I cry. "Are we like that?"

"Well, we're Chinese, and they're Chinese, too, so we must be!" returns my seven-year-old brother.

"Of course you are," puts in a boy who has followed us down the street, and who lives near us and has seen my mother: "Chinky, Chinky, Chinaman, yellow-face, pigtail, rat eater." A number of other boys and several little girls join in with him.

"Better than you," shouts my brother, facing the crowd. He is younger and smaller than any there, and I am even more insignificant than he; but my spirit revives.

"I'd rather be Chinese than anything else in the world," I scream.

They pull my hair, they tear my clothes, they scratch my face, and all but lame my brother; but the white blood in our veins fights valiantly for the Chinese half of us. When it is all over, exhausted and bedraggled, we crawl home, and report to our mother that we have "won the battle."

"Are you sure?" asks my mother doubtfully.

"Of course. They ran from us. They were frightened," returns my brother.

My mother smiles with satisfaction.

"Do you hear?" she asks my father.

"Umm," he observes, raising his eyes from his paper for an instant. My childish instinct, however, tells me that he is more interested than he appears to be.

It is tea time, but I cannot eat. Unobserved I crawl away. I do not sleep that night. I am too excited and I ache all over. Our opponents were so very much stronger and bigger than we. Toward morning, however, I fall into a doze from which I awake myself, shouting:

"Sound the battle cry;
See the foe is nigh."

My mother believes in sending us to Sunday school. She has been brought up in a Presbyterian college.

The scene of my life shifts to eastern Canada. The sleigh which has carried us from the station stops in front of a little French Canadian hotel. Immediately we are surrounded by a number of villagers, who stare curiously at my mother as my father assists her to alight from the sleigh. Their curiosity, however, is tempered with kindness, as they watch, one after another, the little black heads of my brothers and sisters and myself emerge out of the buffalo robe, which is part of the sleigh's outfit. There are six of us, four girls and two boys; the eldest, my brother, being only seven years of age. My father and mother are still in their twenties. *"Les pauvres enfants,"* the inhabitants murmur, as they help to carry us into the hotel. Then in lower tones: *"Chinoise, Chinoise."*

For some time after our arrival, whenever we children are sent for a walk, our footsteps are dogged by a number of young French and English Canadians, who amuse themselves with speculations as to whether we, being Chinese, are susceptible to pinches and hair pulling, while older persons pause and gaze upon us, very much in the same way that I have seen people gaze upon strange animals in a menagerie. Now and then we are stopt and plied with questions as to what we eat and drink, how we go to sleep, if my mother understands what my father says to her, if we sit on chairs or squat on floors, etc., etc., etc.

There are many pitched battles, of course, and we seldom leave the house without being armed for conflict. My mother takes a great interest in our battles, and usually cheers us on, tho I doubt whether she understands the depth of the troubled waters thru which her little children wade. As to my father, peace is his motto, and he deems it wisest to be blind and deaf to many things.

School days are short, but memorable. I am in the same class with my brother, my sister next to me in the class below. The little girl whose desk my sister shares shrinks closer against the wall as my sister takes her place. In a little while she raises her hand.

"Please, teacher!"

"Yes, Annie."

"May I change my seat?"

"No, you may not!"

The little girl sobs. "Why should I have to sit beside a—"

Happily my sister does not seem to hear, and before long the two little girls become great friends. I have many such experiences.

My brother is remarkably bright; my sister next to me has a wonderful head for figures, and when only eight years of age helps my father with his night work accounts. My parents compare her with me. She is of sturdier build than I, and, as my father says, "always has her wits about her." He thinks her more like my mother, who is very bright and interested in every little detail of practical life. My father tells me that I will never make half the woman that my mother is or that my sister will be. I am not as strong as my sisters, which makes me feel somewhat ashamed, for I am the eldest little girl, and more is expected of me. I have no organic disease, but the strength of my feelings seems to take from me the strength of my body. I am prostrated at times with attacks of nervous sickness. The doctor says that my heart is unusually large; but in the light of the present I know that the cross of the Eurasian bore too heavily upon my childish shoulders. I usually hide my weakness from the family until I cannot stand. I do not understand myself, and I have no idea that the others will despise me for not being as strong as they. Therefore, I like to wander away alone, either by the river or in the bush. The green fields and flowing water have a charm for me. At the age of seven, as it is today, a bird on the wind is my emblem of happiness.

I have come from a race on my mother's side which is said to be the most stolid and insensible to feeling of all races, yet I look back over the years and see myself so keenly alive to every shade of sorrow and suffering that it is almost a pain to live.

If there is any trouble in the house in the way of a difference between my father and mother, or if any child is punished, how I suffer! And when harmony is restored, heaven seems to be around me. I can be sad, but I can also be glad. My mother's screams of agony when a baby is born almost drive me wild, and long after her pangs have subsided I feel them in my own body. Sometimes it is a week before I can get to sleep after such an experience.

A debt owing by my father fills me with shame. I feel like a criminal when I pass the creditor's door. I am only ten years old. And all the while the question of nationality perplexes my little brain. Why are we what we are? I and my brothers and sisters. Why did God make us to be hooted and stared at? Papa is English, Mamma is Chinese. Why couldn't we have been either one thing or the other? Why is my mother's race despised? I look into the faces of my father and mother. Is she not every bit as dear and good as he? Why? Why? She sings us the songs she learned at her English school. She tells us tales of China. Tho a child when she left her native land she remembers it well, and I am never tired of listening to the story of how she was stolen from her home. She tells us over and over again of her meeting with my father in Shanghai and the romance of their marriage. Why? Why?

I do not confide in my father and mother. They would not understand. How could they? He is English, she is Chinese. I am different to both of them—a stranger, tho their own child. "What are we?" I ask my brother. "It doesn't matter, sissy," he responds. But it does. I love poetry, particularly heroic pieces. I also love fairy tales. Stories of everyday life do not appeal to me. I dream dreams of being great and noble; my sisters and brothers also. I glory in the idea of dying at the stake and a great genie arising from the flames and declaring to those who have scorned us: "Behold, how great and glorious and noble are the Chinese people!"

My sisters are apprenticed to a dressmaker; my brother is entered in an office. I tramp around and sell my father's pictures, also some lace which I make myself. My nationality, if I had only known it at that time, helps to make sales. The ladies who are my customers call me "The Little Chinese Lace Girl." But it is a dangerous life for a very young girl. I come near to "mysteriously disappearing" many a time. The greatest temptation is in the thought of getting far away from where I am known, to where no mocking cries of "Chinese!" "Chinese!" can reach.

Whenever I have the opportunity I steal away to the library and read every book I can find on China and the Chinese. I learn that China is the oldest civilized nation on the face of the earth and a few other things. At eighteen years of age what troubles me is not that I am what I am, but that others are ignorant of my superiority. I am small, but my feelings are big—and great is my vanity.

My sisters attend dancing classes, for which they pay their own fees. In spite of covert smiles and sneers, they are glad to meet and mingle with other young folk. They are not sensitive in the sense that I am. And yet they understand. One of them tells me that she overheard a young man say to another that he would rather marry a pig than a girl with Chinese blood in her veins.

In course of time I too learn shorthand and take a position in an office. Like my sister, I teach myself, but, unlike my sister, I have neither the perseverance nor the ability to perfect myself. Besides, to a temperament like mine, it is torture to spend the hours in transcribing other people's thoughts. Therefore, altho I can always earn a moderately good salary, I do not distinguish myself in the business world as does she.

When I have been working for some years I open an office of my own. The local papers patronize me and give me a number of assignments, including most of the local Chinese reporting. I meet many Chinese persons, and when they get into trouble am often called upon to fight their battles in the papers. This I enjoy. My heart leaps for joy when I read one day an article signed by a New York Chinese in which he declares "The Chinese in America owe an everlasting debt of gratitude to Sui Sin Far for the bold stand she has taken in their defense."

The Chinaman who wrote the article seeks me out and calls upon me. He is a clever and witty man, a graduate of one of the American colleges and as well a Chinese scholar. I learn that he has an American wife and several children. I am very much interested in these children, and when I meet them my heart throbs in sympathetic tune with the tales they relate of their experiences as Eurasians. "Why did Papa and Mamma born us?" asks one. Why?

I also meet other Chinese men who compare favorably with the white men of my acquaintance in mind and heart qualities. Some of them are quite handsome. They have not as finely cut noses and as well-developed chins as the white men, but they have smoother skins and their expression is more serene; their hands are better shaped and their voices softer.

Some little Chinese women whom I interview are very anxious to know whether I would marry a Chinaman. I do not answer No. They clap their hands delightedly, and assure me that the Chinese are much the finest and best of all men. They are, however, a little doubtful as to whether one could be persuaded to care for me, full-blooded Chinese people having a prejudice against the half white.

Fundamentally, I muse, all people are the same. My mother's race is as prejudiced as my father's. Only when the whole world becomes as one family will human beings be able to see clearly and hear distinctly. I believe that someday a great part of the world will be Eurasian. I cheer myself with the thought that I am but a pioneer. A pioneer should glory in suffering.

"You were walking with a Chinaman yesterday," accuses an acquaintance.

"Yes, what of it?"

"You ought not to. It isn't right."

"Not right to walk with one of my own mother's people? Oh, indeed!"

I cannot reconcile his notion of righteousness with my own.

I am living in a little town away off on the north shore of a big lake. Next to me at the dinner table is the man for whom I work as a stenographer. There are also a couple of business men, a young girl, and her mother.

Someone makes a remark about the cars full of Chinamen that passed that morning. A transcontinental railway runs thru the town.

My employer shakes his rugged head. "Somehow or other," says he, "I cannot reconcile myself to the thought that the Chinese are humans like ourselves. They may have immortal souls, but their faces seem to be so utterly devoid of expression that I cannot help but doubt."

"Souls," echoes the town clerk. "Their bodies are enough for me. A Chinaman is, in my eyes, more repulsive than a nigger."

"They always give me such a creepy feeling," puts in the young girl with a laugh.

"I wouldn't have one in my house," declares my landlady.

"Now, the Japanese are different altogether. There is something bright and likable about those men," continues Mr. K.

A miserable, cowardly feeling keeps me silent. I am in a Middle West town. If I declare what I am, every person in the place will hear about it the next day. The population is in the main made up of working folks with strong prejudices against my mother's countrymen. The prospect before me is not an enviable one—if I speak. I have no longer an ambition to die at the stake for the sake of demonstrating the greatness and nobleness of the Chinese people.

Mr. K. turns to me with a kindly smile.

"What makes Miss Far so quiet?" he asks.

"I don't suppose she finds the 'washee, washee men' particularly interesting subjects of conversation," volunteers the young manager of the local bank.

With a great effort I raise my eyes from my plate. "Mr. K.," I say, addressing my employer, "the Chinese people may have no souls, no expression on their faces, be altogether beyond the pale of civilization, but whatever they are, I want you to understand that I am—I am a Chinese."

There is silence in the room for a few minutes. Then Mr. K. pushes back his plate and standing up beside me, says:

"I should not have spoken as I did. I know nothing whatever about the Chinese. It was pure prejudice. Forgive me!"

I admire Mr. K.'s moral courage in apologizing to me; he is a conscientious Christian man, but I do not remain much longer in the little town.

I am under a tropic sky, meeting frequently and conversing with persons who are almost as high up in the world as birth, education, and money can set them. The environment is peculiar, for I am also surrounded by a race of people, the reputed descendants of Ham, the son of Noah, whose offspring, it was prophesied, should be the servants of the sons of Shem and Japheth. As I am a descendant, according to the Bible, of both Shem and Japheth, I have a perfect right to set my heel upon the Ham people; but tho I see others around me following out the Bible suggestion, it is not in my nature to be arrogant to any but those who seek to impress me with their superiority, which the poor black maid who has been assigned to me by the hotel certainly does not. My employer's wife takes me to task for this. "It is unnecessary," she says, "to thank a black person for a service."

The novelty of life in the West Indian island is not without its charm. The surroundings, people, manner of living, are so entirely different from what I have been accustomed to up north that I feel as if I were "born again." Mixing with people of fashion, and yet not of them, I am not of sufficient importance to create comment or curiosity. I am busy nearly all day and often well into the night. It is not monotonous work, but it is certainly strenuous. The planters and business men of the island take me as a matter of course and treat me with kindly courtesy. Occasionally an Englishman will warn me against the "brown boys" of the island, little dreaming that I too am of the "brown people" of the earth.

When it begins to be whispered about the place that I am not all white, some of the "sporty" people seek my acquaintance. I am small and look much younger than my years. When, however, they discover that I am a very serious and sober-minded spinster indeed, they retire quite gracefully, leaving me a few amusing reflections.

One evening a card is brought to my room. It bears the name of some naval officer. I go down to my visitor, thinking he is probably someone who, having been told that I am a reporter for the local paper, has brought me an item of news. I find him lounging in an easy chair on the veranda of the hotel—a big, blond, handsome fellow, several years younger than I.

"You are Lieutenant ———?" I inquire.

He bows and laughs a little. The laugh doesn't suit him somehow—and it doesn't suit me, either.

"If you have anything to tell me, please tell it quickly, because I'm very busy."

"Oh, you don't really mean that," he answers, with another silly and offensive laugh. "There's always plenty of time for good times. That's what I am here for. I saw you at the races the other day and twice at King's House. My ship will be here for ——— weeks."

"Do you wish that noted?" I ask.

"Oh, no! Why—I came just because I had an idea that you might like to know me. I would like to know you. You look such a nice little body. Say, wouldn't you like to go out for a sail this lovely night? I will tell you all about the sweet little Chinese girls I met when we were at Hong Kong. They're not so shy!"

I leave eastern Canada for the Far West, so reduced by another attack of rheumatic fever that I only weigh eighty-four pounds. I travel on an advertising contract. It is presumed by the railway company that in some way or other I will give them full value for their transportation across the continent. I have been ordered beyond the Rockies by the doctor who declares that I will never regain my strength in the East. Nevertheless, I am but two days in San Francisco when I start out in search of work. It is the first time that I have sought work as a stranger in a strange town. Both of the other positions away from home were secured for me by home influence. I am quite surprised to find that there is no demand for my services in

San Francisco and that no one is particularly interested in me. The best I can do is to accept an offer from a railway agency to typewrite their correspondence for five dollars a month. I stipulate, however, that I shall have the privilege of taking in outside work and that my hours shall be light. I am hopeful that the sale of a story or newspaper article may add to my income, and I console myself with the reflection that, considering that I am limp and bear traces of sickness, I am fortunate to secure any work at all.

The proprietor of one of the San Francisco papers, to whom I have a letter of introduction, suggests that I obtain some subscriptions from the people of Chinatown, that district of the city having never been canvassed. This suggestion I carry out with enthusiasm, tho I find that the Chinese merchants and people generally are inclined to regard me with suspicion. They have been imposed upon so many times by unscrupulous white people. Another drawback—save for a few phrases, I am unacquainted with my mother tongue. How, then, can I expect these people to accept me as their own countrywoman? The Americanized Chinamen actually laugh in my face when I tell them that I am of their race. However, they are not all "doubting Thomases." Some little women discover that I have Chinese hair, color of eyes and complexion, also that I love rice and tea. This settles the matter for them—and for their husbands.

My Chinese instincts develop. I am no longer the little girl who shrunk against my brother at the first sight of a Chinaman. Many and many a time, when alone in a strange place, has the appearance of even an humble laundryman given me a sense of protection and made me feel quite at home. This fact of itself proves to me that prejudice can be eradicated by association.

I meet a half-Chinese, half-white girl. Her face is plastered with a thick white coat of paint and her eyelids and eyebrows are blackened so that the shape of her eyes and the whole expression of her face is changed. She was born in the East, and at the age of eighteen came West in answer to an advertisement. Living for many years among the working class, she had heard little but abuse of the Chinese. It is not difficult, in a land like California, for a half-Chinese half-white girl to pass as one of Spanish or Mexican origin. This the poor child does, tho she lives in nervous dread of being "discovered." She becomes engaged to a young man, but fears to tell him what she is, and only does so when compelled by a fearless American girlfriend. This girl, who knows her origin, realizing that the truth sooner or later must be told, and better soon than late, advises the Eurasian to confide in the young man, assuring her that he loves her well enough not to allow her nationality to stand, a bar sinister, between them. But the Eurasian prefers to keep her secret, and only reveals it to the man who is to be her husband when driven to bay by the American girl, who declares that if the half-breed will not tell the truth she will. When the young man hears that the girl he is engaged to has Chinese blood in her veins, he exclaims: "Oh, what will my folks say?" But that is all. Love is stronger than prejudice with him, and neither he nor she deems it necessary to inform his "folks."

Since the Americans have for many years manifested a much higher regard for the Japanese than for the Chinese, several half-Chinese young men and women, thinking to advance themselves, both in a social and business sense, pass as Japanese. They continue to be known as Eurasians; but a Japanese Eurasian does not appear in the same light as a Chinese Eurasian. The unfortunate Chinese Eurasians! Are not those who compel them to thus cringe more to be blamed than they?

People, however, are not all alike. I meet white men, and women, too, who are proud to mate with those who have Chinese blood in their veins, and think it a great honor to be distinguished by the friendship of such. There are also Eurasians and Eurasians. I know of one who allowed herself to become engaged to a white man after refusing him nine times. She had discouraged him in every way possible, had warned him that she was half Chinese; that her people were poor, that every week or month she sent home a certain amount of her earnings, and that the man she married would have to do as much, if not more; also, most uncompromising truth of all, that she did not love him and never would. But the resolute and undaunted lover swore that it was a matter of indifference to him whether she was a Chinese or a Hottentot, that it would be his pleasure and privilege to allow her relations double what it was in her power to bestow, and as to not loving him—that did not matter at all. He loved her. So, because the young woman had a married mother and married sisters, who were always picking at her and gossiping over her independent manner of living, she finally consented to marry him, recording the agreement in her diary thus:

"I have promised to become the wife of ——— ——— on ——— ———, 189, because the world is so cruel and sneering to a single woman—and for no other reason."

Everything went smoothly until one day. The young man was driving a pair of beautiful horses and she was seated by his side, trying very hard to imagine herself in love with him, when a Chinese vegetable gardener's cart came rumbling along. The Chinaman was a jolly-looking individual in blue cotton blouse and pantaloons, his rakish-looking hat being kept in place by a long queue which was pulled upward from his neck and wound around it. The young

woman was suddenly possest with the spirit of mischief. "Look!"
she cried, indicating the Chinaman. "There's my brother. Why
don't you salute him?"

The man's face fell a little. He sank into a pensive mood. The
wicked one by his side read him like an open book.

"When we are married," said she, "I intend to give a Chinese
party every month."

No answer.

"As there are very few aristocratic Chinese in this city, I shall fill
up with the laundrymen and vegetable farmers. I don't believe in
being exclusive in democratic America, do you?"

He hadn't a grain of humor in his composition, but a sickly smile
contorted his features as he replied:

"You shall do just as you please, my darling. But—but—consider
a moment. Wouldn't it be just a little pleasanter for us if, after we
are married, we allowed it to be presumed that you were—er—
Japanese? So many of my friends have inquired of me if that is not
your nationality. They would be so charmed to meet a little Japanese lady."

"Hadn't you better oblige them by finding one?"

"Why—er—what do you mean?"

"Nothing much in particular. Only—I am getting a little tired of
this," taking off his ring.

"You don't mean what you say! Oh, put it back, dearest! You
know I would not hurt your feelings for the world!"

"You haven't. I'm more than pleased. But I do mean what I say."

That evening the "ungrateful" Chinese Eurasian diaried, among
other things, the following:

"Joy, oh, joy! I'm free once more. Never again shall I be untrue
to my own heart. Never again will I allow any one to 'hound' or
'sneer' me into matrimony."

I secure transportation to many California points. I meet some
literary people, chief among whom is the editor of the magazine that
took my first Chinese stories. He and his wife give me a warm
welcome to their ranch. They are broad-minded people, whose
interest in me is sincere and intelligent, not affected and vulgar. I
also meet some funny people who advise me to "trade" upon my
nationality. They tell me that if I wish to succeed in literature in
America I should dress in Chinese costume, carry a fan in my hand,
wear a pair of scarlet beaded slippers, live in New York and come of
high birth. Instead of making myself familiar with the Chinese
Americans around me, I should discourse on my spirit acquaintance
with Chinese ancestors and quote in between the "good mornings"
and "how d'ye dos" of editors,

> "Confucius, Confucius, how great is Confucius. Before Confucius, there never was Confucius. After Confucius, there never came Confucius," etc., etc., etc.,

or something like that, both illuminating and obscuring, don't you know. They forget, or perhaps they are not aware that the old Chinese sage taught "The way of sincerity is the way of heaven."

My experiences as an Eurasian never cease; but people are not now as prejudiced as they have been. In the West, too, my friends are more advanced in all lines of thought than those whom I know in eastern Canada—more genuine, more sincere, with less of the form of religion, but more of its spirit.

So I roam backward and forward across the continent. When I am East, my heart is West. When I am West, my heart is East. Before long I hope to be in China. As my life began in my father's country it may end in my mother's.

After all I have no nationality and am not anxious to claim any. Individuality is more than nationality. "You are you and I am I," says Confucius. I give my right hand to the Occidentals and my left to the Orientals, hoping that between them they will not utterly destroy the insignificant "connecting link." And that's all.

The Story of One White Woman Who Married a Chinese

Why did I marry Liu Kanghi, a Chinese? Well, in the first place, because I loved him; in the second place, because I was weary of working, struggling, and fighting with the world; in the third place, because my child needed a home.

My first husband was an American fifteen years older than myself. For a few months I was very happy with him. I had been a working girl—a stenographer. A home of my own filled my heart with joy. It was a pleasure to me to wait upon James, cook him nice little dinners and suppers, read to him little pieces from the papers and magazines, and sing and play to him my little songs and melodies. And for a few months he seemed to be perfectly contented. I suppose I was a novelty to him, he having lived a bachelor existence until he was thirty-four. But it was not long before he left off smiling

at my little jokes, grew restive and cross when I teased him, and
when I tried to get him to listen to a story in which I was interested
and longed to communicate, he would bid me not bother him. I was
quick to see the change and realize that there was a gulf of differences between us. Nevertheless, I loved and was proud of him. He
was considered a very bright and well-informed man, and although
his parents had been uneducated working people he had himself
been through the public schools. He was also an omnivorous reader
of socialistic and new-thought literature. Woman suffrage was one
of his particular hobbies. Whenever I had a magazine around he
would pick it up and read aloud to me the columns of advise to
women who were ambitious to become comrades to men and walk
shoulder to shoulder with their brothers. Once I ventured to remark
that much as I admired a column of men keeping step together, yet
men and women thus ranked would, to my mind, make a very
unbeautiful and disorderly spectacle. He frowned and answered that
I did not understand him, and was too frivolous. He would often
draw my attention to newspaper reports concerning women of marked
business ability and enterprise. Once I told him that I did not
admire clever business women, as I had usually found them, and so
had other girls of my acquaintance, not nearly so kind-hearted,
generous, and helpful as the humble drudges of the world—the
ordinary working women. His answer to this was that I was jealous
and childish.

But, in spite of his unkind remarks and evident contempt for
me, I wished to please him. He was my husband and I loved him.
Many an afternoon, when through with my domestic duties, did I
spend in trying to acquire a knowledge of labor politics, socialism,
woman suffrage, and baseball, the things in which he was most
interested.

It was hard work, but I persevered until one day. It was about six
months after our marriage. My husband came home a little earlier
than usual, and found me engaged in trying to work out problems in
subtraction and addition. He laughed sneeringly. "Give it up, Minnie," said he. "You weren't built for anything but taking care of
kids. Gee! But there's a woman at our place who has a head for
figures that makes her worth over a hundred dollars a month. *Her*
husband would have a chance to develop himself."

This speech wounded me. I knew it was James's ambition to write
a book on social reform.

The next day, unknown to my husband, I called upon the wife of
the man who had employed me as a stenographer before I was
married, and inquired of her whether she thought I could get back
my old position.

"But, my dear," she exclaimed, "your husband is receiving a good salary! Why should you work?"

I told her that my husband had in mind the writing of a book on social reform, and I wished to help him in his ambition by earning some money towards its publication.

"Social reform!" she echoed. "What sort of social reformer is he who would allow his wife to work when he is well able to support her!"

She bade me go home and think no more of an office position. I was disappointed. I said: "Oh! I wish I could earn some money for James. If I were earning money, perhaps he would not think me so stupid."

"Stupid, my dear girl! You are one of the brightest little women I know," kindly comforted Mrs. Rogers.

But I knew differently and went on to tell her of my inability to figure with my husband how much he had made on certain sales, of my lack of interest in politics, labor questions, woman suffrage, and world reformation. "Oh!" I cried. "I am a narrow-minded woman. All I care for is for my husband to love me and be kind to me, for life to be pleasant and easy, and to be able to help a wee bit the poor and sick around me."

Mrs. Rogers looked very serious as she told me that there were differences of opinion as to what was meant by "narrow-mindedness," and that the majority of men had no wish to drag their wives into all their business perplexities, and found more comfort in a woman who was unlike rather than like themselves. Only that morning her husband had said to her: "I hate a woman who tries to get into every kink of a man's mind, and who must be forever at his elbow meddling with all his affairs."

I went home comforted. Perhaps after a while James would feel and see as did Mr. Rogers. Vain hope!

My child was six weeks old when I entered business life again as stenographer for Rutherford & Rutherford. My salary was fifty dollars a month—more than I had ever earned before—and James was well pleased, for he had feared that it would be difficult for me to obtain a paying place after having been out of practice for so long. This fifty dollars paid for all our living expenses, with the exception of rent, so that James would be able to put by his balance against the time when his book would be ready for publication.

He began writing his book, and Miss Moran, the young woman bookkeeper at his place, collaborated with him. They gave three evenings a week to the work, sometimes four. She came one evening when the baby was sick and James had gone for the doctor. She looked at the child with the curious eyes of one who neither loved nor understood children. "There is no necessity for its being sick," said she. "There must be an error somewhere." I made no answer, so she went on: "Sin, sorrow, and sickness all mean the same thing. We have no disease that we do not deserve, no trouble which we do not bring upon ourselves."

I did not argue with her. I knew that I could not; but as I looked at her standing there in the prime of her life and strength, broad-shouldered, masculine-featured, and, as it seemed to me, heartless, I disliked her more than I had ever disliked anyone before. My own father had died after suffering for many years from a terrible malady, contracted while doing his duty as a physician and surgeon. And my innocent child! What had sin to do with its measles?

When James came in she discussed with him the baseball game which had been played that afternoon, and also a woman suffrage meeting which she had attended the evening before.

After she had gone he seemed to be quite exhilarated. "That's a great woman!" he remarked.

"I do not think so!" I answered him. "One who would take from the sorrowful and suffering their hope of a happier existence hereafter, and add to their trials on earth by branding them as objects of aversion and contempt, is not only not a great woman but, to my mind, no woman at all."

He picked up a paper and walked into another room.

"What do you think now?" I cried after him.

"What would be the use of my explaining to you?" he returned. "You wouldn't understand."

How my heart yearned over my child those days! I would sit before the typewriter and in fancy hear her crying for her mother. Poor, sick little one, watched over by a strange woman, deprived of her proper nourishment. While I took dictation from my employer I thought only of her. The result, of course, was, that I lost my place. My husband showed his displeasure at this in various ways and as the weeks went by and I was unsuccessful in obtaining another position, he became colder and more indifferent. He was neither a drinking nor an abusive man, but he could say such cruel and cutting things that I would a hundred times rather have been beaten and ill-used than compelled, as I was, to hear them. He even made me feel it a disgrace to be a woman and a mother. Once he said to me: "If you had had ambition of the right sort you would have perfected yourself in your stenography so that you could have taken cases in court. There's a little fortune in that business."

I was acquainted with a woman stenographer who reported divorce cases and who had described to me the work, so I answered:

"I would rather die of hunger, my baby in my arms, than report divorce proceedings under the eyes of men in a court house."

"Other women, as good as you, have done and are doing it," he retorted.

"Other women, perhaps better than I, have done and are doing it," I replied, "but all women are not alike. I am not that kind."

"That's so," said he. "Well, they are the kind who are up to date. You are behind the times."

One evening I left James and Miss Moran engaged with their work and went across the street to see a sick friend. When I returned I let myself into the house very softly for fear of awakening the baby, whom I had left sleeping. As I stood in the hall I heard my husband's voice in the sitting room. This is what he was saying:

"I am a lonely man. There is no companionship between me and my wife."

"Nonsense!" answered Miss Moran, as I thought a little impatiently. "Look over this paragraph, please, and tell me if you do not think it would be well to have it follow after the one ending with the words 'ultimate concord,' in place of that beginning with 'These great principles.' "

"I cannot settle my mind upon the work tonight," said James in a sort of thick, tired voice. "I want to talk to you—to win your sympathy—your love."

I heard a chair pushed back. I knew Miss Moran had arisen.

"Good night!" I heard her say. "Much as I would like to see this work accomplished, I shall come no more!"

"But, my God! You cannot throw the thing up at this late date."

"I can and I will. Let me pass, sir."

"If there were no millstone around my neck, you would not say, 'Let me pass, sir,' in that tone of voice."

The next I heard was a heavy fall. Miss Moran had knocked my big husband down.

I pushed open the door. Miss Moran, cool and collected, was pulling on her gloves, James was struggling to his feet.

"Oh, Mrs. Carson!" exclaimed the former. "Your husband fell over the stool. Wasn't that stupid of him!"

James, of course, got his divorce six months after I deserted him. He did not ask for the child, and I was allowed to keep it.

2

I was on my way to the waterfront, the baby in my arms. I was walking quickly, for my state of mind was such that I could have borne twice my burden and not have felt it. Just as I turned down a hill which led to the docks, someone touched my arm and I heard a voice say:

"Pardon me, lady, but you have dropped your baby's shoe!"

"Oh, yes!" I answered, taking the shoe mechanically from an outstretched hand, and pushing on.

I could hear the waves lapping against the pier when the voice again fell upon my ear.

"If you go any further, lady, you will fall into the water!"

My answer was a step forward.

A strong hand was laid upon my arm and I was swung around against my will.

"Poor little baby," went on the voice, which was unusually soft for a man's. "Let me hold him!"

I surrendered my child to the voice.

"Better come over where it is light and you can see where to walk!"

I allowed myself to be led into the light.

Thus I met Liu Kanghi, the Chinese who afterwards became my husband. I followed him, obeyed him, trusted him from the very first. It never occurred to me to ask myself what manner of man was succoring me. I only knew that he was a man, and that I was being cared for as no one had ever cared for me since my father died. And my grim determination to leave a world which had been cruel to me, passed away—and in its place I experienced a strange calmness and content.

"I am going to take you to the house of a friend of mine," he said as he preceded me up the hill, the baby in his arms.

"You will not mind living with Chinese people?" he added.

An electric light under which we were passing flashed across his face.

I did not recoil—not even at first. It may have been because he was wearing American clothes, wore his hair cut, and, even to my American eyes, appeared a good-looking young man—and it may have been because of my troubles; but whatever it was I answered him, and I meant it: "I would much rather live with Chinese than Americans."

He did not ask me why, and I did not tell him until long afterwards the story of my unhappy marriage; my desertion of the man who had made it impossible for me to remain under his roof; the shame of the divorce, the averted faces of those who had been my friends; the cruelty of the world; the awful struggle for an existence for myself and child; sickness followed by despair.

The Chinese family with which he placed me were kind, simple folk. The father had been living in America for more than twenty years. The family consisted of his wife, a grown daughter, and several small sons and daughters, all of whom had been born in America. They made me very welcome and adored the baby. Liu Jusong, the father, was a working jeweler; but, because of an accident by which he had lost the use of one hand, he was partially incapacitated for work. Therefore, their family depended for maintenance chiefly upon their kinsman, Liu Kanghi, the Chinese who had brought me to them.

"We love much our cousin," said one of the little girls to me one day. "He teaches us so many games and brings us toys and sweets."

As soon as I recovered from the attack of nervous prostration which laid me low for over a month after being received into the Liu home, my mind began to form plans for my own and my child's maintenance. One morning I put on my hat and jacket and told Mrs. Liu I would go downtown and make an application for work as a stenographer at the different typewriting offices. She pleaded with me to wait a week longer—until, as she said, "your limbs are more fortified with strength"; but I assured her that I felt myself well able to begin to do for myself, and that I was anxious to repay some little part of the expense I had been to them.

"For all we have done for you," she answered, "our cousin has paid us doublefold."

"No money can recompense your kindness to myself and child," I replied; "but if it is your cousin to whom I am indebted for board and lodging, all the greater is my anxiety to repay what I owe."

When I returned to the house that evening, tired out with my quest for work, I found Li Kanghi tossing a ball with little Fong on the front porch.

Mrs. Liu bustled out to meet me and began scolding me in motherly fashion.

"Oh, why you go downtown before you strong enough? See! You look all sick again!" said she.

She turned to Liu Kanghi and said something in Chinese. He threw the ball back to the boy and came towards me, his face grave and concerned.

"Please be so good as to take my cousin's advice," he urged.

"I am well enough to work now," I replied, "and I cannot sink deeper into your debt."

"You need not," said he. "I know a way by which you can quickly pay me off and earn a good living without wearing yourself out and leaving the baby all day. My cousin tells me that you can create most beautiful flowers on silk, velvet, and linen. Why not then you do some of that work for my store? I will buy all you can make."

"Oh!" I exclaimed. "I should be only too glad to do such work! But do you think I can earn a living in that way?"

"You certainly can," was his reply. "I am requiring an embroiderer, and if you will do the work for me I will try to pay you what it is worth."

So I gladly gave up my quest for office work. I lived in the Liu Jusong house and worked for Liu Kanghi. The days, weeks, and months passed peacefully and happily. Artistic needlework had always been my favorite occupation, and when it became a source both of remuneration and pleasure, I began to feel that life was worth living, after all. I watched with complacency my child grow amongst the little Chinese children. My life's experience had taught me that the virtues do not all belong to the whites. I was interested in all that concerned the Liu household, became acquainted with all their friends, and lost altogether the prejudice against the foreigner in which I had been reared.

I had been living thus more than a year when, one afternoon as I was walking home from Liu Kanghi's store on Kearney Street, a parcel of silks and floss under my arm, and my little girl trudging by my side, I came face-to-face with James Carson.

"Well, now," said he, planting himself in front of me, "you are looking pretty well. How are you making out?"

I caught up my child and pushed past him without a word. When I reached the Liu house I was trembling in every limb, so great was my dislike and fear of the man who had been my husband.

About a week later a letter came to the house addressed to me. It read:

Dear Minnie,—If you are willing to forget the past and make up, I am, too. I was surprised to see you the other day, prettier than ever—and much more of a woman. Let me know your mind at an early date.

Your affectionate husband,
James

I ignored this letter, but a heavy fear oppressed me. Liu Kanghi, who called the evening of the day I received it, remarked as he arose to greet me that I was looking troubled, and hoped that it was not the embroidery flowers.

"It is the shadow from my big hat," I answered lightly. I was dressed for going downtown with Mrs. Liu, who was preparing her eldest daughter's trousseau.

"Someday," said Liu Kanghi earnestly, "I hope that you will tell to me all that is in your heart and mind."

I found comfort in his kind face.

"If you will wait until I return, I will tell you all tonight," I answered.

Strange as it may seem, although I had known Liu Kanghi now for more than a year, I had had little talk alone with him, and all he knew about me was what he had learned from Mrs. Liu; namely, that I was a divorced woman who, when saved from self-destruction, was homeless and starving.

That night, however, after hearing my story, he asked me to be his wife. He said: "I love you and would protect you from all trouble. Your child shall be as my own."

I replied: "I appreciate your love and kindness, but I cannot answer you just yet. Be my friend for a little while longer."

"Do you have for me the love feeling?" he asked.

"I do not know," I answered truthfully.

Another letter came. It was written in a different spirit from the first and contained a threat about the child.

There seemed but one course open to me. That was to leave my Chinese friends. I did. With much sorrow and regret I bade them good-bye, and took lodgings in a part of the city far removed from the outskirts of Chinatown, where my home had been with the Lius.

My little girl pined for her Chinese playmates, and I myself felt strange and lonely; but I knew that if I wished to keep my child I could no longer remain with my friends.

I still continued working for Liu Kanghi, and carried my embroidery to his store in the evening after the little one had been put to sleep. He usually escorted me back but never asked to be allowed, and I never invited him, to visit me, or even enter the house. I was a young woman, and alone, and what I had suffered from scandal since I had left James Carson had made me wise.

It was a cold, wet evening in November when he accosted me once again. I had run over to a delicatessen store at the corner of the block where I lived. As I stepped out, his burly figure loomed up in the gloom before me. I started back with a little cry, but he grasped my arm and held it.

"Walk beside me quietly if you do not wish to attract attention," said he, "and by God, if you do, I will take the kid tonight!"

"You dare not!" I answered. "You have no right to her whatever. She is my child and I have supported her for the last two years alone."

"Alone! What will the judges say when I tell them about the Chinaman?"

"What will the judges say!" I echoed. "What can they say? Is there any disgrace in working for a Chinese merchant and receiving pay for my labor?"

"And walking in the evening with him, and living for over a year in a house for which he paid the rent. Ha! ha! ha! Ha! ha! ha!"

His laugh was low and sneering. He had evidently been making inquiries concerning the Liu family, and also watching me for some time. How a woman can loathe and hate the man she has once loved!

We were nearing my lodgings. Perhaps the child had awakened and was crying for me. I would not, however, have entered the house, had he not stopped at the door and pushed it open.

"Lead the way upstairs!" said he. "I want to see the kid."

"You shall not," I cried. In my desperation I wrenched myself from his grasp and faced him, blocking the stairs.

"If you use violence," I declared, "the lodgers will come to my assistance. They know me!"

He released my arm.

"Bah!" said he. "I've no use for the kid. It is you I'm after getting reconciled to. Don't you know, Minnie, that once your husband, always your husband? Since I saw you the other day on the street, I have been more in love with you than ever before. Suppose we forget all and begin over again!"

Though the tone of his voice had softened, my fear of him grew greater. I would have fled up the stairs had he not again laid his hand on my arm.

"Answer me, girl," said he.

And in spite of my fear, I shook off his hand and answered him: "No husband of mine are you, either legally or morally. And I have no feeling whatever for you other than contempt."

"Ah! So you have sunk!"—his expression was evil—"The oily little Chink has won you!"

I was no longer afraid of him.

"Won me!" I cried, unheeding who heard me. "Yes, honorably and like a man. And what are you that dare sneer at one like him. For all your six feet of grossness, your small soul cannot measure up to his great one. You were unwilling to protect and care for the woman who was your wife or the little child you caused to come into this world; but he succored and saved the stranger-woman, treated her as a woman, with reverence and respect; gave her child a home, and made them both independent, not only of others but of himself. Now, hearing you insult him behind his back, I know what

I did not know before—that I love him, and all I have to say to you is, Go!"

And James Carson went. I heard of him again but once. That was when the papers reported his death of apoplexy while exercising at a public gymnasium.

Loving Liu Kanghi, I became his wife, and though it is true that there are many Americans who look down upon me for so becoming, I have never regretted it. No, not even when men cast upon me the glances they cast upon sporting women. I accept the lot of the American wife of an humble Chinaman in America. The happiness of the man who loves me is more to me than the approval or disapproval of those who in my dark days left me to die like a dog. My Chinese husband has his faults. He is hot-tempered and, at times, arbitrary; but he is always a man, and has never sought to take away from me the privilege of being but a woman. I can lean upon and trust in him. I feel him behind me, protecting and caring for me, and that, to an ordinary woman like myself, means more than anything else.

Only when the son of Liu Kanghi lays his little head upon my bosom do I question whether I have done wisely. For my boy, the son of a Chinese man, is possessed of a childish wisdom which brings the tears to my eyes; and as he stands between his father and myself, like yet unlike us both, so will he stand in after years between his father's and his mother's people. And if there is no kindliness nor understanding between them, what will my boy's fate be?

Her Chinese Husband

Sequel to The Story of One White Woman
Who Married a Chinese

Now that Liu Kanghi is no longer with me, I feel that it will ease my heart to record some memories of him—if I can. The task, though calling to me, is not an easy one, so throng to my mind the invincible proofs of his love for me, the things he has said and done. My memories of him are so vivid and pertinacious, my thoughts of him so tender.

To my Chinese husband I could go with all my little troubles and perplexities; to him I could talk as women love to do at times of the past and the future, the mysteries of religion, of life and death. He was not above discussing such things with me. With him I was never strange or embarrassed. My Chinese husband was simple in his tastes. He liked to hear a good story, and though unlearned in a sense, could discriminate between the good and bad in literature. This came of his Chinese education. He told me one day that he thought the stories in the Bible were more like Chinese than American stories, and added: "If you had not told me what you have about it, I should say that it was composed by the Chinese." Music had a soothing though not a deep influence over him. It could not sway his mind, but he enjoyed it just as he did a beautiful picture. Because I was interested in fancy work, so also was he. I can see his face, looking so grave and concerned, because one day by accident I spilt some ink on a piece of embroidery I was working. If he came home in the evenings and found me tired and out of sorts, he would cook the dinner himself, and go about it in such a way that I felt that he rather enjoyed showing off his skill as a cook. The next evening, if he found everything ready, he would humorously declare himself much disappointed that I was so exceedingly well.

At such times a gray memory of James Carson would arise. How his cold anger and contempt, as exhibited on like occasions, had shriveled me up in the long ago. And then—I would fall to musing on the difference between the two men as lovers and husbands.

James Carson had been much more of an ardent lover than ever had been Liu Kanghi. Indeed it was his passion, real or feigned, which had carried me off my feet. When wooing he had constantly reproached me with being cold, unfeeling, a marble statue, and so forth; and I, poor, ignorant little girl, would wonder how it was I appeared so when I felt so differently. For I had given James Carson my first love. Upon him my life had been concentrated as it has never been concentrated upon any other. Yet—!

There was nothing feigned about my Chinese husband. Simple and sincere as he was before marriage, so was he afterwards. As my union with James Carson had meant misery, bitterness, and narrowness, so my union with Liu Kanghi meant, on the whole, happiness, health, and development. Yet the former, according to American ideas, had been an educated broad-minded man; the other, just an ordinary Chinaman.

But the ordinary Chinaman that I would show to you was the sort of man that children, birds, animals, and some women love. Every morning he would go to the window and call to his pigeons, and they would flock around him, hearing and responding to his whispering and cooing. The rooms we lived in had been his rooms ever since he had come to America. They were above his store, and large and cool. The furniture had been brought from China, but there was nothing of tinsel about it. Dark wood, almost black, carved and antique, some of the pieces set with mother-of-pearl. On one side of the inner room stood a case of books and an ancestral tablet. I have seen Liu Kanghi touch the tablet with reverence, but the faith of his fathers was not strong enough to cause him to bow before it. The elegant simplicity of these rooms had surprised me much when I was first taken to them. I looked at him then, standing for a moment by the window, a solitary pigeon peeking in at him, perhaps wondering who had come to divert from her her friend's attention. So had he lived since he had come to this country—quietly and undisturbed— from twenty years of age to twenty-five. I felt myself an intruder. A feeling of pity for the boy—for such he seemed in his enthusiasm— arose in my breast. Why had I come to confuse his calm? Was it ordained, as he declared?

My little girl loved him better than she loved me. He took great pleasure in playing with her, curling her hair over his fingers, tying her sash, and all the simple tasks from which so many men turn aside.

Once the baby got hold of a set rat trap, and was holding it in such a way that the slightest move would have released the spring and plunged the cruel steel into her tender arms. Kanghi's eyes and mine beheld her thus at the same moment. I stood transfixed with horror. Kanghi quietly went up to the child and took from her the trap. Then he asked me to release his hand. I almost fainted when I saw it. "It was the only way," said he. We had to send for the doctor, and even as it was, came very near having a case of blood poisoning.

I have heard people say that he was a keen business man, this Liu Kanghi, and I imagine that he was. I did not, however, discuss his business with him. All I was interested in were the pretty things and the women who would come in and jest with him. He could jest too. Of course, the women did not know that I was his wife. Once a woman in rich clothes gave him her card and asked him to call upon her. After she had left he passed the card to me. I tore it up. He took those things as a matter of course, and was not affected by them. "They are a part of Chinatown life," he explained.

He was a member of the Reform Club, a Chinese social club, and the Chinese Board of Trade. He liked to discuss business affairs and Chinese and American politics with his countrymen, and occasionally enjoyed an evening away from me. But I never needed to worry over him.

He had his littlenesses as well as his bignesses, had Liu Kanghi. For instance, he thought he knew better about what was good for my health and other things, purely personal, than I did myself, and if my ideas opposed or did not tally with his, he would very vigorously denounce what he called "the foolishness of women." If he admired a certain dress, he would have me wear it on every occasion possible, and did not seem to be able to understand that it was not always suitable.

"Wear the dress with the silver lines," he said to me one day somewhat authoritatively. I was attired for going out, but not as he wished to see me. I answered that the dress with the silver lines was unsuitable for a long and dusty ride on an open car.

"Never mind," said he, "whether it is unsuitable or not. I wish you to wear it."

"All right," I said, "I will wear it, but I will stay at home."

I stayed at home, and so did he.

At another time, he reproved me for certain opinions I had expressed in the presence of some of his countrymen. "You should not talk like that," said he. "They will think you are a bad woman."

My white blood rose at that, and I answered him in a way which grieves me to remember. For Kanghi had never meant to insult or hurt me. Imperious by nature, he often spoke before he thought— and he was so boyishly anxious for me to appear in the best light possible before his own people.

There were other things too: a sort of childish jealousy and suspicion which it was difficult to allay. But a woman can forgive much to a man, the sincerity and strength of whose love makes her own, though true, seem slight and mean.

Yes, life with Liu Kanghi was not without its trials and tribulations. There was the continual uncertainty about his own life here in America, the constant irritation caused by the assumption of the white men that a white woman does not love her Chinese husband, and their actions accordingly; also sneers and offensive remarks. There was also on Liu Kanghi's side an acute consciousness that, though belonging to him as his wife, yet in a sense I was not his, but of the dominant race, which claimed, even while it professed to despise me. This consciousness betrayed itself in words and ways which filled me with a passion of pain and humiliation. "Kanghi," I would sharply say, for I had to cloak my tenderness, "do not talk to me like that. You *are* my superior. . . . I would not love you if you were not."

But in spite of all I could do or say, it was there between us: that strange invisible—what? Was it the barrier of race—that consciousness?

Sometimes he would talk about returning to China. The thought filled me with horror. I had heard rumors of secondary wives. One afternoon the cousin of Liu Kanghi, with whom I had lived, came to see me, and showed me a letter which she had received from a little Chinese girl who had been born and brought up in America until the age of ten. The last paragraph in the letter read: "Emma and I are very sad and wish we were back in America." Kanghi's cousin explained that the father of the little girls, having no sons, had taken himself another wife, and the new wife lived with the little girls and their mother.

That was before my little boy was born. That evening I told Kanghi that he need never expect me to go to China with him.

"You see," I began, "I look upon you as belonging to me."

He would not let me say more. After a while he said: "It is true that in China a man may and occasionally does take a secondary wife, but that custom is custom, not only because sons are denied to the first wife, but because the first wife is selected by parents and guardians before a man is hardly a man. If a Chinese marries for love, his life is a filled-up cup, and he wants no secondary wife. No, not even for sake of a son. Take, for example, me, your great husband."

I sometimes commented upon his boyish ways and appearance, which was the reason why, when he was in high spirits, he would call himself my "great husband." He was not boyish always. I have seen him, when shouldering the troubles of kinfolk, the quarrels of his clan, and other responsibilities, acting and looking like a man of twice his years.

But for all the strange marriage customs of my husband's people, I considered them far more moral in their lives than the majority of Americans. I expressed myself thus to Liu Kanghi, and he replied: "The American people think higher. If only more of them lived up to what they thought, the Chinese would not be so confused in trying to follow their leadership."

If ever a man rejoiced over the birth of his child, it was Liu Kanghi. The boy was born with a veil over his face. "A prophet!" cried the old mulatto Jewess who nursed me. "A prophet has come into the world."

She told this to his father when he came to look upon him, and he replied: "He is my son, that is all I care about." But he was so glad, and there was feasting and rejoicing with his Chinese friends for over two weeks. He came in one evening and found me weeping over my poor little boy. I shall never forget the expression on his face.

"Oh, shame!" he murmured, drawing my head down to his shoulder. "What is there to weep about? The child is beautiful! The feeling heart, the understanding mind is his. And we will bring him up to be proud that he is of Chinese blood; he will fear none and, after him, the name of half-breed will no longer be one of contempt."

Kanghi as a youth had attended a school in Hong Kong, and while there had made the acquaintance of several half Chinese half English lads. "They were the brightest of all," he told me, "but they lowered themselves in the eyes of the Chinese by being ashamed of their Chinese blood and ignoring it."

His theory, therefore, was that if his own son was brought up to be proud instead of ashamed of his Chinese half, the boy would become a great man.

Perhaps he was right, but he could not see as could I, an American woman, the conflict before our boy.

After the little Kanghi had passed his first month, and we had found a reliable woman to look after him, his father began to take me around with him much more than formerly, and life became very enjoyable. We dined often at a Chinese restaurant kept by a friend of his, and afterwards attended theaters, concerts, and other places of entertainment. We frequently met Americans with whom he had become acquainted through business, and he would introduce them with great pride in me shining in his eyes. The little jealousies and suspicions of the first year seemed no longer to irritate him, and though I had still cause to shrink from the gaze of strangers, I know that my Chinese husband was for several years a very happy man.

Now, I have come to the end. He left home one morning, followed to the gate by the little girl and boy (we had moved to a cottage in the suburbs).

"Bring me a red ball," pleaded the little girl.

"And me too," cried the boy.

"All right, chickens," he responded, waving his hand to them.

He was brought home at night shot through the head. There are some Chinese, just as there are some Americans, who are opposed to all progress, and who hate with a bitter hatred all who would enlighten or be enlightened.

But that I have not the heart to dwell upon. I can only remember that when they brought my Chinese husband home there were two red balls in his pocket. Such was Liu Kanghi—a man.

Anonymous

Translations and commentary by Marlon K. Hom

The Angel Island Immigration Station (1910–1940), on the island that some say looks like a slumbering angel in the middle of San Francisco Bay, was but one white racist humiliation created specifically for the Chinese by the Chinese exclusion laws. Chinese attempting to enter the United States were detained at the station and housed in one wooden building that was divided into men's and women's sections. All immigrants had to prove themselves to be related by blood to a current United States resident. All immigrants underwent long and sometimes repeated interrogations from United States immigration officials whose questions were detailed, if not clever entrapment: "How many steps lead to your front door?" many remember being asked, and laugh. If the immigrant was indeed a "paper son," a man who had bought a family history and a ticket to America, his paper father would have sold him the answers to all the questions Immigration would ask, and he would have memorized them. Their stories, their sorrows, their fears, and their spirit—much of it informed by and evoking the fairy tale and the strategies of the heroic tradition—are carved deep into the walls of the wooden building that still stands today.

Marlon K. Hom's translations of these Angel Island poems in "Immigration Blues" and his "Lamentations of Stranded Sojourners" form an important link in the study of Chinese American literary history. These poems and rhymes represent the visions of the early Chinese immigrant in America in the late-nineteenth and early twentieth century. Hom states in the introduction to *Songs of Gold Mountain*, "the language used in the rhymes is colloquial Cantonese. It is folksy, somewhat vulgar, and at times erotic. Some of the pieces contain faultily written characters, either unintentional mistakes by writers or typographical errors. The errors reveal the unsophisticated peasant background of some of the writers, who became very uninhibited behind the mask of anonymity."

Marlon K. Hom is a professor of Asian American studies at San Francisco State University.

Songs of Gold Mountain

Immigration Blues

The Chinese Exclusion Act of 1882 opened an infamous chapter in United States immigration history, one that brought insurmountable hardship to the Chinese. The moment that their ship docked at the San Francisco pier, the Chinese immigrants were herded into the notorious detention center known to all the Chinese as the "Muk uk" (Mu wu), or "Wooden Barracks," to be processed for immigration. Before 1910, detainees were sent to a wooden building alongside the Pacific Mail Steamship Company pier that was known as the "Tongsaan Matau" (Tangshan Matou), the China Dock (now Pier 50 on the San Francisco waterfront). Because of rampant corruption and the facility's poor physical condition, it ceased to be used in 1910. Instead, the government put into operation the newly built Angel Island Immigration Station in San Francisco Bay to process immigrants and returnees from Asia. This station was sometimes called the Ellis Island of the West Coast.

At Angel Island, the Chinese had to submit to a battery of physical examinations and harsh interrogations. Those who passed were ferried to San Francisco to begin their new life; those who did not were deported back to China permanently. Detainees at the Wooden Barracks were not allowed to go beyond the compound or to meet any outside visitors. It was not uncommon to be detained in the Wooden Barracks for several weeks, even over a year, while awaiting processing. The facilities were minimal, without any consideration for privacy. Suicides were not unknown.

Many of the Chinese at the Angel Island Wooden Barracks wrote poems expressing their agony, frustration, anger, and despair. They would scribble the lines all over the walls of the barracks where they slept. In the 1930s, two detainees copied these scribbles and brought them to San Francisco. However, this genre of Chinese immigration poetry remained unknown to most people until recently.

In 1940, a fire destroyed the administration building of the Angel Island Immigration Station, and the use of the facility was soon halted. Detainees were moved to another detention center in San Francisco. Barrack 37, the housing compound, survived the fire, but was forgotten for thirty years. Finally in the early 1970s, when the building was targeted for demolition, the Chinese scribbles on the walls caught the attention of the Chinese in San Francisco. Community efforts from Chinatown saved Barrack 37, and it has since become a historical site, augmented by an exhibit on the island's Chinese immigration history. Over 135 Wooden Barracks poems are extant today.

The Cantonese folk rhymes on immigration in the 1911 anthology represent the earliest collection of published poems dealing with the Chinese immigration experience. They are different from the poems on the Wooden Barracks walls. Not only do these rhymes protest the harsh treatment at the Wooden Barracks; they also show that Angel Island with its Wooden Barracks was not a euphoric Ellis Island for the Chinese immigrants. Instead, it was a contradiction of the principles of liberty that testified to injustice. The criticism, so pronounced in the rhymes, reveals that the Chinese immigrants did have an appreciation of the American principles of justice and democracy. They expected to be treated on that level and they believed that they should be accorded such rights. This was, I believe, the first crude sign of their Americanization.

1

As soon as it is announced
　　the ship has reached America:
I burst out cheering,
　　I have found precious pearls.
How can I bear the detention upon arrival,
Doctors and immigration officials refusing
　　to let me go?
All the abuse—
I can't describe it with a pen.
I'm held captive in a wooden barrack, like King Wen
　　in Youli:*
No end to the misery and sadness in my heart.

一話（一）
話船到美。歡同得寶珠。

那堪抵埠受羈縻，醫生稅員未準紙（三）。

受太氣。筆尖難以紀。

板樓困入如羑里，無限凄涼心裡悲。

（三）（二）（一）
準：作「准」；未准紙：
稅員：海關官員
一話：一說

不發准許入境證件

---

*King Wen (ca. 1200 B.C.), the first ruler of the Zhou dynasty, was detained in Youli for being an adversary of the ruling Shang.

2

The moment I hear
    we've entered the port,
I am all ready:
    my belongings wrapped in a bundle.
Who would have expected joy to become sorrow:
Detained in a dark, crude, filthy room?
What can I do?
Cruel treatment, not one restful breath of air.
Scarcity of food, severe restrictions—all
    unbearable.
Here even a proud man bows his head low.

一聞入港口。打起個伏包⑴。

誰知歡喜反爲愁。闇室受困更濁陋。

冇能較⑵。殘酷氣難哮。

缺食不堪嚴掣肘。英雄到此也垂頭。

（一）伏：作「袱」

（二）冇能較：沒法計較，無可奈何

3

In search of a pin-head gain,
I was idle in an impoverished village.
I've risked a perilous journey to come to the Flowery
　Flag Nation.
Immigration officers interrogated me;
And, just for a slight lapse of memory,
I am deported, and imprisoned in this barren
　mountain.
A brave man cannot use his might here,
And he can't take one step beyond the confines.

欲蒐蠅頭利。窮鄉沒作置(二)。

乘危履險走花旗(一)。遇着稅員盤詰汝

稍忘記。撥禁荒島裡。

好漢眞無用武地。不能一步越雷池。

（三）撥：：驅逐

（二）稅員：：參看歌#1

（一）花旗：：美國

4

At home I was in poverty,
    constantly worried about firewood and rice.
I borrowed money
    to come to Gold Mountain.
Immigration officers cross-examined me;
    no way could I get through.
Deported to this island,
    like a convicted criminal.
Here—
Mournful sighs fill the gloomy room.
A nation weak; her people often humiliated
Like animals, tortured and destroyed at others'
    whim.

家貧柴米患。貸本來金山(一)。
關員審問脫身難。撥往埃崙如監犯
到此間。闇室長嗟嘆。
國弱被人多辱慢。儼然畜類任摧殘。

（一）金山：美國

（二）撥：參看歌#3

（三）埃崙：音譯「島」；
　　指天使島．

5

Wooden barracks, all specially built;
It's clear they're detention cells.
We Chinese enter this country and suffer
All sorts of autocratic restrictions made at
    whim.
What a disappointment—
Cooped up inside an iron cage;
We have an impotent ambassador who cannot
    handle matters.
We knit our brows and cry for heaven gives no
    recourse for our suffering.

板樓特別起。明白係監羈。

華人入境受凄其。種種專制由在彼。

冇爭氣。困埋鐵籠裡。

雖有使臣難料理。呼天無路皺埋眉。

（一）係：是

（二）困埋：困在一起

6

The wooden cell is like a steel barrel.
Firmly shut, not even a breeze can filter
  through.
Over a hundred cruel laws, hard to list
  them all;
Ten thousand grievances, all from the
  tortures day and night.
Worry, and more worry—
How can I sleep in peace or eat at ease?
There isn't a cangue, but the hidden
  punishment is just as weighty.*
Tears soak my clothes; frustration fills my
  bosom.

雖無枷鎖陰刑重。淚滿衣裳悶滿胸。

愛忡忡。寢膳遑安用。

百般苛例講唔窮。朝夕被凌悲萬種。

室板如鐵桶。嚴關不漏風。(一)

(一)唔窮‥不盡

*A cangue consists of two locked wooden boards with holes for the neck and hands.
A convict wears it around his neck, with his hands bound in front of him and his feet
in chains.

7

Detention is called "awaiting review."
No letter or message can get through to me.
My mind's bogged down with a hundred frustrations
  and anxieties,
My mouth balks at meager meals of rice gruel.
O, what can I do?
Just when can I go ashore?
Imprisoned in a coop, unable to breathe,
My countrymen are made into a herd of cattle!

為留名審候。信息不通透。

百般抑鬱在心頭。水飯一些難入口。

乜能較(一)。幾時得上埠(二)。

闇室監禁氣莫哮(三)。嗟我同胞作馬牛。

(一) 乜能較：無奈何；參看歌#2

(二) 上埠：登岸進城

(三) 氣莫哮：不能平靜休息

8

America, I have come and landed,
And am stranded here, for more than a year.
Suffering thousands upon thousands of
   mistreatments.
Is it in retribution for a past life that I
   deserve such defilement?
It is outrageous—
Being humiliated repeatedly by them.
I pray my country will become strong and
   even the score
Send out troops, like Japan's war against
   Russia!*

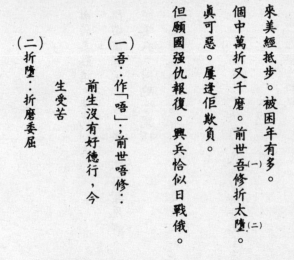

*In the Russo-Japanese War of 1903, Japan defeated Russia in Manchuria, in northeastern China, and emerged from this war as a world power.

9

A weak nation can't speak up for herself.
Chinese sojourners have come to a foreign
　country.
Detained, put on trial, imprisoned in a hillside
　building;
If deposition doesn't exactly match: the case is dead
　and in a bind.
No chance for release.
My fellow countrymen cry out injustice:
The sole purpose is strict exclusion, to deport
　us all back to Hong Kong.
Pity my fellow villagers and their flood of tears.

國弱真難講。華僑到異邦。
阻留候審困山房。供一不符案死鄉。
總唔放。同胞呼寃枉。
志在嚴禁撥返港，可憐梓里淚汪汪。

（三）撥：參看歌#3
（二）供：口供
（一）山房：天使島移民拘留所背山面海，
　　　　　故曰「山房」

10

The mighty power rescinds her treaty;
The weak race suffers oppression from the mighty.
I am jailed unjustly across the bay.
Enduring the unendurable tyranny of immigration
    officials.
Doors: firmly shut.
Guards and officers: watching me closely, like wolves.
News and letters: not permitted.
O, it's hard to bear the hundred cruel regulations
    they devise at will.

強權廢約例。弱種受他掣。
無辜困我隔江涯。關吏橫行眞譽抵(一)。
門緊閉。狼差嚴密睇(二)。
音信不容驛使遞。苛條百出確難捱。

(三)(二)(一)
苛睇譽
條：抵
：監：
指守難
排　以
華　抵
苛　受
例

11

American laws, more ferocious than tigers:
Many are the people jailed inside wooden walls,
Detained, interrogated, tortured,
Like birds plunged into an open trap—
   What suffering!
To whom can I complain of the tragedy?
I shout to Heaven, but there is no way out!
Had I only known such difficulty in passing
   the Golden Gate . . .
Fed up with this treatment, I regret my journey here.

美例苛於虎。人困板璧多。
所留候審受摯磨。鳥入樊籠折太陸(一)。
慘莫訴。呼天嘆無路。
闖過金門難若此。飽嘗況味悔奔波。

（一）折陸：參看歌#8

12

So, liberty is your national principle;
Why do you practice autocracy?
You don't uphold justice, you Americans,
You detain me in prison, guard me closely.
Your officials are wolves and tigers,
All ruthless, all wanting to bite me.
An innocent man implicated, such an injustice!
When can I get out of this prison and free
   my mind?

自由爲國例。何事學專制。

不持公理美人兮。困我監牢嚴密睇(一)。

狼虎差。橫行更欲噬。

罪及無辜眞惡抵(二)。幾時出獄開心懷。

（二）惡抵：難以抵受，參看歌#10

（一）睇：參看歌#10

13

Fellow countrymen, four hundred million
    strong;
Many are great, with exceptional talents.
We want to come to the Flowery Flag Nation
    but are barred;
The Golden Gate firmly locked, without even
    a crack to crawl through.
This moment—
Truly deplorable is the imprisonment.
Our hearts ache in pain and shame;
Though talented, how can we put on wings and
    fly past the barbarians?

同胞四萬萬。豪傑在其間。

花旗⁽一⁾欲入被他攔。緊鎖金門無路趨。

這一番。拘囚眞可恨。

縱有奇才心痛報。怎能插翼越夷蠻。

（一）花旗：：參看歌 #3

14

I roam America undocumented.
White men blackmail me with many demands.
I say one thing, and they, another;
I want to complain of injustice, but my tongue
    stutters.
At a loss for words—
I wrack my brain for a solution, to no avail.
Thrown into a prison cage, I cannot fly away.
Don't you think this is cruel? Don't you think
    this is cruel?

遊美因冇冊⁽⁻⁾。洋人多索勒。

我講南時佢⁽⁻⁾講北。欲訴寃情又語塞。

口嘿嘿。思量無計策。

被困牢籠飛不得⁽⁻⁾。汝話刻唔刻。

（一）冊：指「冊紙」；身份證明文件；
　　冇冊：沒有證件

（二）佢：他

（三）話：說，認爲，覺得

15

I am a man of heroic deeds;
I am a man with pride and dignity.
My bosom encompasses the height of Heaven
  and the brilliance of Earth;
Everywhere they know me as a truly noble
  man.
In search of wealth—
Greed led me on the road to Golden Mountain.
Denied landing upon reaching the shore, I am
  filled with rage.
With no means to pass the border, what can a
  person do?

處世豪傑士。堂堂大丈夫。

高明天地胸全羅。四處傳名眞君子。

欲愛富。貪走金山路。

抵岸難登氣滿肚。越界無策奈誰何。

16

Stay at home and lose opportunities;
A hundred considerations lead me to sojourn
  in Mexico.
Political parties are like wolves and tigers eliminating
  each other;
Hatred and prejudice against foreigners take away our
  property and many lives.
Unable to stay on—
I sneak across the border to the American side,
But bump into an immigration officer who sternly
  throws the book at me
And orders my expulsion back to China.

守家多失策。百謀方旅墨。
政黨相持狼虎革。仇視外人財命索。
唔棲得〔一〕。偷關過美域。
撞着稅員嚴拉冊〔二〕。令我回華申逐客。

（一）稅員··參看歌#1

（二）拉冊··審查「冊紙」及拘捕無
　　冊紙者；參看歌#14

17

A transient living beneath a stranger's
   fence.
Cruelties increase day by day.
Though innocent, I am arrested and thrown
   in jail;
Pathetic the lonely bachelors stranded in a
   foreign land.
O, let's all go home.
Spare ourselves of this mighty tyrant.
The outside world may be entertaining at times;
But life at home is just as bustling.

寄居人籬下。苛刻日日加。

無辜被拘禁監衙。覊留異地憐孤寡。

歸去罷。免受他強霸。

外國世界雖樂也。故園風景却繁華。

Lamentations of Stranded Sojourners

Economic hardship is the theme of the rhymes contained in this section. In recruiting Cantonese to work as laborers in America's West, Western capitalists preached the promise and glory of economic advancement. The possibility of attaining a better life was an irresistible temptation in southeastern China during the mid-nineteenth century, as many of the inhabitants of the region had been reduced to a marginal existence by natural and human disasters. Therefore, the news of economic opportunity was a welcome relief, and the discovery of gold in California only further encouraged the desperate Cantonese natives to rush to the United States. The promise of a steady income by working on the construction of the transcontinental railroads was also readily accepted by the impoverished men. Thus, they made the journey, thousands of miles across the perilous Pacific Ocean, pursuing their Gold Mountain Dream of success, a dream not too different from that of their European immigrant counterparts.

The Chinese immigrants worked hard at their jobs. They reclaimed California land and laid the foundation for the state to become the salad bowl of America. They mined claims that had been abandoned by white miners, paying a hefty foreign miners' tax. They worked on railroad construction, handling the most dangerous assignments, at a cost of thousands of lives. The wages they were paid, however, were lower than those of white workers. When they struck to demand better pay, their employer cut off their food supplies and the white workers did not support them. In the winter season, they lived and worked literally in the snow while laying track through the Sierra mountains. An avalanche could claim many lives without warning. When spring finally arrived, the bodies would emerge from the melting snow, intact, still holding picks and shovels, as a frozen testimony to their hardships.

Hardship and labor in the United States were an accepted reality for these Cantonese men, but the rampant racial prejudice of American society only made their lives more miserable. Even in urban San Francisco, their economic opportunities were limited. Many became disillusioned upon realizing that, after years of toiling in pain, there was not one sign of relief. Increasing their plight was the agony and frustration that they felt when they recognized the fact that their journey to America was not made just for themselves. Their sense of duty to their families back in China, who depended on them for survival, became an ever-present reminder, pushing them to the edge of desperation. A man's ability to achieve economic success and to provide for his family was the ultimate judgment of his success in the American sojourn. Anything less than that would be considered a failure. Thus, the most poignant reference in these rhymes is not to hardship or physical labor, but to the lack of economic reward. When their labor went unrewarded, many of these men became resigned to fate and disillusioned; others still desperately continued trying. Regardless of their differing responses to this harsh reality, all were haunted by the Gold Mountain Dream.

18

Dispirited by life in my village home,
I make a journey specially to the United States
  of America.
Separated by mountains and passes, I feel an
  extreme anxiety and grief;
Rushing about east and west does me no good.
Turning in all directions—
An ideal opportunity has yet to come.
If fate is indeed Heaven's will, what more can
  I say?
'Tis a disgrace to a man's pride and dignity.

失志居鄉黨。特來遊美邦。

關山阻隔極悽惶。東走西奔無善狀。

遍四方。未逢佳景況。

命實由天真譽講。男兒應愧貌堂堂。

(一)譽講：難說

19

Born into a rotten life,
Coming or going, all without leaving my mark.
Even after leaving the village for a foreign
    country,
Running about east and west, I've gained nothing.
Everything's turned upside down;
It's more disconcerting being away from home.
I have gone to the four corners of the world;
Alas, I am neither at ease while resting nor
    happy while moving.

一生條命薄。來去都冇作⁽一⁾。

縱使離鄉往外國。東走西奔無所獲。

陰陽錯。出門更落索⁽二⁾。

轉過天涯四個角。居弗安兮行弗樂。

(二)(一)
落冇
索作
：：
孤沒
伶有
失成
意就

20

Pitiful is the twenty-year sojourner,
Unable to make it home.
Having been everywhere—north, south, east,
    west—
Always obstacles along the way, pain knitting
    my brows.
Worried, in silence.
Ashamed, wishes unfulfilled.
A reflection on the mirror, a sudden fright:
    hair, half frost-white.
Frequent letters from home, all filled with much
    complaint.

廿年悲作客。猶未返故宅。

遍歷東南又西北。所爲報阻常慼額。

愁默默。自慙志不得。

對鏡乍驚頭半白。家書屢接頻交謫。

21

Come to think of it, what can I really say?
Thirty years living in the United States—
Why has life been so miserable and I, so frail?
I suppose it's useless to expect to go home.
My heart aches with grief;
My soul wanders around aimlessly.
Unable to make a living here, I'll try it in the East,
With a sudden change of luck, I may make it back to
 China.

想來無可講。卅年居美邦。

爲何命蹇咁懷惶。料必歸家未使望(一)。

心愴愴。神魂多飄蕩。

覓食難求東走往。忽然運轉就回唐(二)。

(一)未使望：沒有希望

(二)唐：即「唐山」，中國；四邑
人稱中國故鄉爲「唐山」

22

Stranded in a lodge: a delay;
Old debts up to my ears: here to stay.
No sign of relief, only a pain stealing through
    my heart.
And nagged by worry for my aged parents.
I want to go home;
But what can I do without money in my purse?
Determined to shape up and shake loose, I move
    elsewhere;
But I am still stuck with rotten luck, as life only
    gets worse.

逗遛羈旅郎。依舊滿身債。

毫無振作暗傷懷。每念高堂年紀邁。

欲歸計。囊中冇文解。(一)

發奮圖強來他徙。仍然屯寒事無諧。

(一)冇文：沒有一分錢

23

I have walked to the very ends of the earth,
A dusty, windy journey.
I've toiled and I'm worn out, all for a miserable lot.
Nothing is ideal when I am down and out.
I think about it day and night—
Who can save a fish out of water?
From far away, I worry for my parents, my wife,
    my boy:
Do they still have enough firewood, rice, salt, and
    cooking oil?

走盡天涯路。風塵跋涉多。
勞勞碌碌爲窮途。景遇未逢眞不妥。
朝夕思。憑誰救涸鮒。
遠念高堂妻共子。柴米油鹽尚有無。

24

Toiling in pain, east and west, all in vain;
Hurrying about, north and south, still more
   rushing.
What can a person do with a life full of mishap?
Searching, scheming, on all four sides, not
   one good lead in sight.
Eyes brimming with tears:
O, I just can't get rid of the misery.
My belly is full of frustration and grievance;
When life is at low ebb, I suffer dearly.

東西徒勤苦。南北更奔波。

命途多舛奈誰何。四邊求謀無好路。

眼悰悰。淒涼有計度。

抑鬱牢騷堆滿肚。人生當晦受磋磨。

(一) 有計∶沒有辦法

25

Drifting around, all over the place,
Seeking food everywhere, in all four directions.
Turning east, going west, always on an
  uncertain road;
Toiling, rushing about, much ado for nothing.
Fed by wind and frost,
I search for wealth, but all in vain.
If fate indeed has excluded me so, what more can
  I say?
After years of sojourn, I sigh in fear.

遍地飄流蕩。覓食走四方。

東轉西至路渺茫。勞碌奔馳冤太柱。

飽風霜。求財空虛望。

命裡唔凑真謷講。客途歲月嗟悽惶。

(二)(一)
謷講：不吻合
凑：參看歌 #18

26

Look at that face in the mirror:
My appearance so completely changed.
Hair white as frost, long beard hanging;
Disheartening are the bald spots sparkling
　　like stars.
Old age has arrived.
No longer is my face young and handsome.
Without my noticing, I am already over forty.
Shame is toiling in hardship, across the vast
　　and distant oceans.

照吓個容像（一）。看來變細（二）。

皓首如霜鬚又長。惱煞星星光掩映。

老至將。唔似靚仔樣（三）。

不覺年登四十上。自羞勞碌遠飄洋。

（一）吓：一下

（二）細：作「唔」；變唔相：容貌完全
　　　改變了

（三）靚仔：美少年

27

My ambition wouldn't allow me to stay cooped up
   in humility.
I took a raft and sailed the seas.
Rising early at dawn, with the stars above me,
   I traveled deep into the night, the moon my
   companion.
Who could have known it would be a journey full of
   rain and snow?
Winds pierced through my bones.
Hugging a blanket, my thighs trembling.
I wish to buy a fox-fur coat, but lack the
   money—
Right now I don't have the means even to fight
   the cold!

志不甘蝼屈。乘槎浮海出。
早起披星夜戴月。誰識客途多雨雪。
風刺骨。擁衾雙股慄。
欲購狐裘銀又缺。此際禦冬真無術。

28

The Flowery Flag Nation is deep in frost and heavy
with snow.
No one can withstand its winter without a fur
coat.
Traveling is not at all like staying at home:
In thin clothing on wintry days, my shoulders and
arms shrug and shiver in the cold.
Even if you are brave and strong,
The fierce wind will bend your back into a bow.
Prepare a cotton-padded gown and rush it to me!
Don't make this distant traveler wait anxiously
for the journeying geese!*

整備綿袍早遞送。免教遠客盼征鴻。

雖壯勇。風狂腰亦拱。

出外居家總不同。衫少歲寒肩膊聳。

花旗霜雪重。非裘莫絮冬。

*Journeying geese—a metaphor for news messengers.

29

Men on the remote frontier, all terrified:
In autumn, north winds begin to blow.
Sojourners from faraway places share the same
    thought:
O, how can this little bit of clothing be enough
    in deep frost and heavy show?
Once winter comes—
A fur coat is needed all the more in the
    freezing cold.
I can buy one at a clothing store,
But it's not the same as the one sewn by my dear wife
    or my mother.

（一）當‧‧作「擋」

遠塞人心悚。因秋起朔風。
退方旅客念相同。衫少怎當霜雪重。
一交冬。更需裘絮凍。
服店雖能加購用。奚如慈母與妻縫。

30

Life is like a vast, long dream
Why grieve over poverty?
A contented life soothes ten thousand matters.
Value the help from other people.
In all earnest, just endure:
You can forget about cold and hunger, as you
    see them often.
After lasting through winter's chill and snow's
    embrace,
You will find joy in life when happiness comes
    and sorrow fades.

處世若大夢。胡爲怨恨窮。

人生安份萬事通。玉汝於成雖珍重。

耐忍衷。見慣忘飢凍。

捱過歲寒和雪擁。苦盡甜來樂在中。

31

A brave man meeting an untimely adversity,
All day long, unable to eat or sleep.
Rushing about over ten thousand miles,
   deep in sorrow,
Every hour, every minute, mind and body
   toil in pain.
Heaven's will is extreme!
This big roc wants to spread its wings.*
Yet scores are not evened up; the mind is not
   at ease.
Alas, I can't rest in peace, I just can't rest
   in peace.

前　天　萬　烈
仇　意　里　士
未　極　奔　運
報　。　馳　達
真　大　愁　逆
唔　鵬　戚　。
值　就　戚　終
。　振　。　朝
難　翼　時　忘
安　。　刻　寢
息　　　勞　食
兮　　　心　。
難　　　兼
安　　　勞
息　　　力
。　　　。

---

*"Big roc," an allusion from *Zhuang zi,* commonly refers to a person who is about to
seek out a great future.

32

To be hard-pressed by poverty is truly disgusting.
Yet it's all due to fate.
Since antiquity, great men have often had to contend
　with adversity;
Remember, the cycle of life is Heaven's way.
So there's no need to complain.
All matters will turn around in the end, they
　always do;
One day, Heaven's eyes will no longer wink at me,*
And we'll go back to South China with enough
　money.

困窮眞可恨。皆因命所關。
自古英雄多受難。須知天道有循環。
唔使⑴嘆。物極終須反。
一日天公來生眼。自然富足返唐山⑵
　。

（二）（一）
唐　唔
山　使
：　：
參　不
看　必
歌
#21

* A Cantonese expression meaning positive retribution for a good deed.

33

In dire need of food and clothing,
I took my chances and came to Mexico alone.*
Savages rob and loot with frequent violence.
I ask Heaven: Why is there hatred against the
    yellow race?
On a journey,
It's hard to go anywhere without money.
With deep sorrow we Chinese sojourners must
    face many calamities,
Wondering when we can expect to go home in
    triumph and in grace.

只為衣食窮。挺身來呂宋(一)。
番奴掠劫屢行兇。問天何事厭黃種。
旅途中。無錢身難動。
深惜華僑遭劫重。那知方許望旋東。

（一）呂宋：照歌中內容，不應指
菲律賓，該為墨西哥

*For the Chinese in America, *Leuisung* refers to the Philippines or Mexico, or
sometimes Cuba, probably because Spanish is spoken in these places. Here, the term
refers to Mexico, as the poem depicts the turmoil of the Mexican Revolution of 1910,
as also seen in song 16.

34

Since coming to the frontier land,
I have taken all kinds of abuse from the
    barbarians.
I have come across the horizon to the Flowery
    Flag Nation;
The surroundings still fill me with thoughts
    of home.
Don't despair:
All we need is profit and money.
Should our purses be stuffed with gold,
We'll pick out a date and have our homebound
    whip ready.

自到邊疆地。受盡番奴欺。

天涯走過至花旗(一)。觸景依然懷故里。

莫傷氣。祇爭財與利。

黃金擲入荷包裡。整定歸鞭有日期。

(一)花旗：參看歌#3

Shawn Wong

(1949–   )

Shawn Wong was born in Oakland, California, and raised in Berkeley. His novel, *Homebase,* won both the Pacific Northwest Booksellers Award and a Washington State Governor's Writers Day Award. A German edition of *Homebase* was published in 1982. In addition to co-editing *Aiiieeeee!* and *The Big Aiiieeeee!*, he has edited two other volumes of Asian American literature. Wong is also a recipient of a National Endowment for the Arts creative writing fellowship. A graduate of the University of California at Berkeley and San Francisco State University, Wong has taught at Mills College, University of California at Santa Cruz, and San Francisco State University. He is a former chairman of the Seattle Arts Commission and is presently a professor in the American Ethnic Studies department at the University of Washington.

Homebase

The night train stopped at the edge of the ocean, the engine steaming into the waves that lapped against the iron wheels. The ocean was humbled in front of the great steaming engine, its great noise was iron; the moonlight on the ocean gave the sea its place, made the water look like waves of rippling steel. There was a low mumble heard beneath the sound of the waves, whose constant voice muted itself against fine sand; the voices of the men came towards me. I could not see their faces smeared with soot, charcoal faces. Their voices moved past me, towards the ocean, yet I was not afraid, I knew them. They had worked all day on the railroad, but at night they built the great iron engine that brought them to the sea's edge, pointed them home, the way west. They climbed down from the engine, faces black with soot, disguised, to dive into the ocean and swim home, but the moonlight hit the waves and made the surf like bones, white in their faces. Their swimming was useless, their strokes made in a desert of broken bones, of bone hitting bone, hollow noises to men who believed in home and hollow noises to men whose black faces held in their souls. But the engine waited in the iron night. And by morning the sun came up like the hot pulsating engine, the earth steams dry as I walk and kneel and wash my face with the earth's breathing, and the Chinamen rise all around me, their faces clean and grim, rising like swiftly rising steam to walk farther into their forest.

They go back to work, their eyes red with sea salt, their hands red from swimming with the broken bone sea. The black from the iron rails comes off on their hands.

I run through a thick night, that night of black soot mixing with my sweat to drip like tears from my face; my heart is the engine's red iron and if I stop running I will be burned. Now the night driver is me. The old night train filled with Chinamen, my grandfathers, fathers, all without lovers, without women, struggling against black iron with hands splintered from coarse cross ties. I am driving my car, moving out of a narrow side road at ninety onto a highway. With my father's spirit I am driving at night. No music. No more dreams. There is only the blur of the white line, the white guard rail at the edges of my sight as I outrun the yellow glare of lights, an ache at the temples and a pulse in the whites of my palms, knowing what is in front of me. I am speaking to the road with the green lights of the car's instruments touching my face, no dreams, just talk, like an ocean's talk, constant, muted against sand, immediate, suffocating. My fingers moving from the steering wheel, through glass, to grab at the blurs of white at one hundred miles an hour. My hands lift me out of my seat to stoop over and grab at the bleached bones of the road. I reach out to take the road in my hands, the blur of bones, no blood, someone speaks and I do not recognize the voice. Piano music rising in my ears like the winds that move across the plains and sweep like rivers, its waves of voice nearing my ear. The memorized picture fades and I am again speaking to myself with my lovers there, mother and father, and I remind myself what I call them. They begin to move. I give her all my weight, my father gives me his hand to hold saying, "We have to run, hold on." And I hold on for the chase, flying, my feet touching ground every six feet, like giants marching over the earth, my father, the track star, the runner giving me all the soul of his life.

I was never old enough to write a letter to my father to tell him how he had shaped my life. So on a night like this I write him a letter. Standing there on the beach, the night train easing up to me, the engine blacker than the night, is blowing steam out to sea. So I write. Dear Father, I am now at home. At our home on the range, our place. It is April. Tonight I remember a humid night on Guam when I held your forehead in my small hands as I rode on your shoulders. My hands felt your ears, the shape of your chin, and the shape of your nose until you became annoyed and placed my hands back on your forehead and shifted my weight on your shoulders. Like a blind man, I remember your face in the darkness. I remember you now with urgency. In this night here I heard the same sounds of a tropical night; the clicking of insects, the scrape of a lizard's claws on the screen door. Because I am now the same age as you are, Father, I remember how you showed me the button holes and buttons of my clothes, the loops needed to tie my shoes. I do not remember whether you admired me then, or remarked to yourself how much I looked like you, or felt satisfied that I would grow into the athlete you were. Tonight I took a long look into your face and saw you smiling. You are twenty-eight years old. At fifteen, when my mother died, I thought my terror would increase with age. The terror that I would not be like you, the terror that I would never admit where my home stood rooted. A woman I love, Father, told me that identity is a word full of the home. Identity is a word that whispers, not whispers, but *gets* you to say, "ever, ever yours."

The night train is beside me, spewing steam. I hear iron gates and doors opening and closing, I feel the heat of the engine beside me. The cold ocean waves boil against the hot iron beneath the engine. The waves wet my shoes and my pants at the ankles. The train fills the whole night. It is a wall between the dry beach and the edge of the ocean. Under the legend of this train, the heart of this country lies in immovable granite mountains, and lies in the roots of giant trees. Those roots are sharp talons in the earth of my country. I stand my ground and wave the train on. The train inches by me, heaving up steam, heat, sand, and sea water. The last thing I remember doing tonight is raising my hand to signal the train on. I walk back to the dock where I am making my stand in the night and see the train gather speed, feel it brush by me. I count every car pulled by the engine until all the noise of the night is gone.

Now I have the loneliness of fathers. To work from my soul, the heart speaking and pledging a feeling and commitment that gives like my father's giving to his lover, my mother. Not in self-pity, since the dream of Great-Grandfather, whose crying left scars on his face, Dear Father, I say, I write, I sing, I give you my love, this is a letter whispering those words, "ever, ever yours." But you are dead, there is nothing that keeps me, no voice, except that voice plagued by memory and objects of no value, a watch, a ring, a sweater, no movement, "keep it close to the skin," I say to myself. Father, I have dreams of departures, people leaving me, of life losing ground. I cannot control the blood that rushes to my head in the night and makes my dreams red.

I am driving at night and the whine of the car's engine rips through second and third gears. The straight road at last, that familiar white blur. A shift at a hundred and ten, deafening my ears. No sound now except for the building whine of my engine, my knees go weak, no blood there. I am too busy for fear, checking oil, rpm's, engine heat, speed at a glance, hands and arms working at the wheel, correcting for wind gusts.

I am pointing the car's sloping blue nose at a hundred into the blur of moons. What my eye sees becomes a scream, the scream of moonlight. I take my hands off the road, out of the ocean of bones, my sight returns to that yellow glare of headlights, the car slows to a stop, trembling like the blood at my knees. I move across America picking up ghosts. . . .

In the late nights of spring, 1957, my mother drove home from Oak Knoll Naval Hospital, thrashing the night traffic, pushing the little car through its gears, and somehow returned home away from the sleepless daze and the edge of crash. She came home joking about amazing dog stories, traveling across the desert, oceans, freezing mountains all in the night without food. Her driving at night seemed to her like swimming the currents of a flooded street, her eyes unfocused on the black night, still seeing the white hospital bed, father's pale skin and the light in the hospital's solarium that signaled his dying.

And one night she came home early, not joking, not ready to gather me up in her arms to play. She asked what color I wanted my room painted. And in her black expression I knew that father had died. I started crying. She became angry, not looking at me, and started calling out colors.

My mother taught me how to iron clothes that night. She had a basket full of clothes that had been around for years. The basket never grew or decreased in size. She ironed only what we needed. So when I was seven she told me to iron the back of the collar on my shirt so that the collar won't show wrinkles on the top part that shows. Next, to iron the shoulder area. Then the sleeves. The flap that the buttons are sewn to. Then the left front, the back, and the right front. Hang it up and button the top two buttons. A family tradition had been passed on to me. I don't remember how long I was ironing that night but I ironed all my own shirts. When I had finished ironing my shirts I noticed she had fallen asleep on the couch. I could see her from the kitchen. That was when I started ironing my father's shirts. Most of them were at the bottom of the basket. My father used to send his shirts out to be cleaned and ironed. He would let me put on his huge shirt before he put it on so that I could hear the sound of my hand working its way down the sleeve with that tearing sound because the starch had glued the sleeves shut. He had shirt pockets that held both my hands. I didn't have any starch that night so I ironed his shirts like mine. I folded them all neatly on the kitchen table, ten white shirts, five light blue shirts, two khaki work shirts, two plaid ones. I reached down into the basket and found myself a set of flannel pajamas. I ironed them and put them on. I took the blanket off my bed and squeezed into a small space next to my mother on the couch and fell asleep with her, the blanket trapped the smells of clean and warm cotton with her perfume and her warm breath.

I had said before that I am violent, that I had become a father to myself. But it was my mother that controlled my growing until she too died eight years after my father's death. Not a startling revelation except when I saw her burial and I discovered that she had shaped the style of my manhood in accordance with her own competitive and ambitious self. I grew up watching my mother's face for direction, the movements of her body. The features of her face shaped me. She was thirty-two years old when my father died and I was seven, and when I think of her now I remember her as a young woman and how her growing kept pace with mine. She would not let me be present at my father's funeral, she did not want to be the object of everyone's pity, the mother of a fatherless child, and she did not want my childhood shaped around the ceremony and ritual of a funeral. And now, after I had witnessed her dying in another hospital eight years later and became the prominent figure at her funeral, I did not cry. I did not want everyone's pity for an orphaned fifteen-year-old boy, but kept my eyes on the casket, kept my hands in my pockets and walked quickly through the ceremony of her death.

After she died I was no longer anyone's son . . . I was alone, but I did not cry. My sleep tore me apart, and gave her flesh back to me in pieces, her voice with no substance, and finally nothing but a hollow sound would wake me, her jade bracelet knocking against the house as she moved around, cleaning, cooking, writing. It had become for me, in those dreams, the rhythmic beating of her heart. There was no need for me to put my head against her chest to hear the beating of her heart; the cold stone, jade in my eyes, filled my youth and kept time with the unsteady beating of my own heart. . . .

"Drifting alone in the ocean it suddenly passed autumn."
                                                    —Angel Island

Now after seeking out all the wrong names to call myself, I've
been to those places that can destroy me, I've felt those places
overcome me without violence, only my own dreaming brought it on
until I was able to say that I am violent and I sought out these
places, making them mine.

Now I knew that my grandfather's land was an island. He was
born in San Francisco but his father, my great-grandfather, sent him
back to China for safety. It was 1917 when he came back. And in
1917 Grandfather's island was called Angel Island.

My grandfather's land sits in the middle of San Francisco Bay
directly in the path of the fog that flows in from the Golden Gate.
The fog meets Angel Island and moves around it to hold it and
silence it. When the fog lifts and retreats to the sea it will often
leave a halo around the peaks of Angel Island.

On the north side of the island at Winslow Cove there is a
building called P-317—the U.S. Justice Department Immigration
detention center for Chinese immigrants. A chain link fence surrounds the building. All the windows are broken yet the frames for
the small panes of glass are still in position. Some windows are half
open.

There is a movement about the place that gives off sound like
sleeping gives off dreams, like a haunted house moves people to
realize that life still exists within. The sounds I heard as a child in
dreams made me deaf but never woke me. Hearing voices waked
me.

I have to bend back the fence to get near the building. I walk
through and release the fence and it springs back into place and
rattles against the pole that holds it. There is broken glass everywhere, even on the stairs leading to the door. After I make my way
past the sounds under my feet of old wood rotten from the ocean air
mixed with breaking glass, I am standing at an open door looking
in.

Once inside, you will see that the room is lit with bare bulbs hung
from the ceiling. You will see that the room is filled with men,
women, and children. There are two lines—men and young boys in
one and women and a few very young children in the other. An
officer stands between the two lines. Behind a large counter there is
an officer for each line. There is some shuffling but no talking
except for the two officers behind the counter. You will see that we
are dressed in drab jackets, some men are wearing long coats with

black pants underneath, others are wearing regular work clothes, and many are wearing flat brim black hats.

You will know why you're standing in line with me. I am my grandfather come back to America after having been raised in China. My father is dead so I've had to assume someone else's name and family in order to legally enter the country. All this information about my new family has been memorized. All my sons after me will have my assumed name.

I was not allowed to ever leave the building, even to go outside. Husbands were not allowed to see their wives or children, who were kept in another part of the building. We ate in different shifts. There were riots in the mess hall and the main building. We had given up everything to come to this country. Many were former citizens. If you run your fingers across the walls at night in the dark, your fingers will be filled with the splinters of poems carved into the walls. Maybe there is a dim light to help see what your fingers feel. But you can only read, "Staying on this island, my sorrow increases with the days/my face is growing sallow and body is getting thin," before your fingers give out following the grooves and gouges of the characters.

Sometimes the morning will show you someone has hung themselves in the night, someone who could no longer bear the waiting, or the interrogation, or failing the interrogation—someone waiting to be sent back to China. Everyone knows how to hang yourself. There are no nails or hooks high enough to hang a piece of cloth from and leap from a stool to a quick death. There is only one way—to tie your piece of cloth on one of those big nails about four and a half feet off the floor, lean against the wall to brace yourself, and bend your knees and hold them up off the floor. Then your bones will be collected and placed on the open seas.

I have memorized someone else's family history, taken someone else's name, and suppressed everything that I have chronicled for myself. The questions begin in the Interrogation Room. It is a room blocked off from the light. The windows are painted black. One immigration officer has a list of questions in his hand and the other has a file folder in front of him with the data given by relatives years ago.

Question: How large is your village?
Answer: It has fifty houses.
Question: How many rows of houses are there?
Answer: Ten rows.
Question: Which way does the village face and where is the
          head?

Answer: It faces east and the head is south.

Question: Where is your house located?

Answer: Second house, third row, counting from the south.

Question: Do you know who lived in that house before your family?

Answer: I do not remember.

Question: How many houses in your row?

Answer: Five.

Question: Do all of the houses in your row touch each other?

Answer: None of them do.

Question: How far apart are they?

Answer: About six feet.

Question: What were the sleeping arrangements in your house when you were last in China?

Answer: My mother, all my brothers, and I occupied the south bedroom.

Question: How many beds are in the south bedroom?

Answer: Sometimes two, and sometimes three.

Question: Please explain that statement.

Answer: When the weather gets warm, we use three.

Question: How many steps lead to your front door?

Answer: None.

Question: Is there a clock in your house?

Answer: Yes.

Question: Describe it.

Answer: It is wood on the outside. It is brass with a white porcelain face. It has brass numbers.

Question: Where did your mother buy provisions?

Answer: She buys at the Tin Wo Market.

Question: How far and in what direction is that from your village?

Answer: One or two lis west.

Question: How many of your brothers have attended school?

Answer: All my brothers.

Question: Did they attend the same school with you?

Answer: Yes.

Question: When did your youngest brother start school?

Answer: The beginning of this year.

Question: When did your oldest brother start school?

Answer: When he was eleven years old.

Question: When did you quit school?

Answer: I attended school for six months this year, then I quit.

Question: Who told you to quit?

Answer: My mother. She told me to prepare myself to go to the United States.

Question: When did you first learn that you were to come to the United States of America?

Answer: About the time my mother told me to quit school.

The officer asking the questions stops for a moment. He puts down the paper he's been reading from and draws out a tobacco pouch and begins to roll a cigarette for himself. He rises from his chair and goes to the window. He licks his cigarette and draws a match out from his pocket and lights his cigarette. The second officer has stopped writing whatever he was writing and puts down his pencil. The first one begins scraping the black paint from a small section of the window. He pulls out his pocket knife, unfolds it, and continues scraping until he has a small peephole. "It's a nice day outside," he says to no one. The room fills with the cigarette smoke. He continues to look out the hole in the window and, absentmindedly, is folding and unfolding his pocket knife. "Where does your mother receive her mail?" He asks with his back still turned to me.

"I don't know."

"Who goes after the mail?"

"My mother."

"Where do you suppose she goes to get it?"

"I don't know."

"Describe your mother."

"She is medium in height and slim in build. She has black hair. She is exuberant, graceful, and stubborn." I see her on no particular day in my mind. Her hair is set in a fashionable wave. She always wore red lipstick, not brilliant red but a darker shade. She used eyebrow pencil even though she didn't need it. She was always looking at her clothes to see if everything was in place, picking lint off, brushing her hand over the material as if to smooth out a wrinkle. She was doing that now as she crossed the street. She had extravagant taste in clothes, not flashy, but suits made of Italian knits, cashmere sweaters, elegant slips.

"Does your mother wear any jewelry?"

"Yes."

"Describe it."

"It is a dark green jade bracelet. She wears it on her right wrist. I can hear her working around the house when she has it on because it knocks against everything she touches. I've felt it touching my skin many times."

The officer turns from the window to face me. He steps towards me, but I do not see him move towards me. I'm gazing out of the small hole he's carved in the window.

"Have you ever seen a photograph of your father?"

"Yes. Yes, it was taken on a day like today. He is seated in a wooden chair on a lawn somewhere next to a wooden table with a heart-shaped hole. . . ." I see my father sleeping on a cot. It is night and the air around me is brilliantly cold. There is snow outside.

Then the poor men filled the island with their smells, filled the yellow glow of the bare light in the building. Their fists rose like clubs. Then I smelled the rotting wood of the building and I rose with them. I moved with them through the barracks screaming at the doors until the taste of metal came to my tongue. We beat at the steel doors until they broke loose from the wooden building. Then water came rushing in pushing us back. Ocean water from a fire hose pushed at us until we were all huddled in the corners of the bunk room. The doors closed again.

After the riot of blood, a man was beaten and thrown into isolation. And beaten again and again until I could hear his flesh break like glass, cutting him deeper and the salt of his sweat moved like dark worms in his wound.

On days like today, the glass is merely under my feet and I pick the pieces up like I'm collecting bones. This is my home base, my Rainsford, California. I place the glass in a small pile on the floor and rise up to the window. On days like today, I will remember the time I took the rotting wooden windowsill in my hands and tore it to shreds. It crumbled like bone marrow. The window is open.

On days like today, I hear someone moving through the chain link fence, something she's wearing strikes a note on the fence post and as the vibration fades away, she moves through.

Kazuo Miyamoto

(1897–1988)

Kazuo Miyamoto was born on the Hawaiian island of Kauai in 1897, attended Stanford University, and studied medicine at Washington University Medical School in St. Louis, Missouri. He practiced medicine in Honolulu before and after World War II. A doctor by profession, a man of history and conscience by nature, in *Hawaii: End of the Rainbow* he attempted the epic history of his people out of the necessity of his nature. The wartime relocation and internment of the Japanese Americans threatened Japanese American history and drove Miyamoto to defend it.

How much of a threat the camps posed, to Nikkei in general and Kazuo Miyamoto specifically, the good doctor may never have known. His mail was censored while he was a physician in the camp hospital at Tule Lake. One letter was so full, the censor copied it, in its entirety, duplicating every hurried misspelling and typo, for the censor's files.

Dr. Miyamoto's letter to a friend recuperating in an army hospital in Honolulu reveals a Nisei of vigorous opinions, a roiling conscience, and sentiment. The letter is stamped with a notice from the director of censorship:

SPECIAL NOTICE—This contains information taken from private communications, and its extremely confidential character must be preserved. The information must be confined only to those officials whose knowledge of it is necessary to prosecution of the war. In no case should it be widely distributed or copies made, or the information used in legal proceedings or in any other public way without express consent of the Director of Censorship.

BYRON PRICE, Director

The letter, dated August 12, 1944, opens with the salutation "My dear Chicken Hearted Friend." Miyamoto jokes about being wounded, as only a doctor can to a friend. Then he mentions a pro-Japan group the camp authorities, the social scientists, the FBI, and all of American intelligence are watching very carefully:

Last night, I was not so busy at the hospital and went to the opening of the So Koku kenkyo seinen kai. There were about seven or eight hundred young men. I leave it up to your imagination what the scene was like . . .

A chatty letter to a friend gives us Miyamoto the man:

Araki is a Gila Relocation center in Arizona. It seems to be beastly hot in Arizona at present. We are fortunate in this respect as I probably told you in the last letter.

Yoshi got a grazing wound in the neck early this year but he is still going strong. Raymond, my wife's brother, is awaiting his furlough at some embarkation point in Europe and advised us not to write to him anymore. We shall be waiting for him. He is supposed to have been shot through the thigh but vital structures were missed fortunately. He will I am sure return to the islands on his days off.

I sent some telegrams through the Red Cross. There is a chance of the message going through Russia. I am going to write to Mr. Kishi through that channel in a few days and will drop a word about you. . . .

Summer will be gone pretty soon. With fall and winter in the offing, I am dreading the work that will pile up on us. Right now we are just about working as we should. There is a little time for reading and study, but once there is a cold spell this tranquility will be shattered.

Take courage and don't brood. We shall meet again under better circumstances with me playing the host again. So much do I have confidence in the lucky star under which you have been born. The sun shines upon her children. Sun is the healer of many ailments.

Sincerely,
Kazuo

The return address was 716-C, Newell, California. The airmail postage was six cents. The postmark was August 15, 1944, 9 A.M., Tule Lake, California.

A Farmer's Life

Anti-Japanese feeling in California was being fanned by politicians every election year, and the bungling, historic "grave consequence" utterance of the Japanese ambassador at Washington, D.C., so ired the Congress that the Japanese Exclusion Act was enacted in 1924. Prior to that fateful year there was a complete hamstringing of legal residents lawfully entered and actively contributing to California economy by a law that forbade leasing of any farm land to any "person ineligible to United States citizenship." Primarily aimed at alien Japanese, the majority of whom dwelt on farms either as lessees or farm hands, this law of 1920 reduced at one stroke all of them to the status of day laborers. The sword, however, was double-edged, and the white landowners were equally hit hard. How to get around this newly enacted law (which was ruled unconstitutional in 1946 by the United States Supreme Court and also removed by a referendum in 1956) was the pressing need in the winter of 1921.

Children of California Japanese were too young to step in to utilize their legal rights to help carry on the farms that their fathers had so laboriously improved and cultivated. A year-to-year basis of tenure was too precarious to make any investment, and a long-term agreement was desired by both landowners and tenants. To lay out a fruit ranch and plant and care for young trees needed a lot of expenditure both in capital and work, and a guarantee of a lease for at least ten years was imperative. Knowing the loyalty, industry, and ability of Japanese farmers, independent white ranchers and absentee landlords were eager to have them remain and continue as tenants. The fall of 1921 was thus a very dark, depressing, almost hopeless one for the Japanese community.

"A telephone call for you. Long distance."

"For me? I wonder who from?" Minoru was surprised, for there was no particular person that he knew in California.

"This is Kawano of Oakland. You are Minoru Murayama of Waipunalei, Hawaii, and your father is Torao Murayama?"

"Yes sir."

"I am a cousin to your mother, and I left Waipunalei when you were about five years old. Lately I discovered from one of your fellow students that you are now at Stanford University. By the way, how old are you now?"

"I became twenty-one years old in April of this year."

"Can you come to my store in Oakland right away? I have a very important piece of business which may be of great interest and help to you. I heard that you are working your way through college. This proposition may solve your problem."

The summer was a very unproductive one due to low farm wages and scarcity of work. Being faced with the beginning of the fall term and increased expenses (he was beginning his first year in medicine), he was mentally debating whether it would not be a wise thing to stay out of school for a year. He was just back at the university from a frustrating three days on the island of Rindge at Stockton. He worked at onion harvesting, but the fine dust hurt his eyes so badly he had to flee. The outlook was extremely dismal. Any legitimate way to add to his scant coffer was welcome. He proceeded to Oakland immediately.

"This is Mr. Tom Tanaka of Courtland in the delta district of the Sacramento River. He is about the biggest Japanese farmer of northern California and is well known to all in that district. He is related by marriage to us. Mrs. Kawano, my wife, is first cousin to Mrs. Tanaka. Now, you being my third cousin will make this a talk among relatives, and whatever can come out of this discussion will be within the family so to speak."

This introduction was made after the usual handshakes, at Mr. Kawano's fruit stand on Franklin St., Oakland. Proffering cups of green tea and delicious Japanese candies, talk dealt with generalities and Minoru instinctively sensed that he was being sized up. From his side, he was also trying to form some sort of evaluation of these people who suddenly appeared in his life. He was sure they were shaping a definite milestone in the course of his destiny. Mr. Kawano, he vaguely remembered, came to visit the family at Waipunalei just before he left for California. Only he was then much slimmer. His wife was a jolly extrovert, rare among Japanese women. Mr. Tanaka had a strong Kumamoto brogue but he seemed to be very worldly wise for he never contradicted anyone. But one could sense the strong undertone of his character even in his acquiescence and adaption to the talk going on.

"You have no doubt read in the papers in what plight the Japanese farmers are. After the recent law that forbids even a one-year lease of farmland goes into effect, there can be no farming done in this state. Mr. Tanaka not only farms himself, but has several tenants who sublease acres for different crops. His present interest is in beans and he has been working about fifteen hundred acres on a new island called Holland Tract. His tenants take care of the fruit ranch, the seed crops, potato, celery, and onions. There is a need for someone to lease these lands. The landlord is a very honest man known to Mr. Tanaka after twelve years of intimate business dealings. Because he is honest and upright, he wants Tom to be protected legally by a lease. It can be legally done. The whole crux of the arrangement is in the getting of a trustworthy citizen who will not betray the Japanese farmers. Since you are twenty-one years old, you can lease these farms for us. What do you think? In return Mr. Tanaka will guarantee the expense to put you through medical school. Isn't that what you will do if you both can agree in this matter, Tom?"

Mr. Tanaka became serious and said, looking straight into Minoru's eyes, "The subject has been covered well by Mr. Kawano and there is not much for me to add, except to say that we shall be most grateful if you can sacrifice a year or two of your life and come to the farm. We have to show the neighbors that you are farming even if the actual thing is done by us farmers. You will be doing a lot for us with families, and we in turn will see to it that you will also profit by this arrangement. Please give it deep thought."

It was a very unusual turn of events and nobody could have planned anything more convenient at such an opportune time. No matter how hard he worked, it was impossible to raise enough money to finance medical school and he had already discovered that to work through the last four years was an almost impossible task. Now, out of a clear sky, he was offered a way to achieve his ambition. He could very well afford to stay out of college a few years if such a guarantee was in the offing. He might have had to do just that anyway without that assurance.

Wakako Yamauchi

(1924–   )

Wakako Yamauchi's first play, *And the Soul Shall Dance*, is the most honored and celebrated work in Asian American theater. It won the Los Angeles Critics' Circle Award for best new play of 1977 and was named the best new play in regional theater. It has also been produced for public television. The play was developed and first presented at the East/West Players in Los Angeles, with Mako directing.

And the Soul Shall Dance was the first Asian American work to dramatize an Asian American search for identity without rhetoric and to face the white racism of the period without polemics. It grew out of a story of the same name, first published in *Aiiieeeee! An Anthology of Asian American Writers* (1974). In Act One, Mr. Oka, the cloddish peasant Issei farmer, is married to a woman who has schemed for two years to flee her forced marriage and go back to her true lover in Japan. These tragically bound people are two of the great characters in Asian American theater. They burn onstage, before our eyes, raging great unspoken passions that will destroy them both. The fascination the young Nisei girl, Masako, has for the crazy and graceful Mrs. Oka is a hauntingly accurate expression of the American-born's feelings of attraction, revulsion, and mystery for the immigrant generation.

Wakako Yamauchi, like Masako, through whose eyes we see the world, was a farmer's daughter, born in California's Imperial Valley. In 1942, she and her family were interned at the concentration camp at Poston, Arizona. In camp she and Nisei writer Hisaye Yamamoto became lifelong friends. Yamauchi's short fiction appeared in the holiday editions of the Japanese American newspaper *Rafu Shimpo* and numerous anthologies and magazines of Asian American writings.

And the Soul Shall Dance

CHARACTERS

MASAKO, a young girl. She is slim, eleven, wears her hair combed back behind her ears and fastened with a large metal clip. She wears clothes of the early thirties, country vintage.

MURATA, a first-generation Japanese immigrant of about forty. He is a quiet man; tall, thin, typically Japanese in his manner . . . a patriarch. There is an interplay between him and Mrs. Murata; both know how far they can go within this framework (although the balance is tipped toward his side). He asserts himself more freely in the company of Oka.

MRS. MURATA (HANA), about thirty-five. She plays a submissive Japanese wife reluctantly, and with some dignity. She is moral, sympathetic, has all the human frailties.

MR. OKA, a simple humble man, about forty-five. He is short and rather stout. He enjoys his association with the Muratas, a somewhat restricted relationship, but the only social one he has in the limited environment. He apparently accepts his small piece of life, but we do not see the seething passion of his frustrations that his loveless marriage engenders. He makes effective use of his ultimate weapon, Kiyoko.

MRS. OKA, about twenty-eight, thin and small. The calico she wears doesn't hide her delicate femininity. She abhors the situation she has become heir to. Coping with life with the only instruments she possesses, she manages to live just above the level of emotional survival. Until Kiyoko disrupts the pattern.

KIYOKO OKA, a fifteen-year-old girl, a physical counterpart of her father, Japan-born and -trained. She giggles and bows a lot. Battered by life's injustices, she scratches out a place for herself, in the process displacing her stepmother.

TRUCK DRIVER, a young Caucasian swamper. He finds Japanese are a strange bunch.

GLOSSARY

chan   an endearing suffix for children
eh   a feminine expression of acknowledgment, accompanied with a nod
furo-ba (foo-ro-bah)   a bathhouse
kun   an intimate masculine suffix

nnn   an expression of acknowledgment

oba-san (oh-bah-san)   like "ma'am"; also means "aunt"

oi   hey; hello

ondo (ohn-do)   music, very gay, usually danced to during festivals

sah   now then

sake (sah-keh)   Japanese wine

san   a respectful suffix

yah   an expression of resignation

yoshi (yoh shi)   an arrangement by which a man marries into a family of daughters and takes on the family name

yukata (yoo-kah-tah)   an evening robe

zori (zoh-ri)   Japanese sandals

Act 1. Scene 1

TIME: 1935, day

On Rise: The interior and exterior of the MURATAS' *house and yard. Left stage is the interior. Two rooms are visible: the kitchen and the bedroom. The other bedroom is behind a doorway covered with home-made curtains. Upstage is the wall of the house, with a narrow single bed or cot made to look like a couch. A lamp sits on a nightstand next to it. On the wall hangs a calendar from a fertilizer company. Downstage is a table with an oilcloth cover and three chairs. There is a rough cabinet containing a saucepan, a bottle of* sake, *and a jar of chiles. A kerosene stove stands next to the cabinet. On the kitchen wall hang two towels. The interior of the house is raised slightly above the exterior or there is some other demarcation line. A wooden bench stands outside.*

Offstage we hear the excited voices of MURATA, *his wife,* HANA, *and daughter,* MASAKO, *putting out the bathhouse fire. There are sounds of fire crackling and hissing, and ad-libbed cries of: More water, Fire's starting out over there, It's out of control, Let it burn itself out, etc.*

The MURATAS *enter from stage left:* MURATA, *forty, wearing work clothes;* HANA *thirty-five, in a housedress;* MASAKO *also in a summer dress. They are disheveled and exhausted.* HANA *is talking as they walk in.*

HANA: My God, I don't know how such a thing could happen! How could you be so careless, Masako? When you stoke a fire, you should see that everything is swept . . .

MURATA: This kind of weather dries everything. The shack went up like a match box . . .

HANA: Swept into the fireplace. How many times have I told you that?

(*MASAKO is petulant. The three dust themselves and enter the house.*)

MURATA (*sighing audibly*): No use crying about it now. That's it. It's burned to the ground. No more bathhouse. That's all there is to it.

HANA (*whining*): You got to tell her. Otherwise she'll make the same mistake. You'll be building a bath every year.

(*MURATA removes his shirt and wipes off his face. He throws his shirt on a chair and sits at the table. HANA stands by him.*)

MURATA: Ridiculous!

MASAKO (*sulking*): I didn't do it on purpose.

(*MASAKO goes directly to the bed. She plumps a pillow and opens a book. HANA follows her.*)

HANA: I know that, but you know what this means? It means we bathe in a bucket—inside the house. Carry water in from the pond, heat it on the stove . . .

MURATA: The tub's still there. And the fireplace. We can still build a fire under the tub . . .

HANA (*shocked*): But no walls! Everyone in the country can see us.

MURATA: Wait 'til dark. Wait 'til dark then.

HANA: We'll be using a lantern. They'll still see us.

MURATA (*irritated*): Anghh! Who? Who'll see us? You think everyone around the country wants to watch us take a bath? You know how stupid you sound? My God, woman . . .

HANA: It'll be inconvenient . . .

(*HANA is saved by OKA, who enters from the right. He is forty-five, short and stout. He's dressed in faded work clothes.*)

OKA: Hello, hello! Hey! What's going on here? Hey! Was there some kind of fire?

(*HANA rushes to the door to let OKA in. He stamps the dust from his shoes.*)

HANA: Oka-san. You just wouldn't believe . . . we had a terrible thing happen.

OKA: Yeah. Saw the smoke from down the road. Thought it was your house . . . came rushing over.

(*MURATA half rises and sits back again. He is exhausted.*)

MURATA: Oi, oi. Come in . . . sit down. No big problem. It was just the bathhouse.

OKA: Just the bathhouse, eh? Good. Thought it was your house.

MURATA (*muttering*): Nah, nah. Just the bath.

OKA: Well, let me help you with it.

MURATA: What . . . now? Now?

OKA: Yeah, long as I'm here . . .

HANA: Oh, Papa. Aren't we lucky to have such friends?

MURATA (*turning to his wife*): Hell, we can't work on it now. The ashes are still hot.

(*OKA is embarrassed not to have thought of this.*)

MURATA (*continuing*): I just now put the damned fire out. Let me rest a while. (*He turns to OKA.*) Oi, how about some *sake*? Hey, sit a while. (*He gestures to HANA.*) Make *sake* for Oka-san.

(*OKA sits at the table. HANA goes to the cabinet, pulls out a bottle of wine, pours some in a saucepan, and sets it on the stove to heat.*)

MURATA (*continuing*): I am tired . . . I am *tired.*

HANA (*glancing over to Murata*): But Papa, Oka-san has so generously offered to help . . .

(*OKA is uncomfortable. He looks around for something to help him. He sees MASAKO sitting on the bed.*)

OKA: Hello there, Masako-chan. You studying?

MASAKO: No, it's summer vacation.

MURATA (*sucking in his breath*): Kids nowadays . . . no manners . . .

(*HANA serves the wine.*)

HANA: She's mad because I had to scold her . . .

MURATA (*gesturing*): Drink up, Oka. Eh, you don't have work to do today?

OKA (*nodding his thanks and taking a swallow*): Ah, that's good. No, no . . . I took the day off today. I was driving over to Nagata's when I saw this big black cloud of smoke coming from your yard. I rushed over, thinking it was your house . . .

MURATA (*chuckling*): No, not my house. What's up at Nagata's? (*MURATA drinks from his cup and addresses his wife.*) Get the chiles out. Oka loves chiles.

(*HANA walks back to the cabinet and opens a jar of chiles. She arranges some on a plate and serves the men. She gets her mending basket and walks over to MASAKO. MASAKO makes room for her on the bed.*)

OKA (*helping himself*): Ah, chiles . . . Well, I thought I'd see him about my horse. I'd like to sell him my horse.

MURATA (*pretending to choke*): Sell your horse!

OKA (*scratching his head*): The fact is, I need some money. Nagata's the only one around made money this year, and I'm thinking he might want another horse.

MURATA: Yeah, he made a little this year. And he's talking big. Big. Says he's leasing twenty more acres this fall. Yeah, he might want another horse.

OKA (*whistling*): Twenty acres . . .

MURATA: That's what he says . . .

OKA: I better get over there . . .

MURATA: Why the hell you selling your horse? You pulling out of here?

OKA: No . . . no . . . I need cash . . .

MURATA: Yeah, I could use some too. Seems like everyone's getting out of the depression but the poor farmers.

HANA: Papa, do you have lumber for the bathhouse?

MURATA (*over his shoulder*): Don't worry about that. We need more *sake.* (*He indicates his cup is empty.*)

(*HANA hurries over to serve him.*)

OKA: You sure Nagata's working twenty more acres?

MURATA: Yeah. But what the hell: if you need a few bucks, I can loan . . .

OKA: A few hundred. I need a few hundred dollars.

MURATA: Oh, a few hundred. But what the hell you going to do without a horse? A man's horse is as important as his wife here.

OKA: I don't think Nagata will buy my wife. (*The men laugh and enjoy the joke. HANA doesn't find it quite so funny. MURATA glances at his wife. She fills the cups again. OKA makes a half-hearted gesture to stop her.*) I better get moving.

MURATA: What's the hurry?

OKA: Like to get the horse business done.

MURATA: Relax. Do it tomorrow . . . He ain't going to die, is he?

OKA (*laughing*): Hey, he's a good horse. I better get it settled today. If Nagata won't buy, I have to find someone else. You think Kawaguchi . . .

MURATA: Not Kawaguchi. Maybe Yamamoto.

HANA: What is all the money for, Oka-san? Does Emiko-san need an operation?

OKA (*chuckling*): Nothing like that.

HANA: Sounds very mysterious . . .

OKA: No mystery, ma'am, no mystery. No sale, no money, no story . . .

MURATA (*laughing*): That's a good one. "No sale, no money, no . . ." Eh, Mama . . . (*He points to the cups.*)

(*HANA fills the cups and goes back to MASAKO.*)

HANA (*muttering*): I see we won't be doing any work today. (*She looks at MASAKO critically.*) Are you reading again? Maybe you ought to stop all that and put your mind to real things. Maybe we'd still have a bath if you . . .

MASAKO: I didn't do it on purpose.

MURATA (*loudly*): I sure hope you know what you're doing, Oka. What'd you do without a horse?

OKA: I was hoping you'd lend me yours now and then . . .

MURATA (*emphatically*): Sure!

OKA: The fact is I need that money. I got a daughter in Japan, and I just got to send for her this year.

(*HANA puts down her mending and comes back to the table. She seats herself.*)

HANA: A daughter? You have a daughter in Japan? Why, I didn't know you had children. Emiko and you . . . I thought you were childless.

OKA: We are. I was married before.

MURATA: You son-of-a-gun . . .

HANA: Oh. Is that so? How old is your daughter?

OKA: Kiyoko must be fifteen now. Yeah, fifteen.

HANA: Fifteen! Oh, that *would* be too old to be Emiko's daughter. Is Kiyoko-san living with relatives now?

OKA (*reluctantly*): Yeah, with grandparents. Well, the fact is, Shizue, that's my first wife, and Emiko were sisters. They come from a family with no sons. I was a boy when I went to work for the family—they're blacksmiths. I was an apprentice there. Later I married Shizue and took on the family name—you know, because they had no sons. My real name is Sakakihara.

MURATA: Sakakihara. That's a great name!

OKA: No one knows me by that here.

MURATA: You should have kept that—Sakakihara . . .

OKA (*muttering*): I don't even know myself by that name . . .

HANA: And Shizue died? And you married Emiko?

OKA: Oh, yeah. Well, Shizue and I lived with the family for a while . . . and we had the baby—that's you know, Kiyoko. (*He pauses, recollecting the past. The liquor has affected him and he is less inhibited.*) Well, while I was serving apprenticeship with the family, they always looked down on me. After I married, it got worse . . . That old man was terrible—always pushing me around, making me look bad in front of my wife and kid. That old man was mean . . . Ugly!

MURATA: Yeah, I heard about that apprentice work. Heard it was goddamn bloody . . . humiliating . . .

OKA: That's the God's truth!

MURATA: Never had to do it. I came to America instead.

OKA: I hated the work. I hated them! Well, Shizue and I talked it over, and we decided the best thing was for me to go to America, make some money and send it to her, and when we had enough, I'd go back and we'd leave the family. You know, move to another province . . . start a small business—maybe in the city—a noodle shop or something . . .

MURATA: That's everyone's dream. Make money, go home, and live like a king.

OKA: I worked like a dog here. Sent every penny to Shizue. And then she died—died on me!

HANA: Oh, so you married Emiko.

OKA: *I* didn't marry her. They married her to me! Right after Shizue died, the old man wrote me they were arranging a marriage by proxy for me and Emiko. They said she'd grown to be a beautiful woman and would serve me well.

HANA: So that's how . . .

OKA: And they sent her to me. Took care of everything: immigration, fare, everything . . .

HANA: Well, if she was your sister-in-law . . . after all Emiko is Kiyoko-san's aunt . . . it's good to keep the family together . . .

OKA: That's what I thought. But hear this: Emiko was the favored one. Shizue was not so pretty, not so smart. They were grooming Emiko for a rich man—his name was Yamato—lived in a grand house in the village. They sent her to schools; you know, the culture thing: the dance, the tea ceremony, you know, all that. They didn't even like me, and suddenly they married her to me.

MURATA: Yeah, you don't need all that formal training to make it over here. Just a strong back.

HANA (*looking meaningfully at her husband*): And a strong will . . .

OKA: It was all arranged. I couldn't do anything about it.

HANA (*reassuringly*): It'll be all right. Now with Kiyoko coming . . .

OKA (*dubiously*): I hope so. (*He sips his wine and reflects on it.*) I never knew human beings could be so cruel. You know how they mistreated my daughter? You know after Emiko came over, things got from bad to worse, and I *never* had enough money to send to Kiyoko.

MURATA: They don't know what it's like here. They think money's picked off the ground here.

OKA: They treated Kiyoko so bad. They told her I forgot about her. They told her I didn't care—they said I abandoned her. Well, she knew better. She wrote to me all the time, and I always told her I'd send for her . . . soon as I got the money. (*He shakes his head.*) I just got to do something this year . . .

HANA: She'll be happier here. She'll know her father cares . . .

OKA: Kids tormented her for not having parents.

MURATA (*nodding*): Kids are cruel . . .

HANA: Masako will help her. She'll help her get started at school and . . . she'll be all right.

OKA: I hope so. She'll need friends. (*He considers what Kiyoko's life might be like in America.*) What could I say to her? Stay there?

It's not what you think over here? I can't help her? I just have to do this thing. I just have to do this one thing for her.

MURATA: Don't worry. It'll work out fine. Eh, Mama . . . (*He gestures to* HANA. *She fills the cups.*) You talk about selling your horse, I thought you were pulling out.

OKA: I wish I could. But there's nothing else I can do.

MURATA: Without money, yeah . . .

OKA: You can go into some kind of business with money, but a guy like me—no education—there's no kind of job I can do. I'd starve in the city.

MURATA: Dishwashing, maybe. Janitor . . .

OKA: At least here we can eat. Carrots maybe, but we can eat.

MURATA (*shaking his head*): All the carrots we been eating 'bout to turn me into a rabbit.

(*They laugh.* HANA *starts to pour more wine for* OKA, *but he stops her.*)

OKA: I better not drink any more. Got to drive to Nagata's yet. (*OKA rises and walks over to* MASAKO.) You study hard, don't you? You'll teach Kiyoko to read too, eh?

(*MASAKO looks up from her book and smiles.*)

HANA: Oh, yes. She will. It'll be good for Masako to have a friend.

MURATA: Kiyoko could probably teach her a thing or two.

(*OKA moves toward the door, and the* MURATAS *accompany him.*)

OKA: Well, thanks for the *sake*. I guess I talk too much when I drink. (*He rubs his head and laughs.*) Oh. I'm sorry about your fire. By the way, come to my house for your bath. Until you build yours again.

HANA (*hesitantly*): Oh, uh . . . thank you. I don't know . . .

MURATA: Good. Thanks a lot. I need a good hot bath tonight.

OKA: Tonight then.

MURATA: We'll be there.

HANA (*bowing*): Good-bye, and thank you very much.

OKA: See you tonight.

(*OKA leaves, and* HANA *faces her husband.*)

HANA: Papa, I don't know about going over there.

MURATA (*surprised*): Why?

HANA: Well, Emiko . . .

MURATA (*irritated*): What's the matter with you? We need a bath, and Oka's invited us over.

HANA (*calling over her shoulder to* MASAKO): Masako, help me clear the table. (*MASAKO leaves her book and goes to the kitchen.*) Papa, you know we've been neighbors already three, four years, and Emiko has never been very hospitable.

MURATA: She's shy, that's all.

HANA: Not just shy . . . secretive . . . inhospitable . . . a loner . . . Never put out a cup of tea . . . If she had all that training in the graces, why, a cup of tea . . .

MURATA: So if you want tea, ask for it.

HANA (*offended*): I can't do that, Papa. I say she's strange . . . very strange . . . I don't know . . . (*She turns to* MASAKO.) When we go there, be very careful not to say anything wrong.

MASAKO: I never saw anything anyway.

HANA: Just be careful. (*She looks around.*) We'll have to take something . . . (*She thinks.*) There's nothing to take . . . Maybe you can dig up some carrots . . .

MURATA: God, Mama, be sensible. They got carrots. Everybody's got carrots . . .

HANA: Something . . . Maybe I should make something . . .

MURATA: Hell, they're not expecting anything.

HANA: It's not good manners to go empty-handed.

MURATA: I'll take the *sake*.

MASAKO: We can take the Victrola! We can play records for Mrs. Oka. Then nobody has to talk.

(*The* MURATAS *laugh, and* HANA *pats* MASAKO'S *head.*)

(*Fade out*)

Act 1. Scene 2

TIME: That evening

On Rise: Outside the OKAS' *house and yard. We see on stage right the wall of a weathered house. There is a screen door and one very large screened window. Through this window,* MRS. OKA *can be seen walking erratically back and forth. In the yard there is a low wide bench* (dai) *where several people can sit together. There is one weathered wooden chair.* MR. OKA *is sitting on the bench cross-legged. He fans himself with a round Japanese fan. The last rays of the sun light the area with a soft golden glow. This light grows gray as the scene progresses; it is quite dark at the end of the scene. The* MURATAS *enter from stage left with towels,* yukatas, *and a portable Victrola and records.*

OKA (*standing to greet his guests*): You've come. Hello!

MURATA: Hello, hello.

OKA: Yah . . . Glad to see you.

HANA: Good evening, Mr. Oka. Thank you for your concern this afternoon, and thank you for inviting us to bathe here. Such an imposition. Say thank you, Masako.

MASAKO: Thank you.

OKA: Don't worry about it—between friends, between friends. Sit down. (*He makes room on the bench and half turns toward the house.*) Emi!

(*MRS. OKA's dark form is seen silently on the scene. She doesn't move.*)

OKA: Emi!

HANA: Please don't call Mrs. Oka. She must be busy. Please don't disturb her. (*She flutters her hand.*)

OKA (*mutters and half stands*): Emiko!

(*MRS. OKA joins the guests.*)

HANA: Oh, Mrs. Oka. Good evening. I didn't mean to disturb you. We're sorry to be such an imposition . . . but our Masako here—say "hello," Masako . . .

MASAKO: Hello, Mrs. Oka.

HANA: She was careless with the fire, and our bathhouse burned down. Today. To the ground—right to the ground. Mr. Oka happened by and was kind enough to invite us to use your bath. (*MRS. OKA says nothing.*) I hope you don't mind. It burned to the ground. There's only this charred tub left. Papa says we can still use the tub, but I, well . . . I hope it won't be long before we get . . .

MURATA: My God, Mama, it only burned down today. I'll get to it soon. (*Looks at OKA and smiles sheepishly.*)

OKA (*rubbing his head*): Don't worry about it. You're welcome here. Heh, heh . . .

MURATA: So what happened? Did you see Nagata? Did he buy the horse?

OKA (*glancing at his wife*): No, I didn't get around to it. Had too much to drink this afternoon, heh, heh. I came home and went to sleep. I'll go tomorrow.

MURATA: It was some day for me too. (*He lays the Victrola on the bench and sits with OKA.*)

OKA: What's this? You brought a Victrola?

HANA: Oh, yes. Masako wanted to bring the records over. She loves to play the Victrola. Papa likes these songs too.

MURATA: Yeah, I do. I get lonesome for Japan, and these records take me back. Heh, heh. That's the only way I can get back there. In my mind.

OKA: Yeah.

HANA: I thought Mrs. Oka might enjoy them too. It will be a little relaxation for all of us . . .

(*MRS. OKA sits very primly on the separate chair while the others gather near the record player.*)

HANA: Maybe you'd like to look through the records, Mrs. Oka. There may be some you're familiar with.

(MRS. OKA *nods, but doesn't move. She extracts a sack of Bull Durham from her dress pocket and very carefully rolls a cigarette.* HANA *turns her attention to the Victrola, but* MASAKO *stands by* MRS. OKA *and watches her intently.*)

HANA: I hope you like music, Mrs. Oka. Some of these are very old. You might remember hearing them in Japan.

(MRS. OKA *smiles and tilts her head. She blows puffs of smoke.*)

HANA: Would you like to look through some of these? (HANA *extends some records to* MRS. OKA, *but the lady does not respond.*)

HANA: Oh, if you'd rather not, we don't have to play . . .

OKA: Play. Play them. (*He rubs his head and avoids looking at anyone.*)

MURATA: (*He pretends to notice nothing. He calls* MASAKO *over to the bench.*) Masako, did you bring the needles?

(MASAKO *goes to the bench, finds the needles, gives them to her father, and returns to watching* MRS. OKA. *Melancholy strains of the theme song begin.* MRS. OKA *listens. Tears well in her eyes.*)

MASAKO (*whispers to her mother*): She's crying, Mama . . .

HANA (*gives* MASAKO *a small pinch*): The smoke is in her eyes, Masako.

(MRS. OKA *rises abruptly and enters the house.*)

HANA: Oh, Masako, I'm afraid we've offended her.

OKA: No-no. Pay no attention. (*He listens to the song.*) Nice . . .

MURATA: Yeah, makes me homesick for Japan . . .

HANA: Ah, Japan . . . It's so lovely on a summer evening—the fireflies, the flutes. Masako, in the evening all the flutes of Shizuoka begin to sound. Sweet, haunting . . . Fireflies glow, the children chase them—laughing . . . Happy laughter, warm voices of our parents . . . peaceful, secure . . . like life would go on forever this way. After our bath, my mother serves melons chilled in the well—cold from the bottom of the well . . .

(HANA'S *words drift off and she begins to hum along with the record. Everyone slips into his private nostalgia. Only* MASAKO *sees* MRS. OKA *dancing to the music. She seems to be dancing for* MASAKO. HANA *notices* MASAKO *and turns to the window.* MRS. OKA *ducks out of sight.*)

HANA: Masako, I think you should take your bath now.

(MASAKO *picks up her towel and robe, still reluctant to leave. The music continues.*)

MURATA: Change the record, Mama. I had enough of that one.

OKA: Heh, heh . . .

(HANA *stops the player and shuffles through the records.* MASAKO *peers over her shoulder.*)

MASAKO: Play that one.

HANA: Oh, that's a child's record. Go take your bath. Ah, here's one you might like, Oka-san.

(*MASAKO leaves, HANA has selected a lively* ondo. *The remaining three start clapping hands and tapping feet to the infectious music. From the side of the house, MRS. OKA emerges dancing. Her hair is down, she wears an old straw work hat. Everyone is momentarily startled, but HANA recovers quickly and resumes her clapping. The men stop. OKA looks grieved, clears his throat, sets down his fan, aggravated. He rises. MRS. OKA, now close to the door, jumps inside. OKA mutters, settles down, and HANA begins to hum. MURATA looks off to the horizon. The record stops. MASAKO returns.*)

HANA: You're finished already?

MASAKO: I wasn't very dirty. The water was too hot.

MURATA: That's good. Just the way I like it. (*He picks up his towel and* yukata.) Come on, Mama; scrub my back.

HANA (*laughing*): Now don't forget, Masako: crank the machine and change the needle now and then.

(*They exit.*)

OKA: You don't like hot baths, Masako?

MASAKO: Not too hot.

OKA: Oh. I thought you liked it hot. Hot enough to burn down the house. Heh, heh. That's a little joke.

(*MASAKO laughs, but not too heartily.*)

OKA: I hear you're good in school. When Kiyoko comes to live here, you'll take care of her for me, eh? A favor for me?

MASAKO: Okay, Mr. Oka. (*She cranks the Victrola and busies herself.*)

OKA: Kiyoko won't be speaking English. You'll take her to school and be her friend, eh?

OKA: She's smart. Masako-chan. Like you. She'll soon be a little American—like you.

(*MASAKO laughs, politely.*)

OKA: What grade you in now?

MASAKO: Sixth grade, this September.

OKA: That's good. Very smart. Good. (*He stands, yawns, and stretches.*) Heh, heh. I'll go for a little walk now. Have to go for a little walk now and then, heh, heh . . . (*He exits to the right, unbuttoning his fly.*)

(*MASAKO, her back to the house, is engrossed reading labels and trying to identify them. The door opens silently, MRS. OKA emerges and sits on the separate chair. She smiles and watches MASAKO. She moves to the bench.*)

MRS. OKA: Masako-chan, do you like Japanese songs? (*MASAKO is startled, MRS. OKA reaches for her hand. MASAKO draws back.*) Do you like to sing?

MASAKO: Oh, sometimes. (*She cranks the Victrola.* MRS. OKA *touches her hand.* MASAKO *stops the activity.* MRS. OKA *smiles.*)

MRS. OKA: I used to sing. Once long ago. I was very young. Older than you. (*She begins to move her hands, head, and arms in dance movements and starts to sing.*) *Akai kuchibiru/ Kappu ni yosete/ Aoi sake nomya/ Kokoro ga odoru* . . . Do you know what that means, Masako-chan?

MASAKO: That the soul shall dance?

MRS. OKA: Yes, yes . . . The soul shall dance. Red lips press against a glass/ Drink the purple wine/ And the soul shall dance . . .

(MRS. OKA *remembers another time and is quite overcome.* MASKAKO *watches her closely.* MR. OKA *returns, buttoning his fly.* MRS. OKA *rises quickly and ducks into the house.* OKA *sits on the bench, fans himself, and tries to think of something to say to this little girl.*)

OKA: Yeah, Kiyoko and you will have good times together. How old did you say you are?

MASAKO: Eleven.

OKA: Well, well. Kiyoko is fifteen. You'll get along good together. Like I told you, she won't know any English . . .

(*While they are talking, they are startled by a loud crash coming from the house. They resume their conversation, pretending to hear nothing.* MASAKO *is uncomfortable. She fiddles with the record player. There is another crash.* OKA *sucks in his breath, jumps from the bench, stomps into the house, and slams the door behind. There are violent sounds.* MASAKO *nervously stands, sits, and finally goes to the window and peers in. She reacts to what she sees, protecting her face, etc. Just before* OKA *comes out again, she jumps back to the bench and starts the cranking.* OKA *returns, smoothing his hair. Sounds of wailing are heard from the house.*)

OKA: It's getting darker. Do you want me to light a lamp?

MASAKO: No. That's all right.

(*The* MURATAS *return from their bath. They are in good spirits. They wear* yukatas.)

MURATA: Ahhhhh, nothing like a good hot bath.

HANA: Yes, refreshing. A bath must be taken leisurely. I don't know how Masako gets through so fast.

MURATA: She probably doesn't get in the tub.

MASAKO: I do. I do.

(*Everyone laughs.* MRS. OKA *appears again through the screen door. Her hair is loose. She has purple welts on her face. She sits on the separate chair, hands folded, and quietly watches the* MURATAS. *They look at her with alarm.* OKA *engages himself with his fan.*)

HANA: Oh. Oh . . . Mrs. Oka . . . what, ah ah . . . (*She takes a deep breath.*) Oh, Mrs. Oka, we had such a lovely bath. We do appreciate it. Thank you ever so much.

MRS. OKA: It's a very warm evening, isn't it?

HANA: Yes, yes, it is . . . very . . . It's a very warm evening.

MURATA: Sah, we'd better be going . . .

HANA: Yes, tomorrow is a busy day. Come, Masako, gather our things.

MRS. OKA: Why, so soon? Please stay a little longer.

HANA: Thank you, but we must . . .

MRS. OKA: It's still quite early . . .

OKA (*stands*): Yah, enjoyed the music.

MRS. OKA: The records are very nice. Makes me remember my girlhood in Japan. I used to sing some of these very songs. Did you know I used to sing?

HANA (*with polite interest*): No, no . . . I didn't know that. You must have a beautiful voice. Oh, no, I didn't know that. That's very interesting.

MRS. OKA: Yes, I used to sing. My parents were very strict and they didn't like it, but I sang. I sang. (*She nods her head, assuring herself that she did indeed sing.*) Yes, I sang.

HANA: Yes, yes, I understand. In those days, singing was not for proper young la . . . What a shame you couldn't continue with it.

MRS. OKA: I came to America.

HANA: Yes, of course.

MRS. OKA: I came to America . . . I came to America . . .

MURATA (*turns to OKA and slaps his back*): Oka! So you're going to see Nagata tomorrow.

OKA: Yeah.

MURATA: He'll like your horse. Did I tell you he's working twenty more acres next season? Hey, want me to come along with you? I'll vouch for the animal.

OKA (*looks uneasy*): You won't be too busy?

MURATA: Hell, I'd better come along with you. You got to know how to deal with Nagata. First you talk to his wife . . . tell a few jokes . . . soften her up, you know.

OKA: Ho-ho. I'm not too good at that.

MURATA: You know, she's got the power there.

OKA: Well, that's what I hear. You got to hand it to her. It's pretty hard to hang on to power.

HANA (*sniffs*): Well, if it's a matter of that or no power at all . . .

MURATA: I'll pick you up tomorrow morning. Better get to it before it gets too hot; while the old lady's in a good mood. Hahaha.

MRS. OKA: I used to sing all those songs. I danced too. (*She makes dance movements.*) My parents were against it.

MURATA: Pick up the things, Masako.

HANA (*bowing*): Many, many thanks. We'll bring the records again sometime, Mrs. Oka.

MRS. OKA: They made me stop. That was a long time ago . . .

(*MURATA nudges his wife, and she pulls away, bowing again and again, murmuring her apologies and thanks. MASAKO carries the Victrola and records; OKA enters the house, and MRS. OKA goes out to the desert, exiting to the left. She moves as though in a trance. MURATA walks offstage to the right. It grows dark everywhere except for a dim light on HANA and MASAKO, who walk slowly behind.*)

MASAKO: Mama! You should have seen what happened! Did you hear it?

HANA: Shhh. No, no, we heard nothing. Papa was singing in the bath. We heard nothing.

MASAKO: It was just awful, awful. I was frightened.

HANA: Shhh. There, there; it'll be all right.

MASAKO: You know, after you left? First Mrs. Oka came out and tried to talk to me, then Mr. Oka came back from the toilet, and she went back into the house, and there was this awful crash. (*She makes like she's ready to fling the Victrola to the ground.*)

HANA: Watch out!

MASAKO: And Mr. Oka pretended nothing happened. And then there were more crashes, and more and more, and Mr. Oka finally ran into the house. He was so mad! That was the terrible part. I heard this loud thumping and crashing. Mr. Oka was hitting her. Did you see those marks on her face?

HANA: She probably fell and hurt herself.

MASAKO: No! He was hitting her!

HANA: Masako! I hope you weren't looking through the window.

MASAKO: I was so scared!

HANA: You weren't looking through the window, were you?

MASAKO: No. No . . .

HANA: I know you weren't looking through the window. Because you *know* it's not your business, don't you? Now, try to forget it. All right?

MASAKO: Did you see how she danced? Did you see her face?

HANA: No, Masako. I didn't see her dance. I heard her sing. I sang too, Masako. You must understand this is private business. The Okas have lived a long time together, probably just like this. It's just one of those things: not everyone gets along well together—all the time. They'll be all right, Masako. Don't worry.

MASAKO: I think she's crazy, Mama.

HANA: Shhh. Don't say that. Mrs. Oka is not crazy.

MASAKO: She *acts* crazy. I think she's crazy.

HANA: Well, that's the way some people get when they drink too much.

MASAKO: She drinks?

HANA: Yes.

MASAKO: And she smokes cigarettes like Papa does.

HANA: Yes, yes. Well, she's a little different from most Japanese women—at least around here—but she did say she sang and danced. Maybe she was an entertainer in Japan. (*aside*) No, no, she was too young.

MASAKO: You mean like in the movies?

HANA: Something like that. In Japan women are paid to sing and dance in tea houses and restaurants. But she would have been quite young. (*She shrugs.*) What do we know? Who can tell how hard it is for her to live out here in the middle of a desert—no company, no children, no life at all except this . . . this . . . her husband, and he, well . . . I guess it's not easy for anyone . . . She's probably very lonely for Japan. It'll be different when their daughter comes. She probably misses her family in Japan . . . We all do.

MASAKO: Mama, do you want to go back to Japan?

HANA: Everyone does, Masako.

MASAKO: Not me, not me . . .

(*Far off,* MRS. OKA *is singing the song: Akai kuchibiru/ Kappu ni yosete/ Aoi sake nomya/ Kokoro ga odoru . . .*)

HANA: Well, Papa will just have to build the bathhouse. We simply can't come over like this for long. He'll just have to work on it as soon as possible.

MASAKO: Mama, you don't like Mrs. Oka, do you?

HANA: It's not that. I like her. I don't really know her. It's not that at all.

(*Fade out*)

Act 1. Scene 3

TIME: Two weeks later, late morning

On rise: Interior of the MURATAS' *house and yard. The day is bright and warm.* MASAKO *is in the kitchen reading.* HANA *is offstage.* MURATA *and* OKA *are in the yard working on plans for the new bathhouse. The "blueprint" is a piece of torn cardboard.*

MURATA: I'm building it over the old tub—same place. The old lady's cleaned it. Hell, she set fire to what was left, raked away

the ashes, took care of everything. Heh, heh. I'll be glad to get
this done. Been hearing about it for the past two weeks. (*He
slaps his ear a couple of times.*)

OKA: Ha, ha . . .

MURATA: Getting tired of washing in a bucket too . . .

OKA: You should have come over for your bath. You never came
back after the first time.

MURATA: Well, she didn't think we should impose on you. Maybe
this was her way of getting me on the job. She knows how I love
a good full bath. Got to get up pretty early in the morning to
keep up with her.

OKA: Hahaha. Well, this shouldn't take too long. Tonight, you'll be
sitting in your *furo-ba*. You using the tin sheets?

MURATA: Nnnn. That'll save time too. Might be pretty hot in summer, yeah, and cold in winter, but it sure as hell won't burn
down again. Want to come in for a drink first? I have some port
wine.

OKA: Port wine?

MURATA: Got it for the old lady. She's been having trouble getting
to sleep; she gets these headaches. But she doesn't like the taste
of it. Hahaha. Maybe I'll get her some white wine. Maybe she'll
like that better.

OKA: Ah, no . . . It's no good for a woman to drink. Once they
start, they got no sense to stop. No good.

(*MURATA is silent. They both enter the house, and* MURATA *finds
the wine. He fills two small glasses.* MASAKO *is sitting at the table.
She looks up.*)

OKA: Hello, Masako-chan. Studying?

MASAKO: It's summer vacation. I'm not studying.

MURATA (*good-naturedly*): She's always reading, reading. American
school seems to be more fun than Japanese school. I hated
school. Never read any more than I had to.

OKA: Me too. Guess that's why we're doing this kind of work now.
Masako-chan will be a great scholar.

MURATA: Hahaha. No need for a woman to know too much. Not
much chance to get anywhere. Well, no harm in dreaming, I
guess.

(*MASAKO tosses her head indignantly.*)

OKA: You know, Nagata's very happy with that horse. Thanks for
helping me in that deal.

MURATA: Wasn't that something? That woman of his really pulls the
strings—all the strings.

OKA: He came over yesterday and bought my tiller. No use to me
now without a horse.

MURATA: Yeah, you can use mine.

OKA: He expects to make a killing next year.

MURATA: He might at that. That woman will keep him at it 'til he does. She's ambitious. I knew they'd like the horse. First when you told me you wanted to sell him, I thought you were pulling out. Quitting farming.

OKA: I'd like to, but what else could I do? A man like me has no skills. There's nothing else I can do.

MURATA: I'm in the same boat. I hear there aren't too many jobs in the city open to Japanese. With a family, it's better here on a farm. You can't starve on a farm. You can always eat—pull up a carrot when you're hungry. Haha. And I don't have enough capital to start a business. I'd have to wash dishes in a restaurant or sweep floors or something.

OKA: I have a friend doing that—washing dishes. But he's a single man.

MURATA: No family.

OKA: Yeah, no family. Happy-go-lucky. Oh, by the way, I bought a ticket for Kiyoko. I sent it down right after I got the money.

MURATA: You did that, eh?

OKA: Can't keep money like that around. I'd spend it before I knew what was happening.

MURATA: That's the truth.

OKA: Yeah, she'll be coming down about the middle of September. (*He looks toward* MASAKO.) Masako-chan, my daughter will be here before school starts. Remember what I asked you? I'm counting on you to help her.

MASAKO: All right, Mr. Oka.

MURATA: More likely she'll be helping Masako. Heh, heh. (*He pours more wine in their glasses.*)

OKA: That poor kid.

MURATA: Poor kid?

OKA: Kiyoko. My daughter. God, she's been reared by that family—my first wife's family—all her life, and they've been making life miserable for her. How can they do that? Like one of their own and so mean to her.

MURATA: Mean to her?

(*OKA looks toward* MASAKO.)

MURATA: Can't you do that somewhere else?

(*MASAKO moves to the bedroom, now very alert to the conversation.*)

OKA (*lowers his voice*): The fact is Shizue, that's my first wife, and Emi, you know, they come from a family with no sons. So when I married Shizue I took on the Oka name. Oka is not my real name. My true name is Sakakihara.

MURATA: Sakakihara. That's got a good sound to it. A name of substance.

OKA: No one knows me by that here. Well, the family was, you know . . . I should never have consented to the arrangement, the *yoshi* . . . That old man Oka was so . . . domineering—a tyrant. Always pushing me around and humiliating me in front of my wife and kid. I couldn't stand it; I hated the old man's guts. Anyway, everyone was talking about America then—all the money to be picked off the ground here . . .

MURATA: Ha! (*He rolls a cigarette and passes the sack to* OKA.)

OKA: And I wanted to get out of the house, come to America, make some money, go back and take my wife and child away to another village. I was thinking: with money I could open a shop, a fish market, a noodle counter—I was thinking all the time, I was thinking how to get out of the old man's grip. You know?

MURATA: Nnnnn. That's rough.

OKA (*rubs his head*): Well, I left the wife and kid and came to America. You know how it is: I worked—mostly day labor— sent all the money home. No more than two years later, my wife died. She died on me! And I was stuck with their name. (*The wine has loosened him up. He looks like he's ready to cry.* MURATA *gazes out the window.*) Well, I was always sending money to them. Lived like a beggar here, thinking my wife was putting the money away like we planned. I don't know what happened: everything went wrong. Right after she died, before I knew it, they wrote me they were arranging a marriage by proxy for me and Emiko. They said she'd grown to be a beautiful woman and would serve me well.

MURATA: Nnnn.

OKA: I should have suspected something was wrong then. That Emiko was their pride and joy. Shizue was not so pretty, not so smart, you know? I should have known something was wrong right then. They didn't like me, why would they want to give me their precious Emiko? But you know me, I'm gullible. So that was all right with me, after all, we were kin. My first wife was not the favored one. They'd sent Emiko to a girls' school. They groomed her for someone special—maybe a rich man. Anyway, me, I'm gullible; I was flattered. It would be good for Kiyoko too, almost like a real mother . . . and the kid needed a mother, especially with me so far away. I would go on with my plans, sending money and saving for the little shop. In another village.

MURATA: Yeah, that's every man's dream. Mine too . . . I wanted to . . .

OKA: But that wasn't what the family had in mind. They meant to send Emiko out of the country to me here in America. I didn't know what was happening . . . I got a telegram saying to pick her up in San Francisco. Just like that. Just like that. They took care of everything.

MURATA: Immigration papers and all?

OKA: Everything. They took care of everything. I found out why later. Did I ever! (*He draws a deep breath from his cigarette.*) It seems Emiko had a lover that the family couldn't accept. See, they'd sent her to some relatives in the city so she could attend this fancy school. They had great marriage plans for her. But see, in the city—well— (*He rubs his head.*) She's a good-looking woman, and she met this man. The relatives complained they couldn't keep an eye on her. She was out all the time with this man—drinking, singing, dancing—God knows what else . . .

MURATA: A young girl like that? They couldn't hold her down?

OKA: Singing, dancing, and drinking with this man . . . I don't know what kind of man he was . . . Maybe he was a good man, or maybe a good-for-nothing . . . Maybe just too poor. The family tried to break it up, but looks like it wasn't that easy. So they took care of all the details, the paperwork, everything, and they just put her on a boat and sent her to me. I guess they thought better *me* than him. Maybe they thought *I* had money. You know, all the money I'd been sending . . . I don't know. Dumb guy like me can't figure them out. They outsmart me every time. Maybe they thought I was rich.

MURATA: Nnnn. They think everyone's rich out here.

OKA: So they sent me Emiko. Well, I can see what trouble they had with her. She's got a streak you wouldn't believe. She blames me for the way things turned out for her. God! I had nothing to do with it. Nothing! They tricked me! They tricked her too. You'd think she'd understand this. Sometimes I think she's nuts. Maybe the whole family's . . .

MURATA: Nnnn. (*Looks out the window.*)

OKA: I guess you want to get started on the house. (*He half stands but obviously has more to say.*)

MURATA: That's all right; finish your wine first.

OKA: You know how it is. If I had the money, I'd have sent her back that first year. She's got a stubborn streak—mean—like her father. Pretty and smart is nothing. (*He rubs his head.*) They sure tricked me. But between trying to make a living and sending money for the kid . . . you know how it is . . .

MURATA: Nnnn. It's not easy. That's for sure. They think the money's here to be picked . . .

OKA (*snorts*): I wonder who started that big lie. (*He sips his wine.*) After a while there wasn't enough to send even that little bit home. For the kid. This woman has been pure bad luck for me. Well, I didn't have the money; that's all. As soon as Kiyoko learned to write, she's sent me letters and pictures. As she grew older, she told me the kids teased her for not having parents— for being abandoned— Where do kids get that kind of talk? From old man Oka, that's where. She said the kids tormented her.

MURATA: Kids can be cruel . . .

OKA: And the family . . . She said the family grumbled all the time about not having enough money. (*Indignantly*) What kind of talk is that for kin? What did they do with all my money? (*Reasoning*) Well, who can blame them? She's my responsibility . . . they thought I was rich.

MURATA: They think everyone's rich in America. Hell, if I were rich, I'd go back right now. It's easier to swim across than find the money for it.

OKA: Poor Kiyoko. I know how mean they can get. Anyway, the past year she's been writing asking when she could come to America. Every letter. What could I say? It's not what you think it is out here? It's worse? (*He draws on his cigarette.*) Well, it's done now. She'll be coming in September.

(*HANA comes through the door. She's wearing a sunbonnet and is carrying a basket of greens. She removes her hat and fans herself with it. She's caught the last of the conversation and is very excited.*)

HANA: She's coming in September? Oh, Mr. Oka! What exciting news! I'm so happy for you. And Mrs. Oka. And for us, too, especially Masako.

OKA (*grinning*): Yeah, she'll be here in September. I'll be counting on you and Masako-chan to help her. She'll be awful lonely— homesick.

HANA: But of course, of course. We'll do all we can.

OKA: I'll be much obliged to you.

HANA: And it'll do Mrs. Oka a lot of good. Mrs. Oka . . .

MURATA: Masako can take her to school. (*He rises.*) Sah, are you ready?

OKA (*gulps down the last drop*): Yeah, yeah, I'm ready.

(OKA *and* MURATA *exit.*)

HANA: Masako! Did you hear that? Isn't that good news? Kiyoko-san will be coming from Japan soon! Now you'll have a friend. You won't be all by yourself day after day reading all the time. You'll have a best friend!

MASAKO: She's not Mrs. Oka's daughter, Mama.

HANA: I know that. But that won't make a bit of difference. To me, or you, or Mrs. Oka. After all, she's Mrs. Oka's niece. Blood relative.

MASAKO: Mrs. Oka had a boyfriend in Japan. A lover.

HANA: Masako! Don't talk like that!

MASAKO: It's true, Mama. I heard Mr. Oka say so. Ask Papa.

HANA: I said you shouldn't be talking like that. It isn't nice. (*Changes her tone.*) Masako, think how nice it'll be for you. You can have her over and you can try out some of those recipes . . . the American ones . . .

MASAKO: You have to have chocolate and cream and things like that.

HANA: We'll get them. And you can sew together . . . She can probably teach you a lot in that department. You know, in Japan, little girls learn all those arts very early—so they can be good wives and mothers.

MASAKO: (*MASAKO sets her book down; she is interested.*) You'll get us some material too? Would you really let me cut and sew?

HANA (*nods*): And you can teach her to read some of those books you like so well; she'll go to church with us . . .

MASAKO: And movies. Will Papa take us to the movies?

HANA: Well, I don't know. You'll have to ask him about that. You know how he is. Maybe sometimes. I don't like you to go to the movies. They're not good for you.

(*There is the sound of hammering. The bathhouse is on the way. HANA is happy.*)

HANA: We'll soon have our *furo-ba*. No more washing in the kitchen, Masako. Isn't that wonderful?

(*Fade out*)

Toshio Mori

(1910–1980)

Toshio Mori was born in Oakland, California. "The Seventh Street Philosopher" is from *Yokohama, California*, his collection of short stories about Oakland and San Leandro in the twenties and thirties, which was published in 1949. His work appeared in several anthologies, including *New Directions* and *Best American Short Stories of 1943*, and in periodicals such as *Pacific Citizen, Public Welfare, Common Ground, The Coast, Writer's Forum, Current Life, Clipper, Matrix*, and *Iconograph*. While interned at Topaz concentration camp in Utah, Mori, along with other writers and artists, started the camp magazine, *Trek*.

His fiction was rediscovered by Asian American readers when his short stories were reprinted in literary anthologies in the seventies. *The Chauvinist and Other Stories* was published by the Asian American Studies Center at UCLA in 1978. A novel, *Woman from Hiroshima*, was published in 1980 by Isthmus Press and won the Honor Award from the Women's International League for Peace and Freedom in 1981.

The Seventh Street Philosopher

He is what our community calls the Seventh Street Philosopher. This is because Motoji Tsunoda used to live on Seventh Street sixteen or seventeen years ago and loved even then to spout philosophy and talk to the people. Today he is living on an estate of an old lady who has hired him as a launderer for a dozen years or so. Every once so often he comes out of his washroom, out of obscurity, to mingle among his people and this is usually the beginning of something like a furore, something that upsets the community, the people, and Motoji Tsunoda alike.

There is nothing like it in our community, nothing so fruitless and irritable which lasts so long and persists in making a show; only Motoji Tsunoda is unique. Perhaps his being alone, a widower, working alone in his sad washroom in the old lady's basement and washing the stuff that drops from the chute and drying them on the line, has quite a bit to do with his behavior when he meets the people of our community. Anyway when Motoji Tsunoda comes to the town and enters into the company of the evening all his silent hours and silent vigils with deep thoughts and books come to the fore and there is no stopping of his flow of words and thoughts. Generally, the people are impolite when Motoji Tsunoda begins speaking, and the company of the evening either disperse quite early or entirely ignore his philosophical thoughts and begin conversations on business or weather or how the friends are getting along these days. And the strangeness of it all is that Motoji Tsunoda is a very quiet man, sitting quietly in the corner, listening to others talk until the opportunity comes. Then he will suddenly become alive and the subject and all the subjects in the world become his and the company of the evening his audience.

When Motoji Tsunoda comes to the house he usually stays till one in the morning or longer if everybody in the family are polite about it or are sympathetic with him. Sometimes there is no subject for him to talk of, having talked himself out but this does not slow him up. Instead he will think for a moment and then begin on his favorite topic: What is there for the individual to do today? And listening to him, watching him gesture desperately to bring over a point, I am often carried away by this meek man who launders for an old lady on weekdays. Not by his deep thoughts or crazy thoughts but by what he is and what he is actually and desperately trying to put across to the people and the world.

"Tsunoda-san, what are you going to speak on tonight?" my mother says when our family and Motoji Tsunoda settle down in the living room.

"What do you want to hear?" Motoji Tsunoda answers. "Shall it be about Shakyamuni's boyhood or shall we continue where we left off last week and talk about Dewey?"

That is a start. With the beginning of words there is no stopping of Motoji Tsunoda, there is no misery in his voice nor in his stance at the time as he would certainly possess in the old washroom. His tone perks up, his body becomes straight, and in a way this slight meek man becomes magnificent, powerful, and even inspired. He is proud of his debates with the numerous Buddhist clergymen and when he is in fine fettle he delves into the various debates he has had in the past for the sake of his friends. And no matter what is said or what has happened in the evening Motoji Tsunoda will finally end his oration or debate with something about the tradition and the blood flow of Shakyamuni, St. Shinran, Akegarasu, and Motoji Tsunoda. He is not joking when he says this. He is very serious. When anyone begins kidding about it, he will sadly gaze at the joker and shake his head.

About this time something happened in our town which Motoji Tsunoda to this day is very proud of. It was an event which has prolonged the life of Motoji Tsunoda, acting as a stimulant, that of broadcasting to the world in general the apology of being alive.

It began very simply, nothing of deliberation, nothing of vanity or pride but simply the eventual event coming as the phenomenon of chance. There was the talk about this time of Akegarasu, the great philosopher of Japan, coming to our town to give a lecture. He, Akegarasu, was touring America, lecturing and studying and visiting Emerson's grave, so there was a good prospect of having this great philosopher come to our community and lecture. And before anyone was wise to his move Motoji Tsunoda voluntarily wrote to Akegarasu, asking him to lecture on the night of July 14 since that was the date he had hired the hall. And before Motoji Tsunoda had received an answer he went about the town, saying the great philosopher was coming, that he was coming to lecture at the hall.

He came to our house breathless with the news. Someone asked him if he had received a letter of acceptance and Akegarasu had consented to come.

"No, but he will come," Motoji Tsunoda said. "He will come and lecture. Be sure of that."

For days he went about preparing for the big reception, forgetting his laundering, forgetting his meekness, working as much as four men to get the Asahi Auditorium in shape. For days ahead he had all the chairs lined up, capable of seating five hundred people. Then the word came to him that the great philosopher was already on his way to Seattle to embark for Japan. This left Motoji Tsunoda very flat, leaving him to the mercy of the people who did not miss the opportunity to laugh and taunt him.

"What can you do?" they said and laughed. "What can you do but talk?"

Motoji Tsunoda came to the house, looking crestfallen and dull. We could not cheer him up that night; not once could we lift him from misery. But the next evening, unexpectedly, he came running in the house, his eyes shining, his whole being alive and powerful. "Do you know what?" he said to us. "I have an idea! A great idea."

So he sat down and told us that instead of wasting the beautiful hall, all decorated and cleaned and ready for five hundred people to come and sit down, he, Motoji Tsunoda would give a lecture. He said he had already phoned the two Japanese papers to play up his lecture and let the world know he is lecturing on July 14. He said for us to be sure to come. He said he had phoned all his friends and acquaintances and reporters to be sure to come. He said he was going home now to plan his lecture, he said this was his happiest moment of his life and wondered why he did not think of giving a lecture at the Asahi Auditorium before. And as he strode off to his home and to lecture plans, for a moment I believed he had outgrown the life of a launderer, outgrown the meekness and derision, outgrown the patheticness of it and the loneliness. And seeing him stride off with unknown power and unknown energy I firmly believed Motoji Tsunoda was on his own, a philosopher by rights, as all men are in action and thought a philosopher by rights.

We did not see Motoji Tsunoda for several days. However in the afternoon of July 14 he came running up our steps. "Tonight is the big night, everybody," he said. "Be sure to be there tonight. I speak on a topic of great importance."

"What's the time?" I said.

"The lecture is at eight," he said. "Be sure to come, everybody."

The night of July 14 was like any other night, memorable, fascinating, miserable; bringing together under a single darkness, one night of performance, of patience and the impatience of the world, the bravery of a single inhabitant and the untold braveries of all the inhabitants of the earth, crying and uncrying for salvation and crying just the same; beautiful gestures and miserable gestures coming and going; and the thoughts unexpressed and the dreams pursued to be expressed.

We were first to be seated and we sat in the front. Every now and then I looked back to see if the people were coming in. At eight-ten there were six of us in the audience. Motoji Tsunoda came on the platform and sat down and when he saw us he nodded his head. He sat alone up there, he was to introduce himself.

We sat an hour or more to see if some delay had caused the people to be late. Once Motoji Tsunoda came down and walked to the entrance to see if the people were coming in. At nine-eighteen Motoji Tsunoda stood up and introduced himself. Counting the two babies there were eleven of us in the audience.

When he began to speak on his topic of the evening, "The Apology of Living," his voice did not quiver though Motoji Tsunoda was unused to public speaking and I think that was wonderful. I do not believe he was aware of his audience when he began to speak,

whether it was a large audience or a small one. And I think that also
was wonderful.

Motoji Tsunoda addressed the audience for three full hours without intermission. He hardly even took time out to drink a glass of
water. He stood before us and in his beautiful sad way, tried to
make us understand as he understood; tried with every bit of finesse
and deep thought to reveal to us the beautiful world he could see
and marvel at, but which we could not see.

Then the lecture was over and Motoji Tsunoda sat down and
wiped his face. It was wonderful, the spectacle; the individual standing up and expressing himself, the earth, the eternity, and the
audience listening and snoring, and the beautiful auditorium standing ready to accommodate more people.

As for Motoji Tsunoda's speech that is another matter. In a way,
however, I thought he did some beautiful philosophizing that night.
No matter what his words might have meant, no matter what gestures and what provoking issues he might have spoken in the past,
there was this man, standing up and talking to the world, and also
talking to vindicate himself to the people, trying as hard as he could
so he would not be misunderstood. And as he faced the eleven
people in the audience including the two babies, he did not look
foolish, he was not just a bag of wind. Instead I am sure he had a
reason to stand up and have courage and bravery to offset the
ridicule, the nonsense, and the misunderstanding.

And as he finished his lecture there was something worthwhile for
everyone to hear and see, not just for the eleven persons in the
auditorium but for the people of the earth: that of his voice, his
gestures, his sadness, his patheticness, his bravery, which are of
common lot and something the people, the inhabitants of the earth,
could understand, sympathize and remember for a while.

Monica Sone
(1919–   )

Monica Sone was born in Seattle's Carrollton Hotel, which her father and mother owned and operated in the Pioneer Square district—known as skid row then, when the pioneers roamed the streets. Originally published in 1953 by Little, Brown, *Nisei Daughter*, Sone's memoir was reprinted by the University of Washington Press in 1979 at an important time in Nikkei history: the beginning of the redress campaign. In the preface of the 1979 edition, Monica Sone writes:

> The Nikkeis are telling the nation about 1942, a time when they became prisoners of their own government, without charges, without trials. . . . Most astounding of all, the Supreme Court chose not to touch the issue of the Niseis' civil liberties as American citizens. . . . Justice Robert Jackson, in dissent, wrote, "The Supreme Court for all time has validated the principle of racial discrimination in criminal procedure."

The early chapters of *Nisei Daughter* portray a Seattle Japanese American community before the war and the evacuation that destroyed and divided the community.

Monica Sone completed her undergraduate education at Hanover College in Hanover, Indiana, and received a master's degree in clinical psychology from Western Reserve University in Cleveland, Ohio, in 1949. She lives and works in Canton, Ohio, with her husband, Gary.

Nisei Daughter

The first five years of my life I lived in amoebic bliss, not knowing whether I was plant or animal, at the old Carrollton Hotel on the waterfront of Seattle. One day when I was a happy six-year-old, I made the shocking discovery that I had Japanese blood. I was a Japanese.

Mother announced this fact of life to us in a quiet, deliberate manner one Sunday afternoon as we gathered around for dinner in the small kitchen, converted from one of our hotel rooms. Our kitchen was cozily comfortable for all six of us as long as everyone remained in his place around the oblong table covered with an indestructible shiny black oilcloth; but if more than Mother stood up and fussed around, there was a serious traffic jam—soy sauce splattered on the floor and elbows jabbed into the pot of rice. So Father sat at the head of the table, Kenji, Henry, and I lined up on one side along the wall, while Mother and baby Sumiko occupied the other side, near the kitchen stove.

Now we watched as Mother lifted from a kettle of boiling water a straw basket of steaming slippery noodles. She directed her information at Henry and me, and I felt uneasy. Father paid strict attention to his noodles, dipping them into a bowl of fragrant pork broth and then sprinking finely choped raw green onion over them.

"Japanese blood—how is it I have that, Mama?" I asked, surreptitiously pouring hot tea over my bowl of rice. Mother said it was bad manners to wash rice down with tea, but rice was delicious with *obancha*.

"Your father and I have Japanese blood and so do you, too. And the same with Henry, Ken-chan, and Sumi-chan."

"Oh." I felt nothing unusual stirring inside me. I took a long cool sip of milk and then with my short red chopsticks I stabbed at a piece of pickled crisp white radish.

"So, Mama?" Henry looked up at her, trying to bring under control with his chopsticks the noodles swinging from his mouth like a pendulum.

"So, Papa and I have decided that you and Ka-chan will attend Japanese school after grammar school every day." She beamed at us.

I choked on my rice.

Terrible, terrible, terrible! So that's what it meant to be a Japanese—to lose my afternoon play hours! I fiercely resented this sudden intrusion of my blood into my affairs.

"But, Mama!" I shrieked. "I go to Bailey Gatzert School already. I don't want to go to another!"

Henry kicked the table leg and grumbled, "Aw gee, Mama, Dunks and Jiro don't have to—why do I!"

"They'll be going, too. Their mothers told me so."

My face grew hot with anger. I shouted. "I won't, I won't!"

Father and Mother painted glowing pictures for me. Just think, you'll grow up to be a well-educated young lady, knowing two languages. One of these days you'll thank us for giving you this opportunity.

But they could not convince me. Until this shattering moment, I had thought life was sweet and reasonable. But not anymore. Why did Father and Mother make such a fuss just because we had Japanese blood? Why did we have to go to Japanese school? I refused to eat and sat sobbing, letting great big tears splash down into my bowl of rice and tea.

Henry, who was smarter and adjusted more quickly to fate, continued his meal, looking gloomy, but with his appetite unimpaired.

Up to that moment, I had never thought of Father and Mother as Japanese. True, they had almond eyes and they spoke Japanese to us, but I never felt that it was strange. It was like one person's being red-haired and another black.

Father had often told us stories about his early life. He had come from a small village in the prefecture of Tochigi-ken. A third son among five brothers and one sister, Father had gone to Tokyo to study law, and he practiced law for a few years before he succumbed to the fever which sent many young men steaming across the Pacific to a fabulous new country rich with promise and opportunities.

In 1904 Father sailed for the United States, an ambitious young man of twenty-five, determined to continue his law studies at Ann Arbor, Michigan. Landing in Seattle, he plunged into sundry odd jobs with the hope of saving enough money to finance his studies. Father worked with the railroad gang, laying ties on virgin soil, he toiled stubbornly in the heat of the potato fields of Yakima, he cooked his way back and forth between Alaska and Seattle on ships of all sizes and shapes, but fortune eluded him. Then one day he bought a small cleaning and pressing shop on Tenth and Jackson Street, a wagon, and a gentle white dobbin, Charlie. The years flew by fast, but his savings did not reflect his frenzied labor. With each passing year, his dream of Ann Arbor grew dimmer.

At last Father's thoughts turned toward marriage. About this time the Reverend Yohachi Nagashima—our grandfather —brought his family to America. Grandfather Nagashima was a minister of a Congregational church in Sanomachi, about twenty miles north of

Tokyo in Tochigi-ken prefecture. He had visited the United States twice before on preaching missions among Japanese. Grandfather had been impressed with the freedom and educational opportunities in America. He arrived in Seattle with his wife, Yuki, three daughters, Yasuko, my mother Benko, and Kikue, twenty-two, seventeen, and sixteen years of age respectively, and two little round-eyed sons, Shinichi and Yoshio, six and four years.

Mother and her sisters sailed into the port looking like exotic tropical butterflies. Mother told us she wore her best blue silk crepe kimono, Yasuko chose a deep royal purple robe, and Kikue, a soft rose one. Their kimonos had extravagantly long, graceful sleeves, with bright red silk linings. Over their kimonos, the girls donned long, plum-colored, pleated skirts, called the *hakama*, to cover the kimono skirts that flipped open as they walked. Shod in spanking white *tabis*—Japanese stockings—and scarlet cork-soled slippers, the young women stood in tense excitement at the rails of the ship. Yasuko, the eldest, held a picture of a young man in her hand, and she could hardly bring herself to look down at the sea of faces below on the dock where her prospective husband, whom she had never met, stood waiting. Mother told us she and Kikue scanned the crowd boldly and saw hundreds of young, curious masculine faces turned upward, searching for their picture brides.

Father heard of the Nagashimas' arrival. He immediately called to pay his respects. Seeing three marriageable daughters, Father kept going back. Eventually he sent a mutual friend to act as go-between to ask for the hand of the first daughter, Yasuko, but the friend reported that Mr. Nagashima had already arranged for Yasuko's marriage to a Mr. Tani. Undaunted, Father sent his friend back to ask for the second daughter, Benko. Mother said that when her father called her into his study and told her that a Mr. Itoi wanted to marry her, she was so shocked she fled to her room, dived under her bed, and cried in protest, "I can't, Otoh-san, I can't. I don't even know him!"

Her father had got down on his hands and knees and peered at her under the bed, reprimanding her sternly. "Stop acting like a child, Benko. I advise you to start getting acquainted with Mr. Itoi at once."

And that was that. Finally Mother gave her consent to the marriage, and the wedding ceremony was performed at the Japanese mission branch of the Methodist Episcopal Church on Fourteenth and Washington Street. Years later, when Henry and I came upon their wedding picture in our family album, we went into hysterics over Mother's face, which had been plastered white and immobile with rice powder, according to Japanese fashion. Only her piercing black eyes looked alive. In deference to Occidental tradition, she wore a white gown and bridal veil in which she looked tiny and doll-like beside Father, who stood stiff and agonized in formal white tie and tails.

For about a year Mother helped Father haphazardly at his dry-cleaning shop, intent on satisfying the customer's every whim. She scribbled down the strangely garbled phone messages. More than once Mother handed Father an address at which he was supposed to pick up clothes, and he found himself parking his wagon in front of an empty, weed-choked lot or cantering briskly out of the city limits as he pursued phantom house numbers.

In January 1918, their first child was born, Henry Seiichi—Son of Truth. Shortly after, Father sold his little shop and bought the Carrollton Hotel on Main Street and Occidental Avenue, just a stone's throw from the bustling waterfront and the noisy railroad tracks. It was, in fact, on the very birth site of Seattle when the town began its boisterous growth with the arrival of pioneer Henry Yesler and his sawmill on the waterfront. In its early days, the area south of Yesler Hill, where we lived, was called Skid Road because loggers used to grease the roads at intervals to help the ox teams pull the logs down to the mills. Nearly a hundred years later, the district bore the name Skidrow, a corrupted version of Skid Road, with its shoddy stores, decayed buildings, and shriveled men.

The Carrollton had seen its heyday during the Alaskan gold rush. It was an old-fashioned hotel on the second floor of an old red brick building. It had twenty outside rooms and forty inside ones, ar-ranged in three block formations and separated by long corridors. The hallways and inside rooms were lighted and ventilated by the ceiling skylight windows. During the cold of winter, these inside rooms were theoretically warmed by a potbellied stove in the lobby, which was located just at the left of the top stair landing. There was only one bathroom, with a cavernous bathtub, to keep sixty-odd people clean. A separate rest room, For Gents Only, eased the bathroom congestion somewhat. For extra service all the rooms were equipped with a gigantic pitcher of water, a mammoth-sized washbowl, and an ornate chamber pot.

When Father took over the hotel in 1918, the building fairly burst with war workers and servicemen. They came at all hours of the day, begging to sleep even in the chairs in the hotel lobby. Extra cots had been set up in the hallways.

Father and Mother loved to tell us how they had practically rejuvenated the battered, flea-ridden Carrollton by themselves. Fa-ther had said firmly, "If I have to manage a flophouse, it'll be the cleanest and quietest place around here." With patience and care, they began to patch the aches and pains of the old hotel. The tobacco-stained stairways were scrubbed, painted, and lighted up. Father varnished the floors while Mother painted the woodwork. New green runners were laid out in the corridors. They repapered the sixty rooms, one by one. Every day after the routine room-servicing had been finished, Mother cooked up a bucket of flour and water and brushed the paste on fresh new wallpaper laid out on a long makeshift work table in the hall.

All the while Father tried to build up a choice selection of customers, for even one drunkard on a binge always meant fistfights and broken furniture. Father quickly found that among the flotsam of seedy, rough-looking characters milling around in Skidrow were men who still retained their dignity and self-respect. There were lonely old men whose families had been broken up by the death of wives and departing children, who lived a sober existence on their meager savings or their monthly pension allotment. Father also took in sea-hardened mariners, shipyard workers, airplane workers, fruit pickers, and factory workers. He tried to weed out petty thieves, bootleggers, drug peddlers, perverts, alcoholics, and fugitives from the law. At first glance it was hard to tell whether a stubble-bearded, wrinkled, and red-eyed man had just returned from a hard day's work or a hard day at the tavern. Father had a simple technique. If the man smelled of plain, honest-to-goodness perspiration, he was in. But if he reeked of wood alcohol or bay rum, the office window came crashing down in front of his nose.

Shortly after the Armistice of World War I was signed, I was born and appropriately named Kazuko Monica, the Japanese name meaning "Peace." (Mother chose Monica from her reading about St. Augustine and his mother, St. Monica.) Two years later Kenji William arrived, his name meaning "Healthy in Body and Spirit." Mother added "William" because she thought it sounded poetic. And two years after that, Sumiko, "The Clear One," was born.

For our family quarters, Mother chose three outside rooms looking south on Main Street, across an old and graying five-story warehouse, and as the family increased, a fourth room was added. Father and Mother's small bedroom was crowded with a yellow brass bed that took up one wall. Mother's dainty white-painted dresser and small square writing table piled with her books and papers occupied another wall. Father's brown dresser stood off in another corner, its only ornament a round, maroon-lacquered collar box. A treadle sewing machine squatted efficiently in front of the window where Mother sat in the evenings, mending torn sheets and pillowcases. Their closet was a pole slung against the fourth wall, covered with a green, floral-print curtain.

The living room was large, light, and cheerful-looking, with a shiny mahogany-finished upright piano in one corner. Right above it hung a somber picture of Christ's face which looked down upon me each time I sat in front of the piano. Depending on my previous behavior, I felt restless and guilty under those brooding eyes or smugly content with myself. Against another wall, next to the piano, stood an elegant-looking, glass-cased secretary filled with Father's Japanese books, thick hotel account books, a set of untouched, glossy-paged encyclopedias, and the back numbers of the *National Geographic*. In the corner, near the window, was a small square table, displaying a monstrous, iridescent half of an abalone shell and a glass ball paperweight filled with water, depicting an underwater scene with tiny corals and sea shells lying on the ocean bottom. In front of the other two windows was a long, brown leather davenport with a small gas heater nearby. A round dining table in the center of the room was surrounded by three plain chairs.

The children's bedrooms were simply furnished with brown iron cots and old-fashioned dressers. Although rugs were laid out in the living room and our parents' bedroom, our rooms had toe-chilling, easy-to-keep-clean linoleum. Sumiko and I occupied the room next to the living room while Henry and Kenji had the last room.

At first glance, there was little about these simple, sparse furnishings to indicate that a Japanese family occupied the rooms. But there were telltale signs like the *zori*, or straw slippers, placed neatly on the floor underneath the beds. On Mother's bed lay a beautiful red silk comforter patterned with turquoise, apple green, yellow, and purple Japanese parasols. And on the table, beside the local daily paper, were copies of the *North American Times*, Seattle's Japanese-community paper, its printing resembling rows of black multiple-legged insects. Then there was the Oriental abacus board which Father used once a month to keep his books.

Our kitchen was a separate room far down the hall. The kitchen window opened into an alley, right above the Ace Café. An outdoor icebox, born of an old apple crate, was nailed firmly to our kitchen window sill.

Father had put in a gas stove next to the small sink. The huge stove took up nearly all the floor space. He had nailed five layers of shelves against the opposite wall almost up to the ceiling, and next to this, he installed a towering china cabinet with delicate, frosted glass windows. A large, oblong table was wedged into the only space left, in a corner near the door. Here in the kitchen were unmistakable Oriental traces and odors. A glass tumbler holding six pairs of red and yellow lacquered chopsticks, and a bottle of soy sauce stood companionably among the imitation cut glass sugar bowl and the green glass salt and pepper shakers at the end of the table. The tall china cabinet bulged with bright hand-painted rice bowls, red lacquered soup bowls, and Mother's precious *somayaki* tea set.

The tea set was stunningly beautiful with the uneven surface of the gray clay dusted with black and gold flecks. There was a wisp of soft green around the rim of the tiny cups, as if someone had plucked off grass from the clay and the green stain had remained there. At the bottom of each teacup was the figure of a galloping, golden horse. When the cup was filled with tea, the gold horse seemed to rise to the surface and become animated. But the tea set was only for special occasions and holidays, and most of the time we used a set of dinnerware Americana purchased at the local hardware store and a drawerful of silver-plated tableware.

In the pantry, the sack of rice and gallon jug of *shoyu* stood lined up next to the ivory-painted canisters of flour, sugar, tea, and coffee. From a corner near the kitchen window, a peculiar, pungent odor emanated from a five-gallon crock which Mother kept filled with cucumbers, *nappa* (Chinese cabbage), *daikon* (large Japanese radishes), immersed in a pickling mixture of *nuka*, consisting of rice polishings, salt, rice, and raisins. The fermented products were sublimely refreshing, delicious, raw vegetables, a perfect side dish to a rice and tea mixture at the end of a meal.

Among the usual pots and pans stood a dark red stone mixing bowl inside of which were cut rows and rows of minute grooves as on a record disc. The bowl was used to grind poppy seeds and *miso* (soybeans) into soft paste for soups and for flavoring Japanese dishes. I spent many hours bent over this bowl, grinding the beans into a smooth, fine paste with a heavy wooden club. For all the work that went into making *miso shiru*, soybean soup, I thought it tasted like sawdust boiled in sea brine. Mother told me nothing could be more nutritious, but I could never take more than a few shuddering sips of it.

In our family we ate both Western and Oriental dishes. Mother had come to America just fresh out of high school and had had little training in Japanese culinary art. In the beginning, Father taught Mother to cook all the dishes he knew. Father had a robust, mass-cooking style which he had learned in the galleys of Alaska-bound ships and he leaned heavily toward ham and eggs, steaks and potatoes, apple and pumpkin pies. Later Mother picked up the technique of authentic Japanese cooking herself and she even learned to cook superb Chinese dishes. Although we acquired tastes for different types of food, we adhered mostly to a simple American menu.

So we lived in the old Carrollton. Every day, amidst the bedlam created by four black-eyed, jet-propelled children, Father and Mother took care of the hotel. Every morning they went from room to room, making the beds and cleaning up. To help speed up the chores, we ran up and down the corridors, pounding on doors. We brutally woke the late sleepers, hammering with our fists and yelling, "Wake up, you sleepyhead! Wake up, make bed!" Then someone would think of pushing the linen cart for Father and the rest of us would rush to do the same. We usually ended up in a violent tussle. One of our favorite games, when neither Father nor Mother was looking, was "climbing the laundry." We vied with each other to see who could climb highest on an ill-smelling mountain of soiled sheets, pillowcases, and damp towels, piled high to the ceiling. Henry always reached the top by giving himself a running start halfway down the hall. He flew light-footed up the mound like a young gazelle. He hooted scornfully when I scrambled up, red-faced and frantic, grabbing at the sheets and tumbling down when I snatched a loose pillowcase. Kenji and Sumiko squealed happily at the foot of the linen pile and slapped each other with the sopping wet towels. Whenever Mother discovered us, she shrieked in dismay, "*Kita-nai, mah, kita-nai koto!* It's dirty and full of germs. Get right out of there!"

Yes, life to us children was a wonderful treat—especially during hot summer nights when Father slipped out to a market stand down the block and surprised us with an enormous, ice-cold watermelon. It was pure joy when we first bit into its crisp pink succulence and let the juice trickle and seeds fall on old newspapers spread on the round table in the parlor. Or sometimes on a wintry evening, we crowded around the kitchen table to watch Father, bath towel–apron draped around his waist, whip up a batch of raisin cookies for us. It wasn't everybody's father who could turn out thick, melting, golden cookies. We were especially proud that our father had once worked as a cook on romantic Alaska-bound freighters.

Life was hilarious whenever Mother played *Jan-ken-pon! Ai-kono-hoi!* with us. This was the game played by throwing out paper, scissors, and rock symbols with our hands, accompanied by the chant. The winner with the stronger symbol had the privilege of slapping the loser's wrist with two fingers. Mother pretended to cry whenever our small fingers came down on her wrist. With her oval face, lively almond-shaped eyes, and slender aquiline nose, Mother was a pretty, slender five feet of youth and fun.

I thought the whole world consisted of two or three old hotels on every block. And that its population consisted of families like mine who lived in a corner of the hotels. And its other inhabitants were customers—fading, balding, watery-eyed men, rough-tough bearded men, and good men like Sam, Joe, Peter, and Montana who worked for Father, all of whom lived in these hotels.

It was a very exciting world in which I lived.

I played games with a little girl I liked, Matsuko, who lived in Adams Hotel, two blocks away. Sometimes Henry and his friends Dunks and Jiro joined us to explore dingy alleys behind produce warehouses, looking for discarded jars of candies. Sometimes we fished from Pier Two, dipping a long string with bread tied to its end in the briny, moldy-green water. It was pleasant to sit on the sun-warmed old timber which creaked with the waves, and bask in the mellow sun, waiting for the shiners to nibble.

Our street itself was a compact little world, teeming with the bustle of every kind of business in existence in Skidrow. Right below our living quarters was a large second-hand clothing store. It was guarded by a thin, hunchbacked, gray wooly-bearded man who sat napping on a little stool at the entrance. Its dust-misted windows were crammed with army and navy surplus clothes, blanket bath-robes, glistening black raincoats, stiff lumber jackets which practi-cally stood up by themselves, and a tangled heap of bootery from romeo house slippers to hip-length fishing boots. Oddly, the shop was very susceptible to fire, and every now and then smoke would seep up through our bedroom floor boards and we would hear fire engines thundering down our street. After each such uproar, the old man would put up huge, red-lettered signs: *Mammoth Fire Sale . . . practically a giveaway!*

Next to the clothing store was the tavern, the forbidden hall of iniquity, around which we were not supposed to loiter. The swinging door was sawed off at the bottom, but with our heads hanging down we managed to get an upside down view of it. All we could see were feet stuck to brass rails. A nickelodeon played only one song, day in and day out, a melancholy, hillbilly tune of which we could make out just one phrase: "When they cut down that old pine tree. . . ." It was drowned out by the heaven-splitting songs from the mission hall next door, which was filled with hollow-eyed, gray-ing old men, sitting impassively with battered hats balanced on their knees.

Next to our hotel entrance, Mr. Wakamatsu operated the Ace Café. We liked him, because he was such a tall, pleasant-mannered, handsome man. He had a beautiful clear tenor voice which floated out into the alley up to our kitchen as he called out, "Veal, French fries on the side . . . !" Mr. Wakamatsu's window display was always a splendid sight to see. There would be a neat row of purple strawberry shortcakes, or a row of apple pies shining with the luster of shellac, or a row of rigid, blood-red gelatin puddings planted squarely in the center of thick white saucers.

Next to the Ace Café was Dunks's father's small barbershop. Then there was the little white-painted hot-dog stand where we bought luscious hot dogs and hamburgers smothered with onions and the hottest of chili sauce, which brought tears brimming to our eyes. The hot-dog man was constantly swatting flies on the meat board, and I hate to think how many mashed flies were in the red ground meat.

Then came another forbidden place, the burlesque house. A brunet-haired woman with carefully powdered wrinkles sat in the ticket booth, chewing gum. She always winked a shiny purple eyelid at us whenever we passed, and we never knew for sure whether we should smile back at her or not. The theater marquee was studded with dingy yellow light bulbs, spelling out the "Rialto," and the doors were covered with life-size paintings of half-naked girls, about to step out from behind feathers, balloons, and chiffon scarves.

On the corner of Occidental and Washington Street stood a small cigar shop. We were sure that the storekeeper, who constantly rattled dice in a dirty leather cylinder box, had been a big-time gambler in the past. He was just the type, with his baggy eyes, cigar stuffed in his mouth, and his fingers covered with massive jeweled rings.

Just around the corner was a teamsters' union office. Hairy-armed, open-shirted, tattooed men clomped continually in and out of the smoke-filled room. Twice a day, a man hustled out of there carrying a wooden cratebox. He beckoned to the men loafing on the corner to gather near and listen to what he had to say. We stood watching on tiptoes at the fringe of the crowd until the orating man had worked himself into a passion, alternatingly purring at and berating his apathetic audience.

". . . tell me, my friends, what the hell are you anyway . . . men or beasts? To the goddamned capitalist, you're nothin' but beasts! Are you going to grovel under their feet the rest of your life? CRUMBS? That's all they give you . . . CRUMBS! Are you going to be satisfied with that? I say 'NO!' None of that for us anymore. We have to break them now . . . now!"

"Hallelujah," someone would respond dryly.

Across on the opposite corner there was another small crowd, gawking at a man with flowing, silver-white hair and full beard. Tears would be rolling down his uplifted face and disappear into his beard as he pleaded with his audience to "repent before it is too late." Listening to him, I always felt the urgency to repent before it was too late, but I was never sure which of my sins was worth confessing.

The Salvation Army was always there, marching along the street, keeping in time with the brass drum. Wheeling expertly into semi-circle formation near the curb, the uniformed men and women would lift their bugles and trumpets and blare out a vigorous hymn. When the tambourine was passed around for our offering, we would move on guiltily, having already spent our nickles for hot dogs.

This was the playground where I roamed freely and happily. And when I finally started grammar school, I found still another enchanting world. Every morning I hurried to Adams Hotel, climbed its dark flight of stairs, and called for Matsuko. Together we made the long and fascinating journey—from First Avenue to Twelfth Avenue—to Bailey Gatzert School. We always walked over the bridge on Fourth Avenue where we hung over the iron rails, waiting until a train roared past under us, enveloping us completely in its hissing, billowing cloud of white, warm steam. We meandered through the international section of town, past the small Japanese shops and stores, already bustling in the early morning hour, past the cafés and barbershops filled with Filipino men, and through Chinatown. Then finally we went up a gentle sloping hill to the handsome low-slung, red-brick building with its velvet green lawn and huge play yard. I felt like a princess walking through its bright, sunny corridors on smooth, shiny floors. I was mystified by a few of the little boys and girls. There were some pale-looking children who spoke a strange dialect of English, rapidly like gunfire. Matsuko told me they were *"hagu-jins,"* white people. Then there were children who looked very much like me with their black hair and black eyes, but they spoke in high, musical singing voices. Matsuko whispered to me that they were Chinese.

And now Mother was telling us we were Japanese. I had always thought I was a Yankee, because after all I had been born on Occidental and Main Street. Montana, a wall-shaking mountain of a man who lived at our hotel, called me a Yankee. I didn't see how I could be a Yankee and Japanese at the same time. It was like being born with two heads. It sounded freakish and a lot of trouble. Above everything, I didn't want to go to Japanese school.

Milton Murayama

(1923–   )

Milton Murayama was born in Lahaina, on the Hawaiian island of Maui. He graduated from the University of Hawaii in 1947 with a bachelor of arts degree in English and philosophy, and in 1950 graduated from Columbia University with a master of arts degree in Chinese and Japanese. He lives and works in San Francisco, California. In addition to his award-winning novel, *All I Asking For Is My Body*, Murayama has written a play, *Yoshitsune*, which was produced by the University of Hawaii in 1982.

All I Asking For Is My Body

There was something funny about Makot. He always played with guys younger than he and the big guys his own age always made fun of him. His family was the only Japanese family in Filipino camp and his father didn't seem to do anything but ride around in his brand-new Ford Model T. But Makot always had money to spend and the young kids liked him.

During the summer in Pepelau, Hawaii, the whole town spends the whole day at the beach. We go there early in the morning, then walk home for lunch, often in our trunks, then go back for more spearing fish, surfing, or just plain swimming, depending on the tide, and stay there till sunset. At night there were the movies for those who had the money and the Buddhist Bon dances and dance practices. The only change in dress was that at night we wore Japanese *zori* and in the day bare feet. Nobody owned shoes in Pepelau.

In August Makot became our gang leader. We were all at the beach and it was on a Wednesday when there was a matinee, and

Makot said, "Come on, I'll take you all to the movies," and Mit, Skats, and I became his gang in no time. Mit or Mitsunobu Kato and Skats or Nobuyuki Asakatsu and I were not exactly a gang. There were only three of us and we were all going to be in the fourth grade, so nobody was leader. But we were a kind of a poor gang. None of us were in the Boy Scouts or had bicycles, we played football with tennis balls, and during basketball season we hung around Baldwin Park till some gang showed up with a rubber ball or real basketball.

After that day we followed Makot at the beach, and in spearing fish Skats and I followed him across the breakers. We didn't want to go at first, since no fourth-grader went across the breakers, but he teased us and called us yellow, so Skats and I followed. Mit didn't care if he was called yellow. Then at lunchtime, instead of all of us going home for lunch, Makot invited us all to his home in Filipino Camp. Nobody was home and he cooked us rice and canned corned beef and onions. The following day there was the new kind of Campbell soup in cans, which we got at home only when we were sick. So I began to look forward to lunchtime, when we'd go to Makot's home to eat. At home Father was a fisherman and so we ate fish and rice three times a day, and as my older brother Tosh, who was a seventh-grader always said, "What! Fish and rice again! No wonder the Japanese get beriberi!" I was sick of fish and rice too.

Mother didn't seem too happy about my eating at Makot's. About the fourth day when I came home at sunset, she said in Japanese, "You must be famished, Kiyo-chan, shall I fix you something?"

"No, I had lunch at Makoto-san's home."

"Oh, again?"

Mother was sitting on a cushion on the floor, her legs hid under her, and she was bending over and sewing a kimono by hand. It was what she always did. I sat down cross-legged. "Uh-huh. Makoto-san invited me. I ate a bellyful. Makoto-san is a very good cook. He fixed some corned beef and onions and it was delicious."

"Oh, are you playing with Makoto-san now? He's too old for you, isn't he? He's Toshio's age. What about Mitsunobu-san and Nobuyuki-san?"

"Oh, they still with me. We all play with Makoto-san. He invited all of us."

"Makoto-san's mother or father wasn't home?"

"No, they're usually not home."

"You know, Kiyo-chan, you shouldn't eat at Makoto-san's home too often."

"Why? But he invites us."

"But his parents didn't invite you. Do you understand, Kiyo-chan?"

"But why? Nobuyuki-san and Mitsunobu-san go."

"Kiyo-chan is a good boy so he'll obey what his mother says, won't he?"

"But why, Mother! I eat at Nobuyuki's and Mitsunobu's homes when their parents aren't home. And I always thank their parents when I see them. I haven't thanked Makoto's parents yet, but I will when I see them."

"But don't you see, Kiyoshi, you will bring shame to your father and me if you go there to eat. People will say, 'Ah, look at the Oyama's number two boy. He's a *hoitobo*! He's a *chorimbo*! That's because his parents are *hoitobo* and *chorimbo*!' "

Hoitobo means beggar in Japanese and *chorimbo* is something like a bum, but they're ten times worse than beggar and bum because you always make your face real ugly when you say them and they sound horrible!

"But Makoto invites us, Mother! Once Mitsunobu didn't want to go and Makoto dragged him. We can always have Makoto-san over to our home and repay him the way we do Mitsunobu-san and Nobuyuki-san."

"But can't you see, Kiyo-chan, people will laugh at you. 'Look at that Kiyoshi Oyama,' they'll say, 'he always eats at the Sasakis'. It's because his parents are poor and he doesn't have enough to eat at home.' You understand, don't you, Kiyo-chan? You're a good filial boy so you'll obey what your parents say, won't you? Your father and I would cry if we had two unfilial sons like Toshio . . ."

"But what about Nobuyuki and Mitsunobu? Won't people talk about them and their parents like that too?"

"But Kiyoshi, you're not a monkey. You don't have to copy others. Whatever Nobuyuki and Mitsunobu do is up to them. Besides, we're poor and poor families have to be more careful."

"But Mitsunobu's home is poor too! They have lots of children and he's always charging things at the stores and his home looks poor like ours!"

"Nemmind! You'll catch a sickness if you go there too often." She made a real ugly face.

"What kind of sickness? Won't Mitsunobu-san and Nobuyuki-san catch it too?"

She dropped her sewing on her lap and looked straight at me. "Kiyoshi, you will obey your parents, won't you?"

I stood up and hitched up my pants. I didn't say yes or no. I just grunted like Father and walked out.

But the next time I went to eat at Makot's I felt guilty and the corned beef and onions didn't taste so good. And when I came home that night the first thing Mother asked was, "Oh, did you have lunch, Kiyo-chan?" then, "At Makoto-san's home?" and her face looked as if she was going to cry.

But I figured that that was the end of that so I was surprised when Father turned to me at the supper table and said, "Kiyoshi . . ." Whenever he called me by my full name instead of Kiyo or Kiyo-chan, that meant he meant business. He never punched my head once, but I'd seen him slap and punch Tosh's head all over the place till Tosh was black and blue in the head.

"Yes, Father." I was scared.

"Kiyoshi, you're not to eat anymore at Makoto-san's home. You understand?"

"But why, Father? Nobuyuki-san and Mitsunobu-san eat with me too!"

"Nemmind!" he said in English. Then he said in Japanese, "You're not a monkey. You're Kiyoshi Oyama."

"But why?" I said again. I wasn't being smart-alecky like Tosh. I really wanted to know why.

Father grew angry. You could tell by the way his eyes bulged and the way he twisted his mouth. He flew off the handle real easily, like Tosh. He said, "If you keep on asking 'Why? Why?' I'll crack your head *kotsun*!"

Kotsun doesn't mean anything in Japanese. It's just the sound of something hard hitting your head.

"Yeah, slap his head, slap his head!" Tosh said in pidgin Japanese and laughed.

"Shut up! Don't say uncalled-for things!" Father said to Tosh and Tosh shut up and grinned.

Whenever Father talked about this younger generation talking too much and talking out of turn and having no respect for anything, he didn't mean me, he meant Tosh.

"Kiyoshi, you understand, you're not to eat anymore at Makoto's home," Father said evenly, his anger gone now.

I was going to ask "Why?" again but I was afraid. "Yes," I said.

Then Tosh said across the table in pidgin English, which the old folks couldn't understand, "You know why, Kyo?" I never liked the guy, he couldn't even pronounce my name right. "Because his father no work and his mother do all the work, thass why! Ha-ha-ha-ha!"

Father told him to shut up and not to joke at the table and he shut up and grinned.

Then Tosh said again in pidgin English, his mouth full of food; he always talked with his mouth full, "Go tell that *kodomo taisho* to go play with guys his own age, not small shrimps like you. You know why he doan play with us? Because he scared, thass why. He too *wahine*. We bust um up!"

Wahine was the Hawaiian word for woman. When we called anybody *wahine* it meant she was a girl or he was a sissy. When Father said *wahine* it meant the old lady or Mother.

Then I made another mistake. I bragged to Tosh about going across the breakers. "You *pupule* ass! You wanna die or what? You want shark to eat you up? Next time you go outside the breakers I goin' slap your head!" he said.

"Not dangerous. Makot been take me go."

"Shaddup! You tell that *kodomo taisho* if I catch um taking you outside the breakers again, I going bust um up! Tell um that! Tell um I said go play with guys his own age!"

"He never been force me. I asked um to take me."

"Shaddup! The next time you go out there, I goin' slap your head!"

Tosh was three years older than me and when he slapped my head, I couldn't slap him back because he would slap me right back, and I couldn't cry like my kid sister because I was too big to cry. All I could do was to walk away mad and think of all the things I was going to do to get even when I grew up. When I slapped my sister's head she would grumble or sometimes cry but she would always talk back, "No slap my head, you! Thass where my brains stay, you know!" Me, I couldn't even talk back. Most big brothers were too cocky anyway and mine was more cocky than most.

Then at supper Tosh brought it up again. He spoke in pidgin Japanese (we spoke four languages: good English in school, pidgin English among ourselves, good or pidgin Japanese to our parents and the other old folks). "Mama, you better tell Kyo not to go outside the breakers. By-'n'-by he drown. By-'n'-by by the shark eat um up."

"Oh, Kiyo-chan, did you go outside the breakers?" she said in Japanese.

"Yeah," Tosh answered for me, "Makoto Sasaki been take him go."

"Not dangerous," I said in pidgin Japanese; "Makoto-san was with me all the time."

"Why shouldn't Makoto-san play with people his own age, *ne*?" Mother said.

"He's a *kodomo taisho,* thass why!"

Kodomo taisho meant General of the kids.

"Well, you're not to go outside the breakers anymore. Do you understand, Kiyo-chan?" Mother said.

I turned to Father, who was eating silently. "Is that right, Father?"

"*So,*" he grunted.

"Boy, your father and mother real strict," Makot said. I couldn't go outside the breakers, I couldn't go eat at his place. But Makot always saved some corned beef and onions and Campbell soup for me. He told me to go home and eat fast and just a little bit and come over his place and eat with them and I kept on doing that without Mother catching on. And Makot was always buying us pie, ice cream, and chow fun, and he was always giving me the biggest share of the pie, ice cream, or chow fun. He also took us to the movies now and then and when he had money for only one treat or when he wanted to take only me and spend the rest of the money on candies, he would have me meet him in town at night, as he didn't want me to come to his place at night. "No tell Mit and Skats," he told me and I didn't tell them or the folks or Tosh anything about it, and when they asked where I was going on the movie nights, I told them I was going over to Mit's or Skats'.

Then near the end of summer the whole town got tired of going to the beach and we all took up slingshots and it got to be slingshot season. Everybody made slingshots and carried pocketsful of little rocks and shot linnets and myna birds and doves. We would even go to the old wharf and shoot the black crabs which crawled on the rocks. Makot made each of us a dandy slingshot out of a guava branch, as he'd made each of us a big barbed spear out of a bedspring coil during spearing-fish season. Nobody our age had slingshots or spears like ours, and of the three he made, mine was always the best. I knew he liked me the best.

Then one day Makot said, "Slingshot waste time. We go buy a rifle. We go buy .22."

"How?" we all said.

Makot said that he could get five dollars from his old folks and all we needed was five dollars more and we could go sell coconuts and mangoes to raise that.

"Sure!" we all said. A rifle was something we saw only in the movies and Sears Roebuck catalogues. Nobody in Pepelau owned a rifle.

So the next morning we got a barley bag, two picks, and a scooter wagon. We were going to try coconuts first because they were easier to sell. There were two bakeries in town and they needed them for coconut pies. The only trouble was that free coconut trees were hard to find. There were trees at the courthouse, the Catholic church, and in Reverend Hastings' yard, but the only free trees were those deep in the cane fields and they were too tall and dangerous. Makot said, "We go ask Reverend Hastings." Reverend Hastings was a minister of some kind and he lived alone in a big old house in a big weedy yard next to the kindergarten. He had about a dozen trees in his yard and he always let you pick some coconuts if you asked him, but he always said, "Sure, boys, provided you don't sell them." "Aw, what he doan know won't hurt um," Makot said.

Makot said he was going to be the brains of the gang and Mit and Skats were going to climb the trees and I was going to ask Reverend Hastings. So we hid the wagon and picks and bags and I went up to the door of the big house and knocked.

Pretty soon there were footsteps and he opened the door. "Yes?" He smiled. He was a short, skinny man who looked very weak and who sort of wobbled when he walked, but he had a nice face and a small voice.

"Reverend Hastings, can we pick some coconuts?" I said.

Makot, Mit, and Skats were behind me and he looked at them and said, "Why, sure boys, provided you don't sell them."

"Thank you, Reverend Hastings," I said, and the others mumbled, "thank you."

"You're welcome," he said and went back into the house.

Mit and Skats climbed two trees and knocked them down as fast as they could and I stuck my pick in the ground and started peeling them as fast as I could. We were scared. What if he came out again? Maybe it was better if we all climbed and knocked down lots and took them somewhere else to peel them, we said. But Makot sat down on the wagon and laughed, "Naw, he not gonna come out no more. No be chicken!" As soon as he said that the door slammed and we all looked. Mit and Skats stayed on the trees but didn't knock down any more. Reverend Hastings jumped down the step and came walking across the yard in big angry strides! It was plain we were going to sell the coconuts because we had more than half a bagful and all the husks were piled up like a mountain! He came up, his face red, and he shouted, "I thought you said you weren't going to sell these! Get down from those trees!"

I looked at my feet and Makot put his face in the crook of his arm and began crying, "Wah-wah . . ." though I knew he wasn't crying.

Reverend Hastings grabbed a half-peeled coconut from my hand and, grabbing it by a loose husk, threw it with all his might over the fence and nearly fell down and shouted, "Get out! At once!" Then he turned right around and walked back and slammed the door after him.

"Ha-ha-ha!" Makot said as soon as he disappeared. "We got enough anyway."

We picked up the rest of the coconuts and took them to the kindergarten to peel them. We had three dozen and carted them to the two bakeries on Main Street. But they said they had enough coconuts and that ours were too green and six cents apiece was too much. We pulled the wagon all over town and tried the fish markets and grocery stores for five cents. Finally we went back to the first bakery and sold them for four cents. It tooks us the whole day and we made only $1.44. By that time, Mit, Skats, and I wanted to forget about the rifle, but Makot said, "Twenty-two or bust."

The next day we went to the tall trees in the cane fields. We had to crawl through tall cane to get to them, and once we climbed the trees and knocked down the coconuts we had to hunt for them in the tall cane again. After the first tree we wanted to quit but Makot wouldn't hear of it, and when we didn't move he put on his *habut*. *Habut* is short for *habuteru,* which means to pout the way girls and children do. Makot would blow up his cheeks like a balloon fish and not talk to us. "I not goin buy you no more chow fun, no more ice cream, no more pie," he'd sort of cry, and then we would do everything to please him and make him come out of his *habut*. When we finally agreed to do what he wanted he would protest and slap with his wrist like a girl, giggle with his hand over his mouth, talk in the kind of Japanese which only girls use, and in general make fun of the girls. And when he came out of his *habut* he usually bought us chow fun, ice cream, or pie.

So we crawled through more cane fields and climbed more coconut trees. I volunteered to climb too because Mit and Skats grumbled that I got all the easy jobs. By three o'clock we had only a half a bag, but we brought them to town and again went all over Main Street trying to sell them. The next day we went to pick mangoes, first at the kindergarten, then at Mango Gulch, but they were harder to sell so we spent more time carting them around town.

"You guys think you so hot, eh," Tosh said one day. "Go sell mangoes and coconuts. He only catching you head. You know why he pick on you guys for a gang? Because you guys the last. That *kodomo taisho* been leader of every shrimp gang and they all quit him one after another. You, Mit, and Skats stick with him because you too stupid!"

I shrugged and walked away. I didn't care. I liked Makot. Besides, all the guys his age were jealous because Makot had so much money to spend.

Then several days later Father called me. He was alone at the outside sink, cleaning some fish. He brought home the best fish for us to eat but it was always fish. He was still in his fisherman's clothes.

"Kiyoshi," he said and he was not angry, "you're not to play with Makoto Sasaki anymore. Do you understand?"

"Buy why, Father?"

"Because he is bad." He went on cleaning fish.

"But he's not bad. He treats us good! You mean about stealing mangoes from kindergarten! It's not really stealing. Everybody does it."

"But you never sold the mangoes you stole before?"

"No."

"There's a difference between a prank and a crime. Everybody in town is talking about you people. Not about stealing, but about your selling mangoes and coconuts you stole. It's all Makoto's fault. He's older and he should know better but he doesn't. That's why he plays with younger boys. He makes fools out of them. The whole town is talking about what fools he's making out of you and Nobuyuki and Mitsunobu."

"But he's not really making fools out of us, Father. We all agreed to make some money so that we could buy a rifle and own it together. As for the work, he doesn't really force us. He's always buying us things and making things for us and teaching us tricks he learns in Boy Scout, so it's one way we can repay him."

"But he's bad. You're not to play with him. Do you understand?"

"But he's not bad! He treats us real good and me better than Mitsunobu-san or Nobuyuki-san!"

"Kiyoshi, I'm telling you for the last time. Do not play with him."

"But why?"

"Because his home is bad. His father is bad. His mother is bad."

"Why are his father and mother bad?"

"Nemmind!" He was mad now.

"But what about Mitsunobu-san and Nobuyuki-san? I play with them too!"

"Shut up!" He turned to face me. His mouth was twisted. "You're not a monkey! Stop aping others! You are not to play with him. Do you understand! Or do I have to crack your head *kotsun*!"

"Yes," I said and walked away.

Then I went inside the house and asked Mother, "Why are they bad? Because he doesn't work?"

"You're too young to understand, Kiyo-chan. When you grow up you'll know that your parents were right."

"But whom am I going to play with then?"

"Can't you play with Toshi-chan?"

"Yeah, come play with me, Kyo. Any time you want me to bust up that *kodomo taisho* I'll bustum up for you," Tosh said.

That night I said I was going to see Mit and went over to Makot's home. On the way over I kept thinking about what Father and Mother said. There was something funny about Makot's folks. His father was a tall, skinny man and he didn't talk to us kids the way all the other old Japanese men did. He owned a Model T when only the *haoles,* or whites, had cars. His mother was funnier yet. She wore lipstick in broad daylight, which no other Japanese mother did.

I went into Filipino Camp and I was scared. It was a spooky place, not like Japanese Camp. The Filipinos were all men and there were no women or children and the same-looking houses were all bare, no curtains in the windows or potted plants on the porches. The only way you could tell them apart was by their numbers. But I knew where Makot's house was in the daytime, so I found it easily. It was the only one with curtains and ferns and flowers. There were five men standing in the dark to one side of the house. They wore shoes and bright aloha shirts and sharply pressed pants, and smelled of expensive pomade. They were talking in low voices and a couple of them were jiggling so hard you could hear the jingle of loose change.

I called from the front porch. "Makot! Makot!" I was scared he was going to give me hell for coming at night.

Pretty soon his mother came out. I had never spoken to her though I'd seen her around and knew who she was. She was a fat woman with a fat face, which made her eyes look very small.

"Oh, is Makoto-san home?" I asked in Japanese.

"Makotooooo!" she turned and yelled into the house. She was all dressed up in kimono. Mother made a lot of kimonos for other people but she never had one like hers. She had a lot of white powder on her face and two round red spots on her cheeks.

"Oh, Sasaki-san," I said, "I've had lunch at your home quite a few times. I wanted to thank you for it but I didn't have a chance to speak to you before. It was most delicious. Thank you very much."

She stared at me with her mouth open wide and suddenly burst out laughing, covering her mouth and shaking all over, her shoulders, her arms, her cheeks.

Makot came out. "Wha-at?" he pouted in Japanese. Then he saw me and his face lit up. "Hiya, Kiyo, old pal, old pal, what's cookin'?" he said in English.

His mother was still laughing and shaking and pointing at me.

"What happened?" Makot said angrily to his mother.

"That boy! That boy!" She still pointed at me. "Such a nice little boy! Do you know what he said? He said, 'Sasaki-san . . .' " And she started to shake and cough again.

"Aw, shut up, Mother!" Makot said. "Please go inside!" and he practically shoved her to the door.

She turned around again. "But you're such a courteous boy, aren't you? 'It was most delicious. Thank you very much.' A-ha-hahaha. A-hahahaha . . ."

"Shut up, Mother!" Makot shoved her into the doorway. I would never treat my mother like that but then my mother would never act like that. When somebody said, "Thank you for the feast," she always said, "But what was served you was really rubbish."

Makot turned to me. "Well, what you say, old Kiyo, old pal? Wanna go to the movies tonight?"

I shook my head and looked at my feet. "I no can play with you no more."

"Why?"

"My folks said not to."

"But why? We never been do anything bad, eh?"

"No."

"Then why? Because I doan treat you right? I treat you okay?"

"Yeah. I told them you treat me real good."

"Why, then?"

"I doan know."

"Aw, hell, you can still play with me. They doan hafta know. What they doan know won't hurt them."

"Naw, I better not. This time it's my father and he means business."

"Aw, doan be chicken Kiyo. Maybe you doan like to play with me."

"I like to play with you."

"Come, let's go see a movie."

"Naw."

"How about some chow fun. Yum-yum."

"Naw."

"Maybe you doan like me, then?"

"I like you."

"You sure."

"I sure."

"Why, then?"

"I doan know. They said something about your father and mother."

"Oh," he said and his face fell and I thought he was going to cry.

"Well, so long, then, Kiyo," he said and went into the house.

"So long," I said and turned and ran out of the spooky camp.

Taro Yashima

(1908–   )

Taro Yashima, artist and author, is a Japanese American original, a seminal force in Asian American arts. Born a country boy in Kagoshima, Japan, Yashima went to the big city, Tokyo, to study art at the conservatory. Distressed by the increasing oppressiveness of the militarists' control of Japan, he dropped out of the conservatory to band together with a group of resistance artists to propagandize against the Fascists.

In Kobe he married a young art student, Mitsu Sasako. They bore two children and two children died. At that time Japan was deeply committed to wars of conquest on the Asian continent. All the young men were being drafted into the war machine and being devoured. Yashima wanted to stay out of the Imperial Japanese Army and continue his art studies. He wanted to apply his art as an instrument of war against the militarists' corruption of Japan's humanity. Attracted by the French "wild beasts of color," or fauves, led by Henri Matisse, Yashima sought to develop the direct emotional appeal of color and use it to promote world peace.

This much of his life is told in his first book, *The New Sun,* an autobiographical picture book. Published in 1943 by Henry Holt, it was the first book by a Japanese American published during the war. It was the only book published by one legally designated as a pariah, an "enemy alien." The form of this picture book was influenced by horizontal Japanese narrative scrolls, French picture books, and haiku. The top half of each page is a drawing in black ink, below are one or two lines in English, followed by the Japanese equivalent. The ideal line, Yashima says, would have been three words long.

His second book, *Horizon Is Calling,* was also published by Henry Holt, in 1947. It tells of the birth of his third child, Makoto, and includes pictures by the boy, drawn when soldiers were marching off to war and the boy was four or five. The book ends with Yashima's decision to leave his son with his in-laws and answer the call of the horizon by fleeing with his artist wife to America in 1939.

Yashima feels the end of *Horizon Is Calling* demands a third book, one that describes his work in America for the Office of Strategic Services (OSS) during the war and his return to Japan after the war to search for his son. Japan was smoldering when he arrived there. Two panic-stricken weeks later, he found his son "at the top of a mountain."

Taro Yashima's place in the history of Asian American arts is unique. He is the head of Japanese America's first family in the arts. Mitsu Yashima is an accomplished artist who lives in San Francisco. His daughter, Momo, is an actress in Los Angeles. His son is Mako, the actor, Oscar nominee for *The Sand Pebbles,* Tony nominee for *Pacific Overtures,* and founder and artistic director of the East/West Players. Mako's East-West Players is the only professional Asian American theater and has generated the bulk of Asian American dramatic literature. Yashima himself is an internationally acclaimed painter and author/illustrator of children's books. His *Crow Boy* and *Momo's Umbrella* are classics of the genre.

Taro Yashima is a permanent resident of the United States but not a citizen. He considers himself an expatriate. The militarists no longer rule Japan. The Japanese are building a museum in the town of his birth to house his works. He is preparing, slowly, to return home to the Japan he fled in the thirties.

Taro Yashima

Horizon Is Calling

Unfinished Portrait

未完成肖像画

I longed to paint before I was called into the army at least one portrait of Kiyoshi, who had moved me more than anyone else.

自分が出征するまでに、誰よりも心をうつ清の肖像をせめて一枚は描きあげたいと、思ふやうになつた。

In the days when he had been a pig-iron smasher, he had been unable, after sending an allowance to his mother, to buy even a package of cigarettes.

ズク割りしてゐるころは、母に送金すれば煙草一つ買へない彼であつた。

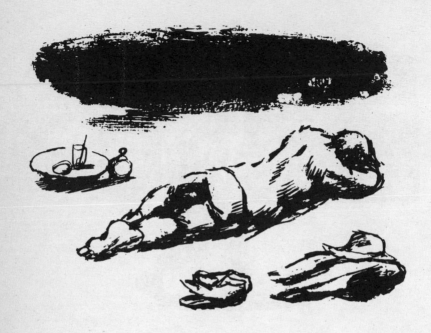

He used to sleep as if dead and as soon as he awoke the all-day labor awaited him.

死んだやうに眠り、覺めればズク割りの終日勞働が待つわ
た。

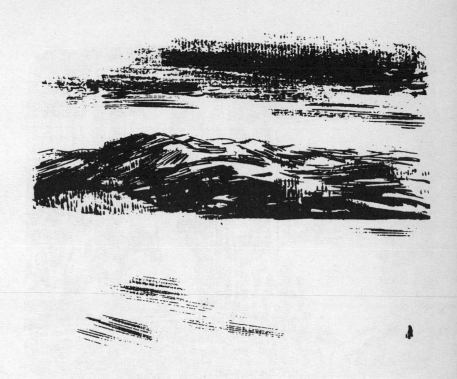

He said he almost despaired in the hopelessness and loneliness,
which neither heaven nor earth could help.

天にも地にも救ひなき孤獨と絶望のなかで、彼は慟哭せん
ばかりであつたといふことである。

Finally the foreman of the foundry gave him a helping hand, and
he began to learn the technique.

しかし、鑄物場の職長は救ひの手をさしだし、彼は技術を
ならふこととなつた。

The foreman had come to like his spirit, for he endured the burns on his muscles in order to keep his partner from getting hurt.

協働者をきずつけぬために、自分の筋肉が燒けるのを我慢してはたらく彼の精神を、職長は愛した。

With deep love the foreman tried to help him become an independent technician as soon as possible.

職長はふかい愛をもつて、彼がはやく一本だちの技術家に
なれるやう骨折つてくれた。

An acquaintance in the machine shop became the guide who revealed conditions in the large cities to him and made his future seem brighter.

知りあひになつた機械場の友は、大都會の現實をあきらか
にしてくれ、未來をあかるくしてくれる水先案内であつた。

Only these valuable friendships made it possible for him to easily
pass the entrance examination for skilled workers in the Kawasaki
shipyard.

ねうち高い友愛こそが、彼に川崎造船所の熟練工試験をや
すやすとパスさせたのであつた。

Also his brother from the country became the head of his class at
a lathe school.

よびよせた弟は、また、旋盤學校の一席をしめる生徒とな
つた。

The book in Kiyoshi's hand now was a "holy" book, for he had
got it after long perseverance.

彼の手にする本は、かうした永い忍耐ののちに得られた實
典であつたのだ。

Then later he passed the highest skilled workers' examination, which would entitle his mother to half of his pay even after he was called to war.

そして彼は、まもなく、出征後にも月給半額が家族にゆく最高熟練工試験にもパスしたのであつた。

One night at the rest and nutrition gathering he put his hand upon his brother's shoulder and said, "'This fellow will acquire knowledge much sooner than me."

ある晩、滋養と休息の會で——こいつは、わしより早く智識がもてますよと、彼は弟の肩に手をおいた。

His mother, in the country, called him "Treasure Son," and was praying for his health morning and night.

郷里の母は、彼を寶子とよび、彼の健在を朝に晩に祈つてゐた。

The farmers in the settlement were calling him "Hero of the Settlement."

部落の農夫たちは、彼を『部落の英雄』とよんでゐた。

One Sunday when we went fishing, I too sensed in his figure "a great man of the future."

魚つりにいつたある日曜日に、なにげない彼のすがたの中に、私もまた、「未來の偉人」をみた氣がした。

A portrait of the most highly skilled foundryman!

最高熟練鋳物工の像！

But his striking progress overwhelmed the technique of my art,
and I made only a few unsatisfactory sketches of him.

だが、かうしためざましい彼の成長は私の技術を圧倒する
ものであり、私は、不満足な下圖をいくらか作つたにすぎ
なかつた。

Winter deepened; the shadows of women asking people to help embroider good luck sashes for their husbands were growing thinner.

冬がふかまるにつれて、戦野にある夫のために千人針を乞ふひとの影もうすまつてゐた。

Civilians no longer had even a shred of freedom of speech since the disciplinary rumor law had been issued by urgent Imperial order.

勅令による流言ヒゴ取締法の發布以來、もはや市民は、一分一厘の言論の自由もなかつた。

A student who said, watching the parade of ashes, "The number of widows will be increased," was caught by that law.

遺骨行列をながめながら——ヤモメがふえるなアと言つた
學生は、その法律にひつかけられた。

Even a girl student's murmuring, "I got so tired," after she had
had to stand half a day in the line of welcome for the Emperor's
visit, was not good.

行幸奉迎行列に半日もたちつくさされた一女學生が——あ
あ、つかれたとつぶやいただけでもいけなかつた。

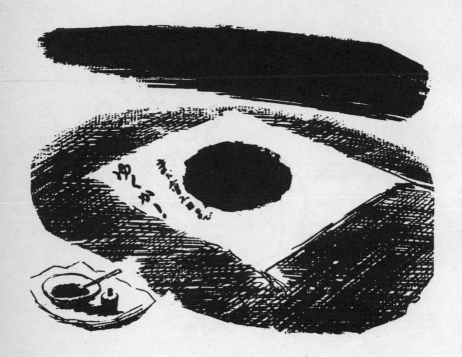

Members of our nourishment and rest group were called by the army one after another.

滋養と休息の會のメムバアも、つぎからつぎへと召集され
ていつた。

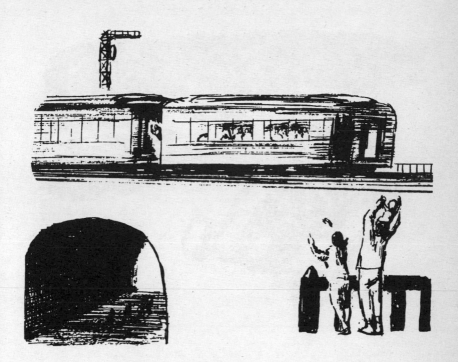

There was only in our minds the hope that we should see each other again alive and well.

ぶじで再會したい願望のほかには、何一つ、おたがひの心の中にあるわけはなかつた。

After we received a card from Hara's brother, the first of us called, that he was in a hospital with a bullet wound in his neck, we did not get news from anyone else.

最初に出征した原の弟から、首に貫通銃創を負つて入院してゐるハガキがきたきり、誰からも便りがなかつた。

Another card from him: "I am leaving for the front. I would rather be with the fellows than in the hospital"... then nothing more.

彼からは——また一線にゆく、病院にゐるより皆と一しよ
がいゝといふハガキがきて、それつきりになつた。

In Kiyoshi's room his young brother was studying, alone.

清の部屋では、兄のゐなくなつた弟が、ひとりさびしく勉
強してゐた。

One night I had the lucky chance to visit Kiyoshi's regiment which was to leave Kobe City the next morning.

ある夜のこと、翌朝神戸を出發する清の部隊を見送る機會が、私にめぐまれた。

When I found the regiment, it was in roll-call and as I approached
I felt some abnormal tension.

そして、私が彼の部隊をみつけた時は人員點呼の最中であ
つたが、近づくと、何か異常な空氣がながれてゐた。

A lieutenant was insulting a sergeant who had said that all his men were present when two of them were still in a bar.

酒場にゐる二人の兵士をかばつて、人員異常なしと報告した軍曹を少尉が罵倒してゐる。

"Why not excuse them? Our fate is to die anyway," the sergeant answered back to the lieutenant. Look out! The battalion commander has come!

——勘辨できねえのか、どうせ死ぬ身だぞ！軍曹は少尉にたてついた。あぶない！大隊長が下りてくる！

The battalion commander took the sergeant's hand, then he grasped both hands, said, "You are a warmhearted man. The lieutenant was wrong."

大隊長は、軍曹の手をとつた、両手でにぎつた、そして言つた──君は、人情のある人だ、少尉がわるかつた。

". . . Day after tomorrow we are going to pass through a curtain
of bullets. Let's stop fighting among ourselves." The commander's
voice was pleading, which I had never heard before.

——明後日は、彈丸フスマをくぐるのだ、日本人同志の爭
ひはやめやう、大隊長の態度は、まだ見たこともない懇願
であつた。

The sergeant answered, "I understand," and the battalion commander said, "I thank you for understanding me."

軍曹は──わかりますと答へ、大隊長は──わかつてくれ
て感謝しますと言つた。

But angry voices rose from the soldiers going to their billets.
"Beat the life out of those fellows!" "The bullets don't come only
from the front!"

それでも、宿舎にむかふ兵士たちの中からは怒声があげら
れた——奴らを叩つころしちめえ！弾丸は前からばかり来
やしねぇぞ！

All I could say when I found Kiyoshi was, "You must live through it."

清をさがしあてた私は ──どうしても生きぬいてくれとい
ふほかに言葉がない。

. . ."Didn't you think it strange that I did not sell my house when
I was trying hard to become a worker?" Kiyoshi inquired calmly.

——村をでるのにあんなに苦勞してゐた私が、家を賣却し
なかつたのを、あんたは不思議に思はなかつたですかと、
清がしづかに言ふ。

"That was . . . that was because I planned to donate it to the villagers, for the time when the villagers had to fight for themselves." Tears were shining in Kiyoshi's eyes.

あれは、あれは、いつか村のひとたちが戦ふ日がきたら、提供するつもりなのです —— 清の目に涙が光つてゐる。

Oh, how we want to live! We cannot die! Our handclasp con-
veyed this thought, one to the other.

あゝどんなに生きたいか！死んでたまるものか！にぎつた
手と手とは、この思ひをつたえ合つてゐた。

In my mind the light in Kiyoshi's house, kept burning by his mother, was flickering.

私の頭には、清の母が家をまもつてゐる光りが明滅してゐ
た。

After a while I sent to an exhibition in Tokyo a painting called "Farewell."

その後私は、東京の展覽會に、『別離』と題する作品を送
つた。

But it was sad; it was a shameful picture that showed nothing but
my slow progress.

しかし、かなしいかな、それは私の立後れを語る羞辱の作
でしかなかつた。

マコの作品

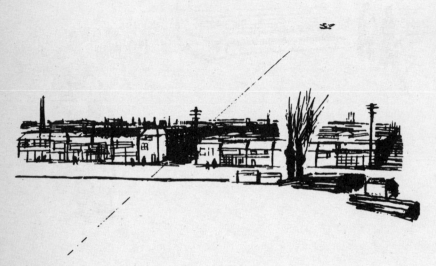

New Year's came again. I was playing with Mako every day.

あたらしい年がふたたびきた。私は、毎日、マコと遊んで
ゐる。

His progress both in ideas and in technique since his drawings of dogs when he was a year and a half old had been far better than mine.

一歳半のとき描いた『犬』以來の彼の思索と表現の發展は、
父親の比ではない。

He thought that carrots grew on branches and were colored by the sun, and that the farmers waited beside the trees in easy chairs.

人参は枝になり、太陽が色づけてくれ、農夫は椅子をすえて待つてゐると彼は思つた。

As the war began, many things he had not known became objects for understanding.

戦争がはじまると、みたこともない品物のかずかずが認識の對象となつた。

"The commander is a superman who orders the crossing of the waterways in spite of piercing bullet wounds."

『部隊長は、貫通銃創をうけても、クリークを渡れと命令するスーパーマンにちがひない 』

Sometimes he thinks the soldiers in the wilds of China must be lonely.

時々、兵隊さんは支那の荒地でさびしからうと思ふことがある。

He comforts wounded soldiers, who are coming home in heart-rending condition, by painting a pot of flowers on his picture.

せつないすがたで歸つてくる負傷兵を、彼は、病院車の窓に花瓶を描きいれて慰問する。

"What will happen to the Chinese children who have lost their parents? Butterflies will amuse them, and other grown-up men and women will take care of them."

『父母をうしなつた支那の子供は、どうなるだらう？蝶々が
なぐさめ、よそのおぢさんやおばさんが育てゝやつてくれ
るだらう。』

If we live in an old train attached to an automobile, he dreams,
no one will ever die in the flood.

もし、自動車に古列車をくつつけた家に住んでをれば、い
ざ水害さいふときにも誰も死なないのだと彼は夢みる。

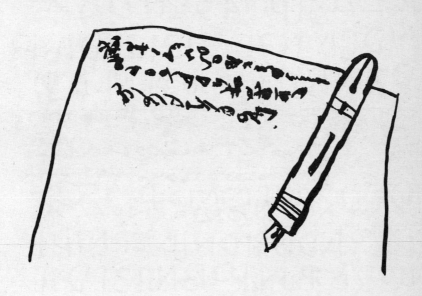

"Taro, my father, has a fountain pen, writes characters with it. But he is in the bathroom now."

『父親の太郎は、萬年筆をもつてゐる、字を書く、書きかけ
のまゝで便所にゆく。』

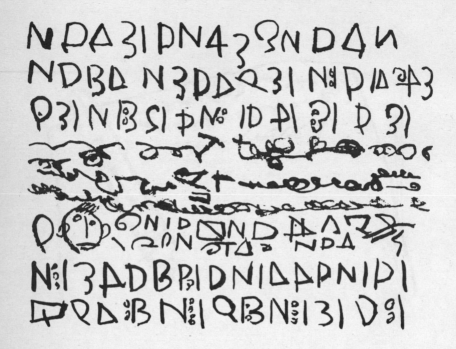

Sometimes he wants to send a letter to children in foreign countries. A self-portrait is necessary on it in order to introduce himself.

あるときは、外國の子供に手紙をおくつてみたくなる、自
喬像を入れて自己紹介する必要がある。

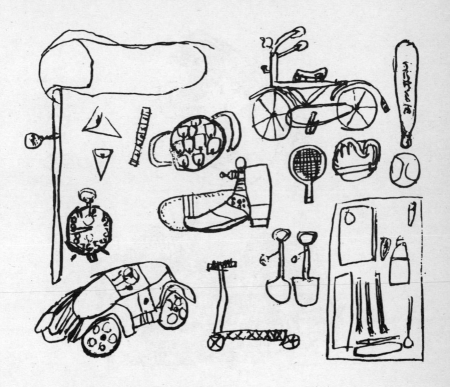

There are lots of things he wants but since his parents are poor he bears up by making pictures.

ほしいものが一ぱいある。父母はびんぼうで買つてくれないから、絵に描いて我慢する。

"Kiyoshi is a strong man who makes toothed wheels and even machines. There are 'roads of blood' all over his arms."

『清さんは、歯車でも機械でもつくる強いおぢさんだ。腕には、血の通る道が一ばいついてるぞ。』

He wishes he could be the operator of a racing train shaking the earth.

地ひびきをたててはしる汽車の機關士になれたらと思ふ。

"A truck driver is not too bad either. A truck rushes even in the rain."

トラックの運轉手もわるくはない。雨のなかでもゴンゴン
はしれる。

When we are wrestling, I say, pushing my face on him, "You're wonderful!" In embarrassed defense the little da Vinci retorts, "You stinky nose!"

ある日、相撲をとつだとき、私は彼に顔をおしつけて――
こいつ、すばらしいぞ！と言ふ、小さきダヴインチは――
おまえ、鼻くさいぞ！と應酬する。

Lonny Kaneko

(1939–   )

The Seattle-born Sansei Lonny Kaneko is an award-winning writer of short fiction, a poet, and a playwright. During the war, he and his family were removed from their home to the assembly center at Puyallup, Washington, then interned at Minidoka, the concentration camp in Idaho. "The Shoyu Kid" is a story of childhood behind the American barbed wire.

With Amy Sanbo, he wrote the play *Lady Is Dying,* which won the Henry Broderick Playwright Prize at the Pacific Northwest Writers Conference in 1977. It also won the Asian American Playwright Search Award of the Asian American Theatre Workshop in San Francisco, where it was first staged in 1977, with Frank Chin directing.

Kaneko's fiction and poetry have appeared in *Playboy* and several literary magazines. He is the recipient of a National Endowment for the Arts Fellowship in poetry.

The Shoyu Kid

We were ready for him. The three of us were crouched in the vines expecting the Kid to come stumbling into the garden. Itchy was to my right trying to tell me about what he'd seen earlier in the morning. Something about the sun rising from the wrong direction. I was too busy looking for the Kid to pay much attention. Jackson was in front of Itchy, ready to close off the Kid's escape in case he should see us before we could jump him. He came this way every day. Usually when there was nothing else to do, he would wander into the patch and sit down in the heat of the late morning sun and pull out a chocolate bar and eat it slowly, so that by the time he finished, his face and hands were streaked gooey brown. There was a dark lingering haze on the western horizon, and I wondered if it would rain.

"Here he comes."

"Shhh."

"Get your butt down. Shit, I think he heard us."

The Kid had stopped at the edge of the walk and was looking around. His dirty cotton bib coveralls billowed loosely over bare, unwashed feet. I couldn't see his eyes, but I knew they were watery. They always were. The Kid was always on the verge of crying. And he usually had his arms full of dog, his skinny weiner dog that Jackson nicknamed Kraut.

"Shutup."

The Kid stopped about six feet in front of Jackson, still too far away for Jackson to nab him. I heard him drawing the snot back into his nose. It was his trademark, that sniffing. He sounded like the old men who snuff tobacco. Itchy flattened his face in the dirt, and I did the same, holding my breath, trying not to inhale the dust that rose over the ground. It was already coating my tongue. The vines coiled around my right wrist and reached inside the back of my shirt.

We waited a long time. When I looked up, the Kid was gone.

"Hey, where'd he go?"

"I donno."

"That way. Around the building." Jackson was up and flying down the edge of the garden with Itchy and me not far behind. At the corner of the building, he pulled up, flattened himself against the wall and like a soldier in a war movie, peered around the corner. We pulled up behind him, puffing, and he turned and put a finger to his lips and inched an eye like a periscope around the corner. His body relaxed, and he turned back to us. "He's gone."

"Which way'd he go?"

"Maybe he turned up one of the rows."

So we ran half the length of the block, checking the walkways between the barracks to see if the Kid had turned up one of them. Nothing but a couple of girls the Kid's age trying to skip rope and Glenn Miller music from the window of one of the barracks. We skirted three old women, who, like old women, stood in the shade of the barracks talking. It was already too hot for them to be out weeding the gardens. Jackson always greeted the women smoothly.

"Good morning, *obasan*," and they in return flashed smiles, and as if on cue made some comment in Japanese about Ichiro and Hiroshi and Masao growing up to be fine lads. Jackson hated to be called Hiroshi and would make a face or thumb his nose as soon as they turned their backs, but today he was too puzzled about the Kid's disappearing to remember his ritual.

"Hey, let's try over there." Itchy was pointing to the large garage and storage area that stood at right angles to the rows of barracks. We ran across the road to the garage—I guess that's what it was, because Furuta, the cop, used to leave his car there. Beyond the garage was a road that was part of the system that connected all of the blocks of barracks and beyond that was the fence that surrounded our whole camp. When we first arrived, soldiers used to march around the fence. In the distance were hills that stretched as far as we could see. The past few days the hills had been covered with sheep so white that the hills had blended with the clouds. But this morning the sheep were gone, leaving us alone in the middle of a wide saucer of gray, overgrazed rangeland.

"C'mon. The Kid must be behind the building." Itchy pulled at my arm.

"But we aren't supposed to go over there."

"You're chicken. There aren't any more soldiers patrolling that fence."

"Geez, I know that."

"Well, I'm going to look." Itchy took off and pressed up against the side of the garage as Jackson had done before. Jackson followed, crouching like a cat stalking prey. And I went, too.

Itchy was already peering around the corner like an Indian from behind a tree, when his body went stiff. He motioned us back, but he stayed fixed at the corner for another minute; then he took off past us running as hard as he could. Jackson and I turned and ran too. Itchy turned the corner of the garage, cut across the street, zagged past the second row of barracks and cut into the walkway in front of the third, almost hitting the old women and stumbling over one of the girls with the rope. We followed as fast as we could. I heard a shout and a dog barking behind us and urged my palomino to even greater speeds, following Itchy's dust. At the end of the third barracks we cut down the middle of the block and slipped into the side door of the laundry room, where Jackson slowed so suddenly I almost galloped over him.

Mrs. Furuta had her little girl in a cast-iron laundry tub, giving her a bath, and Jackson, as he always did, stopped to take a look at the girl's naked body. Not obviously. He just strolled past Mrs. Furuta, said, "Good morning, is Joyce having a bath?" just as if he couldn't tell what was happening in front of his eyes, and Mrs. Furuta said in Japanese, "Go. Get out of here. You aren't supposed to play here," and we turned and ran on through and out the back door. At the door Jackson stopped and gave Mrs. Furuta's bent back the finger.

Jackson circled the laundry building, peered in through the window to get another look, then went into a cowboy pose, his thumbs hooked into his pockets.

Itchy, who had run straight through the building, was waiting for us. "Is anybody following us?"

"Nyaa."

"Hey, Itchy, what were we running for?"

"Nothing."

"Nothing?"

"C'mon, what happened?"

"Did you see Joyce?" Itchy was changing the subject. "Little girls are sure funny to look at, aren't they?"

"Itchy, you act like you ain't never seen a naked girl before."

"Well, have you? I mean really seen one, Jackson? Seen what kind of prick they have?"

"They don't have one."

"That's what I mean. Do you know what to do with it?"

"Everyone knows. You get this hard-on, see, and . . ."

"Jackson, you got a hard-on?" Itchy's face was tight.

"Yeah, don't you? You're supposed to."

"N-no."

"What are you, Itchy, some kind of queer or something? Don't you know you're supposed to have a hard-on when you see a naked girl?" Jackson was getting wound up on his favorite subject. I sneaked a look at Jackson, and I think he as lying.

"Hey, Itchy, what'd you see?" I was still curious what we were running from. "Was the Kid back of the garage?"

"Kinda."

"What do you mean, kinda?"

"There was a soldier back there."

"A soldier? And the Kid?"

"He was there, too."

"Yeah?"

"And he had a chocolate bar."

"So that's where he gets them."

"Yeah."

"Maybe we can get some, too." Jackson was coming to life again. "Who was the soldier?"

"That red-headed one."

"What the hell was he doing way over here?" Jackson took great pains to sound like his older brother sometimes. "They don't patrol here anymore. They're supposed to stay by the gate. Let's check it out tomorrow. Maybe he'll give us some, too."

"Uh, no thanks."

"Why not, Itchy? Chicken?"

"Kinda."

"Whaddayou mean, Itchy? Shit, talk plain will you?" Jackson was leaning into Itchy.

"There's something strange about that guy. I mean that's the same red-headed soldier who used to stand there at the fence and point his gun at me like he was going to shoot."

I remembered that, too. So did Jackson. It was enough to make us nervous. "Well, how does the Kid do it? Maybe the guy's changed. Let's ask the Kid."

"Are you kidding? That snot-nosed brat. Makes me nervous to look at him, too."

I knew what Itchy meant. The Kid always had that heavy snot dripping from his nose. Like a perpetual cold. Except that the snot was the color of soy sauce. Jackson's older brother told him the reason the Kid had brown snot was because he used too much soy sauce, and it just dripped out of his nose. We all stopped using shoyu when we heard that.

The Kid used to follow us around all the time as if he were a pet. And Jackson would get him to bring food from the lunch line or steal pies. Then the Kid quit hanging around like he used to and he started showing up with the chocolate candy every now and then. His mother used to make him wear white shirts and polished shoes, but I guess the dust must have gotten to her, and she gave up. Later, I thought it was the chocolate that made the Kid's snot brown because it didn't used to be when he trailed after us.

"Ichirooo! Ichirooo!" It was Itchy's mother calling him for lunch, so we decided to meet later at the clubhouse. Actually there was no house, just a place by the bridge over the irrigation ditch, on the far edge of the garden, that we had marked with a couple of stolen signs. I was sure Itchy hadn't told us everything; so after he left, Jackson and I made a pact to be sure to get Itchy to spill what he had seen.

The sky was noticeably cloudier after lunch. A gray haze had drifted in front of the sun, but the heat had gotten physical, like a weight around my chest. I heard the shouting while I was eating lunch, and when I came out there was a crowd gathered behind our barrack. The kids were jumping up and down and cheering. The women were shouting and laughing. I looked for Itchy and Jackson but didn't see them, so I squeezed through to see what was going on. My cousin Aya's grandfather was scurrying between the hollyhocks, leaping awkwardly every now and then as if he were stepping on nails. He was a skinny old man whose feet seemed to be moving in two directions at once while his body was heading in a third. His arms, weighted by a heavy, blunt spade, seemed to be confused about moving in a fourth direction. His khaki shirt was open and his ribbed cotton undershirt was stained by sweat and the flying dust. Suddenly a group of women and children along the sidewalk leaped almost in unison. "There he is!" "He's there!" "Get him!" "Kill him!" They were screaming and laughing at the same time and I saw something brown dart past then and head directly toward me. It stopped still for a moment, its eyes wide and staring blankly. It darted sharply to the left and headed straight for the Shoyu Kid, who was standing at the corner of the first barrack. He kicked out with his foot and jumped back at the same time, blinking wildly to keep back his tears, and almost falling over backward. Meantime, Oisan had figured out which direction the animal had gone and took a shortcut across a patch of hollyhocks and sunflowers, leaving them bent and broken. The spade arched over his head and clanged dully as it struck at the furry blur and banged against the base of the barrack instead.

"He's gone underneath!" someone next to me shouted.

"Did you see the size of that rat?"

"Is that what it is?" Jackson shouldered up beside me as everyone spread out and surrounded the barrack.

I tried peering into the hole through which the animal had entered and saw only the faint glow of daylight haloing the inky dark. I wondered how dark and frightening it must be to be trapped underneath a barrack with no way out.

"What are we going to do?"

"Hey, kid, get away from there." Someone was pulling me back.

"We can't just stand around here all day. It's too hot. Besides, at night it'd slip away."

"We've got to kill it."

The voices were insistent. "Kill it. Kill it." The old man looked bewildered. Somehow he had gotten started in a chase that now had ended with a colony of people laughing and rattling the baseboards that both penned and protected the victim. We were a tribe readied for a primitive hunt.

Jackson came up with a solution. "Plug all the holes to the crawl space, Oisan, and then send the weiner dog in."

The old man's face lit up. "And then we can wait for it here at the hole where it entered, eh? Smart boy."

"But Oisan, it's not a rat." It was the Shoyu Kid. "I saw it, Oisan, and it was really scared."

The old man patted the Kid on the head, then wiped his hand unconsciously on his trouser leg. We took the Kid's dog and shoved him under the barrack anyway and waited for some sound or sign of movement. The Kid might have been right. It had been big as a rabbit when it stopped in front of me. After a while, the old man went up and put his eye to the hole, then he went to the crawl-space door and unhooked it. We hung back as if the beast would come charging out. No sign. Not even the dog. A few people started drifting back to their homes, but a sizeable group still crowded around the old man, who hunched there on his heels, holding his spade ready like an executioner's ax. After a while he said, "Maybe it is a jack rabbit and it has a burrow under the barrack." Maybe calling it a jack rabbit was better than believing it was a rat that had just shimmied up into your bedroom.

Jackson tugged at my elbow and motioned to the Shoyu Kid. He was still standing at the corner where the rat had entered the building.

"Let's get him now."

And we casually worked our way over to the Kid.

"Was it a rat, Kid?"

"If it wasn't, what was it, Kid?"

He started to back away from us, but he knew it would be useless to run.

"You got any chocolate, Kid?"

"Hope your dog didn't get lost under there, Kid."

Then Jackson was close enough and was on him and swung him around the corner of the barrack before the Kid could yell and half carried him across the road and to the west side of the garage.

"Jeez, it's hot today." Itchy had seen us and came around the corner complaining.

Jackson smiled his John Wayne smile and took the Kid by the overall straps where the lapels should be and shoved the kid up against the side of the garage. "You'd better shape up and talk, Kid."

The Kid's face was twisted open and the tears were already rolling down his face. He seemed to have stopped breathing.

"Where'd you get your chocolate bars, Kid?"

No answer.

Again. This time I grabbed his other arm and twisted it up behind his back.

"C'mon, Kid, you better talk if you know what's good for you." Jackson's face was dead serious, his eyes narrowed into black flickering jets of hate. "We'll tear you limb from limb if you don't talk, Kid. We know you got them from the soldier, so you may as well speak up." He was the cavalry colonel threatening a turncoat Indian scout; he was a police interrogator breaking a burglar; he was an army intelligence officer ripping into a prisoner of war. His face was impassive. Perfect.

The Kid looked up, then bent his head moaning and sniffling snot, which now was a brown ribbon between his nose and lips.

Jackson took the Kid's other arm and started to give him an Indian burn, rubbing his palms tightly over the Kid's wrists until they turned pink. The Kid started to scream and his body slumped to the dirt so suddenly the arm I held slipped free. But still he hadn't admitted to anything. He was moaning for us to stop. The pain was getting to him. Jackson's face was suddenly animated. He lost his John Wayne pose and was beginning to enjoy his job.

"Listen, Kid," he continued, "we know the soldier gives you candy. We seen you with it every day. Why does he give it to you? C'mon. Speak up. Or we'll take it away from you next time. Every time." Then suddenly he changed his tactic. "You. You're a spy, aren't you, Kid? Admit it. You give the soldier our military secrets."

The Kid started to say something about Mommy, but just then Jackson twisted the wrist again and it was bright red, shining brightly, a blood-red band burning the surrounding grayish flesh of his arm. "We just," the Kid blurted, "we just play games."

The Kid slumped and sobbed great breaths.

"Let's pants him." Jackson reached for the Kid's grimy pants and I flipped open the flaps of the coverall suspenders. Jackson grabbed the cuffs and tugged.

"No." The Kid tried to cover up.

When Jackson tugged again the pants gave way around the Kid's hipless waist and bagged at his knees, the bib still covering him decently. "No," the Kid was saying, "I didn't do anything. I just played with his chimpo like he asked."

Jackson stopped, his mouth dropped open. "You what? You whore! Queer!" He was shouting "Queer! Queer!" and yanking at the pants at the same time and there staring at us with its single eye squinting in Jackson's face was a little white prick like a broken pencil between equally white but shapeless thighs. Jackson was immobilized, his face slack in surprise, and Itchy moved away.

And then Jackson was at him again. "You played with the sonofabitch soldier? Goddamn queer!" and Jackson's hands were fumbling for the Kid's prick and he was pulling as if he were going to pull it off and the Kid was convulsing on the ground, trying to roll away, his face smeared brown. Jackson's face was set, his eyes were distant, as if he were remembering the Kid standing there in front of him in white shirt and short pants, pie in hand, waiting for Jackson to pat him on the head for a job well done, or Jackson remembering how he would give the soldiers the finger as they marched around the fence, how he had made Itchy and me accompany him down to the gate one night to steal the hastily painted government signs. The Kid was a traitor to a lost cause and though he couldn't really blame the Kid, he didn't have to let him do it, either.

"I didn't do nothing, honest. I didn't." But I couldn't tell whether in his convulsions the Kid was crying or laughing.

Jackson stood up abruptly and looked at his hands. He wiped them on his pants. Then we heard it. "Geooooogie. Geooooogie" It was the Kid's mother.

When Jackson looked up, Itchy was already heading down the length of the garage, planning to come out onto the main street from the other end of the building. "You better not say nothing about this or we'll cut it off, Kid." It was pure Bogey. Just then Kraut came barking around the corner and Jackson grabbed my arm and pushed me stumbling after Itchy.

I stopped at the corner of the garage to catch my breath and kicked at the dog. The Kid was pulling up his pants, a lone figure almost as gray as the desert. Far to the west, the land met with a sky that now was even darker, more ominous than nightfall.

We met again after dinner. The sun had gone down, but there was still a strange glow in the horizon that had never before been there. The air had a definite odor to it. Jackson was sitting at the edge of the clubhouse, next to the irrigation ditch, looking out at the strange, lingering sunset. Itchy was off to one side, sitting by himself.

"What do you think it is? The end of the world?"

"Nyaa," said Jackson. "My brother says there's a fire out there."

"I saw it this morning, too. It looked like a sunrise when I got up to pee. But I knew the sun never comes up from over there."

"It's a fire, Itchy." Jackson's voice was soft, tired. "And they're fighting it out there. My brother went out this afternoon with a group of fathers to help. It'll be out pretty soon."

We sat there in silence and watched it glowing red, an ember that seemed to burn without flickering, without warmth.

Jackson was rubbing his palms into the dirt.

"Jeez." Itchy was talking more to himself than to Jackson or me. "I thought the guy was just taking a leak behind the garage. Goddam queers. Jeezus, everyone's queer." He stood up and threw a rock at the Off Limits sign we had taken. And missed. He picked up another and missed again. "Do you think the Kid will squeal?"

"Nyaa. Who cares." Jackson's voice was quiet, almost a curse. He threw a stone at the other sign. It hit the wood above the words MINIDOKA RELOCATION CENTER. Jackson continued to stare at the red glow, his face pale in the spotlight from the fence a hundred yards off. He was sitting very still, and his eyes were soft and wide like a rabbit's.

Hiroshi Kashiwagi

(1922–   )

Hiroshi Kashiwagi was born in Sacramento, California, and raised in the intellectual resonance of Berkeley, California, when it was tweedy with leather patches on the elbows. Kashiwagi is a quiet, soft-spoken librarian with a taste for the classics. One is not surprised at the quiet ordinariness of the tone, characters, and subjects of his light comedies of Nikkei manners. What is surprising is the boiling anger, the working bitterness that forms the bed of all that seems lighthearted and comical about life in the camps of his plays.

The ethnical and moral corruption of the Nisei is so common and accepted as a fact of life in the concentration camps that having to pay bribes and be victimized by fellow "pariah" internees arouses no hard feelings. Hard stuff for a light comedy, but a light comedy of manners is what Kashiwagi's one-act play, *Laughter and False Teeth,* pretends to be.

Kashiwagi's concentration camp is populated by a people in a state of moral deterioration. Self-pity and self-contempt are the perverse life blood of the place. Everyone steals. Everyone bribes. In *Laughter and False Teeth*, the Nisei dentist refuses to do even inadequate work without a bribe. The comedy and gentle veneer soften the edges and points of a very grim vision of Nisei camp reality. Kashiwagi states the intent and effect of his play through the voice of a character called the Boiler Man:

> I suppose they have to laugh. It may seem abnormal, but we have an abnormal situation here. Sixteen thousand Japanese living in this camp, which is actually a prison. So we have to laugh in order to sustain ourselves, to keep alive our hopes that some day we'll be free again, and back to normal. But oh the price we pay to laugh, the price we pay.

Hiroshi Kashiwagi is the only Japanese American writer to write beyond the stereotype of the Japanese American internee as helpless, innocent victim and to explore the dark side of Japanese

America. *Laughter and False Teeth* is the first exploration of the moral ramifications of the Nikkei acceptance of betrayal. In the camp universe, the fact that all have been betrayed leads inexorably to one individual's betrayal of another, until everyone is a traitor and everyone is betrayed.

Laughter and False Teeth

(A play in four scenes)

CHARACTERS

MADAME, an attractive woman, except for her missing teeth, in her late thirties.

BOILER MAN, a determined man, forty-five, whose purpose is to keep the furnace going

FIRST BOY, a boy of thirteen

YOSHIO, an earnest, slender boy of fourteen

OFFSTAGE FEMALE VOICE, strident and demanding

CHORUS, four women, three of whom double as PATIENTS A, B, C (in their thirties and forties)

WINE-WOMAN, a woman in her fifties, beyond caring about her appearance

TOJO, a slender, proud man with a fierce mustache

MP, a man who could be from the South

OFFSTAGE VOICE, an official

FOUR DANCERS, two couples in their late teens and early twenties

SECRETARY, at the clinic, dressed in a white uniform

MR. WINE-WOMAN, a philosophic, somewhat eccentric man in his late fifties

JANITOR, at the clinic, a slow, methodic mopper

DENTIST YOKOMICHI, a camp dentist who won't do even substandard work without a bribe.

PLACE: Wartime camp for Japanese, USA
TIME: World War II, winter

Scene 1

After dark

On rise of curtain MADAME *is seated on a chair at center. At down-stage left* BOILER MAN *is shoveling coal into a furnace. Along stage right is a row of chairs. Chorus of laughter is heard offstage and two boys, both about fourteen, enter.*

YOSHIO (*screaming and chasing* FIRST BOY). I'll kill you! I'll kill you!

(*They run around at center;* BOILER MAN *rushes over and stops* YOSHIO, *who struggles.*)

YOSHIO. Let me go. I want to kill him.

FIRST BOY (*going off to stage right*). Yoshio's mother is crazy. Yoshio's mother is cra-zy. (*He exits; laughter is heard offstage.*)

(*YOSHIO tries to break free.*)

BOILER MAN. Stop it, boy. There's no need for killing here. Stop it, I say.

(*YOSHIO finally stops;* BOILER MAN *brings him downstage left.*)

YOSHIO. Do you think my mother is crazy?

BOILER MAN. No.

YOSHIO. I know she acts funny. She walks around holding a handkerchief in front of her and spends all her time in the laundry room washing the handkerchief. Oh sometimes I wish she weren't my—

BOILER MAN. No, Yoshio, you mustn't say that; you mustn't ever say that.

YOSHIO. But why won't she talk? She just looks and looks at me and won't say anything.

BOILER MAN. Your mother is a fine woman.

YOSHIO. They say she got that way after I was born. But she used to talk. I remember she used to scold my brother when he made me cry.

BOILER MAN. When did your mother stop talking?

YOSHIO. It was after Pearl Harbor when the FBI took away my father. He was feeding the chickens when they came for him. My mother shouted and screamed and wouldn't stop. Papa barely had time to pack a few things in his suitcase, and there was Mama screaming all the while, so finally my brother had to hit her to make her stop. Oh it was terrible.

BOILER MAN (*gently*). How's your brother in the army?

YOSHIO. Oh he's fine. He writes us every week.

BOILER MAN. What does he say?

YOSHIO. He's in the mountains somewhere in Italy; it's winter there and very cold. He always talks about back home in Whittier and the chicken ranch.

BOILER MAN. The war will be over soon, and you'll all be together again in Whittier.

YOSHIO. Do you think so? (*BOILER MAN nods.*) Boy, I can hardly wait to get home. My brother will be home from the war, and my father will be released from Santa Fe, and mother and I will be there to meet them.

BOILER MAN. You're lucky to have a home to go back to.

YOSHIO. Don't you have a home, Boiler Man?

BOILER MAN. No.

YOSHIO. Oh . . . then why don't you come with us; we have lots of room; we have a big house, and you can help us on the chicken ranch. Promise you'll come with us, Boiler Man.

BOILER MAN. Thank you, Yoshio. I promise, but I hope I can live that long. This work is strenuous for an old man, and I'm getting tired.

OFFSTAGE FEMALE VOICE. The water's cold, Boiler Man; we want some hot water. Hurry up with the hot water.

BOILER MAN. You see, this keeps up day and night.

YOSHIO. I'll get the coal. Boiler Man, why don't you let somebody else do this work? (*Shoveling coal.*)

BOILER MAN. Nobody wants the job; it's too menial and dirty.

YOSHIO (*thoughtfully*). Do you think my mother will talk again?

BOILER MAN. Of course she'll talk again.

(*YOSHIO continues to shovel coal into the furnace; a CHORUS comes in laughing and dances around MADAME. As the CHORUS goes over to the chairs, stage right, MADAME stands and raises her arm as if imploring them to stay. She drops her arm, moans.*)

YOSHIO. Why are they laughing?

BOILER MAN. I suppose they have to laugh. It may seem abnormal, but we have an abnormal situation here. Sixteen thousand Japanese living in this camp, which is actually a prison. So we have to laugh in order to sustain ourselves, to keep alive our hopes that some day we'll be free again, and back to normal. But oh the price we pay to laugh, the price we pay.

YOSHIO. But why are they laughing at Madame?

BOILER MAN. Because she's afraid to laugh. I know she wants to laugh. I've tried to explain to her but I've failed. I'm afraid I've had no experience with beautiful women.

WINE-WOMAN (*comes in running*). Boiler Man, Boiler Man, **BOILER MAN!**

BOILER MAN. What is it, Wine-Woman?

WINE-WOMAN. Have you seen Madame lately?

BOILER MAN. For the last time, no I have not seen Madame lately.

WINE-WOMAN (*in a gentler tone*). Tell me, Boiler Man, what's wrong with Madame?

BOILER MAN. I don't know.

WINE-WOMAN (*in a gentler tone*). Tell me, Boiler Man, what's wrong with Madame?

BOILER MAN. I don't know.

WINE-WOMAN. Ah surely, Boiler Man, you must know. They told me you were quite a wise man. Huh! (*She turns away.*) I haven't seen Madame in two months; I wonder if she's ill.

BOILER MAN. Don't tell me you're concerned about her.

WINE-WOMAN. Of course I'm concerned about her. Why else would I be asking?

BOILER MAN. You could be curious.

WINE-WOMAN. I wouldn't bother myself with you except that I want to help Madame.

BOILER MAN. You help Madame . . . ha ha hhh

WINE-WOMAN. What's so funny?

BOILER MAN. You and your wine.

WINE-WOMAN. What's wrong with my wine?

BOILER MAN. I know, I know. It's the best wine in camp. But it's the only wine I know that costs two dollars a pint.

WINE-WOMAN. It's cheap enough, and people are willing to pay; it's really a bargain for all the happiness it brings.

BOILER MAN. Men getting drunk and making fools of themselves in front of women and children, you call that happiness? No, Wine-Woman, with or without your wine, you couldn't help Madame.

WINE-WOMAN. Why don't you open your eyes and find out where you are?

BOILER MAN. I know where I am. Look up there. See those searchlights from the tower? They follow you around every corner.

WINE-WOMAN. I know we're in jail, and who knows for how long we'll be here. Probably for the duration of the war. But the time I spend here is still part of my life, and I'm not going to throw it away. Life's too precious. I'm going to live it—every minute of it. Did you hear me? I said I'm going to live it.

BOILER MAN. I heard you. But the police . . .

WINE-WOMAN. Oh the police—they are no happier than we are. They are here because they were sent here. They like it better when they have something to do.

BOILER MAN. Thanks to you they're kept busy every night.

WINE-WOMAN. I always forget you're not a drinking man. There's something rigid about a teetotaler. You know, I worry about you. I think you need a healthy slug of wine. Here—take some—

BOILER MAN. Take that vile thing away.

WINE-WOMAN. What can we expect of a boiler man, a dirty old janitor cleaning up after—

BOILER MAN. Your mess.

WINE-WOMAN. I believe you're proud of your job. Oh well, someone has to clean up. It might as well be someone who enjoys doing it. (*Starts to go, then stops in front of* MADAME'*s apartment, suddenly.*) Does Madame ever take a shower? (*Sniffing.*) She must be filthy; why, she's a disgrace to our block.

BOILER MAN. And what about you?

WINE-WOMAN. I'm Japanese; I believe in cleanliness and I take a shower every day.

BOILER MAN. You need it, Wine-Woman.

WINE-WOMAN (*walking deliberately down to* BOILER MAN). We know something about you, Boiler Man.

BOILER MAN. Go ahead, say it.

WINE-WOMAN. All the women are saying it.

BOILER MAN. They're full of gossip.

WINE-WOMAN. Oh such evil you hide behind your righteousness.

BOILER MAN. Evil? What do you mean?

WINE-WOMAN (*giggly and delaying*). Whenever the women are in the shower room taking a shower—you know, soaping themselves, making themselves clean and beautiful—they feel someone watching them.

BOILER MAN. Why, I never heard anything so cheap. (BOILER MAN *shakes his stoking iron, and* WINE-WOMAN *jumps back in glee*). Get back to your stinking wine cellar where you belong. Go! Go!

(*He chases her off;* WINE-WOMAN *runs laughing and clapping her hands. Then the* CHORUS *is heard laughing and clapping offstage.* BOILER MAN *comes back breathing hard.*)

YOSHIO. Are you all right, Boiler Man?

BOILER MAN. Oh, I forgot that you were still here. You better get home now; it's late.

(YOSHIO *exits;* BOILER MAN *looks to make sure no one is around then goes to* MADAME'*s apartment and knocks;* MADAME, *who was half asleep, suddenly comes to life.*)

BOILER MAN. Madame, Madame. Would you like to take a shower tonight?

MADAME (*runs to the door; opens it a bit*). Is it all right? I thought I heard some voices.

BOILER MAN. I just chased her away.

MADAME. Was she talking about me?

BOILER MAN. Oh, no. She was just carrying on about things in general. Madame, the water's good and hot if you care to—

(*TOJO, in white trousers and black mackinaw, comes running in. He makes several turns onstage and then runs toward the women's room.*)

BOILER MAN. (*closes MADAME's door and runs out in front of TOJO*). Wait! You can't go in there. Madame is going to taker her shower.

TOJO (*trying to push BOILER MAN aside*). I don't care who's taking a shower. I want to get in.

BOILER MAN. But this is a women's room, and you're a man.

TOJO. That's exactly why I want to go in. The police are after me.

BOILER MAN. The police? Just what've you been doing after curfew?

TOJO. There's no time for explanations. They'll be here any minute.

BOILER MAN. No, you hide in the men's room.

TOJO. All right, I'll tell you. I was working late at the hospital and I forgot about the curfew. On my way home the police saw me and started to chase me.

BOILER MAN. A likely story; I believe every word of it. Who are you anyway?

TOJO. You're worse than the police. (*Loudly.*) They call me Mr. Tojo.

BOILER MAN. Tojo? I mean Mr. Tojo. Why didn't you say so in the first place. By all means, Mr. Tojo. (*BOILER MAN opens the door for TOJO; TOJO goes in; BOILER MAN takes a deep breath, sighs; at stage right an MP appears.*)

MP. Did you see a man come running by here?

BOILER MAN (*in Issei accent*). Man? Ohhh. He have white pants?

MP. Yeah, that's him.

BOILER MAN. Yes, yes, I see. He Mr. Tojo.

MP. Who?

BOILER MAN. Mr. Tojo.

MP. That's what I thought you said. Mr. Tojo, heh? (*bursts out laughing*) Which way did he go?

BOILER MAN. Go? Oh yes, yes. (*motioning to MP while going upstage*) Come this way. He go over there, way over there.

MP. You sure?

BOILER MAN. Yes sah, Captain sah!

MP. Okay, ole man. (*smiles*) Mr. Tojo, heh? (*exits laughing*)

BOILER MAN (*after making sure MP has gone, opens door to women's room*). Mr. Tojo, the policeman has gone. You can come out now.

TOJO. Can't I stay in her while Madame takes her shower.

BOILER MAN. No, no, Mr. Tojo. Please!

TOJO. I won't make myself conspicuous; I'll stay behind this partition, and she'll never know I'm here.

BOILER MAN. If the police ever found out I lied, they will take me in. Please, Mr. Tojo.

TOJO. Oh come, Boiler Man, don't be so timid.

BOILER MAN. Hear me, Mr. Tojo. I'm all alone in this world but I'm happy because I have a purpose in life.

TOJO. And what is your purpose?

BOILER MAN. I keep the boiler going so people can bathe.

TOJO. Your purpose is to keep the boiler going so people can bathe?

BOILER MAN. Yes, and stay clean.

TOJO. How very noble.

BOILER MAN. Please don't mock, Mr. Tojo. It's not as simple as you think. There's so much dust here that people must bathe every day—sometimes twice a day, and if the water's cold they scream at me. Just a boiler man but—

TOJO. Enough of that woman talk. (*comes out*) But tell me, who is this Madame who takes a shower at this time of night?

BOILER MAN. Madame . . .

TOJO. Well?

BOILER MAN. Madame is a widow.

TOJO. Yes, go on.

BOILER MAN. A beautiful woman.

TOJO. A widow and beautiful! This is very good, very excellent good.

BOILER MAN. But I'm afraid she is very unhappy.

TOJO. A beautiful widow unhappy? Hmmm. Interesting. We must do something about that.

BOILER MAN. No, there's nothing you can do—I mean—

TOJO. You mean there's nothing I cannot do, especially where beautiful, unhappy widows are concerned.

BOILER MAN. Yes, Mr. Tojo. I meant there's nothing you can do tonight. It's much too late, and besides, the police may come again.

TOJO. The police have been here . . . now's the best time for making whoopee . . .

BOILER MAN. Please, Mr. Tojo, won't you go now?

TOJO. All right, if you insist, but I want to meet this—Madame someday.

BOILER MAN. Yes, of course, Mr. Tojo, someday.

(*TOJO starts upstage, and BOILER MAN stops him.*) No no, not that way. This way. Good-bye Mr. Tojo. (*runs to* MADAME's *door*) Madame, Madame.

MADAME. (*coming to the door*). Yes.

BOILER MAN. I'm sorry to bother you again, but I'm sure there won't be any more interruptions.

MADAME. Who was that man going into the women's room?

BOILER MAN. A strange man I couldn't understand at all. He kept insisting that it was all right for him to go in the women's room.

MADAME. Did you stop him?

BOILER MAN. Yes. After a struggle I managed to send him on his way. Oh, Madame, the water is still hot if you—

MADAME. No thank you, Boiler Man. Some other time.

BOILER MAN (*turns to go*). Yes.

MADAME. Boiler Man, you're the only friend I have.

BOILER MAN. I'm proud to be your friend.

MADAME. You're more than kind.

BOILER MAN. I'm an old man, Madame, and I only want to help you. (*pauses, somewhat awkwardly*) I hope you won't think me a meddler if I told you that I—

MADAME. What is it, Boiler Man?

BOILER MAN. It wasn't difficult for me to see why you were unhappy, so I arranged an appointment with the dentist—

MADAME. Dentist!

BOILER MAN. You don't have to keep the appointment, but I thought—

MADAME. No, I can't; I can't bare to look at another dentist.

BOILER MAN. But you are so unhappy, Madame, and—

MADAME. Please cancel the appointment.

BOILER MAN. Very well, I shall call Yokomichi in the morning.

MADAME. Yokomichi? Not the Dentist Yokomichi?

BOILER MAN. Do you know him?

MADAME. How well I know him. But I don't understand. I thought he was in the army. He told me a year ago in San Francisco that he was going to be a lieutenant in the United States Army. I remember he said it very proudly.

BOILER MAN. Apparently he wasn't accepted by the army.

MADAME. He wasn't accepted by the army; well, that proves he's a beast.

BOILER MAN. All dentists are beasts once they peer into your mouth. But if you already know this Yokomichi, it will be that much easier.

MADAME. I'm afraid you don't know Dentist Yokomichi as well as I do. Why, he was in such a hurry to become a lieutenant that he extracted all my teeth in one afternoon and bled me half to death.

BOILER MAN. I'm sorry to hear that. But how could he hurt you now, even Yokomichi? Madame, you haven't any teeth left. I mean . . .

MADAME (*brings hand over mouth*). Ohh . . .

BOILER MAN. I'm sorry, I didn't mean . . .

MADAME (*stopping him, just above a whisper*). You are right. I haven't any teeth and he can't hurt me anymore. Of course.

BOILER MAN. Then you will keep the appointment? (*MADAME looks at BOILER MAN and nods quickly.*) Everything will be all right after tomorrow.

MADAME. Yes, after tomorrow.

(*MADAME closes the door; BOILER MAN, smiling, comes downstage and sits on chair.*)

(*Lights dim*)

Scene 2

The following morning

Slow lights and sound of loud mess-hall bell. BOILER MAN is in boiler room. MADAME has just finished dressing. Adjusting her veil, she comes to the door.

MADAME. Boiler Man, is it all right?

BOILER MAN. The regulars have all gone to the mess hall, and we don't have to worry about the rest; they never get up for breakfast. But hurry, Madame.

MADAME. Please show me the way to the clinic.

BOILER MAN. You take this road as far as the canteen; then turn left and cross the firebreak and you'll come to the green barracks. That's the clinic. You can't miss it. Good luck, Madame. (*MADAME starts outside, then stops.*) What's the matter, Madame?

MADAME. I can't.

BOILER MAN. You aren't afraid, are you? (*MADAME nods slowly.*) Courage, Madame. Remember, it takes courage to live.

MADAME. Yes, you are right, you are always so right.

BOILER MAN. Not always, Madame, but I try.

(*MADAME leaves; she walks about the stage and finally stops in front of the CHORUS, who are dental patients waiting in the hallway of the clinic.*)

MADAME. Is this the dental clinic? (*CHORUS nods, holding swollen cheeks.*) But why are you carrying packages? (*CHORUS points to cheeks; shakes hands in front of faces.*)

(*MADAME sits in last chair; SECRETARY walks in from stage left; MADAME rises; both exchange greetings; CHORUS remains silent.*)

SECRETARY. The doctor will be here shortly. (*She sits on chair upstage; DENTIST strides in from stage left; CHORUS jumps to feet and bows.*)

CHORUS. Good morning, Dr. Yokomichi.

(*DENTIST glares at CHORUS and goes inside.*)

SECRETARY. Good morning, Doctor.

DENTIST. All right, I'm ready.

(*SECRETARY comes to hall and motions to PATIENT A, who jumps up and goes inside.*)

PATIENT A. The doctor told me it was my teeth.

DENTIST. Never mind the talk, just sit down. (*PATIENT A sits on high stool; DENTIST looks into her mouth.*) There's nothing wrong with your teeth.

PATIENT A. But the doctor said it was my teeth.

DENTIST. What doctor?

PATIENT A. It was Dr. . . . I forgot his name. He examined my ear.

DENTIST. Your ear?

DENTIST. You go back and tell your ear doctor there's nothing the matter with your teeth. (*Whisks PATIENT off chair.*)

PATIENT A. But Doctor, I had a toothache all last night.

DENTIST. You must have dreamt it. (*Loudly.*) Next!

(*PATIENT A leaves sadly.*)

PATIENT B (*with a large package*). Doctor Yokomichi, I hear you are leaving for the army soon.

DENTIST (*brightly*). Yes. Of course, it isn't definite yet, but I should know in two weeks.

PATIENT B. We'll certainly miss you, Doctor.

DENTIST. Thank you. But my duty as a good American comes first.

PATIENT B. Yes, of course. Will you be an officer?

DENTIST (*beaming*). I shall be a lieutenant.

PATIENT B. That sounds very important.

DENTIST. It's what I've waited for for a long time—lieutenant in the United States Army. (*Carried away for a moment.*) Lieutenant Eizo Yokomichi. No. I think I'll use my American name—Lieutenant Ace Yokomichi! (*Faintly the playing of Taps is heard.*)

PATIENT B. Oh, Lieutenant, I mean, Dr. Yokomichi, I brought you something. It's a very humble thing, please take it.

(*DENTIST pulled back from his fantasy, takes the package.*)

PATIENT B. A side meat of pork.

DENTIST. A side meat of pork! Oh, but I can't take this.

PATIENT B. Please, Doctor. I brought it for you.

DENTIST. Very well. (*To SECRETARY.*) Will you put this away—someplace where it'll be safe. (*Helping PATIENT B to chair.*) Tell me, lady, how did you ever get hold of the pork?

PATIENT B. Oh, my son-in-law works at the hog farm.

DENTIST. Oh, I see. You must have a fine daughter to have such a resourceful son-in-law. (*PATIENT B giggles.*) Now let's see what we can do for you. Oh, oh, we'll have to pull this one out. It might hurt a bit, lady. Hold on now.

PATIENT B (*with mouth wide open*). I will, Doctor.

(*DENTIST yanks out tooth; PATIENT B jumps out of the chair, washes out her mouth a few times, bows several times, and goes out holding her hand over her mouth.*)

DENTIST. Next.

PATIENT C. I couldn't help overhearing, Doctor. Are you really going to be a captain?

DENTIST. No, a lieutenant.

PATIENT C. Oh, is that better?

DENTIST. It's a rank lower than a captain.

PATIENT C. I must confess I'm very ignorant about these things. Oh Doctor, this is a very humble thing, but please take it. (*hands package.*)

DENTIST. What is it, may I ask?

PATIENT C. It's a sack of sugar.

DENTIST. Sugar! But I can't take all this sugar.

PATIENT C. Please take it, Doctor. You'll make me very happy.

DENTIST. Well, this is my lucky day. (*To SECRETARY.*) Will you put this away in my locker? How did you manage to get so much sugar?

PATIENT C. Oh, I work in the mess hall.

DENTIST. In the mess hall? How interesting.

PATIENT C. I borrowed it, so to speak, a little at a time whenever the chef was busy boasting about his cooking.

DENTIST. Ah, clever woman. Now this may hurt a little. I'll try to be as gentle as possible. Are you brave, lady?

PATIENT C. I think so.

(*DENTIST yanks out tooth; PATIENT C, after rinsing out her mouth, bows several times and goes out.*)

DENTIST. NEXT!

MADAME. I'm sorry I didn't know you were going away to the army. I thought you were a lieutenant long ago. You told me so when you extracted my tooth.

DENTIST. Who are you?

MADAME. My name is Madame.

DENTIST. You put on some weight. (*Lifts her veil.*)

MADAME. Then you do remember me.

DENTIST. You look well enough. What do you want?

MADAME. Doctor, I wondered if . . . that is . . .

DENTIST. Well, what is it?

MADAME. I haven't any teeth and I would like a set of false teeth.

DENTIST. A set of false teeth. Of course, why couldn't I think of that before? Just leave your name with the secretary.

MADAME. Then you will make my denture.

DENTIST. Lady, in two weeks I expect to be in the army so I can't make you any promises right now.

MADAME. But Dr. Yokomichi, couldn't you make it before you go in the army?

DENTIST. No, I'm sorry. Now if you don't mind, I have other patients waiting. NEXT!

(*It takes a while for* MADAME *to understand; then, humiliated, she hurries out; as* MADAME *comes back to her apartment the* BOILER MAN *runs to her, but* MADAME *ignores him and hurries inside. She takes a dark blanket and covers herself.* BOILER MAN *turns away sadly;* WINE-WOMAN *enters.*)

WINE-WOMAN. Hello, Boiler Man. What's the matter?

BOILER MAN. Go and sell you wine.

WINE-WOMAN. I believe there's something really wrong. I've never seen you look so miserable. Have a sip of my newest wine; it will kill whatever that's ailing you. Here.

BOILER MAN. The vile thing will kill me. (*Grabs bottle and hurls it on coal pile.*)

WINE-WOMAN. Oh my wine, my newest wine. I try to be kind with you, and this is how you thank me.

BOILER MAN (*recovering self*). I'm sorry, Wine-Woman. I was out of my mind. I too tried to help someone this morning and failed.

WINE-WOMAN. Who did you try to help? Could it be Madame? Ah, yes. (*Runs over to apartment.*)

BOILER MAN. Come back, Wine-Woman!

(WINE-WOMAN *breaks into* MADAME'S *apartment startles her;* WINE-WOMAN *screams, seeing figure in dark covering move; she tries to go.*)

MADAME (*within cover*). Wait, please don't go. (WINE-WOMAN *trembles.*)

WINE-WOMAN. Is it really you, Madame? (MADAME *nods.*) Then please come out of there. I feel so funny talking to you like that. It's like talking to the dead. (MADAME *moans.*) Can you hear me? Are you all right, Madame?

MADAME. I don't know.

WINE-WOMAN. Do you have a headache?

MADAME. No.

WINE-WOMAN. Then you are not ill, and I'm glad of that. Perhaps you are unhappy. Arc you unhappy, Madame?

MADAME. Yes, very unhappy.

WINE-WOMAN. We can all be unhappy. Now look at me. Oh I forgot you cannot see me. I wish you would take that off. I'm an old wine-woman now, but do you know that back in Portland I used to grow roses in my garden—can you picture me—a lady with prize-winning roses while my good-for-nothing was a million-dollar insurance man?

MADAME. Then why are you the wine-woman now?

WINE-WOMAN. Because my husband is a good-for-nothing. Do you know it's the first time in thirty years I've seen him really happy? You won't believe this, but he has discovered a talent for music in his old age. He plays every day. Between his flute and my wine, we are driving the neighbors crazy. Having come from a long line of wine drinkers, I also know the secret of good wine. But the real reason is for this. (*Grabs her money belt.*) I forgot again you cannot see. (*Whispering.*) It's money.

MADAME. Isn't that dangerous, making and selling wine? Suppose the police catch you.

WINE-WOMAN. Not a chance. The police are very stupid and very understanding. Do you know that more and more men are caught wandering after curfew and taken to jail? (*Laughs.*)

MADAME. Don't you care?

WINE-WOMAN. If I cared, I would be like you with a blanket over my head, pretending to be dead.

MADAME. Ohhh . . .

WINE-WOMAN. I'm sorry, Madame, but that's what I mean. If I cared, I would be unhappy, so why should I care? (*laughs again.*) Why don't you laugh, Madame?

MADAME. Can't you see why I can't? (*Throws off the blanket, startling* WINE-WOMAN.)

(*WINE-WOMAN studies* MADAME, *looks puzzled.*)

MADAME. (pointing to her open mouth) Look!

WINE-WOMAN (*claps and laughs*). But did you expect an ugly, old one like me to notice? And what have you done about it?

MADAME. This morning I went to see the dentist.

WINE-WOMAN. Not Yokomichi.

MADAME. Yes. It seems that every time I go see Dentist Yokomichi, he's going into the army.

WINE-WOMAN. Then you're an old patient of his?

MADAME. Yes.

WINE-WOMAN. And he wouldn't make your teeth?

MADAME. He couldn't make any promises.

WINE-WOMAN. Why, he should be batted over the head.

MADAME. Yes, that's right. No. I mustn't even think it. I suppose I should resign myself to being a toothless old hag.

WINE-WOMAN. What are you saying, Madame? Even if you said that about me, I'd put up a fight. A toothless old hag indeed!

MADAME. But what is there to do?

WINE-WOMAN. Tojo! Have you seen Tojo?

MADAME. Who is Tojo?

WINE-WOMAN. He claims to be a great leader of men, which he is, and a gentleman, which I doubt. He still owes me money for the wine. Just because he has a big mustache and people call him "Mr. Tojo" he thinks I should keep him supplied with wine.

MADAME. Is he a dentist?

WINE-WOMAN. He is everything he wants to be. Right now he works at the laboratory, and I must say he makes beautiful teeth.

MADAME (*excited*). Do you suppose he will make mine?

WINE-WOMAN. Of course he will make yours, but it will take this. (*Grabs money belt.*)

MADAME. Money?

WINE-WOMAN. What else?

MADAME (*thinks a moment*). I have money.

WINE-WOMAN. Then there's nothing to worry about. I will bring Tojo right away. I know he's at home expecting a delivery of wine. Well, just this once I'll take him some and bring him here.

MADAME. Thank you, Wine-Woman; you are very kind.

WINE-WOMAN. Don't thank me, Madame. Remember, I don't care. (*Exits laughing.*)

MR. WINE-WOMAN (*enters from stage right*). Oh there you are, Boiler Man, busy as always. Why do you work so hard? But I suppose you can't help it. To some men a job becomes his life, and I'm afraid you are one of those unfortunate ones. You know, Boiler Man, I'm starting a campaign.

BOILER MAN. A campaign.

MR. WINE-WOMAN. Yes, a campaign to save you.

BOILER MAN. All right, all right. That's enough.

MR. WINE-WOMAN. Listen, this is good, I just thought of it. It will be a campaign to limit our shower-takings to once a week. Of course, this will only apply to the men as nothing is more offensive than a smelly woman. But just think if all the males in this block took one shower a week, won't that give you time to rest? And you, if no one else, deserve a rest. Why, you're the hardest-working boiler man in this block.

BOILER MAN. I'm the only boiler man in this block.

MR. WINE-WOMAN. Then you're the hardest-working boiler man in this whole camp.

BOILER MAN. If you're leading up to something—I can't loan you money. You still owe me ten from last week.

MR. WINE-WOMAN. You didn't tell the old bag?

BOILER MAN. I made a promise once—

MR. WINE-WOMAN. I trust you completely, Boiler Man. Why, even if I were selling insurance again I wouldn't sell one to you. For the life of me I couldn't mention dying to you. I couldn't see you dying. You should live on and on forever.

BOILER MAN. I still can't loan you any money.

MR. WINE-WOMAN. Who mentioned money? I came looking for the old bag. Have you seen her around?

BOILER MAN. Yes, I saw her going in there a while ago. (*MR. WINE-WOMAN starts for apartment.*) You can't go in there.

MR. WINE-WOMAN. Why not? I'm looking for my wife. (*BOILER MAN shrugs, lets him go; MR. WINE-WOMAN knocks, and MADAME opens the door.*) Just let me in, and I'll drag that old bag away from you.

MADAME. If you are talking of the Wine-Woman, she left a few minutes ago.

MR. WINE-WOMAN. Then I'm too late.

MADAME. Are you—

MR. WINE-WOMAN. Yes, I'm the good-for-nothing.

MADAME. Please come in and play something for me.

MR. WINE-WOMAN. So she has told you all about me. Sometimes I believe the old one is rather fond of me. Of course I'll play for you.

MADAME. Do you have your instrument with you?

MR. WINE-WOMAN. Oh, yes, right here in my pocket. Always where it's handy and convenient. I hope you're not particular because I just know one song and that's a short one. It took me months to learn to play it properly, but that's not so bad, considering it took thirty years to discover this talent. (*Makes a false start.*) Did you know I have another talent, one I also discovered in my old age?

MADAME. No.

MR. WINE-WOMAN. Good. The old bag doesn't know yet.

MADAME. What is the other talent?

MR. WINE-WOMAN. That is a secret. But first the song you wanted me to play. (*Plays on flute; music is high, shrill, tender, and understanding.*)

MADAME. It's beautiful. It's sad and faraway and beautiful.

MR. WINE-WOMAN. It's not sad and faraway. It's supposed to be happy and full of life. (*He gets up to do a little dance, but MADAME doesn't notice.*) You don't understand.

MADAME. It's sad and faraway. It almost made me remember the days of my childhood in Japan.

MR. WINE-WOMAN. It's no use. I admit it is only a cry of an old man, shrill and weak, trying to call back all the foolish years. You see, for thirty years I depended on other people's fears. My success depended on their fear of insecurity, and I had a million clever ways to feed this fear and make it big. But now this fear . . . (*He picks up flute and plays; music is very sad, very lonely; he stops suddenly.*)

MADAME. You haven't told me the secret. What about your other talent?

MR. WINE-WOMAN (*brightly*). Oh yes. It's not really a talent because I'm a very poor gambler, but I play as recklessly as I please. Already I've lost all my savings, but I still play with any money I can get my hands on. The good old bag . . .

MADAME. But how can you? She wears her money belt next to her skin.

MR. WINE-WOMAN. Remember, all this is secret. When the old bag goes to bed she never wears a thing, not a stitch.

MADAME. How Western of her.

MR. WINE-WOMAN. You mean, how considerate of her.

MADAME. And doesn't she miss the money?

MR. WINE-WOMAN. She's too busy making the money that she doesn't care what happens to it—that is, she doesn't know yet. (*Begins to look at* MADAME.)

MADAME. Why are you looking at me like that? (*Brings hand over her mouth.*)

MR. WINE-WOMAN (*laughs*). You have no teeth.

MADAME. Please.

MR. WINE-WOMAN. Everybody laughs at me. The fool is taking music lessons in his old age, they say.

MADAME. I will be laughing with you soon because your wife is bringing Mr. Tojo here. She has been very kind.

MR. WINE-WOMAN. Kind, you say? Well, you'll be paying dearly for this kindness. I better go before they come. I don't want to be here when Mr. Tojo arrives.

MADAME. Why do you say that?

MR. WINE-WOMAN. Because he gambles with his mustache. Even when I know I have a good hand, across the table I see this mustache—big and black—and I forget my hand and make foolish blunders. I don't like that mustache.

MADAME. Is it so frightening?

MR. WINE-WOMAN. It just makes me nervous.

MADAME. Thank you for playing me your song, Mr. . . . . ?

MR. WINE-WOMAN. Wine-Woman, Mr. Wine-Woman, that's my name. (*Leaves.*)

(*MADAME* walks around room humming the song softly.)

BOILER MAN. I see you had some visitors.

MADAME. It has been wonderful. Two visitors and more coming.

BOILER MAN. What did that good-for-nothing say to you?

MADAME. He just played me a song on his flute. It was beautiful, so sad and faraway.

BOILER MAN. And what about that old woman? What did that vile one have to say?

MADAME. She's not vile; she's very kind. She's bringing Mr. Tojo here.

BOILER MAN. So that's it. Oh Madame, is this really what you want?

MADAME. I want to laugh, Boiler Man. Laugh like the rest of the people.

BOILER MAN. Yes, you want to laugh like the rest of the people. (*Walks away weakly.*)

MADAME. Boiler Man, you're my friend, please say I'm doing right. Please say it. Please—

YOSHIO (*enters*). What's the matter, Boiler Man? Are you ill? Here, let me help you.

BOILER MAN. Thank you, Yoshio. It's getting to be too much for me, and I'm tired. (*YOSHIO throws coal into furnace.*)

YOSHIO. Look, here comes Wine-Woman with Mr. Tojo. (*He starts to go.*)

BOILER MAN (*calling*). Yoshio, don't go yet. Before it's too late, make me a promise. If anything should happen to me, promise that you'll take over my job and tend the boiler.

YOSHIO. Yes, Boiler Man, I promise, but why?

(*Laughter is heard offstage.*)

WINE-WOMAN. Get back to your apartments and humor your husbands before they think of some mischief.

(*MADAME, hearing a knock at the door, jumps; takes step, hesitates, finally opens the door.*)

TOJO. I'm what they call Tojo. I heard from the Wine-Woman.

MADAME. Please come in. The Wine-Woman talked much of you too, Mr. Tojo.

TOJO. She did? I wouldn't trust everything she says. She has a weak mind.

MADAME. But she's very kind.

(*WINE-WOMAN returns, listens to the conversation.*)

TOJO. Oh anyone can be kind. Now let's have a look at those jaws. Hmm, the gums are good and firm . . . fine jaw. (*Outside,*

WINE-WOMAN *nods approval;* MADAME *stands, turns around, goes to her purse;* TOJO *studies her.*) Very attractive . . . jaw.

MADAME. About the payment, Mr. Tojo—

TOJO. Oh we won't bother with that now.

MADAME. But the Wine-Woman said . . .

TOJO. Never mind what she said. I'll trust you; that is, if you'll trust me. You do trust me?

MADAME (*with a suggestion of a smile.*) How soon will you be able to make the teeth?

TOJO. For you, Madame, I'll have them in two weeks. But you'll have to come to the clinic at twelve o'clock when Yokomichi is out to lunch.

MADAME. Are you sure it's all right . . . about Dr. Yokomichi, I mean?

TOJO. Yokomichi never misses his lunch, but don't worry about him. I'll take care of everything. Then I'll see you tomorrow at noon.

MADAME. Yes, and thank you Doctor, I mean Mr. Tojo.

TOJO. I'm afraid Mr. Tojo can never be called a doctor. (*He leaves laughing, discovers* WINE-WOMAN *and chases her offstage.*)

(*Lights dim*)

Scene 3

Two weeks later, late afternoon

CHORUS *is composed of patients at clinic again:* SECRETARY *is at her station.*

DENTIST (*enters, followed by* JANITOR). I want this place looking like a dental clinic.

JANITOR (*speaking in Issei accent*). But Doctor, I scrubbed the whole floor last night.

DENTIST. That was last night. Look at the floor now.

JANITOR (*shaking head*). It's highly irregular . . .

DENTIST. I want no arguments from the janitor.

JANITOR. Yes, Doctor. (*Leaves.*)

CHORUS (*standing and bowing*). Good afternoon, Doctor Yokomichi.

DENTIST (*walking past* CHORUS). Where did all these patients come from? Do they have appointments? (SECRETARY *nods.*) I told you before not to crowd too many appointments.

SECRETARY. But Doctor, these appointments were made weeks ago, and you agreed—

DENTIST. I don't remember agreeing to anything . . . like that. I'm only human, only human.

PATIENT A. Only human, he says.

PATIENT B. He's acting like a beast.

PATIENT C. I think he had a quarrel with his wife.

PATIENT A. I'd hate to be his wife.

(*TOJO walks in; CHORUS stands.*)

CHORUS. Good afternoon, Mr. Tojo.

TOJO (*very gallantly, walks into laboratory*). Good afternoon, ladies.

DENTIST. Tojo!

TOJO (*surprised*). What's the matter, Doc?

DENTIST. Nothing's the matter. I was just cleaning out the dirt that's been piling up.

TOJO (*walking away*). There's dirt everywhere, Doc.

DENTIST (*more quietly*). Tojo, there's something I want to discuss with you.

TOJO. Okay, Doc. I'll be right there, as soon as I get this out of the drawer. (*Takes out false plate from drawer, wraps it in cloth, and puts in pocket.*)

DENTIST (*to SECRETARY*). Tell them I'm not taking any more patients today, and you better go too.

SECRETARY (*nods and goes to CHORUS*). Doctor isn't taking any more patients today. Please come back tomorrow.

CHORUS. But why?

SECRETARY. I don't know. He's not feeling well, I guess.

CHORUS (*leaves grumbling; SECRETARY follows*). Oh my aching tooth!

(*TOJO sits in chair.*)

DENTIST. I don't know what you've been doing in the laboratory, but whatever it was, it couldn't have been much.

TOJO. That's right, Doc. There's been nothing to do.

(*JANITOR comes in mopping the floor.*)

DENTIST. Never mind about the floor. Never mind what I said. (*Janitor, shaking head, leaves, dragging mop behind him.*) Yes, there hasn't been much to do. Now Tojo, I've been thinking of starting on the false plates.

TOJO. You . . . are going to make false teeth?

DENTIST. With your help, yes. Is there anything wrong with that?

TOJO. No, nothing at all. (*Fumbles in pocket.*)

DENTIST. I want to begin with one patient in particular.

TOJO. Not your wife?

DENTIST. Oh thank goodness no. No, this patient came to me a couple of weeks ago, and I'm afraid I was rather abrupt with her, and it's been bothering me a lot lately.

TOJO. Could this patient by any chance be Madame?

DENTIST. Why yes. Do you know her?

TOJO (*putting hand in pocket*). She's a . . . friend of mine, a good friend.

DENTIST. Friend? How is she?

TOJO. Just fine, Doc. I saw her yesterday.

DENTIST. She's not a woman who forgets so easily.

TOJO. Oh Doc, I wouldn't worry any more about her.

DENTIST. But Madame has no teeth.

TOJO. She's perfectly happy as she is. (*Fumbles in pocket.*)

DENTIST (*becoming suspicious*). I don't understand you, Tojo, Madame is your friend, and she needs teeth.

TOJO. I know that, Doc, but why start now when you're almost in the army? Why, in a few days you'll be a lieutenant.

DENTIST. Tojo, what have you got in your pocket?

TOJO (*momentary silence*). It's a plate of false teeth.

DENTIST. Plate of false teeth! I can't believe it. I knew you were up to something in there, but I didn't think you would go as far as to make false plates behind my back. You—without license, without training.

TOJO. Careful what you say, Doc. I was trained in Japan.

DENTIST (*suddenly*). Give it to me.

TOJO. Oh no. It's not for you. It's for Madame—your old patient, the one you're worried about, the one you bled half to death.

DENTIST. That's a lie.

TOJO. Let's not get excited, Doc. In a few day you'll be in the army—a lieutenant in the U.S. Army. What was it? Lieutenant Ace Yokomichi?

DENTIST. You won't get away with this; it's much too serious an offense. I can make it mighty tough for you, Tojo.

TOJO. You are going to be a lieutenant, aren't you, Doc?

DENTIST. Shut up about that!

TOJO. Please Doc, you don't want to excite me, do you, Doc? So the army refused you, heh?

DENTIST. I didn't say that.

TOJO. Don't take it so hard. Stick around a while, and the Imperial Army will be here.

DENTIST. That's what you think.

TOJO. What's the difference? It's the same military. They need good citizens like you—loyal, patriotic, and conscientious. Why, you'll be a captain in the Imperial Army.

DENTIST. You're fired, fired! GET OUT! (*A moment of tension as both glare at each other; then Tojo walks off.*)

(*Lights dim*)

Scene 4

Late evening of same day
WINE-WOMAN enters.

BOILER MAN. Wine-Woman. Wine-Woman.

WINE-WOMAN. I can't be bothered with you. I have something important to tell Madame.

BOILER MAN. Rumors, more rumors, nothing but rumors.

WINE-WOMAN. This one is true. (*She goes to MADAME'S apartment. MADAME opens door, and WINE-WOMAN enters.*) Oh Madame, there's something I must tell you. I could barely hold it this far. I heard it straight from the woman at the hospital laundry.

MADAME. But what is it? Is it bad news?

WINE-WOMAN. It depends on how you look at it.

MADAME. Oh my teeth . . .

WINE-WOMAN. No. This doesn't concern you at all. Please, Madame.

MADAME. Then tell me quickly.

WINE-WOMAN. Yokomichi . . . (*Bursts into laughter.*)

MADAME. Dentist Yokomichi? Is he in the army at last?

WINE-WOMAN. No, far from it. He got it on the head late this afternoon.

MADAME. Got what on the head?

WINE-WOMAN. Oh Madame, do I have to tell you all the bloody details? Someone hit him on the head when he wasn't looking.

MADAME. But who would do such a thing?

WINE-WOMAN. No one knows. No one even dares to make a guess. But Madame, isn't it wonderful? Just think, Yokomichi, that beast, lying there with a terrible, terrible headache.

MADAME. I suppose he had it coming to him.

WINE-WOMAN. Sure, he asked for it long ago. But Madame, isn't Tojo bringing your teeth tonight?

MADAME. Yes, he should be here any minute. I hope nothing has happened to him.

WINE-WOMAN. Don't worry about him. Oh I'm happy for you. (*Starts the laughter dance.*) Let's have a little wine.

MADAME. It's too early for that.

WINE-WOMAN. Please, Madame, let me enjoy this happiness with you.

MADAME. All right. Just a little. (*WINE-WOMAN pours.*) That's enough. (*Knock at the door.*) Mr. Tojo!

WINE-WOMAN. I'll get the door. (*Bowing low.*) Please come in, Mr. Tojo.

MADAME. Oh come in, Boiler Man.

WINE-WOMAN. I was expecting Mr. Tojo, not you, Boiler Man.

BOILER MAN (*notices drinks*). What's going on here? Madame, you are not drinking her wine?

MADAME. Yes, I'm drinking her wine. She was kind enough to offer it to me. Please understand, Boiler Man.

BOILER MAN. I certainly understand.

MADAME. Please let me explain.

BOILER MAN (*leaving hastily*). You can take your shower with the rest. You need it now.

MADAME. Ohhh.

WINE-WOMAN. Don't mind that old fool. Don't let him spoil this night for you. Here, drink this wine, it's wonderful for the soul. (*Exits, leaving the bottle.*)

(*MADAME walks about her room; TOJO approaches.*)

TOJO (*to BOILER MAN*). Well, how's my good Boiler Man? What's the matter, why don't you answer?

BOILER MAN. Go away, I'm tired, very tired.

TOJO. You look it. Well, cheer up, good man.

BOILER MAN. You're drunk.

TOJO. I've been celebrating a little. This is a day for celebration. Well, I have some business with my beautiful Madame. (*Knocks; MADAME hesitates, then opens door.*) I'm sorry to be late, Madame, but this has been quite a day.

MADAME. Please come in. (*Motioning him to a chair.*)

TOJO (*sitting and heaving a great sigh*). It's good to sit down and relax.

MADAME. Do you have my teeth, Mr. Tojo?

TOJO. Of course, Madame. Right here in my pocket. I almost lost it, though.

MADAME. How, Mr. Tojo?

TOJO. That Yokomichi found out.

MADAME. Ohh.

TOJO. It's all right. He's well taken care of. (*Very ceremoniously unravels teeth, then hands her mirror.*) Here, let's put them on right now. Madame, you know, you are very lucky.

MADAME (*looking in the mirror*). Oh, Mr. Tojo, it's perfect.

TOJO. Madame, I said you are lucky.

MADAME. I know I'm lucky.

TOJO. Listen, Madame, that false plate you have in your mouth is the last. There'll be no more.

MADAME. Why no more, Mr. Tojo?

TOJO (*laughing*). Laugh, Madame, laugh and show me those beautiful teeth.

(*MADAME tries but has difficulty; she goes to get envelope of money.*)

MADAME. Here is the money.

TOJO. No, no.

MADAME. Please take it, Mr. Tojo. You have made me happy.

TOJO (*taking envelope*). Are you really happy now?

MADAME. I think so. Would you care for some wine? The good Wine-Woman left me her bottle.

TOJO. Wonderful. Now we can celebrate. (*MADAME pours.*) Ah, to be served by a lady again. You know, we celebrate many things tonight. First your new teeth.

MADAME. Yes, my new teeth.

TOJO. You know, Madame, you are quite attractive.

MADAME. What else are we celebrating, Mr. Tojo?

TOJO. Oh yes. First we are celebrating your new teeth. I said that. Then next we are celebrating . . . (*Bursts into laughter; MADAME pours again.*) Aren't you drinking any more?

MADAME. I've had quite enough.

TOJO. Why, you only had one. Come, Madame, you must have another. (*TOJO grabs bottle, pours over MADAME's protest, and spills wine.*)

MADAME. What are we celebrating, Mr. Tojo?

TOJO. First your new teeth. I said that twice already, didn't I? You see, I still remember.

MADAME. But what else?

TOJO. I almost forgot. We are also celebrating the loss of my job. (*MADAME looks at him strangely.*) Please, Madame, don't look at me like that.

MADAME. Then did you—

TOJO. Of course not. Remember they call me Mr. Tojo. I wouldn't do a thing like that. Please, Madame, another. (*She pours again.*) This one is to Yokomichi and his poor swollen head. (*Beams at MADAME.*) Madame, you are beautiful.

MADAME. It must be the new teeth.

TOJO. No, it's you, Madame, you are very beautiful.

MADAME. Oh, Mr. Tojo, you cannot mean that.

TOJO. Of course I mean it. (*Reaches into pocket, pulls out envelope, and slaps it on table.*) I did not make the teeth for your money.

MADAME. But Mr. Tojo . . .

TOJO. I made it for you, Madame. (*MADAME tries to press envelope on TOJO, who refuses; he grabs MADAME and envelope falls to floor; MADAME struggles; TOJO speaks emotionally.*) Madame, Madame.

MADAME. CURFEW! (*Breaks free from TOJO.*) You must leave immediately! (*TOJO makes no move; MADAME grabs broom and begins to hit TOJO on head; TOJO staggers to door, opens it, and now*

MADAME *sweeps him out; she stands trembling; outside,* TOJO, *cursing, goes toward* BOILER MAN.)

TOJO. That woman threw me out. I said that woman threw me out. Are you listening?

(BOILER MAN *does not answer.*)

TOJO (*grabs* BOILER MAN). Remember, I'm still Mr. Tojo.

(MP *enters.*)

MP. What's going on here? You there, you live in this block?

TOJO. I'm still Mr. Tojo. I'll always be Mr. Tojo. Police, I just came out of that apartment. There's a woman in there.

MP. You stay where you are. (*Goes over to apartment.*) Did a man called Tojo leave your apartment a few minutes ago?

MADAME. Tojo? No.

TOJO (*shouting*). I left some money in there; tell her that, police.

MP. He says he left some money here.

MADAME. Money? I don't know.

MP. Are you sure now?

MADAME. Quite sure.

MP (*to* TOJO). Okay, pop. Come along, you can cool 'er off in jail.

TOJO (*as he leaves*). You goddamn woman!

MADAME. Who ever heard of a man called Tojo? (*She breaks into laughter, runs outside:* CHORUS *enters laughing and begins to dance; now* MADAME *joins them.*)

PATIENT C. Why don't you join us, Boiler Man? (*Dancing continues.*)

PATIENT A. Come on, Boiler Man. (BOILER MAN *slumps in a chair.*)

PATIENT B. Boiler man, Boiler Man.

PATIENT C. Boiler Man is dead. (*Runs to* CHORUS; *dancing stops;* MADAME *rushes over to* BOILER MAN.)

MADAME. Oh Boiler Man. Oh Boiler Man.

CHORUS. The good Boiler Man is dead. The good Boiler Man is dead.

MADAME. Oh, what have I done? Why didn't I listen to him? Now he's gone. (*Flute music up.*)

YOSHIO (*enters shouting*). Boiler Man, Boiler Man, I've something to tell you, something good. Boiler Man—what's the matter?

CHORUS (*softly*). The good Boiler Man is dead.

YOSHIO. Oh no. And I had good news, happy news. Boiler Man, my mother can talk again. For the first time in three years she looked at me, she really looked at me and said, "Baby."

MADAME (*places her hand on* YOSHIO's *head*). Oh Yoshio, Yoshio.

(*Lights dim slowly*)

Hisaye Yamamoto

(1921–   )

Born in Redondo Beach, California, Hisaye Yamamoto wrote and published seven short stories between 1948 and 1961. Since 1961 the duties of wife and mother have kept her from writing any new fiction. Today her writing is confined to poetry for the holiday editions of the *Rafu Shimpo*. Her modest body of fiction is remarkable for its range and gut understanding of Japanese America. The questions and themes of Asian American life are fresh. Growing up with foreign-born parents, mixing with white and nonwhite races, racial discrimination, growing old, the question of dual personality— all were explored in the seven stories of Hisaye Yamamoto. Technically and stylistically, hers is among the most highly developed of Asian American writing. Her sense of humor, precisely Japanese American, is unlike that of better-known Asian American writers because it does not reinforce the reader's sense of the superiority of white culture. Her jokes about an Issei's garbled understanding of American slang do not demean the foreign-born, as when the Issei asks a young Nisei about his wife. He is told she "took a powder." "Poison?" the Issei asks. Instead of crudely illuminating the ignorance of the old man from Japan, she illuminates a whole linguistic process. In her work we see how language adapts to new speakers, new experience, and becomes new language. Hisaye Yamamoto's people speak a fluid language that is in a constant state of change. Her seven stories form the only portrait of prewar rural Japanese America in existence. She now lives in Los Angeles with her husband and five children. In 1989 her stories and essays were published in one volume, *Seventeen Syllables and Other Stories*, by Kitchen Table: Women of Color Press.

The Legend of Miss Sasagawara

Even in that unlikely place of wind, sand, and heat, it was easy to imagine Miss Sasagawara a decorative ingredient of some ballet. Her daily costume, brief and fitting closely to her trifling waist, generously billowing below, and bringing together arrestingly rich colors like mustard yellow and forest green, appeared to have been cut from a coarse-textured homespun; her shining hair was so long it wound twice about her head to form a coronet; her face was delicate and pale, with a fine nose, pouting bright mouth, and glittering eyes; and her measured walk said, "Look, I'm *walking*!" as though walking were not a common but a rather special thing to be doing. I first saw her so one evening after mess, as she was coming out of the women's latrine, going toward her barracks, and after I thought she was out of hearing, I imitated the young men of the Block (No. 33), and gasped, "Wow! How much does *she* weigh?"

"Oh, haven't you heard?" said my friend Elsie Kubo, knowing very well I had not. "That's Miss Sasagawara."

It turned out Elsie knew all about Miss Sasagawara, who with her father was new to Block 33. Where had she accumulated all her items? Probably a morsel here and a morsel there, and, anyway, I forgot to ask her sources, because the picture she painted was so distracting: Miss Sasagawara's father was a Buddhist minister, and the two had gotten permission to come to this Japanese evacuation camp in Arizona from one farther north, after the death there of Mrs. Sasagawara. They had come here to join the Rev. Sasagawara's brother's family, who lived in a neighboring Block, but there had been some trouble between them, and just this week the immigrant pair had gotten leave to move over to Block 33. They were occupying one end of the Block's lone empty barracks, which had not been chopped up yet into the customary four apartments. The other end had been taken over by a young couple, also newcomers to the Block, who had moved in the same day.

"And do you know what, Kiku?" Elsie continued. "Oooh, that gal is really temperamental. I guess it's because she was a ballet dancer before she got stuck in camp, I hear people like that are temperamental. Anyway, the Sasakis, the new couple at the other end of the barracks, think she's crazy. The day they all moved in, the barracks was really dirty, all covered with dust from the dust storms and everything, so Mr. Sasaki was going to wash the whole barracks down with a hose, and he thought he'd be nice and do the Sasagawaras' side first. You know, do them a favor. But do you know what? Mr. Sasaki got the hose attached to the faucet outside and started to go in the door, and he said all the Sasagawaras' suitcases and things were on top of the army cots and Miss Sasagawara was trying to clean the place out with a pail of water and a broom. He said, 'Here let me flush the place out with a hose for you; it'll be faster.' And she turned right around and screamed at him, 'What are you trying to do? Spy on me? Get out of here or I'll throw this water on you!' He said he was so surprised he couldn't move for a minute, and before he knew it, Miss Sasagawara just up and threw that water at him, pail and all. Oh, he said he got out of that place fast, but fast. Madwoman, he called her."

But Elsie had already met Miss Sasagawara, too, over at the apartment of the Murakamis, where Miss Sasagawara was borrowing Mrs. Murakami's Singer, and had found her quite amiable. "She said she was thirty-nine years old—imagine, thirty-nine, she looks so young, more like twenty-five; but she said she wasn't sorry she never got married, because she's had her fun. She said she got to go all over the country a couple of times, dancing in the ballet."

And after we emerged from the latrine, Elsie and I, slapping mosquitoes in the warm, gathering dusk, sat on the stoop of her apartment and talked awhile, jealously of the scintillating life Miss Sasagawara had led until now and nostalgically of the few ballets we had seen in the world outside (how far away Los Angeles seemed!), but we ended up as we always did, agreeing that our mission in life, pushing twenty as we were, was first to finish college somewhere when and if the war ever ended and we were free again, and then to find good jobs and two nice, clean young men, preferably handsome, preferably rich, who would cherish us forever and a day.

My introduction, less spectacular, to the Rev. Sasagawara came later, as I noticed him, a slight and fragile-looking old man, in the Block mess hall (where I worked as a waitress, and Elsie, too) or laundry room or going to and from the latrine. Sometimes he would be farther out, perhaps going to the post office or canteen or to visit friends in another Block or on some business to the Administration building, but wherever he was headed, however doubtless his destination, he always seemed to be wandering lostly. This may have been because he walked so slowly, with such negligible steps, or because he wore perpetually an air of bemusement, never talking directly to a person, as though, being what he was, he could not stop for an instant his meditation on the higher life.

I noticed, too, that Miss Sasagawara never came to the mess hall herself. Her father ate at the tables reserved for the occupants, mostly elderly, of the end barracks known as the bachelors' dormitory. After each meal, he came up to the counter and carried away a plate of food, protected with one of the pinkish apple wrappers we waitresses made as wrinkleless as possible and put out for napkins, and a mug of tea or coffee. Sometimes Miss Sasagawara could be seen rinsing out her empties at the one double tub in the laundry that was reserved for private dishwashing.

If any one in the Block or in the entire camp of fifteen thousand or so people had talked at any length with Miss Sasagawara (everyone happening to speak of her called her that, although her first name, Mari, was simple enough and rather pretty) after her first and only visit to use Mrs. Murakami's sewing machine, I never heard of it. Nor did she ever willingly use the shower room, just off the latrine, when anyone else was there. Once, when I was up past midnight writing letters and went for my shower, I came upon her under the full needling force of a steamy spray, but she turned her back to me and did not answer my surprised hello. I hoped my body would be as smooth and spare and well turned when I was thirty-nine. Another time, Elsie and I passed in front of the Sasagawara apartment, which was really only a cubicle because the once-empty barracks had soon been partitioned off into six units for families of two, and we saw her there on the wooden steps, sitting with her wide, wide skirt spread splendidly about her. She was intent on peeling a grapefruit, which her father had probably brought to her from the mess hall that morning, and Elsie called out, "Hello there!" Miss Sasagawara looked up and stared, without recognition. We were almost out of earshot when I heard her call, "Do I know you?" and I could have almost sworn that she sounded hopeful, if not downright wistful, but Elsie, already miffed at having expended friendliness so unprofitably, seemed not to have heard, and that was that.

Well, if Miss Sasagawara was not one to speak to, she was certainly one to speak of, and she came up quite often as topic for the endless conversations which helped along the monotonous days. My mother said she had met the late Mrs. Sasagawara once, many years before the war, and to hear her tell it, a sweeter, kindlier woman there never was. "I suppose," said my mother, "that I'll never meet anyone like her again; she was a lady in every sense of the word." Then she reminded me that I had seen the Rev. Sasagawara before. Didn't I remember him as one of the three *bhikshus* who had read the sutras at Grandfather's funeral?

I could not say that I did. I barely remembered Grandfather, my mother's father. The only thing that came back with clarity was my nausea at the wake and the funeral, the first and only ones I had ever had occasion to attend, because it had been reproduced several times since—each time, in fact, that I had crossed again the actual scent or a suspicion of burning incense. Dimly I recalled the inside of the Buddhist temple in Los Angeles, an immense, murky auditorium whose high and huge platform had held, centered in the background, a great golden shrine touched with black and white. Below this platform, Grandfather, veiled by gauze, had slept in a long, grey box which just fitted him. There had been flowers, oh, such flowers, everywhere. And right in front of Grandfather's box had been the incense stand, upon which squatted two small bowls, one with a cluster of straw-thin sticks sending up white tendrils of smoke, the other containing a heap of coarse, grey powder. Each mourner in turn had gone up to the stand, bowing once, his palms touching in prayer, before he reached it; had bent in prayer over the stand; had taken then a pinch of incense from the bowl of crumbs and, bowing over it reverently, cast it into the other, the active bowl; had bowed, the hands praying again; had retreated a few steps and bowed one last time, the hands still joined, before returning to his seat. (I knew the ceremony well for having been severely coached in it on the evening of the wake.) There had been tears and tears and here and there a sudden sob.

And all this while, three men in black robes had been on the platform, one standing in front of the shining altar, the others sitting on either side, and the entire trio incessantly chanting a strange, mellifluous language in unison. From time to time there had reverberated through the enormous room, above the singsong, above the weeping, above the fragrance, the sharp, startling whang of the gong.

So, one of those men had been Miss Sasagawara's father. . . . This information brought him closer to me, and I listened with interest later when it was told that he kept here in his apartment a small shrine, much more intricately constructed than that kept by the usual Buddhist household, before which, at regular hours of the day, he offered incense and chanted, tinkling (in lieu of the gong) a small bell. What did Miss Sasagawara do at these prayer periods, I wondered; did she participate, did she let it go in one ear and out the other, or did she abruptly go out on the steps, perhaps to eat a grapefruit?

Elsie and I tried one day of working in the mess hall. And this desire for greener fields came almost together with the Administration announcement that henceforth the wages of residents doing truly vital labor, such as in the hospital or on the garbage trucks that went from mess hall to mess hall, would be upped to nineteen dollars a month instead of the common sixteen.

"Oh, I've always wanted to be a nurse!" Elsie confided, as the Block manager sat down to his breakfast after reading out the day's bulletin in English and Japanese.

"What's stopped you?" I asked.

"Mom," Elsie said. "She thinks it's dirty work. And she's afraid I'll catch something. But I'll remind her of the extra three dollars."

"It's never appealed to me much either," I confessed. "Why don't we go over to garbage? It's the same pay."

Elsie would not even consider it. "Very funny. Well, you don't have to be a nurse's aide, Kiku. The hospital's short of all kinds of help. Dental assistants, receptionists. . . . Let's go apply after we finish this here."

So, willy-nilly, while Elsie plunged gleefully into the pleasure of wearing a trim blue-and-white-striped seersucker, into the duties of taking temperatures and carrying bedpans, and into the fringe of medical jargon (she spoke very casually now of catheters, enemas, primiparas, multiparas), I became a relief receptionist at the hospital's front desk, taking my hours as they were assigned. And it was on one of my midnight-to-morning shifts that I spoke to Miss Sasagawara for the first time.

The cooler in the corridor window was still whirring away (for that desert heat in summer had a way of lingering intact through the night to merge with the warmth of the morning sun), but she entered bundled in an extraordinarily long black coat, her face made petulant, not unprettily, by lines of pain.

"I think I've got appendicitis," she said breathlessly, without preliminary.

"May I have your name and address?" I asked, unscrewing my pen.

Annoyance seemed to outbalance agony for a moment, but she answered soon enough, in a cold rush, "Mari Sasagawara. Thirty-three-seven C."

It was necessary also to learn her symptoms, and I wrote down that she had chills and a dull aching at the back of her head, as well as these excruciating flashes in her lower right abdomen.

"I'll have to go wake up the doctor. Here's a blanket, why don't you lie down over there on the bench until he comes?" I suggested.

She did not answer, so I tossed the army blanket on the bench, and when I returned from the doctors' dormitory, after having tapped and tapped on the door of young Dr. Moritomo, who was on night duty, she was still standing where I had left her, immobile and holding on to the wooden railing shielding the desk.

"Dr. Moritomo's coming right away," I said. "Why don't you sit down at least?"

Miss Sasagawara said, "Yes," but did not move.

"Did you walk all the way?" I asked incredulously, for Block 33 was a good mile off, across the canal.

She nodded, as if that were not important, also as if to thank me kindly to mind my own business.

Dr. Moritomo (technically, the title was premature; evacuation had caught him with a few months to go on his degree), wearing a maroon bathrobe, shuffled in sleepily and asked her to come into the emergency room for an examination. A short while later, he guided her past my desk into the laboratory, saying he was going to take her blood count.

When they came out, she went over to the electric fountain for a drink of water, and Dr. Moritomo said reflectively, "Her count's all right. Not appendicitis. We should keep her for observation, but the general ward is pretty full, isn't it? Hm, well, I'll give her something to take. Will you tell one of the boys to take her home?"

This I did, but when I came back from arousing George, one of the ambulance boys, Miss Sasagawara was gone, and Dr. Moritomo was coming out of the laboratory where he had gone to push out the lights. "Here's George, but that girl must have walked home," I reported helplessly.

"She's in no condition to do that. George, better catch up with her and take her home," Dr. Moritomo ordered.

Shrugging, George strode down the hall; the doctor shuffled back to bed; and soon there was the shattering sound of one of the old army ambulances backing out of the hospital drive.

George returned in no time at all to say that Miss Sasagawara had refused to get in the ambulance. "She wouldn't even listen to me. She just kept walking and I drove alongside and told her it was Dr. Moritomo's orders, but she wouldn't even listen to me."

"She wouldn't?"

"I hope Doc didn't expect me to drag her into the ambulance."

"Oh, well," I said. "I guess she'll get home all right. She walked all the way up here."

"Cripes, what a dame!" George complained, shaking his head as he started back to the ambulance room. "I never heard of such a thing. She wouldn't even listen to me."

Miss Sasagawara came back to the hospital about a month later. Elsie was the one who rushed up to the desk where I was on day duty to whisper, "Miss Sasagawara just tried to escape from the hospital!"

"Escape? What do you mean, escape?" I said.

"Well, she came in last night, and they didn't know what was wrong with her, so they kept her for observation. And this morning, just now, she ran out of the ward in just a hospital nightgown and the orderlies chased after her and caught her and brought her back. Oh, she was just fighting them. But once they got her back to bed, she calmed down right away, and Miss Morris asked her what was the big idea, you know, and do you know what she said? She said she didn't want any more of those doctors pawing her. *Pawing* her, imagine!"

After an instant's struggle with self-mockery, my curiosity led me down the entrance corridor after Elsie, into the longer, wider corridor admitting to the general ward. The whole hospital staff appeared to have gathered in the room to get a look at Miss Sasagawara, and the other patients, or those of them that could, were sitting up attentively in their high, white, and narrow beds. Miss Sasagawara had the corner bed to the left as we entered and, covered only by a brief hospital apron, she was sitting on the edge with her legs dangling over the side. With her head slightly bent, she was staring at a certain place on the floor, and I knew she must be aware of that concentrated gaze, of trembling old Dr. Kawamoto (he had retired several years before the war, but he had been drafted here), of Miss Morris, the head nurse, of Miss Bowman, the nurse in charge of the general ward during the day, of the other patients, of the nurse's aides, of the orderlies, and of everyone else who tripped in and out abashedly on some pretext or other in order to pass by her bed. I knew this by her smile, for as she continued to look at that same piece of the floor, she continued, unexpectedly, to seem wryly amused with the entire proceedings. I peered at her wonderingly through the triangular peephole created by someone's hand on hip, while Dr. Kawamoto, Miss Morris, and Miss Bowman tried to persuade her to lie down and relax. She was as smilingly immune to tactful suggestions as she was to tactless gawking.

There was no future to watching such a war of nerves as this, and besides, I was supposed to be at the front desk, so I hurried back in time to greet a frantic young mother and father, the latter carrying their small son who had had a hemorrhage this morning after a tonsillectomy yesterday in the outpatient clinic.

A couple of weeks later, on the late shift, I found George, the ambulance driver, in high spirits. This time he had been the one selected to drive a patient to Phoenix, where special cases were occasionally sent under escort, and he was looking forward to the moment when, for a few hours, the escort would permit him to go shopping around the city and perhaps take in a new movie. He showed me the list of things his friends had asked him to bring back for them, and we laughed together over the request of one plumpish nurse's aide for the biggest, richest chocolate cake he could find.

"You ought to have seen Mabel's eyes while she was describing the kind of cake she wanted," he said. "Man, she looked like she was eating it already!"

Just then one of the other drivers, Bobo Kunitomi, came up and nudged George, and they withdrew a few steps from my desk.

"Oh, I ain't particularly interested in that," I heard George saying.

There was some murmuring from Bobo, of which I caught the words, "Well, hell, you might as well, just as long as you're getting to go out there."

George shrugged, then nodded, and Bobo came over to the desk and asked for pencil and paper. "This is a good place . . . ," he said, handing George what he had written.

Was it my imagination, or did George emerge from his chat with Bobo a little ruddier than usual? "Well, I guess I better go get ready," he said, taking leave. "Oh, anything you want, Kiku? Just say the word."

"Thanks, not this time," I said. "Well, enjoy yourself."

"Don't worry," he said. "I will!"

He had started down the hall when I remembered to ask, "Who are you taking, anyway?"

George turned around. "Miss Sa-sa-ga-wa-ra," he said, accenting every syllable. "Remember that dame? The one who wouldn't let me take her home?"

"Yes," I said. "What's the matter with her?"

George, saying not a word, pointed at his head and made several circles in the air with his first finger.

"Really?" I asked.

Still mum, George nodded in emphasis and pity before he turned to go.

How long was she away? It must have been several months, and when, toward late autumn, she returned at last from the sanitarium in Phoenix, everyone in Block 33 was amazed at the change. She said hello and how are you as often and easily as the next person, although many of those she greeted were surprised and suspicious, remembering the earlier rebuffs. There were some who never did get used to Miss Sasagawara as a friendly being.

One evening when I was going toward the latrine for my shower, my youngest sister, ten-year-old Michi, almost collided with me and said excitedly, "You going for your shower now, Kiku?"

"You want to fight about it?" I said, making fists.

"Don't go now, don't go now! Miss Sasagawara's in there," she whispered wickedly.

"Well," I demanded. "What's wrong with that, honey?"

"She's scary. Us kids were in there and she came in and we finished, so we got out, and she said, 'Don't be afraid of me. I won't hurt you.' Gee, we weren't even afraid of her, but when she said that, gee!"

"Oh, go on home and go to bed," I said.

Miss Sasagawara was indeed in the shower and she welcomed me with a smile. "Aren't you the girl who plays the violin?"

I giggled and explained. Elsie and I, after hearing Menuhin on the radio, had, in a fit of madness, sent to Sears and Roebuck for beginners' violins that cost five dollars each. We had received free instruction booklets, too, but, unable to make heads or tails from them, we contented ourselves with occasionally taking the violins out of their paper bags and sawing every which way away.

Miss Sasagawara laughed aloud—a lovely sound. "Well, you're just about as good as I am. I sent for a Spanish guitar. I studied it about a year once, but that was so long ago I don't remember the first thing and I'm having to start all over again. We'd make a fine orchestra."

That was the only time we really exchanged words, and some weeks later, I understood she had organized a dancing class from among the younger girls in the Block. My sister Michi, becoming one of her pupils, got very attached to her and spoke of her frequently at home. So I knew that Miss Sasagawara and her father had decorated their apartment to look oh, so pretty, that Miss Sasagawara had a whole big suitcase full of dancing costumes, and that Miss Sasagawara had just lots and lots of books to read.

The fruits of Miss Sasagawara's patient labor were put on show at the Block Christmas party, the second such observance in camp. Again, it was a gay, if odd, celebration. The mess hall was hung with red and green crêpe-paper streamers and the grayish mistletoe that grew abundantly on the ancient mesquite surrounding the camp. There were even electric decorations on the token Christmas tree. The oldest occupant of the bachelors' dormitory gave a tremulous monologue in an exaggerated Hiroshima dialect, one of the young boys wore a bow tie and whispered a popular song while the girls shrieked and pretended to be growing faint, my mother sang an old Japanese song, four of the girls wore similar blue dresses and harmonized on a sweet tune, a little girl in a grass skirt and superfluous brassiere did a hula, and the chief cook came out with an ample saucepan and, assisted by the waitresses, performed the familiar *dojosukui,* the comic dance about a man who is merely trying to scoop up a few loaches from an uncooperative lake. Then Miss Sasagawara shooed her eight little girls, including Michi, in front, and while they formed a stiff pattern and waited, self-conscious in the rustly crêpe-paper dresses they had made themselves, she set up a portable phonograph on the floor and vigorously turned the crank.

Something was past its prime, either the machine or the record or the needle, for what came out was a feeble rasp but distantly related to the Mozart minuet it was supposed to be. After a bit I recognized the melody; I had learned it as a child to the words

When dames wore hoops and powdered hair,
And very strict was e-ti-quette,
When men were brave and ladies fair,
they danced the min-u-et. . . .

And the little girls, who might have curtsied and stepped gracefully about under Miss Sasagawara's eyes alone, were all elbows and knees as they felt the Block's 50 or more pairs of eyes on them. Although there was sustained applause after their number, what we were benevolently approving was the great effort, for the achievement had been undeniably small. Then Santa came with a pillow for a stomach, his hands each dragging a bulging burlap bag. Church people outside had kindly sent these gifts, Santa announced, and every recipient must write and thank the person whose name he would find on an enclosed slip. So saying, he called by name each Block child under twelve and ceremoniously presented each eleemosynary package, and a couple of the youngest children screamed in fright at this new experience of a red-and-white man with a booming voice.

At the last, Santa called, "Miss Sasagawara!" and when she came forward in surprise, he explained to the gathering that she was being rewarded for her help with the Block's younger generation. Everyone clapped and Miss Sasagawara, smiling graciously, opened her package then and there. She held up her gift, a peach-colored bath towel, so that it could be fully seen, and everyone clapped again.

Suddenly, I put this desert scene behind me. The notice I had long awaited, of permission to relocate to Philadelphia to attend college, finally came, and there was a prodigious amount of packing to do, leave papers to sign, and good-byes to say. And once the wearying, sooty train trip was over, I found myself in an intoxicating new world of daily classes, afternoon teas, and evening concerts, from which I dutifully emerged now and then to answer the letters from home. When the beautiful semester was over, I returned to Arizona, to that glowing heat, to the camp, to the family, for although the war was still on, it had been decided to close down the camps, and I had been asked to go back and spread the good word about higher education among the young people who might be dispersed in this way.

Elsie was still working in the hospital, although she had applied for entrance into the cadet nurse corps and was expecting acceptance any day, and the long conversations we held were mostly about the good old days, the good old days when we had worked in the mess hall together, the good old days when we had worked in the hospital together.

"What ever became of Miss Sasagawara?" I asked one day, seeing the Rev. Sasagawara go abstractly by. Did she relocate somewhere?"

"I didn't write you about her, did I?" Elsie said meaningfully. "Yes, she's relocated all right. Haven't seen her around have you?"

"Where did she go?"

Elsie answered offhandedly. "California."

"California?" I exclaimed. "We can't go back to California. What's she doing in California?"

So Elsie told me: Miss Sasagawara had been sent back there to a state institution, oh, not so very long after I had left for school. She had begun slipping back into her aloof ways almost immediately after Christmas, giving up the dancing class and not speaking to people. Then Elsie had heard a couple of very strange, yes, very strange things about her. One thing had been told by young Mrs. Sasaki, that next-door neighbor of the Sasagawaras'.

Mrs. Sasaki said she had once come upon Miss Sasagawara sitting, as was her habit, on the porch. Mrs. Sasaki had been shocked to the core to see that the face of this thirty-nine-year-old woman (or was she forty now?) wore a beatific expression as she watched the activity going on in the doorway of her neighbors across the way, the Yoshinagas. This activity had been the joking and loud laughter of Joe and Frank, the young Yoshinaga boys, and three or four of their friends. Mrs. Sasaki would have let the matter go, were it not for the fact that Miss Sasagawara was so absorbed a spectator of this horseplay that her head was bent to one side and she actually had one finger in her mouth as she gazed, in the manner of a shy child confronted with a marvel. "What's the matter with you, watching the boys like that?" Mrs. Sasaki had cried. "You're old enough to be their mother!" Startled, Miss Sasagawara had jumped up and dashed back into her apartment. And when Mrs. Sasaki had gone into hers, adjoining the Sasagawaras', she had been terrified to hear Miss Sasagawara begin to bang on the wooden walls with something heavy like a hammer. The banging, which sounded as though Miss Sasagawara were using all her strength on each blow, had continued wildly for at least five minutes. Then all had been still.

The other thing had been told by Joe Yoshinaga, who lived across the way from Miss Sasagawara. Joe and his brother slept on two army cots pushed together on one side of the room, while their parents had a similar arrangement on the other side. Joe had standing by his bed an apple crate for a shelf, and he was in the habit of reading his sports and western magazines in bed and throwing them on top of the crate before he went to sleep. But one morning he had noticed his magazines all neatly stacked inside the crate, when he was sure he had carelessly thrown some on top the night before, as usual. This happened several times, and he finally asked his family whether one of them had been putting his magazines away after he fell asleep. They had said no and laughed, telling him he must be getting absentminded. But the mystery had been solved late one night, when Joe gradually awoke in his cot with the feeling that he as being watched. Warily, he had opened one eye slightly and had been thoroughly awakened and chilled, in the bargain, by what he saw. For what he saw was Miss Sasagawara sitting there on his apple crate, her long hair all undone and flowing about her. She was dressed in a white nightgown and her hands were clasped on her lap. And all she was doing was sitting there watching him, Joe Yoshinaga. He could not help it, he had sat up and screamed. His mother, a light sleeper, came running to see what had happened, just as Miss Sasagawara was running out the door, the door they had always left unlatched, or even wide open in summer. In the morning, Mrs. Yoshinaga had gone straight to the Rev. Sasagawara and asked him to do something about his daughter. The Rev. Sasagawara, sympathizing with her indignation in his benign but vague manner, had said he would have a talk with Mari.

And, concluded Elsie, Miss Sasagawara had gone away not long after. I was impressed, although Elsie's sources were not what I would ordinarily pay much attention to—Mrs. Sasaki, that plump and giggling young woman who always felt called upon to explain that she was childless by choice, and Joe Yoshinaga, who had a knack of blowing up, in his drawling voice, any incident in which he personally played even a small part (I could imagine the field day he had had with this one). Elsie puzzled aloud over the cause of Miss Sasagawara's derangement, and I, who had so newly had some contact with the recorded explorations into the virgin territory of the human mind, sagely explained that Miss Sasagawara had no doubt looked upon Joe Yoshinaga as the image of either the lost lover or the lost son. But my words made me uneasy by their glibness, and I began to wonder seriously about Miss Sasagawara for the first time.

Then there was this last word from Miss Sasagawara herself, making her strange legend as complete as I, at any rate, would probably ever know it. This came some time after I had gone back to Philadelphia and the family had joined me there, when I was neck deep in research for my final paper. I happened one day to be looking through the last issue of a small poetry magazine that had suspended publication midway through the war. I felt a thrill of recognition at the name, Mari Sasagawara, signed to a long poem, introduced as ". . . the first published poem of a Japanese-American woman who is, at present, an evacuee from the West Coast making her home in a War Relocation center in Arizona."

It was a *tour de force,* erratically brilliant and, through the first readings, tantalizingly obscure. It appeared to be about a man whose lifelong aim had been to achieve Nirvana, that saintly state of moral purity and universal wisdom. This man had in his way certain handicaps, all stemming from his having acquired, when young and unaware, a family for which he must provide. The day came at last, however, when his wife died and other circumstances made it unnecessary for him to earn a competitive living. These circumstances were considered by those about him as sheer imprisonment, but he had felt free for the first time in his long life. It became possible for him to extinguish within himself all unworthy desire and consequently all evil, to concentrate on that serene, eight-fold path of highest understanding, highest-mindedness, highest speech, highest action, highest livelihood, highest recollectedness, highest endeavor, and highest meditation.

This man was certainly noble, the poet wrote, this man was beyond censure. The world was doubtless enriched by his presence. But say that someone else, someone sensitive, someone admiring, someone who had not achieved this sublime condition and who did not wish to, were somehow called to companion such a man. Was it not likely that the saint, blissfully bent on cleansing from his already radiant soul the last imperceptible blemishes (for, being perfect, would he not humbly suspect his own flawlessness?), would be deaf and blind to the human passions rising, subsiding, and again rising, perhaps in anguished silence, within the selfsame room? The poet could not speak for others, of course; she could only speak for herself. But she would describe this man's devotion as a sort of madness, the monstrous sort which, pure of itself and so with immunity, might possibly bring troublous, scented scenes to recur in others' sleep.

Violet Kazue Matsuda de Cristoforo
(1917–   )

Born Violet Kazue Yamane, in Ninole, Hawaii, January 3, 1917, she began her education in Japan at the age of eight. She returned to America when she was thirteen, attending Theodore Roosevelt High School in Fresno, California, and went on to San Jose State College, Monterey Peninsula College, and, after World War II, Sophia University (Jochi Daigaku) in Tokyo, Japan. Having married Shigeru Matsuda, she was living in Fresno in late 1941.

As a member of the Kaikoo Valley Ginsha, she wrote free-form haiku; haiku free of the five-, seven-, and five-syllable lines; and haiku free of the traditional restriction to natural—meaning non-human—subject matter. The free-form Haiku does keep the traditional requirement of including something to indicate a specific season.

She writes: "Prior to the war, Valley Ginsha haiku were published by the Northern California Japanese-language newspapers, as well as by the Kaikoo monthly haiku magazine in Tokyo, Japan. The post-war period saw several former Valley Ginsha members expatriated or repatriated to Japan, others scattered throughout the United States and a handful back in Central California. The forced evacuation of persons of Japanese ancestry into the government-operated detention camps brought tragedies to the Japanese ethnic communities, including the death of their culture."

The Matsudas were evacuated to Fresno Assembly Center, where Violet gave birth to a daughter. She and her family were then evacuated to Jerome Relocation Center, a War Relocation Authority concentration camp in Arkansas. In 1943, Shigeru refused to answer questions 27 and 28 of the Leave Clearance registration form. He simply left the spaces blank. Blank. Blank, to the government, merit the same as no, and Shigeru was sent to a Justice Department camp at Santa Fe, New Mexico. Violet and her three children were sent to the notorious Tule Lake concentration camp near Newell, California. In 1944, at Tule Lake, she was befriended by a duplicitous social scientist, Rosalie Hankey Wax. Violet writes:

"under those oppressive conditions I became more and more intro-spective and found solace in my Haiku as the humble expression of the dejection experienced by a lonely young mother with small children."

Never charged, never tried, never convicted, Violet Kazue Matsuda was expatriated to Japan. Her proficiency in both English and Japanese led to her employment by the Allied forces as an interpreter/translator of technical materials and as the confidential secretary to the U.S. Atomic Energy Commission.

Shigeru had never registered his American marriage to Violet in Japan. Japanese law did not recognize it. So when he married a Japanese woman in Japan, Violet became, if not exactly divorced, certainly unmarried. In Japan she wed Wilfred H. de Cristoforo and returned to the United States after the war.

In the Japanese Evacuation and Relocation Study (JERS) and in *The Spoilage* and in Rosalie Hankey Wax's *Doing Fieldwork* Violet Kazue Matsuda is portrayed as "Mrs. Tsuchiraua," the conduit of pro-Japan sentiment and plotting at Tule Lake. After forty years, having suffered violations of her constitutional rights and physical exile from her American homeland, and having ended the vile, false portrayal by social scientists in their attempt to posit false history, social ostracism, obscurity, and dismissal from the world of real considerations, Violet Kazue Matsuda de Cristoforo, like Yuranouske Oishi, who let his sword get rusty to convince his enemies he was not one to be afraid of, is back with a warm vengeance. For her brother Tokio Yamane, who was falsely accused and brutally beaten at Tule Lake, then expatriated to Japan; for her first husband Shigeru; and for Kinzo Ernest Wakayama and other Nisei and Kibei, forced to renounce their U.S. citizen-ship, who suffered the brutality and corruption of the concentration camp at Tule Lake, Violet's impeccably researched, if idiosyn-cratically written and told, self-published *A Victim of the Japanese Evacuation and Resettlement Study (JERS): An AFFIDAVIT chal-lenging the inaccurate, misleading and denigrating references and accusations made by Rosalie Hankey Wax in Doing Fieldwork: Warnings and Advice, and in The Spoilage, at Tule Lake, California, 1944–45.* Signed, notarized, and dated June 30, 1987, in Monterey County, California, the *AFFIDAVIT* forces all of today's students of Japanese American camp history and social science to recon-sider the authenticity of the social science done at Tule Lake and the ethics of all the social science done in all of the camps by all of the anthropologists and sociologists, and all the clichés about camp history and Issei and Nisei behavior that have resulted from their work. Her *AFFIDAVIT* independently and unexpectedly corroborates sociologist Peter Suzuki's work on JERS and Hankey Wax.

In her zeal for justice and the completion of history, and in her poetry, Violet Kazue Matsuda de Cristoforo is remarkable for distinguishing between the real and the fake. The object of the free-form haiku she wrote in camp was an emphatic expression of the fleeting deep emotion of a specific flashing moment. In concrete images of the big and little phenomena about camp she gives us both the flashing moment and the fleeting deep emotion. Of the hundreds of haiku de Cristoforo wrote in Tule Lake concentration camp, only these fifteen survive. The moment and the emotion and more reach the reader, with poetic effect and the heavy reality of her subject, even in the way she signs her name:

Violet Kazue de Cristoforo
formerly Kazue Matsuda, Internee ID No. 29001

Poetic Reflections of the Tule Lake Internment Camp 1944

Many Dandelions Are Stepped On Only One Blooming Properly

Dandelions

The Tule Lake "Segregation Center" was built on volcanic ashes in the desolate lava beds of northern California, near the Oregon border. During the spring and summer it was very dry and dusty, and in the winter it was a muddy swamp, making it impossible for the internees to walk to the mess hall and to the communal washroom and toilet facilities. This condition made it necessary for the internees to build wooden catwalks connecting the barracks and the facilities serving them.

After the long and harsh winter dandelions sprang up between the wooden planks of the catwalks only to be stepped on by passers-by. One day, as if by a miracle, I found just one perfect dandelion among the many which had been crushed—as the down-trodden internees had been trampled underfoot by circumstances. As each day was a reminder of the humiliating and oppressive existence we were forced to endure, this one perfectly blooming dandelion was a symbol which inspired and fortified me. The pleasure I derived from this one blossom filled me with determination to endure the harsh conditions of camp life and to overcome all obstacles and difficulties.

"あるは踏まれたんぽぽ一つ正しく咲いた"

　ツール・レイク「隔離センター」は、オレゴン州境に近いカリフォルニア北部にある火山帯の熔岩と火山灰の上に建てられていた。春から夏にかけては空気は乾燥して埃っぽく、冬は泥沼のようになり、収容者は、食堂や、自分達の便所へ行くことも出来なかった。従って、収容者達は自分の手で建物とこれらの施設をつなぐ、すの子式の狭い板の通路を作って使用した。

　長く厳しい冬が終わる頃、タンポポが通路の板の隙間から芽を出したが、通る人に踏まれてしまった。ほとんどのタンポポが打ちのめされた収容者と同じように踏みにじられた中で、或る日私はまるで奇跡のように完全な姿のタンポポを見つけた。我慢を強いられ、忍従の毎日だっただけにこの完全な姿の一輪の花は私を勇気づけ力づけてくれるシンボルになった。この花を見つけた喜びは私にあらゆる困難を克服して、辛い収容生活に耐え抜いて行こうという固い決心を与えてくれたのだった。

Strong Sunrays Barracks Are All
Low and Dark

Sun Rays

The arrival of spring and summer is typically late in the high plains of Tule Lake, the largest of the ten internment camps built to house more than eighteen thousand detainees on about six square miles of black volcanic ash.

After the long, gloomy winter days the intense glare of summer creates a strong contrast and makes the low, dark, tar-papered barracks seem even more dismal and disheartening for the internees.

"強き日の光り家みな低し家みな黒し"

六千方マイルの火山灰の中に一万八千人を収容する最大のツール・レイク収容所にも春や夏が訪れた。けれどもそれは高地であるが故に極端に遅かった。

長く重苦しかった冬の後の夏の直射日光はきつく、タール紙を貼りつけた宿舎に濃い影を投げかけ、それは宿舎を一層低く、黒いものに見せて、尚更惨めで希望のない建物に見せていた。

Flowers on Tule Reeds and Sandy Flats
Brother Confined over 200 Days

Brother's Imprisonment

The November 4, 1943, warehouse incident, caused by reports of thefts of food for the internees by War Relocation Authority (WRA) personnel, resulted in confrontations and disturbances at Tule Lake.

Brother Tokio, an innocent bystander, had been asked to help restore order among the agitators. As he was about to do so, he was arrested by WRA Internal Security personnel and accused of taking part in the disorder. During a night of brutal interrogation he was cruelly beaten and, not only was he denied medical treatment for his injuries, but he was imprisoned in the "Bull Pen" of the camp stockade—a place of maximum punishment for serious offenders.

Following the occurrence army troops took over control of the camp and martial law was declared at Tule Lake.

Then came spring, the snow melted and the Tule reeds sprouted and grew. By July the reeds even had blossoms. Brother Tokio was still confined in the "Bull Pen," after nine months of imprisonment without trial or a hearing. Fall was about to come again and, under those conditions of dark uncertainty and desperation, everything was measured in terms of the growth and death of the Tule reeds.

弟等　監禁　久し

"蘭の花や砂っ原や二百余日"

　一九四三年十一月四日の倉庫事件は、収容所当局の役人によって食糧盗難事件として報告され、収容所内を対立と暴動に導いた。

　事件に関与せずただ居合わせただけの弟トキヲは暴動を鎮めるよう頼まれた。彼がそうしようとした矢先に当局によって逮捕された。一晩中の残忍極まる詰問の間に彼は酷く殴打された。彼は傷の手当ても受けさせて貰えず、それどころか最も重い刑罰として"ブルペン"と呼ばれる獄舎に入れられた。間もなく暴動鎮圧軍隊が収容所を統治し非常事態宣言が発令された

　やがて春が訪れ、雪解けと共に蘭が茂り始め、七月に入ると花も咲いた。弟のトキヲ外十六人は、相変わらず二百日間もブルペンに入れられたままで、その間、事情聴取も釈明も許されなかった。再び秋が訪れようとしていたが、この暗い不安な時間の経過はただ蘭の成長と枯れて行く様子でしか計れなかった。

Harsh Summer Ground
Being Ill Day After Day

Harsh Summer

After a short spring, the severe summer heat of the high plateau reflected from the black volcanic ash became unbearable, especially to one allergic to the wild grasses, weeds, and to the abundant dust to Tule Lake.

Every day was one of emotional and physical illness, of inner struggle, and of resignation.

"夏の地面きびしく少し病んでいるにちにち"

短い春の後に来る夏の強烈な日差しは、黒い火山灰に反射して、耐え難いものになっていた。特にツール・レイクの野草や埃に対してアレルギー体質の者にはたまらなかった。

毎日精神的にも肉体的にいためられて病人が続出し、ストレスと失望が充満した。

A Visitor Brings Me Tranquility and Happiness
The Summerly Ground Is Flat

Visitor

A priest friend was finally transferred to Tule Lake after being incarcerated in several isolation camps as a result of reports by WRA informers, including some of the so-called community analysts and researchers.

His visit to me brought happiness and tranquility, but also the realization that the summertime ground was still monotonously flat— that nothing had really changed.

"人を迎え心なごみて夏めきし地面平ら"

　僧職にある友人が、あちこちの収容所を廻された後、ツール・レイクへ配置された。彼の収容所たらい廻しは「調査官」という名目で収容者の動向を見張っていた幾人かの人の密告の結果だった。

　彼の来訪は私の心に幸せと平静さを与えてくれた。しかし、真夏の荒野は相変わらず平坦で単調であり、この幸福感も心の平安も、いつこわれるか分からない頼りないものであることに思い至った。それはまたこの現実は「結局、何一つ変わらないのだ」ということを思い起こさせた。

White Bare Feet
The Endless Wave of Wild Grass

Bare Feet

I frequently walked the lonely path leading to the hospital area to visit my dying mother-in-law terminally ill with cancer.

One day, while kicking the black volcanic ash off my sandals, I noticed for the first time my bare white feet. With aching heart, and challenging the war and the elements, I realized the monotony and the futility of our existence.

"素足が白くそして穂草がつづく"

　私は、ガンで死期の近かった義母を見舞う為に、病院に通じる淋しい道をよく歩いていた。

　或る日サンダルについた黒い火山灰を振り落として自分の素足の白さに初めて気が付いた。そして痛む心をかかえながら、戦争や他のことと戦っている自分達の存在が何と単純で無意味なものであるかを実感した。

Depressing Autumn Sky
Thinking About the War

Autumn Sky/War

Fall comes early to the lava beds of Tule Lake and by September the weather turns blustery, with sudden storms blanketing the area. The dismal autumn sky relates to my thoughts about the war and I become aware that it is the war our lives depend on. What is happening to the war? How many tears must I shed until it ends? What is befalling my parents in Hiroshima City?

"一帯秋の空せきばくみ戦を念ふ"

ツール・レイクの熔岩帯への秋の訪れは早い。九月になると天候は荒々しくなり突風が来て一帯に吹きまくる。秋の空は私に戦争のことを想わせる。この戦争は私達の生命を左右するものだ。この戦争は一体どうなっているのだろう。戦争が終わるまで私はどれだけの涙を流すことになるのだろう。広島にいる私の両親の身には何か困難が振りかかっているのだろうか。

Spider Web Turned Black
Confined Three Years

Spider Web

My baby is taking a nap and soon I shall leave for the camp hospital to see my dying mother-in-law, who is still waiting to hear from her only son interned in the Santa Fe camp. Letters to my husband and his letters to me, and to his mother, are censored and news is scanty. What shall I tell her today?

This is the third year the Tule Lake Segregation Center has been in operation and even the spider webs have turned black. What a long confinement it has been in our barren room where even a spider web focuses my attention!

"蜘蛛の巣くろみみとせ住ふ"

幼子は昼寝の眠りについた。死期の近い義母を見舞って来よう。彼女はサンタ・フェ収容所にいる一人息子からの消息を心待ちにしているのだ。夫への手紙、夫から私や義母への手紙は全部検閲を受けている。だから情報は乏しい。今日は義母に何と言おうかしら。

ツール・レイク収容所が出来て三年、蜘蛛の巣までが黒くなっている。蜘蛛の巣さえも私の注意をひく程の無聊な部屋でいつまで抑留されるのだろう。

A Man Picking and Discarding Cosmos Flowers His Face Ever So Gentle

Cosmos Flowers

One autumn day, on my way to the hospital, I saw an elderly man tending his flower garden. He was picking and discarding the wilting cosmos flowers, wrenching them out at times but with no visible signs of emotion. Ojisan probably had only the flowers for solace, as many of us did during the four years of confinement. I watched him awhile then walked away without saying anything to him, but a sense of compassion and affinity permeated me as I left him in his own world of nature.

"小父さんコスモスもぎ捨てる面ざしすなを"

秋の或る日、病院へ行く道すがら、年輩の小父さんが花畑の手入れをしているのを見かけた。彼はしおれたコスモスの花をちぎっては捨て、時には引き抜いていた。彼の顔は無表情だった。多分小父さんは花だけが唯一の慰めと思っていたのだろう。四年間の拘留生活で私達は皆そうだったもの。

暫 く 彼 の 様 子 を 見 て い た が 、 私 は 一 言 も 声 を 掛 け る で も

な く 立 ち 去 っ た 。 し か し 彼 を 彼 一 人 の 自 然 の 世 界 の 中 に 置

い た ま ま 立 ち 去 り な が ら 、 何 と も 言 え ぬ 温 か さ と 親 近 感 が

ひ し ひ し と 湧 い て 来 る の を 禁 じ 得 な か っ た 。

Memorized Shape of the Mountain Walk in the Same Direction on Winter Days

Shape of the Mountain

Castle Rock Mountain, the last battleground of the Modoc Indians, was my inspiration during my Tule Lake days. The Castle Rock area was also the location of the WRA Administration Office, the camp hospital, the military police, and the infamous "Bull Pen" of the stockade.

It was in the "Bull Pen" that my brother Tokio was imprisoned for ten months, without due process of law, in the most severe and degrading conditions, after being falsely accused of inciting the November fourth food riots.

I made numerous visits to this area to appeal to the camp authorities for the release of my brother from the "Bull Pen," to plead that my husband, who was being detained in the Santa Fe camp, be permitted to visit his dying mother, and later, that he be allowed to attend her funeral. All to no avail because the authorities were insensitive and indifferent to our plight and branded me a trouble-maker for my pains.

How abandoned I felt! How I longed to have the authorities heed my pleas for justice and humane treatment! How I ached for my relatives caught in the web of man's inhumanity to man! And always my vision and my thoughts were drawn to Castle Rock, comparing our fate to the Modoc Indians' last stand in their Lava Bed Campaign of 1872–73.

"山のかたち覚え冬の日歩く一方へ"

モ ド ッ ク ・ イ ン デ ィ ア ン の 最 後 の 戦 場 と な っ た キ ャ ッ ス ル ・ ロ ッ ク ・ マ ウ ン テ ン は ツ ー ル ・ レ イ ク 時 代 の 私 に は 印 象 的 で あ っ た 。 又 、 キ ャ ッ ス ル ・ ロ ッ ク 地 区 に は 収 容 所 当 局 の 本 部 や 病 院 、 軍 警 察 等 が あ り 、 そ し て 悪 名 高 い 極 悪 犯 隔 離 所 、 "ブ ル ペ ン" も こ こ に あ っ た 。

この"ブルペン"で弟のトキヲは十一月四日の食糧盗難
騒ぎの煽動者として誤認逮捕され、十ヵ月もの間、法の保
護を受けることもなく、屈辱的な獄中生活を強いられたの
だ。私はこの地区へ何度足を運んだことだろう。

私は弟を"ブルペン"から出して貰うよう陳情に行った
り、病気で余命いくばくもない義母を見舞う為に、そして
後には義母の葬儀参列の為にサンタ・フェから夫を帰して
貰うよう請願した。しかし、総ては徒労に終わった。当局
は、私達の苦境と心情には全く無理解で、とうとう私に煽
動者の烙印を押すことで終わった。

どんなに見捨てられたと嘆いたことだろう。どんなに当
局が私達の正義のための訴えと、人間らしい扱いを望む声
を聞き届けてくれるよう願ったことだろう。私は家族が人
間の作った蜘蛛の巣にかかり、非人間的な扱いを受けてい
ることにどんなに心を痛めたことだろう。そして私の視線
と想いはいつもキャッスル・ロックへ向けられ、1872年か
ら73年にかけて最後まで戦ったモドック族の運命と自分達
の運命を比べずにはいられなかった。

Two Summers Forced to Be Here
I Hold This Year's Flower Seeds in My Hand

Forced to Be Here

Forced to be in Tule Lake for two summers. I have already
gathered the seeds of this year's flowers. How many more years
must I keep doing this?

"二夏を遂はれ今年の花の種掌にする"

ツール・レイクに収容されて二夏が過ぎた。

私はもう今年の花の種を集め終わった。

この後、何年同じことを続けなければならないのだろう。

Autumn Grass Not Yet Tall
Fall Comes Earlier on the High Plains

Autumn Grass

It is not yet autumn by the calendar yet the fall weather is here. The stunted Tule reeds already have tassels and we are heading for another long and gloomy winter of confinement and uncertainty. Fall comes too soon in captivity. Where do I turn to lament my fate?

"秋草高からず秋が早い高原"

暦の上ではまだなのに、ここにはもう秋がきている。伸び悩みの蘆はもう花を持っている。私達はまた長く重苦しい冬を目前に、拘束と不安の長い時期を過ごさねばならない。囚われの身に秋は早い。私は運命に対する嘆きを何処に転じたら良いのだろう。

An Autumn Day Flowers with Thorns
A Lump in My Heart

Autumn Day

Brother Tokio, a U.S. citizen by birth, and many of his companions, are being sent to the Justice Department camp for enemy aliens in Santa Fe, New Mexico.

After much pleading with U.S. government agencies and with the Spanish consulate, the neutral protective power for enemy aliens, my kindly mother-in-law was finally sent to the hospital in Oregon for radium treatment—escorted by two armed soldiers with rifles and fixed bayonets. On the train one sat beside her and the other on the opposite seat. They stood guard over her when she used the train lavatory, and outside her hospital room. What danger did she pose to U.S. security?

Having been treated so shabbily by the government, was it a crime that she had requested repatriation to Japan so she could die in her native country and be buried by her family?

How do I express my feelings of repugnance, except to talk to my flowers? How do I suppress my pride? For whom do I shed my tears?

"秋の日花に棘あり女かたくな心で"

生まれながらの米国市民である弟のトキヲは、他の仲間達大勢と一緒にニュー・メキシコ州サンタ・フェの敵国人収容所に移された。

政府に対する度重なる懇願と中立国による敵国人保護をスペイン領事館に申し出て、義母はやっとオレゴンの病院でラジウム治療を受けることになった。ライフルと付け刃で武装した兵二人に監視されながら．．．。汽車の中では一人が隣に、一人が向かいの席に座って監視を続け、車中や病院のトイレでも監視を怠らなかった。米国の安全を乱す為に義母に何が出来るというのだろう。

政府によってこんな屈辱的な扱いを受けている義母や家族が日本への送還を願うことは罪なのだろうか。母国で死に母国の家族に葬られるよう願うことが。

それを否定せずにはいられない私のこの感情をどこに、どう表現できるのか。花に語るより他にないのか。私の誇りはさんざんに踏みにじられて、その悔しさをどう処理すればよいのか。私の涙は誰の為に流せばよいのだろう。考えれば考えるほど私の心はかたくなに閉ざされてしまう。

Flowers Are Good
I Endure a Long Time Raising Flowers

Flowers Are Good

How am I to endure these hardships? My young children and I are constantly ill. Yesterday's "friends" have become informers for the WRA and other government agencies. The constant harassment by WRA Internal Security personnel are creating "disloyals" to justify their tactics of "divide and conquer."

Again, I turn to my flowers for solace so I can endure the indignity, inhumanity, and injustice.

My lovely flowers—I love you!

"花はよきもの花作りて耐えくらすひさし"

どうやってこの苦しみに耐えればよいのだろう。私と幼い子供達はいつも病気を患っている、昨日までの友達は当局への通報者となっている。WRAの所内警備員の終わりのないいやがらせは彼等の作戦、"分離して征服"するために「不忠誠者」をでっち上げる。

再び私は、花に慰めを求め、屈辱と非人間性と不正に立ち向かっていかなければならない。

Death Brings Deep Thoughts
No Breeze on the Hilltop Today

Death

Many tragedies happened during my four years of internment, but one of the most cruel was the suicide of my haiku pal following her relocation to the Midwest. She was to have been the "prize" for her husband's gambling debts so she took her own life instead.

Hatsujo had helped me during my child-bearing days in Fresno, and later, in caring for my young children in the Jerome Internment

Center. She was an exceptional Kibei and there was a remarkable perception in the things she saw and the elegance of the haiku she wrote.

When news of Hatsujo's suicide reached me in Tule Lake, I sank into an uncontrollable depression, unable to rationalize her death although, deep in my heart, I felt it was the result of the harsh realities of the internment.

Then I realized we must all die sooner or later, whether today, tomorrow, or later on, and peace came to my tormented soul as I dedicated this haiku to her memory.

悼初女

"人は死ぬものとして物思ふ高原今日無風"

四年前の収容生活の間に無数の悲劇を経験したが、最も残酷だったのは、俳句仲間が中西部へ再転住した直後に自殺をしたことだった。彼女は、夫が自分を賭博の借金のかたにしていることを知り、自からの生命を断ったとのこと。

初女は、フレスノ時代、私の妊娠中に面倒を見てくれたり、ジェローム収容所では幼い子供達の世話をしてくれた。彼女は教養のある帰米二世で、彼女の眼を通して見た物事を俳句に表す優雅さとその観察力は抜群であった。

彼女の死は私を仰天させ、私はどうしようもない落胆に襲われた。彼女の死に対する正当な理由付けも出来なかったが、心の奥では、この収容所生活の悲惨さが彼女の夫の正常心を歪め、彼女を死に追いやったのだと思った。

やがて私達は皆遅かれ早かれ死ぬ運命にあるのだ。今日か明日か、百年後かということが判りかけて来た。そ〇して、この句を彼女の想い出として捧げようとした時、私の打ちひしがれた心に平和が甦った。

Peter T. Suzuki

(1928–   )

Peter T. Suzuki is an anthropologist who has turned his scientific tools on the anthropologists and sociologists who worked for the government in the American concentration camps. He finds the War Relocation Authority (WRA) social scientists wanting in science, ethics, and honesty. In his statement before the Commission on Wartime Relocation and Internment of Civilians chaired by Joan Bernstein in 1981, Suzuki concluded:

> The camp experience was a corrupting one for those social scientists, who under the pretext of scientific research, undertook such activities as spying, informing, and intelligence work. It also shows the extent to which the government attempted to manipulate and control the inmates.

Today, the social scientists who did their dirty work on human subjects in the camps are the honored and *emeriti* of their profession. They occupy the distinguished chairs of their sciences at the most holy universities and colleges in America.

Former anthropologists of the WRA's Community Analysis Section control the *American Anthropologist* and successfully kept Suzuki's study of their malfeasance, "The War Relocation Authority and an Anthropology of the Absurd," from sullying the pages of this self-aggrandizing journal. The work subsequently appeared in *Dialectical Anthropology*.

The Spoilage by Dorothy Swaine Thomas and Richard S. Nishimoto and the University of California Japanese Evacuation and Resettlement Study (JERS) that Dorothy Swaine Thomas headed are sacred monuments to the science of sociology. The works produced by Thomas and the scientists working with her represent the canon of scientific literature on the life and society of the Nikkei living in the concentration camps. Peter T. Suzuki was the first to openly charge Thomas's work with being unethical and fake science, with being bad science, with using fake data, and with reflecting racist paranoia and racist stereotyping. If he is right, virtually everything in print by an anthropologist/sociologist since the end of the war is suspect. If he is right, it means that the adventure of recovering Japanese American history, started by Michi Weglyn's *Years of Infamy,* has just begun.

Suzuki was born and raised in Seattle. He and his family were interned at the Puyallup Assembly Center in Washington State and at Minidoka concentration camp in Idaho. At fifteen he left Minidoka by himself to get a better education. In 1951 he graduated from Columbia University and the following year received an M.A. in anthropology at Columbia. He began his doctoral studies at Yale, won a Fulbright scholarship, and attended Leiden University in the Netherlands, where he received a second M.A. degree and his Ph.D. in anthropology in 1959. Suzuki is presently on the faculty of the Urban Studies Department at the University of Nebraska at Omaha, where he has taught since 1973.

The University of California Japanese Evacuation and Resettlement Study: A Prolegomenon

One's opinions regarding the effort and efficacy of the congressionally sponsored Commission on Wartime Relocation and Internment of Civilians (CWRIC) and of its report aside,[1] there is no gainsaying that the hearings the commission held in 1981 and 1982 throughout the United States, including Alaska, have compelled many to examine or reexamine the significant scientific literature on the wartime camps for Japanese Americans. Certainly a corpus of such studies on these camps[2] will include *The Spoilage* by Dorothy Swaine Thomas and Richard S. Nishimoto (with contributions by Rosalie A. Hankey, James M. Sakoda, Morton Grodzins, and Frank Miyamoto).[3] This 1946 publication was the first volume published of the University of California Evacuation and Resettlement Study.

The purpose of this paper is to examine certain aspects of *The Spoilage* and of the Evacuation and Resettlement Study (ERS) based upon published and unpublished materials (the latter in the National Archives, Washington, D.C.). Additionally, some materials recently submitted to CWRIC will be used to aid in the analysis that follows; and a basic and fundamental concept in anthropology will be used to help elucidate certain figures who were associated with ERS.

ERS was a major social science research project which was financed by the following institutions: the University of California, the Giannini Foundation, the Columbia Foundation, and the Rockefeller Foundation.[4] The magnitude of the funding can be imagined by the contributions which were made to support the study: the University of California, $29,554; the Rockefeller Foundation, $38,750; and the Columbia Foundation, $30,000.[5] Thus, almost $100,000 went into the project,[6] which was begun in February 1942 and concluded in July 1948.[7] Given the cost of living and the purchasing power of the dollar in this period, Carey McWilliams's characterization of ERS as "a lavishly financed research project"[8] remains indisputable.

The project was headquartered in Room 207 of Giannini Hall on the campus of the University of California at Berkeley and was headed by the sociologist Dorothy Swaine Thomas, who was also Lecturer in Sociology for the Giannini Foundation and a professor of rural sociology.

In addition to *The Spoilage*, a companion volume, *The Salvage*, published in 1952, dealing with those who had moved from the camps to the Chicago area, was a product of ERS.[9] It was hoped that a third volume, on the "residue," i.e., those who had returned to the West Coast from the camps, would be written. The two volumes published were the only ones on the social aspects which were definitely projected and realized.[10] However, 1954 saw the publication of *Prejudice, War and the Constitution,* a work that concerned itself with the political characteristics and legal consequences of the evacuation.[11] All three books were published by the University of California Press.

ERS had an ambitious goal even for the large-scale interdisciplinary research project that it was. Each of the major social sciences— sociology, social anthropology [sic], political science, social psychology, and economics—was intended to intermesh and converge upon the "evacuation, detention, and resettlement of the Japanese minority in the United States."[12]

One can readily agree with the statement by the authors of *The Spoilage* that "the ambitious conceptualization was never realized to the full."[13] This was especially true of the economic aspect of the project, a point which did not escape its critics.[14]

It is not only in ERS's failure to deal with one of the aspects of the stated goal of the project that *The Spoilage* falls short of its goal, however. There are other significant omissions which have the cumulative effect of raising serious questions regarding the study's effectiveness.

As an example, consider the statement that follows regarding the camps where research was done.

> Our three major "laboratories" were at Tule Lake project [camp] in northern California, the Poston project in Arizona, and the Minidoka project in Idaho. We were able, also, to make spot observations in five of the other seven War Relocation Authority [the government agency which ran the camps] projects.[15]

Despite the last statement of the citation above, the reader will look in vain within the covers of *The Spoilage* for the names of the five camps (projects) where "spot observations" were made. Moreover, extremely confusing is the use of the collective pronouns. As applied in the first statement of the passage cited, the plural form obviously refers to the entire ERS, a fact which can be deduced from the paragraph which precedes the cited passage. However, the use of "we" in the second statement could be interpreted to mean the co-authors, Thomas and Nishimoto. To further confound the clarity of the first statement is the issue of the criteria which were used to determine the selection of Minidoka, Poston, and Tule Lake as the "major laboratories."

As regards ERS fieldworkers in the camps, Gila, also in Arizona, at one time or another (depending upon the sources) had upwards of seven, the largest contingent of ERS fieldworkers. On the other hand, Minidoka, one of the "major laboratories," had only one (and that person moved from Tule Lake to Minidoka in mid-1943 [Minidoka had been in existence since the summer of 1942]); Poston, another "major laboratory," had but two (perhaps only one, after mid-1944); and Tule Lake had upwards of six.

Furthermore, inasmuch as Minidoka, Poston, and Tule Lake were the "major laboratories," one wonders why an inordinate portion of *The Spoilage* was given over to Tule Lake. Correspondingly, considering that they were viewed as "major laboratories," Poston and Minidoka receive scant attention. Specifically, coverage of these two camps in *The Spoilage* is, in the case of Poston, limited to approximately five pages (pages 45–49; 67–68), while in the case of Minidoka, not quite three pages are devoted to this Idaho camp (pages 65–68) in a 388-page volume. Of those where, presumably, "spot observations" were made and which may be considered the "minor laboratories," and where there were ERS fieldworkers, we have the following page figures: Manzanar, California: some five pages (pages 49–52; 70–71); Topaz, Utah: one and a half pages (pages 64–65); Gila, Arizona: one and three-fourths pages (pages 68–69); and Jerome, Arkansas: three-fourths of a page (pages 71–72). (Assuming that these are where "spot observations" were made—by Thomas and Nishimoto (?)—there is no indication which camp might have been the fifth where "spot observations" were made.) It should be noted that the print-type on the four camps in the pages cited is half the size of the regular print-type of the book; but even taking this into account, the fact of the paucity of information on all but Tule Lake remains an issue.

Moving to the topic of ERS personnel, Thomas and Nishimoto have this to say: "Most of the staff observers were evacuees; at one time as many as twelve Japanese Americans were employed as technical or research assistants in the camps."[16] Yet, there is no systematic listing of the names of these individuals. The normal protocol observed by a scientific research project—of recognizing in its published results those who have participated—is ignored in this book.[17] By examining closely the index of names and the pages in which the persons listed for their studies are referenced, one might be able to compile a list of such Japanese American researchers. Nevertheless, even by using this cumbersome method, an accurate listing cannot be compiled.

In point of fact, only by studying assiduously a not readily accessible mimeographed catalog of the General Library of the University of California listing ERS materials which appeared twelve years after *The Spoilage,*[18] or by doing research at the National Archives in Washington, D.C.,[19] can one learn the names of the Japanese American personnel. But these are largely hit-or-miss processes because inference and deduction must be used.

Just as negligent as omitting the study's Japanese American researchers in the WRA camps is the omission in *The Spoilage,* and subsequent ERS volumes, of the names of Japanese American ERS fieldworkers who did studies in the so-called assembly centers. There were sixteen in all, including Manzanar, a camp which later became a WRA camp. In general, these sixteen detention camps were in or near large urban areas (but included one in Arizona) along the West Coast and were the temporary camps where internees were incarcerated before being transferred to the more permanent WRA camps.

The authors acknowledge that there were such researchers, but not until the footnote at the bottom of page 23 can the observant reader, one fully conversant with the types, names, and history of the camps, for the first time infer from the citation, "Field Notes, August, 1942," that material from Japanese American researchers in the detention camps was used. Again, either by combing Barnhart's General Library catalog or by doing research in Washington, D.C.,[20] the persistent student might succeed in compiling a list of such researchers and where they worked. There is, of course, the direct method, which is to say, journeying to the Bancroft Library of the University of California at Berkeley, where the ERS materials are deposited.

Parenthetically, with regard to ERS collection and accessibility to its archival materials at Berkeley, the following odd circumstance must be noted.

Although Alexander H. Leighton was a lieutenant commander in the U.S. Navy while he was head of the Poston camp's Bureau of Sociological Research, the entire bureau file was moved to Bancroft after the war. Consequently, for the student who wishes to do archival research on the WRA camps, in addition to doing it at the National Archives in Washington, D.C., he/she must also travel to Berkeley for the Leighton file. Yet, because Leighton was a government employee, his materials should have been deposited in the National Archives in the first instance, as was the case of WRA materials (copies of which were deposited at Berkeley, among other places).[21]

Japanese American ERS personnel in the detention camps ("assembly centers"):

Manzanar (Owens Valley, California):
  Mari Okazaki
  Togo Tanaka
Santa Anita (Santa Anita Racetrack, Arcadia, Los Angeles County):
  Tamie Tsuchiyama
Tanforan (Tanforan Park Racetrack, San Bruno, San Mateo County, California):
  Doris Hayashi
  Fred Hoshiyama
  Ben Ijima
  Charles Kikuchi
  Michio Kimutani
  Tamotsu Shibutani
  Haruo Najima
  Henry Tani
  Kay Ushida
  Fujii Ushida
  Earle T. Yusa

Tulare (Tulare County Fairgrounds, Tulare, California):
 James Sakoda
Japanese-American ERS personnel in the WRA camps:
 Gila, Arizona:
 Shotaro Hikida
 Inoue (first name unknown) [22]
 Charles Kikuchi[23]
 Y. Okuno
 Joe Omachi
 Tamie Tsuchiyama[24] (see also under Poston, below)
 Earle T. Yusa[25]
 Manzanar, California:
 Mari Okazaki
 Togo Tanaka
 Minidoka, Idaho:
 James Sakoda[26] (see also under Tule Lake, below)
 Poston, Arizona:
 Richard N. Nishimoto
 Tamie Tsuchiyama (see also under Gila, above)
 Tule Lake, Newell, California:
 Frank S. Miyamoto[27]
 James Sakoda (see also under Minidoka, above)
 Tamotsu Shibutani[28]
 Tetsuo Najima (worked for the Giannini Foundation)
 Chet Yamauchi
 Topaz, Utah:
 Doris Hayashi
 Frederick Hoshiyama
Japanese-American ERS personnel in the Midwest:
 Chicago:
 M. Ishida
 Charles Kikuchi
 Frank Miyamoto
 R. S. Nishimoto
 Tamotsu Shibutani
 Togo Tanaka
 St. Louis:
 Setsuko Matsunaga
 No city identified:
 M. Ikeda

For some individuals listed above the complete names could not
be found. Aside from the silence regarding the Japanese American
ERS personnel in the detention camps in *The Spoilage*, it would

appear from the above that there may have been at least four more than the "twelve" in the WRA camps mentioned by Thomas and Nishimoto[29]

Still on the topic of ERS personnel, if the focus is now shifted to the non-Japanese staff, an equally ambiguous accounting is found in *The Spoilage*.

> In addition to the Japanese-American staff observers, three "Caucasian" members of our staff resided for long periods in the [WRA] camps we were studying. Two of these were graduate students in anthropology; one was a sociologist, with graduate training in political science.[30]

These "Caucasians" remain equally nameless; likewise where they were assigned is not revealed except by references in footnotes. Of the anthropologists, one was Robert Francis Spencer, a Berkeley graduate student who spent from July 1942 to June 1943 at Gila.[31] One comes across his name in a reference note at the bottom of page 68 as the author of a report. This is the only reference to Spencer, despite numerous reports he had filed during his tenure with ERS.[32] The second anthropologist was Rosalie A. Hankey (later Rosalie Hankey Wax),[33] who is listed on the title page as one of contributors to the book. This is the only instance in which her name appears in the book. The third was Robert H. Billigmeier.[34] One learns, also only indirectly, that he was the third "Caucasian." His name appears three times in three separate footnotes.

With regard to Billigmeier, the unknowing reader could readily assume that it was Morton Grodzins rather than Billigmeier who was the third "Caucasian." Grodzins is listed as one of the contributors on the title page of *The Spoilage* (just as is Hankey). Furthermore, the description of the third person, as one who had training in political science, could apply to Grodzins equally. Truth to tell, in 1945 he received his Ph.D. in political science at Berkeley.[35] A secondary source—namely, the book review by Marvin Opler, the WRA community analyst who did in-depth studies of all aspects of the Tule Lake camp—confirms that it was Billigmeier (rather than Grodzins) who did some field research at the camp of Tule Lake.[36]

Beyond those issues raised thus far, which might be excused as lapses, very serious ones emerge relating to the quality of *The Spoilage*. As Marvin Opler has pointed out, the first eighty-three pages contain rather straightforward material pertaining to the internees before the war and materials up to, and including, the loyalty oath ("registration") period in Tule Lake. These first eighty-three pages he considers "excellent."[37] The remainder of the volume is devoted to Tule Lake exclusively. This was the WRA camp in northern California, which, from the middle of 1943, became the "segregation center" for those who had been removed from the nine other camps because they had not passed the loyalty-oath test or had wanted to return to Japan for one reason or another. It also housed those who had been placed there originally and had not wanted to make another move to still another camp when Tule Lake was being converted to the segregation camp.

Marvin Opler's review of *The Spoilage* reveals that there is much to be desired in its section on Tule Lake, based upon Wax's observations. One major shortcoming, according to Opler, is Wax's lack of objectivity.

In order to understand the lengthy passages from *The Spoilage* which follow, the following must be stated. Wax initially became deeply involved with a group of internees—the segregants; that is, those who had selected to go to Tule Lake rather than those who had been there before the camp became a segregation camp—who were "pro-Japan." Then, after a murder of a "pro-America" member, she turned against the members of the former group. The following, therefore, reveals her subjective approach to some of the Tule Lake segregants, many of whom she came to despise. The passages are excerpts from pages 370 through 379 in *The Spoilage*.

Abe, Shozo (pseudonym). Of medium height and slender; physically unattractive. Manner forbidding in general and arrogant toward WRA officials and other Caucasians.

Kuratomi, George Toshio. Of medium height and slender. Quick intelligence; somewhat high-strung; dignified manner; an effective speaker. . . .

Kato, Bill (pseudonym). Of medium height, heavy set; affected *bozu* haircut. Boastful of leadership qualities. . . .

Seki, Johnny (pseudonym). Short and plump; gentle-mannered; genial and courteous. . . .

Tada, Mitsugu (pseudonym). Slender and extremely tall for a Japanese; often addressed by nickname, "Slim." High-bridged nose; moustache; in appearance more like a person of Mexican extraction than a Japanese.

Sasaki, Milton (pseudonym). Short and slender; distinguished appearance; dressy and dandified.

Watanabe, Taro (pseudonym). Heavy set; of medium height; impressive manner.

Noma, Takeo (pseudonym). Taller than average and well built. Considered arrogant and blunt in manner. . . .

Yamashita, Koshiro (pseudonym). Of medium height and stout; large "handle-bar" moustache. Pompous and condescending manner. . . .

Kira, Stanley Masanobu (pseudonym). Short and stout; effeminate appearance; small features; beard.

Ishikawa, Torakichi (pseudonym). Tall and well built. Argumentative and self-assertive.

Yamada, Nobuo (pseudonym). Of medium height and slender. Arrogant and self-assertive.

Tsuchikawa, Mrs. Hanako (pseudonym). Very short and slender; physically attractive; often called "Madame Chiang Kaishek" by fellow evacuees. Proud and stubborn; argumentative.

Wakida, George (pseudonym). Short and well built.

Niiyama, Sam (pseudonym). Short and somewhat stout. Practical and cynical.

Tsuruda, Bob (pseudonym). Medium height and slender; attractive in appearance. Conceited, but good sense of humor; talkative.

Kurusu, Isamu (pseudonym). Tall and slender. Gentle in manner and courteous.

Higashi, Thomas (pseudonym). Short, medium build.

Itabashi, Kazuhiko (pseudonym). Short and slender. Neat in appearance; spry and alert. Straightforward; kind manner.

The descriptions in themselves—some of which can be found word for word in Wax's *Doing Fieldwork*—not only are gratuitous, they also amply support Marvin Opler's criticism of Wax, regarding lack of objectivity, in his review of *The Spoilage*.

What is striking about the descriptions is that for none are standard measurements applied. Yet, Wax, an anthropologist, who, having studied in one of the world's foremost departments of anthropology, surely must have had at least one course in physical anthropology, which, if it was a standard course, taught use of simple objective measurements of body height in feet and inches and of body weight in pounds.

Withal, the most serious infelicity by Wax had to do with Stanley Masanobu Kira (pseudonym), an alleged Tule Lake terrorist. After she had turned against the "pro-Japan" group, the faction with which she had great empathy and sympathy prior to the murder of a Tulean of the opposing view (a "pro-America" member), and a faction with which she had ingratiated herself in order to get information, she began to abhor the "pro-Japan" group and its leaders, especially Kira. In her new "anti-fanatic" role she accepted as true what the leaders of the group to which she had switched her allegiance had to say about Kira. She asserted that Kira was a "selfish and dangerous man who wished only to become a big shot," and that Kira was nothing more than a gangster.[38] It came to a point where she felt so enraged about Kira, owing to the allegations of terrorism she had heard charged against him, that she pictured herself running to the section of the camp where Kira lived "like a berserk and beating up Mr. Kira."[39] She then plotted to get vengeance on Kira.[40]

Wax ultimately wreaked her vengeance on Kira in another, more effective, way. She informed on Kira to the Federal Bureau of Investigation at Tule Lake.

Not surprisingly, her hatred of Kira can be seen in the most denigrating and pejorative description with which one can label a man, a description she reserved for Kira: "effeminate."

What is most disquieting about the entire episode revolving around the Kira incident, aside from the ethics of an anthropologist turning informer, is this: in *The Spoilage*, perhaps one of the most astounding facts of the entire evacuation is buried in an appendix and laconically stated—in an incomplete sentence, no less—because it had to do with Stanley Masanobu Kira: "Filed suit against General DeWitt [commander of the Western Defense Command, and the general who was ordered to implement the evacuation], contesting legality of evacuation."[41]

The precious few Japanese Americans who contested in the courts one aspect or another of the martial law, evacuation, and incarceration have become landmark cases in legal history, irrespective of the outcomes of the cases, and the plaintiffs have become folk heroes in contemporary Japanese American culture.

What student of the Japanese American experience or of constitutional law has not heard of the Yasui, Hirabayashi, Endo, and Korematsu cases?[42] However, one wonders how many have heard of Kinzo Ernest Wakayama (Wax's "Kira")? Yet, had "Kira" not been turned in by Wax there is a good possibility that Wakayama would be as well known and as highly respected as the other four, a thesis which will be explored in greater detail shortly.

Before proceeding further, however, consider Wax's words on Kira's fate after she had informed the Federal Bureau of Investigation (FBI) about him. She

> suggested that they [the FBI] call in Mr. Kira and question him about his loyalties in the presence of some of the young *Hokoku* [a group of Tuleans who had renounced their American citizenship] officers [because Kira himself had not renounced

his citizenship]. Mr. Kira applied for denationalization. Subsequently, he was sent to Japan with the other expatriates. . . .[43]

Wax's matter-of-fact observation hardly reveals what then happened to "Kira." Thanks to the remarkable research and study by Michi Weglyn, one learns firsthand what actually took place during the FBI's "questioning." (Information on the source of Weglyn's section dealing with Wakayama precedes that portion in her book specifically dealing with him.)

Ted Nakamura, a Nisei attorney . . . recently recalled that in a Gestapo-style predawn raid, government officers forced themselves into the apartment of Kinzo Wakayama—a World War I veteran and embittered extremist leader—and compelled him to sign away his citizenship at gunpoint. Nakamura explains in a letter of June 25, 1973: "I interviewed him [Wakayama] during the summer of 1957 in Hakata, Japan. At which time he stated to me that he was rudely awakened about 3 or 4 in the morning. The FBI came to his quarter with a pistol brandishing, and the officer that accompanied the FBI compelled him to renounce.
Mr. Wakayama told the Justice Department official that he will only sign the renunciation document under protest. The officer stated to him that he may do so. Consequently, Kinzo Wakayama signed the renunciation document under protest. This means that the document so obtained would not be valid, and was obtained by duress."[44]

In neither *The Spoilage* nor in any of Wax's other writings are the central facts about Wakayama's life mentioned, facts which would have raised serious doubts in the readers' minds that he was a "fascist," as he was painted to be. It remained for his son, Junro Edgar Wakayama, presently assistant professor in a school of medicine of a western state university, to carry on the fight to clear his father's name.[45] Dr. Wakayama (born in the camp of Manzanar) and his younger brother were successful in making it possible for Kinzo Ernest Wakayama, at age eighty-six, to fly from a home for senior citizens near Fukuoka, Japan, to San Francisco in order to testify before CWRIC on August 11, 1981.[46]
The outstanding fact about Wakayama, and relegated to an incomplete statement in the Appendix of *The Spoilage,* and never again raised in any of Wax's writings or in any ERS publication, is that Kinzo Ernest and his wife Toki Wakayama challenged the constitutionality of the internment in "An Application of Wakayama, Ernest and Toki, for a Writ of *Habeas corpus.* No. 2376-H and 2380-OC

(Civil). The District Court of the United States Southern District of California. September 23, 1942."[47] Both were supported in their efforts by the American Civil Liberties Union of Southern California.

It would be only fair to have Kinzo Ernest Wakayama present his story, as outlined in autobiographical form and submitted to CWRIC prior to his actual appearance before the commission in 1981.

Brief Personal history. Incidents and Opinion [sic]

1. American citizen of Japanese ancestry—Born at Kohala, Hawaii, on June 16, 1895.

2. Enlisted in the United States Army—First World War.

3. Secretary—Republican Party, 2nd Precinct, 2nd Representative District—Island of Hawaii.

4. Clerk—United States Post Office—Kohala, Hawaii.

5. Bookkeeper—People's Bank, Kohala Branch, Hawaii.

6. Interpreter—Kohala District Court—Hawaii.

7. Candidate for the West Hawaii Board of Supervisors primary election from Republican Party.

8. Secretary-Treasurer of Fishermen's Union of Los Angeles Harbor Area, Los Angeles, California, affiliated with the American Federation of Labor.

9. Statement of loyalty, an article published in the San Pedro Pilot—newspaper, California—written by me and was introduced in Congress—recorded in Congressional Record of June or July issue 1940 or 1941 (exact date, month and year not clear).

10. Submitted request to General DeWitt, West Coast Defense Commander, to make a separate camp for First World War Veterans (American Legionnaires) of Japanese ancestry if removal of every person of Japanese blood is necessary for defense purpose, to avoid criticism later if dumped together with others, which will be taken up as racial issue and abridge [sic] of Constitutional Rights. The reply was as we all know, "Jap is Jap," which greatly hurt my heart because I believed that I was a loyal American regardless of race, creed or color.

11. The above request was sent by me, acting adjutant of Commodore Perry Post, American Legion of Southern California, and in behalf of Townsend Harris Post of San Francisco, California, but the reply as mentioned above to my disappointment.

12. I rejected evacuation at Terminal Island, California, because I am an American citizen, but was ordered to obey the removal under the point of a machine gun by armed sailors.

13. Filed writ of *Habeas Corpus* through the [American] Civil Liberties Union of Southern California in the United States

District Court to challenge our (wife included) Constitutional Rights. Attorneys Edgar Camp, [A. L.] Wirin and O'Zrand and others handled this case.

14. I was illegally imprisoned without due process of law twice—approximately 72 days in the Los Angeles County Jail and 2 weeks at Lone Pine Jail near Manzanar Relocation Center, California.

15. Arraignment at Los Angeles Jail read as follows: "Knowingly and willingly attempt to over-throw the United States Government" which was very ridiculous when heard.

16. I was handcuffed from Santa Anita Segregation Center to Los Angeles County Jail and this photo appeared in the next morning which was read by thousands of people.

17. I was blended [sic] [branded] as a traitor, my reputation injured greatly beyond words expressed because of my loyalty to the country of my birth, which was demonstrated by serving as a good soldier with the United States Army became regrettable after a number of years passed by and my above written personal record was not given any consideration at all.

18. Nothing has been done during my imprisonment except once taken to court for 10 minutes and was released without explanation or decision given after 2 months of confinement.

19. I was taken to Pomona Camp [Pomona Assembly Center, Pomona, California], Manzanar, Tule Lake, Santa Fe [Internment Camp] and Crystal City [Texas] Camps thereafter.

20. I was kicked and pushed around and taken to the stockade for questioning countless number of times, told to drop the case of *Habeas Corpus* otherwise there will be other method to curtail my movement hereafter which was a vengeance cleverly planned by the authorities of the Justice Department, also based on racial prejudice.

21. There were few Japanese in Lone Pine Jail and the Mexican [sic] [Spanish] Government Consul (neutral country represented Japan) came to see them but I was refused when asked to interview my case because he had nothing to do with American citizen. Mr. Gaffrey (spelling might be wrong) came to Manzanar at that time so my wife requested why should my husband be taken in prison and no protection given to a person of American citizen while the aliens are taken care of by the Mexican [sic] Consul. Reply was, "If your husband needs protecting tell him to become an alien," which was very astonishing and disappointing—forced me to become an alien and give up my American citizenship which I have valued greatly for many, many years and was a great shock to me.

22. Over 110,000 Americans of Japanese blood were sent to segregation [sic] centers by forceful evacuation. However, none of the enemy aliens of Italy and Germany were taken in—this biased act clearly demonstrated racial discrimination; abridge [sic] of Constitutional Rights of the Nisei, American citizens of Japanese ancestry; and unfair treatment to veterans of the First World War of American Legion which stated above.

23. I was glad to hear the good news of the heroism of Nisei soldiers of 442nd Infantry from Hawaii—my nephew was injured but returned—who fought gallantly to preserve American democracy but on the other hand I felt sorry for those who died and to those who came back not knowing that some day in the future these boys will experience what I am now going through and be too late to regret.

24. I denounced my citizenship under threat and duress of war plus in fear of unlawful imprisonment again and illegal questioning thereafter in consideration of my declining health if I refused to do so.

25. I still believe that I am a good American citizen compared with those who waved patriotic flag and did not care to fight for their rights in time of peace or at war. As an example, I have preached my 3 sons to render their service with the Armed Forces of the United States to show their loyalty to which they have done so regardless of what have [sic] happened to their father, because some day, the government will realize the black page in the brilliant American history and correct it by someone, though it may take many years hereafter.

26. My first son was discharged from the United States Army in 1970 was a Captain and my third son served overseas at Vietnam.

27. I would like to see this great mistake of injustice done to me and other 110,000 Americans of Japanese ancestry by the United States Government authorities be corrected if the true spirit of democracy is to be preserved and if the United States of America is still claimed to be the land of the free and justice for all the people. For this reason I sent a claim and letter to my sons who are presently attending University of Oregon Medical School and San Francisco State College.

I had gall bladder extracted at the age of 77 and I am now recuperating at an Old Age People's Home in Japan. I desire settlement before I pass away, may be not to [sic] far in the future, to rest my soul in peace.

signed/ Ernest Kinzo Wakayama
October 16, 1972 [48]

The especially harsh treatment which had been meted out to Wakayama at various stages and places of his incarcerations lend credence to his Point 20 of the statement above. That an anthropologist, perhaps unwittingly, may have occupied a key position by playing into the hands of those who had a larger plan—to be rid of Ernest and Toki Wakayama and their children by banishment to Japan—is quite disconcerting to contemplate. What is established is that Wax knew exactly what the consequences of her informing on Wakayama would mean.

In the circumstances that make up *The Spoilage* chronicle, an interesting but revealing aside is presented by the pseudonym selected by Wax for Wakayama. The rich allegorical imagery is revealed when the plot of one of Japan's classic and most beloved tales, *Chushingura* (Tale of the Forty-Seven Ronin), is recounted.

In brief, it is a tale of feudal Japan revolving around the villainous Lord Kira and the hero Retainer Oishi. Lord Kira, a corrupt and greedy figure, fails to instruct Lord Asano properly on court etiquette and dress because the latter had not plied Lord Kira with lavish gifts. Ultimately, Lord Asano is forced to commit *seppuku* (ritual suicide). To avenge his death the Lord Asano's retainer Oishi develops a plot which culminates in avenging his lord's death. *Chushingura* is a tale of greed, power, perfidy, face, honor, and revenge.[49]

By the use of the particular pseudonym and the descriptions of Kira and of his alleged activities, Wax leaves no room for doubt that, in Wax's eyes, the morality play unfolded in Tule Lake while she was there, and the choice of "Kira" for Wakayama, was more than fortuitous.[50]

Although seemingly quite unrelated, there is still another significant aspect of ERS, which is to say, a book by one of its principal researchers, Morton Grodzins.

Grodzins was a young graduate student in political science who joined ERS in early 1942 and who was, in many respects, Dorothy Thomas's right-hand man.[51] Based upon his research while with ERS, as has been reported already, he wrote his Ph.D. dissertation in political science in 1945 for the University of California. "The Effects of the Japanese Evacuation."

Four years later, while teaching in the political science department of the University of Chicago, he had a book published by the University of Chicago which stemmed from his research with ERS, *Americans Betrayed: Politics and the Japanese Evacuation.*

Although this book is now remembered more for its analysis of the Japanese evacuation, *Americans Betrayed* was a brilliant *tour de force* for the field of political science, breaking barriers in theory, methodology, and policy analysis. Nonetheless, the basic thesis of this comprehensive tome is that pressure groups and politicians were behind the unjust evacuation.

An important consequence of the publishing of *Americans Betrayed*, and neglected to date by students of the evacuation, was the alteration of ERS's publication plans.

As will be recalled, had there been a third volume, it was to have been entitled *The Residue,* a book on the returnees from the camps to the West Coast. That *The Residue* was to be the third volume was also clear to the most knowledgeable person about ERS not connected with it, Marvin Opler. "The third [ERS volume, after *The Salvage*], already titled *The Residue*, will concern that population segment which ultimately returned to coastal areas."[52]

In the words of the authors of the third volume of ERS which did come off the press, *Prejudice, War and The Constitution: Causes and Consequences of the Evacuation of the Japanese Americans in World War II,* published in 1954:

> Before leaving the University of California and the directorship of the Evacuation and Resettlement Study in 1948, Professor Thomas, together with Professor [Charles] Aiken, prevailed upon Professor [Jacobus] tenBroek to undertake the preparation of the present volume. The latter invited Professor [Edward N.] Barnhart to participate in the enterprise, and subsequently Floyd Matson was asked to join as collaborator.
>
> The present work is concerned with the evacuation in terms of its historical origins, its political characteristics, the responsibility for it, and the legal implications arising from it. Thus it is less a study of the Japanese in particular than of Americans in general.[53]

However, it is clear that one of the major goals of this book had to do with Grodzins's *Americans Betrayed* in a very direct way. Thus:

> Some of the original file material bearing on the political aspects of the evacuation had been collected by Morton Grodzins in his position as research assistant for the study. Utilizing this as well as other study materials, he prepared and published a book on the subject. . . . Although Dr. Grodzins and the authors of the present work have all drawn upon the file material of the study, the present authors differ substantially from him in their assessment of the reliability, relevance, and significance of much of the data, and have supplemented these resources

with much additional material. Accordingly, their ultimate conclusions are different from his, and sometimes flatly contradict
them.[54]

The authors then reveal their position very early in the book. This
paragraph is found on page 4.

A number of students of liberal persuasion have attributed the
principal responsibility for the evacuation to pressure groups
and politicians. Thus Bradford Smith declares that "the prepon-
derantly loyal Japanese minority were rounded up in an illegal
fashion, chiefly in response to pressure from a bluntly intoler-
ant, grasping element on the Pacific Coast." Smith also observes that "this was an election year" and "anti-Orientalism
was a staple product on the Pacific Coast." According to Carey
McWilliams, "the Federal Government was pressured, or perhaps more accurately, 'stampeded' " into undertaking the evacuation "by the noisy clamor of certain individuals, groups, and
organizations in the three western states," by "groups that had
an obvious and readily acknowledged economic interest in evacuation," by "politicians and political units" exerting pressure
directly on General DeWitt as well as indirectly "through the
technique of an organized campaign." Morton Grodzins—though
his conclusions as to responsibility for evacuation vary from
chapter to chapter of *Americans Betrayed*—adheres, in the main,
to the pressure group and political theory.

Veritably an entire chapter (chapter 4) is set aside in the book by
tenBroek, Barnhart, and Matson to criticize Grodzins's *Americans
Betrayed*.[55]

Notwithstanding the then startling thesis posited by the three
authors, and increasingly substantiated by heretofore classified documents as they are declassified (especially those pertaining to
Roosevelt)[56]—that Roosevelt, his civilian aides, Henry Stimson, the
Congress, and the Supreme Court were to bear the heaviest burden
of responsibility[57]—a major question remains. Why did an unplanned
book, or one which, at the most, was to be a "monograph" to "deal
with political and administrative aspects of evacuation and resettlement"[58] come to be a cornerstone of ERS?

A clue to the answer—providing yet another twist to the history
of ERS—may be found in reactions by specific institutions of higher
education to *Americans Betrayed*.

On page 27 of the December 15, 1950, issue of *The New York
Times* can be found this news item, cited here in its entirety.

William Terry Couch charged today that he lost his job as director of the University of Chicago Press last month because he had published a book that Chancellor Robert M. Hutchins, at the request of the University of California, had sought to suppress.

Mr. Couch quoted Chicago's president, Ernest C. Colwell, as telling him in effect two years ago, during the controversy over the book, that "inter-university comity" was more important than freedom of the press.

He asserted he had decided to disclose the background of his dismissal after waiting three weeks in vain for the university to do so. When the vice president, James A. Cunningham, announced Mr. Couch's discharge on Nov. 21, he said the reason was "private." To Mr. Couch personally, he said it was "inability to get along with your subordinates or superiors."

The book involved in the dispute was *Americans Betrayed,* by Morton M. Grodzins, Assistant Professor of Political Science at the University of Chicago. It was published early last year, and is critical of California's and the Federal Government's handling of the Japanese relocation problem [sic] during the war. The book was written as a thesis by Mr. Grodzins while he was studying at the University of California.

Mr. Couch denied the assertion by the University of California that it had allowed Mr. Grodzins access to material in the book only on his written agreement not to publish it.[59]

There is no denying the sharp criticisms of Californians and of leading California officials contained in the book. Very few Californians and California organizations (or, for that matter, West Coast groups) receive accolades from Grodzins for having tried to prevent the evacuation or for having tried to help Japanese Americans (this follows logically from the fact that there were so few such groups or people). The forthrightness of the author in pointing the finger of blame to Californians and others on the West Coast for culpability in the evacuation obviously did not escape the attention of Grodzins's alma mater.

It appears that the decision to work on a study assigning blame for the evacuation, as was done in *Prejudice, War and the Constitution,* instead of pursuing a study about the lives of former inmates through *The Residue* (for which background research already had been established),[60] was directly connected with the unhappiness of the University of California over the then forthcoming *Americans Betrayed.* Quite clearly the next best policy by those who have been unsuccessful in proscribing a book is to have a team of "experts" write a book to discredit the first. One must bear in mind the following words by a disinterested historian written almost twenty years after the appearance of *Prejudice, War and the Constitution* in order to appreciate better the cogency of the previous statement.

> The highly argumentative tone of the volume [*Prejudice, War and the Constitution*], one suspects, can be explained by the fact that its authors, Edward N. Barnhart, Jacobus Ten Broek [sic], and Floyd W. Matson were quite concerned with refuting the argument of Morton Grodzins in *Americans Betrayed: Politics and the Japanese Evacuation* (Chicago, 1949)[61]

The final twist to this particular episode regarding *Americans Betrayed* is that—in order to mute further criticism of the University of California and the University of Chicago—Grodzins was appointed the director of the University of Chicago Press in 1951, a position he held until 1953.[62]

DISCUSSION

Up to this point the basic facts concerning some shortcomings and odd developments of ERS have been indicated. Some interpretation of the facts has been made as well. It now remains to try to understand in greater depth some of the facts. This will be done by looking more closely at several of the principals who were associated with ERS by applying a standard and basic anthropological concept as a basis for interpretation. This concept is enculturation.[63]

The first of these principals is Morton M. Grodzins. With reference to a passage by tenBroek, Barnhart, and Matson cited earlier, the reader will recall that Grodzins, because of his "liberal persuasion" (along with Smith and Carey McWilliams), as averred by the three authors, offered the thesis that he did in *Americans Betrayed*. This kind of approach is facile and obfuscates what this observer considers to be a more important reason. However, before proceeding to Grodzins, a few observations on Carey McWilliams are in order.

According to William Petersen, Carey McWilliams, strongly influenced by communists, had, after all, backed the evacuation, had even tried to organize a group that would endorse the evacuation, and then had praised the efficiency with which the evacuation had been undertaken.[64] After he had switched positions and had come out against the evacuation and incarceration, it would hardly have been seemly to have criticized those (i.e., government officials) whom he had praised earlier. Moreover, for McWilliams, blaming agribusinesses, chambers of commerce, and "rightwing groups" (such as the army, the American Legion, nativists, etc.) provided a good stratagem; it helped deflect blame from his idol, Franklin D. Roosevelt. Thus, lumping Grodzins with McWilliams and Smith (about whose political ideology there is little information) provides little elucidation.

Regarding *Americans Betrayed* and Roosevelt, however, it is interesting what one astute reviewer, writing in *Columbia Law Review,* had to say as a major criticism of the book: "the major omission in the work [*Americans Betrayed*] is the almost complete failure to mention the part, if any, played by the president. . . ."[65]

The key to understanding Morton Grodzins's attack on West Coast organizations and officials is not that he was a "liberal" (he may well have been). Rather, the underpinning clue is found in the following statement on page ix of his book. "As a relative newcomer to California, I was unfamiliar with the Japanese problem when I began my work in the early spring of 1942."

Here was a young doctoral student (he was twenty-five when he arrived in California) who had not been raised on the West Coast and therefore had not been enculturated to and sullied by hatred of and prejudice against Japanese Americans so endemic on the West Coast, even infecting academia.[66]

Grodzins was born in Chicago in 1917, and had studied for his undergraduate and M.A. degrees at the University of Louisville.[67] In neither Chicago nor even the South—Kentucky—had he been enculturated to dislike Japanese, because there had been no set anti-Japanese ideology rampant in these places in contrast to the West Coast. (Therefore it was no accident that Chicago welcomed Japanese Americans from the camps when many moved out of them. Eventually the Japanese American community grew from next to nothing to some twenty thousand in a few short years.) His stay in California was brief, from 1942, to 1945, and some of this time was spent in Washington, D.C., for ERS.[68]

It may have been Grodzins's anger and indignation over the evacuation and over the long history of the mistreatment of the Japanese on the West Coast, culminating in the evacuation, rather than liberalism, which steered him to seek to put the blame on those whom he felt were most immediately responsible for the injustice— ranging from the Magnolia Study Club of Anaheim and the University of Oregon Mothers to Earl Warren.[69]

The validity of the enculturation thesis in understanding Grodzins's *Americans Betrayed* can be apprehended more successfully by looking at another white male researcher who had been with ERS.

Like Grodzins, Robert F. Spender was a graduate student at

Berkeley (his field was anthropology). He had spent from July 1942 to June 1943 at the camp of Gila, in Arizona, as a fieldworker for ERS. Like Grodzins, Spencer was born in 1917.[70] Like Grodzins, Spender received his Ph.D. from Berkeley (in 1946, in anthropology), and also based his dissertation on some of the work he had done as field researcher for ERS, much as Grodzins had done.

However, the similarities end there. Spencer was born in San Francisco and received his B.A. degree from Berkeley in 1937. For his M.A. degree he went to Albuquerque, New Mexico, where he received the degree in 1940. He taught at Reed College, Portland, Oregon, from 1946 to 1947 and then from 1947 to 1948 he taught at the University of Oregon. It is clear that he was a product of the West Coast (Arizona certainly could be considered a West Coast state, and New Mexico, a western state).[71]

It is apparent that the enculturation of typical West Coast prejudicial and pejorative attitudes toward that region's Japanese population had taken place for Spencer along the lines of the classic model.[72] Despite the training he had received in one of the world's finest departments of anthropology and under the tutelage of world-renowned anthropologists Robert H. Lowie and Alfred L. Kroeber,[73] his training in anthropology was of little aid in helping him transcend the values and attitudes with which he had been enculturated. The good Pacific Coast citizen that he was first and foremost, he wrote two articles in the immediate postwar years which showed how effective the enculturation process had been for him and how ineffectual his Berkeley training in anthropology had been in competing against it.

Nineteen forty-eight saw the appearance in print of his article "Social Structure of a Contemporary Japanese-American Buddhist Church."[74] The languid state of the Berkley Buddhist Church in the immediate postwar period is analyzed without proper reference to the devastating effects of the evacuation, incarceration, and resettlement or to the pervasive anti-Japanese attitudes and discriminatory acts before, during, and after the war. Additionally, Spencer leaves the reader with the distinct impression that the priest and the Japanese congregation (Issei, Nisei, Kibei) were somewhat deficient and therefore were to blame for the pathetic state of affairs of the church. In his 1948 article is embodied a textbook case of the critic blaming the victim.[75]

Two years later, and one year after the publication of Grodzins's *American Betrayed,* he made known his position even more forthrightly. In a journal publication on the speech of Japanese Americans—based upon those whom he had studied in the camp of Gila and those in Berkeley—he observed, "Not only is this American-born segment [Nisei and Kibei] of considerable interest as bilingual, *but, more significantly, the development of English follows a somewhat distinct aberrant path."* A few pages later is found this statement: "One cannot but agree with Swadesh when he implies that a bilingualism which prevents mastery of either language reflects not psychic confusion, as a behavioristic psychologist might claim, *but rather feeble-mindedness."*[76]

A good case for enculturation can be made as a basis for understanding Rosalie H. Wax as well.

The chief writer of *The Spoilage* was born in Des Plaines, Illinois, in 1911.[77] During the depression years, from about 1930 to 1938, her fatherless family, composed of her mother, two brothers, two sisters, and Rosalie, lived in a Mexican slum *(barrio)* of Los Angeles. During this period she did housework, was on relief, and worked on several Works Project Administration (WPA) jobs.

Despite her working-class background, she had enculturated the following value, as expressed in her own words.

> During this period I had come to accept hard work as one of the essential elements of life and I had also developed an imperviousness to obstacles, disappointments, and discouragements. If I thought a task worth doing and finishing, I would stick with it.[78]

This is borne out by her subsequent upwardly mobile, success-oriented achievements. She completed junior college at age twenty-seven in an era when adult college students that old were a rare phenomenon. She then received a modest scholarship for study at the University of California, from which she received her bachelor's degree in 1942.

While at Berkeley she had heard that Professor Alfred L. Kroeber, the great anthropologist, was hostile to the idea of women becoming anthropologists. Fearful that he would tell Wax to leave the Department of Anthropology, she avoided him for a year. When she did take a course with him, she "worked like a demon and he seemed to find [her] . . . phenomenal energy baffling and amusing." He never made an attempt to discourage her interest in anthropology; she did work very hard as a graduate student.[79] Indeed, it was Kroeber who notified Wax of a position with ERS when another Berkeley anthropology student, Spencer, had resigned.[80]

She notes that ERS originally had a number of social scientists. "But the war gradually drew all of the male planners out of the study, and its directorship fell upon Dorothy Swaine Thomas. . . ."[81]

For her part, the latter was very pleased to have Wax as Spencer's replacement.[82]

Fieldwork at Gila, Arizona, was difficult for Wax and discouraging from the very start.[83]

Obviously, Thomas was a demanding taskmistress, requiring of Wax "voluminous data about attitudes and events that she desired." She kept asking Wax for these data on a regular basis.[84]

At the same time, Thomas told Wax "on no account to give any information or 'data' to the WRA,"[85] but Wax did have contact with G. Gordon Brown, the community-analyst anthropologist at Gila.

Even after a month at Gila, Wax had obtained "almost no data of the type that Dr. Thomas considered valuable."[86]

During her early months at Gila, quite understandably, Wax felt discouraged because she could not conform to Thomas's expectations[87] in terms of field data, and because Thomas became dissatisfied with Wax.[88] However, Wax was not the only ERS fieldworker who felt this way. Tamie Tsuchiyama ("Miss K" in Wax's *Doing Fieldwork*), a Japanese American anthropologist, "worried Dr. Thomas because she [Tsuchiyama] sent in so few field notes."[89]

Thomas gave Wax the charge of getting at the attitudes of the internees in Gila who had passed the loyalty test, but Wax felt that it was not possible to get this kind of information using the participant-observation method.

In order to gain the confidence of these people (the "loyals"), Wax began a series of survey and interview studies. These studies, which Wax terms "red-herring studies," were useful in gaining entrée into the lives of the inmates, and also presented her "in the role of a conscientious scholar collecting data on relatively harmless matters. They also provided the opportunity for a return visit to discuss specific problems . . ." and "gave respondents a reasonable story to tell curious neighbors."[90]

The red-herring studies also provided her with an opportunity to learn to be a competent friend and fieldworker and taught her respondents to be useful and competent respondents.[91]

I doggedly submitted my red-herring studies to Berkeley and described the attempts I was making to reach the point where I could get the kind of information needed. As the return letters [from Thomas] grew increasingly critical, I grew increasingly stubborn. I knew I was not doing a good job, and this distressed me very much. But in my more optimistic moments I hoped I was making progress.[92]

Then Thomas told Wax quite clearly, "sternly and . . . even harshly," ordering Wax to abandon her "time-wasting" red-herring studies and "to report what was going on."[93] (She learned some time later, though not after this particular letter, that Thomas had considered firing Wax.[94]) In the meantime, Wax had submitted a report on the shooting of a young internee by an army guard, an event which had taken place just before she had received the warning letter from Thomas. In this incident and events surrounding it, Wax

> found it possible for the first time to prepare a detailed, reasonably accurate, and well-balanced report, which presented a comprehensive picture of the dynamics of an event and the attitudes it produced.

This report was enclosed in a letter replying to Thomas's warning letter. "Dr. Thomas praised the report and did not again complain about my field techniques."[95]

The shooting incident also had the effect of structuring the relationship of the inmates to Wax as respondents and fieldworker, and the knowledge that Wax had prepared a good report helped her self-confidence and morale. "From this point forward it was relatively easy to keep informed on the salient political and social developments."[96]

The salience of what has been brought to the fore on Wax, based almost exclusively upon information in her book *Doing Fieldwork,* toward understanding her is clear. To recapitulate, Wax was a highly motivated, success-oriented person who, through enculturation, firmly believed in hard work and had developed an imperviousness to obstacles and disappointments. By practicing what she believed, she had received her bachelor's degree from an elite university at an age when most Americans of that period, especially women, were resigned to a lesser status. Having encountered another obstacle, Kroeber, a purported sexist, she waited until she felt she was ready to tackle him, and when she did, she so impressed him through hard work that he even notified her of a position (as researcher for ERS), and took a solicitous interest in her health while undergoing preparations for Gila.[97]

Despite extremely adverse physical, cultural, psychological, and social conditions at Gila, and under manifestly inordinate pressure from the director of ERS to produce results, Wax persevered. To compound her difficulties, ERS was directed by a woman (with whom she had very little in common because Thomas was a demographer, rural sociologist, and statistician[98]), who, Wax implied, became director through default rather than through hard work and merit because all the original male planners (including the anthropologist Robert H. Lowie) were called upon to do other things owing to wartime exigencies.

She persevered through doggedness and recourse to red-herring studies. Also, she worked "furiously" to get data[99] and was aided by a fortuitous circumstance. An extraordinary event—the shooting of an inmate—took place. It was an event ". . . *of the type on which the study particularly desired data.*"[100] The report on it not only enhanced her rapport with the internees; it also shut off all criticisms of her field research methods from Thomas from then on.

It appears Wax interpreted the significance of the report in the following way. The way to satisfy Thomas was to keep her apprised of events beyond the prosaic and mundane, beyond reports on "Japanese language and Japanese customs."

Seen from Thomas's perspective, the demand for data on extraordinary events also made sense. As a female who had been given the vast responsibility, albeit by "default" (although she was a professor in a major university), of heading what up to that time had been one of the largest social science research projects affiliated with a stellar university, she had to prove herself in a sexist world and prove to others her uniqueness and individuality (that she was not "just" the wife of W. I. Thomas, the world-famous sociologist). One way to make ERS a landmark project was to immortalize it with field data even Japanese-American researchers could not attain. Quite possibly Wax would be the one capable of obtaining such data. This was vindicated, as can be seen in the statement that follows from *The Spoilage*: "One of the Caucasian observers—a contributor to this volume—obtained confidential reports from a group of determined 'disloyals' with whom no Japanese-American staff member could possibly have established contact."[101]

It was in keeping with this, therefore, that Thomas in January 1944 asked Wax to make an exploratory visit to Tule Lake, where there had been a major disturbance in the previous fall.[102] After Wax's visit to Tule Lake, Gila seemed "quiet and dull" and boring. Consequently she was pleased when requested by Thomas to make a ten-day return visit to Tule Lake.[103] A third visit, lasting six days, like the previous two visits, centered on the political activities of various factions.[104]

By her third visit she had good working relationships with "more than a dozen of the segregated residents [v. those who had been at Tule Lake from the start] . . . ."[105]

She moved permanently to Tule Lake in May 1944 and remained there a year.

At Tule Lake, Wax became more and more involved with the people she was to be detachedly observing.[106] Her assignment at Tule Lake was "to gather information in two areas, past history and current events . . . ,[107] whereas at Gila, the stress had been more upon what the internees "were doing and detailed—if possible, verbatim—accounts of what they were saying . . . ."[108]

Through a white administrator Wax was put in touch with an "underground group," one of the many factions within the camp,[109] and one which was "pro-Japan." The close identification with this group[110] precipitated a state whereby she became "once again a little crazy," and became a "fanatic"[111] (i.e., "pro-Japan," "anti-America"). However, after one of the "pro-America" group members was murdered, and she had taken satisfaction in this death, she changed her mind and became an "anti-fanatic."[112] She "came to believe that observing and recording what went on at Tule Lake was [her] . . . transcendental task, and . . . went about this task with an unflagging energy and relish that today seems rather frightening."[113] However, she did not confine herself to observing and reporting data. In her "anti-fanatic" stage, she came to loathe Kira (Wakayama), as noted before.

As for myself, I had privately decided to do all that I could to stop Kira's (and Kato's) policy of terrorism and violence. And I also decided that, if I ever got the opportunity, I would pay Kira back. If anyone had told me that I was about to "interfere" in a field situation and that I was thereby breaking a primary rule of scientific procedure, I think I would have laughed, or, perhaps, told the admonisher to go to hell.[114]

She consulted with some of her anti-Kira informants on how best to see that Kira could be denounced to the proper authorities, and suggested to one of them to denounce him before any more violence would take place. This suggestion was rejected. The person to whom she had made this suggestion was able to get at Kira in another manner, the end result of which was the resignation of Kira from the leadership position he had held.[115]

Quite obviously, having shorn power from Kira was not enough for Wax, because she followed the action up by informing the FBI about Kira, a fact to which reference already has been made.

The values Wax had enculturated help explain her singleminded devotion to doing good fieldwork, gathering data, and satisfying Thomas, or, in other words, overcoming whatever obstacles were in her path and succeeding in the assigned tasks and proving to herself and to others that she was a competent anthropologist.[116] Regrettably, this devotion to her enculturated values overrode her role as objective scientist. Participant-observation could have been achieved by studying the other aspects of the Tuleans' lives,[117] which would have given her a better and healthier perspective on those issues which were of such consuming interest to her.

The particular tragedy of the Wax case is not just her having attempted to alter the course of events; her having lost all objectivity; her having sided with one faction and then another; her having turned against a group from whom she had won trust; or her having informed the FBI on Wakayama. The major tragedy is that, because she was expelled from Tule Lake by the WRA (among other reasons, for having contacted the FBI), she could not report on the major events in Tule Lake subsequent to her expulsion.

> Ending with renunciation [the topic of the final chapter of *The Spoilage*] rather than with Center [Tule Lake] closure, the entire final chapter of Center history is missing, *including the complete transformation of Tule Lake to the most relocation-minded Center of all.*[118]

Consequently, not only was a certain family (the Wakayamas) victimized by Wax's enculturated values, infelicitously actuated at Tule Lake, but the entire Tule Lake population and the scientific community as well. Even today, in the Japanese American community there is a definite stigma surrounding former Tuleans. And even today, what precisely took place at Tule Lake, not only in connection with factionalism but also with regard to the total culture of the community, remains open to research.[119]

In the framework of contemporary events, the Wax case has an all too familiar ring. From the laboratories of the most prestigious universities (e.g., Boston, Cornell, Harvard, Sloan-Kettering, and Yale, to name a few) has come the following kind of case (presented in composite form): young scientist recruited for his promising research talents; under great pressure to produce spectacular results; manipulates data to meet the high expectations.

That Wax's report on Tule Lake (a "major laboratory" for ERS) in *The Spoilage* distressingly fits into the same pattern can be concluded from the observations of the greatest authority on all aspects of Tule Lake, Marvin Opler, as seen in some of the excerpts from his book review.

> Dependence upon one person [Wax] for major contributions led, in turn, to undue credence afforded about two dozen factional leaders who happened to impress the fieldworker [Wax],

during the year period, as knowing the Center [Tule Lake]. . . . [T]he penchant for quoting "an Issei," "Kibei," or "Nisei" stands out since context is generally lacking; on pages 101–102, for example, "Kibei" are stereotyped and oversimplified on the basis of two short quotations from two of their members.

The reliance of one fieldworker [Wax] upon testimony of a few dozen persons among thousands available is, of course, a highly vulnerable method; and, since the technique of description is governed by quotations from these individuals rather than by analytical procedures, there is a certain amount of careless interpretation specifically resulting from overstress on one set of factional leaders . . . and the boundless credence afforded them which reifies their rationalization. On page 103, the authors remark "a tendency among large numbers of Tuleans toward narrowly opportunistic decisions to hold to status of 'disloyalty' "—the term "Tuleans" here referring to a rival faction apparently. . . . [W]e pointed out carefully that pontifications about "opportunism," based on the "loyalty-disloyalty" labels were actually misleading since these labels had long since lost any objectively significant meaning in the maelstrom of emotionalized reactions to consistently discriminatory treatment. . . . [W]e argued against it [segregation], predicted its immediate and long-range results, and finally indicated that the only valid distinctions which could be sought within this population would be cultural identifications and socio-economic stati, not political determinations; family typologies, not loyalties; emotionalized reactions, not consistent international programs. It is surprising to find the old labels applied, amid pontifications, years later.

With social, cultural, economic and psychological analysis lacking at points in the record, a factional interpretation threads through the final three hundred pages. On page 110, the same Tuleans of the rival faction are castigated for an alleged control of the Co-operative Enterprises of the Center: "There were no major positions left unfilled" when people arrived from other centers [during the segregation process]. On page 168, this inaccuracy is swallowed with the rumor, "residents had noted that fruits . . . on purchase by (the government) were conspicuously absent from the messhalls but were on sale in the (Co-operative's) canteens." This last refers to a million-and-a-half-dollar enterprise undergoing regular, periodic audit by both a governmental agency and reputable private firms. In the event the reader remains unconvinced by these allegations of opportunism, job monopoly and the supposed dishonesty rampant among six thousand Tuleans, their factional leader receives the sociological description of "dressy and dandified" and his chief cohort is implied to have been "opportunistic" in decisions to safeguard a son "of draft age." A Mr. Tada (pseudonym) of a more-favored rival faction likewise had a son of draft age, but this fact is not adduced in accounts of his heroics. On pages 117–119, this favored faction is described as having duly elected a representative body "in about the proper proportions, but some blocs of transferees [those who had moved to Tule Lake from the other camps] were markedly over-represented and were soon able to obtain and hold positions of control in the organization"; on page 142, this curious contradiction is doubly confounded when we learn that the elections of October 16th, "in proper proportions" yet "markedly over-represented" by some blocs of transferees, were completed on November 4th by "arrangements for selecting the permanent representative body." Staff members and Center contacts who were selected into this representative body give no indication of a *bona fide* elective process.

The contradictions of *The Spoilage* arise from credence given to accounts written up and mimeographed by the favored faction months later. On page 131, the favored faction is credited with community support of the now-famous November 1st Incident, contrary to all evidence in print. On page 140, Mr. Myer, Director of the [War Relocation] Authority is alleged to have unwillingly attended a staff meeting in the nearby town of Tule Lake; there was no such meeting outside Center confines. At another point, the favored faction is credited with having eluded administrative notice while "organizing their protest movement" (p. 120) whereas, in truth, there was practically daily contact. On pages 153, 157, and 158, the Center mimeographed newspaper is quoted first as calling, later as cancelling, a meeting between Daihyo Sha Kai (Negotiating Committee) and the Army and WRA; again the Daihyo Sha Kai position is presented approvingly, unmindful of the fact that for several issues, following Army control of the center, the paper was published under direct and exclusive control of the Negotiating Committee alone and that no meeting with the Committee had been sanctioned by the Colonel in command and certainly none cancelled. The point of these corrections, and of scores of others for which there is neither time nor space, is that well-heated attempts to play sides in factional disputes which rend any aggrieved and disaffected community are only possible where the proper interpretation of factionalism in general is lacking.

. . . Tule Lake is given too much the cast of a "disloyal" center where "disloyals" were treated badly. *The Spoilage* becomes an excellent source-book on government documents, but the treatment of daily rumors and the ebb and flow of opinion are subordinated to the presentation of factional claims; and there is practically nothing on Center art and religion, recreation, welfare and economic status. Obviously, the 19,000 men, women and children cramped in a square mile of tar-papered "theater of operations" barracks do not emerge as people. The effects of discriminatory and racist treatment are only in part reflected. And the need in social science apparently is to know the possible limitations of a few dozen informants or where the document ends and broad social analysis begins.[120]

CONCLUSION

I have here attempted to identify, clarify, and explain certain aspects of ERS which, to date, have not been examined by others.

For various reasons ERS remains a puzzle.

1. Four of the five camps where "spot observations" were made have been identified, but published data do not reveal enough to help in identifying the fifth.

2. On what bases Minidoka, Poston, and Tule Lake were identified as the "major laboratories" cannot be determined. Why Tule Lake came to be the focus of *The Spoilage*, it now seems certain, was because of expediency. This is where, to one field observer, the extraordinary events were taking place, and the accounts in that researcher's reports were accepted at face value.[121] By the same token, in Thomas's desire for reports on such events all other camps came to be of secondary importance.

Even one of the stated aspects of the goal of ERS, a study of the economic impact, diminished in significance to the sensationalistic reports on the political events which were taking place at Tule Lake.[122]

3. ERS staff (Japanese Americans and whites) have been identified, a listing of whom cannot be found in ERS publications. Japanese American staff in the detention camps ("assembly centers")—an issue hardly dealt with in ERS publications—have been identified as best could be, through inference and deduction. Both lists of Japanese American staff require further confirmation.

4. Why the complete Leighton file relating to the Bureau of Sociological Research at Poston was sent to Berkeley instead of the National Archives, Washington, D.C., has yet to be fathomed. As the situation now stands the researcher interested in the Leighton

file pertaining to the Bureau of Sociological Research must rely upon the Bancroft collection at Berkeley. Whereas for all other WRA materials the National Archives have been the repository, the kind of easy usufruct offered by the National Archives is denied the researcher interested in the Leighton file. In this case, federal property has been appropriated by the State of California, and the University of California in particular.[123]

5. In a prefatory section of *The Salvage*, the second volume of ERS, Thomas has this to say in the first paragraph.

In 1946, the University of California Press published *The Spoilage*. . . . Publication of *The Salvage* completes the plan, announced at that time, for a two-volume work on social aspects of the wartime evacuation, detention, segregation, and resettlement of the Japanese American minority.[124] Nonetheless, had the third volume been published as had been anticipated, it was to have been a book on the return of the internees to the West Coast. Two minor "monographs" also were to have been published "concurrently with the two main volumes. One . . . [on] political and administrative aspects of evacuation and resettlement; the other . . . [on] the ecology of 'disloyalty.' "[125]

Prejudice, War and the Constitution, the third volume of ERS which actually came off the press, was commissioned by the University of California to discredit Grodzins's *Americans Betrayed* and to assuage the devastating criticisms, accurate or inaccurate, of Californians in his book.[126]

6. An anthropological concept, enculturation, has been useful to help explain the thrust of the writings of three former ERS members: Grodzins, Spencer, and Wax.[127]

Given the powerful, but not subtle, influence used to exert pressure in suppressing the publication of *Americans Betrayed*, and the *raison d'être* of *Prejudice, War and the Constitution*, the particular documents and sources cited by tenBroek, Barnhart, and Matson in criticizing Grodzins must be reexamined for their validity by an objective, disinterested researcher.

Because of the politics which gave rise to *Prejudice, War and the Constitution*, the three ERS publications must be reexamined in their entirety for the same reason. That is to say, what roles, if any, the backers of ERS, other than the University of California, played in determining the results of ERS must be examined. Attention of the reader is called again to two foundations in particular which supported ERS. Both the Giannini Foundation (presently known as the Bank of America–Giannini Foundation) and the Columbia Foundation have been San Francisco-based organizations.[128]

The section in *The Spoilage* on Tule Lake (pages 84–380) cannot be relied upon for accurate information regarding factionalism and the personalities involved during the period covered.

A complete and objective history of Tule Lake, including its operation in the postwar period and the social and cultural life of the people after it became a segregation camp, has yet to be written and therefore must be undertaken. Such an enterprise will require not only use of ERS file materials[129] and unpublished data by Marvin Opler and his staff,[130] but interviews of survivors who experienced Tule Lake life.[131]

Because I have not utilized archival materials at Berkeley, this paper must be viewed as a prolegomenon to the larger undertaking of analyzing ERS and its publications (including *Americans Betrayed*) and of writing a dispassionate history of Tule Lake.

Withal, such an undertaking can never adequately help restore those like Wakayama and his family who have been irreparably damaged by ERS.

A final, and ineluctable conclusion flows from the previous statements in this section. ERS was a failure. This fiasco is quite unique in the annals of American social-science research projects. Granted, there is a small portion in *The Spoilage* which is reliable, *The Salvage* contains useful information,[132] and *Prejudice, War and the Constitution* is hard-hitting. Nevertheless, ERS clearly represents a disturbing misappropriation of lavish funds, rich talent, precious time, and boundless energy.

NOTES

1. Joan Z. Bernstein et al., *Personal Justice Denied: Report of the Commission on Wartime Relocation and Internment of Civilians* (Washington, D.C.: Government Printing Office, 1982).
2. See, for example, Howard H. Sugimoto, "A Bibliographic Essay on the Wartime Evacuation of Japanese on the West Coast Areas," in Hilary Conroy and T. Scott Miyakawa (eds.), *East Across the Pacific* (Santa Barbara: ABC-Clio Press, 1972), pp. 140–150.
3. D. S. Thomas and R. S. Nishimoto, *The Spoilage* (Berkeley: University of California Press, 1946). CWRIC's *Personal Justice Denied* cites *The Spoilage* in several of its sections.
4. Thomas and Nishimoto, op. cit., 1946, p. xiv.
5. Jacobus tenBroek, Edward N. Barnhart, and Floyd W. Matson, *Prejudice, War and Constitution: Causes and Consequences of the Evacuation of the Japanese Americans in World War II* (Berkeley: University of California Press, 1968 [1954]), p. ix.
6. No figures are cited for the contributions by the Gianinni Foundation.

7. tenBroek, Barnhart, and Matson, op. cit., 1954, p. ix; Thomas and Nishimoto, op. cit., 1946, p.v, merely state "Early in 1942." However, in a letter to the acting president of the University of California, Dorothy S. Thomas, Letter to Morton Deutsch, July 9, 1945, p. 1, states she had been with ERS "since Pearl Harbor." Unless otherwise noted, all documents in this paper are in the National Archives, Washington, D.C., Record Group 210, 61.300 Folder No. 24.

8. Carey McWilliams, "Review of *The Spoilage*," *New York Times Book Review*, February 2, 1947, p. 22. For example, professional anthropologists who worked for the War Relocation Authority (WRA) in one of the camps received an annual salary of $3,800 at the rank of P[rofessional] 4 Class plus overtime during the wartime forty-eight-hour workweek, according to John F. Embree, "Community Analysis —An Example of Anthropology in Government," *American Anthropologist,* vol. 46 (1944), p. 284 and p. 284, fn8.

9. By Dorothy S. Thomas, prepared with the assistance of Charles Kikuchi and James Sakoda (Berkeley: University of California Press, 1952).

10. Thomas and Nishimoto, op. cit., 1946, p. xiii; see also, Marvin K. Opler, "Review of *The Spoilage*," *American Anthropologist,* vol. 50 (1948), p. 307.

11. tenBroek, Barnhart, and Matson, op. cit., 1954.

12. Thomas and Nishimoto, op. cit., 1946, p. v. According to one source, Foster Goss, "Dr. [Dorothy] Thomas' Survey," Memorandum to E. L. Shirrell, June 26, 1942, pp. 1–2, social psychology was not included as one of the disciplines to be investigated.

13. Thomas and Nishimoto, op. cit., 1946, p. v.

14. Opler, op. cit., 1948, p. 308; Constantine Panunzio, "Review of *The Spoilage*," *Annals of the American Academy of Political and Social Science,* vol. 251 (1947), p. 203. The book was also faulted for its lack of breadth in sociological interpretation; see Solon T. Kimball, "Review of *The Spoilage*," *American Journal of Sociology,* vol. 53 (1947), p. 229; Kimball Young, "Review of *The Spoilage*," *American Sociological Review,* vol. 12 (1947), p. 363; Otis D. Duncan, "Review of *The Spoilage*," *Social Forces,* vol. 25 (1947), p. 457. Marvin Opler, op. cit., 1948, is highly critical of the book as an anthropological study. Of the major reviews, only Carey McWilliams, op. cit., 1947, praised it highly.

15. Thomas and Nishimoto, op. cit., 1946, p. vii.

16. Ibid., p. viii.

17. Contrast this with another large-scale interdisciplinary research project on another American minority funded by another foundation and completed the same year that ERS started: Gunnar Myrdal *An American Dilemma* (New York: Pantheon, 1972 [1944]), vol. I, p. li, lists each staff member who was on the project.

18. Edward N. Barnhart, *Japanese American Evacuation and Resettlement: Catalog of Material in the General Library* (Berkeley: General Library, University of California, 1958) (mimeographed).

19. See, for example, Goss, "Dr. Thomas' Survey," op. cit., 1942, pp. 2–3 and Appendix (which lists the addresses of some of the researchers as well).

20. In addition to ibid., see Harvey M. Coverley. Letter to Dillon S. Myer, December 14, 1942, p. 1; Thomas and Nishimoto, op. cit., 1946, p. vii, fn2, "We have, in addition, observational records from four of the temporary assembly centers to which evacuees were moved. . . ."

21. At the meeting which decided the disposition of the Leighton file, Thomas, Letter to Deutsch, op. cit., 1945, p. 2, of the other two making the decision one was Edward H. Spicer, Head, Community Analysis Section, WRA, whose supervisor while he was community analyst at Poston was Leighton. See also, Thomas and Nishimoto, op. cit., 1946, p. xii, fn13; Barnhart, op. cit., 1958, pp. 90–91, on the Leighton file.

22. Listed in Coverley, Letter to Dillon Myer, op. cit., 1942, p. 1, but Inoue's name does not appear in Barnhart, op. cit., 1958.

23. Charles Kikuchi, *The Kikuchi Diary: Chronicle from an American Concentration Camp. The Tanforan Journals of Charles Kikuchi,* John Modell (ed.), (Urbana: University of Illinois Press, 1973). Kikuchi dedicated this book to Dorothy Thomas.

24. An anthropologist, Tsuchiyama originally was at Poston, Arizona, and spent some time at Gila, Arizona. See John F. Embree, "Second Report on Poston, February 4–6, 1943," Washington, D.C.: Community Analysis Section, p. 9; 61.300 Folder No. 2. She is the "Miss K" in Rosalie H. Wax, *Doing Fieldwork: Warnings and Advice* (Chicago: University of Chicago Press, 1971; paperback ed.), p. 74. See, also, Peter T. Suzuki, "Anthropologists in the Wartime Camps for Japanese Americans: A Documentary Study," *Dialectical Anthropology,* vol. 6 (1981), p. 55, n145. Tsuchiyama's Ph.D. dissertation at Berkeley was "A Comparison of the Folklore of the Northern, Southern, and Pacific Athabaskan: A Study in Stabilizing Folklore with a Linguistic Stock," Department of Anthropology, 1947.

25. Yusa, who did author some materials as a researcher for ERS while in Tanforan, had none to his name from Gila, according to Barnhart, op. cit., 1958. However, Goss, "Dr. Thomas' Survey," op. cit., 1942, Appendix, lists him as a researcher for ERS at Gila.

26. James Minoru Sakoda, "Minidoka: An Analysis of Changing Patterns of Social Interaction," Ph.D. dissertation, Department of Psychology, University of California, Berkeley, 1949, pp. 6–7, moved from Tule Lake in 1943 to Minidoka. He remained there until March 1945 and then returned to this camp in June 1945 and again in October, to witness the closure of the camp.

27. Frank Shotaro Miyamoto, "The Career of Intergroup Tensions: A Study of the Collective Adjustments of Evacuees to Crises at Tule Lake Relocation Center," Ph.D. dissertation, Department of Sociology, University of Chicago, 1951; "The Forced Evacuation of the Japanese Minority During World II," *Journal of Social Issues,* vol. 29 (1973), originally had a Social Science Research Council predoctoral fellowship and did some research at the Puyallup Assembly Center, Puyallup, Washington, according to Goss, "Dr. Thomas' Survey," op. cit., 1942, p. 2. According to what Thomas had told Goss, idem., he received the fellowship " 'provided he works under sponsorship of our University [ERS] group.' " He then resigned from the fellowship to work for ERS (he was at Tule Lake) to head up its Chicago "office," for which see Dorothy S. Thomas, Letter to John F. Embree, June 4, 1943.

28. Tamotsu Shibutani, "Rumors in a Crisis Situation," M.A. thesis, Department of Sociology, University of Chicago, 1944; "The Circulation of Rumors as a Form of Collective Behavior," Ph.D. dissertation, Department of Sociology, University of Chicago, 1949; *Improvised News: A Sociology of Rumor* (Indianapolis: Bobbs-Merrill, 1966), esp. pp. 64–68; *The Derelicts of Company K: A Sociological Study of Demoralization* (Berkeley: University of California Press, 1978), especially p. xiii, with reference to ERS and his praise of Dorothy Thomas.

29. Thomas and Nishimoto, op. cit., 1946, p. viii.

30. Idem.

31. Robert F. Spencer, "Japanese Buddhism in the United States 1940–1946: A Study in Acculturation," Ph.D. dissertation, Department of Anthropology, University of California, Berkeley, 1946, p. ii.

32. Thomas and Nishimoto, op. cit., 1946, pp. 68–69. For a list of Spencer's reports, see Barnhart, op. cit., 1958, pp. 101–102, 167.

33. Rosalie Hankey [Wax], "The Development of Authoritarianism: A Comparison of the Japanese-American Relocation Centers and Germany," Ph.D. dissertation, Department of Anthropology, University of Chicago, 1950; "Reciprocity as a Field Technique," *Human Organization*, vol. 11 (1952), pp. 34–37; "The Destruction of a Democratic Impulse," *Human Organization*, vol. 12 (1953), pp. 11–21; "Twelve Years Later: An Analysis of Field Experience," *American Journal of Sociology*, vol. 63 (1957), pp. 133–142; *Doing Fieldwork*, op. cit., 1971.

34. Robert H. Billigmeier, "Aspects of the Culture History of the Romansh People in Switzerland, 1950–1956," Stanford University, 1951. Billigmeier was offered a position as community analyst at Tule Lake by John F. Embree, a position which he turned down; see John F. Embree, Letter to Dorothy S. Thomas, March 31, 1943.

35. Morton M. Grodzins, "The Effects of the Japanese Evacuation," Ph.D. dissertation, Department of Political Science, University of California, Berkeley, 1945.

36. Marvin Opler, "Review of *The Spoilage*," op. cit., 1948, p. 308. It should be borne in mind that the Barnhart catalog was not compiled until 1958.

37. Ibid, p. 308.

38. Wax, *Doing Fieldwork*, op. cit., 1971, p. 155.

39. Ibid, p. 157.

40. Ibid., pp. 158–162.

41. Thomas and Nishimoto, op. cit., 1946, p. 376.

42. tenBroek, Barnhart, and Matson, op. cit., 1954, cite these four cases quite extensively.

43. Wax, *Doing Fieldwork*, op. cit., 1971, pp. 168–169. See also, Thomas and Nishimoto, op. cit., 1946, p. 339 and 339, fn27. For statements by Japanese Americans Koji Ariyoshi, Karl Yoneda, and James Oda (the second, according to the source, a Communist) to the Naval Intelligence Service informing on internees—one of them, Joe Kurihara, a major figure in *The Spoilage* and *Doing Fieldwork*—see District Intelligence Office, Twelfth Naval District, "Manzanar Relocation Project, conditions at," Memorandum to The Director of Naval Intelligence, February 16, 1943 ("Confidential"; declassified December 14, 1979), pp. 1–2, 4–5. Numerous other internees are denounced by these three informers in this seven-page document. This document is in Record Group 210, Box No. 2, entitled, "Washington Central File *Confidential Files*, Federal Bureau of Investigation. Office of Naval Intelligence, Office of Censorship, Department of Justice, Executive Office of the President, Department of State, Selective Service, Office of Strategic Service, United States Coast Guard, Office of War Information," Folder: Office of Naval Intelligence. On Joe Kurihara, see also Togo Tanaka and Joe Masaoka, "Straws in the Wind: An Inquiry into the course of the recent flare-ups [at Manzanar]," Project Report No. 47, Manzanar Historical Documentation, August 12, 1943 ("Restricted"; declassified February 3, 1975), p. 2.

44. Michi Weglyn, *Years of Infamy: The Untold Story of America's Concentration Camps* (New York: William Morrow, 1976), p. 243.

45. Junro Edgar Wakayama, Letter to CWRIC, July 13, 1981. I thank Michi Weglyn for her generosity in making this letter, the article from the *San Francisco Chronicle* (see Note 46, below), the autobiographical statement by Kinzo Wakayama (see Note 48, below), and the Nielson document (see Note 47, below) available to me.

46. Evelyn Hsu, "War Heroes Testify on the Internment Camps," *San Francisco Chronicle*, August 12, 1981. The article includes a picture of Wakayama.

47. Junro Edgar Wakayama, Letter to CWRIC, July 13, 1981, p. 2. According to a government report, Western Defense Command, "History of Litigation Involving Western Defense Command" (no date; 1945?), p. 1, Record Group 338, in a binder with the title, "Chronology of the Western Defense Command Exclusion Program, June 26, 1944 to October 10, 1945," the petitions (sic) were filed on August 20, 1942. I thank Edwin R. Coffee, Assistant Chief, Modern Military Headquarters Branch, Military Archives Division, The National Archives, for having located this document upon my request. See Victor Nielson (Director of Information?), Western Defense Command, "The Legal Phases of the Exclusion Program and Other Controls Imposed Pursuant to Executive Order No. 9066" (no date; 1945?), p. 7 (italics added): *"One of the first challenges to the validity of group exclusion of Japanese was made by Ernest Wakayama when he* applied in the United States District Court of the Southern District of California for a Writ of Habeas Corpus to obtain his release from the assembly center [Santa Anita]."

In Western Defense Command, "History of Litigation. . . ," op. cit., no date, p. 1, are found these sentences. "Petitioners (Ernest and Toki Wakayama) moved for dismissal without prejudice. The motion was granted 8 March 1943. It is understood that attorneys for petitioners became uninterested in the case when they discovered that Mr. Wakayama had indicated his desire for expatriation."

The above interpretation does not square with the facts alluded to in connection with what Wax had done. In Audrie Girdner and Anne Loftis, *The Great Betrayal: The Evacuation of the Japanese-Americans During World War II* (London: Macmillan, 1969), p. 183, a more detailed description is provided (see, also, p. 544). "The Southern California branch of the Civil Liberties Union decided to defend several of those charged [in Santa Anita who had been arrested because they had met to discuss camp conditions, including its camouflage factory]. After many months, A.L. Wirin, attorney for the ACLU, succeeded in reducing individual bail from $10,000 to $2,000 each and in securing a writ of *habeas corpus,* the first since the evacuation began, for one of its defendents, Ernest Wakayama, a Nisei Republican, American Legion leader, and former AF of L official, and his wife, Toki. These two were chosen for the purpose of developing a federal test case to challenge the constitutionality of certain aspects of the evacuation. The defense contended that the Army action constituted imprisonment without hearing or trial and that the petitioners were being held solely because of their ancestry and thus were illegally discriminated against. The National ACLU and Walter Tsukamoto of the JACL [Japanese American Citizens League] joined in this particular action which did not challenge the constitutionality of Executive Order 9066 [which enabled the evacuation and incarceration] nor the congressional legislation making disobedience to the military proclamations a crime. The Wakayama case was eventually dropped by the ACLU as other cases which more directly challenged the evacuation came into prominence."

48. Ernest Kinzo Wakayama, "Brief Personal History, Incidents and Opinion (sic)," Certified October 16, 1972, pp. 1–3, attachment to "Redress Questionnaire." The second part of his Point 23 seems particularly haunting today.

49. See Ruth Benedict, *The Chrysanthemum and the Sword: Patterns of Japanese Culture* (New York: New American Library, 1946, Paperback ed.), pp. 199–205, for a cultural analysis of this tale.

50. Correlatively, it is obvious whom Wax had in mind as Oishi. Although there is no mention of this tale in *Doing Fieldwork,* it is apparent that she knew about it, inasmuch as she was exposed to even more arcane Japanese folk tales than

Chushingura while with ERS; see Wax, *Doing Fieldwork,* op. cit., 1971, p. 153, for a summary of one such tale. Also, in the same book, she makes quite a few references to the traditional role of the samurai. On the use of "Kira" for a person at Gila, see Wax, "Shooting of Satoshi Kira" (pseudonym?) as listed in Barnhart, op. cit., 1958, p. 100. (Apparently this was the report which, for the first time, pleased Thomas.)

51. See, for example, John F. Embree, Letter to Dorothy S. Thomas, October 6, 1942, p. 1; Dorothy S. Thomas, Letter to John F. Embree, October 13, 1942, p. 1; Coverley, Letter to Dillon S. Myer, op. cit., 1942, p. 1; Dorothy S. Thomas, Letter to John F. Embree, April 28, 1943, p. 2, in which the various assignments given to Grodzins are mentioned.

52. Marvin Opler, "Review of *The Spoilage,*" op. cit., 1948, p. 307.

53. tenBroek, Barnhart, and Matson, op. cit., 1954, p. x.

54. Ibid, p. xii.

55. In addition to the contents of chapter 4, the endnotes to the chapter contain pointed criticisms of Grodzins. See, for example, tenBroek, Barnhart, and Matson, op. cit., 1954, pp. 374, n229; 376, n50; 377, n61, n62; 378, n73, n88; 381, n111. It is probably for their attacks on Grodzins that one historian, whose major interest is the Japanese American experience, has termed *Prejudice, War and the Constitution* "somewhat tendentious. . . ." John Modell, "Suggestions for Further Reading," in Charles Kikuchi, op. cit., 1973, p. 256.

56. See, for example, R. J. C. Butow, et al., "The FDR Tapes: Secret Recordings Made in the Oval Office of the President in the Autumn of 1940," *American Heritage,* vol. 33, no. 2 (1982), pp. 9–24; "FDR ordered internment of Hawaii Nikkei [persons of Japanese descent] in 1936," *Pacific Citizen,* February 11, 1983, p. 1; New York Times News Service, "Official says Japanese Internment Possibly Not Justified by Cables," *Omaha World-Herald,* May 22, 1983, p. 11.

57. tenBroek, Barnhart, and Matson, op. cit., 1954, pp. 331–334.

58. Thomas and Nishimoto, op. cit., 1946, p. xii, fn10. The other monograph was planned to deal with the "ecology of 'disloyalty.' " Idem.

59. "Ousted Chicago Man Says Book Cost Job," *New York Times,* December 15, 1950, p. 27, col. 4; see, also, "Couch Dismissal Scored," *New York Times,* November 30, 1950, p. 41, col. 3.

60. "This is in sharp contrast to what tenBroek, Barnhart, and Matson had to undertake. For some aspects of their study which came to be *Prejudice, War and the Constitution,* they literally had to start anew because the ERS files were incomplete with reference to certain issues they wanted to pursue; see tenBroek, Barnhart, and Matson, op. cit., 1954, pp. xi–xii.

61. John Modell, in Charles Kikuchi, *The Kikuchi Diary,* op. cit., 1973, p. 256 (italics added). The roles of Dorothy Thomas and Charles Aiken in all this remain areas open to research. Charles Aiken of Berkeley's Department of Political Science was one of the original planners of ERS; see Thomas and Nishimoto, op. cit., 1946, p. vi, fn1. See, also, Grodzins, op. cit., 1949, p. ix.

62. C. Herman Pritchett, "In Memoriam: Morton Grodzins," *American Political Science Review,* vol. 58 (1964), p. 504.

63. See Melville J. Herskovits, *The Study of Man* (New York: Alfred Knopf, 1951), especially pp. 39–42, 491, 625–627, for a basic discussion of this concept.

64. William Petersen, *Japanese Americans: Oppression and Success* (New York: Random House, 1971; paperback ed.), p. 76.

65. "Review of Americans Betrayed," *Columbia Law Review,* vol. 50 (1950), p. 130.

66. As an example, Frank Miyamoto encountered some difficulties in being hired by the Department of Sociology of the University of Washington because one of its members held Miyamoto's Japanese background against him. See John H. Provinse, Letter to Harold S. Fistere, June 7, 1945, pp. 1–2.

67. C. Herman Pritchett, "In Memorian," op. cit., 1964, p. 504.

68. Dorothy Thomas, Letter to John F. Embree, April 28, 1943, p. 2.

69. For a list of some of the West Coast organizations which were for the evacuation, see Grodzins, op. cit., 1949, p. 21. Under what circumstances Grodzins accepted the position of director of the University of Chicago Press can only be speculated. A most revealing case similar to Grodzins's, concerning enculturation, is that of William Petersen, the eminent sociologist, who had been professor of sociology at the University of California at Berkeley. "When the editor of *The New York Times Magazine* proposed that I write an article on Japanese Americans, I supposed that he must have asked other more likely candidates and that they had refused. For at that time, in 1965, I knew less about that subnation than the average long-time resident of the West Coast. Until 1953, when I accepted a position at the Berkeley campus of the University of California, I had never been west of Chicago; and my acquaintances in and around New York included precisely two Nisei. In retrospect, I believe this psychological distance from Japanese Americans . . . was not altogether a disadvantage."

    The upshot was a splendid article on Japanese Americans and, ultimately, his brilliant book on the same group, from which the above quotation is taken: *Japanese Americans,* op. cit., 1971, p. ix.

    Petersen, a political conservative, illustrates in good measure the folly of labeling—as tenBroek, Barnhart, and Matson have done—students of the evacuation as either liberals or conservatives. In the case of evacuation (the evacuation, incarceration, segregation, and resettlement), those who one would think would have fought against it backed it, and vice versa. The critical element appears to be enculturation, with a measure of human decency. In the case of Carey McWilliams, the enculturation thesis can also prove useful, but he represents opportunism *par excellence* (as do Earl Warren and a host of the politicians who originally came out for the evacuation).

70. Jacque Cattell Press (ed.), "Spencer, Robert Francis," *American Men and Women of Science: The Social Sciences,* (New York: Bowker, 1976, 13th ed.), vol. 5, p. 4235.

71. One notion that has to be disabused is that San Francisco and the Bay Area always had been tolerant and liberal places toward a Japanese. On October 11, 1906, San Francisco's Board of Education issued a resolution removing its ninety-three Japanese American students from its regular public schools and ordered them to attend special "Oriental" schools. This idea caught on elsewhere in California. As a result, in 1909 the state legislature sought to establish segregated schools for Japanese and special ghettos to confine California's Asian population.

    As for Oregon, it has an image of being a liberal, tolerant, and humanistic state, with special attention being paid to the environment. And in the postwar era, John Gunther, *Inside America* (New York: Harper & Bros., 1951); revised ed.), pp. 89–100, tried to project the image of this state as one which was libel and tolerant; but the facts show otherwise, so far as Japanese Americans were concerned. See Audrie Girdner and Anne Loftis, *The Great Betrayal: The*

Evacuation of the Japanese-Americans During World War II (London: Macmillan, 1969), pp. 396–399, concerning Hood River, Oregon. Also, note again the University of Oregon Mothers, a group which was for the evacuation. See also, Peter T. Suzuki, "The Enthnolinguistics of Japanese Americans in the Wartime Camps," *Anthropological Linguistics,* vol. 19 (1976). p. 427, n 11, on Hood River, Oregon. For a contemporary study of Hood River, Oregon, see Wallace Turner, "Hatred of 40's Still Vivid to Japanese [of Hood River, Oregon]," *New York Times,* July 20, 1981, p. 6, columns 1–6.

72. For the "classic model," see Melville Herskovits, op. cit., 1951, pp. 40–41.

73. Robert F. Spencer, *Japanese Buddhism in the United States. . . ,* op. cit., 1946, p. ii.

74. *Social Forces,* vol. 26 (1948).

75. Correspondingly, by ignoring what was going on in California and what had taken place on the West Coast before the war, Spencer was exonerating the people and institutions of California and the West Coast. For a more detailed discussion of his paper, see Peter T. Suzuki, "Anthropologists in the Wartime Camps. . . ," op. cit., 1981, pp. 37–38.

76. "Japanese Language Behavior," *American Speech,* vol. 25 (1950), pp. 242, 244 (italics added). See Peter T. Suzuki, "The Enthnolinguistics of Japanese Americans. . . ," op. cit., 1976, on the influence of camp life on Japanese American speech.

77. Jacque Cattell Press (ed.), "Wax, Rosalie Hankey," *American Men and Women of Science: The Social Sciences* (New York: Bowker, 1976, 13th ed.), vol. 6, p. 4736.

78. Wax, *Doing Fieldwork,* op. cit., 1971, p. 64. See also, ibid, p. 53, on her family background. Although of German descent, and this factor was perceived as important by some internees in Tule Lake, this ethnic factor is not significant in other respects.

79. Ibid., p. 64.

80. Ibid., p. 65.

81. Idem.

82. "Luckily, we were able to replace him [Spencer] with a young but highly intelligent graduate student in anthropology, Miss Rosalie Hankey," Dorothy S. Thomas, Letter to John F. Embree, July 9, 1943.

83. Wax, *Doing Fieldwork,* op. cit., 1971, pp. 66–67. However, according to a letter Thomas received from Wax, Dorothy S. Thomas, Letter to John F. Embree, July 14, 1943, p. 2: "Hanky has arrived at Gila, and her first reports are enthusiastic."

84. Wax, *Doing Fieldwork,* op. cit., 1971, p. 69.

85. Ibid., p. 65. See Peter T. Suzuki, "Anthropologists in the Wartime Camps . . . ," op. cit., 1981, p. 39, on Thomas's attitude toward the WRA researchers.

86. Wax, *Doing Fieldwork,* op. cit., p. 70.

87. Idem.

88. Ibid., p. 71.

89. Ibid., p. 74.

90. Ibid., pp. 75–76.

91. Ibid., p. 79.

92. Ibid., p. 81.

93. Ibid., p. 82.

94. Ibid., p. 74.

95. Ibid., p. 82. The passage quoted is also on this page.

96. Ibid., p. 83.

97. Ibid., p. 66.

98. Ibid., p. 63.
 99. Ibid., p. 44.
100. Ibid., p. 81 (italics added).
101. Thomas and Nishimoto, op. cit., 1946, p. viii, fn5. "(Some of the Japanese fieldworkers employed by the study had been accused by their fellow evacuees of being informers or 'spies for the administration.' Some were made so uncomfortable that they left the centers [camps] soon after the registration [loyalty oath] crisis.)," Wax, *Doing Fieldwork,* op. cit., 1971, pp. 94–95.
102. Ibid., pp. 94–95.
103. Ibid., p. 105.
104. Ibid., pp. 118–119.
105. Ibid., p. 123.
106. Ibid., p. 105.
107. Ibid., p. 108.
108. Ibid., p. 63.
109. Ibid., p. 112.
110. On Wax's warnings to the fieldworker, of identifying oneself too closely with his/her informants, see ibid., pp. 47–49.
111. Ibid., p. 139. In her "pro-Japan" stage, she "found the news of these beatings [of alleged "pro-America, pro-administration" internees] exciting and somehow gratifying," ibid., p. 136.
112. Ibid., pp. 152–162. Some of these points have been covered in Peter Suzuki, "Anthropologists in the Wartime Camps. . . ," op. cit., 1981, p. 31.
113. Wax, *Doing Fieldwork,* op. cit., 1971, p. 139.
114. Ibid., p. 158. "One [of the first four] safeguard[s] [of the participant-observation method used by ERS field researchers] was, of course, the competence, intellectual honesty, self-control and self-correction of the observers themselves," Thomas and Nishimoto, op. cit., 1946, p. x.

    Marvin Opler, "Narrative Report on Work of the [Community Analysis] Section by the [Tule Lake] Community Analyst," Tule Lake Community Analysis Section, August 31, 1945, p. 14 (61.319 Folder No. 18), has this observation about Wax. ". . . Miss Hankey, post-incident, again revived the one-way style of pumping appearing regularly with pencils and notebook. . . . The one-way operation proved to be burdensome, week after week, that when it settled in a pattern out of office hours in evening sessions, we bore it for a time, then terminated our contractual, it would seem, obligation to serve as chief 'informant' for the Thomas study."

    He then continues on the same page, still in Connection with Wax: "Some essential material, though not essential to the understanding of the Washington office [of WRA], had thus willfully been secreted in our files, on the assumption that reports labeled 'confidential' were not so treated as regards the Thomas study."
115. Wax, op. cit., 1971, pp. 160–161.
116. See, for example, Wax, op. cit., 1971, pp. 71 ff., 79, 133, 139, 147; op. cit., 1952, pp. 36–37; op. cit., 1957, pp. 140–142, regarding her concern about competent field research and gathering data. It goes without saying that some of the values associated with being a good researcher had been enculturated while a graduate student in one of the world's most research-oriented anthropology departments (sociologists prefer to use the term "socialization," for which, see Harriet Zuckerman, *Scientific Elite* [New York: The Free Press, 1977], pp. 122–132). On enculturating values as an adult, see Melville Herskovits, op. cit., 1951, p. 41.
117. See Peter Suzuki, "Anthropologists in the Wartime Camps. . . ," op. cit., 1981, p. 39.

118. Marvin Opler, "Review of *The Spoilage*," op. cit., 1948, p. 310 (italics added).
119. Notwithstanding the heroic efforts of Michi Weglyn, *Years of Infamy,* op. cit., 1976, which have helped so much to expose the issues.
120. Marvin Opler, "Review of *The Spoilage*," op. cit., 1948, pp. 309–310.
121. Of the "safeguards" which were developed for ERS field workers (see Note 114 above), three of the four "were established and reinforced by frequent conferences of observers and other staff members with the dirctor of the study [Thomas] and its advisors." See Thomas and Nishimoto, op. cit., 1946, p. xi. The other safeguards were as follows. The interdisciplinary approach "which resulted in a situation analogous to 'differential diagnosis.' " A third safeguard was the bicultural composition of the evacuee staff (i.e., Japanese American). "A fourth was the utilization, wherever possible, of administrative and particularly quantitative materials collected independently of the study for checking or revising the generalizations growing out of the materials of the study itself." Idem.
122. On "sensationalistic," see Marvin Opler, "Review of *The Spoilage,* op. cit., 1948, p. 308, as noting the "marked tendency toward incomplete coverage and sensationalistic opinion . . ." of the book's section dealing with Tule Lake after it had become a segregation camp.
123. I have written to my congressman and to the director of the National Archives to see what can be done to have the Leighton file returned to its rightful place.
124. Dorothy S. Thomas, op. cit., 1952, p. v.
125. Thomas and Nishimoto, op. cit., 1946, p. xii, fn10. The monograph on the "ecology of 'disloyalty' " was never written.
126. The article from *The New York Times* quoted in this paper mentions the controversy over *Americans Betrayed* as having taken place "two years ago" (i.e., 1948). According to tenBroek, Barnhart, and Matson, 1948 was the year that tenBroek was given the assignment to write what eventually came to be *Prejudice, War and the Constitution.* In other words, the University of California made the assignment through Thomas and Aiken in 1948, the year of the height of the controversy.
127. The gender factor also has been taken into consideration in the case of Wax (and Thomas).
128. Foundation Center, *Foundation Directory* (New York: The Foundation Center, 1981, 8th ed.), pp. 11, 15. An intriguing aspect in this connection has to do with the fact that in the three ERS publications, but especially in *Prejudice, War and the Constitution,* no attention is paid to the favored treatment of other aliens, especially Italian aliens and Italian Americans, by California and by the Roosevelt administration, over and against Japanese aliens and Japanese Americans. Grodzins, op. cit., 1949, pp. 39, 47, 72–73, 96, 108, 110, 120, 144, 193, 263, 282–283, 318, 322, 362, pursued the invidious treatment relentlessly. On this same issue, see also, Weglyn, op. cit., 1976, pp. 29, 68–69, 73–74, 96, 103, 134, 139–140, 200, 291 n10. The political influence of Italian Americans was marked, especially in the Bay Area; the mayor of San Francisco in 1942 was Angelo Rossi. On his statements regarding Japanese v. Italians and Germans, see Grodzins, op. cit., 1949, p. 110. For detailed studies showing the decided influence of American foundations on research projects they have financed, see the excellent studies in Robert F. Arnove (ed.), *Philanthropy and Cultural Imperialism* (Boston: G. K. Hall, 1980).
129. Curiously, according to Barnhart, op. cit., 1958, p. 158, the only ERS materials at Berkeley by Wax while at Tule Lake are classified as correspondence "with evacuees." Yet, according to ibid., p. 100, the same Berkeley collection has seven titled reports (totaling 170 pages) plus some untitled reports by Wax while

she was at Gila. And Wax herself refers to "Field Notes" throughout *The Spoilage,* or her Tule Lake period. See also, Wax, op. cit., 1971, p. 386, "Wax, Rosalie H. 1943–1945, Field notes, Japanese-American relocation center [Tule Lake]."

130. For statements about Marvin Opler's and the Tule Lake Community Analysis Section's reports, see Peter Suzuki, "Anthropologists in the Wartime Camps. . . ," op. cit., 1981, p. 39. Needless to say, all WRA materials on Tule Lake should be consulted as well.

131. The playwright Frank Chin has been interviewing some of these people for his research project on camp dissidents.

132. It is no mere coincidence that, of the ERS trilogy, the only book which was not born of expediency, *The Salvage,* also happens to be the most solid and the least spectacular.

Michi Weglyn

(1929–   )

Michi Nishiura Weglyn was born in Brentwood, a small farming town in northern California. When the war came, she and her family were evacuated from their home and eventually interned at Gila Relocation Center in Arizona, where she contracted tuberculosis. After her recovery, by designing and constructing costumes for "The Perry Como Show," a weekly network-TV variety show, she proved hard work and talent can win out. The show didn't last forever; neither did her good health.

Very little of this has any bearing on the form, content, or writing of her book, *Years of Infamy: The Untold Story of America's Concentration Camps* (1976). Her book is not an autobiography. *Years of Infamy* is the only Asian American book to change Asian American history. Its significance is described by one of those Nisei she most affected. William Minoru Hohri is organizer and leader of the National Council for Japanese American Redress (NCJAR), which filed a class-action lawsuit against the United States for redress of the constitutional wrongs done Japanese Americans by the evacuation and internment:

When I read *Years of Infamy,* I wrote to Michi Weglyn. Her book was a revelation. She had performed the monumental task of using primary documents to reconstruct the history of our exclusion and detention. She placed responsibility directly on the highest leaders of the U.S. government. She integrated into Japanese American history the horrors of "segregation" and the Tule Lake Segregation Centers as well as the gross injustices suffered by Peruvian Japanese, and by Japanese-Americans who were induced to renounce U.S. citizenship. The book brought new understanding of the events. Besides, she was a lay person, not an academic, a sister Japanese American internee (Gila River), like me a teenager in camp, and an attractive woman. Weglyn didn't take . . . long [to reply] and was, to my good fortune, friendly. By 1979, we'd been exchanging letters regularly. In the movement for redress she became an important mentor of mine.

After all the histories and essays had been written and published by doctors of philosophy from distinguished universities, it took a theatrical costume designer without a degree named Michi Weglyn to enunciate the hostage-reprisal theory. And it was Michi Weglyn who first grasped, then explained, the meaning of the Munson Report, thirty years after it became public.

The chapters that follow, on the Munson Report and hostage reprisal, are the first two chapters of Weglyn's book, and are notable because Weglyn did not hide her Nisei anger in interpreting documents she had accumulated over a period of eight years. Until *Years of Infamy* Japanese American histories of camp had been obsequious.

At Washington State University, during the dedication of a lantern designed by Isamu Noguchi in Michi Weglyn's honor, William Hohri, speaking on behalf of Michi Weglyn, asked the Asian Pacific Students Committee of the university to take Weglyn as "a lesson in the triumph of documented, verifiable truth over false accepted theory. Take her with you as a guide to passionate, yet disciplined, writing flowing into, mingling with and making history."

Hohri's NCJAR lawsuit was finally rejected by the U.S. Supreme Court after an eight-year campaign financed largely by Nisei contributors. But redress, on paper, at least was won in Congress. Thus far not a dollar of redress has been paid out. But money or no money, the confrontation of the Japanese American with the raw stuff of history—the order with the signature on it, the campaign for redress, *corum nobis,* and recognition of the racist purpose and effect of the concentration camps after ten years—has changed Japanese America. The change began in 1976 with Japanese America's embrace of *Years of Infamy.*

Years of Infamy: The Untold Story of America's Concentration Camps

The Secret Munson Report

> One important difference between the situation in Hawaii and the mainland is that if all the Japanese on the mainland were actively disloyal they could be corralled or destroyed within a very short time.
> —Curtis B. Munson, November 7, 1941

By fall of 1941, war with Japan appeared imminent. For well over a year, coded messages going in and out of Tokyo had been intercepted and decoded by Washington cryptoanalysts. With relations between Tokyo and Washington rapidly deteriorating, a desperate sense of national urgency was evidenced in messages to Ambassador Nomura, then carrying on negotiations in the nation's capital. On July 25, Japan had seized south French Indo-China. The activation the following day of the Morgenthau-Stimson plan, calling for the complete cessation of trade with Japan and the freezing of her assets in America—Great Britain and the Netherlands following suit— had resulted in the strangulation and near collapse of the island economy.

By late September, Tokyo's coded messages included demands for data concerning the Pacific Fleet stationed at Pearl Harbor. Of great implication for U.S. Army and Naval Intelligence was the September 24 dispatch directed to Consul Nagao Kita in Honolulu:

HENCEFORTH, WE WOULD LIKE TO HAVE YOU MAKE REPORTS CONCERNING VESSELS ALONG THE FOLLOWING LINES IN SO FAR AS POSSIBLE:

1. THE WATERS OF PEARL HARBOR ARE TO BE DIVIDED ROUGHLY INTO FIVE SUB-AREAS. WE HAVE NO OBJECTION TO YOUR ABBREVIATING AS MUCH AS YOU LIKE. AREA A. WATERS BETWEEN FORD ISLAND AND THE ARSENAL. AREA B. WATERS ADJACENT TO THE ISLAND SOUTH AND WEST OF FORD ISLAND. THIS AREA IS ON THE OPPOSITE SIDE OF THE ISLAND FROM AREA A. AREA C. EAST LOCH. AREA D. MIDDLE LOCH. AREA E. WEST LOCH AND THE COMMUNICATING WATER ROUTES.

2. WITH REGARD TO WARSHIPS AND AIRCRAFT CARRIERS WE WOULD LIKE TO HAVE YOU REPORT ON THOSE AT ANCHOR (THESE ARE NOT SO IMPORTANT), TIED UP AT WHARVES, BUOYS, AND IN

DOCK. DESIGNATE TYPES AND CLASSES BRIEFLY. IF POSSIBLE, WE WOULD LIKE TO HAVE YOU MAKE MENTION OF THE FACT WHEN THERE ARE TWO OR MORE VESSELS ALONGSIDE THE SAME WHARF.

With all signs pointing to a rapid approach of war and the Hawaiian naval outpost the probable target, a highly secret intelligence-gathering was immediately ordered by the President. Mandated with *pro forma* investigative powers as a special representative of the State Department was one Curtis B. Munson. His mission: to get as precise a picture as possible of the degree of loyalty to be found among residents of Japanese descent, both on the West Coast of the United States and in Hawaii.

Carried out in the month of October and the first weeks of November, Munson's investigation resulted in a twenty-five-page report of uncommon significance, especially as it served to corroborate data representing more than a decade of prodigious snooping and spying by the various U.S. intelligence services, both domestic and military. *It certified a remarkable, even extraordinary degree of loyalty among this generally suspect ethnic group.*

Yet, for reasons that still remain obscured, this highest level "double-checking" and confirmation of favorable intelligence consensus—that *"there is no Japanese problem"*—was to become one of the war's best-kept secrets. Not until after the cessation of hostilities, when the report of the secret survey was introduced in evidence in the Pearl Harbor hearings of 1946, did facts shattering all justification for the wartime suppression of the Japanese minority come to light.

What is more remarkable, perhaps, is that to this very day, the unusual significance of these findings has been strangely subdued.

Evidence would indicate that the Munson Report was shared only by the State, War, and Navy departments; yet, paradoxically, Cordell Hull, Henry L. Stimson, and Frank Knox, who then headed up these Cabinet posts, were to end up being the most determined proponents of evacuation. Researchers and historians have repeatedly—and with justification—leveled an accusatory finger at Stimson's War Department cohorts as being the Administration's most industrious evacuation advocates. The question naturally arises: Were aides of the Secretary kept in the dark regarding the "bill of health" given the vast majority of the Japanese American population?

On February 5, 1942, a week before the go-ahead decision for the evacuation was handed down, Stimson informed the Chief Executive in a letter sent along with the President's personal copy of the Munson Report: "In response to your memorandum of November 8 [see Appendix 10], the Department gave careful study and consider-

ation to the matters reported by Mr. C. B. Munson in his memorandum covering the Japanese situation on the West Coast." This
meant that the General Staff had had fully three months to study,
circulate, review, and analyze the contents of the report before it
was returned to the President.

Owing to the wartime concealment of this important document,
few, if any, realized how totally distorted was the known truth in
pro-internment hysterics emanating from the military, with the exception of those in naval intelligence and the FBI, whose surveillance of the Japanese minority over the years had been exhaustive.
Both services, to their credit, are on record as having opposed the
President's decision for evacuation.

To the average American, the evacuation tragedy, well shrouded
as it remains in tidied-up historical orthodoxy and in the mythology
spawned by the "total-war" frenzy, remains no more than a curious
aberration in American history. Only during the civil rights turbulence of the sixties, when personal liberties of unpopular minorities
were once again in jeopardy, was interest sharply rekindled in this
blurred-out episode in America's past. A generation of the nation's
youth, who had grown up knowing nothing or little of so colossal a
national scandal as American-style concentration camps, suddenly
demanded to know what it was that had happened. Noticed also was
an upsurge of interest among the "Sansei" (the children of the
second-generation "Nisei"), some of whom had been born in these
camps, who now wanted to be told everything that their parents and
grandparents, the "Issei," had tried so hard to forget.

Yet the enormity of this incredible governmental hoax cannot
begin to be fathomed without taking into consideration the defini-
tive loyalty findings of Curtis B. Munson, especially in relation to
the rationale that in 1942 "justified" the sending of some 110,000
men, women, and children to concentration camps: namely, that an
"unknown" number of Japanese Americans presented a potential
threat of dire fifth-column peril to the national security; that it
would be difficult to sort out the dangerous ones in so short a time,
so to play it safe all should be locked up.

2

Behind it all was a half century of focusing anti-Asian hates on
the Japanese minority by West Coast pressure groups resentful of
them as being hyperefficient competitors. An inordinate amount of
regional anxiety had also accompanied Japan's rapid rise to power.
Years of media-abetted conditioning to the possibility of war, invasion, and conquest by waves and waves of fanatic, emperor-worshiping

yellow men—invariably aided by harmless-seeming Japanese gar-
deners and fisherfolk who were really spies and saboteurs in disguise—
had evoked latent paranoia as the news from the Pacific in the early
weeks of the war brought only reports of cataclysmic Allied defeats.

In 1941, the number of Japanese Americans living in the continental United States totaled 127,000. Over 112,000 of them lived in
the three Pacific Coast states of Oregon, Washington, and California. Of this group, nearly 80 percent of the total (93,000) resided in
the state of California alone.

In the hyperactive minds of longtime residents of California,
where antipathy toward Asians was the most intense, the very
nature of the Pearl Harbor attack provided ample—and prophetic—
proof of inherent Japanese treachery. As the Imperial Army chalked
up success after success on the far-flung Pacific front, and as rumors
of prowling enemy submarines proliferated wildly, the West Coast
atmosphere became charged with a panicky fear of impending invasion and a profound suspicion that Japanese Americans in their
midst were organized for coordinated subversive activity. From the
myriad anti-Oriental forces and influential agriculturists who had
long cast their covetous eyes over the coastal webwork of rich
Japanese-owned land, a superb opportunity had thus become theirs
for the long-sought expulsion of an unwanted minority.

By enlisting the support of civic leaders, politicians, and their
powerful mass-media allies, with special emphasis on those important in the military, the tide of tolerance which had surprisingly
followed the news of attack was reversed by what soon appeared
like a tidal wave of cries for evacuation. In the more inflammatory
journals, the switch-over from tolerance to mistrust had been as
simple as juxtaposing news of the bestial, despised enemy with that
of "Japs" in their own backyards. The public became totally confused in their hatred.

Because little was known about the minority which had long kept
itself withdrawn from the larger community in fear of rebuff, it was
possible to make the public believe anything. The stereotype of the
Oriental of supercunning and sly intent was rekindled and exploited
in such a manner that Chinese Americans and other Asians began
wearing "I am a Chinese" buttons in fear of being assaulted and
spat upon. The tactics used in manipulating public fears were hardly
different from those used to achieve the cutoff in Chinese immigration in 1882 and in bringing a halt to all Japanese immigration in
1924.

Significant for those maximizing this once-in-a-lifetime opportunity was that although the Japanese minority comprised only a
minuscule 1 percent of the state's population, they were a group

well on their way to controlling one-half of the commercial truck crops in California. Centuries-old agricultural skills which the Japanese brought over with them enabled Issei farmers not only to turn out an improved quality of farm produce but also to bring down prices. The retail distribution of fruits and vegetables in the heavily populated Southern California area was already a firmly entrenched monopoly of Japanese Americans.

And it was in the name of the citizen Nisei that much of the rich growing acreage belonged to the immigrants.

Like the Chinese before them, the immigrant Japanese were denied the right to become American citizens. Because they lacked this right of naturalization, they could not own land. Even the leasing of land was limited by a 1913 land law to three years. But the Issei found ways to get around such laws devised to drive Orientals away from California, the most popular of which was for the Issei to purchase property in the name of their citizen offspring.

It was a common practice among the Issei to snatch up strips of marginal unwanted land which were cheap: swamplands, barren desert areas that Caucasians disdained to invest their labor in. Often it included land bordering dangerously close to high-tension wires, dams, and railroad tracks. The extraordinary drive and morale of these hard-working, frugal Issei who could turn parched wastelands, even marshes, into lush growing fields—usually with help from the entire family—became legendary. In the course of the years, notably during period of ecconomic crisis, a hue and cry arose of "unfair competition" and accusations that "the Japs have taken over the best land!"

Then, with the wild tales of resident Japanese perfidy that Pearl Harbor unleashed, rumors flew back and forth that Issei landowners had settled in stealth and with diabolical intent near vital installations. Their purpose: a "second Pearl Harbor." At the Tolan Committee hearings, then ostensibly weighing the pros and cons of evacuation, impressive documentation was unfurled by the top law officer of California, Attorney General Earl Warren (later to become the Chief Justice of the U.S. Supreme Court), purporting to support his theory of a possible insurrection in the making: that, with malice aforethought, Japanese Americans had "infiltrated themselves into every strategic spot in our coastal and valley counties." Substantiation of this county-by-county penetration read, in part, as follows:

ALAMEDA COUNTY
Japs adjacent to new Livermore Military Airport.
Japs adjacent to Southern Pacific and Western Pacific Railroads.

Japs in vicinity of Oakland Airport.

Japs in vicinity to Holt Caterpillar Tractor Co., San Leandro. . . .

SAN DIEGO COUNTY

Thirty miles of open coast broken by small water courses with a Jap on every water course.

Thirty miles of main railroad and highway easily blocked by slides, etc., with Japs throughout their entire length. . . .

Japs adjacent to all dams supplying water to San Diego and vicinity. . . .

Japs adjacent to all power lines supplying the city of San Diego and vicinity.

There was no possible way of separating the loyal from the disloyal, insisted the Attorney General: "when we are dealing with the Caucasian race we have methods that will test the loyalty of them. . . . But when we deal with the Japanese we are in an entirely different field and we cannot form any opinion that we believe to be sound." Warren urged speedy removal.

Unfortunately for the Nisei and Issei, it was an election year. The tide of "public opinion"—the ferocity of the clamor, at least—indicated total unconditional removal, citizen or not. And all politicians were falling in line.

In a desperate last-ditch effort to halt the mass uprooting, Nisei leaders proposed the formation of a volunteer suicide battalion, with parents as hostages to insure their good behavior. Just one opportunity to demonstrate the depth of Nisei integrity, implored Mike Masaoka, the mystic mainspring behind the audacious proposal. How else could they disprove Attorney General Warren's outrageous assertion that "there is more potential danger among the group of Japanese who were born in this country than from the alien Japanese who were born in Japan"?

Though Masaoka's brash proposal was summarily rejected at the time, it would later be reconsidered and implemented by the military, notwithstanding their initial insistence that America did not believe in the concept of hostages or of a segregated battalion—except, of course, for blacks.

Being one of the outstanding members of the xenophobic brotherhood of the "Native Sons of the Golden West" and not having access to Munson's intelligence summation, Attorney General Warren may have been merely vociferating some widely held concepts of supremacist groups as he readied himself for the gubernatorial race in the fall. But the army, which did have the facts, went on to interpret the surprising lack of disloyal activity among the Japanese minority as proof positive of intended treachery: "The very fact that no sabotage has taken place to date is a disturbing and confirming indication that such action will be taken."

Because the decision for concentrating the Japanese American population was one made in total isolation from the American people, the justifications given for it were often conflicting, varying from authority to authority. Humanitarian groups and civil libertarians who sharply protested the stamping out of due process were assured that it was merely a "protective custody" measure deemed necessary to shelter "these admirable people" from mob action. Yet when violence and intimidation were encountered by families who attempted voluntarily to relocate themselves in the "Free Zone" of California (the eastern half) and in intermountain areas of the American interior, not one move was made by federal authorities to help stem the harassment and vigilantism so that an orderly resettlement might have been made possible. The proven failure of this voluntary movement, halted by a military freezing order on March 27, 1942, was given as one more justification why "drastic measures" were called for. The Nisei who pleaded to be allowed to remain free, and Caucasian friends who attempted to aid them, were reduced to helplessness, since Washington and the military insisted they had knowledge of certain facts not known to the average person, that only the authorities were equipped to know what was best for the "Japanese."

To explore such facts not then known to the U.S. citizenry— indeed, to cut through the morass of long-nurtured, still-persisting myths—is therefore the primary objective of this chapter.

3

Apart from occasional brief references to the Munson Report in works of scholarly research, the eye-opening loyalty findings of Curtis B. Munson have yet to receive merited exposure in the pages of history. As it is a document which brings into better perspective the often grievously misunderstood and misinterpreted 1942 federal action, its more pertinent passages have been excerpted for examination in the pages which follow. For readers interested in studying the report in its entirety, a reprint of the document may be found in the Pearl Harbor hearings of the 79th Congress, 1st session. The original copy of the report may be found at the Franklin D. Roosevelt Library, Hyde Park, New York. A duplicate copy may be found in the files of the assistant Secretary of War, National Archives.

A far greater portion of the allotted investigatory time had been spent by Curtis Munson in probing the West Coast Issei and Nisei;

for the three naval districts (11th, 12th, and 13th) covered in Munson's coastal survey encompassed the full length of the West Coast— Southern California, Northern California, Washington, and Oregon. The report on the findings of the Special Investigator began as follows:

JAPANESE ON THE WEST COAST
Ground Covered

In reporting on the Japanese "problem" on the West Coast the facts are, on the whole, fairly clear and opinion toward the problem exceedingly uniform. . . . Your reporter spent about a week each in the 11th, 12th, and 13th Naval Districts with the full cooperation of the Naval and Army Intelligence and the FBI. Some mention should also be made of the assistance rendered from time to time by the British Intelligence. Our Navy has done by far the most work on this problem, having given it intense consideration for the last ten or fifteen years. . . .

Opinions of the various services were obtained, also for business, employees, universities, fellow white workers, students, fish packers, lettuce packers, farmers, religious groups, etc. The opinion expressed with minor differences was uniform. Select Japanese in all groups were sampled. To mix indiscriminately with the Japanese was not considered advisable chiefly because the opinions of many local white Americans who had made this their life work for the last fifteen years were available . . .

In other words, long before the bombs began to fall on Pearl Harbor, efficient counterintelligence activity along the West Coast of the United States had resulted in all necessary loyalty-disloyalty information on Japanese Americans being evaluated, correlated, and catalogued—an impressive amount of amassed data representing more than a decade's worth of surveillance and intelligence-gathering. What is equally impressive is that this vast accumulation of military and domestic intelligence estimates (including opinions of private organizations, individuals, and informers) was, "with minor differences," in the estimation of the presidential sleuth, "exceedingly uniform."

Yet, with amazing aplomb, the army, whose own intelligence service had been an integral part of the investigative teamwork, was to maintain baldly throughout that the loyalties of this group were "unknown" and that "time was of the essence." If the time factor had, indeed, been so critical as to prevent holding hearings to separate the loyal from the disloyal, it is curious that some eleven months were to elapse before the last of such men, women, and children constituting a special menace were removed from restricted areas.

For the benefit of executive officers deficient in knowledge of the "Japanese background," historical and sociological background data "as [they have] a bearing on the question" were then briefly summarized by Munson. "No estimate of the elements characteristics of the Japanese is complete without a word about 'giri,' " explained the Special Investigator, displaying a keen power of observation for a nonspecialist working under obvious pressure:

> There is no accurate English word for "giri." The nearest approach to an understanding of the term is our word "obligation," which is very inadequate and altogether too weak. Favors of kindnesses done to a Japanese are never forgotten but are stored up in memory and in due time an adequate quid pro quo must be rendered in return. . . . "Giri" is the great political tool. To understand "giri" is to understand the Japanese.

Individuals aware of this ingrained character trait of the Japanese were even then attempting to convince the President that the strategy of tact and civility would prove more constructive than threats, sanctions, and affronts to Japan's pride. Among such individuals concerned for peace was the eminent theologian E. Stanley Jones, who sought repeatedly in the months preceding the attack to convince the President that if America were to revoke its punitive protectionist stance and accord discretionary treatment to a "have-not" nation vexed by problems of an exploding population, Japan would not only doubly reciprocate but also might possibly end up as an ally.

Severely damaging then to the Nisei was the habit of being lumped as "Japanese," or the pejorative "Japs," which also meant "the enemy." Munson was careful to point out to policy makers that "in the United States there are four divisions of Japanese to be considered." A brief definition of each followed:

> 1. The ISSEI—First generation Japanese. Entire cultural background Japanese. Probably loyal romantically to Japan. They must be considered, however, as other races. They have made this their home. They have brought up children here, their wealth accumulated by hard labor is here, and many would have become American citizens had they been allowed to do so. [The ineligibility of Orientals to acquire citizenship through naturalization had been determined by a Supreme Court deci-

sion: *Ozawa v. U.S.*, 260 U.S. 178(1922).] They are for the most part simple people. Their age group is largely 55 to 65, fairly old for a hard-working Japanese.

2. The NISEI—Second generation who have received their whole education in the United States and usually, in spite of discrimination against them and a certain amount of insults accumulated through the years from irresponsible elements, show a pathetic eagerness to be Americans. They are in constant conflict with the orthodox, well disciplined family life of their elders. Age group—1 to 30 years.

3. The KIBEI—This is an important division of the NISEI. This is the term used by the Japanese to signify those American born Japanese who received part or all of their education in Japan. In any consideration of the KIBEI they should be again divided into two classes, i.e. those who received their education in Japan from childhood to about 17 years of age and those who received their early formative education in the United States and returned to Japan for four or five years Japanese education. The Kibei are considered the most dangerous element and closer to the Issei with special reference to those who received their early education in Japan. It must be noted, however, that many of those who visited Japan subsequent to their early American education come back with added loyalty to the United States. In fact it is a saying that all a Nisei needs is a trip to Japan to make a loyal American out of him. The American educated Japanese is a boor in Japan and treated as a foreigner . . .

4. The SANSEI—The Third [sic] generation Japanese is a baby and may be disregarded for the purpose of our survey.

One of the gross absurdities of the evacuation was that a preponderance of those herded into wartime exile represented babes-in-arms, school-age children, youths not yet of voting age, and an exhausted army of elderly men and women hardly capable of rushing about carrying on subversion. The average age of the Nisei was eighteen. The Issei's average age hovered around sixty.

The Nisei generation, the American-born and -educated, had appeared relatively late on the scene, for only after years of saving up from his meager earnings did the early male immigrant send back to Japan for a bride. "Between these first and second generations there was often a whole generation missing," notes sociologist William Petersen in a January 9, 1966, *New York Times Magazine* article, "for many of the issei married so late in life that in age they might have been their children's grandparents." Owing largely to this generational chasm which separated the Issei from their fledgling offspring, the Nisei suffered not only from a serious communication gap—neither group speaking the other's language with any facility—but from the severe demands of an ancestral culture totally alien to the Americanizing influence of the classroom: a culture which emphasized strict conformity as opposed to individuality, duty more than rights.

The Kibei, the return-to-America Nisei, were an extreme product of this paradox. Some eight thousand of these native-born Americans had received three or more years of schooling in prewar Japan, often a desperate and sacrificial move on the part of parents at a time when even the highest level of educational preparation could not break down white employment barriers on the West Coast. Severe maladjustment problems were usually the lot of the Kibei on their return to a Caucasian-dominated society, causing some to withdraw into a shell of timidity. Ostracized not only by whites but also by their more Americanized peers as being too "Japanesey," the Kibei (often the older brothers and sisters in the family) suffered in angry isolation, feeling contemptuous of the Nisei as being a callow, culturally deprived generation whose "kowtowing" to whites they found distasteful. Marched into concentration camps before many had had a chance to readjust to the culture shock, and where the Kibei were subjected to stricter security surveillance, the more strident camp firebrands and disruptive deviants were inevitably to emerge from this group of misfits.

The factor of ethnicity, or "racial guilt" for the crime of adhering to old world cultural patterns, had been another of the bizarre arguments advanced by the military in justification for the preventive detention of a minority. In the words of Colonel Karl Bendetsen, the army architect-to-be of the racial uprooting, it was highly suspect that Japanese Americans were then part of a "national group almost wholly unassimilated and which had preserved in large measure to itself its customs and traditions." In the event of a Japanese invasion, he determined, the Issei and Nisei would hardly be able to "withstand the ties of race."

And for Secretary of War Stimson, mere racial identification with the fiendish Asiatic foe, whose military might had been woefully miscalculated, was cause enough to have little confidence in the American-born Nisei: "The racial characteristics are such that we cannot understand or trust even the citizen Japanese."

In striking contradiction to such insinuations and untruths fabricated of prejudice, a far kindlier assessment of Issei and Niesi acculturation, aspirations, and value priorities had been documented for the President in the weeks prior to the outbreak of hostilities.

Munson's prewar assessment had been strongly positive; his commendation of the Nisei was glowing:

> Their family life is disciplined and honorable. The children are obedient and the girls virtuous. . . .
>
> There are still Japanese in the United States who will tie dynamite around their waist and make a human bomb out of themselves. We grant this, but today they are few. Many things indicate that very many joints in the Japanese set-up show age, and many elements are not what they used to be. The weakest from a Japanese standpoint are the Nisei. They are universally estimated from 90 to 98 percent loyal to the United States if the Japanese-educated element of the Kibei is excluded. The Nisei are pathetically eager to show this loyalty. They are not Japanese in culture. They are foreigners to Japan. Though American citizens they are not accepted by Americans, largely because they look differently [sic] and can be easily recognized. The Japanese American Citizens league should be encouraged, the while an eye is kept open, to see that Tokio does not get its finger in this pie—which it has in a few cases attempted to do. The loyal Nisei hardly knows where to turn. Some gesture of protection or wholehearted acceptance of this group would go a long way to swinging them away from any last romantic hankering after old Japan. They are not oriental or mysterious, they are very American and are of a proud, self-respecting race suffering from a little inferiority complex and a lack of contact with the white boys they went to school with. They are eager for this contact and to work alongside them.

Noting the "degrees to which Americans were willing to believe almost anything about the Japanese," Professor Roger Daniels (*Concentration Camps USA:* Holt, Rinehart and Winston) wonders whether Munson's apocryphal reference to the fanatic-minded Japanese "who will tie dynamite around their waist and make a human bomb out of themselves" might not have contributed to alarming the President.

In 1941, the Japanese American Citizens League (JACL) was still a politically unsophisticated neophyte organization preoccupied with the problems of how to better the status of their own minority in the United States; most Nisei were not yet old enough to belong to it. In an eagerness to gain white approbation, and moved by the deep and unselfish ideals of the Republic, the League had early taken the route of superpatriotism, leading in time to a near-systematic disavowal of things Japanese. This marked compulsion on the part of the minority's youth generation to demonstrate an extraordinary allegiance may have accounted for the excellent bill of health given the Nisei, generally, and the Investigator's positive recommendation to policy makers: "the Japanese American Citizens League should be encouraged." Which military and civilian authorities proceeded to do to such a discriminatory degree that the manifest partiality shown JACL leaders in the stressful removal and adjustment period was to later become the fundamental cause of intracamp ferment.

Contradicting widely held assumptions to the contrary, Munson's following assessment of the immigrant group reveals the personal esteem in which many Issei had been held as individuals, even in the face of mounting prewar feelings:

> The Issei, or first generation, is considerably weakened in their loyalty to Japan by the fact that they have chosen to make this their home and have brought up their children here. They expect to die here. They are quite fearful of being put in a concentration camp. Many would take out American citizenship if allowed to do so. The haste of this report does not allow us to go into this more fully. The Issei have to break with their religion, their god and Emperor, their family, their ancestors and their after-life in order to be loyal to the United States. They are also still legally Japanese. Yet they do break, and send their boys off to the Army with pride and tears. They are good neighbors. They are old men fifty-five to sixty-five, for the most part simple and dignified. Roughly they were Japanese lower middle class, about analogous to the pilgrim fathers.

A strong factor in the Issei's ability to adapt to their inhospitable environment was that most of the immmigrants had come from the lower rung of the social and economic ladder of their highly class-conscious homeland, thus were inured to inequalities in rights. Their self-effacing, uncritical admiration of America despite obvious repudiation was something "short of miraculous," recalls the Reverend Daisuke Kitagawa, an Episcopal priest from Japan who had worked among them in the less populous Pacific Northwest, where a lesser degree of discrimination was experienced than in California.

The Issei's admiration of, and ever-increasing attachment to, their adopted land was profoundly reinforced as the Nisei began to be inducted into the army under the Selective Service Act of 1939, Father Dai notes discerningly:

> When he saw his son standing proudly in a U.S. Army uniform, he knew that he had been wedded to the United States for all these years, even though there had been many in-laws, as it

were, who mistreated him. . . . At that moment the Issei was in
a frame of mind that would easily have led him to fight the
Japanese forces, should they invade the Pacific Coast. Emotionally it would have been an extremely painful thing for him
to do, but he would have done it just the same, for he saw quite
clearly that it was the only thing for him to do as one who had
been "wedded" to the United States. The traditional Japanese
ethic, when faithfully adhered to, would not only justify, but
more positively demand, his taking the side of the United
States.

The Nisei "show a pathetic eagerness to be Americans" had been
Munson's perceptive summation, and it was an apt one; for it
described the state of mind of a substantial majority of draft-age
Japanese Americans when pridefully answering their nation's call to
arms as a heaven-sent opportunity to prove that, first and foremost,
they were Americans —that their love and loyalty were for the Stars
and Stripes.

The report continued: "Now that we have roughly given a background and description of the Japanese elements in the United
States, the question naturally arises—what will all these people do
in case of a war between the United States and Japan?" In other
words, could Japanese Americans be trusted to withstand the ties of
"blood" and "race" in the ultimate test of loyalty, of being pitted
against their own kind? Would there be the *banzai* uprisings, the
espionage and sabotage long prophesied and propagandized by anti-
Oriental hate exploiters? "As interview after interview piled up,"
reported Investigator Munson, "those bringing in results began to
call it the same old tune."

The story was all the same. There is no Japanese "problem" on
the Coast. There will be no armed uprising of Japanese. There
will undoubtedly be some sabotage financed by Japan and
executed largely by imported agents. . . . In each Naval District
there are about 250 to 300 suspects under surveillance. It is easy
to get on the suspect list, merely a speech in favor of Japan at
some banquet being sufficient to land one there. The Intelligence Services are generous with the title of suspect and are
taking no chances. Privately, they believe that only 50 or 60 in
each district can be classed as really dangerous. The Japanese
are hampered as saboteurs because of their easily recognized
physical appearance. It will be hard for them to get near anything to blow up *if it is guarded*. There is far more danger from
Communists and people of the Bridges type on the Coast than

there is from Japanese. The Japanese here is almost exclusively a farmer, a fisherman or a small businessman. He has no entree to plants or intricate machinery.

Despite the restrained intelligence estimate that "only 50 or 60 in each district can be classed as really dangerous," the ferocity of the sneak attack which followed provided apparent justification for a ruthless sweep for suspects, made possible by the blanket authority given the Attorney General by Presidential Proclamation No. 2525, of December 7, 1941. Over five thousand Issei and Nisei were pulled in by the FBI, most of whom were subsequently released after interrogation or examination before Alien Enemy hearing boards. Over two thousand Issei suspects bore the anguish of having businesses and careers destroyed, reputations defiled in being shipped to distant Department of Justice detention camps for an indefinite stay.

Herbert V. Nicholson, a former Quaker missionary to Japan who then headed up a Japanese American congregation in Los Angeles, recalls the haphazardness of the indiscriminate pickups—that the FBI, with the help of law enforcement officers

picked up anybody that was the head of anything. The same thing they did when Lenin and the Communists took over in Russia. . . . Anybody that was a *cho*—that means "head"—he was picked up. Heads of prefectural organizations were picked up. Just because we come from the same country, we get together occasionally, see, and just have a social time and talk about our friends back in Japan. But everybody that was head of anything was picked up, which was a crazy thing. . . . Because of public opinion and pressure, others were picked up later for all sorts of things. Buddhist priests and Japanese language schoolteachers were all picked up later . . . because of public opinion, they picked up more and more.

Since it was assumed that years of social and legislative slights had hopelessly estranged the Japanese American minority, little did authorities then realize that with all their zealotry, not one instance of subversion or sabotage would ever be uncovered among the Issei, or a single case involving the Nisei. James Rowe, Jr., then second-in-command at the Justice Department as the Assistant Attorney General (today a prominent Washington attorney) recently admitted with candor that "we picked up too many . . . some of this stuff they were charged on was as silly as hell."

The four-week probe of the West Coast "problem" had ended up putting the Nisei entirely in the clear. Munson was positive the enemy would look elsewhere for agents: "Japan will commit some sabotage largely depending on imported Japanese as they are afraid of and do not trust the Nisei."

> There will be no wholehearted response from Japanese in the United States. They may get some helpers from certain Kibei. They will be in a position to pick up information on troop, supply and ship movements from local Japanese. . . . [Another salient passage that may have alarmed the President.]
> For the most part the local Japanese are loyal to the United States or, at worst, hope that by remaining quiet they can avoid concentration camps or irresponsible mobs. We do not believe that they would be at the least any more disloyal than any other racial group in the United States with whom we went to war. Those being here are on a spot and they *know* it.

4

A total of nine days were spent by the Special Investigator in Honolulu. As had been done in the Pacific Coast probe of the Japanese minority, an independent check was made with "the full cooperation of Army and Navy Intelligence and the FBI" on intelligence estimates of each agency, culled from years of accumulated surveillance data. Munson's assessment of the Hawaiian-Japanese problem began as follows:

> The concensus of opinion is that there will be no racial uprising of the Japanese in Honolulu. The first generation, as on the Coast, are ideologically and culturally closest to Japan. Though many of them speak no English, or at best only pigeon-English, it is considered that the big bulk of them will be loyal. . . . The second generation is estimated as approximately ninety-eight percent loyal. However, with the large Japanese population in the Hawaiian Islands, giving this the best interpretation possible, it would mean that fifteen hundred were disloyal. However, the F.B.I. state that there are about four hundred suspects, and the F.B.I.'s private estimate is that only fifty or sixty of these are sinister. . . .

Following the Pearl Harbor assault, 980 suspects from the Hawaiian Japanese community were to be pulled in by authorities and penned up at the Hawaiian Detention Center before their removal to mainland Justice Department camps. It is worth noting that the Honolulu-based FBI appears to have exercised far more restraint than its West Coast counterparts, considering that twice as many mainland Issei were to end up in Justice's custody.

A marked difference between the kind of discrimination being practiced on the Islands as compared to that on the mainland caught the attention of the Special Investigator. On the West Coast, there was no mistaking that racial attitudes were at the root of the animosity against the Issei and Nisei: "there are plenty of 'Okies' to call the Japanese a 'Yellow-belly,' when economically and by education the Japanese may not only be their equal but their superior." On the other hand, discrimination as practiced in Hawaii (where the Japanese "fit in" because "the bulk are dark-skinned of one kind or another") struck Munson as being based more on one's financial standing—on whether one fitted in on a social and economic basis.

The result of this is that the Hawaiian Japanese does not suffer from the same inferiority complex or feel the same mistrust of the whites that he does on the mainland. While it is seldom on the mainland that you find even a college-educated Japanese-American citizen who talks to you wholly openly until you have gained his confidence, this is far from the case in Hawaii. Many young Japanese there are fully as open and frank and at ease with a white as white boys are. In a word, Hawaii is more of a melting pot because there are more brown skins to melt—Japanese, Hawaiian, Chinese and Filipino. It is interesting to note that there has been absolutely no bad feeling between the Japanese and the Chinese in the islands due to the Japanese-Chinese war. Why should they be any worse toward us?

More than a few Nisei and Kibei detained by Hawaiian authorities were to end up, with family members, in mainland "relocation centers," where the breezy outspokenness of Hawaiian youths and their uninhibited tendency to be openly resentful of insult was to come as a shock and special vexation to administrators—accustomed, as they were, to the docile, more taciturn mainland Nisei.

However marked the difference in personality makeup, the compelling need to demonstrate love of country and loyalty to the flag was a character trait shared in common by both the Hawaiian and mainland Nisei, or one might gather as much by their positive attitude toward army enlistment—no doubt a moral imperative—"country before self"—passed on to them by their duty-conscious parents. Noted the Investigator:

Due to the preponderance of Japanese in the population of the Islands, a much greater proportion of Japanese have been called to the draft than on the mainland. As on the mainland they are inclined to enlist before being drafted. The Army is extremely high in its praise of them as recruits. . . . They are beginning to feel that they are going to get a square deal and some of them are really almost pathetically exuberant.

Postwar statistics were to dramatize this remarkable *esprit de corps* more tellingly. A higher percentage of Americans of Japanese ancestry ended up serving in the U.S. Army during World War II than any other racial group, divided almost equally between the mainland Nisei (13,528) and those in Hawaii (12,250). "The final count of Hawaiian war casualties revealed that 80 percent of those killed and 88 percent of those wounded throughout the war were of Japanese descent," states Andrew Lind, writing in *Hawaii's Japanese*.

5

Los Angeles, California: December 20, 1941 (or some two weeks *after* the Pearl Harbor attack).

Munson offered no comments or post-mortems on the "surprise" attack which finally came—in obvious anticipation of which he had warned Washington from his Hawaiian vantage point in the early part of November: *"The best consensus of opinion seemed to agree that martial law should be proclaimed now in Hawaii."*

From his post-Pearl (December 20) Los Angeles vantage point, Munson volunteered some strong private opinions on a fast-developing situation which augured no good for the Coastal Japanese.

We desire respectfully to call attention to a statement of the Secretary of the Navy evidently made to some reporter on his return to Washington after the Pearl Harbor attack as printed in the *Los Angeles Times* of December 18. . . . We quote, "I think the most effective Fifth Column work of the entire war was done in Hawaii with the possible exception of Norway," Secretary of the Navy Knox said. . . . Fifth Column activities, such as in Norway, impugns [sic] the loyalty of a certain large proportion of a population. Your observer still doubts that this was the case in Honolulu. . . .

Some reaction of an undesirable nature is already apparent on the West Coast due to this statement of the Secretary's. In Honolulu your observer noted that the seagoing Navy was inclined to consider everybody with slant eyes bad. This thought stems from two sources: self-interest, largely in the economic field, and in the Navy usually from pure lack of knowledge and the good old "eat 'em up alive" school. It is not the measured judgment of 98% of the intelligence services or the knowing citizenry either on the mainland or in Honolulu. . . .

Knox's allegations of foul play were providing the opening wedge for racist forces to begin reactivating slumbering anti-Oriental prejudices along the Pacific Coast. Subsequently, the climate was to take an abrupt turn toward intolerance, notably when the Roberts Commission Report on the attack, released on January 25, 1942, reinforced the misleading impression that the aid of resident traitors had been received by the spy operation then centered in the Japanese Consulate: "some were consular agents and others were persons having no open relations with the Japanese foreign service." Yet Washington was to remain remarkably silent about it. By the time official denials reached the mainland public, the developing fear hysteria had become irreversible.

Even as Munson sought to set the record straight, the President and his Cabinet had agreed, as early as December 19, 1941, to concentrate all aliens of Japanese ancestry on an island other than Oahu. Navy Secretary Knox doubted that the measure went far enough and sought, from the outset, to convince the President that citizens, too, should be included. In a memorandum of February 26, a supremely confident President assured Knox that there would be no problem in removing "most of the Japanese": "I do not worry about the constitutional question, first because of my recent order [West Coast evacuation], second because Hawaii is under martial law. The whole matter is one of immediate and present war emergency. I think you and Stimson can agree and then go ahead and do it as a military project."

Had the island roundup involved only aliens, as originally agreed upon, the Hawaiian evacuation might have proceeded swiftly, without hindrance. Approximately twenty thousand aliens and ninety-eight thousand citizens then lived on the island of Oahu, the Japanese minority then making up one-third of the total island population. The small Issei population might have been readily replaced by an equivalent work force.

But because of Knox's stubborn insistence on a large-scale evacuation, which would have involved some hundred thousand Nisei and Issei (recommended by the Joint Chiefs of Staff on March 11, 1942, and approved by the President on March 13, 1942), the project was to end up becoming unwieldly and unworkable, especially since the Joint Chiefs of Staff ruled on removal to the mainland "utilizing empty ships returning to the west coast" at a time when shipping facilities were being taxed to their utmost.

The Hawaiian evacuation, to begin with the removal of twenty thousand of "the most dangerous" aliens and citizens, was vigorously opposed—later thwarted—by island army and navy authorities closer to the problem as being too costly, logistically complex, and self-defeating. As Munson had prohetically forewarned in his pre–Pearl Harbor report, "it would simply mean that the Islands would lose their vital labor supply by so doing, and in addition to that we would have to feed them . . . it is essential that they should be kept loyal."

Accordingly—and paradoxically—it had become a veritable military necessity for authorities to retain, *not detain,* Hawaii's Japanese population in a battle zone thousands of miles closer to the enemy mainland than the jittery state of California and to do everything possible to encourage their loyalty so that all would stay at their tasks.

It was in sharp contrast to the policy pursued on the West Coast in reference to a people then posing an increasing threat to the prosperity of native farmers and merchants though still an infinitesimal percentage of the population—thus expendable, both politically and economically. Should the "Japanese" on the mainland "prove actively disloyal *they could be corralled or destroyed within a very short time,"* the Special Investigator, in his prewar assessment, had dramatically punctuated this expendability.

But on the basis of the highly favorable impression he had gained during the hurried survey, Munson was moved to submit to the President his own well-considered recommendations with the reassurance "Your reporter, fully believing that his reports are still good after the attack, makes the following observations about handling the Japanese 'problem' on the West Coast."

A. The loyal Japanese citizens should be encouraged by a statement from high government authority and public attitude toward them outlined.

B. Their offers of assistance should be accepted through such agencies as:
   1. Civilian Defense
   2. Red Cross
   3. U.S.O., etc., etc.

This assistance should not be merely monetary, nor should it even be limited to physical voluntary work in segregated Nisei units. The Nisei should work with and among white persons, and be made to feel he is welcome on a basis of equality.

C. An alien property custodian should be appointed to supervise Issei (first generation-alien) businesses, *but* encouraging Nisei (second generation-American citizen) to take over.

D. Accept investigated Nisei as workers in defense industries such as shipbuilding plants, aircraft plants, etc.
E. Put *responsibility* for behavior of Issei and Nisei on the leaders of Nisei groups such as the Japanese American Citizens League.
F. Put the *responsibility* for production of food (vegetables, fish, etc.) on Nisei leaders.

In essence, Munson's power-to-the-Nisei policy was to involve federal control:

> In case we have not made it apparent, the aim of this report is that all Japanese Nationals in the continental United States and property owned and operated by them within the country be immediately placed under absolute Federal control. The aim of this will be to squeeze control from the hands of the Japanese Nationals into the hands of the loyal Nisei who are American citizens. . . . It is the aim that the Nisei should police themselves, and as result police their parents.

Munson's suggested course of governmental action, which would have catapulted the Nisei into a position of leadership and control, might have proved sound had both the Issei and Nisei been permitted to remain at liberty as in Hawaii. But the power-to-the-Nisei policy was to become the root cause of resentment and conflict, when imposed behind barbed wire, in abortively speeding up the process whereby the still fledgling Nisei were taken out from under the control of elders, a generation to whom they owed unlimited deference and obedience.

Regrettably ignored was Munson's strong recommendation that the public's attitude toward the minority be positively led with a reassuring statement by the "President or Vice President, or at least [someone] almost as high"—as was the adopted policy in Hawaii, where the newly appointed military governor acted swiftly to squelch fifth-column rumors while assuring justice and equitable treatment to aliens and citizens alike, if they would remain loyal.

But on the U.S. mainland, where other pressing considerations apparently outweighed justice for so inconsequential a minority, fear and fiction were allowed to luxuriate as part of the total war propaganda. And for reasons that defy easy explanation, Secretary of the Navy Knox was to further crucify a powerless minority by reporting to the Tolan Committee in a letter of March 24, 1942:

. . . There was a considerable amount of evidence of subversive activity on the part of the Japanese prior to the attack. This consisted of providing the enemy with the most exact possible kind of information as an aid to them in locating their objectives, and also creating a great deal of confusion in the air following the attack by the use of radio sets which successfully prevented the commander in chief of the fleet from determining in what direction the attackers had withdrawn and in locating the position of the covering fleet, including the carriers. . . .

It can only be assumed that Knox's tissue of fallacies impugning the fidelity of the resident Japanese was meant merely to divert, to take political "heat" off himself and the administration for the unspeakable humiliation that Pearl Harbor represented. By the convenient redirection of public rage, a nation on the verge of disunity and disaster was finally—and purposefully—united as one.

The actions of Knox and the wartime suppression of the Munson papers, like the more familiar Pentagon Papers, once again make evident how executive officers of the Republic are able to mislead public opinion by keeping hidden facts which are precisely the opposite of what the public is told—information vital to the opinions they hold.

In the case of Japanese Americans, data regarding their character and integrity were positive and "exceedingly uniform," the facts clear-cut. But as once observed by Nobel Peace Prize recipient Sir Norman Angell: "Men, particularly in political matters, are not guided by the facts but by their opinions about the facts." Under the guise of an emergency and pretended threats to the national security, the citizenry was denied the known facts, public opinion was skillfully manipulated, and a cruel and massive governmental hoax enacted. According to one of the foremost authorities on constitutional law, Dr. Eugene V. Rostow: "One hundred thousand persons were sent to concentration camps on a record which wouldn't support a conviction for stealing a dog."

Hostages

I'm for catching every Japanese in America, Alaska, and Hawaii now and putting them in concentration camps. . . . Damn them! Let's get rid of them now!

—Congressman John Rankin,
Congressional Record, December 15, 1941

Since much of Munson's documentation for the President reads more like a tribute to those of Japanese ancestry than a need for locking them up, the question remains: Had the President, having perceived the racist character of the racist character of the American public, deliberately acquiesced in the clearly punitive action knowing it would be rousingly effective for the flagging home-front morale?

Or could factors other than political expedience, perhaps a more critical wartime exigency, have entered into and inspired the sudden decision calling for mass action—made as it was at a time when the Allied cause in the Pacific was plummeting, one reversal following another in seemingly endless succession?

A bit of personal conjecture: Shocked and mortified by the unexpected skill and tenacity of the foe (as the Administration might have been), with America's very survival in jeopardy, what could better insure the more considerate treatment of American captives, the unknown thousands then being trapped daily in the islands and territories falling to the enemy like dominoes, than a substantial *hostage reserve?* And would not a readily available *reprisal reserve* prove crucial should America's war fortune continue to crumble: should the scare propaganda of "imminent invasion" become an actual, living nightmare of rampaging hordes of yellow "barbarians" overrunning and making "free fire zones" of American villages and hamlets—looting, raping, murdering, slaughtering . . .

In an earlier crisis situation which had exacerbated U.S.–Japan relations to the near-breaking point, the very sagacity of such a contingency plan had been forthrightly brought to the attention of the President by Congressman John D. Dingell of Michigan. On August 18, 1941, months before the outbreak of hostilities, the Congressman had hastened to advise the President:

Reports contained in the Press indicate that Japan has barred the departure of one hundred American citizens and it is indicated that the detention is in reprisal for the freezing of Japanese assets in the United States of America.

I want to suggest without encroaching upon the privilege of the Executive or without infringing upon the privileges of the State Department that if it is the intention of Japan to enter into a reprisal contest that we remind Nippon that unless assurances are received that Japan will facilitate and permit the voluntary departure of this group of one hundred Americans within forty-eight hours, the Government of the United States will cause the forceful detention or imprisonment in a concentration camp of ten thousand alien Japanese in Hawaii; the ratio of Japanese hostages held by America being one hundred for every American detained by the Mikado's Government.

It would be well to further remind Japan that there are perhaps one hundred fifty thousand additional alien Japanese in the United States who will be held in a reprisal reserve whose status will depend upon Japan's next aggressive move. I feel that the United States is an ideal position to accept Japan's challenge.

God bless you, Mr. President.

Within two months after the crippling blow dealt by the Japanese at Pearl Harbor, a fast-deteriorating situation in the soon untenable Philippine campaign moved Stimson to call for threats of reprisals on Japanese nationals in America "to insure proper treatment" of U.S. citizens trapped in enemy territory. On February 5, the very day when mass evacuation-internment plans began to be drawn up and formalized within the War Department, Stimson wrote Hull:

General MacArthur has reported in a radiogram, a copy of which is enclosed, that American and British civilians in areas of the Philippines occupied by the Japanese are being subjected to extremely harsh treatment. The unnecessary harsh and rigid measures imposed, in sharp contrast to the moderate treatment of metropolitan Filipinos, are unquestionably designed to discredit the white race.

I request that you strongly protest this unjustified treatment of civilians, and suggest that you present a threat of reprisals against the many Japanese nationals now enjoying negligible restrictions in the United States, to insure proper treatment of our nationals in the Philippines.

If a reprisal reserve urgency had indeed precipitated the sudden decision for internment, the emphasis, as the tide of the war reversed itself, switched to the buildup of a "barter reserve": one sizable enough to allow for the earliest possible repatriation of American detainees, even at the price of a disproportionate number of Japanese nationals in exchange. Behind this willingness on the part of the State Department *to give more than they expected back* may have lurked profound concern that unless meaningful concessions were to be made in the matter of POW exchanges, the whole procedure would get mired in resistance and inertia to the jeopardy of thousands subject to terrible suffering in enemy prison camps.

As revealed in a letter from the Secretary of the Navy to President Roosevelt, the Secretary of State, in Knox's estimate, was being overly disconcerted by the belief that German authorities intended to hold on indefinitely to American detainees "as hostages for captured Germans whom we might prosecute under the war criminal procedure." A similar alarmist concern may have been entertained by Secretary of State Hull as to the intent of Japanese authorities.

The use of the Nisei as part and parcel of this human barter was not totally ruled out in the realm of official thinking. By curious circumstance, such intent on the part of U.S. authorities became starkly evident in the latter part of 1942 and early 1943, when numerous Nisei, to their shocked indignation, were informed by Colonel Karl Bendetsen in a form letter: "Certain Japanese persons are currently being considered for repatriation [expatriation] to Japan. You and those members of your family listed above, are being so considered."

2

The removals in the United States were only a part of forced uprootings which occurred almost simultaneously in Alaska, Canada, Mexico, Central America, parts of South America, and the Caribbean island of Haiti and the Dominican Republic.

Canada's decision to round up and remove its tiny twenty-three thousand West Coast minority, 75 percent of whom were citizens of Canada, preceded America's by about a month and may have had a decisive influence on the War Department's decision to proceed similarly; but, in many ways, discriminatory measures imposed on the Canadian Japanese were more arbitrary and severe. An order of January 14, 1942, calling for the removal of all enemy alien males over sixteen years of age from the area west of the Cascade Mountains resulted in men being separated from women in the initial stage of the evacuation. But a follow-up decree of February 27 demanded total evacuation, of citizens as well as aliens, most of whom were removed to work camps and mining "ghost towns" in mountain valleys of the Canadian interior. Property and possessions not disposed of were quickly confiscated and sold off at public auctions since evacuees were expected to assume some of the internment expenses from the proceeds. Canadian Japanese were not permitted to return to British Columbia and their home communities until March 1949, seven years after the evacuation.

Of the 151 Alaskan Japanese plucked from their homes and life pursuits under color of Executive Order 9066, around fifty were seal- and whale-hunting half Indians and half Eskimos (*one-half* "Japanese blood" was the criterion in Alaska), some of whom were to associate with Japanese for the first time in the camps. Except for a "few fortunate ones with second-generation fathers," families were left fatherless since male nationals suffered mass indiscriminate internment in various Justice Department detention centers. Most ended up in the camp maintained exclusively for Japanese alien detainees in Lordsburg, New Mexico. Remaining family members were airlifted to the state of Washington (following a short initial stay at Fort Richardson, Alaska) and penned up temporarily in the Puyallup Assembly Center near Seattle. In the mass Japanese American exodus out of the prohibited military area during the summer of 1942, the evacuees from Alaska wound up in the relocation center of Minidoka in Idaho.

In Mexico, the Japanese residing in small settlements near the American border and coastal areas (along a sixty-two-mile zone) were forced to liquidate their property and move inland, some to "clearing houses" and resettlement camps, a number of them to concentration camps in Perote, Puebla, and Vera Cruz.

Even less selectivity was exercised in the case of the Japanese then scattered throughout the Central American republics. Many were simply "picked up" by reason of their "hostile origin" and handed over to U.S. authorities, who, in turn, arranged for their transportation by sea or air to the U.S. mainland.

Such gunpoint "relocations" to American concentration camps became quite commonplace on the South American continent in the days and months following the Pearl Harbor attack. The reason: Considerable pressure had been applied by the U.S. State Department on various republics of the Western Hemisphere to impound, with the option of handing over to American authorities for care and custody, persons who might be considered "potentially dangerous" to hemispheric security, with special emphasis on the Japanese. More than a month before the war's outbreak, plans for this unusual wartime action began to take shape. On October 20, 1941, U.S. Ambassador to Panama Edwin C. Wilson informed Under Secretary of State Sumner Welles:

My strictly confidential despatch No. 300 of October 20, 1941, for the Secretary and Under Secretary, transmits memoranda of my conversations with the Foreign Minister regarding the question of internment of Japanese in the event that we suddenly find ourselves at war with Japan.

The attitude of the Panamanian Government is thoroughly cooperative. The final memorandum sets out the points approved by the Panamanian Cabinet for dealing with this matter. Briefly, their thought is this: Immediately following action by the United States to intern Japanese in the United States, Panama would arrest Japanese on Panamanian territory and intern them on Taboga Island. They would be guarded by Panamanian guards and would have the status of Panamanian interns. *All expenses and costs of internment and guarding to be paid by the United States.* The United States Government would agree to hold Panama harmless against any claims which might arise as a result of internment.

I believe it essential that you instruct me by telegraph at once to assure the Foreign Minister that the points which he set out to cover this matter meet the approval of our Government [Italics mine.]

Funds which would be immediately needed, as in the construction of a prison camp which would serve as a staging area for transshipments to U.S. detention facilities, were to be provided by the Commanding General of the Caribbean Defense Command. And from Chief of Staff General George Marshall came the suggestion that a more liberal interpretation of persons to be detained be considered. On October 28, 1941, he wrote Under Secretary Welles:

It is gratifying to know that Panama is prepared to intern Japanese aliens immediately following similar action by the United States.

I suggest, however, that the agreement be enlarged to provide for internment by the Panamanian Government of all persons believed dangerous, who are regarded by the United States as enemy aliens, under similar conditions.

Similarly encouraged to undermine in advance any possibility of Japanese sabotage, subversion, or fifth-column treachery was Panama's neighbor republic of Costa Rica. On December 8, 1941, upon America's declaration of war on Japan, the U.S. Legation in Costa Rica wired the State Department: ORDERS FOR INTERNMENT OF ALL JAPANESE IN COSTA RICA HAVE BEEN ISSUED.

At a Conference of Foreign Ministers of the American Republics held in Rio de Janeiro in January 1942, a special inter-American agency (the Emergency Committee for Political Defense) to coordinate hemispheric security measures was organized, with headquarters subsequently established in Montevideo. The Emergency Committee adopted, without delay, a resolution which had been drafted by the U.S. Department of Justice in conjunction with the Department of State which stressed the need for prompt preventive detention of dangerous Axis nationals and for the "deportation of such persons to another American republic for detention when adequate local detention facilities are lacking." States interested in the collaborative effort were assured that not only detention accommodations but also shipping facilities would be provided by the United States "at its own expense." The State Department offered an additional incentive: It would include any of the official and civilian nationals of the participating republics in whatever exchange arrangements the U.S. would subsequently make with Axis powers.

More than a dozen American states cooperated. Among them: Bolivia, Colombia, Costa Rica, the Dominican Republic, Ecuador, El Salvador, Guatemala, Haiti, Honduras, Mexico, Nicaragua, Panama, Peru, and Venezuela. Three states, Brazil, Uruguay, and Paraguay, instituted their own detention programs (Paraguay, for one, promptly arrested the two Japanese residing within her borders). Since Argentina and Chile held back breaking off diplomatic relations with the Axis powers until much later, both nations took no part in the hemispheric imprisonments.

In time, the State Department was able to claim that "the belligerent republics of the Carribbean area have sent us subversive aliens without limitation concerning their disposition"; but four republics—Venezuela, Colombia, Ecuador, and Mexico—exacted "explicit guarantees" before turning over internees. Panama liberally granted the U.S. "full freedom to negotiate with Japan and agrees to the use of Japanese internees . . . for exchange of any non-official citizen of an American belligerent country."

The concept of hemispheric removals had its origin in the State Department, but responsibility for the success of the operation was shared by the Departments of War, Navy, and Justice. With the safety of the Panama Canal a veritable life-or-death matter after the near annihilation of the Pacific Fleet, it appears that all concerned acted on the conviction that the threat to continental security was so grave as to outweigh the momentary misuse of executive, military, and judicial power.

As a direct result of the hemispheric nations' agreement to "cooperate jointly for their mutual protection," over two thousand deportees of Japanese ancestry were to swell the already impressive U.S. barter reserve by ending up in scattered mainland detention camps, whose existence was virtually unknown then to the American public. Though the deportees were legally in State Department custody, the custodial program for them was supervised by the Immigration and Naturalization Service of the U.S. Justice Department.

3

As for persons of Japanese ancestry residing in the democratic republic of Peru, racial antagonism fed by resentment of the foreign element as being exceedingly successful economic competitors had more to do with the Peruvian Government's spirited cooperation than its concern for the defense of the hemisphere. The steady economic encroachment of the resident Japanese and their alleged imperviousness to assimilation had aroused increasing nativist hostility; and anti-Japanese legislation and restrictive ordinances of the West Coast type had been copied through the years, culminating with the revocation, by executive action, of citizenship rights of Nisei possessing dual citizenship. Racial feelings against the Japanese minority, abetted by the press, had burst into occasional mob action even before the Pearl Harbor attack. And much of the blame for the cut-off of Japanese immigration in 1936 had been attributed to the "social unrest" stirred up by the unwanted minority because, in the words of Foreign Minister Ulloa, "their conditions and methods of working have produced pernicious competition for the Peruvian workers and businessmen."

Accordingly, 80 percent of the Latin American deportees of Japanese ancestry was to be contributed by the government of Peru, an enthusiasm stimulated not only by the opportunity presented to expropriate property and business (Law No. 9586 of April 10 authorized seizure of Axis property) but also to rid the realm of an undesirable element. On July 20, 1942, Henry Norweb, the U.S. Ambassador to Peru, informed the State Department of President Manuel Prado's manifest fervor in this regard:

> The second matter in which the President [Prado] is very much interested is the possibility of getting rid of the Japanese in Peru. He would like to settle this problem permanently, which means that he is thinking in terms of repatriating thousands of Japanese. He asked Colonel Lord to let him know about the prospects of additional shipping facilities from the United States. In any arrangement that might be made for internment of Japanese in the States, Peru would like to be sure that these Japanese would not be returned to Peru later on. The President's goal apparently is the substantial elimination of the Japanese colony in Peru.

Pressure in the name of "mutual protection" had obviously paid off. Only three months earlier, a dispatch from the American Embassy in Lima had underscored the gravity of the subversion potential inherent in the Peruvian Japanese, "whose strength and ability have, in the past, been vastly underestimated and whose fanatic spirit has neither been understood nor taken seriously . . . there appears to be little realization of the actual danger and a reluctance on the part of the Government to take positive measures." Recommendations from the Legation included the removal of key Japanese leaders, the encouragement of "propaganda intended to call attention of the Peruvians to the Japanese dangers," and suggestion that covert assistance might even be rendered by U.S. authorities: "Ways may be found to provide . . . material without of course permitting the source to become known as the Embassy."

In light of such concerns among embassy officials of the Lima legation, the Peruvian president's unexpected eagerness to cooperate to the fullest came as a welcome turn of events and as an instant go-ahead for the core of U.S. advisers to assist in widening the scope of Peruvian expulsions. An intradepartmental State Department memo noted ways in which the operation might be expedited:

> President Prado has officially stated his willingness to have this deportation program carried through. . . . The suggestion that Japanese be removed from strategic areas should be followed and this should be carried on by *well-paid* police; even if this necessitates a loan from this government. All police charged with supervision of Japanese should be well paid. [Legation had warned that Peruvian law officers "are susceptible to Japanese bribes . . . their alertness cannot be depended upon."] The suggestion that Japanese be expelled whether they are naturalized Peruvians or not might be met by a denaturalization law.

Arrests were made in swift, silent raids by the Peruvian police, who first confined detainees in local jails, then turned them over to the custody of U.S. military authorities. Then began the strange odyssey which would take them northward to the United States mainland: "We were taken to the port of Callao and embarked on an American transport under strict guard and with machine gun pointed at us by American soldiers." As it was found that immunity from deportation could be "bought" by a generous bribe unless the removal was swiftly expedited, Army Air Transport planes were used in a number of cases involving the "extremely dangerous," usually the wealthier and influential Peruvian Japanese considered high-priority trade bait. After a short stopover in the Panama-based internment camp used as a staging area, deportees were shipped on to various Department of Justice detention centers in the States, after landing at a Gulf Coast or West Coast port.

More fortunate prisoners enjoyed reunion with family members at the Crystal City Internment Camp in Texas, the only "family camp" operated by the Justice Department where detainees were dealt with as "prisoners of war." Even the voluntary prisoners. The latter were mostly women and children. A total of 1,094 of them, officially designated as "voluntary detainees," answered the State Department's "invitation" to place themselves in war-duration voluntary incarceration with the 1,024 men who had been seized and spirited to the mainland by the U.S. military.

The question of whether the reunion program had been undertaken as a direct means of swelling the U.S. barter stockpile or whether the entire procedure represented a "humanitarian" concession on the part of the State and Justice departments is a matter still shrouded in mystery.

By late October of 1942, fears concerning hemispheric security had greatly diminished. A pounding U.S. counteroffensive in the Solomons had finally begun to check the thrust of the Japanese juggernaut in the Pacific. And with the mass transportation of the coastal subnation to the inland camps nearing completion, Hull hastened to advise the President of what, to the Secretary of State, were still overriding reasons why there should be no letup in the hemispheric removals—at least of "all the Japanese . . . for internment in the United States."

There are in China 3,300 American citizens who desire to return to the United States. Many of them are substantial persons who have represented important American business and commercial interests and a large number of missionaries. They are scattered all through that part of China occupied by the Japanese. Some of them are at liberty, some of them are in concentration camps, and some of them have limited liberty, but all of them subject to momentary cruel and harsh treatment by their oppressors. Under our agreement with Japan which is still operating, we will be able to remove these people. It will take two more trips of the *Gripsholm* to do so. In exchange for them we will have to send out Japanese in the same quantity. . . .

In addition, there are 3,000 non-resident American citizens in the Philippines. We have no agreement for their exchange but it has been intimated that Japan might consider an exchange of them. It would be very gratifying if we could obtain those people from Japanese control and return them to the United States. But to do so we would have to exchange Japanese for them. That would take two more round trips of the *Gripsholm*.

Still, in addition, there are 700 civilians interned in Japan proper captured at Guam and Wake. It is probable that we might arrange for their return. But in order to obtain them we would have to release Japanese. . . .

With the foregoing as a predicate, I propose the following course of action:

. . . Continue our exchange agreement with the Japanese until the Americans are out of China, Japan and the Philippines —so far as possible. . . .

Continue our efforts to remove all the Japanese from these American Republic countries for internment in the United States.

Continue our efforts to remove from South and Central America all the dangerous Germans and Italians still there, together with their families . . . [Reparagraphed by author]

In the Secretary of State's recommended course of action, the precise wording of the directive is significant: Note the qualifying prerequisite, *dangerous,* in reference to hostages-to-be of German and Italian nationalties. In Hull's implied suggestion of more discriminating treatment of non-Oriental Axis nationals, while calling for wholesale removal—dangerous or harmless—of "all the Japanese," evidence again lies tellingly exposed of racial bias then lurking in high and rarefied places in the nation's capital.

4

By early 1943, the Justice Department, in its custodial role in the hemispheric operation, had become greatly alarmed at the number of internees being sent up. Worse, it had come to its attention that many being held under the Alien Enemies Act were not enemy Japanese but Peruvian nationals, thus aliens of a friendly nation, and that little or no evidence supported the Peruvian Government's contention that their deportees were dangerous. "Some of the cases seem to be mistakes," Attorney General Biddle wrote the Secretary of State on January 11, 1943.

Biddle insisted on more conclusive proof that the deportees were in fact "the dangerous leaders among the Japanese population in Peru," and he proposed sending his own representative to Peru and other donor nations to help sort out the people to be sent up. Since barter negotiations between Washington and Tokyo had then come to a standstill, Biddle balked at going along with the indiscriminate internment of bodies being sent up in ever-growing numbers from Peru, insisting that his department had merely agreed to "expediting *temporary* custody" pending repatriation.

The State Department's primary concern was that the competence and sincerity of the donor states would be impugned if Biddle were to challenge the veracity of their criterion of "dangerousness." But the State Department finally gave in, and Raymond W. Ickes (of the Central and South American division of the Alien Enemy Control unit) of the Justice Department was permitted to make on-the-spot reviews of all pending deportee cases. Ickes found little evidence anywhere to support the claims of the participating republics that individuals being held—or targeted—for deportation were "in any true sense of the word security subjects." On turning down the deportation from Venezuela of thirty Japanese, he advised the U.S. legation in Caracas:

> This is the very thing that we have to guard against, particularly in the case of Peru, where attempts have been made to send job lots of Japanese to the States merely because the Peruvians wanted their businesses and not because there was any adverse evidence against them.

All deportations to the United States thereafter ceased.

With the coming of peace, the once felicitous relationship between the U.S. and Peru suffered another setback. While the State Department proceeded to return various ex-hostages to their respective homelands, the government of Peru refused to allow reentry in the case of Japanese. Only a few select citizens were permitted readmission, mostly native-Peruvian wives and Peruvian-citizen children.

The Justice Department thereupon pressed ahead with an extraordinary piece of injustice on the onetime kidnapees no longer needed to ransom off U.S. detainees. With certain hierarchal changes in the department (FDR's death on April 12, 1945, had resulted in Tom Clark, a Truman appointee, becoming attorney general on September 27, 1945), all were scheduled for removal to Japan despite vigorous protest that a sizable number of them had no ties in a country many had never visited; wives and children of many were in fact still living in Peru. The grounds for the second "deportation" of the Peruvian kidnapees was that they lacked proper credentials: they had entered the United States illegally, without visas and without passports.

From despair arising from their prolonged detention without the possibility of return to their homeland or release, a contingent of some 1,700 Peruvian Japanese (700 men and their dependents) allowed themselves, between November 1945 and February 1946, to be "voluntarily" unloaded on Japan. Many had acquiesced in this drastic federal action in the belief that reunion with families left behind in Peru could not otherwise be achieved.

Awaiting a similarly grim fate were 365 remaining Peruvian rejects, whose desperate plight came to the attention of Wayne Collins, a San Francisco attorney then conducting a one-man war against the Justice Department in trying to extricate thousands of Nisei caught in their "renunciation trap" (see chapter 12), another one of the extreme consequences of the evacuation tragedy.

To abort U.S. plans to "dump" this residual Peruvian group on a defeated, war-pulverized enemy hardly able to care for its own starving masses, Collins filed two test proceedings in habeas corpus on June 25, 1946, in a U.S. District Court in San Francisco after the Immigration Department contended that suspension of deportation on a like basis as Caucasians was not permitted, and a subsequent appeal directly to the Attorney General and the President came to no avail. With the removal program brought, by court action, to a forced halt, the detainees were placed in "relaxed internment"—many of them at Seabrook Farms, New Jersey, the well-known frozen-food processing plant where the labor of German POWs had been utilized during the war years, and where evacuee groups from many camps were given employment.

Collins, with the aid of the Northern California office of the American Civil Liberties Union, also sought to bring to public attention what both contended was a "legalized kidnapping" program masterminded by the State Department and sanctioned by the nation's chief guardian of decency and legality, the Attorney General, whose office and the State Department now disclaimed any responsibility for the plight of the unfortunate people.

Interior Secretary Harold Ickes (father of Raymond W. Ickes), the only high-level officer of the FDR Administration to speak out in criticism of the State and Justice departments' highly clandestine proceedings, took issue with Attorney General Clark, then seeking the U.S. vice-presidency spot by paying glowing homage to the nation's democratic ideals of human rights and individual liberty. This did not sit well with former Cabinet officer Ickes, who knew, through and through, the wartime injustices perpetrated on the Issei and Nisei throughout the Western Hemisphere, which, even then, were being perpetuated by Attorney General Clark's zealous pursuance of postwar deportations of "disloyals" and scores of defenseless aliens under arbitrary classification as "dangerous."

Ickes was sharply outspoken:

What the country demands from the Attorney General is less self-serving lip-service and more action. . . .

The Attorney General, in the fashion of the Russian Secret Police, maintains a top-secret list of individuals and organizations supposed to be subversive or disloyal. What are the criteria for judging whether a person is disloyal? . . .

I cannot begin . . . even to call the role of our maimed, mutilated, and missing civil liberties, but the United States, more than two years after the war, is holding in internment some 293 naturalized Peruvians of Japanese descent, who were taken by force by our State and Justice Departments from their homes in Peru.

The resolution of the Peruvian-Japanese dilemma was to take years of unprecedented legal maneuvering on the part of lawyer Collins to untangle the mess in which so many charged with not one specifiable offense found themselves—their lives often mangled beyond repair through the prolonged splitting of families.

Changes in U.S. laws eventually enabled the Peruvian Japanese to apply for suspension of deportation if it could be shown that deportation to Japan would result in serious economic hardship and if "continued residence" in the United States of at least ten years could be proved—with years spent in various concentration camps counting also as "residence."

Peru finally permitted reentry of the deportees in the mid-1950s, but less than one hundred returned. By then the job of reconstructing their lives had begun elsewhere.

Three hundred of the 365 rescued by Collins chose to remain in the United States. An impressive number became American citizens under the amended U.S. naturalization law of 1952, which finally gave immigrants of Asian ancestry the right to become Americans.

Minoru Yasui

(1917–1988)

On May 6, 1942, Japanese American Citizens League (JACL) spokesman Mike M. Masaoka, an activist advocate of Japanese American assimilation by white America, put down the Nikkei cry to mount cases to test the constitutionality of the evacuation and the internment of Japanese Americans. In *JACL Bulletin #142 RE: Test Cases,* he argued that court challenges by Nikkei were unpatriotic and therefore un-American, jeopardizing the acceptance and assimilation of Japanese Americans by creating bad publicity.

Minoru Yasui, a lawyer, an officer in the Oregon National Guard, and the U.S. Army Reserve, and a leading light of the Portland chapter of the JACL, violated the military curfew and was arrested, convicted, and sent to jail to await a hearing in the United State Supreme Court as part of the Gordon Hirabayashi curfew violation case.

In *JACL Bulletin #142* Masaoka declared the JACL to be "unalterably opposed to test cases . . . at this time" and called his JACL colleague a "self-styled martyr out to gain headlines." Masaoka's statement of the JACL's official stand reduced the Nisei response to the concentration camps to a choice between pursuing good publicity and good law. By the JACL's reckoning, good law and good publicity were mutually exclusive.

Yasui answered Masaoka's *JACL Bulletin #142* by distributing his own bulletin among the JACL. He reproduced Masaoka's bulletin and answered it, paragraph by paragraph. The existence of this debate going on inside Japanese America—indeed, inside the JACL—has been suppressed.

Yasui later adopted Masaoka's argument that good publicity was more important than mounting test cases, to turn Nisei away from supporting the organized resistance at Heart Mountain Relocation Center.

The discovery of *JACL Bulletin #142* and Yasui's bulletin embarrassed Masaoka and Yasui. When presented with copies of the bulletins and questioned, they both said the bulletins sounded like them, they had been young, it had been a long time ago, and they didn't remember the documents.

The originals, copies, and drafts of Masaoka's *JACL Bulletin #142* were deposited by the JACL in the University of California's Japanese Evacuation and Relocation Study (JERS) collection in the Bancroft Library. Copies of Yasui's bulletin and personal memorabilia of Portland JACL Nisei interned at Minidoka Relocation Center (Idaho) are in the Special Collections of the University of Washington Library.

The Masaoka–Yasui debate reveals a JACL that was, until the day Yasui was finally made to hew to the Masaoka/ JACL party line, cooking with more life and ideas than is commonly known today. The debate suggests the leadership the JACL might have offered the Nikkei and the man Yasui might have been. And it raises the question of what happened to make Minoru Yasui abandon his cause and sing the song of making good publicity, not good law. In the 1980s, with another change in political climate and the inevitability of redress for internment in the camps, Yasui again changed colors and was the JACL's champion of good law and test cases.

Good Law vs. Good Publicity

(Note: The following is the official stand of the JACL and that of Mr. Minoru Yasui)

April 17, 1942

MASAOKA: "The National JACL Headquarters is unalterably opposed to test cases to determine the constitutionally of military regulations at this time," declared Mike Masaoka, national secretary, in a general bulletin to all chapters in reference to the Minoru Yasui case in Oregon.

"We have reached this decision unanimously after examining all the facts in light of our national policy of 'the greatest good for the greatest number.' "

Masaoka in his statement said: "We recognize that self-styled martyrs who are willing to be jailed in order that they might fight for the rights of citizenship, as many of them allege, captured the headlines and the imagination of many more persons than our seemingly indifferent stand.

"We realize that many Japanese and others who are interested in our welfare have condemned the JACL for its apparent lackadaisical attitude on the matter of defending the rights and privileges of American citizens with Japanese features.

"But we submit that a careful examination of all the facts with the view of doing the greatest good for the greatest number will justify our position on such matters as these."

YASUI: The National JACL Headquarters has announced their unalterable opposition to test cases at this time to determine the constitutionality and enforceability of military regulations. It is recognized that this national policy has been formulated with the sincere purpose of achieving the "greatest good for the greatest number."

However, it is submitted that whether or not such policy is actually conducive to the "greatest good for the greatest number" is nevertheless subject to questions, and moreover, although the National can be convinced, thru legitimate means, that not only a substantial majority, but an overwhelming majority of the individual members, demand certain affirmative actions, that the National would be compelled to take such steps. If such effort is construed to be an usurpation of the prerogatives of National, then it is submitted that National Headquarters would be failing in its primary function of representing the organization. There is no attempt to usurp the functions of the National, but rather a sincere endeavor to supplement and augment the program of the National.

The notice given by National to "self-styled martyrs" seems unacceptably condescending. It is believed that National should be above such pettiness. There has never been any intention or motive to hold myself out as any such "self-styled martyrs" but rather the sincere conviction that the actions of this writer is for the preservation of certain fundamental rights of an American citizen, by the proper legal methods. The motive for such action has always been for the ultimate protection and preservation of the citizenship rights of not only the American citizen of Japanese ancestry, but also for every American citizen.

If the National is willing to sacrifice certain fundamental rights of citizenship establishing a precedent whereby those rights may be deprived of American citizens without protest, then is it not possibly contributing to the destruction of the very fundamental basis of this country? Surely, this country is fighting the tyrannies and dictatorships imposed by any one man or group of men. Surely, even the orders of those in command in the Western Defense Area is nevertheless subject to the Constitutional limitations of this government. It is still contended that we, American citizens of Japanese ancestry, are still an integral part of "we, the people," from whom such governmental leaders still derive their authority. We, as loyal American citizens, can do no less than to do our utmost to preserve and defend our Constitution, and the government which derives its just powers from the people. It is submitted that any American citizen worthy of being called such, would never quietly tolerate the destruction of the essential principle of our nation. If it be tyranny to impose unreasonable restrictions upon the people upon the arbitrary and discriminatory basis of race, then it is just as shameful to submit to such unreasonable restrictions.

There is no advocacy of mass violation of the orders of the duly constituted Army authorities, but rather a plea to the National that they reserve for us, upon the record, that we as American citizens have never given up our citizenship rights. There must be stated that the American citizen of Japanese ancestry have always contended that they are loyal, patriotic American citizens. The danger that some day in the future the statements that the Japanese American thought so little of their citizenship that they sacrificed them without protest must be guarded against, and handled in such a manner that no such precedent can be established. In all that we do, and in all that we shall do in the future must be done with the paramount thought that we are Americans and that our protests are recorded in an American way.

So much for the general points involved. With regard to the specific ten points enumerated, there is still doubt in my mind, and undoubtedly in the minds of a great many people, American citizens of Japanese ancestry and American citizens of Caucasian ancestry. I should like to present my own personal viewpoints in regard to these specific points:

MASAOKA: 1. Our primary consideration as good Americans is the total war effort. Individuals and groups are not important when the life of a nation is at stake. We have been asked to evacuate from the Pacific Coast as a military measure designed to strengthen national defense. We will cooperate in the war effort.

YASUI: 1. It is admitted that it is essential to make a total war effort to strengthen national defense. It is further admitted that the lives of individuals are not important when national interests are at stake. However, it is submitted that if in the prosecution of that war effort, the principles of democracy are destroyed, then indeed we shall be a nation winning the war and losing the peace. It was the Hitlerian theory that the end always justifies the means; in a democracy, such a theory cannot exist. In making that all-out effort, the orderly processes of democratic government must be followed, so that we shall in truth be a united nation against tyrannies and dictatorships of the world. If evacuation be predicated upon any other basis than race, then it might be acceptable as a contribution to national defense.

MASAOKA: 2. As a rational organization and as individuals, we have pledged our wholehearted cooperation to the President without qualifications or reservations in the winning of the war. We will not violate our pledge.

YASUI: 2. We, as American citizens, have pledged ourselves to wholehearted cooperation with the President. That is admitted, and wholly approved. Equally important, we have taken an oath of allegiance to the United States of America, and to the principles for which that nation stands. We have pledged ourselves to preserve and to defend the Constitution of the United States, even as our governmental representatives and leaders. The Army and the President derive their authority from that Constitution. Then, surely it cannot be argued that support to the President must be placed above or regarded as more sacred than our pledge to that fundamental document of human rights. It is submitted that in our efforts to preserve the Constitution, we shall be fulfilling our pledge of cooperation to the President. War or no war, it must be admitted that it is only human to err. If we feel that our President has erred, or if we feel that the Army has overstepped the bounds of its powers, then we must zealously guard those fundamental rights of citizenship. The United States Supreme Court has time and time again stated that the declaration of war does not abrogate these sacred rights.

MASAOKA: 3. We have continually cooperated with the Federal Government on all regulations and orders in the hope that our cooperation would inspire a reciprocal cooperation on their part. Our hopes have been justified. We will continue our policy of cooperation.

YASUI: 3. The National JACL is to be commended in its attitude of cooperation with the Federal government. Such policy should be continued. However, it is submitted that such cooperation must never go to such an extent as to be in derogation of certain fundamental rights. We, American citizens, are willing to have certain specified rights suspended for the duration of the emergency. But, we, as American citizens, must insist and maintain those certain democratic principles which relate to freedom and expression, the inalienable right to vote, the fundamental right to be regarded equally with other American citizens. When the Army or other governmental authorities place us in a less favorable position than that of an ENEMY alien, surely there is basis for protest and redress of our grievances.

MASAOKA: 4. Gracious acceptance of all Army regulations and orders and cooperating with them to the fullest extent is our contribution to the national defense effort. It is the sacrifice which we have been called upon to make. Although our contribution may seem greater than most, it still remains that it must be our share in the program. We will make our contributions to our nation.

YASUI: 4. Gracious acceptance of Army regulations to a certain point is necessary. However, if these regulations contravene the basic principles for which the patriots of this country have fought for and died, then surely such regulations are unacceptable. To reduce the principles of cooperation to an absurdity, if Army regulations require every American citizen of Japanese ancestry to commit suicide to wipe out the disgrace of Pearl Harbor, would National advocate unquestioned obedience to such orders? We must contribute more to our nation than any other American citizens, but even so there is a limit beyond which an American citizen will not go. If we are willing to accept the position of prisoners of war, or perhaps as no longer free men and women, then possibly the position of National can be justified. But, as long as we contend that we are American citizens, even the actions of the military are still [unjustified].

MASAOKA: 5. Public opinion is opposed to any measure which seems to be directed against the Army and its authority. Should we challenge their right to pass such regulations as the five-mile travel limit and the curfew restrictions, we might be damned as fifth columnists who are attempting to sabotage military plans and to embarrass the government at a time when a united front is essential.

We will not take any action which might be construed as an organized effort to sabotage Army measures which are designed for public safety.

YASUI: 5. It is recognized that public opinion is opposed to the Japanese. We, as American citizens, must direct public opinion to the injustices being committed in the name of our government, and point out that our efforts to preserve the democratic forms of government are valuable contributions to our country. There is no attempt to create a divided front; rather, it is submitted that the segregation of the Japanese American in "internment camps" creates a tendency towards such division of objectives and feelings. The American public will come to regard the Japanese American in the same category as the Japanese enemy aliens, in contravention of every principle of law and in derogation of our lawful status. Admittedly, no matter how right we are in our actions we are liable to censure and criticism. Surely, the American citizen who qualms before the possible criticism of unthinking people is certainly a poor American, when we remember the heroic words of American patriots who so gallantly fought for the freedom of this country.

MASAOKA: 6. Even assuming that we should win a test case, which we doubt, we may be in the same position as the nation which wins a war and loses the peace. It will take so long for a case of this nature to run the gamut of the courts from the lowest to the highest that we will, in all probability, be evacuated out of this area before it is finally passed upon by the Supreme Court.

YASUI: 6. It has never been hoped that this test case would be decided in time to prevent evacuation. But, it has always been the paramount motive to make it a matter of record that an American citizen has thought enough of his citizenship to take every legal step to preserve that status. It is doubted whether the people would have resented the fact that an American citizen has appealed to the courts in order to preserve and protect those citizenship rights, not only for himself but for every American citizen. As for the advice that legal actions be left until after the war, it is believed that such action would be of no purpose. After the damage is done, then it is too late to insist upon our rights. It would be as practical as locking the door after the horse has been stolen.

MASAOKA: (continuation of 6.) Even though we should win a legal victory, if the people at large resented our activities, it might have been better either to have lost or not to have attempted a contest. Too, if we should lose the case, which appears likely at this time, we have no further recourses; the law has been settled and cannot be reversed.

It appears more sensible if all legal actions of this nature were left until after the war when public sentiments may have changed and suits may be initiated to recover for damages suffered. Even this latter step is a moot question at this time. We do not intend to attempt to win a case and lose goodwill.

MASAOKA: 7. Attempts to slow up or to question military dictates may result in irritating those in charge so that they may retaliate by instituting stricter regulations. Whatever may be said against the procedure followed by the Army in conducting this evacuation is one thing, but no one can gainsay the statement they have been tolerant, fair and reasonable as possible in their treatment of this problem. We do not intend to force them to change their attitude in this matter.

YASUI: 7. If the legitimate questioning of arbitrary rulings would irritate those in charge, so that they would impose more stringent rulings, then there would be even more cause to object. If we are to accept discriminatory rulings of Army which undoubtedly infringes upon the rights of the people, then we are contributing thereby to the disintegration of the democratic principles of government for which we are struggling to preserve. The Army has not been tolerant and reasonable in handling this problem unless we are willing to accept the designation of being more dangerous than an Italian or German enemy alien. If the fact be unacceptable, then it is submitted that the rulings of the Army has been arbitrary, unfair and unreasonable, as far as it relates to the 8:00 o'clock curfew, restrictions on travel, and compulsory evacuation is concerned.

MASAOKA: 8. If our recollection serves correctly, Attorney General Biddle, one of the greatest defenders of civil rights in this country, declared that there was little chance that the courts would go beyond the military should any person desire to challenge the legality of the President's proclamation which gave the Secretary of War and his military commanders the power to designate zones in which any and all persons might be excluded and to facilitate the removal of the undesirable persons by adopting whatever measures were deemed necessary and proper. We trust that the opinion of the Attorney General represents the majority of the jurists' opinion on this subject.

YASUI: 8. Attorney General Biddle has stated that even the enemy alien should be treated with the greatest consideration and every respect. However, the manner in which such consideration is being demonstrated does not coincide with such statement. The fundamental law of our land acts forth that we have formed this government to "secure the blessings of liberty to ourselves and our posterity." If we yield at this time, then we are not only sacrificing our own liberty, but the liberty and blessings of freedom for our posterity. The basic principle upon which this country has been founded is that every man is created free and equal. When the regulations of the Army violates those principles, then it is submitted that such regulations should be modified or revoked, so as to be consistent with those principles. I feel certain that if the Attorney General be presented with the direct question of whether or not the Army can violate the fundamental laws of this country to the detriment of American citizens his opinion would confirm my stand that such action would be unconstitutional and void. Whether the curfew law or the evacuation program is in fact contradictory to the rights of American citizens is still a question to be decided in the Courts of the United States.

MASAOKA: 9. The American Civil Liberties Union, after polling its members as to whether they should make a test case of the Army orders for evacuation, decided against it.

When the one group of all groups which has most vigorously and consistently battled against great odds for civil liberties in this nation concedes that a court test of legality should not be attempted, we are ready to accept their verdict.

If the general orders should not be challenged, then it seems only logical that the supplementary orders necessary to effect the evacuation should also not be contested. We are not disposed to question the wisdom of the American Civil Liberties Union on questions of this kind.

YASUI: 9. With regard to the particular test case in question, an offer of assistance from the American Civil Liberties Union was received and refused. Moreover, it is noted that the Union has recently written to the office of the Secretary of War stating their objections to the discriminatory and arbitrary rulings of the evacuation program. Surely, if a group of people, not directly concerned with such program and not affected by the rulings, take such an interest in this matter, how much more should be concerned with the regulations which infringe upon our own rights. There is certainly nothing subversive or disloyal in maintaining those rights which are inherent within every American citizen.

MASAOKA: 10. Unfavorable publicity often results from attempting such test cases. The Yasui case is one in point. Editorial comments as well as news reports did not concentrate their attention on the constitutionality of the regulations involved but rather featured the fact that the subject for the test was a former paid propagandist for the Japanese government.

Moreover, from letters sent to the various public opinion sections of the newspapers, we can gather that the majority of those who wrote in were very vicious of their condemnation not only of Yasui but also of all Japanese. This incident just gave them one more excuse for publicity branding us as treacherous and dangerous.

One letter, printed in the *San Francisco Examiner*, for example, declared that "all Japanese-Americans should be discharged from the Army because Yasui, a reserve lieutenant, had deliberately violated regulations." The letter went on to say that "Yasui took advantage of an American education, going to the University of Oregon, and paid that back with the usual Japanese treachery."

Because our motives are too often misunderstood and unfavorable publicity often results which is injurious not only to the person involved but also to all Japanese in America, we believe that test cases should not be made. We do not intend to create any unnecessary excuses for denouncing the Japanese as disloyal and dangerous.

YASUI: 10. Unfavorable publicity unquestionably arises out of cases which involve national interests. However, it is submitted that the National should take steps to correct erroneous views that are held by the general public. Whenever an unfavorable article or letter appears in the newspapers, such articles or letters should be forthwith answered, not so much with the intent of convincing such persons but rather to present the other viewpoint, so as to give such persons something vital to consider in their arguments. When it is pointed out that the efforts of the Japanese Americans are constructively intended for the preservation of the principles of this government, perhaps a more sympathetic attitude can be created.

MASAOKA: (conclusion) Lastly, we are not giving up our rights as citizens by cooperating with the government in the evacuation program. We may be temporarily suspending and sacrificing some of our privileges and rights of citizenship in the greater aim of protecting them for all time to come and to defeat these powers which seek to destroy them.

When the war against the Axis is won, we are confident that all our rights and privileges will be returned to us a hundredfold because we cooperated in the winning of the war. We will consistently adhere to this announced principle of cooperation.

In times like these, let us remember that it is much easier to be a martyr than it is to be a quiet, self-suffering, good citizen who is vitally interested in the winning of the war.

To win this time will require sacrifices beyond those demanded in the First World War, and the sacrifices which we are called upon to make are even greater than those demanded of the majority.

Because our sacrifice is greater, let us trust that our reward in that greater America which is to come will be that much the greater.

YASUI: In conclusion, those points should be kept in mind. The attitude of this writer is not to oppose the reasonable and justifiable regulations of the United States Army. There is no attempt to secure any favored rulings for the Japanese American, but rather to secure for ourselves and our people a fair, unprejudiced, impartial treatment, comparable to the treatment being accorded other people of this country. It is attempted to convince National that the great majority of the Japanese Americans is not in sympathy with the apathetic attitude of the National JACL, and by legitimate means to call attention of our leaders to such sentiments. It is hoped that National will take immediate and affirmative steps to preserve for us the essential attributes of citizenships, so that in the future we cannot and will not be regarded as person of no citizenship, to be cared for on military reservations or to be shipped back to a country to which we owe no loyalty.

There are three fundamental issues at stake: First, are the American citizens of Japanese ancestry to be regarded in a less favorable position then enemy aliens? Second, is the evacuation of such American citizens in "internment centers" whereby potential human energies and manpower is to be impounded and not fully utilized, actually designed for the strengthening of national defense, or is it based upon the distinction of race? Third, is the future of the American citizen of Japanese ancestry to be jeopardized by the establishment of the precedent that the Japanese Americans did not hold their citizenship rights in high enough esteem that it was not worth the effort to preserve?

The policy advocated is to follow the legitimate processes of government, by appealing to the courts, by sending our petitions for a redress of grievances to the proper authorities, by a reservation of our rights with the proper agencies, and by publicizing our particular convictions and the principles for which we stand to the public at large. It is submitted that such methods are the only American way to respond in the face of the present emergency. It is sincerely hoped that the motives of this writer will not be interpreted as an effort to undermine the efforts of our leaders, but rather as an effort to contribute to the preservation of the American way of life. It is hoped that this action is in reality a substantial contribution to a greater America, where every man is free and equal, and may hold high his head among fellow Americans.

Respectfully submitted,
Minoru Yasui

Larry Tajiri

(1914–1965)

Masaharu Hane

(Dates unknown)

Both stories that follow—"Relocation" by Larry Tajiri and "Nurse" by Masaharu Hane (translated by George Kushida)—appeared in Poston concentration camp publications. All that is known about Masaharu Hane is that he was an Issei interned at Poston Arizona, and his story appeared in *Poston Poetry*. Born in Los Angeles, Larry Tajiri was Nisei and the wartime editor of the Japanese American Citizens League (JACL) newspaper, the *Pacific Citizen*, from 1942 to 1953. Tajiri was one of the best Nisei of his time. In his column, "Nisei USA," he wrote plain, strong, and smart against race prejudice in the American press, American literature, and American movies. Tajiri joined the staff of the *Denver Post* in 1954 and was named drama critic in 1956. He died in Denver in 1965.

Both stories were written at the end of the war and are contemplations and visions of the future set on trains. The Issei train of Hane's story is convincingly real, and the Issei is a complex and complete character who makes the cloyingly unreal train of Tajiri's Nisei vision of acculturation, acceptance, and assimilation hollow and sad. The Issei and Nisei stories read side by side, as a pair, are striking in their similiarity and differences. In one, the Issei skeptically observes the behavior of a young Nisei woman. In the other, a narrative voice of the Nisei vision unconvincingly characterizes the Issei and Nisei and all of Japanese American history. The difference between the two is the difference between the real and the fake.

Relocation

Larry Tajiri

The *Sunshine Special*, the express from Houston and the cities of southern Texas, pushes up the Mississippi valley, past the green fields of southern Arkansas where the early corn is already shoulder-high. The train slows down as it nears the little flag stop of Jerome, where a group of young men and women are waiting with their suitcases beside the track. The train stops and the young men and women climb aboard and thread their way through the crowded day coaches in search of a seat. The cars are filled with soldiers on furlough from the great training fields in the pine-forested hills of the Deep South. But there are a few seats and the young men and women, all of whom are Americans of Japanese ancestry, find them and settle down for the long ride ahead.

At the railroad junction of McGhee a half-hour later, the train stops again and another score of Japanese Americans, among whom are several soldiers returning from visits to the Rohwer center, go aboard. They fill the remaining seats in the warm day coaches. The luggage racks are full and their suitcases overflow into the aisles.

The train hurries on into the deepening dusk. Little towns slide by. Little Rock is the next big stop but at some of the way stations a few more passengers come aboard. Some are forced to stand because now all the seats are filled. Some of the evacuees talk of the hopes ahead and the camp life they are leaving behind. One is seriously reading literature which gives advice to persons leaving the relocation center. His face has been deeply tanned by seven months under the Arkansas sun. His hands look strong and capable.

Some of the passengers try to sleep in their backed seats. The train will reach St. Louis in the morning. At St. Louis the two score evacuees aboard the *Sunshine Special* will part in the huge Union Station to take trains for individual destinations. Some are going west for farm work. Others are going to the cities of the Middle West, to Chicago, Cincinnati, Cleveland, and the Twin Cities. Some are going to hostels, where they will have bed and board until they find their own housing. Others are going to waiting homes. The girl in the rose dress with the eight-month-old baby will join her husband at a nursery in Ohio. The youth in the leather jacket has a job promised him in an aircraft plant. A veteran of the production line, he worked at a factory in southern California before evacuation.

For some of the evacuees this train ride up the broad Mississippi valley is the first step toward their reinstatement as free citizens of the American community. A few are hesitant, hypersensitive. But they soon overcome their shyness and their fears evaporate. For in the day coach they become just another group of Americans going somewhere. No questions are asked. No one stares. A woman across the aisle offers to hold the baby while the Nisei mother rests. The white soldier who has the seat next to a Japanese American sergeant shows the Nisei a picture of his "best girl," the girl who will be waiting for him at a station in Pennsylvania. The Nisei brings out his wallet and shows his fellow soldier his girl's picture. "She's at the camp at Rohwer," he captions. "We'll be married soon."

At the Union Station in St. Louis these returning exiles are soon caught up in the ebb and flow of the crowds around the entrance gates and in the waiting rooms. The evacuee with his suitcases, the wife, the sweetheart, the mother waiting for the furlough soldier, the executive with his saddle-leather briefcase, the student home from school are all human props in the daily drama of a big-city rail station, all Americans on the move in a world at war.

To the evacuee, the "outside world" they have looked to with so much apprehension proves to be much the same world they left after the soldiers had posted those evacuation posters on the telephone poles of the western coast and after everyone had been bundled into trains and buses for the long rides and the short rides to the army assembly centers. There are no brass bands for the evacuees but in many of the stations these Americans with Japanese faces will find sympathetic people, usually representing a resettlement committee, who will help them bridge the long gap between camp life and normal living.

Like the *Sunshine Special*, which is a Missouri Pacific express, other trains and buses are similarly bringing evacuees back into the everyday stream of America. And the young men and women, with indefinite leaves and their WRA identification cards in their wallets and purses, wait on desert roadsides and in dust-beaten stations for the transportation which will take them away from the watchtowers and the sentries at the gate. From Topaz and Minidoka, from Rivers and Poston, from Heart Mountain and Granada, from the California and Arkansas camps, from all the giant "Little Tokyos" of war relocation, the exiles of evacuation are returning to the free lives of ordinary Americans.

The knell has sounded for the war relocation centers. The individual resettlement process is in actual motion and the proof may be had by walking down the streets of Denver or Chicago or Cincinnati. You will see Nisei window-shopping, waiting in the lines before movie theaters, in a seat at a major-league ball game and in factories and shops across America, on the farms and in the mills. Japanese Americans are doing their part in the sweaty business of producing for victory.

The War Relocation Authority is proving that it is not a self-perpetuating bureaucracy by its sincere emphasis on outside reloca- tion. The barrack cities of war relocation were conceived as temporary expedients at a time when the individual resettlement of the evacu- ees appeared impossible in view of what was represented at that time to be public sentiment. The initial seasonal work program in the inland west, necessitated primarily by a shortage of labor on sugar beet farms, proved that individual resettlement was possible. Since then the program has been gradually broadened, until now it embraces the major energies of the WRA. The government has also indicated that it is more interested in permanent employment for individual evacuees than in seasonal work on a group basis.

More than fifty WRA field offices are now carrying on an inten- sive program to assist all loyal evacuees in reestablishing themselves in all areas except those from which the evacuees are excluded. Thus all of forty-four states and parts of three others are open for resettlement, while California is the only state from which the evacuees are totally barred.

Already several thousand evacuees have resettled in the Middle West, particularly in urban areas. A substantial number have lo- cated in Chicago, where they are working in war plants as well as domestics, clerks, and in hotel and restaurant work. Demands from hotels and country clubs, apparently hard hit by the fact that many of their workers have left for the higher wages offered by war factories, have been particularly heavy for evacuee workers in the Chicago area, according to the WRA.

With the gradual increase in clearances for the eastern defense command, the possibility for the eventual resettlement of many thousands in New York and other eastern cities can be fore- seen. The WRA has offices operating in New York, Boston, and Baltimore, as well as its national headquarters in Washington. Indicative of the widespread interest in the relocation of Japanese Americans is the fact that a Chinese American businessman has recently been negotiating for two ceramics factories in New Jersey which he hopes to turn over to evacuee workers on a cooperative basis.

Housing, or the lack of it, has been a limiting factor in the resettlement program, particularly in war production centers where jobs are plentiful. The WRA office in Chicago recently announced that the speed of relocation will be governed largely by the ability of the WRA officials to find housing, rather than any limit on the number of jobs available.

The opening of the hostels, which are in effect an extension of the relocation centers, has accelerated resettlement. The warm and friendly hostels, with their sympathetic, informed personnel, have proven invaluable in assisting the readjustment of the evacuees from the barrack–mess hall life of the camps to more normal existence on the outside. The hostels also dramatize the assistance and understanding which the evacuees are receiving from both religious and social organizations. The work of these private agencies has been a necessary supplement to the services supplied by the government through the WRA.

The evacuee passengers of the St. Louis–bound express were almost without exception young men and women. The age composition of the evacuees leaving the relocation centers points up one of the bottlenecks in the relocation program. Few of the older group are leaving the centers for permanent employment, while younger couples with children are hesitant to take the plunge from minimum security of the centers to the unknown hazards of life in the wartime economy on the outside. Unless the older generation and the family groups can be induced to quit the camps, the present program will inevitably bog down. It seems imperative that greater stress be placed on the resettlement of larger family units, although the difficulties attendant to such a plan are evident.

The hostel idea is particularly adapted to the resettlement of larger families, since it is admittedly more difficult to obtain suitable housing for such units. An encouraging factor is that more of these hostels are being contemplated, although even with these in operation only a small percentage of those desiring relocation can be accommodated.

The number of persons relocated up to the present time is small, being less than 10 percent of the total held in the ten WRA camps. A certain resistance is evident against immediate relocation.

This resistance stems from uncertainties regarding Selective Service status, a feeling of fear and insecurity growing out of the intemperate attacks of race baiters and hysteria mongers, and an exaggerated conception of the rise in the cost of living and the necessity to obtain compensatory wages, as well as a hope for an eventual return to the evacuated area.

The importance of immediate relocation, however, cannot be overstressed. Except in the Far West, national sentiment appears definitely favorable to the resettlement of all loyal evacuees. It is obvious that each passing day will make more difficult the physical and psychological adaptations necessary for successful resettlement.

Those resettled during the war will be in a far better position to effect the inevitable changeover from wartime to postwar living and peacetime employment. Furthermore, evacuees leaving the centers today have the benefit of the WRA's intensive effort to assist their adjustment.

An evacuee in Chicago said recently: "What I like about this part of the country is that people let you live like a human being. You begin to forget that you are of Japanese ancestry, or any ancestry, and remember only that you are an American."

Today, this morning, this afternoon, this evening, young Japanese Americans are arriving in bus and railroad stations throughout America, leaving the dust of relocation centers behind and returning to the broad boulevards, the movie palaces, and the skyscrapers of America. And this minute the *Sunshine Special* is on its long journey up from Houston and the cities of southern Texas. It will be flagged down again at the little station at Jerome, where another group of Japanese Americans will be waiting with suitcases in hand. And a half-hour later at McGhee there will be others from Rohwer.

Nurse

Masaharu Hane
translated by George Kushida

It was well past midnight when the Los Angeles–bound train from Denver pulled into Ashfork, Arizona. Sleepy-eyed soldiers with large duffel bags got off the train. This station is the transfer point for Wickenburg (Arizona). A few of us civilians followed them.

"Say, there's a Japanese!" exclaimed Mr. "O," my traveling companion, pointing in a general direction with his chin, since both his arms were loaded with suitcases. On looking, sure enough, there was a small Japanese girl standing behind a group of soldiers.

Around that time, it was quite a novelty to come across a Japanese while traveling by train, and we had longed to see even one. My eyes scanned the area in search of her parents or her brothers, but in vain.

An old conductor, oblivious to the din being created by the soldiers, examined their tickets in minute detail, and herded them onto the coaches. I placed my hand baggage on the shelf, removed my coat, and gave a sigh of relief as I sat down.

As I mopped the perspiration from my brow, I looked around me. Then my gaze met that of the Japanese girl, who was seated across the aisle, and who I presume had been staring in this direction for quite some time. She was not as young as I had imagined the first time I saw her. All my doubts—as to her traveling alone in these times—were completely dispelled when I saw the Caucasian soldier seated next to her. That's it! —The girl was married to a white soldier, and she had come halfway to meet her husband, who was back on furlough!

Since they had come this far, it was a certainty that they were on their way to Poston, but my heart felt heavy, thinking of the feelings of this girl's parents.

As cosmopolitan as I am, I do not yet quite relish the thought of marrying off my own daughter to either a Caucasian or a Negro. With my own conception, I imagined the embarrassment about to be caused her parents by her act of bringing this youth back to camp, and as I speculated on the pending heartache of her parents, I began to feel morose and moody. The train started to move.

"Tickets, please—tickets." The old conductor checked the tickets again. He stuck a small check stub in the windows when he got through and went on to the next passenger. If the stubs were white, it meant that the passenger was getting off at the next transfer station; the red stubs were for through passengers.

After the conductor had gone by, I again looked at the young couple across the aisle. In this long travel by train, I have witnessed many "misbehaviors" on the part of the young people of this country. Naturally, these "misbehaviors" are thought to be so purely from my own point of view; from the standpoint of the people of this country, it could be their ordinary behavior. In any event, the sight of young girls and men seated near me, leaning on each other's shoulders, or using each other's lap for a pillow, disgusted me no end.

Oh well, no matter if Japanese blood coursed through this girl's veins; she was one that would marry a Caucasian. There is no reason to believe that her morality was not estranged from that of a true Japanese. Be that as it may, this girl consistently assumed a correct posture. The soldier, also, carried himself with decorum and deportment.

They were whispering to each other, but contrary to expectations, they did not enact a disgraceful scene.

Not only that, it did not appear that they were on too intimate terms. This caused me to throw overboard my original imagination regarding these two, and I determined anew that they were a brother and sister. I made up my mind that she was the young sister, and that she had an older brother who had features that resembled a Caucasian's. Unconsciously, I began to think that there was no mistaking his Caucasian features, but that somehow—it may have been just my fancy—he betrayed a mannerism characteristic of a Japanese.

At some unknown stop, the train picked up a few passengers, and we were on our way again. By this time, there were no seats for the new passengers. One of them, a middle-aged man, stood in the aisle next to a seat where two middle-aged women were seated.

After examining the tickets of the new passengers, the conductor turned out the lights. Only one small globe was left burning, and the inside of the coach became dark.

It was about three o'clock in the morning. The soldiers were all fast asleep. I, too, being tired from the continuous train trip, began to feel drowsy. Suddenly, sensing a noise resembling someone's suppressed laughter, I awoke with a start. I looked in the direction whence the voice came.

The aforementioned middle-aged man, who was previously standing in the aisle, had just succeeded in squirming himself into the seat between the two middle-aged women. So revolting was the scene that I turned over, and started to close my eyes—but before I did so, I looked once more toward the Japanese girl.

The soldier brother appeared very tired as he slept, resting his head on his clenched fists, which were resting on the windowsill. The girl was seated erect, with her legs trimly together, but her right hand was placed over her forehead, obscuring her face.

I was unable to tell whether she was asleep or awake; [but assuming that she was asleep—trans.] in all my long experiences of train travel, I have never seen a man or woman who slept so correctly and properly as this girl.

Up until then, I felt ashamed, imagining that this girl had, contrary to the wishes of her parents, married a Caucasian, and that therefore, being such a girl, she would carry on in a disgraceful manner like the rest of the Caucasians; but now, on seeing the correct posture of this girl, I suddenly felt a sense of racial pride in being a member of the Japanese race. I smiled sardonically at my egotism, and to my own way of thinking to my own convenience.

However, I became distressed as I thought of the young girl with her odd "brother," and of their parents' feelings. Why did this girl try to avoid my glance? Could it be because she was ashamed of her brother? While thinking of such matters, I became drowsy again.

The aged conductor was shaking me by the arm. He informed me that we were due in Wickenburg in five minutes. Startled, I began to get ready to get off.

Dawn was completely upon us.

The Japanese girl was all prepared, and sitting formally erect. For the first time, I noticed that she was wearing a uniform. It was an extremely conservative neutral uniform in contrast to the WAC's.

I glanced at the check stub by the window. One was white—the other, red. The soldier was *not* getting off here with her.

Passing by the seat where the middle-aged man had squeezed his way between the two middle-aged women, and who was now sleeping with his arm embracing one of the women, I wound my way to the vestibule.

While waiting for the train to come to a complete stop, I asked this girl: "Where did you board this train?"

In clear-cut Japanese the girl answered: "I am on leave from the nurse's school in Colorado Springs."

Joy Kogawa

(1935–   )

Born in Vancouver, British Columbia, Joy Kogawa has served as writer-in-residence at the University of Ottawa, worked as a writer for the Canadian prime minister's office, and published three volumes of poetry. She brought her poetic and lyrical style to her first novel, *Obasan* (1982), the story of a five-year-old Japanese Canadian girl, Naomi Nakane, and her family, who are forcibly evacuated from British Columbia and sent to the bleak interior of Alberta, Canada, during World War II. Along with her brother Stephen, her father, and aunt and uncle, Naomi lives in Slocan, a mining ghost town. Though the novel tells a Japanese Canadian story and is written by a Japanese Canadian, it is presented here because of its rare sense of history and its description of the quality of the relationship between Issei and Nisei.

Naomi's aunt, her *obasan,* is the emotional center of the novel. She protects and coddles the children through the years of exile and hardship and even into the present, when Naomi and Stephen sit before the family as adults. Kogawa portrays the bond between the first generation Issei and the second-generation Nisei, a bond that never breaks. When Naomi's uncle dies, she comes to bury him and to sit with her *obasan:*

> Obasan is small as a child and has not learned to weep. Back and forth, back and forth, her hands move on her knees. She looks at me unsteadily, then hands me the ID card with Uncle's young face. What ghostly whisperings I feel in the air as I hold the card. *"Kodomo no tame*—for the sake of the children—*gaman shi masho*—let us endure.*" The voices pour down like rain but in the middle of the downpour I still feel thirst.

At the insistence of her Aunt Emily, a researcher and writer of the evacuation experience, Naomi relives her past. Aunt Emily tells her, "The past is the future. . . . You have to remember. You are your history. If you cut off any of it you're an amputee. Don't deny the past. Remember everything. . . ."

In the chapter excerpted here, Naomi has just been saved from drowning by Rough Lock Bill, mountain man and friend of children, and taken to the hospital. It is 1943.

Obasan

I am in a hospital. Father is in a hospital. A chicken is in a hospital. Father is a chicken is a dream that I am in a hospital where my neck and chin are covered with a thick red stubble of hair and I am reading the careful table of contents of a book that has no contents.

When I waken fully at last, I am in the Slocan hospital and a nurse is standing beside me smiling. I have been asleep, it seems, forever. Vaguely I remember Rough Lock carrying me here. I also remember Obasan's hand rubbing my back. The nurse starts to comb my tangled hair, pulling so that the roots clinging to the scalp strain the surface of the skin.

"Does it hurt?" she asks me.

"No," I reply. The weeds in the garden do not moan when they are plucked from the skin of the earth. Nor do the trees cry out at their fierce combing as they lie uprooted by the roadside. Rapunzel's long ladder of hair could bear the weight of prince or witch. I can endure this nurse's hands yanking at the knots in the thick black tangles.

The beds are as close together as the desks in the schoolroom where we are jammed two to a seat. If I lean out, I can almost touch the bed of the woman beside me who sits up washing her face in a basin, cupping the water in her hands and rubbing her face up and down, her eyes squeezed shut. The heads of the beds are against a windowed wall and the feet point to the door and the hospital corridor.

Obasan has brought me my blue *Highroads to Reading Book Two* with the bright orange lettering and the happiness inside.

Minnie and Winnie slept in a shell;
Sleep little ladies! And they slept well.

The fairies, white gowned with white-veined wings, sleep wispy as smoke in a blue shell, and the woman in the next bed sleeps, her mouth open, and all the others in the room also sleep and sleep and Father, I was told, is in a hospital too with Grandpa Nakane in New Denver and are they also sleeping in a room full of people like this?

I am in a grade-two reader full of fairies, sitting in the forest very still and waiting for one fairy tiny as an insect to come flying through the tall grasses and lead me down to the moss-covered door on the forest floor that opens to the tunnel leading to the place where my mother and father are hiding.

What does it mean? What can it mean? Why do they not come?

"Daddy is sick, Nomi," Stephen said.

"When will he come home?"

"I don't know. Maybe never."

"Never? Is he going to die?"

The kids in school said that when old Honma-san died in Bayfarm, there was a ball of fire that came out of the house and then moved off up the mountain. The kids know about the place by the mine road where Grandma Nakane was cremated.

The nurse is never going to be finished with my hair. I am quite capable of combing it myself. Why is this spectacle being made of me? If I cry now while I sit on this bed, all the people will turn and look.

"It's old people who die, isn't it, Stephen?"

"Yes."

"Daddy won't die."

"Of course not."

"And Mommy?"

Obasan has also brought me a thin book with a picture of animals in it called *Little Tales for Little Folk*. There is an oversized baby chick called "Chicken Little" standing on the front cover.

What is this thing about chickens? When they are babies, they are yellow. Yellow like daffodils. Like Goldilocks' yellow hair. Like the yellow Easter chicks I lost somewhere. Yellow like the yellow pawns in the Yellow Peril game.

The Yellow Peril is a Somerville Game, Made in Canada. It was given to Stephen at Christmas. On the red-and-blue box cover is a picture of soldiers with bayonets and fists raised high looking out over a sea full of burning ships and a sky full of planes. A game about war. Over a map of Japan are the words:

The game that shows how
a few brave defenders
can withstand a very
great number of enemies

There are fifty small yellow pawns inside and three big blue checker kings. To be yellow in the Yellow Peril game is to be weak and small. Yellow is to be chicken. I am not yellow. I will not cry however much this nurse yanks my hair.

When the yellow chicks grow up they turn white. Chicken Little is a large Yellow Peril puff. One time Uncle stepped on a baby chick. One time, I remember, a white hen pecked yellow chicks to death, to death in our backyard.

There it is. Death again. Death means stop.

All the chickens in the chicken coop, dim-witted pinbrains though they are, know about it. Every day, the plump white lumps are in the chicken yard, scratching with their stick legs and clucking and barkling together. If anything goes overhead—a cloud, an airplane, the King Bird—they all seem to be connected to one another like a string of Christmas tree lights. Their orange eyes are in unison, and each head is crooked at an angle watching the overshadowing death. They stop for a moment, then carry on as death passes by. A little passover several times a day. Sensei said in church, the Death angel passes over at Passover.

Hospitals are places where Death visits. But Death comes to the world in many unexpected places.

There is that day on the way to school. When was it? Just a week ago?

The long walk from Slocan to school in Bayfarm is by way of a path through a heavily wooded forest, past some houses and the white house where the missionaries live, and onto the highway to Lemon Creek. The road curves up in a long slow slope near Bayfarm.

Stephen and I are walking to school that death day, my schoolbag slung over my shoulder, his strapped to his back. In my bag are two new scribblers, one with a picture of a dog and one with two little girls. I have pencils, wax crayons, scissors, a cube eraser, all new in a new pencil case, and my lunch is in a rectangular metal lunch box with a diagonal slot in the lid for a small pair of ivory chopsticks. My lunch that Obasan made is two moist and sticky rice balls with a salty red plum in the centre of each, a boiled egg to the side with a tight square of lightly boiled greens. Stephen has peanut-butter sandwiches, an apple, and a thermos of soup. My schoolbag thumps against my hips as we walk.

We have just come out of the patch of woods near the missionaries' place when I see two big boys, Percy Bower and another boy, running down the road. Stephen sees them too and freezes briefly.

"Don't notice," he whispers, barely moving his mouth.

Percy has a handful of stones and throws them down the road. When he sees us, he calls out, "Hey Gimpy, where ya goin'?"

"Takin' yer girlfriend to school?" the other boy shouts.

They catch up to us and begin dancing in front of Stephen, jabbing him on the shoulder. "Fight, Jap. Fight?"

Stephen stands still as a stone. One of his hands is on the strap of his backpack ready to take it off.

"C'mon, ya gimpy Jap!"

Stephen hands me his lunch box. I step backwards wanting to run away, wanting to stay with Stephen. He is taking his schoolbag off when we hear one of the missionaries shouting at us. She is a thin woman with light brown hair. I see her at Sunday school.

"Here here!" The voice is sharp, like an ax chopping logs into kindling. She is standing at the side of the house, her hands on her hips, her feet apart.

The boys flee, sprinting down the road. Stephen with his schoolbag dangling from one shoulder begins walking rapidly in the opposite direction towards Bayfarm. I catch up to him and hand him his lunch box.

We walk together rapidly and in silence, past the Doukhobor store and across the road to the open field. In the middle of the field stands the school and, behind the school, the rows and rows of small wood huts, each with its stack of wood—round logs, logs chopped in quarters, neat stacks of kindling wood. Miyuki's place is hidden from view by the school. All the houses are the same—fourteen feet wide and twenty-eight feet long. Two families live in each house. Laundry hangs from lines strung on poles. Wooden sidewalks extend out short distances from doorways to outhouses, and around gardens.

"Miyuki's sister likes you," I say to Stephen.

"Hah!" Stephen snorts.

Sometimes, instead of staying at school to eat lunch, I go to Miyuki's house. We sit on a bench by a table that takes up almost all the room. On the other side of a partition is a family with three children. We can all hear each other talking. Miyuki's mother gives me some pickles and a plate of lightly fried vegetable okazu to eat with my rice balls. After the meal she usually hands me a wet cloth to wipe the sticky film of rice off my fingertips.

I am telling Stephen about Miuyki's sister when I turn and see that Stephen is no longer walking beside me. We are about halfway into the open field. I turn around and Stephen is standing still staring past me.

Not far from school, and directly in the line of our walk, is a cluster of boys. It is something about the way they stand there—not moving. Not making a sound.

"C'mon, Steef," I say, feeling curious.

Stephen is shifting back and forth uncomfortably, then turns abruptly and walks away from me.

There are six boys all together. I glance down as I approach them. The circle is tight and their heads are bent, the bodies tense. I peer through a space between two of the boys. At first all that I can see are the hands and the white feather fluttering on the ground. One boy suddenly breaks and runs from the circle.

"Hey Jiro," the boy closest to me shouts after him. None of the others move. I am unable either to move or to avert my eyes.

I recognize two of the boys standing. Tak and Seigo are big boys in grade five. Danny, a small boy in Stephen's class, is kneeling on the ground. Danny is tough. His clothes are always shabbier than everyone else's. His socks hang over his boots or sometimes he has no socks at all.

The boy who is doing the killing is Sho, a shiny-faced boy in grade five, with slippery smooth skin and sharp round eyes.

A hole about the size of both my fists is scooped out of the ground. The hen's neck is held over the hole. Danny grips the white body. Sho holds the head, pulling it taut. Blood drips like a slow nose-bleed into the hole. The chicken's body quivers and jerks, its feet clutching and trembling.

"Got to make it suffer," Sho says. He is sitting on his haunches and his hand squeezes the chicken's tiny head. Its beak is open, but there is no sound. The pocketknife is on the ground beside him, the blade smeared red. Sho's eyes are like the pocketknife, straight, bright, sharp.

"Is it dead yet?" I ask. My question is a prayer. I am paralyzed.

The boys ignore me. I wait, attending the chicken's quivering, the plump body pulsing and beating like a disembodied heart. As long as the moving continues I wait. Sho picks up the knife and cuts into the neck wound. The chicken jerks and Danny loses his grip. It lurches away and flaps drunkenly over the field. Sho jumps up and runs after the chicken as it leaps and flutters high in the air, then comes crashing down to the ground, one wing slapping and dragging on the earth. He grabs the chicken by the wing, clutching its body against his shirt. Its feet stick straight out. The wings flap wildly as Sho grabs the feet. His arm jerks high up over his head and the air stirs even where I stand. The chicken's neck gyrates and it splatters the ground and Sho's face and shirt with its dripping blood. There is no sound from the chicken except a strange squeaking noise from the wings as if they are metal hinges.

"Kill it, Sho."

Although the air is raining with feathers and sudden red splatterings, there is a terrible stillness and soundlessness as if the whole earth cannot contain the chicken's dying. Over and over, like a kite caught in a sudden gust, it plunges.

"Kill it, Sho."

Danny kneels on the ground, his fist clutching the knife. From across the field, I can hear the sound of the school bell and the shouts of the children as they run to their places. Sho begins to run, swinging the bleeding struggling chicken as he goes. I run too, following the boys across the field to the schoolyard, where a loudspeaker is summoning us.

We are late. The singing is already beginning.

O Canada, our home and native land
True patriot love in all thy sons command
With glowing hearts we see thee rise
The true north, strong and free. . . .

We scuttle into place like insects under the floorboards. I am the last child in the single file of children in my class, standing to the left of the main wooden sidewalk in front of the wide stairs. The stairs lead to the center of the long covered platform like a hall connecting the two buildings of Pine Crescent School.

O Canada, glorious and free
O Canada, we stand on guard for thee!

Kenji is in the row ahead of me, behind a girl called Hatsumi, and Miyuki is in front of her. When the principal, Mr. Tsuji, starts to talk, we stand with our hands straight down our sides.

"Good morning, boys and girls," he says.

"Good morning, Mr. Tsuji," we reply in unison. I am barely listening to what Mr. Tsuji is saying. From behind the school, I can see Sho running, then slowing to a walk as we start our school song.

Slocan get on your toes
We are as everyone knows
The school with spirit high!
We all do our best
And never never rest
Till we with triumph cry. . . .

I am wondering where he left the chicken and if it is dead at last. The teacher in front is waving her arms vigorously and urging us to sing. All her gestures are as intense and jerky as a hen and she flutters and broods and clucks over us.

Work with all your might
Come on, rise up, and fight
And never give up hope
The Banner we will hold with pride
As to victory we stride.

Sho is at the end of his line and his smooth face is streaked. His shirt sleeve has a red blotch on it and a small pocketknife dangles from a string tied to a belt loop. He is not singing. I don't sing either.

"Once more," Mr. Tsuji says. "Slocan get on your toes. . . ."

I hate school. I hate running the gauntlet of white kids in the woods close to home. I hate, now, walking through the field where the chicken was killed. And I hate walking past the outhouse where the kitten died. At least it should be dead now.

John Okada

(1923–1971)

John Okada's *No No Boy* (1957) was a forgotten, neglected, and rejected novel about Japanese America that every Japanese American knew about but never read during Okada's lifetime. In the fourteen years that John Okada lived with his book, he saw it slip into obscurity and fail to sell out an edition of fifteen hundred copies. Japanese Americans out to prove to America that they were loyal and perfect Americans after the war sidestepped Okada's realistic portrayal of Seattle's Japanese American community, a community full of pain, depression, suicide, anger, bitterness, and guilt.

Okada was born in the old Merchants Hotel in the Pioneer Square area of Seattle with the help of a Japanese midwife. He received two bachelor's degrees from the University of Washington, one in library science and the other in English, and later received a master's degree in English at Columbia University, where he met his wife Dorothy. He served as a sergeant in the U.S. Air Force during World War II.

Five years after Okada's death of a heart attack in 1971, the Combined Asian American Resources Project reprinted his landmark novel, the only novel written by a Japanese American writer. Its time had come. The book sold out two printings of three thousand each, mainly to Japanese American readers who were ready to look back at themselves. The University of Washington Press has continued to keep *No No Boy* in print with two additional printings.

Earl Miner reviewed *No No Boy* in 1957 in the *Saturday Review* and was one of the few who saw Okada's sensitivity and skill:

> *No No Boy* is an absorbing, if often strained, melodrama based on the injustice and the immemorial problem of harmonizing the guilt of a society with the lesser guilt of the individual. The modern American, of whatever descent, is truly both the hero and the villain of the piece. The heroine is "that faint and elusive insinuation of promise" which is the American's heri-

tage. The problem itself is tragic, and *No No Boy* comes as close as anything in recent fiction to exploring the nature of this tragedy.

In the Spring 1978 issue of *Pacific Affairs*, Professor Gordon Hirabayashi pointed out that

Japanese Americans who were aware of *No-No Boy* seemed to be embarrassed by its appearance and tended vigorously to reject it. That was in the 1950s. In the 1970s, however, during the emergence of Asian American literature as something distinctive—neither Asian nor white American—*No-No Boy* was rediscovered.

What follows is the novel's opening chapter.

No-No Boy

Two weeks after his twenty-fifth birthday, Ichiro got off a bus at Second and Main in Seattle. He had been gone four years, two in camp and two in prison.

Walking down the street that autumn morning with a small, black suitcase, he felt like an intruder in a world to which he had no claim. It was just enough that he should feel this way, for, of his own free will, he had stood before the judge and said that he would not go in the army. At the time there was no other choice for him. That was when he was twenty-three, a man of twenty-three. Now, two years older, he was even more of a man.

Christ, he thought to himself, just a goddamn kid is all I was. Didn't know enough to wipe my own nose. What the hell have I done? What am I doing back here? Best thing I can do would be to kill some son of a bitch and head back to prison.

He walked toward the railroad depot where the tower with the clocks on all four sides was. It was a dirty-looking tower of ancient brick. It was a dirty city. Dirtier, certainly, than it had a right to be after only four years.

Waiting for the light to change to green, he looked around at the people standing at the bus stop. A couple of men in suits, half a dozen women who failed to arouse him even after prolonged good behavior, and a young Japanese with a lunch bucket. Ichiro studied him, searching in his mind for the name that went with the round, pimply face and the short-cropped hair. The pimples were gone and the face had hardened, but the hair was still cropped. The fellow wore green, army-fatigue trousers and an Eisenhower jacket—Eto Minato. The name came to him at the same time as did the horrible significance of the army clothes. In panic, he started to step off the curb. It was too late. He had been seen.

"Itchy!" That was his nickname.

Trying to escape, Ichiro urged his legs frenziedly across the street.

"Hey, Itchy!" The caller's footsteps ran toward him.

An arm was placed across his back. Ichiro stopped and faced the other Japanese. He tried to smile, but could not. There was no way out now.

"I'm Eto. Remember?" Eto smiled and extended his palm. Reluctantly, Ichiro lifted his own hand and let the other shake it.

The round face with the round eyes peered at him through silver-rimmed spectacles. "What the hell! It's been a long time, but not that long. How've you been? What's doing?"

"Well . . . that is, I'm . . ."

"Last time must have been before Peal Harbor. God, it's been quite a while, hasn't it? Three, no, closer to four years, I guess. Lotsa Japs coming back to the Coast. Lotsa Japs in Seattle. You'll see 'em around. Japs are funny that way. Gotta have their rice and saké and other Japs. Stupid, I say. The smart ones went to Chicago and New York and lotsa places back east, but there's still plenty coming back out this way." Eto drew cigarettes from his breast pocket and held out the package. "No? Well, I'll have one. Got the habit in the army. Just got out a short while back. Rough time, but I made it. Didn't get out in time to make the quarter, but I'm planning to go to school. How long you been around?"

Ichiro touched his toe to the suitcase. "Just got in. Haven't been home yet."

"When'd you get discharged?"

A car grinding its gears started down the street. He wished he were in it. "I . . . that is . . . I never was in."

Eto slapped him good-naturedly on the arm. "No need to look so sour. So you weren't in. So what? Been in camp all this time?"

"No." He made an effort to be free of Eto with his questions. He felt as if he were in a small room whose walls were slowly closing in on him. "It's been a long time, I know, but I'm really anxious to see the folks."

"What the hell. Let's have a drink. On me. I don't give a damn if I'm late to work. As for your folks, you'll see them soon enough. You drink, don't you?"

"Yeah, but not now."

"Ahh." Eto was disappointed. He shifted his lunch box from under one arm to the other.

"I've really got to be going."

The round face wasn't smiling anymore. It was thoughtful. The eyes confronted Ichiro with indecision which changed slowly to enlightenment, and then to suspicion. He remembered. He knew.

The friendliness was gone as he said: "No-no boy, huh?"

Ichiro wanted to say yes. He wanted to return the look of despising hatred and say simply yes, but it was too much to say. The walls had closed in and were crushing all the unspoken words back down into his stomach. He shook his head once, not wanting to evade the eyes but finding it impossible to meet them. Out of his big weakness the little ones were branching, and the eyes he didn't have the courage to face were ever present. If it would have helped to gouge out his own eyes, he would have done so long ago. The hate-churned eyes with the stamp of unrelenting condemnation were his cross and he had driven the nails with his own hands.

"Rotten bastard. Shit on you." Eto coughed up a mouthful of sputum and rolled his words around it: "Rotten, no-good bastard."

Surprisingly, Ichiro felt relieved. Eto's anger seemed to serve as a release to his own naked tensions. As he stooped to lift the suitcase, a wet wad splattered over his hand, dripped onto the black leather. The legs of his accuser were in front of him. God in a pair of green fatigues, U.S. Army style. They were the legs of the jury that had passed sentence upon him. Beseech me, they seemed to say, throw your arms about me and bury your head between my knees and seek pardon for your great sin.

"I'll piss on you next time," said Eto vehemently.

He turned as he lifted the suitcase off the ground and hurried away from the legs and the eyes from which no escape was possible.

Jackson Street started at the waterfront and stretched past the two train depots and up the hill all the way to the lake, where the houses were bigger and cleaner and had garages with late-model cars in them. For Ichiro, Jackson Street signified that section of the city immediately beyond the railroad tracks between Fifth and Twelfth avenues. That was the section which used to be pretty much Japanese town. It was adjacent to Chinatown and most of the gambling and prostitution and drinking seemed to favor the area.

Like the dirty clock tower of the depot, the filth of Jackson Street had increased. Ichiro paused momentarily at an alley and peered down the passage formed by the walls of two sagging buildings. There had been a door there at one time, a back door to a movie house which only charged a nickel. A nickel was a lot of money when he had been seven or nine or eleven. He wanted to go into the alley to see if the door was still there.

Being on Jackson Street with its familiar store fronts and taverns and restaurants, which were somehow different because the war had left its mark on them, was like trying to find one's way out of a dream that seemed real most of the time but wasn't really real because it was still only a dream. The war had wrought violent changes upon the people, and the people, in turn, working hard and living hard and earning a lot of money and spending it on whatever was available, had distorted the profile of Jackson Street. The street had about it the air of a carnival without quite succeeding at becoming one. A shooting gallery stood where once had been a clothing store; fish and chips had replaced a jewelry shop; and a bunch of Negroes were horsing around raucously in front of a pool parlor. Everything looked older and dirtier and shabbier.

He walked past the pool parlor, picking his way gingerly among the Negroes, of whom there had been only a few at one time and of whom there seemed to be nothing but now. They were smoking and shouting and cussing and carousing and the sidewalk was slimy with their spittle.

"Jap!"

His pace quickened automatically, but curiosity or fear of indignation or whatever it was made him glance back at the white teeth framed in a leering dark brown which was almost black.

"Go back to Tokyo, boy." Persecution in the drawl of the persecuted.

The white teeth and brown-black leers picked up the cue and jigged to the rhythmical chanting of "Jap-boy, To-ki-yo; Jap-boy, To-ki-yo . . ."

Friggin' niggers, he uttered savagely to himself and, from the same place deep down inside where tolerance for the Negroes and the Jews and the Mexicans and the Chinese and the too short and too fat and too ugly abided because he was Japanese and knew what it was like better than did those who were white and average and middle class and good Democrats or liberal Republicans, the hate which was unrelenting and terrifying seethed up.

Then he was home. It was a hole in the wall with groceries crammed in orderly confusion on not enough shelving, into not enough space. He knew what it would be like even before he stepped in. His father had described the place to him in a letter, composed in simple Japanese characters because otherwise Ichiro could not have read it. The letter had been purposely repetitive and painstakingly detailed so that Ichiro should not have any difficulty finding the place. The grocery store was the same one the Ozakis had operated for many years. That's all his father had had to say. Come to the grocery store which was once the store of the Ozakis. The Japanese characters, written simply so that he could read them, covered pages of directions as if he were a foreigner coming to the city for the first time.

Thinking about the letter made him so mad that he forgot about the Negroes. He opened the door just as he had a thousand times when they had lived farther down the block and he used to go to the Ozakis' for a loaf of bread or a jar of pickled scallions, and the bell tinkled just as he knew it would. All the grocery stores he ever knew had bells which tinkled when one opened the door, and the familiar sound softened his inner turmoil.

"Ichiro?" The short, round man who came through the curtains at the back of the store uttered the name preciously as might an old woman. "Ya, Ichiro, you have come home. How good that you have come home!" The gently spoken Japanese which he had not heard for so long sounded strange. He would hear a great deal of it now that he was home, for his parents, like most of the old Japanese, spoke virtually no English. On the other hand, the children, like Ichiro, spoke almost no Japanese. Thus they communicated, the old speaking Japanese with an occasional badly mispronounced word or two of English; and the young, with the exception of a simple word or phrase of Japanese which came fairly effortlessly to the lips, resorting almost constantly to the tongue the parents avoided.

The father bounced silently over the wood flooring in slippered feet toward his son. Fondly, delicately, he placed a pudgy hand on Ichiro's elbow and looked up at his son who was Japanese but who had been big enough for football and tall enough for basketball in high school. He pushed the elbow and Ichiro led the way into the back, where there was a kitchen, a bathroom, and one bedroom. He looked around the bedroom and felt like puking. It was neat and clean and scrubbed. His mother would have seen to that. It was just the idea of everybody sleeping in the one room. He wondered if his folks still pounded flesh.

He backed out of the bedroom and slumped down on a stool. "Where's Ma?"

"Mama is gone to the bakery." The father kept his beaming eyes on his son who was big and tall. He shut off the flow of water and shifted the metal teapot to the stove.

"What for?"

"Bread," his father said in reply, "bread for the store."

"Don't they deliver?"

"Ya, they deliver." He ran a damp rag over the table, which was spotlessly clean.

"What the hell is she doing at the bakery then?"

"It is good business, Ichiro." He was at the cupboard, fussing with the tea cups and saucers and cookies. "The truck comes in the morning. We take enough for the morning business. For the afternoon, we get soft, fresh bread. Mama goes to the bakery."

Ichiro tried to think of a bakery nearby and couldn't. There was a big Wonder Bread bakery way up on Nineteenth, where a nickel used to buy a bagful of day-old stuff. That was thirteen and a half blocks, all uphill. He knew the distance by heart because he'd walked it twice every day to go to grade school, which was a half-block beyond the bakery or fourteen blocks from home.

"What bakery?"

The water on the stove began to boil and the old man flipped the lid on the pot and tossed in a pinch of leaves. "Wonder Bread."

"Is that the one up on Nineteenth?"

"Ya."

"How much do you make on bread?"

"Let's see," he said pouring the tea, "Oh, three, four cents. Depends."

"How many loaves does Ma get?"

"Ten or twelve. Depends."

Ten loaves at three or four cents' profit added up to thirty or forty cents. He compromised at thirty-five cents and asked the next question: "The bus, how much is it?"

"Oh, let's see." He sipped the tea noisily, sucking it through his teeth in well regulated gulps. "Let's see. Fifteen cents for one time. Tokens are two for twenty-five cents. That is twelve and one-half cents."

Twenty-five cents for bus fare to get ten loaves of bread which turned a profit of thirty-five cents. It would take easily an hour to make the trip up and back. He didn't mean to shout, but he shouted: "Christ, Pa, what else do you give away?"

His father peered over the teacup with a look of innocent surprise.

It made him madder. "Figure it out. Just figure it out. Say you make thirty-five cents on ten loaves. You take a bus up and back and there's twenty-five cents shot. That leaves ten cents. On top of that, there's an hour wasted. What are you running a business for? Your health?"

Slup went the tea through his teeth, slup, slup, slup. "Mama walks." He sat there looking at his son like a benevolent Buddha.

Ichiro lifted the cup to his lips and let the liquid burn down his throat. His father had said "Mama walks" and that made things right with the world. The overwhelming simplicity of the explanation threatened to evoke silly giggles which, if permitted to escape, might lead to hysterics. He clenched his fists and subdued them.

At the opposite end of the table the father had slupped the last of his tea and was already taking the few steps to the sink to rinse out the cup.

"Goddammit, Pa, sit down!" He'd never realized how nervous a man his father was. The old man had constantly been doing something every minute since he had come. It didn't figure. Here he was, round and fat and cheerful-looking and, yet, he was going incessantly as though his trousers were crawling with ants.

"Ya, Ichiro, I forget you have just come home. We should talk." He resumed his seat at the table and busied his fingers with a box of matches.

Ichiro stepped out of the kitchen, spotted the cigarettes behind the cash register, and returned with a pack of Camels. Lighting a match, the old man held it between his fingers and waited until the son opened the package and put a cigarette in his mouth. By then the match was threatening to sear his fingers. He dropped it hastily and stole a sheepish glance at Ichiro, who reached for the box and struck his own match.

"Ichiro." There was a timorousness in the father's voice. Or was it apology?

"Yeah."

"Was it very hard?"

"No. It was fun." The sarcasm didn't take.

"You are sorry?" He was waddling over rocky ground on a pitch-black night and he didn't like it one bit.

"I'm okay, Pa. It's finished. Done and finished. No use talking about it."

"True," said the old man too heartily. "It is done and there is no use to talk." The bell tinkled and he leaped from the chair and fled out of the kitchen.

Using the butt of the first cigarette, Ichiro lit another. He heard his father's voice in the store.

"Mama. Ichiro. Ichiro is here."

The sharp, lifeless tone of his mother's words flipped through the silence and he knew that she hadn't changed.

"The bread must be put out."

In other homes mothers and fathers and sons and daughters rushed into hungry arms after week-end separations to find assurance in crushing embraces and loving kisses. The last time he saw his mother was over two years ago. He waited, seeing in the sounds of the rustling waxed paper the stiff, angular figure of the woman stacking the bread on the rack in neat, precise piles.

His father came back into the kitchen with a little less bounce and began to wash the cups. She came through the curtains a few minutes after, a small, flat-chested, shapeless woman who wore her hair pulled back into a tight bun. Hers was the awkward, skinny body of a thirteen-year-old which had dried and toughened through the many years following but which had developed no further. He wondered how the two of them had ever gotten together long enough to have two sons.

"I am proud that you are back," she said. "I am proud to call you my son."

It was her way of saying that she had made him what he was and that the thing in him which made him say no to the judge and go to prison for two years was the growth of a seed planted by the mother tree and that she was the mother who had put this thing in her son and that everything that had been done and said was exacty as it should have been and that that was what made him her son because no other would have made her feel the pride that was in her breast.

He looked at his mother and swallowed with difficulty the bitterness that threatened to destroy the last fragment of understanding for the woman who was his mother and still a stranger because, in truth, he could not know what it was to be a Japanese who breathed the air of America and yet had never lifted a foot from the land that was Japan.

"I've been talking with Pa," he said, not knowing or caring why except that he had to say something.

"After a while, you and I, we will talk also." She walked through the kitchen into the bedroom and hung her coat and hat in a wardrobe of cardboard which had come from Sears Roebuck. Then she came back through the kitchen and out into the store.

The father gave him what was meant to be a knowing look and uttered softly: "Doesn't like my not being in the store when she is out. I tell her the bell tinkles, but she does not understand."

"Hell's bells," he said in disgust. Pushing himself out of the chair violently, he strode into the bedroom and flung himself out on one of the double beds.

Lying there, he wished the roof would fall in and bury forever the anguish which permeated his every pore. He lay there fighting with his burden, lighting one cigarette after another and dropping ashes and butts purposely on the floor. It was the way he felt, stripped of dignity, respect, purpose, honor, all the things which added up to schooling and marriage and family and work and happiness.

It was to please her, he said to himself with teeth clamped together to imprison the wild, meaningless, despairing cry which was forever straining inside of him. Pa's okay, but he's a nobody. He's a goddamned, fat, grinning, spineless nobody. Ma is the rock that's always hammering, pounding, pounding, pounding in her unobtrusive, determined, fanatical way until there's nothing left to call one's self. She's cursed me with her meanness and the hatred that you cannot see but which is always hating. It was she who opened my mouth and made my lips move to sound the words which got me two years in prison and an emptiness that is more empty and frightening than the caverns of hell. She's killed me with her meanness and hatred and I hope she's happy because I'll never know the meaning of it again.

"Ichiro."

He propped himself up on an elbow and looked at her. She had hardly changed. Surely, there must have been a time when she could smile and, yet, he could not remember.

"Yeah?"

"Lunch is on the table."

As he pushed himself off the bed and walked past her to the kitchen, she took broom and dustpan and swept up the mess he had made.

There were eggs, fried with soy sauce, sliced cold meat, boiled cabbage, and tea and rice. They all ate in silence, not even disturbed once by the tinkling of the bell. The father cleared the table after they had finished and dutifully retired to watch the store. Ichiro had smoked three cigarettes before his mother ended the silence.

"You must go back to school."

He had almost forgotten that there had been a time before the war when he had actually gone to college for two years and studiously applied himself to courses in the engineering school. The statement staggered him. Was that all there was to it? Did she mean to sit there and imply that the four intervening years were to be casually forgotten and life resumed as if there had been no four years and no war and no Eto who had spit on him because of the thing he had done?

"I don't feel much like going to school."

"What will you do?"

"I don't know."

"With an education, your opportunities in Japan will be unlimited. You must go and complete your studies."

"Ma," he said slowly, "Ma, I'm not going to Japan. Nobody's going to Japan. The war is over. Japan lost. Do you hear? Japan lost."

"You believe that?" It was said in the tone of an adult asking a child who is no longer a child if he really believed that Santa Claus was real.

"Yes, I believe it. I know it. America is still here. Do you see the great Japanese army walking down the streets? No. There is no Japanese army anymore."

"The boat is coming and we must be ready."

"The boat?"

"Yes." She reached into her pocket and drew out a worn envelope.

The letter had been mailed from São Paulo, Brazil, and was addressed to a name that he did not recognize. Inside the envelope was a single sheet of flimsy rice paper covered with intricate flourishes of Japanese characters.

"What does it say?"

She did not bother to pick up the letter. "To you who are a loyal and honorable Japanese, it is with humble and heartfelt joy that I relay this momentous message. Word has been brought to us that the victorious Japanese government is presently making preparations to send ships which will return to Japan those residents in foreign countries who have steadfastly maintained their faith and loyalty to our Emperor. The Japanese government regrets that the responsibilities arising from the victory compels them to delay in the sending of the vessels. To be among the few who remain to receive this honor is a gratifying tribute. Heed not the propaganda of the radio and newspapers which endeavor to convince the people with lies about the allied victory. Especially, heed not the lies of your traitorous countrymen who have turned their backs on the country of their birth and who will suffer for their treasonous acts. The day of glory is close at hand. The rewards will be beyond our greatest expectations. What we have done, we have done only as Japanese, but the government is grateful. Hold your heads high and make ready for the journey, for the ships are coming."

"Who wrote that?" he asked incredulously. It was like a weird nightmare. It was like finding out that an incurable strain of insanity pervaded the family, an intangible horror that swayed and taunted beyond the grasp of reaching fingers.

"A friend in South America. We are not alone."

"We *are* alone," he said vehemently. "This whole thing is crazy. You're crazy. I'm crazy. All right, so we made a mistake. Let's admit it."

"There has been no mistake. The letter confirms."

"Sure it does. It proves there's crazy people in the world besides us. If Japan won the war, what the hell are we doing here? What are you doing running a grocery store? It doesn't figure. It doesn't figure because we're all wrong. The minute we admit that, everything is fine. I've had a lot of time to think about all this. I've thought about it, and every time the answer comes out the same. You can't tell me different anymore."

She sighed ever so slightly. "We will talk later when you are feeling better." Carefully folding the letter and placing it back in the envelope, she returned it to her pocket. "It is not I who tell you that the ship is coming. It is in the letter. If you have come to doubt your mother—and I'm sure you do not mean it even if you speak in weakness—it is to be regretted. Rest a few days. Think more deeply and your doubts will disappear. You are my son, Ichiro."

No, he said to himself as he watched her part the curtains and start into the store. There was a time when I was your son. There was a time that I no longer remember when you used to smile a mother's smile and tell me stories about gallant and fierce warriors who protected their lords with blades of shining steel and about the old woman who found a peach in the stream and took it home and, when her husband split it in half, a husky little boy tumbled out to fill their hearts with boundless joy. I was that boy in the peach and you were the old woman and we were Japanese with Japanese feelings and Japanese pride and Japanese thoughts because it was all right then to be Japanese and feel and think all the things that Japanese do even if we lived in America. Then there came a time when I was only half Japanese because one is not born in America and raised in America and taught in America and one does not speak and swear and drink and smoke and play and fight and see and hear in America among Americans in American streets and houses without becoming American and loving it. But I did not love enough, for you were still half my mother and I was thereby still half Japanese and when the war came and they told me to fight for America, I was not strong enough to fight you and I was not strong enough to fight the bitterness which made the half of me which was you bigger than the half of me which was America and really the whole of me that I could not see or feel. Now that I know the truth when it is too late and the half of me which was you is no longer there, I am only half of me and the half that remains is American by law because the government was wise and strong enough to know why it was that I could not fight for America and did not strip me of my birthright. But it is not enough to be American only in the eyes of the law and it is not enough to be only half an American and know that it is an empty half. I am not your son and I am not Japanese and I am not American. I can go someplace and tell people that I've got an inverted stomach and that I am an American, true and blue and Hail Columbia, but the army wouldn't have me because of the stomach. That's easy and I would do it, only I've got to convince myself first and that I cannot do. I wish with all my heart that I were Japanese or that I were American. I am neither and I blame you and I blame myself and I blame the world which is made up of many countries which fight with each other and kill and hate and destroy but not enough, so that they must kill and hate and destroy again and again and again. It is so easy and simple that I cannot understand it at all. And the reason I do not understand it is because I do not understand you who were the half of me that is no more and because I do not understand what it was about that half that made me destroy the half of me which was American and the half which might have become the whole of me if I had said yes I will go and fight in your army because that is what I believe and want and cherish and love . . .

Defeatedly, he crushed the stub of a cigarette into an ashtray filled with many other stubs and reached for the package to get another. It was empty and he did not want to go into the store for more because he did not feel much like seeing either his father or mother. He went into the bedroom and tossed and groaned and half slept.

Hours later, someone shook him awake. It was not his mother and it was not his father. The face that looked down at him in the gloomy darkness was his brother's.

"Taro," he said softly, for he had hardly thought of him.

"Yeah, it's me," said his brother with unmistakable embarrassment. "I see you got out."

"How've you been?" He studied his brother, who was as tall as he but skinnier.

"Okay. It's time to eat." He started to leave.

"Taro, wait."

His brother stood framed in the light of the doorway and faced him.

"How've you been?" he repeated. Then he added quickly for fear of losing him: "No, I said that before and I don't mean it the way it sounds. We've got things to talk about. Long time since we saw each other."

"Yeah, it's been a long time."

"How's school?"

"Okay."

"About through with high school?"

"Next June."

"What then? College?"

"No, army."

He wished he could see his face, the face of the brother who spoke to him as though they were strangers—because that's what they were.

"You could get in a year or two before the draft," he heard himself saying in an effort to destroy the wall that separated them. "I read where you can take an exam now and get a deferment if your showing is good enough. A fellow's got to have all the education he can get, Taro."

"I don't want a deferment. I want in."

"Ma know?"

"Who cares?"

"She won't like it."

"Doesn't matter."

"Why so strong about the army? Can't you wait? They'll come and get you soon enough."

"That isn't soon enough for me."

"What's your reason?"

He waited for an answer, knowing what it was and not wanting to hear it.

"Is it because of me? What I did?"

"I'm hungry," his brother said and turned into the kitchen.

His mother had already eaten and was watching the store. He sat opposite his brother, who wolfed down the food without looking back at him. It wasn't more than a few minutes before he rose, grabbed his jacket off a nail on the wall, and left the table. The bell tinkled and he was gone.

"Don't mind him," said the father apologetically. "Taro is young and restless. He's never home except to eat and sleep."

"When does he study?"

"He does not."

"Why don't you do something about it?"

"I tell him. Mama tells him. Makes no difference. It is the war that has made them that way. All the people say the same thing. The war and the camp life. Made them wild like cats and dogs. It is hard to understand."

"Sure," he said, but he told himself that he understood, that the reason why Taro was not a son and not a brother was because he was young and American and alien to his parents, who had lived in America for thirty-five years without becoming less Japanese and could speak only a few broken words of English and write it not at all, and because Taro hated that thing in his elder brother which had prevented him from thinking for himself. And in his hate for that thing, he hated his brother and also his parents because they had created the thing with their eyes and hands and minds which had seen and felt and thought as Japanese for thirty-five years in an America which they rejected as thoroughly as if they had never been a day away from Japan. That was the reason and it was difficult to believe, but it was true because he was the emptiness between the one and the other and could see flashes of the truth that was true for his parents and the truth that was true for his brother.

"Pa," he said.

"Ya, Ichiro." He was swirling a dishcloth in a pan of hot water and working up suds for the dishes.

"What made you and Ma come to America?"

"Everyone was coming to America."

"Did you have to come?"

"No. We came to make money."

"Is that all?"

"Ya, I think that was why we came."

"Why to make money?"

"There was a man in my village who went to America and made a lot of money and he came back and bought a big piece of land and he was very comfortable. We came so we could make money and go back and buy a piece of land and be comfortable too."

"Did you ever think about staying here and not going back?"

"No."

He looked at his father, who was old and bald and washing dishes in a kitchen that was behind a hole in the wall that was a grocery store. "How do you feel about it now?"

"About what?"

"Going back."

"We are going."

"When?"

"Oh, pretty soon."

"How soon?"

"Pretty soon."

There didn't seem to be much point in pursuing the questioning. He went out to the store and got a fresh pack of cigarettes. His mother was washing down the vegetable stand, which stood alongside the entrance. Her thin arms swabbed the green-painted wood with sweeping, vigorous strokes. There was a power in the wiry, brown arms, a hard, blind, unreckoning force which coursed through veins of tough bamboo. When she had done her work, she carried the pail of water to the curb outside and poured it on the street. Then she came back through the store and into the living quarters and emerged once more dressed in her coat and hat.

"Come, Ichiro," she said, "we must go and see Kumasaka-san and Ashida-san. They will wish to know that you are back."

The import of the suggested visits made him waver helplessly. He was too stunned to voice his protest. The Kumasakas and the Ashidas were people from the same village in Japan. The three families had been very close for as long as he could recall. Further, it was customary among the Japanese to pay ceremonious visits upon various occasions to families of close association. This was particularly true when a member of one of the families either departed on an extended absence or returned from an unusually long separation. Yes, he had been gone a long time, but it was such a different thing. It wasn't as if he had gone to war and returned safe and sound or had been matriculating at some school in another city and come home with a sheepskin *summa cum laude*. He scrabbled at the confusion in his mind for the logic of the crazy business and found no satisfaction.

"Papa," his mother shouted without actually shouting.

His father hastened out from the kitchen and Ichiro stumbled in blind fury after the woman who was only a rock of hate and fanatic stubbornness and was, therefore, neither woman nor mother.

They walked through the night and the city, a mother and son thrown together for a while longer because the family group is a stubborn one and does not easily disintegrate. The woman walked ahead and the son followed and no word passed between them. They walked six blocks, then six more, and still another six before they turned into a three-story frame building.

The Ashidas, parents and three daughters, occupied four rooms on the second floor.

"Mama," screamed the ten-year-old who answered the knock, "Mrs. Yamada."

A fat, cheerful-looking woman rushed toward them, then stopped, flushed and surprised. "Ichiro-san. You have come back."

He nodded his head and heard his mother say, with unmistakable exultation: "Today, Ashida-san. Just today he came home."

Urged by their hostess, they took seats in the sparsely furnished living room. Mrs. Ashida sat opposite them on a straight-backed kitchen chair and beamed.

"You have grown so much. It is good to be home, is it not, Ichiro-san?" She turned to the ten-year-old, who gawked at him from behind her mother: "Tell Reiko to get tea and cookies."

"She's studying, Mama."

"You mustn't bother," said his mother.

"Go, now. I know she is only listening to the radio." The little girl fled out of the room.

"It is good to see you again, Ichiro-san. You will find many of your young friends already here. All the people who said they would never come back to Seattle are coming back. It is almost like it was before the war. Akira-san—you went to school with him I think—he is just back from Italy, and Watanabe-san's boy came back from Japan last month. It is so good that the war is over and everything is getting to be like it was before."

"You saw the pictures?" his mother asked.

"What pictures?"

"You have not been to the Watanabes'?"

"Oh, yes, the pictures of Japan." She snickered. "He is such a serious boy. He showed me all the pictures he had taken in Japan. He had many of Hiroshima and Nagasaki and I told him that he must be mistaken because Japan did not lose the war as he seems to believe and that he could not have been in Japan to take pictures because, if he were in Japan, he would not have been permitted to remain alive. He protested and yelled so that his mother had to tell him to be careful and then he tried to argue some more, but I asked him if he was ever in Japan before and could he prove that he was actually there and he said again to look at the pictures and I told him that what must really have happened was that the army only told him he was in Japan when he was someplace else, and that it was too bad he believed the propaganda. Then he got so mad his face went white and he said: 'How do you know you're you? Tell me how you know you're you?' If his mother had not made him leave the room, he might even have struck me. It is not enough that they must willingly take up arms against their uncles and cousins and even brothers and sisters, but they no longer have respect for the old ones. If I had a son and he had gone in the American army to fight Japan, I would have killed myself with shame."

"They know not what they do and it is not their fault. It is the fault of the parents. I've always said that Mr. Watanabe was a stupid man. Gambling and drinking the way he does, I am almost ashamed to call them friends." Ichiro's mother looked at him with a look which said I am a Japanese and you are my son and have conducted yourself as a Japanese and I know no shame such as other parents do because their sons were not really their sons or they would not have fought against their own people.

He wanted to get up and dash out into the night. The madness of his mother was in mutual company and he felt nothing but loathing for the gentle, kindly looking Mrs. Ashida, who sat on a fifty-cent chair from Goodwill Industries while her husband worked the night shift at a hotel grinning and bowing for dimes and quarters from rich Americans whom he detested, and couldn't afford to take his family on a bus ride to Tacoma but was waiting and praying and hoping for the ships from Japan.

Reiko brought in a tray holding little teacups and a bowl of thin, round cookies. She was around seventeen with little bumps on her chest which the sweater didn't improve and her lips heavily lipsticked a deep red. She said "Hi" to him and did not have to say look at me, I was a kid when you saw me last but now I'm a woman with a woman's desires and a woman's eye for men like you. She set the tray on the table and gave him a smile before she left.

His mother took the envelope from São Paulo out of her dress pocket and handed it to Mrs. Ashida.

"From South America."

The other woman snatched at the envelope and proceeded to read the contents instantly. Her face glowed with pride. She read it eagerly, her lips moving all the time and frequently murmuring audibly. "Such wonderful news," she sighed breathlessly as if the reading of the letter had been a deep emotional experience. "Mrs. Okamoto will be eager to see this. Her husband, who goes out of the house whenever I am there, is threatening to leave her unless she gives up her nonsense about Japan. Nonsense, he calls it. He is no better than a Chinaman. This will show him. I feel so sorry for her."

"It is hard when so many no longer believe," replied his mother, "but they are not Japanese like us. They only call themselves such. It is the same with the Teradas. I no longer go to see them. The last time I was there Mr. Terada screamed at me and told me to get out. They just don't understand that Japan did not lose the war because Japan could not possibly lose. I try not to hate them but I have no course but to point them out to the authorities when the ships come."

"It's getting late, Ma." He stood up, sick in the stomach and wanting desperately to smash his way out of the dishonest, warped, and uncompromising world in which defeated people like his mother and the Ashidas walked their perilous tightropes and could not and would not look about them for having to keep their eyes fastened to the taut, thin support.

"Yes," his mother replied quickly, "forgive us for rushing, for you know that I enjoy nothing better than a visit with you, but we must drop in for a while on the Kumasakas."

"Of course. I wish you could stay longer, but I know that there will be plenty of opportunities again. You will come again, please, Ichiro-san?"

Mumbling thanks for the tea, he nodded evasively and hurried down the stairs. Outside, he lit a cigarette and paced restlessly until his mother came out.

"A fine woman," she said without stopping.

He followed, talking to the back of her head: "Ma, I don't want to see the Kumasakas tonight. I don't want to see anybody tonight. We'll go some other time."

"We won't stay long."

They walked a few blocks to a freshly painted frame house that was situated behind a neatly kept lawn.

"Nice house," he said.

"They bought it last month."

"Bought it?"

"Yes."

The Kumasakas had run a dry-cleaning shop before the war. Business was good and people spoke of their having money, but they lived in cramped quarters above the shop because, like most of the other Japanese, they planned some day to return to Japan and still felt like transients even after thirty or forty years in America and the quarters above the shop seemed adequate and sensible since the arrangement was merely temporary. That, he thought to himself, was the reason why the Japanese were still Japanese. They rushed to America with the single purpose of making a fortune which would enable them to return to their own country and live adequately. It did not matter when they discovered that fortunes were not for the mere seeking or that their sojourns were spanning decades instead of years and it did not matter that growing families and growing bills and misfortunes and illness and low wages and just plain hard luck were constant obstacles to the realization of their dreams. They continued to maintain their dreams by refusing to learn how to speak or write the language of America and by living only among their own kind and by zealously avoiding long-term commitments such as the purchase of a house. But now, the Kumasakas, it seemed, had bought this house, and he was impressed. It could only mean that the Kumasakas had exchanged hope for reality and, late as it was, were finally sinking roots into the land from which they had previously sought not nourishment but only gold.

Mrs. Kumasaka came to the door, a short, heavy woman who stood solidly on feet planted wide apart, like a man. She greeted them warmly but with a sadness that she would carry to the grave. When Ichiro had last seen her, her hair had been pitch black. Now it was completely white.

In the living room Mr. Kumasaka, a small man with a pleasant smile, was sunk deep in an upholstered chair, reading a Japanese newspaper. It was a comfortable room with rugs and soft furniture and lamps and end tables and pictures on recently papered walls.

"Ah, Ichiro, it is nice to see you looking well." Mr. Kumasaka struggled out of the chair and extended a friendly hand. "Please, sit down."

"You've got a nice place," he said, meaning it.

"Thank you," the little man said. "Mama and I, we finally decided that America is not so bad. We like it here."

Ichiro sat down on the sofa next to his mother and felt strange in this home which he envied because it was like millions of other homes in America and could never be his own.

Mrs. Kumasaka sat next to her husband on a large, round hassock and looked at Ichiro with lonely eyes, which made him uncomfortable.

"Ichiro came home this morning." It was his mother, and the sound of her voice, deliberately loud and almost arrogant, puzzled him. "He has suffered, but I make no apologies for him or for myself. If he had given his life for Japan, I could not be prouder."

"Ma," he said, wanting to object but not knowing why except that her comments seemed out of place.

Ignoring him, she continued, not looking at the man but at his wife, who now sat with head bowed, her eyes emptily regarding the floral pattern of the carpet. "A mother's lot is not an easy one. To sleep with a man and bear a son is nothing. To raise the child into a man one can be proud of is not play. Some of us succeed. Some, of course, must fail. It is too bad, but that is the way of life."

"Yes, yes, Yamada-san," said the man impatiently. Then, smiling, he turned to Ichiro: "I suppose you'll be going back to the university?"

"I'll have to think about it," he replied, wishing that his father was like this man who made him want to pour out the turbulence in his soul.

"He will go when the new term begins. I have impressed upon him the importance of a good education. With a college education, one can go far in Japan." His mother smiled knowingly.

"Ah," said the man as if he had not heard her speak, "Bobbie wanted to go to the university and study medicine. He would have made a fine doctor. Always studying and reading, is that not so, Ichiro?"

He nodded, remembering the quiet son of the Kumasakas, who never played football with the rest of the kids on the street or appeared at dances, but could talk for hours on end about chemistry and zoology and physics and other courses which he hungered after in high school.

"Sure, Bob always was pretty studious." He knew, somehow, that it was not the right thing to say, but he added: "Where is Bob?"

His mother did not move. Mrs. Kumasaka uttered a despairing cry and bit her trembling lips.

The little man, his face a drawn mask of pity and sorrow, stammered: "Ichiro, you—no one has told you?"

"No. What? No one's told me anything."

"Your mother did not write you?"

"No. Write about what?" He knew what the answer was. It was in the whiteness of the hair of the sad woman who was the mother of the boy named Bob and it was in the engaging pleasantness of the father which was not really pleasantness but a deep understanding which had emerged from resignation to a loss which only a parent knows and suffers. And then he saw the picture on the mantel, a snapshot, enlarged many times over, of a grinning youth in uniform who had not thought to remember his parents with a formal portrait because he was not going to die and there would be worlds of time for pictures and books and other obligations of the living later on.

Mr. Kumasaka startled him by shouting toward the rear of the house: "Jun! Please come."

There was the sound of a door opening and presently there appeared a youth in khaki shirt and wool trousers, who was a stranger to Ichiro.

"I hope I haven't disturbed anything, Jun," said Mr. Kumasaka.

"No, it's all right. Just writing a letter."

"This is Mrs. Yamada and her son Ichiro. They are old family friends."

Jun nodded to his mother and reached over to shake Ichiro's hand.

The little man waited until Jun had seated himself on the end of the sofa. "Jun is from Los Angeles. He's on his way home from the army and was good enough to stop by and visit us for a few days. He and Bobbie were together. Buddies—is that what you say?"

"That's right," said Jun.

"Now, Jun."

"Yes?"

The little man looked at Ichiro and then at his mother, who stared stonily at no one in particular.

"Jun, as a favor to me, although I know it is not easy for you to speak of it, I want you to tell us about Bobbie."

Jun stood up quickly. "Gosh, I don't know." He looked with tender concern at Mrs. Kumasaka.

"It is all right, Jun. Please, just this once more."

"Well, okay." He sat down again, rubbing his hands thoughtfully over his knees. "The way it happened, Bobbie and I, we had just gotten back to the rest area. Everybody was feeling good because there was a lot of talk about the Germans surrendering. All the fellows were cleaning their equipment. We'd been up in the lines for a long time and everything was pretty well messed up. When you're up there getting shot at, you don't worry much about how crummy your things get, but the minute you pull back, they got to have inspection. So, we were cleaning things up. Most of us were cleaning our rifles because that's something you learn to want to do no matter how anything else looks. Bobbie was sitting beside me and he was talking about how he was going to medical school and become a doctor—"

A sob wrenched itself free from the breast of the mother whose son was once again dying, and the snow-white head bobbed wretchedly.

"Go on, Jun," said the father.

Jun looked away from the mother and at the picture on the mantel. "Bobbie was like that. Me and the other guys, all we talked about was drinking and girls and stuff like that because it's important to talk about those things when you make it back from the front on your own power, but Bobbie, all he thought about was going to school. I was nodding my head and saying yeah, yeah, and then there was this noise, kind of a pinging noise right close by. It scared me for a minute and I started to cuss and said, 'Gee, that was damn close,' and looked around at Bobbie. He was slumped over with his head between his knees. I reached out to hit him, thinking he was fooling around. Then, when I tapped him on the arm, he fell over and I saw the dark spot on the side of his head where the bullet had gone through. That was all. Ping, and he's dead. It doesn't figure, but it happened just the way I've said."

The mother was crying now, without shame and alone in her grief that knew no end. And in her bottomless grief that made no distinction as to what was wrong and what was right and who was Japanese and who was not, there was no awareness of the other mother with a living son who had come to say to her you are with shame and grief because you were not Japanese and thereby killed your son but mine is big and strong and full of life because I did not weaken and would not let my son destroy himself uselessly and treacherously.

Ichiro's mother rose and, without a word, for no words would ever pass between them again, went out of the house which was a part of America.

Mr. Kumasaka placed a hand on the rounded back of his wife, who was forever beyond consoling, and spoke gently to Ichiro: "You don't have to say anything. You are truly sorry and I am sorry for you."

"I didn't know," he said pleadingly.

"I want you to feel free to come and visit us whenever you wish. We can talk even if your mother's convictions are different."

"She's crazy. Mean and crazy. Goddamned Jap!" He felt the tears hot and stinging.

"Try to understand her."

Impulsively, he took the little man's hand in his own and held it briefly. Then he hurried out of the house which could never be his own.

His mother was not waiting for him. He saw her tiny figure strutting into the shadows away from the illumination of the street-lights and did not attempt to catch her.

As he walked up one hill and down another, not caring where and only knowing that he did not want to go home, he was thinking about the Kumasakas and his mother and kids like Bob who died brave deaths fighting for something which was bigger than Japan or America or the selfish bond that strapped a son to his mother. Bob, and a lot of others with no more to lose or gain then he, had not found it necessary to think about whether or not to go in the army. When the time came, they knew what was right for them and they went.

What had happened to him and the others who faced the judge and said: You can't make me go in the army because I'm not an American or you wouldn't have plucked me and mine from a life that was good and real and meaningful and fenced me in the desert like they do the Jews in Germany and it is a puzzle why you haven't started to liquidate us though you might as well since everything else has been destroyed.

And some said: You, Mr. Judge, who supposedly represent justice, was it a just thing to ruin a hundred thousand lives and homes and farms and businesses and dreams and hopes because the hundred thousand were a hundred thousand Japanese and you couldn't have loyal Japanese when Japan is the country you're fighting and, if so, how about the Germans and Italians that must be just as questionable as the Japanese or we wouldn't be fighting Germany and Italy? Round them up. Take away their homes and cars and beer and spaghetti and throw them in a camp and what do you think they'll say when you try to draft them into your army of the country that is for life, liberty, and the pursuit of happiness? If you think we're the same kind of rotten Japanese that dropped the bombs on Pearl Harbor, and it's plain that you do or I wouldn't be here having to explain to you why it is that I won't go and protect sons-of-bitches like you, I say you're right and *banzai* three times and we'll sit the war out in a nice cell, thank you.

And then another one got up and faced the judge and said meekly: I can't go because my brother is in the Japanese army and if I go in your army and have to shoot at them because they're shooting at me, how do I know that maybe I won't kill my own brother? I'm a good American and I like it here but you can see that it wouldn't do for me to be shooting at my own brother; even if he went back to Japan when I was two years old and couldn't know him if I saw him, it's the feeling that counts, and what can a fellow do? Besides, my mom and dad said I shouldn't and they ought to know.

And after the fellow with the brother in the army of the wrong country sat down, a tall, skinny one sneered at the judge and said: I'm not going in the army because wool clothes give me one helluva bad time and them O.D. things you make the guys wear will drive me nuts and I'd end up shooting bastards like you which would be too good but then you'd only have to shoot me and I like living even if it's in striped trousers as long as they aren't wool. The judge, who looked Italian and had a German name, repeated the question as if the tall, skinny one hadn't said anything yet, and the tall, skinny one tried again only, this time, he was serious. He said: I got it all figured out. Economics, that's what. I hear this guy with the stars, the general of your army that cleaned the Japs off the coast, got a million bucks for the job. All this bull about us being security risks and saboteurs and Shinto freaks, that's for the birds and the dumbheads. The only way it figures is the money angle. How much did they give you, judge, or aren't your fingers long enough? Cut me in. Give me a cut and I'll go fight your war single-handed.

Please, judge, said the next one. I want to go in your army because this is my country and I've always lived here and I was all-city guard and one time I wrote an essay for composition about what it means to me to be an American and the teacher sent it into a contest and they gave me twenty-five dollars, which proves that I'm a good American. Maybe I look Japanese and my father and mother and brothers and sisters look Japanese, but we're better Americans than the regular ones because that's the way it has to be when one looks Japanese but is really a good American. We're not like the other Japanese who aren't good Americans like us. We're more like you and the other, regular Americans. All you have to do is give us back our home and grocery store and let my kid brother be all-city like me. Nobody has to know. We can be Chinese. We'll call ourselves Chin or Yang or something like that and it'll be the best thing you've ever done, sir. That's all, a little thing. Will you do that for one good, loyal American family? We'll forget the two years in camp because anybody can see it was all a mistake and you didn't really mean to do it and I'm all yours.

There were others with reasons just as flimsy and unreal and they had all gone to prison, where the months and years softened the unthinking bitterness and let them see the truth when it was too late. For the one who could not go because Japan was the country of his parents' birth, there were a thousand Bobs who had gone into the army with a singleness of purpose. In answer to the tall, skinny one who spouted economics, another thousand with even greater losses had answered the greetings. For each and every refusal based on sundry reasons, another thousand chose to fight for the right to continue to be Americans because homes and cars and money could be regained but only if they first regained their rights as citizens, and that was everything.

And then Ichiro thought to himself: My reason was all the reasons put together. I did not go because I was weak and could not do what I should have done. It was not my mother, whom I have never really known. It was me, myself. It is done and there can be no excuse. I remember Kenzo, whose mother was in the hospital and did not want him to go. The doctor told him that the shock might kill her. He went anyway, the very next day, because though he loved his mother he knew that she was wrong, and she did die. And I remember Harry, whose father had a million-dollar produce business, and the old man just boarded everything up because he said he'd rather let the trucks and buildings and warehouses rot than sell them for a quarter of what they were worth. Harry didn't have to stop and think when his number came up. Then there was Mr. Yamaguchi, who was almost forty and had five girls. They would never have taken him, but he had to go and talk himself into a uniform. I remember a lot of people and a lot of things now as I walk confidently through the night over a small span of concrete which is part of the sidewalks which are part of the city which is part of the state and the country and the nation that is America. It is for this that I meant to fight, only the meaning got lost when I needed it most badly.

Then he was on Jackson Street and walking down the hill. Through the windows of the drugstore, the pool hall, the cafés and taverns, he saw groups of young Japanese wasting away the night as nights were meant to be wasted by young Americans with change in their pockets and a thirst for Cokes and beer and pinball machines or fast cars and de luxe hamburgers and cards and dice and trim legs. He recognized a face, a smile, a gesture, or a sneer, but they were not for him, for he walked on the outside and familiar faces no longer meant friends. He walked quickly, guiltily avoiding a chance recognition of himself by someone who remembered him.

* * *

Minutes later he was pounding on the door of the darkened grocery store with home in the back. It was almost twelve o'clock and he was surprised to see his father weave toward the door fully dressed and fumble with the latch. He smelled the liquor as soon as he stepped inside. He had known that his father took an occasional drink, but he'd never seen him drunk and it disturbed him.

"Come in, come in," said the father thickly, moments after Ichiro was well inside. After several tries, his father flipped the latch back into place.

"I thought you'd be in bed, Pa."

The old man stumbled toward the kitchen. "Waiting for you, Ichiro. Your first night home. I want to put you to bed."

"Sure. Sure. I know how it is."

They sat down in the kitchen, the bottle between them. It was half empty. On the table was also a bundle of letters. By the cheap, flimsy quality of the envelopes, he knew that they were from Japan. One of the letters was spread out before his father as if he might have been interrupted while perusing it.

"Ichiro." His father grinned kindly at him.

"Yeah?"

"Drink. You have got to drink a little to be a man, you know."

"Sure, Pa." He poured the cheap blend into a water glass and took a big gulp. "God," he managed to say with the liquor burning a deep rut all the way down, "how can you drink this stuff?"

"Only the first one or two is bad. After that, it gets easier."

Ichiro regarded the bottle skeptically: "You drink all this?"

"Yes, tonight."

"That's quite a bit."

"Ya, but I finish."

"What are you celebrating?"

"Life."

"What?"

"Life. One celebrates Christmas and New Year's and Fourth of July, that is all right, but life I can celebrate any time. I celebrate life." Not bothering with a glass, he gurgled from the bottle.

"What's wrong, Pa?"

The old man waved his arm in a sweeping gesture.

"Nothing is wrong, Ichiro. I just celebrate you. You are home and is it wrong for me to be happy? Of course not. I am happy. I celebrate."

"Things pretty tough?"

"No. No. We don't get rich, but we make enough."

"What do you do with yourself?"

"Do?"

"Yeah. I remember you used to play Go with Mr. Kumasaka all the time. And Ma was always making me run after you to the Tandos. You were never, home before the war. You still do those things?"

"Not so much."

"You go and visit them?"

"Once in a while."

He watched his father, who was fiddling with the letter and avoiding his gaze. "Many people think Japan won the war?"

"Not so many."

"What do you think?"

"No."

"Why?"

"I read, I hear, I see."

"Why don't you tell Ma?"

The old man looked up suddenly and Ichiro thought that he was going to burst out with laughter. Just as quickly, he became soberly serious. He held up the thick pile of letters. "Your mama is sick, Ichiro, and she has made you sick and I am sick because I cannot do anything for her and maybe it is I that is somehow responsible for her sickness in the first place. These letters are from my brothers and cousins and nephews and people I hardly knew in Japan thirty-five years ago, and they are from your mama's brother and two sisters and cousins and friends and uncles and people she does not remember at all. They all beg for help, for money and sugar and clothes and rice and tobacco and candy and anything at all. I read these letters and drink and cry and drink some more because my own people are suffering so much and there is nothing I can do."

"Why don't you send them things?"

"Your mama is sick, Ichiro. She says these letters are not from Japan, that they were not written by my brothers or her sisters or our uncles and nephews and nieces and cousins. She does not read them anymore. Propaganda, she says. She won't let me send money or food or clothing because she says it's all a trick of the Americans and that they will take them. I can send without her knowing, but I do not. It is not for me to say that she is wrong even if I know so."

The father picked up the bottle and poured the liquor into his throat. His face screwed up and tears came to his eyes.

"I'm going to sleep, Pa." Ichiro stood up and looked for a long time at his drunken father who could not get drunk enough to forget.

"Ichiro."

"Yeah?"

His father mumbled to the table: "I am sorry that you went to prison for us."

"Sure. Forget it." He went to the bedroom, undressed in the dark, and climbed into bed wondering why his brother wasn't sleeping.

Louis Chu

(1915–1970)

Louis Chu was born in Toishan, China, on October 1, 1915. Immigrating to the United States when he was nine years old, he completed his high school education in New Jersey and went on to receive a bachelor's degree from Upsala College, a master's degree from New York University, and postgraduate training at the New School for Social Research. He was employed by New York City's Department of Welfare and became director of a social center. He served as executive secretary for the Soo Yuen Benevolent Association and was a well-known figure in New York's Chinatown, where he hosted a radio program called "Chinese Festival." He died in 1970, survived by his wife and four children.

First published in 1961, *Eat a Bowl of Tea* is partly a satire on the manners and mores of Chinatown's bachelor society, a community that lay moribund at the close of the Second World War, enclaves of old men trapped by racist immigration laws to live out their days in San Francisco, Seattle, Los Angeles, Boston, and New York City. With allegiances tied to wives and family barred from entering the United States, they found refuge in the back rooms of barbershops and restaurants, at the local tong, in the repartee and rivalries exchanged over a game of mah jongg. In this tale of adultery and comic retribution, Louis Chu captures their vanities and illusions. These exiles become the vestiges of those who toiled in agriculture and mining, built the Transcontinental Railroad, and funded the Chinese Republican Revolution of 1911. He finds them fifty years later, bound by popular prejudice and the law to an aging, inflexible fraternity living in New York's Chinatown.

Eat a Bowl of Tea

27

When Ben Loy first learned that his wife was pregnant, he was not impressed. In fact he was a little irritated because Mei Oi had called him when he was busy at the restaurant.

Upon further reflection, however, he became elated over the news. He remembered the encounters he had had with friends: Is Auntie going to have a baby? Is there any good news? Heh, heh, what are you waiting for? And from his father: How is Ah Sow these days? Is she well? The old man did not come right out and ask it, but Ben Loy knew what he meant. Wing Sim's wife was no exception: When are you going to invite us to the happy banquet? From his mother Lau Shee, writing to his father: Ben Loy and Lee Shee have been married more than a year. I should think it's time that they have a little one.

Only a week earlier he had seen no way out of his predicament. He had reconciled himself to remaining childless, and he would defend himself with: We don't want children. He consoled himself that in America many couples are childless. But being Chinese, he supposed that his parents would insist, sooner or later, that he and Mei Oi adopt a little boy to carry on the ancestral name, so that someone will cry at his and her funerals. In China, if the children were all girls, the parents would eventually adopt a boy. They want to keep the family name in the tablet house forever, and only a boy could make that possible. A daughter would merely become somebody else's wife.

Ben Loy told himself that, if the baby was a girl, he would not go looking for a boy to adopt. Boy or girl, what's the difference? In America, girls are looked upon with more love and affection than boys anyway.

He was happy because it was the most natural thing for a married couple to do, to have a baby.

When he thought of his youthful foolishness, he despised himself. He felt guilty for speaking sharply to Mei Oi when she called to tell him about the baby. But he would have been more courteous if it had not been so unexpected.

Mixed with this glad tiding, the father-to-be experienced an emotional shock. He had not believed that he was capable of becoming a father. The many months that it took for his wife to become pregnant certainly did not add to his manly pride. With some exceptions, during his year and a half of marriage to Mei Oi, he had been sexually incompetent. He knew he had not been a successful husband. He had left his wife unrewarded.

He kept trying to ignore questions in his own mind. Where did the baby come from? Could it be his? If not his, whose? At first, Ben Loy scoffed at the idea of confiding his problem to another. Nevertheless, he considered as a possible confidant his old roommate, Chin Yuen. Chin Yuen had been a schoolteacher in China. But how could Ben Loy bring up the subject without embarrassment to himself? Say, my wife is going to have a baby and I think it's someone else's? That would be enough to start the laughter rolling. Where would he hide his face then? He certainly could not mention the matter to his father. No doubt a non-Chinese son would take such a matter up with his father. Only last week Ben Loy had overheard in the restaurant a son calling his father George and his mother Beatrice. From his agonized predicament he envied and admired the outspoken American. On second thought, however, he dismissed this outspokenness as animal behaviorism. A Chinese would never confide to his own father that he suspected his wife of infidelity.

"Hey, waiter!" called out the man in booth four. "We ordered subgum chow mein." He lifted the lid off. "This is shrimp chow mein." He replaced the metal lid quickly and looked up at Ben Loy, who meekly took the dish away.

In the same evening two other customers complained: I ordered barbecue spareribs. Is this barbecue spareribs? One customer ordered egg rolls and Ben Loy brought him an order of roast pork.

A boy about six wanted vanilla ice cream and Ben Loy made the mistake of bringing him chocolate. The parents could not persuade the little boy to change his mind. When Ben Loy finally arrived with a dish of vanilla, the mother said: "He's just being disagreeable. Lots of times at home he eats chocolate ice cream. You can't tell me he doesn't like chocolate ice cream!"

That was no solace to Ben Loy. Because of his confused mind, he decided to see Dr. Long on his next day off. "I'm nervous, Doctor," he said. "I kept making mistakes in the orders."

The doctor prescribed some pills for his nerves and told him to take a few days off from work. On the way out of the doctor's office, Ben Loy, sounding as casual as he could, asked: "Say, Doc, could a fellow who has trouble in getting an erection become a father?"

"Sure, why not?" replied the doctor.

That was enough for Ben Loy. His face glowed as he walked home.

When he got home, he called his friend Chin Yuen. "Work a few days for me, will you?" Ben Loy asked.

"What's the matter, sick or something?"

"Yes, sick," he replied. "Nothing much, just a little sick."

28

When Ben Loy left the Chinese Theater the next day, he intended to get a haircut. But when he peered through the plate glass of a nearby barbershop and saw there were others waiting and only one barber in attendance, he did not go in. He swung into Mott Street.

As he descended the stairs of the Wah Que Barber Shop, strands of Cantonese opera music floated from inside the shop. Blocks and cymbals. A shrill voice called out. A heightened cadence of the drums. Excited dialogue which he did not make out. As he neared the door, the music became louder. Some more dialogue. It was *Gim Peng Moy*, a well-known Chinese classic, a story about a housewife married to the older of two brothers. When the Second Uncle returned from the wars, she impetuously fell in love with him and subsequently, through wiles and trickery, seduced him. Ben Loy purposely slowed his steps and listened intently. He immediately compared Mei Oi to Gim Peng Moy. Are they the same type of woman? But I have no brother, he consoled himself.

Next he found himself seated in the barber's chair. "What's the name of the record that's playing now?" he inquired.

"That's *Gim Peng Moy*. A good record." The barber wrapped a towel around Ben Loy's neck.

"Oh, is that a popular record?" pursued Ben Loy.

"Yes, I guess so," said the barber, now flipping an apron on the customer. "I guess people like it because of the sexy story. Everybody likes sex, you know."

Ah Mow knew who Ben Loy was, but he refrained from revealing this knowledge in his conversation. Very often he would come up from his shop and stand at the top of the stairs and watch people go by. He didn't know his name was Ben Loy, but he knew he was Wang Wah Gay's son.

Expertly guiding the clippers around the edges, the barber looked for strands of grey on Ben Loy's head, but he could find none. Looking for grey hair on a customer's head was a sort of hobby with him. He allowed himself the observation that many young folks, men and women, get grey prematurely.

"You're still very young," he finally remarked. "Not a strand of grey hair on you."

"Yeah?" replied Ben Loy unenthusiastically.

"Some people get grey pretty young. Even in their early twenties."

The record player continued with *Gim Peng Moy*. Second Uncle was about to be seduced by his brother's wife. The crashing of cymbals and blocks testified to the urgency of the action. Even the barber stopped his barbering momentarily to concentrate on the climax of this opera. Ben Loy was listening attentively too; but it was obvious that he was not enjoying it as much as he should.

"Many years ago when they had the opera house right here on the Bowery," volunteered Ah Mow, "whenever they played *Gim Peng Moy,* they played to standing room only."

"Everybody is interested in sex," cut in Ah Sing, who had kept quiet up to now.

"Everybody but you, you dead boy. You're dead," said Ah Mow pleasantly to his employee. Then the cymbals and blocks became so loud that talk was impossible and they waited for the music to subside. "Some girls nowadays aren't worth a copper penny," he resumed expectantly. "Just like Gim Peng Moy." He watched for any change of expression on Ben Loy's face. His eyes almost touched the customer's face, who seemed to wince. The proprietor waited for him to say something. Then he saw the lips slowly part. But Ben Loy opened them only to compress them. He began to hate himself for having come into this hole of a basement. He should have waited at the other barbershop, he told himself. But how could they be talking about him? They don't even know him. They certainly don't know Mei Oi.

He closed his eyes tightly and tried to relax, pretending to listen intently to the long-playing record. But his thoughts took him back to the conversation at hand. He could hear the . . . *chop . . . chop* . . . of the scissors. . . . Girls nowadays aren't worth a copper penny. Just Gim Peng Moy . . .

Is Mei Oi like Gim Peng Moy? Is she? No, she can't be!

When he got home, he told his wife he was tired and wanted to lie down and rest.

"Yes, you must be tired," said his wife tenderly. "You'll feel much better after a rest." Immediately she was sorry she had said it. She wished she had asked him to go out to buy something for her so she could call Ah Song. She would ask him yet. She got up and tiptoed to the bedroom and gently pushed open the door. Her husband was curled up in bed in street clothes, minus his shoes, apparently already asleep. Let him sleep. With another wifely glance at Ben Loy, she walked brusquely back to the living room and put away the knitting needles. She must hurry. Ah Song had no set date to drop in to see her. All he knew was that Wednesday was Ben Loy's day off. What if he should show up today, Thursday? As noiselessly as she could, she dialed Ah Song's number. The silence between rings seemed endless, like the Pacific Ocean. The moments ticked away like a whole lifetime until finally someone answered the phone.

"Hello?"

"Uncle Song?" Mei Oi whispered. Her heart pounded hard and fast, and she began to perspire. "This is Mei Oi. Ben Loy is home. Yes, he's taking a few days off. Don't come up to the house until you hear from me. No, I can't talk to you anymore. Bye." She hung up. She was frightened. It was the first time she had ever called Ah Song. The mere thought of it made her feel ashamed. She gently pushed open the bedroom door. Ben Loy was still asleep. Seeing him there, sound asleep, she felt safe and undiscovered.

For many weeks Ah Song had been bringing Mei Oi chickens, pork chops, herbs and Ng Gar Pai, all deemed nutritious for the expectant mother. There was always a pot or two boiling on the range in Mei Oi's apartment. When Ben Loy came home at night, he would walk over to the range, lift up the lid, and sniff at the concoction.

"That's pig tail," Mei Oi would call out. "It's good for my back."

He never asked her where she got the pig's tail; he assumed she bought it herself. Ben Loy himself had gone out once and bought a pullet when Mei Oi complained of dizziness. Chicken and herbs and whiskey, brewed in a double boiler, would be very beneficial to her. Not being a drinking woman, a few drops would make her face like Quon Gung's, the red-faced hero of the *Three Kingdoms*. Even sipping the soup brewed with whiskey made her face red. But she liked these things. She liked even more the attentions that came with them. She enjoyed being sick and eating these liquid foods. And it made her especially happy when Ah Song came with all these things.

As she resumed her knitting in the living room, her heart continued to throb rapidly. The great pleasures she got from her indiscretions were worth the risk, she assured herself. Later when she walked into the bedroom, Ben Loy stirred.

"What's the matter, can't you sleep?" Mei Oi asked softly.

"No, I can't sleep," he replied drowsily. Slowly he brought himself up to a sitting position, with his feet dangling from the edge of the bed. "I think I'll go see a movie."

"But you have just come back from one," Mei Oi protested.

"I'm going uptown to see an American movie."

"Eat something before you go. I'm going to cook now."

"I'm not hungry." With that he walked out of the room.

Once out on the street, instead of going uptown, he turned north on East Broadway and headed for the Chinese Theater. He purchased a ticket without bothering to find out what was playing. After an hour or so in the theater, he couldn't keep his mind on the screen. He didn't know what was playing and he didn't care. The ghost of Gim Peng Moy kept hammering at his consciousness. Is Mei Oi the same type of woman as Gim Peng Moy? Does she belong to the "nowadays women are no good" brand of human beings? What is she doing at this very moment?

On the screen, the leading man was singing a love song.

Ben Loy got up abruptly and bolted out of the theater. He sped home as fast as his legs could carry him. As he inserted his key to the apartment door, he was full of violence and suspicion. The next minute he was calm, sheepish, and full of good will. Mei Oi was on the couch, knitting, just as he had left her.

29

The next day, during the lull between lunch and dinner, Chin Yuen called from the restaurant to find out how his old friend, Ben Loy, was getting along. Mei Oi answered the phone.

"Hello, is Ben Loy home?" asked Chin Yuen.

"No, he is not home. Who is this?"

"This is Chin Yuen," he announced. The voice at the other end sounded soothing and exciting to the former schoolmaster.

"Oh, Mr. Chin, you're working for Ben Loy."

"Yes, I'm calling to find out how he is."

"He's much better. Thank you. You need not worry."

"I hope he'll be able to come back to work soon." Chin Yuen made his voice as pleasant as he possibly could.

"He's all right now," assured Mei Oi. "There's nothing the matter with him. You have a very kind heart to call."

"Kind of you to say that," said Chin Yuen, delighted at her sweet voice. He smiled into the receiver.

"You have a kind heart. Thank you." A gleam appeared in Chin Yuen's eyes as he hung up. "Please come and visit us." He wondered if Ben Loy's wife still remembered him from the brief meeting when he had dropped in to welcome them on their arrival in New York. Ben Loy had introduced him to his wife as an old friend. He had been asked to stay for dinner, but had found it necessary to decline. Ever since then Chin Yuen had regretted his inability to accept this dinner engagement. For, if he had stayed for dinner, he would have had the opportunity to become more familiar with Mei Oi. He hoped for another such invitation, but none had come.

Perhaps an invitation to dinner was too big a face to expect; so he began to entertain the thought that some day his old friend might invite him to his home for tea. He supposed that, after all, there was much work involved in the preparation of a dinner. But tea . . . was different.

Chin Yuen went to an empty booth in the rear of the dining room and sat down. A few moments later another waiter joined him.

"How is Ben Loy today?" asked the waiter.

"I just called his home. His wife said he is much better."

"His wife? Did you talk to his wife?"

"Sure. What's wrong with that?"

"Nothing, except . . . except that . . . that people say his wife is seeing another man. Oop—I shouldn't have talked."

Chin Yuen shook his head in disbelief, startled at the disclosure. To him Ben Loy seemed a little boy, lost in the wilderness, not knowing which way to turn. That first night with Ben Loy at the Hotel Lansing flashed back to him. The night of the big snow. Ben Loy then was a naive, likable lad. He hadn't changed much. . . . But who could this other fellow be? Chin Yuen thought he was the only one, aside from Ben Loy's father and father-in-law, to have set foot inside his apartment. There was a scintilla of jealousy on the part of Chin Yuen, who admitted to himself that he might have been the other man in the love theft if it had not been for his friendship for the husband. Now, with the revelation of Mei Oi's infidelity, he felt a personal challenge in the situation.

30

Inadvertently one Sunday, Lee Gong overheard snatches of conversation drifting from a nearby table while sipping coffee at the Coffee Cup on Bayard Street. The stools at the counter were all taken. Lee Gong was at the end stool, and the five tables were occupied. The gossipers were three men sitting at a table next to the end of the counter.

"Did you know that Wang Wah Gay's son is wearing a *green hat* and he doesn't even know it?" said the thin man whose back was turned to Lee Gong. While his hand, now a little shaky, brought the cup's brim to his mouth, Lee Gong did not drink it. His ears strained for the conversation at the table.

"Nowadays girls are no damned good," said the second man.

"Yeah," said the third, "a stinky fish matched with a stinky shrimp."

Lee Gong toyed with his coffee. When he replaced the cup on the saucer, he drew out a cigarette, but his shaking hands made lighting it difficult.

"They say this guy goes up to her apartment when her husband is at work."

A steady stream of customers kept pressing through the door, coming and going. Finally, with one gulp, Lee Gong finished his coffee and left hurriedly. He was afraid of meeting someone he knew who might have heard the conversation. The very thought made his face darken. The veins stood out around the temples.

Outside the coffee shop, the fresh air was a welcome relief. Slowly he walked on Mott Street, with bowed head. . . . These sonovabitches are liars . . . I like to cup open their bellies . . . Mei Oi would do no such things . . . troublemakers . . . these people are troublemakers . . . the name of the man involved was not mentioned. . . . Liars. . . . Could this happen to me, Lee Gong? . . . A good thing it had not been Wah Gay who was sitting there . . . listening . . . for he patronized the place several times a day . . .

Someone called "Uncle Gong" to him on the street but he did not hear him and continued walking toward his apartment. He climbed the stairs slowly, sighing heavily with each step. . . . Mei Oi . . . why did you do this to me? . . . to your mother? . . .

He fumbled for the key and finally he stuck the wrong one in the key hole. He cursed furiously. Once inside he sank down on his single folding bed and buried his head in the pillow. . . . If Ben Loy were a bad boy . . . a husband who goes after other women . . . it might be excusable . . . but Ben Loy is a good boy . . . a good husband . . . a good provider . . . a conscientious worker . . . he's the kind of son-in-law anyone would pick . . . no vice of any kind . . .

He flopped over and lay on his back. He was breathing heavily, like a physically wounded man. It was strange to find himself in his room at this time of day. He should be at Wah Gay's clubhouse playing mah-jong, which was what he had planned to do after his cup of coffee. He stared absently at the coal stove with its blackened chimney sticking into the wall.

He had lived in this room for more than twenty years. Twenty years is a long time. Maybe this room is unlucky. . . . Look what happened to his old roommate Lee Sam . . . still at the hospital somewhere on Long Island. . . .

Sam was working in a laundry when one night two men came in to beat and rob him . . . after that he was never the same . . . he kept saying that someone was after him . . . someone was looking through the plate glass at him with a butcher knife . . . finally they had to come and take him away . . . maybe this room brings bad luck . . . Sooner or later the scandal about Mei Oi will get back to the village . . . the whole village will hear about it . . . Lee

Gong's daughter . . . hardly two years in America . . . look what has happened to her . . . I don't care for myself because I'm here in New York . . . just feel sorry for the old female rice cooker in the village . . . she has no place to hide . . . no place to go . . . in New York it is different . . . maybe . . . maybe all this talk is nonsense . . . still why should people make up such a story? . . .

After a long while he got up and walked over to the window facing Mott Street. Directly across from him was the Congregational church. Lee Gong had never gone inside that church except to try his luck on the dice tables when the church ran a bazaar. He stared down at the church for a full minute, picturing himself going to church for any other reason than to play dice. This thought almost brought a suppressed chuckle. . . . Had she been a little older, she would have been in a better position to judge things for herself . . . she was like a child lost in thick forest . . . perhaps it would have been better if she had been permitted to marry a schoolteacher instead of marrying Ben Loy and coming to New York . . .

But like all fathers in the village, Lee Gong had wanted to do the right thing, marry his daughter off to a *gimshunhock*. And in Wang Ben Loy, he thought he had found the most eligible bachelor. He knew Ben Loy was a good boy and a conscientious worker. A handsome lad without vice. What more could a prospective father-in-law want in a son-in-law? Ben Loy was the embodiment of the perfect son-in-law. Who could have forecast what was going to happen in less than two short years? In another two years maybe Lee Gong himself would be dead and buried, dead of a heartache. But even his death would not prevent people from talking: Lee Gong's daughter knitted a nice green hat for her husband to wear and it fitted him perfectly.

Slowly Lee Gong rose from his bed again. It was his usual time to eat but he was not hungry. He didn't think he would feel like eating for many days to come. He could never sleep tonight if he didn't hear from the lips of Mei Oi what had happened.

He walked across the converging traffic at Chatham Square without noticing the lights or the traffic and a north-bound car on Park Row screeched to a stop. The driver shouted, "Hey, why don't you watch where you're goin'!" But Lee Gong continued on to the sidewalk without so much as turning his head.

He became confused as to which street to turn to for Mei Oi's apartment. He seldom had been on this side of Chatham Square. The last time was when he visited Mei Oi upon her arrival in New York. It was only when he came upon the school building that he knew that Mei Oi's apartment was close by. He remembered the little candy store on the ground floor. Satisfied that he was at the right place, he wearily climbed the stairs. His feet dragged. He mounted the steps as if he were carrying a hundred pounds of rice on his back. He had to grab at the railing to pull himself up.

Although there was a button for the bell, he knocked on the glass panel of the door and called out hoarsely, "Mei Oi, Mei Oi!" Through the glass panel he could see the lights come on in the apartment. Then he could hear the shuffling of feet.

"Who are you?" a woman's voice called from inside.

"Mei Oi, open the door. This is your papa." The voice sounded urgent in the darkened hallway.

The door swung open. "Papa, come in," invited Mei Oi in a surprised tone.

Lee Gong walked in without saying anything. Mei Oi led him into the living room, where he sank down on the big armchair. "Mei Oi," the father began accusingly, "why did you do this to me?"

"Do what?" asked Mei Oi. "What are you talking about, Papa?"

"Today when I was having a cup of coffee at the Coffee Cup, I overheard three people talking about Wah Gay's daughter-in-law. *You* are Wang Wah Gay's daughter-in-law, aren't you?" Lee Gong stared fiercely at his daughter. "They said this Wang Wah Gay's daughter-in-law knitted a *green hat* for her husband to wear!" he roared.

"Where did you get such a story?" demanded Mei Oi, shaken by the accusation.

"I just told you where I got it from. Are you deaf?"

"Propaganda," said Mei Oi. "Rumors. Just many-mouthed birds spreading rumors." She was terrified of her father.

"If it's not true, why should people talk like that about you?" retorted Lee Gong.

"I don't know." Mei Oi searched frantically for an appropriate answer, trying to pull her thoughts together, fearing that her father might be enraged enough to strike her. Her mind was a blank. She couldn't think. After a long time, she added uneasily, "I have no control over their mouths."

"Such talk will ruin me. Ruin you. Ruin Ben Loy and Wah Gay," said Lee Gong, his face flushed. He waved a menacing finger at Mei Oi. "Have you no shame?"

"Papa, I did nothing wrong," she sobbed. She had never seen her father this angry before. "Don't listen to what others say."

He had no proof of Mei Oi's infidelity. As a father, Lee Gong was already experiencing a mixture of bitterness and pity. He was bitter because he felt his own daughter had brought disgrace upon himself. He was condescendingly compassionate because Mei Oi was so young, so naive and ignorant of life-things.

"If you didn't do anything wrong, why do people talk this way?" growled the father.

"I told you I don't know." Mei Oi's heart sank and she was full of shame.

"If you did do anything wrong, consider yourself no longer my daughter," said Lee Gong. "I have no such daughter."

"Please don't be angry, Father," said Mei Oi. "I'll make you some coffee." She got up to go to the kitchen.

"Don't bother," said the father. "I just had a cup before I came up."

"Maybe you'll stay for dinner then," said the daughter, trying frantically to change the subject. How could she confess such a faceless thing to her own father? It might have been easier if she had known him all her life.

"No. I'm leaving!" Lee Gong jumped up and, without saying another word, stalked out of the apartment.

"Don't worry, Papa," Mei Oi called after him. "You don't have to worry about anything." Then she burst into tears.

31

Mei Oi's vehement denial left Lee Gong unconvinced of his daughter's innocence. He kept asking himself: If it isn't true, why do people say such things about my daughter? Why did they mention Wang Wah Gay's daughter-in-law and not someone else's? He wondered how many people had heard of this face-losing affair of Mei Oi. What hurt the old man most was that Mei Oi was an only child, a son and daughter rolled into one. In a family of many children, one should expect some bad ones, but an only child such as Mei Oi—she is her parents' whole world. A father with many children could take solace in the soundness of the good ones. But Lee Gong had no other children to turn to. At a time when he needed the comfort and sympathy of his wife most, she was many thousands of li away. His whole body shook with anguish. Who is this scoundrel who had wronged his daughter? He wanted to pump his body full of bullets. Then he could die peacefully.

Lee Gong grabbed the bottle of Ng Gar Pai from the table next to the bed and poured himself a full glass. He downed it quickly. He kept it there for mild insomnia. When he tossed in bed and found it impossible to sleep, he would reach for the bottle and pour himself a drink. Then he would sleep like a child. But never before had he felt the urge to resort to the bottle during the day. Even when he drank at night, it was done in moderation. He never downed a full glass in one gulp.

An hour later, the bottle was empty. He decided to write a note to Ah Song; for he had concluded that Ah Song was the number one suspect. . . . Mei Oi had been in New York less than two years. . . . During that period, who could have had the chance to know her well enough to bring on the scandal? . . . Ben Loy had been a good boy, above reproach. . . . If Mei Oi had married an old man, as some girls do, it might have been excusable for her to seek a young lover. . . . But Ben Loy and Mei Oi were the same age and they had every reason to be happily married. . . .

He poured some thick black ink into the dried inkwell, which held a piece of black-stained cotton. He used the writing brush only when he wrote to his wife Jung Shee. But now he wanted to impress Ah Song with his businesslike determination, and he thought a writing brush and blank ink would convey his feelings with added dignity. He began to write with strong, steady strokes, quickly and without hesitation.

Ah Song, you dead boy: In accordance with our Chinese culture, you have committed an unpardonable sin. Kung-fu-tze had said "male and female are not to mix socially." You have brought shame and dishonor to an otherwise honorable family. If you do not stop seeing this housewife immediately, you will have an unfortunate ending. You will not be warned again. You know what I mean. If you value your life, leave this woman alone! From one who fights injustice.

He paused and reread the message before inserting it in an envelope and addressing it. Unsteadily he made his way downstairs to mail the letter. After he dropped the letter into the mailbox at the corner of Mott and Bayard streets, he felt a sense of great accomplishment. He would now sit back and watch for the results of his missive.

As he walked back to his lonely room on the top floor, Lee Gong's shoulders sagged noticeably. Dusk was fast descending upon Chinatown, and a sudden, sharp wind twirled in the sky. Lee Gong grabbed at his left shoulder with his right hand and then banged his fist against it several times, futilely. Damned rheumatism! He looked up at the threatening sky. He breathed deeply, defiantly, the rain-filled air. Yes, he said to himself, it will rain tonight.

32

The president of the Wang Association glanced at his watch and it was only a quarter to one. He would wait until one o'clock and then call Wah Gay. His cousin was not one to get up early, Wang Chuck Ting thought to himself.

His mind flashed back to the day of the Grand Opening of the Wang Association Building in 1934. The chair and desk set where he now sat was a gift from the Ping On Tong on that auspicious occasion. Back in the thirties he had been president of Ping On Tong, and during those years he had appointed Wah Gay a member of the deliberating committee. Now after so many active years in Tong politics, he enjoyed the status of an elder statesman. No longer a candidate for any Tong office, he was a friend of everybody. He had a reputation for fair dealing and everybody respected him for this. His China Pagoda in Stanton served as a semiretirement hangout for him. He was perennially elected president of the Wangs, although he himself had declared he did not want the job.

In another moment he was angry. Angry that his cousin Wah Gay should have the misfortune to be involved in a scandal. It wasn't his cousin's fault, of course, but the good name of the family was at stake. Not only Wah Gay's family, but all the Wangs would lose face if some means could not be found to hush this whispering campaign that was finding its way into attentive and eager ears in the shops and rooms of Chinatown. He consulted his watch again and deftly picked up the receiver and dialed a number.

"Hello? Elder brother Wah Gay? This is Chuck Ting."

"How are you, Chuck Ting *gaw*?" answered Wah Gay gleefully. "What is it now?"

"There is a small matter I'd like to talk to you about," he said.

"Where are you now?"

"I'm at the social club."

"Okay. I'll come up in a few minutes."

Wah Gay had no idea what the president wanted him for. As he walked toward the five-story Wang Association Building on Mott Street, he wondered if his cousin might want him to act as co-signer for some cousin who wanted to borrow money. Two months ago Chuck Ting had called him for just such a purpose. Why can't he get someone else for a co-signer this time?

The social club was filled with smoke and people when Wah Gay opened the door to what was formerly apartments two and three. Their common wall had been torn down to convert them into a social gathering place for the Wangs and their friends in New York. He heard the clack of mah-jonggs even before the door was opened. The mah-jongg table was in the center of the room. Several elbow-rubbers sat watching and kibitzing. Ah Ton was preparing dinner in the tiny alcove to the right. A heavy blue apron hung loosely on his person.

"Ah Ton gaw, cooking rice so early?" asked Wah Gay when he saw Ah Ton with a dipper in his hand.

"Not early, brother. Not early," replied Ah Ton. He was a dark and lanky man in his early sixties.

"Want to play a game?" someone invited Wah Gay.

"Come here and take my place," enticed another.

"No, thank you," said Wah Gay, raising his hand in mild protest. "I'm busy. I'm here to see the president."

"He's in there," said someone, pointing to an inner office.

Without knocking, Wah Gay pushed open the door. He backed out quickly when he saw the president was engaged in conversation with someone else. He turned to while away the time by joining the kibitzers and putting his nose close to the mah-jong table. He lit a cigar and contributed to the smoke floating about the room.

"Wow your mother, I should have won this hand!"

"You illegitimate boy, consider yourself lucky."

"You guys would rather talk than play."

Smoke clouds filled the room and the aroma of cigars and cigarettes vied with the odors of Ah Ton's cooking.

The door to the inner office opened and a man stepped out, followed by Chuck Ting. The latter motioned for Wah Gay to enter.

He indicated a chair for him. "I have a little bad news for you," began Chuck Ting painfully. He interlocked his fingers and twirled his thumbs. He swung on the swivel chair and came face-to-face with his visitor. "It concerns your daughter-in-law."

"*My* daughter-in-law?" asked Wah Gay, startled. He tried not to look alarmed. "What about her?" He was more curious than shocked.

"I got my story from my boy, and he got it from his wife," continued Chuck Ting. "He came out here and told me about it the other day. Said something about his wife hearing about it in a beauty salon on Mulberry Street last Sunday. . . ."

Wah Gay sat numbed and speechless. His earlier nonchalance was gone. But, as serious as the matter sounded, he was confident that there was nothing to it. What could his daughter-in-law do wrong? After all, she had been in New York only a year and a half. What could be so terribly bad about her? And Ben Loy was a good boy too. . . .

"I'm talking to you as a brother. As an elder brother, not as president of the Association. There's nothing official about this. . . ." He paused to light a cigar and began puffing on it until it glowed. Then, as if he had committed an unpardonable sin, he hurriedly pulled another cigar out of his inside pocket and apologetically offered it to Wah Gay, who accepted it with thanks. "I hope this matter will never be taken up by the Association," continued Chuck Ting. "It would be too much of a disgrace. Maybe a little talk will smooth out this whole thing. But it has to be confidential."

Wah Gay did not interrupt. He waited for his cousin to continue.

"Nowadays the young are not like what they used to be," resumed Chuck Ting. "They have no respect for their elders. They are all out for a good time. They don't know right from wrong."

He paused to throw out a stream of smoke from his cigar. His face tensed and a pained expression appeared. The easy flow of language was no longer there. "That sonovabitch Ah Song is absolutely useless!" he roared. Only the fear that someone outside the office might hear him made him lower his voice. "He has a history of being a stinky dead snake. Everybody knows that. It has gotten out that your daughter-in-law and Ah Song are seeing each other. Now you see how this thing has gotten around. Even in Connecticut people have heard about it. You can see how far this thing has gone."

"Ah Song?" Wah Gay refused to believe it. "Ah Song and my daughter-in-law?" He was stunned. "If someone else were to tell me this, I would not believe it. We all know he's a rascal but I would never have thought he would do this to me. I have known him for more than twenty years. Every day he plays mah-jong in my basement. . . ."

"There are all sorts of people," said Chuck Ting. "The bad will always be bad. A person like Ah Song would gouge out his father's eyes."

"I'm going to wrench his head off," said Wah Gay angrily.

"His type you should no longer allow in your basement," said Chuck Ting. "Don't even let him set foot inside your threshold."

"I wish we had some proof. Some proof that he is seeing this good-for-nothing daughter-in-law of mine!"

"Women cannot be trusted," said Chuck Ting. "I've always told my boy to run his family with a firm hand."

"And we always say that *jook sing* girls are no good," sighed Wah Gay. "That's why everybody goes back to China to get married. A village girl will make a good wife, they say. She will not run around. She can tell right from wrong. She will stay home and cook rice for you."

After the initial outburst against Ah Song, the crimson on the president's face had disappeared and he was now calmer. "No one can foretell everything," he said, once more swinging on his chair. "We'll have to keep this quiet. At least as quiet as we can."

"I have no face to meet my friends," said Wah Gay sadly.

"I don't think you should say anything to Lee Gong about it yet. What has happened, has happened. As soon as I heard of this thing, I thought I would let you know first. I don't want you to be the last to find out."

"You have always been a good brother," said Way Gay. "And I know you will always do the right thing."

"You can go back now." Chuck Ting got up and stretched his arms. "Keep everything quiet."

On his way out, Wah Gay waved good-bye perfunctorily to those gathered at the table. The moment he stepped out of sight, voices began talking all at once in hushed tones.

"I'll bet he was talking about his daughter-in-law," whispered someone at the table.

"He always said what a fine boy his son was," said another.

"What's the boy got to do with it?" demanded another. "It's the girl, the wife."

"Yeah, it's that good-for-nothing bitch!"

"Someone should make an example of that Ah Song or whatever his name is," said the third man.

"We ought to hang him."

"No, it would be better to cut his throat."

Just then the president emerged from his office, and an unusual silence fell. He stuck his hands in his pants pockets and started to make light talk. "Who's winning? Who is going to buy coffee?"

"Hey, Uncle Ton," said the man who had the most chips in front of him, "go and get some coffee, will you?" He toyed with the chips and then dug into his pocket and pulled out two singles. "Here, get us some coffee and pastry."

"Wow your mother," said the man opposite him. "We're going to eat soon. Why do we have to get coffee now? They say a cup of coffee spoils a bowl of rice."

"Wow his mother. He's jealous because someone is spending a couple of dollars."

Without saying a word, Ah Ton came over and, hurriedly wiping clean his hands on the apron, grabbed the two dollars that were extended to him.

Over coffee the cousins continued to discuss the case of the *green hat,* after one of them had broken the ice by cautiously saying, "By the way, Chairman, did you hear about a recent scandal involving one of our own members?"

But Chuck Ting cautioned his cousins not to discuss the matter with outsiders, adding, "Family shame is not for the outsider."

33

Shortly after his return to work, Ben Loy received a call from his father, asking him to come to see him on his day off. Ben Loy had asked his father to talk over the phone, but the elder

Wang replied that the matter could not be discussed over the telephone.

The following Wednesday Ben Loy steeled himself for the ordeal of meeting his father. He had always dreaded talking to the old man; for there existed a stern relationship between a Chinese father and his son. The prevailing practice is for neither to speak to the other unless he has to. As he walked toward the Money Come Club, the thought foremost on his mind was to get out of his father's place as soon as possible. Perhaps his father had another one of those letters from his mother. What could a letter from Lau Shee contain? The usual things: "Need more money, send more home." Or: "What is Ben Loy and Lee Shee waiting for? I'm getting old. I want a grandchild before I close my eyes . . ."

When he tried the door, it was locked. He took a quarter from his pocket and knocked on the glass panel. Tap . . . tap . . . tap. There was no movement within. Then he put his nose against the glass, and he could see the silhouette of his father in the darkened interior hurrying to open the door.

"Come in," the elder Wang greeted.

"Did I wake you up?" Ben Loy stepped inside.

"No, I woke up a long time ago. I didn't bother to get up. I was reading the papers in bed." The father fiddled with the belt of his bathrobe. "Sit down. I'll be with you in a moment."

Even with the hundred-watt bulb burning in the middle of the room directly above the mah-jongg table, the room looked dingy. To Ben Loy, having just come in from the sunlight, the room was like a dimly lit tunnel. As the minutes ticked by, he began to discern the various objects in the room. He felt a dampness coursing through his body. This he attributed to his unfamiliarity with the place. This was really the first time he had sat in the room. Previously he had been in and out, like a mailman. He wrinkled his nose. "It's like a dungeon," he said to himself. Only an old man like his father cound stand a shut-in dingy place like this. It seemed a long time before Wah Gay came out.

"Ben Loy," he began slowly, taking a seat almost opposite from his son. "I've heard some very distressing news. Do you have any idea what it is?"

"No," he replied sulkily.

"I've heard from reliable sources that Ah Sow is running around with another man. Is that true?" His voice was stern but his manner was not unpleasant. He placed his palms on his lap and leaned forward. "I want to listen to the truth."

The question exploded on Ben Loy like ten thousand firecrackers. It took him several seconds to recover from the shock. "This is the

first time I've heard of it," he said nervously but defiantly. He
pursed his lips. His first reaction was to dash out of the place, but he
changed his mind and waited.

"It is your business to find out!" Wah Gay raised his voice,
jumping to his feet. "She's *your* wife, not mine." He gestured
vigorously with his hands. "It's a disgrace. Maybe you feel no
shame, but I do!" He started pacing the floor. He whirled and faced
his son. "People will say Wang Wah Gay's daughter-in-law is running around. They don't say *your* wife is running around!"

"Where did you get the news from?" demanded Ben Loy, not
knowing what else to say. "It's all a lie," he added weakly.

"I hope it is," Wah Gay growled. "I hope it is. But when people
talk like that, it's my business to find out!"

"People can say anything they want," retorted the son.

"But why should people say such a thing if it's not true?" the
father demanded impatiently, clenching his fists. "Can you tell me
that?"

"How should I know?" Ben Loy shot back. "I have no control
over other people's mouths."

"No, but you can find out if it's true or not." Wah Gay shook a
finger at his son. "People just don't talk for nothing. There must be
a reason." He paused for an answer, but there was none. "Some
people are stupid, but they are stupid only to a degree," continued
the exasperated father. "Not like you. Unless your wife is no good,
people don't say she's no good!"

Ben Loy stormed out of the clubhouse and slammed the door
behind him.

"Wow your mother," Wah Gay shouted after him, his face red
and his veins bulging with anger. "You think because you can open
and shut your eyelids, you're a human being? You dead boy!" He
rushed up to the door and flipped the latch on the lock. "Sonava-
bitch!" His whole body shook with rage. Foolish. How foolish it was
to get this no-good dead son to this country in the first place! Should
have left him in the village to work the fields . . .

The end of the world came crashing down upon the shoulders of
Wah Gay. He saw in his son a renegade. A no-good loafer. A
stupid, useless youth. A son who would disgrace his own father. He
had lost his one and only son. He and his wife had lived for the boy.
The hopes of grandparenthood were just emerging over the horizon
and they could see in their future many grandchildren. Wah Gay
had enjoyed thoroughly the pleasant task of writing to his wife Lau
Shee, informing her that Ah Sow was at last with child. This, he
assumed, had only been the first of such missives. For indeed, in
America, with the best possible nutrition, babies would come as

regularly as the harvest. Lau Shee would announce proudly to their cousins in the village: Our Ben Loy has another son. And then there would be celebrations. There would be thanksgiving at the temples for Mei Oi's mother. Tiny feet and tiny voices would come in to see Grandpa. . . .

But this beautiful picture was only a dream, a dream mirrored in the subconscious fantasy of the man. A mirror shattered by the alleged scandal of Ben Loy's wife. A mirror shattered and irreparable. The destruction of a beautiful picture. Wah Gay sighed an agonizing sigh, alone and to himself. What was there for him to do? Ben Loy had denied any wrongdoing by his wife. If Ben Loy did not care, why should the old man care?

The private meeting with Chuck Ting flooded his mind. But how could *he* stop it? He had just tried . . . with Ben Loy. What about Lee Shee? Could he talk to her? No. That would be out of the question. She is much closer to her husband than to her father-in-law. But the old man would be the first to feel the brunt of scandal-talk. Once this hushed whispering burst into lively coffee shop topics, where could an old-timer like Wah Gay hide? Get out of town? He would have to! The father-in-law gets out of town because the daughter-in-law misbehaves. What a farce that would make. One would think the father-in-law was a party to this misconduct.

If he hadn't sunk such deep roots in New York, Wah Gay would find it easier to pull up his stakes and disappear. After more than forty years in the community, a sudden uprooting would be bound to have repercussions. If he were to go elsewhere, say Boston or Washington, D.C., he had many friends there too. How could he face them? Through his membership in the Ping On Tong, he had made many contacts with out-of-town delegates when they came to New York for their conventions. Frequently these friends had come in and played mah-jong at his clubhouse. They had sipped coffee together. Now when he needed to get out of town, the choice of site for his exile became agonizingly difficult. What would he say to his friends if they should ask him: Why did you leave New York after so many years? His type of business demanded a large enough city to have a number of mah-jong players. True, he could always go back to the restaurant business, but he was not yet ready for such a drastic move. At his age he would consider that only as a last resort. The prospect of returning to manual labor made the old man shake his head, more in shame than in self-pity. He had worked hard and long to leave the drudgery of the restaurant business for the semiretirement of the mah-jong game. Returning to it now would be humiliating.

To write to his wife, Lau Shee, informing her of what had happened to her daughter-in-law, would be an insurmountable task. What words could he compose that would not bring tears and heartache to the recipient? That his own son is the wearer of a *green hat*? The mere words *green hat* would strike terror and shame to anyone capable of human emotions. Like typhoid or polio.

His head spun with pains. Big pains. As big as a boulder. Now this boulder came tumbling out of the sky, like an exhausted satellite, and crash-landed on Wah Gay's head. The basement clubhouse suddenly was dark and empty.

34

When Ben Loy bolted out of his father's clubhouse that afternoon, he was fuming. Although he had long feared the possibility of an erring wife, he had not expected to hear of it from the lips of his own father. First he was shocked, then angry. He was all the more enraged because he had been told by the old man. This made it somehow official.

Anything that is officially reported must be acted upon. If it had been just a rumor, he might have been able to turn the other way, pretending he was deaf. But to be informed by one's own father of his wife's infidelity, that was the end of all pretense. How could he deny the allegations when he himself had no basis for this denial? He had planned to take Mei Oi to a movie uptown after his visit to his father, but now he did not feel like taking her to anything. In his mind he tried to formulate something concrete, something sensible to say to her. If his wife had to go to bed with another man, why did she have to be discovered? The discovery of an act is even more humiliating than the act itself. Impotency, when it is confined to the bedroom, may be condoned; but when it becomes public gossip, it is mortifying. Ben Loy was most concerned about any publicity over the cause of his wife's infidelity. Try as he would to dismiss the subject matter as inconsequential, the humiliation and jealousy that raged within him could not be tamed.

When Ben Loy arrived home, Mei Oi was getting dressed to go out with her husband. She had on one of her long Chinese gowns, which she had grown fond of wearing lately. As he rushed into the bedroom, she was applying makeup to her face and neck.

"You don't have to doll up so much now," he jeered sarcastically.

The startled Mei Oi turned to meet his eyes. At first she hoped he was joking. After one look at him, she knew he was not. "Loy Gaw," she said uncertainly, "I don't understand. Are you angry?"

"You want me to draw a picture for you?" he retorted.

"Not a picture," she said, "but at least tell me what's troubling you." She moved toward him to throw her arms around him, but Ben Loy pushed her away.

"Keep away from me!" he shouted. "You dirty my hands."

"Whatever it is, please tell me," pleaded Mei Oi. "I hope my husband is not an insane man."

"Insane?" Ben Loy rushed up and stared fiercely at her, showing his teeth. "Is that what you call it, insane?" Shaking with anger, he clenched his fists.

"I was merely saying I hope you're not insane because of the way you act."

"The way I act! If a man objects to his wife sleeping with another man, is that insane? Tell me! Is that insane?"

"I . . . I don't know what you're talking about . . ."

"You knitted a nice green hat for me, that's what."

"It's not true."

"You're lying!"

"I'm not! You're the one who's lying."

"You lying sonovabitch!" He slapped her across the face.

She bowed her head and started to whimper, first softly, then loudly, then uncontrollably.

"You wife-beater, that's the only thing you know how. What kind of a husband have you been? Why don't you ask yourself that? Why don't you . . ."

"Who was it? Tell me who was the sonovabitch who slept with you. Are you trying to protect him? Sooner or later I'll find out, and when I do, I'll kill him! You just wait and see. I'll kill him!"

"I didn't do anything wrong . . . I didn't do anything wrong . . . I thought I've married a young man . . . but it turns out that I've married an old man . . . an old man who's too old to make love to me. . . ."

"Shut up, you useless woman!" Ben Loy backed out of the room. "If it were not for your pregnancy, I would have beaten you to death. Just remember that."

She continued to sob uncontrollably, with her head buried in her arms, lying on the bed. Ben Loy wished he could make her tell him who the guilty man was. He would put a hole through his body. He would. The invasion of his privacy was unbearable. He felt that the violation of something as sacred as his marriage, if permitted to go unchallenged, would make his the greenest and biggest hat of them all.

Still fuming, he returned to the bedroom.

"That baby you've got there, it's not mine! Whose is it?"

There was no answer. Mei Oi was lying on her side, facing away from the doorway, sobbing. The slits on her long dress exposed her thighs.

"That baby! Whose is it?" Ben Loy roared. Anger took reign within him. He rushed up to the bed and picked up his leather slipper from the floor. His hand must have come down at least half a dozen times. Then, perspiring, spent, and dazed, he walked out of the apartment, leaving behind the wailing and terrified Mei Oi.

Frank Chin
(1940–   )

In his anthology, *Asian American Heritage,* editor David Wand
called Frank Chin "the conscience of Asian American writing."
Others have called him "the Godfather" of Asian American writing
or have dismissed him as a relic of the sixties emulating black
revolutionaries.

Frank Chin is the most outspoken and controversial Asian American writer working. Critic, essayist, fiction maker, playwright, Chin
has called himself a Chinaman writer. He is the author of two plays,
The Chickencoop Chinaman and *The Year of the Dragon*, both
produced in New York at The American Place Theatre and published in one volume in 1981 by the University of Washington Press.

A volume of eight short stories and an afterword by Frank Chin,
The Chinaman Pacific & Frisco R.R. Co., was published by Coffee
House Press (Minneapolis) in 1988.

The Only Real Day

The men played mah-jong or passed the waterpipe, their voices low
under the sound of the fish pumps thudding into the room from the
tropical fish store. Voices became louder over other voices in the
thickening heat. Yuen was with his friends now, where he was
always happy and loud every Tuesday night. All the faces shone of
skin oily from the heat and laughter, the same as last week, the
same men and room and waterpipe. Yuen knew them. Here it was
comfortable after another week of that crippled would-be Hollywood Oriental-for-a-friend in Oakland. He hated the sight of cripples on his night and day off, and one had spoken to him as stepped

off the A train into the tinny breath of the Key System Bay Bridge Terminal. Off the train in San Francisco into the voice of a cripple. "Count your blessings!" The old white people left to die at the Eclipse Hotel, and the old waitresses who worked there after said, "Count your blessings" over sneezes and little ouches and bad news. Christian resignation. Yuen was older than many of the white guests of the Eclipse. He washed dishes there without ever once counting his blessings.

"That's impossible," Huie said to Yuen.

Yuen grinned at his friend and said, "Whaddaya mean? It's true! You don't know because you were born here."

"Whaddaya mean 'born here'? Who was born here?"

"Every morning, I woke up with my father and my son, and we walked out of our house to the field, and stood in a circle around a young peach tree and lowered our trousers and pissed on the tree, made bubbles in the dirt, got the bark wet, splattered on the roots and watched our piss sink in. That's how we fertilized the big one the day I said I was going to Hong Kong tomorrow with my wife and son, and told them I was leaving my father and mother, and I did. I left. Then I left Hong Kong and left my family there, and came to America to make money," Yuen said. "Then after so much money, bring them over."

"Nobody gets over these days, so don't bang your head about not getting people over. What I want to know is did you make money?"

"Make money?"

"Yes, did you make money?"

"I'm still here, my wife is dead . . . but my son is still in Hong Kong, and I send him what I can."

"You're too good a father! He's a big boy now. Has to be a full-grown man. You don't want to spoil him."

Yuen looked up at the light bulb and blinked. "It's good to get away from those *lo fan* women always around the restaurant. Waitresses, hotel guests crying for Rose. Ha ha." He didn't want to talk about his son or China. Talk of white women he'd seen changing in the corridor outside his room over the kitchen, and sex acts of the past, would cloud out what he didn't want to talk about. Already the men in the room full of fish tanks were speaking loudly, shouting when they laughed, throwing the sound of their voices loud against the spongy atmosphere of fish pumps and warm-water aquariums. Yuen enjoyed the room when it was loud and blunt. The fish tanks and gulping and chortling pumps sopped up the sound of the clickety clickety of the games and kept the voices, no matter how loud, inside. The louder the closer, thicker, fleshier, as the night wore on. This was the life after a week of privacy with the only real

Chinese speaker being paralyzed speechless in a wheelchair. No wonder the boy doesn't speak Chinese, he thought, not making scnse. The boy should come here sometime. He might like the fish.

"Perhaps you could," Huie said, laughing. "Perhaps you could make love to them, Ah Yuen gaw." The men laughed, showing gold and aged yellow teeth. "Love!" Yuen snorted against the friendly laugh.

"That's what they call it if you do it for free," Huie said.

"Not me," Yuen said, taking the bucket and water pipe from Huie. "Free or money. No love. No fuck. Not me." He lifted the punk from the tobacco, then shot off the ash with a blast of air into the pipe that sent a squirt of water up the stem. "I don't even like talking to them. Why should I speak their language? They don't think I'm anything anyway. They change their clothes and smoke in their slips right outside my door in the hallway, and don't care I live there. So what?" His head lifted to face his friends, and his nostrils opened, one larger than the other as he spoke faster. "And anyway, they don't care if I come out of my room and see them standing half naked in the hall. They must know they're ugly. They all have wrinkles and you can see all the dirt on their skins and they shave their armpits badly, and their powder turns brown in the folds of their skin. They're not like Chinese women at all." Yuen made it a joke for his friends.

"I have always wanted to see a real naked American woman for free. There's something about not paying money to see what you see," Huie said. "Ahhh and what I want to see is bigger breasts. Do these free peeks have bigger breasts than Chinese women? Do they have nipples as pink as calendar girls' sweet suckies?" Huie grunted and put his hands inside his jacket and hefted invisible breasts. "Do they have . . . ?"

"I don't know. I don't look. All the ones at my place are old, and who wants to look inside the clothes of the old for their parts? And you can't tell about calendar pictures . . ." Yuen pulled at the deep smoke of the waterpipe. The water inside gurgled loudly, and singed tobacco ash jumped when Yuen blew back into the tube. He lifted his head and licked the edges of his teeth. He always licked the edges of his teeth before speaking. He did not think it a sign of old age. Before he broke the first word over his licked teeth, Huie raised his hand. "Jimmy Chan goes out with *lo fan* women . . . blond ones with blue eyelids too. And he smokes cigars," Huie said.

"He smokes cigars. So what? What's that?"

"They light his cigars for him."

"That's because he has money. If Chinese have money here,

everybody likes them," Yuen said. "Blue nipples, pink eyelids, everybody likes them."

"Not the Jews."

"Not the Jews," Yuen said. "I saw a cripple. Screamed 'Count your blessings!' Could have been a Jew, huh? I should have looked . . . Who cares? So what?"

"The Jews don't like anybody," Huie said. "They call us, you and me, the Tang people, 'Jews of the Orient.' Ever hear that?"

"Because the Jews don't like anybody?"

"Because nobody likes the Jews!" Huie said. He pulled the tip of his nose down with his fingers. "Do I look like a Jew of the Orient, for fuckin out loud? What a life!" The men at the mah-jong table laughed and shook the table with the pounding of their hands. Over their laughter, Yuen spoke loudly, licking the edges of his teeth and smiling, "What do you want to be Jew for? You're Chinese! That's bad enough!" And the room full of close men was loud with the sound of tables slapped with night-pale hands and belly laughter shrinking into wheezes and silent empty mouths breathless and drooling. "We have a Jew at the Eclipse Hotel. They look white like the other *lo fan gwai* to me," Yuen said, and touched the glowing punk to the tobacco and inhaled through his mouth, gurgling the water. He let the smoke drop from his nostrils and laughed smoke out between his teeth, and leaned back into the small spaces of smoke between the men and enjoyed the whole room.

Yuen was a man of neat habits, but always seemed disheveled with his dry mouth, open with the lower lip shining, dry and dangling below yellow teeth. Even today, dressed in his day-off suit that he kept hung in his closet with butcher paper over it and a hat he kept in a box, he had seen people watching him and laughing behind their hands at his pulling at the shoulders of the jacket and lifting the brim of his hat from his eyes. He had gathered himself into his own arms and leaned back into his seat to think about the room in San Francisco; then he slept and was ignorant of the people, the conductor, and all the people he had seen before, watching him and snickering, and who might have been, he thought, jealous of him for being tall for a Chinese, or his long fingers, exactly what he did not know or worry about in his half-stupor between wakefulness and sleep with his body against the side of the train, the sounds of the steel wheels, and the train pitching side to side, all amazingly loud and echoing in his ears, through his body before sleep.

Tuesday evening Yuen took the A train from Oakland to San Francisco. He walked to the train stop right after work at the restaurant and stood, always watching to the end of the street for the train's coming, dim out of the darkness from San Francisco. The train came, its cars swaying side to side, and looked like a short snake with a lit strip of lights squirming past him, or like the long dragon that stretched and jumped over the feet of the boys carrying it. He hated the dragon here, but saw it when it ran, for the boy's sake. The train looked like that, the glittering dragon that moved quickly like the sound of drum rolls and dangled its staring eyes out of its head with a flurry of beard; the screaming bird's voice of the train excited in him his idea of a child's impulse to run, to grab, to destroy.

Then he stood and listened to the sound of the train's steel wheels, the sound of an invisible cheering crowd being sucked after the lights of the train toward the end of the line, leaving the quiet street more quiet and Yuen almost superstitiously anxious. Almost. The distance from superstitious feeling a loss or an achievement, he wasn't sure.

He was always grateful for the Tuesdays Dirigible walked him to the train stop. They left early on these nights and walked past drugstores, bought comic books, looked into the windows of closed shops and dimly lit used bookstores, and looked at shoes or suits on dummies. "How much is that?" Yuen would ask.

"I don't know what you're talking," Dirigible, the boy of the unpronounceable name, would say. "I don't know what you're talking" seemed the only complete phrase he commanded in Cantonese.

"What a stupid boy you are; can't even talk Chinese," Yuen would say, and "Too moochie shi-yet," adding his only American phrase. "Come on, I have a train to catch." They would laugh at each other and walk slowly, the old man lifting his shoulders and leaning his head far back on his neck, walking straighter, when he remembered. The boy. "Fay Gay" in Cantonese, Flying Ship, made him remember.

A glance back to Dirigible as he boarded the train, a smile, a wave, the boy through the window a silent thing in the noise of the engines. Yuen would shrug and settle himself against the back, against the seat, and still watch Dirigible, who would be walking now, back toward the restaurant. Tonight he realized again how young the Flying Ship was to be walking home alone at night through the city back to the kitchen entrance of the hotel. He saw Dirigible not walking the usual way home, but running next to the moving train, then turning the corner to walk up a street with more lights and people. Yuen turned, thinking he might shout out the door for the boy to go home the way they had come, but the train was moving, the moment gone. Almost. Yuen had forgotten something. The train was moving. And he had no right. Dirigible had heard his mother say that Yuen had no right so many times that Dirigible was saying it too. In Chinese. Badly spoken and bungled, but Chinese. That he was not Yuen's son. That this was not China. Knowing the boy was allowed to say such things by his only speaking parent made Yuen's need to scold and shout more urgent, his silence in front of the spoiled punk more humiliating. Yuen was still and worked himself out of his confusion. The beginning of his day off was bad; nothing about it right or usual; all of it bad, no good, wrong. Yuen chewed it out of his mind until the memory was fond and funny, then relaxed.

"Jimmy Chan has a small Mexican dog too, that he keeps in his pocket," Huie said. "It's lined with rubber."

"The little dog?" Yuen asked. And the men laughed.

"The dog . . ." Huie said and chuckled out of his chinless face, "No, his pocket, so if the dog urinates . . ." He shrugged. "You know."

"Then how can he make love to his blond *fangwai* woman with blue breasts if his pocket is full of dogpiss?"

"He takes off his coat!" The men laughed with their faces up into the falling smoke. The men seemed very close to Yuen, as if with the heat and smoke they swelled to crowding against the walls, and Yuen swelled and was hot with them, feeling tropically close and friendly, friendlier, until he was dizzy with friendship and forgot names. No, don't forget names. "A Chinese can do anything with *fangwai* if he has money," Yuen said.

"Like too moochie shi-yet, he can," Huie shouted, almost falling off his seat. "He can't make himself white!" Huie jabbed his finger at Yuen and glared. The men at the table stopped. The noise of the mah-jong and voices stopped to the sound of rumps shifting over chairs and creaks of table legs. Heavy arms were leaned onto the tabletops. Yuen was not sure whether he was arguing with his friend or not. He did not want to argue on his day off, yet he was constrained to say something. He knew that whatever he said would sound more important than he meant it. He licked his teeth and said, "Who want to be white when they can have money?" He grinned. The man nodded and sat quiet a moment, listening to the sound of boys shouting at cars to come and park in their lots. "Older brother, you always know the right thing to say in a little pinch, don't you."

"You mother's twat! Play!" And the men laughed and in a burst of noise returned to their game.

The back room was separated from the tropical fish store by a long window shade drawn over the doorway. Calendars with pictures of Chinese women holding peaches the size of basketballs, calendars with pictures of nude white women with large breasts of all shapes, and a picture someone thought was funny, showing a man with the breasts of a woman, were tacked to the walls above the stacked glass tanks of warm-water fish. The men sat on boxes, in chairs, at counters with a wall of drawers full of stuff for tropical fish, and leaned inside the doorway and bits of wall not occupied by a gurgling tank of colorful little swimming things. They sat and passed the waterpipe and tea and played mah-jong or talked. Every night the waterpipe, the tea, the mah-jong, the talk.

"Wuhay! Hey, Yuen, older brother," a familiar nameless voice shouted through the smoke and thumping pumps. "Why're you so quiet tonight?"

"I thought I was being loud and obnoxious," Yuen said. "Perhaps it's my boss's son looking sick again."

"The boy?" Huie said.

Yuen stood and removed his jacket, brushed it, and hung it on a nail. "He has this trouble with his stomach . . . makes him bend up and he cries and won't move. It comes and goes," Yuen said.

"Bring him over to me, and I'll give him some herbs, make him well in a hurry."

"His mother, my boss, is one of these new-fashioned people giving up the old ways. She speaks nothing but American if she can help it, and has *lo fan* women working for her at her restaurant. She laughs at me when I tell her about herbs making her son well, but she knows . . ."

"Herbs make me well when I'm sick."

"They can call you 'mass hysteria' crazy in the head. People like her mean well, but don't know what's real and what's phony."

"Herbs made my brother well, but he died anyway," Huie said. He took off his glasses and licked the lenses.

"Because he wanted to," Yuen said.

"He shot himself."

"Yes, I remember," Yuen said. He scratched his Adam's apple noisily a moment. "He used to come into the restaurant in the mornings. I'd fix him scrambled eggs. He always use to talk with bits of egg on his lips and shake his fork and tell me that I could learn English good enough to be cook at some good restaurant. I could too, but the cook where I wash dishes is Chinese already, and buys good meat, so I have a good life."

Huie sighed and said, "Good meat is important I suppose." Then put his mouth to the mouth of the waterpipe.

"What?" Yuen asked absently at Huie's sigh. He allowed his eyes to unfocus on the room now, tried to remember Huie's brother's face with bits of egg on the lips and was angry. Suddenly an angry old man wanting to be alone screamed. He wiped his own lips with his knuckles and looked back to Huie the herbalist. Yuen did not want to talk about Huie's brother. He wanted to listen to music, or jokes, or breaking bones, something happy or terrible.

"His fine American talk," Huie said. "He used to go to the Oakland High School at night to learn."

My boss wants me to go there too," Yuen said. "You should only talk English if you have money to talk to them with . . . I mean, only fools talk buddy buddy with the *lo fan* when they don't have money. If you talk to them without money, all you'll hear is what they say behind your back, and you don't want to listen to that."

"I don't."

"No."

"He received a letter one day, did he tell you that? He got a letter from the American immigration, and he took the letter to Jimmy Chan, who reads government stuff well . . . and Jimmy said that the immigration wanted to know how he came into the country and wanted to know if he was sending money to Communists or not." Huie smiled wanly and stared between his legs. Yuen watched Huie sitting on the box; he had passed the pipe and now sat with his short legs spread slightly apart. He was down now, his eyes just visible to Yuen. Huie's slumped body looked relaxed, only the muscles of his hands and wrists were tight and working. To Yuen, Huie right now looked as calm as if he were sitting on a padded crapper. Yuen smiled and tried to save the pleasure of his day-off visit that was being lost in morbid talk. "Did he have his dog with him?" he asked.

"His dog? My brother never had a dog."

"I mean Jimmy Chan with his rubber pocket."

"How can you talk about Jimmy Chan's stupid dog when I'm talking about my brother's death."

"Perhaps I'm worried about the boy," Yuen said. "I shouldn't have let him wait for the train tonight."

"Was he sick?"

"That too maybe. Who can tell?" Yuen said without a hint, not a word more of the cripple shouting "Count your blessings!" at the end of the A train's line in Frisco. It wouldn't be funny, and Yuen wanted a laugh.

"Bring the boy to me next week, and I'll fix him up," Huie said quickly, and put on his glasses again. Yuen, out of his day-off, loud, cheerful mood, angry and ashamed of his anger, listened to Huie. "My brother was very old, you remember? He was here during the fire and earthquake, and he told this to Jimmy Chan." Huie stopped speaking and patted Yuen's knee. "Yes, he did have his little dog in his pocket . . ." The men looked across to each other, and Yuen nodded. They were friends, had always been friends. They were friends now. "And my brother told Jimmy that all his papers had been burned in the fire and told about how he came across the bay in a sailboat that was so full that his elbows, just over the side of the boat, were in the water, and about the women crying and then shouting, and that no one thought about papers, and some not even of their gold."

"Yes. I know."

"And Jimmy Chan laughed at my brother and told him that there was nothing he could do, and that my brother would have to wait and see if he would be sent back to China or not. So . . ." Huie put his hands on his knees and rocked himself forward, lifting and setting his thin rump onto the wooden box, sighed and swallowed, "my brother shot himself." Huie looked up to Yuen; they licked their lips at the same moment, watching each other's tongues. "He died very messy," Huie said, and Yuen heard it through again for his friend, as he had a hundred times before. But tonight it made him sick.

The talk about death and the insides of a head spread wet all over the floor, the head of someone he knew, the talk was not relaxing; it was incongruous to the room of undershirted men playing mah-jong and pai-gow. And the men, quieter since the shout, were out of place in their undershirts. Yuen wanted to relax, but everything was frantic that should not be; perhaps he was too sensitive, Yuen thought, and wanted to be numb. "You don't have to talk about it if it bothers," Yuen said.

"He looked messy, for me that was enough . . . and enough of Jimmy Chan for me too. He could've written and said my brother was a good citizen or something . . ." Huie stopped and flicked at his ear with his fingertips. "You don't want to talk any more about it?"

"No," Yuen said.

"How did we come to talk about my brother's death anyhow?"

"Jimmy Chan and his Mexican dog."

"I don't want to talk about that anymore, either."

"How soon is Chinese New Year's?"

"I don't think I want to talk about anything anymore," Huie said. "New Year's is a long ways off. Next year."

"Yes, I know that."

"I don't want to talk about it," Huie said. Each man sat now, staring toward and past each other without moving their eyes, as if moving their eyes would break their friendship. He knew that whatever had happened had been his fault; perhaps tonight would have been more congenial if he had not taken Dirigible to the used bookstore, where he found a pile of sunshine and nudist magazines, or if the cripple had fallen on his face, or not been there. Yuen could still feel the presence of the cripple, how he wanted still to push him over, crashing to the cement. The joy it would have given him was embarrassing, ncw, unaccountablc, likc bcing in love.

"Would you like a cigar, ah-dai low?" Huie asked, with a friendly Cantonese "older brother."

"No, I like the waterpipe." Yuen watched Huie spit the end of the cigar out onto the floor.

"You remind me of my brother, Yuen."

"How so?"

"Shaking your head, biting your lips, always shaking your head . . . you do too much thinking about nothing. You have to shake the thinking out to stop, eh?"

"And I rattle my eyes, too." Yuen laughed, knowing he had no way with a joke, but the friendliness botched in expression was genuine, and winning. "So what can I do without getting arrested?"

"I don't know," Huie said and looked around. "Mah-jong?"

"No."

"Are you unhappy?"

"What kind of question is that? I have my friends, right? But sometimes I feel . . . Aww, everybody does. . . ."

"Just like my brother . . . too much thinking, and thinking becomes worry. You should smoke cigars and get drunk and go help one of your *lo fan* waitresses shave her armpits properly and put your head inside and tickle her with your tongue until she's silly. I'd like to put my face into the armpit of some big fangwai American woman . . . with a big armpit!"

"But I'm not like your brother," Yuen said. "I don't shoot myself in the mouth and blow the back of my head out with a gun."

"You only have to try once."

Yuen waited a moment, then stood. "I should be leaving now," he said. Tonight had been very slow, but over quickly. He did not like being compared to an old man who had shot himself.

Huie stood and shook Yuen's hand, held Yuen's elbow, and squeezed Yuen's hand hard. "I didn't mean to shout at you, dai low."

Yuen smiled his wet smile. Huie held on to Yuen's hand and stood as if he was about to sit again. He had an embarrassingly sad smile. Yuen did not mean to twist his friend's face into this muscular contortion; he had marred Huie's happy evening of gambling, hoarse laughter, and alcoholic wheezings. "I shouted too," Yuen said finally.

"You always know the right things to say, older brother." Huie squeezed Yuen's hand and said, "Goodnight, dai low." And Yuen was walking, was out of the back room and into the tropical fish store. He opened the door to the alley and removed his glasses, blew on them in the sudden cold air to fog them, then wiped them clean.

For a long time he walked the always-damp alleys, between glittering streets of Chinatown. Women with black coats walked with young children. This Chinatown was taller than Oakland's, had more fire escapes and lights, more music coming from the street vents. He usually enjoyed walking at this hour every Wednesday of every week. But this was Tuesday evening, and already he had left his friends, yet it looked like Wednesday with the same paper vendors coming up the hills, carrying bundles of freshly printed Chinese papers. He walked down the hill to Portsmouth Square on Kearney Street to sit in the park and read the paper. He sat on a wooden bench and looked up the trunk of a palm tree, looking toward the sounds of pigeons. He could hear the fat birds cooing over the sound of the streets, and the grass snap when their droppings dropped fresh. Some splattered on the bronze plaque marking the location of the birth of the first white child in San Francisco, a few feet away. He looked up and down the park once, then moved to the other side of the tree out of the wind and sat to read the paper by the streetlight before walking. Tonight he was glad to be tired; to Yuen tiredness was the only explanation for his nervousness. Almost anger. Almost. He would go home early; there was nothing else to do here, and he would sleep through his day off, or at least, late into the morning.

He entered the kitchen and snorted a breath through his nose. He was home to the smell of cooking and the greasy sweat of waitresses. His boss wiped her forehead with the back of her arm and asked him why he had come back so early; she did not expect him back until dinnertime tomorrow and was he sick? He answered, "Yes," lying to avoid conversation. All warfare is based on deception, he thought, quoting the strategist Sun Tzu, the grandson. He asked the young woman where her son the Flying Ship was, and she said he was upstairs in his room sleeping, where he belonged. Yuen nodded. "Of course, it's late isn't it," he said, avoiding the stare of her greasy eyes, and went upstairs to his room across the hall from the waitresses' wardrobe. He looked once around the kitchen before turning the first landing. He saw the large refrigerators and the steam table, and realized he was truly tired, and sighed the atmosphere of his day off out of his body. "You're trying to walk too

straight, anyway, ah-bok," his boss, Rose, said, calling him uncle
from the bottom of stairs. He did not understand her joke or
criticism or what she meant and went on up the stairs.

At the top of the stairs he turned and walked down the hall, past
the room of his boss and her paralyzed husband, and past Dirigible's
room, toward his own room across the hall from the wardrobe and
next to the bathroom. Facing the door was the standup wardrobe, a
fancy store-bought box with two doors, a mirror on the inside, and a
rack for clothes, where the waitresses kept their white-and-black
uniforms and changed. A redheaded waitress was sitting inside the
wardrobe smoking a cigarette. She sat between hanging clothes with
her back against the back of the wardrobe, her legs crossed and
stretched out of the box. One naked heel turned on the floor, back
and forth, making her legs wobble and jump to the rhythm of her
nervous breathing.

Yuen walked slowly down the hall, his head down, like a car full
of gunmen down a dark street, his fingers feeling the edges of his
long hair that tickled the tops of his ears. He looked down to the
floor but could no longer see the bare legs jutting from out of the
box, the long muscles under the thighs hanging limp and shaking
slowly to the turning heel. He knew she was ugly. He snorted and
walked close to the far wall; he would walk past her and not look at
her. She did not move her legs. He stopped and leaned against the
wall and lifted one foot after the other and gingerly swung them
over the waitress's legs. As his second foot went over her ankles, he
glanced into the box and saw her pull a strap over her shoulder and
giggle. Dry rock and unnatural white teeth in there. He hopped to
keep his balance. She kicked. "Hiya, Yuen," she said to him stumbling down. He felt his shoe scrape the waitress's leg, skin it a little,
heard her yelp, and fell on her. "Oh, my God!" she growled and
went crazy, tangling her legs and arms with his, jumping into the
box to stamp out the cigarette she had let fall from her mouth
laughing. The smell was sweet, dusty, and flowery inside the box,
like a stale funeral. Huie wanted to stuff his head into a *fangwai*
woman's armpit, did he? Yuen looked, as he stumbled to his feet
out of the sweet choking smell, and could not make out any distinct
armpits in the flurry of flesh and shiny nylon slip and uniforms, and
flying shoes, shouting and pounding after her cigarette. He couldn't
find his hat. He looked under the waitress.

The waitress stood from out of the wardrobe up to her skinny and
flabby self and pulled her slip straight around her belly. She looked
down to Yuen, his head nodding and dangling on his neck. He
looked like a large bird feeding on something dead, and the waitress
laughed. "Come on there, Yuen," the waitress said. "I was just

playing." She bent to help the man up. She took his shoulders with her hands and began pulling gently. The door to the bathroom was open and the light through the doorway shone white on the front of her powdered face. Yuen saw her face looking very white with flecks of powder falling from light hairs over her grin, a very white face on a gray wrinkled neck and a chest warped with skin veined like blue cheese. He did not like her smiling and chuckling her breathing into his face or her being so comfortably undressed in front of him.

"Are you all right now, Yuen?" she asked. He did not understand. He felt her holding him and saw her smiling and saw her old breasts quiver and dangle against her slip and the skin stretch across her ribs, not at all like the women in the calendars and magazines, Yuen thought. He took his shoulders closer to his body and she still held him, squeezing the muscle of his arm with strong hands, and pulled him toward her and muttered something in her rotten-throated voice. He leaned away from her and patted his head to show her he was looking for his hat. He chanced a grin.

She looked at his head and moved her fingers through his hair. "I don't see a bump, honey. Where does it hurt?"

Her body was too close to his face for him to see. The smell of her strong soap, stale perfume, layers of powder hung into his breathing. He was angry. "My hat! My hat!" he shouted in Chinese. He took an invisible hat and put it on his head and tapped the brim with his hands.

The waitress, also on her knees now, moved after him and felt his head. "Where does it hurt?" she said. "I don't feel anything but your head."

He stood quickly and leaned against the wall and glared stupidly at her.

"I was just trying to see if you're hurt, Yuen," the waitress said. "Did I touch your sore or something?" She held her arms out and stood. A strap fell from her shoulder; she ignored it and stretched her neck and reached toward him with her fingers. "I was just joking when I kicked you, honey. I thought it was funny, the way you were stepping over me, see?" All Yuen heard were whines and giggles in her voice. He shook his head. He held his coat closed with his hands and shoved at her with his head. "*Chiyeah!* Go way! *Hooey la!*"

A door opened and Dirigible stepped into the hall in his underwear. "What'sa wrong?" he asked. The waitress turned then, fixed her slip, and brushed her dry hair out of her face. "Make him understand, will you?" she said pointing at Yuen. She jabbed her arm at Yuen again. "Him. He's . . ." She crossed her eyes and pointed at her head.

"She's drunk!" Yuen said. "Tell her to go away."

"I was joking! Tell him I didn't mean to hurt his old head."

"Don't let her touch you, she's crazy tonight. Ask her why she here so late. What's she been doing here all night?"

"Do something! I can't."

"What? What?" Dirigible said. "What? I don't know what you're talking," sounding as if he were being accused of something.

The waitress was in front of the boy now and trying to explain. Yuen stepped quickly down the hall and pushed the boy into his room and closed the door. "Go to sleep . . . you'll get a stomach ache," he said.

"What'd you push me for?" the boy asked in English. He kicked the door and tried to open it, but Yuen held the knob. The boy shouted. His anger burst into tears.

"Coffee," Yuen said to the waitress and pointed at her, meaning that she should go have coffee. The waitress nodded quickly, took a robe from the wardrobe, and went downstairs.

Yuen went to his room without looking for his hat. The boy opened his door and followed the old man. He stood in the doorway and watched Yuen hang his overcoat in his closet. Yuen did not notice the boy and locked the door in his face.

The old man put a hand under his shirt and rubbed the sweat under his armpit. He loosened his belt and flapped the waist of his underwear before lying on top of his bed. He felt under the pillow for his revolver; it was big in his hand. Then he swallowed to slow his breath and sat up to take off his shoes and socks.

He saw the dark stain of blood on the heel of his right shoe, and dropped it onto the floor. I guess, I can't tell, he thought. She'll say I kicked her. He rapped the wall to speak to Dirigible. "*Wuhay! Ah-Fay Shurn ahh,* don't tell nutting, okay?"

"I don't know what you're talking. You . . ." Yuen heard nothing through the wall. He wished that Dirigible spoke Chinese better than he did. What the hell was he learning at that Chinese school if not Chinese?

"You hit me in the face," Dirigible said.

"I did not."

"You did, and it hurt," the boy said. Dirigible. The flying ship that doesn't fly anymore. The boy had the name of an extinct species. He was playing himself more hurt and younger than he was. "Don't be a baby," Yuen said.

"You hit me in the face."

"Uhhh," Yuen groaned, and rolled away from the wall. He would buy the little Dirigible a funnybook in the morning. He would buy

Dirigible a dozen funnybooks and a candy bar in the morning. He leaned back into bed and began unbuttoning his shirt.

He stopped and blinked. Someone knocked at his door again. He'd almost heard it the first time. He almost felt for his revolver. He heard, "Ah Yuen bok, ahhh! I got some coffee, uncle. Are you all right? Anna says you hurt your head?" Rose, his boss, Dirigible's mother.

"Go away, I'm sleeping."

"But Anna says you asked for coffee. Have you been drinking?"

"I don't want any coffee."

"Since you're here, I told the colored boy not to come in tomorrow morning. . . . What's your hat doing in the bathroom?"

"Leave it," Yuen said. "Just leave it. I'll get it in the morning." He coughed and rolled over on the bed and coughed once into the pillow.

"By the way, you got a letter today. Your American name on it. Nelson Yuen Fong . . . Your name looks nice," the voice outside said.

"What?"

"Nothing. I'll keep it until tomorrow for you."

He coughed phlegm up from his chest, held it in his mouth, then swallowed it. His face was warm in his own breath against the pillow. He relaxed the grip of his lids on his eyes for sleep. The hat was probably all dirty if it was in the bathroom, he thought, and did not get up to urinate, get his hat, or shut off the light.

The hallway outside was quiet now. He felt his eyes smarting and felt stale and sour. He was not sure whether or not he was asleep. It was late; the night was wider, higher without lights on the horizon or lengths of sound stretching down the streets. The air was not silent but excited, jittery without noise. Yuen heard sounds on the edge of hearing, and listened for them, the small sounds of almost voices and cars somewhere. He occasionally heard nothing. Perhaps he was sleeping when he heard nothing. If he opened his eyes now, he would know . . . but he could not open his eyes now. He decided he was asleep, and was sleeping, finally.

What had the waitress been doing up here all this time? Entertaining the man who would never play a Japanese general or Chinese sissy sidekick who dies in the movies ever again, if he ever did, by inflicting her flesh on his mute, immobile, trapped, paralyzed self? Or perhaps a show, a long striptease for the boy to watch from his room through his keyhole. Or had she been inside his room? He had no right. How had they met? Come up the stairs one day from a smoke of the waterpipe in the cool dry room where the potatoes and onions were kept and peeled, looking forward to an hour on his bed with one or two picture magazines full of strippers showing their breasts. The sight of the boy, nine or ten years old, holding his revolver stopped the man from stepping into his own room. The unexpected boy caught Yuen dirty-minded, his mental pecker hanging out. He had a loaded gun in his hand, between Yuen and his girlic magazines. His son. The knees. The boy's knees. That was funny. That was laughable now.

Tomorrow he would buy Dirigible a dozen funnybooks and a big candy bar, even if he was not angry or scared anymore.

And now truly asleep, he was sitting at a table with this boy, but the boy was his son, then Huie's dead brother with bits of scrambled eggs drying on his lips. The flesh all over the skull looked as if it had been boiled in soup to fall off the bone. Yuen wiped the boy's lip but more egg came up where he had wiped the egg off. Then the lips were gone. The lipless boy laughed, took Yuen's hand, and pulled him up. They walked from the table and were in a field with not a bird in the sky above them, smooth as skin, blue as veins. The boy pointed, and there, on the edge of the world, was the peach tree. They dropped their trousers, aimed their peckers to the horizon, and pissed the long distance to the tree and watched the streams of their yellow liquid gleam and flash under the bright sky before it arched into the shadow of the mountains. They pissed a very long time without beginning to run out. Yuen was surprised he was still pissing. He squinted to see if he was reaching the tree. The boy was laughing and pissing on Yuen's feet. Yuen was standing in a mud of piss. "What are you doing?"

"Coffee," the boy answered in the waitress's voice and laughed. Birds. They were in the sky out of nowhere and dove on him, silent except for their wings breaking the dive. I'm going to die. Too moochie shi-yet. I'm going to die. And continued fertilizing the peach tree on the horizon. He had not shouted. "It's true!" He woke up to the sound of his voice, he was sure, and heard only the curtains shuffling in front of his open window. He felt under the sheets around his ankles to see if there was any wet. There was not. He hadn't wet the bed. He got up and spat into the washbasin in the corner. He didn't curse the spring handles on the taps. He turned out the light, sat on the edge of his bed, and listened for a hint of waitresses lurking in the silence outside his door, then returned to sleep.

He bathed with his underwear on this morning and plugged the keyhole with toilet paper. He combed his hair and returned to his room. He had found his hat on the lid of the toilet. He did not like the hat any longer; it was too big and the band was dirty. The dream had left him by the time he went downstairs for breakfast, but he knew he had dreamed.

He sat down at a table at the end of the long steam table. He could hear a waitress laughing shrilly outside in the dining room, not the same waitress as last night, he knew, for the breakfast waitresses were different from the ones at dinner. He took a toothpick from a tin can nailed to the end of the steam table and put it in his mouth and sucked the taste of wood and read his Chinese paper. He did not goodmorning his boss. She was younger and should be the first to give greetings, out of respect. But she was his boss. So what. He was reading about Chiang Kai-shek making a speech to his army again. He liked Chiang Kai-shek. He decided he liked Chiang Kai-shek. Chiang Kai-shek was familiar and pleasant in his life, and he enjoyed it. "He made another speech to his army," Yuen said.

Dirigible said, "He made one last week to the army."

He's forgotten last night, Yuen thought, and answered, "That was to the farmers. This time it's to the army. Next week to everybody." This was part of every morning also.

Rose wiped her hands on her apron and sat down next to Yuen. She took an envelope from her pocket and unfolded it. Before removing the letter, she turned to Dirigible and said, "Go upstairs, change your pants. And comb your hair for a change."

"I'll be late for school. I gotta eat breakfast."

"Go upstairs, huh? I don't have time to argue!" Rose said.

"Can I use your comb, ah-bok?"

"You have your own comb. Don't bother people. I wanta talk to ah-bok."

Yuen gave Dirigible his comb, which he kept in a case. Rose watched the boy go past the first landing and out of sight and then took the letter out of the envelope. "I read this letter of yours," she said. She looked straight at Yuen as she spoke, and Yuen resented her look and the way she held his letter. "Who said you could?" he asked. "It might have been from my son. What do you want to read my mail for, when you don't care what else I do?"

"Now, you know that's not so!" Rose said. "Anyway, it's addressed to your American name, and it's from the U.S. immigration."

"Well . . . What did Anna tell you about last night? You know what she was really trying to do, don't you? I'll tell you I don't believe a word that woman says. She eats scraps too. Right off the dirty dishes."

"Oh, Yuen bok, you're so old, your brain's busting loose. She was just trying to see if you had a cut or a hurt on your head was all."

"Aww, I don't like her no matter what," Yuen said. He went to the steam table and ladled cream of wheat into a bowl and sat down to eat it. "What are you looking at? You never seen me eat before?"

"Don't you use milk?" Rose asked.

"No, you should know that."

"But your letter, Yuen bok. You're in trouble."

"What for?"

"It's from the immigrators, I told you. They want to know if you came into this country legally."

Yuen looked up from his cereal to the powder and rouge of her face. The oil from her Chinese skin had soaked through and messed it all up. She smiled with her lips shut and cheeks pulled in as if sucking something in her mouth. He did not like Rose because she treated him with disdain and made bad jokes, and thought she was beautiful, a real femme fatale behind the steam table with an apron and earrings. And now she did not seem natural to Yuen, being so kind and trying so to soften the harshness in her voice. "That's a bad joke," Yuen said.

"I'm not joking. Do I look like I'm joking, ah-bok? Here, you can read it for yourself if you don't believe me." She shoved the letter to him. He pushed his cereal bowl aside and flattened the letter on the table. He put his glasses on, then without touching the letter, bent over it and stared. He saw a printed seal with an eagle. The paper was very white, and had a watermark that made another eagle. He removed his glasses and licked his teeth. "You know I don't read English."

"I know," Rose said. "So why don't you eat your breakfast and I'll tell you what the letter says. Then you can get the dishes done."

Yuen nodded and did as she said. She wiped her hands on her apron and told him that the letter said the immigrators wanted to know if he had any criminal record with the police in the city of Oakland and that he was to go to the Oakland police and have his fingerprints taken and get a letter from them about his criminal record yes or no. "I will talk to Mrs. Walker, who was a legal secretary, and she can help me write a watchacall, a character reference for you."

"Why tell people?"

"They ask for letters making good references about you, don't they? You want to stay in this country, don't you?" She folded the letter and ran her thumb along the creases, leaving gray marks where her fingers had touched. Yuen took the letter and unfolded it again and put on his glasses again and stared down at the piece of paper. He took a pencil and copied something he saw in the letter on a napkin. "What's this?" he asked, pointing at the napkin.

"That's a *t*," Rose said.

"What's it mean?"

"It doesn't mean anything. It's just a *t*."

"Did I make it right?"

"You are not going to learn to read and write English before this afternoon, ah-bok."

Yuen lost interest in his *t* and wiped his face with his napkin. "T Zone wahh. Camel cigarette!" he mumbled. He remembered cigarette ads with the pictures of actors' heads with a *t* over their mouths and down their throats. Rose didn't know everything. She was not his friend. He sighed and straightened in his seat. He was sure Rose heard all the little gurgles and slopping sounds inside him. It ached to sit straight. He had to sit straight to feel any strength in his muscles now. The ache gave a certain bite to the fright. He thought about aching and wanting to ache, like nobody else. Every white muscle in his body felt raw and tender, from the base of his spine, and the muscles from his neck down to his shoulder, and the hard muscles behind his armpit. He was conscious of every corner and bend in his body, and all this was inside him, private, the only form of reliable relaxation he had. He wanted to sit back and enjoy himself, ignore the letter, and travel the countries of his aches. He looked to Rose. She looked away. He saw she knew he was frightened. He did not want her pity, her face to smile some simpering kindly smile for his sake, for he had always pitied her, with her reasonable good looks, her youth, and a husband she keeps in a room like a bug in a jar, who won't be going to Hollywood after all. He didn't want to need her English, her letter full of nice things about him, her help.

Rose patted Yuen's shoulder and stood up and went to the foot of the stairs and called for Dirigible to come down. "You'll be late for school!" Then to the old man, "I'm going to have to tell him, you know."

"Dritchable?" Yuen said, botching the name.

"Everyone will know sooner or later. They come and ask people questions. The immigrators do that," Rose said. They could hear Dirigible stamping on the floor above them.

Yuen put the letter in his shirt pocket and removed his glasses and put them and the case in the tin can with the toothpicks. His place. He went around the steam table to the dishwashing area, lit the fires under the three sinks full of water, and started the electric dishwashing machine slung like an outboard motor in the well of the washing sink.

He put a teaspoonful of disinfectant into the washwater, then a cup of soap powder. He watched the yellow soap turn the water green and raise a cloud of green to the top of the water. He turned and saw Dirigible sitting at the table again. "*Wuhay!* Good morning, kid," he shouted over the noise of the dishwashing machine.

Dirigible looked up and waved back, then looked back at the breakfast his mother had set in front of him. "Come here, Dritch'ble, I got money for funnybooks!" Yuen switched off the machine and repeated what he'd said in a lower voice.

"Dirigible's late for school. He has to eat and run," Rose said. She turned to Dirigible and said, "Be sure you come right home from school. Don't go to Chinese school today, hear?"

"It's not my day to read to Pa."

"Just come home from school, like I told you, hear me? She leaned through a space between a shelf and the steam table to see the boy, and steam bloomed up her face and looked like a beard.

"Oh, boy!" Dirigible said, and Yuen saw that the boy was happy.

"What did you tell him?" he asked Rose.

"That he didn't have to go to Chinese school today."

"Why? Don't you want him to be able to talk Chinese?"

"I want him to take you to the city hall this afternoon and do what the letter says," Rose said. She lifted her head back on her neck to face Yuen, and Yuen looking at her without his glasses on saw her face sitting atop the rising steam.

"I don't want a little boy to help me," he said. "You think I'm a fool? I'll call Jimmy Chan and ask him to help me. Dritch'ble too young to do anything for me."

Rose flickered a smile then twisted herself out from between the shelf and the steam table. "You've been watching too much television, ah-bok. Chinatown's not like that anymore. You can't hide there like you used to. Everything's orderly and businesslike now."

"How do you know Chinatown? You watch television, not me. I know Chinatown. Not everybody talks about the Chinese like the *lo fan* and you. You should know what you're talking about before talking sometimes. Chie!"

"Ham and!" a waitress shouted through the door.

"Ham and!" Rose repeated. "I'm just as much Chinese as you, ah-bok, but this is America!"

"The truth is still the truth, in China, America, on Mars. . . . Two and two don't make four in America, just because you're Chinese."

"What?" the waitress said, jutting her head through the kitchen door, in the rhythm of its swing.

"Eggs how?" Margie asked.

"Oh, basted."

"Basted," Margie said, and reached for the eggs. "Listen, ah-bok. I don't want to get in trouble because of you. I worked hard to get this restaurant, and I gave you a job. Who else do you think would give you a job, and a room? You're too old to work any-

where else, and you'd have to join the union and learn English. You
don't want to learn English. That's your business, but if you get in
trouble here, I'm in trouble too. Now just do what the letter says.
And just don't argue with me about it. No one is trying to hurt
you." She brought three cooking strips of bacon from the back of
grill toward the center, where she kept the iron hot.

"Me make trouble for you? You said I am in trouble already."

"I am trying to help you the best way I can. Now let me alone to
cook, and you get back to the dishes. Can't you see I'm nervous?
Listen, take the day off. I'll call the colored boy. I shouldn't have
told him not to come in. I don't know what I was thinking. . . .
Now, please, ah-bok, leave me finish breakfast, will you?"

"I'm sorry, I'll get the dishes . . ." Yuen said.

"I said take the day off," Rose said. "Please." She quickly slid
the spatula under another egg order on the griddle and flopped
them onto a plate. She forgot the bacon.

"The bacon," Yuen said.

She ignored him and said, "Dirigible, you don't have time to
finish your breakfast. Take that little pie in the icebox for your
teacher and go to school now."

Dirigible looked to Yuen. "I'll walk you to school," Yuen said.
Rose snapped, "Be back in time for the dinner dishes. . . . Oh,
what . . . Forget I said that, but both of you be back after school."

Looking down the street, they could see the morning sun shattered in the greasy shimmer of Lake Merritt. The grass on the shore
was covered with black coots and staggering sea gulls. Yuen had his
glasses on and could see the trees on the other side of the lake and
sailors walking with girls, and he could smell the stagnant water as
he walked the other way with Dirigible.

The boy watched the ground and stayed inside Yuen's shadow as
they walked. Yuen glanced at the boy and saw him playing his game
with his shadow and knew the boy had forgotten last night, the
waitress. They were beyond the smell of the lake now and inside the
smell of water drying off the sides of washed brick buildings, and
Yuen's morning was complete and almost gone. "What're you carrying there?" Yeun asked.

"A pie for teacher," Dirigible said.

Yuen smiled his wet smile. They stopped at the street that had the
train tracks in the center. "Mommy said your hat was in the toilet."

"Do you want to go to San Francisco with me?"

"I can't. I have to go home right after school. You too."

"I mean right now. Would you like to go to San Francisco on the
train, right now?"

"I have to go to school."

"I'll take you to my friend's and he'll give you some herbs that will make your stomach stop hurting again." Yuen put a hand on the boy's shoulder and stood in front of him. What happens to boys born here? Are they all little bureaucrats by ten years old? They no longer dreamed of the Marvelous Traveler from the outlaws of Leongsahn Marsh come to deliver an invitation to adventure? "I'll buy you five funnybooks and a candy bar."

"But it doesn't hurt."

"For when your stomach does hurt. These herbs and it won't hurt again." Then inspiration in his instinct had the words out of his mouth before they'd come to mind. "How about I buy you special Chinese funnybooks? Chinese fighters with swords and bows and arrows, spears, big wars, heads cut off. And the head cut off spits blood in the face of its killer. You'll like them."

There were more people on the train now than at night. The train was dirtier in the day. They caught the A train at the end of the line near Dirigible's school. As the train started to pull, it rang its electric bell, screeching like a thousand trapped birds. They hummed and rattled across Oakland, onto the lower level of the Bay Bridge toward San Francisco. Dirigible ate the little pie and Yuen put his arm over the boy's shoulders when people boarded, and let go on the bridge. He was glad to have the boy with him. Good company. He was young and didn't have to know what Yuen was doing to have a little adventure. Yuen enjoyed being with the boy. That was something he could still enjoy.

The train moved quickly, swaying its cars side to side over the tracks. Yuen looked only once out of the window to the street full of people. He had been in Oakland for twenty years now, and he still felt uncomfortable, without allies in the streets. On the train he could sit and did not have to walk among people with hands out of their pockets all around him. The train moved him quickly out of the moldy shadows between tall buildings, and was moving down a street lined with low wooden houses now. He could see Negro women with scarves around their large heads. Elephant-hipped women with fat legs walking old and slow down the street. The feelings he had for them were vague and nothing personal, but haunted him. The train passed them, and now there were no more houses. They whirred into the train yards, and the A screamed its crazed electric birds toward the bridge.

They passed broken streetcars and empty trains in the yards, and saw bits of grass growing up between the crossties. Beyond the yards they saw the flat bay and the thick brown carpet of dung floating next to the shore. And they could smell the bay, the cooking sewage, the oily steel. Last night he slept past this part of the trip. "Shi-yet," he said sniffing. The boy smiled. Yuen realized now what he was doing. He was trying to be brave, and knew he would fail. He felt the letter in his coat pocket without touching the letter and thought of how he would take the letter from his pocket to show Jimmy Chan.

The sounds of the wheels on the rails changed in pitch and they were on the bridge now, with shadows of steelwork skipping over their faces. They were above the bay and could see the backs of sea gulls gliding and soaring parallel to them, their beaks split in answer to the electric bell. Yuen could see the birds stop and hang on the air with their wings stiff, then fall and keep falling until the bridge blocked his vision, and in his mind he counted the splashes on the bay the sea gulls made. He looked down to Dirigible again and saw pie on the boy's lips. Dirigible took his hand out of the paper bag and grinned. "That's bad for your stomach," Yuen said. Too nervous to smile. No, not nervous, he thought, angry. Calm, numbly angry. It wasn't unpleasant or aggravating or lonely, but moving very fast, train or no train, he without a move felt himself hurtling home. The electric birds screamed and they were moving in a slow curve toward the terminal at the San Francisco end of the line.

Chinatown was very warm and the streets smelled of vegetables and snails set out in front of the shops. Among the shopping Chinese women, Yuen saw small groups of *lo fan* white tourists with bright neckties and cameras pointing into windows and playing with bamboo flutes or toy dragons inside the curio shops. Yuen stopped in front of a bookstore with several different poster portraits of a red-faced potbellied, long bearded soldier in green robes. "Know him?" Yuen asked. The boy glanced. "Sure, I've seen him around."

"Who is he?"

"He's you," the boy said, looking caught again. Yuen took him inside and bought an expensive set of paperbound Chinese funnybooks that looked like little books and came in a box. Yuen opened up one of the books to the pictures and chuckled, delighted. "See, here?" He snatched at the tale of the 108 outlaw heroes of legendary Leongsahn Marsh in curt, chugging Cantonese babytalk the boy might understand. "Heh heh, look like a Buddhist monk fella, huh? Very bad temper this guy. . . . Now this guy, look. He catch cold, get drunk on knock out 'Mickey Finn' kind of booze, not knock out, and gotta cross the mountain. *Don't cross that mountain alone!* they say. *Fuck you!* he says. *Oooh, big tiger eat you up there. Better not go!* they say him. *Don't try to fool me!* he says and he goes and they can't stop him go. Up the mountain at night. The tiger jump him! Whoo! He gotta sniffle and sneeze. Runny eyes and cough. And he drunk too much wine suppose to knock people out. And he thinks

maybe he should not have come up to the mountaintop after all, but
gotta fight anyway, and *kawk kawk kawk kawk!* punch and kick and
push the tiger's face in the dirt and punch and kick 'em and kill that
tiger. They call that one Tiger Jung. He's my favorite of the 108
heroes," Yuen said and sighed, smiling. "One by one, you know, all
the heroes are accused of crimes by the government. They say he
commit a crime he didn't and they make him run, see? And one by
one, all the good guys made outlaw by the bad government come to
Leongsahn Marsh and join the good guy, Soong Gong. Yeah, sure.
Sam Gawk Yun Yee, Sir Woo Jun, I memorize 'em all. All the boys
like to see who know more. Then you see them in the opera, and
. . ." Yuen sighed again and wouldn't finish that thought. "Soong
Gong. They call him the Timely Rain, Gup Sir Yur. Every boy like
you in the world for a while is like these guys. Before you lie, before
you betray, before you steal. You know if you stay honest, don't sell
out, don't betray, don't give up even if it means you run all alone,
someday, someone will tap you on the shoulder and, *You!* the
Marvelous Traveler will say. *Our leader, the Timely Rain, has long
admired your gallantry. Soong Gong says he is a man of no talent,
but asks you to join us and our rebel band and do great things.* But
you grow up. You sell out, you betray, you kill . . . just a little bit.
But too much to expect the Marvelous Traveler to come with any
message from the Timely Rain."

The dining room of Jimmy Chan's restaurant was dark with the
shadows of chairs stacked and tangled on the tabletops. A white-
jacketed busboy led Yuen and the boy between the tables sprouting
trees of chairs to the office. Yuen left Dirigible outside to read his
funnybooks, then went inside after removing his hat. Rose's lessons
in American servility got to him at the oddest times.

Jimmy Chan's bow tie was very small against his fat bellying
throat. The tie wriggled like the wings of a tropical moth when he
spoke. Jimmy Chan's dog walked all over his desk and Jimmy
laughed at it when Yuen came in. Instead of greeting Yuen, he
said, "It's a chee-wah-wah. How about that? Please, have a
seat."

"How are you?" Yuen asked. "I've been trying to catch you to
ask you out for coffee and see how you are. But a busy man about
town, like Jimmy Chan . . ." Yuen said, opening with a courtesy, he
hoped. The knack for saying the right thing. Huie said Yuen had it.
Or had Huie just been saying the right thing himself?

"I'm busy all right. Busy going bankrupt to hell and damn."

Yuen nodded, then too quickly put his hand into his coat pocket,
as if he'd been bitten there. Then, "I got a letter from the United
States of America," Yuen said.

"I can't help with letters from the government. I can't tamper with the government. I'm going to be naturalized next year, but I know people who think I'm a Communist. Why? Because I have a big restaurant. What kind of Communist owns a restaurant with a floor show and a fan dancer? I'm going bust, I tell you the truth. People say Jimmy Chan is a smuggler. I'm not a goddamn-all-to-hell smuggler any more than you are. But what the hellfuck are my problems compared to yours? Where's a crooked cop when you need one, huh? You need money for a lawyer? What you need is a lawyer to tamper with the government, you know that?"

"Maybe you could read the letter?" Yuen held the letter out. Jimmy Chan put a cigar into his mouth and took the letter. The dog walked over to sniff Jimmy's hands and sniffed at the letter. "Don't let the dog dirty the letter," Yuen said.

"You should let him piss on it. Ha ha. It's a chee-wah-wah. You think I'd let my chee-wah-wah walk on my desk if it was going to dirty things up? You think these papers I have on my desk mean nothing? . . . I'm sorry if I seemed short-tempered just then, uncle, you asked with such force. You see, men with letters like this have come in before, and never, ever, have they ordered me or asked me anything straight out. I was surprised. You should be in business. You should be a general!" Jimmy turned and held the letter up to the light and started at the watermark. "Fine paper they use," he said, and patted the dog.

"I thought you could give me some advice,"

"You don't want advice," Jimmy Chan said. "You want me to help you. Perform a miracle. But you said advice. I'll take you on your word and give you advice. If you have no criminal record, you have nothing to worry about. There is no advice to give you. Just do what the letter says. Want me to translate it? It says go to the police. Get your fingerprints made and sent to Washington. Get your record of arrests and have the police send a copy to the government. It says it's only routine. Right here, just like this. I am routine."

"They might send me back to China."

"Not if you're all legal."

"Well, still . . ."

"Uncle, my sympathy is free. My advice too. I sympathize with you. You can't hide from them. They even have Chinese working for them, so you can't hide. I sympathize with you, but the only Chinese that get ahead are those who are professional Christian Chinese, or, you know, cater to that palate, right? You didn't know that when you came here, and now you're just another Chinaman that's all Chinese and in trouble. I can't help you."

"You could write a letter for me telling them I'm all right," Yuen said. He leaned back as Jimmy Chan pushed papers to both sides with his hands and elbows.

"Uncle, I don't know you're all right. And I don't want to know. I can help when I can help because I don't ask for secrets, I don't ask questions, and I don't trust anybody. I'd like to help you. I'm grateful to your generation, but your day is over. You could have avoided all your trouble if you had realized that the *lo fan* like the Chinese as novelties. Toys. Look at me. I eat, dress, act, and talk like a fool. I smell like rotten flower shop. And the *lo fan* can't get into my restaurant fast enough. They all call me Jimmy. I'm becoming an American citizen, not because I want to be like them, but because it's good business. It makes me wealthy enough to go bankrupt in style, to make the *lo fan* think I belong to them. Look! They like the Chinese better than Negroes because we're not many and we're not black. They don't like us as much as Germans or Norwegians because we're not white. They like us better than Jews because we can't be white like the Jews and disappear among the *lo fan*. But! They don't like a Chinaman being Chinese about life because they remind them of the Indians who, thirty-five thousand years ago, were Chinese themselves, see? So . . . !" Jimmy Chan clapped his hands together and spread them with the effect of climaxing a magic trick and looked about his office. He adjusted his bow tie and grinned. "This is being a professional Christian Chinese!"

"Indians?" was all Yuen could say that made sense.

"But helping you would be bad for me. So I write a letter for you. I get investigated, and then I get a letter. I don't want to be investigated. I want to become a citizen next year. Nobody likes me. Your people don't like me anymore because I'm really nobody, and you'll say I stepped on you to become a citizen and a professional Chinese. I have no friends, you see? I'm in more trouble than you."

"I'm going then. Thanks," Yuen said, and stood.

"Listen, uncle," Jimmy said from his seat, "don't do anything goddamn silly. If I can help with anything else, I'll be happy to do it. Want a loan? A job?"

"No," Yuen said and started to leave.

"Uncle, I trust you. You know what I mean. I know you have a job and keep your word and all that." Jimmy stood and took a long time to walk around his desk to Yuen's side. He put an arm around his shoulders. "You are a wise man. . . . If you die, die of old age. I feel bad when I can't help, and I feel real bad when men die." He grinned and opened the door for the old man. "But you are a wise man."

"Didn't even offer a drink," Yuen said outside with the boy.

Pigeons dropped from the sky to walk between the feet of people and peck at feed dropped from the cages of squabs and chickens in front of the poultry shops. "Stupid birds," Yuen said. "Someone will catch one and eat it." He laughed and the boy laughed.

"I'm hungry," Dirigible said.

As they left the restaurant, Yuen walked quickly. He held Dirigible's hand and pulled him down the streets and pointed at fire escapes and told him what Tongs were there and what he had seen when he had been at parties there, and he walked over iron gratings in the sidewalk and pointed down inside and told Dirigible that at night music could be heard down there. They passed men sitting next to magazine stands and shook hands. Then Yuen went to the bank and withdrew all his money in a money order and borrowed a sheet of paper and an envelope, and in Chinese wrote his song: "This is all the money I have. You will not get any more. I'm dead. Your father," and signed it. He put the letter and the money order in the envelope, addressed it, then went to the post office branch and mailed it. San Francisco was nothing to him now. He had said good-bye to his friends and seen the places he used to visit. They were all dirty in this daylight. The value of his death, to himself, was that nothing in his life was important; he had finished with his son that he hadn't seen in twenty years or more, and his friends, and San Francisco. Now he was going home. The tops of the buildings sparkled with their white tile and flags, Yuen saw. Jimmy Chan was wrong, he thought. But he helped me start the finish. The grandson, Sun Tzu, the strategist says, "In death ground, fight." I am. I'm a very lucky man to know when all I am to do in life is done and my day is over. Jimmy Chan is too professional to know that. He doesn't see the difference between me and Huie's dead brother. Too bad. No cringing. No excuses. He walked quickly down the hill, believing himself to the bus stop. Dirigible had to run to keep up with him.

"What did you take him to San Francisco for? And why go to San Francisco, anyway? Do you know I had to wash all the dishes and cook, too? That colored boy wasn't home, you know," Rose said. "Criminey sakes, you think I'm a machine or something?"

"I'm sorry," Yuen said. Rose wouldn't understand anything he said right now. Better she not know what good shape he was in. No explanations.

"Well, you have to hurry, if you're going to get back in time to help me with the dinner dishes. I'm sorry, I didn't mean that, ah-bok, I'm just worried. All right?" She put a hand on his shoulder.

"All right."

Rose took the letter from Yuen's pocket and sat down at the kitchen table and read it over. Yuen sat down next to her and put a toothpick in his mouth. Rose stared down at the letter and began scratching a slow noisy circle around her breast. She talked to Dirigible without looking at the boy. "Uncle's in trouble, dear, I mean ah-bok has to go to the police and get his pictures taken. And you have to take him there and help him answer the questions the police will ask in this letter."

"I've been walking all day, Mommy. I don't wanta walk no more," Dirigible said. "Why don't you go?"

"You got a car," Dirigible said, stepping backward.

"Listen," Rose said. "You take this letter." She lifted the letter and pinned it with a safety pin inside Dirigible's coat. "And you go to where the fingerprint place is and you tell them to read the letter, that the United States immigrators want them to read it, and that everybody, everybody, likes Yuen bok, okay? And you take him." She gave the boy some crackers to eat on the way and helped Yuen to his feet.

"Do you know how to get there?" Yuen asked at every corner. They walked streets full of rush-hour traffic, walked past parking meters and a bodybuilding gymnasium. Yuen put an arm about Dirigible and held him. "Where are we in all this?" Yuen asked and pushed Dirigible toward the edge of the sidewalk with each word.

"We have to go fast now, ah-bok, or the police will close," the boy said.

The streets were not crowded, but everywhere on the sidewalks along the sides of the buildings Yuen saw people walking, all of their eyes staring somewhere beyond him, the pads of fat next to their stiff mouths trembling with their steps. They all moved past him easily, without actually avoiding him. Yuen held the boy's hand and walked, numbing himself to the people.

The long corridor of the city hall was full of the sound of feet and shaking keys against leather-belted hips, and waxed reflections of the outside light through the door at the corridor's end, shrunk and twisted on the floor, as they walked farther down, past men with hats on and briefcases, policemen picking their noses, newspaper vendors with aprons. "Where do we go?" Yuen asked.

"I don't know," Dirigible said. "I can't read all the doors."

In a low voice, almost as smooth as an old woman's, Yuen said, "Do you see any Chinese around? Ask one, he'll help us." His hand rested on the back of the boy's neck, and was very still there as they walked.

"Excuse me . . ." a large man said, walking into them. They all tried to walk through each other a moment, then fell with the large man holding Dirigible's head and shouting a grunted "excuse me." Their legs all tangled, and they fell together in a soft crash. The man stood and brushed himself off. "I'm terribly sorry. Just barged out of my office, not thinking. Or thinking when I should have been watching my step. Are you all right? Your father looks a little sick."

"I have a letter," Dirigible said, and opened his jacket to show the letter pinned to the inside of his lapel.

"What's this?" the man asked, bending again. "A safety pin. All you people are safety pinning each other, my god!" he muttered. He took the letter and took a long grunt to stand up. Dirigible turned and helped Yuen, who was still on the floor, waiting, and staring with drool over his lip up at the strange *lo fan*. Yuen lifted himself to a crouch, rested, then stood and held himself steady, leaning on the boy.

"Immigration people want him fingerprinted," the man said. "You poor kid." He brushed his hair under his hat as he spoke. "I'll take you there. It's upstairs. Don't worry, if things go badly, you can call me, Councilman Papagannis." He adjusted his hat with his fat fingertips and walked quickly upstairs, swinging his arms with each step. They walked into a narrow hall with benches. At a desk, sitting on a high stool, in front of a typewriter, his sleeves rolled sloppily over his elbows, was a police sergeant, typing. "You can wash that ink stuff off your fingers in there, through that office, you see?" he was saying as they walked up to his desk. "What do you want? You'll have to wait in line. All these men here are in a hurry to get fingerprinted too."

"But I got a letter and supposed to tell you how people like Yuen bok. Him." Dirigible pulled Yuen to the desk.

"What?" the police sergeant asked.

"Immigration people want him fingerprinted, photographed, and a copy of his record," Councilman Papagannis said. "Here's the letter. I'm Councilman Papagannis. I'd like to see them out of here in a hurry, you know, for the boy's sake." The councilman shook the sergeant's hand, then removed his tight-fitting hat.

"It says here, they want a copy of his record, too," the sergeant said.

"Well, do it!" the councilman said, stuffing himself between Yuen and the boy. The police sergeant took out a form and put it in the typewriter; then he picked up the telephone and asked for the city's record on Nelson Yuen Fong. He put the telephone down and looked up to the councilman. "Never heard of him," he said.

"Surely you have a form for that contingency, sergeant."

"Surely."

"Who said, 'The mills of the gods grind slow, but they grind exceedingly fine'? or something like that. The mills of the system are a-grinding, young man," the councilman said, marveling at the sergeant's checking boxes on a form. The police sergeant removed Yuen's hat with a short motion of his arm, "Hair color, gray," he said and began typing. He dropped the hat onto Yuen's head.

Yuen took the hat from his head and looked inside the brim. "What for?" he asked.

"Nothing," Dirigible said and took the hat and held it. Yuen watched now, his eyes wide with the lids almost folding over backward. This was a fine joke for Yuen now. They were all so somber for his sake, and he had finished already. He could say anything and they would not understand, but Dirigible might understand a little, and Dirigible was too young to see the humor of the situation. Dirigible shouldn't be here, Yuen thought. I'll buy him a funnybook on the way home. He'll like that and won't feel so bad.

Dirigible yanked Yuen up to the edge of the police sergeant's desk and held his sleeve tightly. "How much do you weigh?" the police sergeant asked.

"He don't talk American," Dirigible said.

"What is he?"

"He's alien," Dirigible said.

"I mean, is he Filipino, Japanese, Hawaiian?"

"He's Chinese."

"Fine people, the Chinese," the councilman said.

"Fine," the police sergeant said and typed. "Now ask him how much he weighs."

Dirigible pulled at Yuen's coat until the man half knelt. Dirigible's first word was in English and jittery. Yuen frowned, then smiled to relax the boy. The boy stamped his foot and snapped his glare burning from the police sergeant to Yuen. Yuen should have known the boy would hate him for not being able to speak English Longtime Californ'.

"You how heavy?" Dirigible said, blushing, sounding stupid to everybody, and cracked the accent on the *choong* word for "heavy" in a flat accent, but meaning "onion" when high-toned. Both the boy and Yuen heard "heavy" waver into "onion" and blushed. "What do you mean?" Yuen asked instead of laughing. "Take it easy, kid."

"You are how many pounds?"

"What's your old man say, boy?"

"We don't talk good together yet," Dirigible said, crunching his tongue into English, while still lugging his tongue in gutless Chinese. "You are *how many pounds*?" The boy stood straight and shouted, *"How heavy the pounds?"* as if shouting made it more Chinese.

"Oh, how many pounds do I weigh?" Yuen grinned and nodded to the police sergeant and the councilman. The police sergeant nodded and pointed at Yuen's stomach then patted his own belly. "Hundred and thirty pounds heavy," Yuen said.

"One hundred and thirty pounds," Dirigible said. The police sergeant typed.

After the questions, the police sergeant stepped down from his high stool and held Yuen's arms. "Tell him we're going to take his picture now, boy." Dirigible told Yuen what he'd heard old Chinese say to children all the time, and Yuen asked Dirigible to ask the police sergeant if he could comb his hair before being photographed. The men laughed when Dirigible asked.

Dirigible stepped away from Yuen and snuck a pinch of the blue stripe of the police sergeant's trousers, to see if what looked like shiny wire was metallic to the fingertips and wasn't sure. Yuen turned his head and combed his hair with his pocket comb.

The police sergeant kicked a lever that turned Yuen's seat around. He snapped a picture. Yuen yelled once as the chair spun ninety degrees with the snap and stunned hum of a huge spring in the floor. "Atta boy, Nelson!" the police sergeant cheered. "Now for the fingerprints." He took the frames from the camera and tapped Dirigible next to the ear. "Tell your father to get down now."

"Ah-bok ahhh, get down now."

They walked home with the first blue of the dark night coming. Yuen patted the boy's shoulder and kept asking him to stop and buy some funnybooks, but the boy pulled Yuen's sleeve and walked on quickly, saying he was hungry and wanted to get back to the hotel kitchen. "Come on, ah-bok. I'm hungry," Dirigible said whenever the old man stopped to sit on a garbage can and nod his head at every streetcorner with a city trash can. He sat as if he would sit forever, without moving his body or fixing the odd hairs the wind had loosened, his head nodding slowly like a sleeping pigeon's. "Are you mad at me?"

"No," the boy said in a hurry.

"Your mother's waiting for us, isn't she?" Yuen said. He stood and walked a little and said, "You're a funny son. . . . ." He muttered to himself louder as they neared the Eclipse Hotel. All his old age shook and fattened up the veins in his hands as he tried to touch Dirigible's nose or his ears or poke the soft of the boy's cheeks. "You're almost as tall as me. . . . Did you see the policeman's face when he saw me?" In his slouching walk Yuen and the boy were very close to the same height. Yuen took a breath and tried to straighten up a thousand years, then sighed. He was too tired. Not important. "And that chair . . ."

He walked slower as they came to the back door of the restaurant. He looked up to the light over the door with pigeon droppings painting the hood. That light had gone out only once while he lived here, and he had changed the bulb himself. He had polished the hood and wiped the bulb. It was his favorite light in the whole restaurant, perhaps because it was the light that helped him open the door when he returned tipsy from San Francisco, or perhaps because it was the only light outside, back of the building. Thinking about a light bulb is stupid, he thought. He could enjoy stupidity now, after all this time of trying to be smart, trying to be tall; stupidity was inevitably on the way to rounding out the circle and resting it in silence.

Yuen could hear Margie shouting the names of foods back to the waitresses as if cussing them out and didn't seem to hear a thing. He could hear the little screech of ice-cold meat slapped flat onto a hot steel griddle before the grease cackles, running water, the insulated door of the walk-in refrigerator stomping shut, and didn't hear a thing. He held Dirigible's wrists together with one hand. Then to his horror, both his hands and all his strength, which felt considerable, twisted Dirigible's wrists. He could see from the ease with which the boy moved his arms that his considerable strength was nothing. "Help me upstairs," he said. "I don't feel well."

He leaned heavily on the boy, pushed himself upright against the wall as they climbed. Dirigible was very strong, Yuen felt, very strong. And very angry. The boy pushed at Yuen, upping the old man onto the next step up, up the stairs to his room.

In his room, Yuen did nothing but sigh and sigh and fall backward onto his bed. He stared a moment at the ceiling. The boy did not leave the room. Yuen closed his eyes and pulled at his nose and wiped it with his fingers and stared at the boy. He saw the boy clearly now, and the smile on his face closed shut, then the mouth opened to breathe. It no longer felt like his face he was feeling, no part of him. The old man's fingers, nothing felt like anything of his now. It all felt like old books in old stores. "I have an idea," he said slowly, and took the gun from under his pillow. "We used to try to swallow our tongues to choke ourselves when we were scared, but we always spit them out, or couldn't get them down. I want you to watch so you can tell them I wanted to."

"I don't know what you're talking." Dirigible eyed the gun.

"I'm going to die by myself," Yuen attempted in Chinese for dummies.

The boy stared, eyes big as black olives. "Who? You . . . what are you doing?"

"Your mother can find another dishwasher. She's a good business-woman."

"Who'll buy me books?"

Yuen pointed the gun at one ear, then switched hands, and pointed the gun at the other ear. He looked at the gun and held it with both hands and pointed it at his mouth, aiming it into his mouth, toward the bulge at the back of his head. He could be angry at the boy, even knowing the boy knew nothing else to say, he could be angry, but wasn't. Dirigible hit himself with a fist and shouted, "Ah-bok!" Dirigible leaned and fell backward, stepped once toward the old man before stopping against the towel rack. The boy was weeping and groaning, holding an imaginary pain in his shoulder.

Yuen looked over the gun and watched the boy's rhythmless stumblings in the close room. He eased the hammer to safe and sighed a longer sigh than he had breath. He went to the boy and pulled him to the bed and sat him and wiped his face with his hand. "It's all right, Dritch'ble." Yuen worked for enough breath to speak. "Get up. Go downstairs, now." He bent to untie his shoe-laces, dropping the gun to the floor when his fingers could not work them. "Wait. Will you help me bathe? I feel very weak." He'd failed. But he had known he would. He'd expected it.

"Yes."

"I have soap. All kinds. You can have some. . . ."

"I have soap too."

He patted the boy's shoulders with his hands and clutched into them with his fingers as he pulled himself to standing. "You're an odd son," Yuen said, before turning to undress. "Help me with this."

Dirigible held a towel about Yuen's pale waist as he took him out of his room to the bathroom and helped him into the tub. Dirigible plugged the tub and turned on the water, with Yuen curled up on the bottom, waiting. He didn't complain about the temperature. He leaned forward and asked the boy to scrub his back. His body was loose over his bones, and the same color as his colorless wrists with fat spongy veins piping through the skin. He took the boy's hand and looked into his face with eyes covered with raw egg white. "You didn't write me," he said clearly and, his body quivering, rippling water away from his waist, Yuen died. He closed his eyes with his mouth opening to breathe or sigh, and at the end, his chest was low, his ribs showed, and he was dead. There was no more for him. He had finished it.

Dirigible lifted his hands from the water and put his cheek on the edge of the tub. Yuen's death had seemed nothing special, nothing personal. He had given up the boy also. The boy tried to work a tear loose. He felt he should. Tears not all for Yuen, but for himself, because Yuen had been *his.*

Rose came up the stairs and walked down the hall noisily, saying, "Well, how did it go, you two?" before she leaned her head into the bathroom.

Jeffery Paul Chan

(1942–   )

Jeffery Chan was born in Stockton, California. He is a professor of Asian American studies at San Francisco State University. Chan's fiction and essays have appeared in *Yardbird Reader, West, Amerasia Journal,* and numerous other periodicals. His play, *Bunny Hop,* was produced by the East/West Players in Los Angeles, and he is the former drama critic of Marin County's newspaper, *Independent Journal.* His short story "The Chinese in Haifa," which appeared in *Aiiieeeee! An Anthology of Asian American Writers* (1974), is one of the most talked about and thought-provoking pieces of fiction in Asian American literature. He lives in Marin County, north of San Francisco, with his wife, Janis, and his children, Jennifer and Aaron Bear.

Cheap Labor

The men were on their way to a stand of oak where they could gather tan bark quickly and where a trail wide enough for Uncle Pius to maneuver his stake truck lay convenient. The winter and spring had been unusually dry, which meant small fruit and no harvest work to speak of, and the valley winds blew hot and dusty, spreading fever, a peculiar contagion that struck the children's mother, who returned to San Francisco on the bus, her legs swollen and her arms covered with a scabrous eczema where doctors at the Chinese Hospital could wonder at this rural disease in her own dialect. They were Der or Tse or See or, in their native village, Cheh, or even Kim when a given name had been confused with their family name by some spelling ritual of baptism, citizenship or entry at the island in San Francisco harbor. Originally, the family had settled in the Sacramento valley, at first in the foothills, then migrating to the flood plain become orchards and rice fields, though they were never farmers. They held to business, a restaurant in Tinkers Rest, a dry goods store in Knights Bridge. After the father had been accidently crushed by a water wagon during a particularly raucous Firemen's Muster in Yuba City, put down to postwar exuberance, a fraternal order among the brigades (founded in the early history of the region as a vigilance committee) offered financial compensation, which became a dry-cleaning plant on the outskirts of the sleepy capital of the state and allowed the twins to attend Catholic schools in San Francisco, where their mother preferred to live.

Uncle Pius had title to land bought in an especially barren section of the buttes called Eden and camped there in a summer with no harvest, contracting small crews of illegals he could busy when the plant was closed, catching snakes, gathering tan bark, hunting doves in the stubbled fields scorched by the summer drought. Uncle said it was good for his sister's children to swim in the shallow spill of the Feather River or the Yuba's south fork and its shallow tributaries before it drained to mud and the feverish swamps in the delta. Uncle called this time in his yearly cycle "vacation," but the twins in their privacy viewed their month in the country as a term in purgatory.

As usual, Uncle had spent the entire evening in Marysville parked in front of the Hop Sing Tong offering a few days' work to the stumbling parade that ambled listlessly from the gambling parlors to the cantinas. Clouds of midges and mayflies swirling in the light and smoke rose from the open transoms. In the dark alleyways the drunks sprawled against the buildings singing chorus after chorus *de mis ranchos y borrachos* the twins called the Mexican blues. In the heat of the evening, Eva's dog hid beneath the truck from the bright moon as if from the sun as they lay on top of the cab watching a dark-faced woman draped in an enormous wool blanket collide against solitary figures in the empty lot across D Street.

Fat Adam, Uncle's cook, perched on the tailgate talking with Fong Sook, who'd stepped from his barbershop to beg a ride to Sacramento. A'Sook greeted the children in Chinese as he removed his hat and mopped his head with his handkerchief, carefully wiping the sweatband with a flourish, coloring the air around him with the smell of bay rum and tiger balm he shook from his gingham rag. He spoke slowly, using the stock phrases these children would understand.

Fat Adam reassured him they wouldn't be riding to Sacramento this night. Maybe in a few days, he promised. He took a'Sook by the arm, and they joined the small crowd toting their losses at the entrance to the Hop Sing listening to the martial opera from the second floor echoing in the tiled stairwell.

"Joey, you think she's trying to pick a fight? She must really be drunk," Eva whispered.

"I think she's a whore trying to get his attention," he replied loudly.

Eva sat up and pointed. "Look, that guy took her blanket."

"It's love," he said in a confident voice. "They'll make their bed in the river." Joe rolled over to his back, staring at the waxing moon. "You'll see their figures caught momentarily at the top of the levee, moonlit silhouettes locked in an embrace."

"They kiss," she giggled.

"They turn into frogs," he echoed. "They'll cure warts."

"You're awful." She slid down the windshield and slapped the dust from her pants. "I'm going to get something to eat. Adam's making *siu yeh* for the slaves before we leave town." She slipped past a'Pok guarding the door to the mah jong table and squirmed through the crowd, avoiding an occasional hand that reached out to tug at her hair or kick at the dog that trailed her footsteps.

A train whistle sounded in the distance. Joe walked to the trestle spanning Hobo Gulch and counted nearly a mile of flatbed cars hauling heavy equipment for the Central Valley Water projects at Oroville and further north at Shasta. As the cars slowed, Joe could pick out men on the corners waiting for their car to clear the steel bridge before chancing a leap into the dark of the gravel embankment. He heard a shout break above the clack and squeal, and a man tending a campfire in the gulch answered, "Marysville. This is Marysville and Mary's gone to hell."

When Uncle Pius had counted seven men eating in the kitchen of the Hop Sing, he ordered the children to the truck. Already well past midnight, they slept the hour's ride to Eden.

Joe first woke up hearing what he thought was the Yuba cresting, water rushing past the dry locks holding the river back, a steady hiss of rain beating against the river willows, the sound of sand tumbling in the boiling waters melting the levee. But when he opened his eyes, there was only a vast stretch of night sky freckled with stars fading and no sound but the mountain stream sliding over the gravel bed, the sigh of water spilling a distance and the faint roar from the granite cistern far below, a dark abyss that swallowed at least this Sierra stream quite whole. The chill air held only a hint of moisture, and his bedding was lightly fissured with dust, the alluvium of night's passing, the leaves of the bay trees graying by the water as the sun lit the rim of the barren canyon. Something, a chipmunk or squirrel, bent and broke dry wood, and came a warning from a songbird answered by a raspy jay. Dusty brown doves rustled beneath the live oak, where Eva slept, kicking leaves aside them, and the dog whined impatiently, still tied to the post of the sleeping deck, her tree house. Fat Adam was already dipping water for coffee, and Joe heard him spit clear his throat and spit again. Joe snuggled deep into his sleeping sack. The men would leave before sunlight reached high enough to warm him, so it wasn't until Uncle's truck backfired on the steep track halfway up the hill that would he wake again.

"Jesu love me, yeah he do, 'caus da bibo tell him to." Fat Adam knelt before an old milled beam rescued from a collasped mine upstream he'd suspended between two convenient rocks beside the cooking fire, paring rind from a lump of leftover pork, feeding Eva's dun rat terrier and singing hymns.

Up, Joe searched among a heap of pots and pans for a bucket. "Jesus, Uncle Adam, Jesus."

"Mut wha?" Flies buzzed warily about a piece of waxy yellow tendon he offered the dog.

Eva had spent another restless night and snapped irritably at him. "Uncle, don't feed her that stuff. She'll get worms." Her bowl of rice gruel was swept into the dirt as she tried to bundle the dog into the blanket she wore to breakfast. Then she kicked it as Toto scrambled from her grasp, circled the fire and began lapping the rice up.

Fat Adam laughed indifferently. "Dog know how to eat bettah den you. *Siu yuk juk* in de morning. You wan' sa'more?" He stood up stiffly and rolled his apron up, wiping his hands on the underside.

"Don't give her any more. She'll just waste it on the dog again or throw up."

"You shut up, Joe."

"Shut up yourself and put some clothes on. You're dragging your blanket in the dirt. What'd you do? Sleep in the river?"

She glared at her brother. "You're the one who knows about stuff like that. I washed my underwear, and it's not dry yet. You wanna look? Wah Gay and what's his face, Mickey Mouse, run around in their underpants. What privacy have I got?"

"A'Mee Kee?" Adam smiled. "Mickey Mouse?"

"The one who's always drooling," she said.

"He lisps. He doesn't drool," Joe countered.

"He drools when he lisps!" she screamed.

Fat Adam cackled and spit. "You know what a'Chinee peeble say wit twins, *a'seung bau toi*? Dey say you two marry in anudder life. You two fight jus' likee you marry."

"I am Chinese," Eva snapped. "I am a'Chinee peeble."

"Mut wha?"

"You know what I said. Just because I don't talk funny like you. *Mut wha, mut wha.* I know what you're saying."

"Dass nice. I sing you Chinee opera song. Teach you sa'more."

She grabbed the dog by one hind leg and yanked it to her. "No, Toto! That stuff'll make you sick." She walked away kicking dust but turned, ignoring Fat Adam. "Uncle Pius said we'd have church tomorrow if we wanted," she smirked.

Joe groaned. "Uncle doesn't care about church. What for?"

"It's Sunday, stupid, that's why. You live out here like a savage and you just lose all track, don't you. Besides, he promised Ma we wouldn't forget our prayers. I bet we could find Billy Sunday on the crystal set. He'd teach Uncle Adam the bibo don't tell Jesus to love him." Toto yelped in pain, held by the scruff as Eva slipped a string leash around its neck. "Come, Toto," she enjoined pleasantly, dragging the dog away.

Fat Adam picked her bowl up and put it to boil with the rest of the morning's dishes, spit into the fire and raised his eyes to Joe. "You eat?"

"*Sic bau law,* thank you, Uncle."

"You' sistah don' eat enough. Always in a bat moot."

"She's just a bitch. I guess she still doesn't feel too good yet, and she misses Ma. Nobody here to talk to for her. Just the guys." He looked at the old man bent over the fire. "You know. We really can't talk with them too well anyway."

"How come yoah ma don' put you in a' Chinee skoo?"

"We have to learn American."

"Shiyet."

"Well, we do. This isn't China."

"Don' be stupid, *a' doy,*" Adam scoffed. "You born here. You are 'Mellican. Shiyet. What you learn for?"

Joe flushed. "I meant English. *Ying mun.*"

Adam sighed and pulled a cigarette from the pack he carried in his waistband. He jabbed it in his mouth, bent down to light it in the fire, then sat back against the makeshift table, blowing a cloud of smoke. "*Ying mun.* Shiyet." He closed his eyes, dismissing his efforts with the boy.

Shiyet, Joe murmured to himself. Eva stayed in her tree house with the earphones clapped over her head. He moved upstream looking for likely crevices where potholes (Uncle Pius confided to anyone that would listen) concealed placer gold washed down the stream bed from the collapsed mine, settling beneath the gravel debris.

"Course now, any speck of gold is heavier than the gravel and there's a lot a' rocks and sand sitting on top of it. So it's just a matter of moving the right rock. And the right rock is a rock nobody else's moved."

"How much could I get?" Joe'd demanded.

Uncle waved his hand at the entire length of the stream, the glow of the campfire reflected in his spectacles, the stub of a cold cigar clenched between his teeth. They stood apart from the crew watching Fat Adam perform, but Uncle was bundled like the rest against the evening chill in field boots, a sweater with his outer vest, and still sporting canvas cuffs up to his elbows. He wore work denims stiff with tree sap and a short knife suspended by a loop of rawhide he used to notch his cigars. "*Gum daw suey*? Heh, heh, all that water? Must be enough there to fill a couple of teeth, anyway." Uncle wanted Joe to become a dentist. So many of the men he imported had poor teeth like himself. Mr. Kwock, who wore a cowboy hat his every waking moment, didn't have any teeth at all and carried a set of dentures in a cotton bag slung to his belt.

"Is that all?"

"That all? *A'doy*, that's fifty, sixty dollars. More'n I pay any of 'em in a month."

Shiyet. He poked through a pile of wood Adam took for the fire, the remains of a collasped lean-to looking for square nails. The air stank of creosote and rotting manzanita as the sun beat down on the scrub and smooth rock. Out of sight and alone, he tracked his own footprints in the fine silt dusting the perimeter of camp and imagined himself killing snakes with a chain whip he improvised with baling wire, parodying the *kung fu* set he'd watched Fat Adam dance in the firelight, howling with Eva's dog for the amusement of the crew.

"What if I find a big piece, Uncle? How big does it have to be?"

Fat Adam had flipped the end of his rope whip through the coals of the fire and set the tail glowing. He raised it slowly then cracked it above his head as he whirled away from the bright tip chasing him, his howling becoming the sound of machine-gun bullets exploding as the fire snapped at his face, twirling a stiff baton that slapped bullets aside as he passed the whip from one hand to the other, rolling on his back, then kipping to his feet to freeze at the ready, dry grass in his hair, bits of rock and dirt patterning the sweat on his shirt, the whip now straight as a stick.

Uncle Pius opened his mouth and pointed to a gold tooth, shouting above the crew applauding Fat Adam's performance. "Don't have to be too big. See?"

Adam held stock-still, the effort to keep his stance as strenuous as movement. The whip pulled wire taut between his outstretched fists, his eyes fixed to the tip of burning rope, his breath stoking the coal end. He slid one hand up the length of rope, using both hands to choke the fire of a writhing snake. Then he straddled it and waved the glowing end at Eva's treehouse, which made them laugh. It became a yard of lit fuse as he raised one foot slowly, pivoting on the other, an expression of mock terror lighting his perspiring face as he puffed his angry red cheeks trying to blow the fire out. He cocked his head, and his lips split in a ghastly smile as the men collasped in laughter.

"Ai ya!" he cried in mock anguish and fell on his face. *"Yup bun pow jeung."*

Shiyet.

"What's a Japanese firecracker anyway?" Eva dangled her feet in the pool where Joe worked to clear a pothole, reaching beneath the boulder where she perched. "If you wanna know what I think personally, Uncle Fatso's mentally retarded and belongs in a looney bin."

"Move your damn feet or I'll pull you in," he gasped, then ducked under the cold water, finding handholds along the mossy underside of the rock to brace against his own buoyancy and the shallow current. He pulled the larger stones from the hole and netted the fine gravel at the bottom with a kitchen strainer, emptying the debris into an improvised sluice box until there was enough for a bucketful. Then, with a rusted frying pan, he could pan the silt he had carefully screened, watching for the lead shot he added to the tailings as markers to tell him if he was washing too vigorously. The lighter debris would rinse away, leaving a fine black grit at the bottom where specks of gold dust occasionally appeared.

"I bet it's dirty."

"Help me move this rock. I can't get to the bottom of the hole." Joe stood up, the water reaching nearly to his shoulders.

"I'm sitting on this rock. It's too heavy anyway. Get the fat lunatic to help you."

"He's gonna hear you say that." Joe rested in the water, surveying the boulder. "Besides which he's not a lunatic."

"Mentally retarded, then. He looks just like those guys who live out of garbage cans in Chinatown. I bet that's what'll happen when he stops working for Uncle. He's a wetback if you wanna know. Just like you," she giggled.

"Uncle says he was a solider in China and fought the Japanese. Some missionaries brought him to Honolulu because he saved their lives. He wasn't in a regular army, some warlord's," Joe offered. Uncle Pius often bragged of the contract labor he'd brought through Hawaii to skirt the exclusion laws, a trick he said he'd learned from the first president of China, who had actually slept in a bed right in Marysville, so the locals claimed.

"Wah Gay called him a rice Christian and a bandit," she countered.

"Who said that?"

"You know who. I think he likes me because he wanted to listen to the radio."

"Sounds like a breakfast food."

"What does?"

"Rice Christians."

"Anyway, Wah Gay said there's no war with the Japanese, at least not yet. Who fights wars before there's a war?"

"Well, he knows *kung fu*. You watched him last night."

"Sure," she said scornfully, "the Japanese firecracker set. You watch him do white crane for supper and we'll all have to eat it." She stood up on the rock and flailed her arms, then throttled an imaginary crane's neck, squinting and puffing her cheeks. *"Mut wha! Mut wha! Ngaw ah say nay wha!"*

Joe laughed out loud, then shot a guilty glance toward the camp, the heat of midday shimmering over the water. Fat Adam waded knee deep, gathering watercress floating in the roots of the bay trees married to the shallow steam flat at camp for several yards before narrowing. His shirt and apron were knotted around his waist. His pants warmed on a rock nearby. He reached under the scrub around the trees, pulling the watercress up in a tangle of roots and tendrils. He rinsed and shook each clump before stuffing it in a burlap bag dripping at his side.

"Stop that. He'll hear you," she whispered. "What's he picking up now? It a good thing Uncle keeps him in the country so he doesn't eat garbage in front of everybody. So humiliating."

"It's just for the soup."

"I know it's for soup," she said, sitting resignedly. "We had it last night, green scum complete with snails. He eats bugs, you know. Mickey Mouse dared him and he ate it."

"Cooked búgs."

"Nope. Live bugs. When I told Uncle, he said it was good Chinese medicine." She laughed, then shuddered. She folded her hands, unfolding and refolding them, coiled some hair around her finger and chewed on the ends. "Joe?"

"Yeah?"

"I miss Ma," she sniffed and seemed to want to cry.

He looked up to see if she was serious. "She'll be okay. She's in a hospital. Doctors know what to do. Don't be a crybaby or I'll tell Wah Gay."

"Sure," she said, her voice cracking. "How?"

"What d'ya mean how?"

"You don't know the word for crybaby." She tried to smile. "But I miss Ovaltine, poached eggs and toast. I want to hear the 'Breakfast Club.' I heard 'Little Orphan Annie' for just a minute last night, but it drifted away."

"We're in a canyon."

"Joey?"

"Still here."

"You think Wah Gay likes me?" Tears streamed in earnest down her face as she hiccoughed and laughed at the same time. "I didn't show you what he gave me after I threw up last night." She held a huge flying beetle in the palm of her hand and struck a light tattoo with her fingertips against its brass-colored back, the chitin shell thick as her thumbnail. "He says it's a goldbug."

He dried his hands against the rocks. "Let me see. There's no such thing as a gold bug." He turned it carefully in the sunlight. "It's a big June beetle. But how come it doesn't have any feet?"

"When he caught it, he pulled the legs off because he didn't want me to feel it wiggle in my hand. Wasn't that sweet?" She mopped her eyes with her shirt tail. "He says I should dip it in lacquer so the color won't fade."

"That's very nice. Kind of a get-well present. Is it dead?" he asked.

"It never moved a muscle."

"Well, it feels heavy." He dropped it in her outstretched hand. "It's probably not dry yet."

"Dry?"

"You know. Inside."

Eva set it carefully on the rock beside her. "I guess I'll let it dry first. But it was sweet of Wah Gay to give it to me. He's kind of old-fashioned and romantic. You know he's only seventeen and he's a gambler and a poet."

"And he's in love with the boss's daughter."

"He said he wants to be my big brother." She smiled, twisting a braid of hair around her finger and brushing her lips with it. "Why Mr. Wah Gay, I'm only thirteen and much too young to know the love of a man, you handsome rogue, you."

"Melly me, a' Eva an' we liff happ fo'evah. You be my *gum sahn paw*."

She clapped her hands together and drew them to the side of her face. "I'm sorry, Wah Gay, you must live with a broken heart. I could never marry a coolie."

"Damn American-born girls. Stop chewing your hair and help me pan that bucket of sand." Joe shuddered violently, then plunged into the water.

Eva climbed down from her perch and grabbed the pan and bucket. "It's a whole bucket of gold," she crowed.

"Not until we move this damn rock."

She scooped the tailings into the pan and tipped it into the stream. "Damn rock," she agreed fiercely.

Upstream, Fat Adam gave a short cry, stumbling, and swore. He hobbled his way around the tangle of tree roots to a wide base of flat granite to rest his foot against the warm rock face.

Joe yelled across to him, but he didn't look up. Instead, Adam scrutinized his foot with an offended air, kneading it methodically, separating his toes and working his knuckles against the arch.

"Hey, Uncle," Joe cried again. "Come here and help us move this rock."

Fat Adam squinted against the glare of sun on the water, then shook his head. "Why? I don' wan' it. Got plenty here."

"Come on," Joe pleaded, "we need your big muscles. Maybe there's gold under it. Make you a rich man."

"Shiyet. I am a rich man. You see me workin'?" He continued massaging his foot.

Eva joined in. "Please, Uncle?" Then, loud enough that Joe winced, "Uncle Asshole."

Adam looked up and spat into the water. "Watch dat, now. Ma spit it stick to gol'," he chortled.

Eva stood up, spilling the pan, and screamed in fury. "You asshole!"

Joe threw water at her. "Cut it out, Eva."

"You talk to you' papa dat way, Jesu gonna hear you." Fat Adam laughed deep in his throat, choked, then spit hugely. "*Bok juk!*" Without hurry, he picked up his pants, drying his legs and feet, then walked slowly back, disappearing into the shadows of the camp marked by smoke coiling above the trees.

The twins stayed by the water panning the tailings Eva collected in the bucket as Joe rinsed the sand and gravel with water, patiently swirling the remains and collecting a heavy grit the color of chewing gum that stayed with the lead shot at the bottom of the frying pan. And it wasn't until they heard the sound of Uncle's truck that they felt the heat of the windless afternoon emanating from wherever the water did not touch, as all around them the dry rubble and eroding fissures caught the bright sun grilling the canyon granite. They waded back to camp, then, keeping to the shallow edges, soaking their hair with quick splashes, mindless of the water dripping in their eyes and down their backs, feeling with their feet for smooth stepping stones. The men sat in the middle of the stream kicking water at each other. Mr. Kwock saluted them with his cowboy hat.

Wah Gay and Mee Kee wrestled in their underpants and hooted as Eva looked away and moved gingerly up the bank of hot sand. Uncle Pius sat on the running board of the stake truck, the hood up and the radiator blowing steam. He waved to them.

"Find anything, boy?" His vest and jacket hung on the mirror attached to the truck door. Joe was anxious to test the grains and twisted bits of white metal they'd collected, when Pius hefted the weight of the cloth pouch and whistled. "Well, that feels heavy enough to be something."

Fat Adam sat by the cooking fire with the dog lapping at a tin bowl of water at his feet. It still trailed a length of broken string Eva had used to tie it to her tree house.

Pius explained, "We'll cook your rocks over the fire. If the white stuff burns off, that's the quicksilver they used in the mines to separate the gold out. It took to the gold when they crushed the ore. You see, they'd wash it just like you washed it, but they probably had a ton. The water carried little bits into the stream bed. So maybe that's what you got here, the leftovers. Put it in a pan and we'll heat it up."

Eva called to her dog, but the animal merely looked up to scratch.

"Is there any fire, Uncle?" Joe asked Adam cautiously.

"Goot cook got fire aw da' time, a'bossy," he answered and spit on the grate, the spittle dancing on the hot metal.

Pius emptied the dog's water bowl on the stove, sending up a cloud of steam, and gave it to Joe. Unnerved by the explosion of steam, the dog ran toward Eva and was brought up short when she stepped on its trailing leash.

"A'dok need water on hot day," Pius said irritably.

"Thank you, Uncle Adam. I just forgot all about her. *Daw jeh sai.*" The dog cowered as she dragged it back to the tree house and hoisted it up, securing its leash to a branch.

"Shiyet," Adam muttered.

Returning, she stood apart as Adam threw fresh wood on the coals and Pius finished explaining that Joe was trying to melt rocks that might be gold. Adam beat the flames with his apron, and they all fell back from the heat. "Hot stuff," he exclaimed.

Uncle Pius laughed. "It's the fate of cooks and soldiers to be near the fire on a hot day."

"Fate worse den be Eva's dok," Adam replied smiling.

"Won't the gold get burned up if it's too hot, Uncle?" Joe asked.

Pius shook his head. "Naah. Gold is an immutable substance, boy. Just like the soul. Says so in the Bible even."

Fat Adam kicked at a falling log, choking as the smoke swirled around him. *"Jun gum but pa hung low foh,"* he said to Pius. "A'Pius, *nay hai m'hai wah,* go' like da' so'? Bibo say dat?"

"Sure," Uncle Pius said. "Best kind. Just like the heart of the mother of the Chinese Revolution, solid gold."

"Mut wha?"

"Gap min gee mo gaw sum hai gum laih ga."

"Bing gaw mo? M'hai ngaw'ga!" Then, they both laughed.

"Hai law, jun gum hai law." Pius wiped the tears from his eyes as much from smoke as from good humor. "Your Uncle Adam, here, always knew we had hearts of gold. Now he wants to see some, I think."

Joe pushed the bowl to one corner of the fire and peered at the dark grit. "Uncle, it's all black. It didn't melt, but it doesn't look like gold either."

Eva said, "Maybe it's the cook."

Adam plucked a piece the size of a fingernail paring with chopsticks and spit on it. They all gathered to watch as he rubbed it against a rough whetstone, then held it up for them all to marvel.

"That's it, boy," Uncle pius beamed. "That's the right stuff."

The right stuff, less than an ounce, Pius estimated, could bring as much as twenty dollars, but the gold itself should be melted down to make jewelry, a ring or perhaps earrings, he advised, as the rest of the men, hearing about Joe's find, congratulated his luck. Joe took them all downstream and together, Fat Adam barking orders, they were able to move the boulder. But in the failing light, they missed or carelessly washed away what little there might have been. Mee Kee and Wah Gay wandered back to camp, and the rest walked further down to where the stream bed fell away and the water disappeared into a natural cistern. Pius and Adam waited until Joe emptied the last pan of tailings, then, in the dark, they felt their way back to camp empty-handed, misplacing Adam's bucket.

"Dass aw'right," he said genially, "no light now. You rich bossy now. You bet make gol' ring for you' wife," he said, nodding at the tree house.

Reminded, Joe was about to call to his sister when suddenly a figure dropped from the branches and came running toward them. It was Wah Gay. He was carrying his shirt in one hand, and when he saw them he waved it like a flag.

"Mo sien din gong a'Jung Gok tung Yup Bun dah jeung la!" he shouted in their faces.

Adam caught him by the arm and meant to hold him there, but the young man twisted free and ran past them without stopping, as if to inform the men downstream. *"Hai jun ga."* They heard him splash into the water, his voice rippling through the canyon as he spread his news.

"What did he say?" Joe asked.

"The radio told him China is at war with Japan," Pius answered.

"*Mut yea* radio?" Adam asked suspiciously.

"The crystal set," Joe concluded. "He found a station. Eva," he called, "Eva."

She sat in the dark of the tree, the dog in her lap, staring at the mantle of evening descending from the rim of the canyon to meet the darkness, touching the pale shadows of the campfire against the granite wall directly across the water. Joe stepped up on a low branch and touched her feet dangling shoeless over the edge of the deck. "Did you hear it too? China's declared war on Japan?"

"I'm the only one who heard it," she whined listlessly. "I found Drew Pearson. Wah Gay wouldn't know what he was saying anyway. I told him." She was wrapped in her sleeping bag, and he could see she had wound the string leash around her hand to keep Toto close.

"How did you tell him?"

"*War* has the same last sound as *firecracker*," she said, annoyed. "You remember, *pow jeung, ah jeung*. At least I did. He was laughing at me, but when I said it, he stopped. Then I said, 'Take me with you to China, fair knight.' But he didn't understand that," she giggled.

"You don't wanna go to China. What for?"

"So's Toto will miss me, won't you, Toto," she said, nuzzling the dog. "Can't take you to China, no, no. They'd eat you there, put you in a pot for stew."

Dinner lay in a line of steaming pots, and Fat Adam and Uncle Pius were already at the soup. Pius bent over the soup kettle, pinching a bit of watercress, and blew furiously on it before lowering it into his mouth.

"Eva, come drink some soup while it's still hot," he called.

"Uncle Adam spits in the river and draws the same water to make soup," she replied distantly. "I want Ovaltine."

"Everybody can hear you," Joe hissed. "What's the matter with you."

Fat Adam belched loud and long. "*Ho may, wah,*" he said to no one in particular, all of the men hunkered around the fire. "Tess goot, Eva."

"That's what makes it taste so good," Pius laughed, embarrassed.

"He eats bugs, too. I saw him eat a worm for breakfast." Eva's voice, a flat monotone, carried over the noise of dinner.

"Goot Chinee medicine," Adam said genially.

"Eva. Come down here and eat some rice. You'll get sick if you don't eat." Pius set his bowl down and walked to the tree.

"Uncle, I wanna go home now."

He looked up at Joe, questioning. "Not now. It's too dark."

"I wanna go home," she repeated.

Adam stood up and followed Pius to the tree, heedless of the men talking around him. He stepped over Mee Kee and Wah Gay talking to Mr. Kwock about the need to return to China. "A'Eva," he called gently, "a'bossy Joe gonna make gol' earrings for you. You like dat? Ain' no bugs dere. You come eat now."

Joe boosted himself to the deck and sat beside her, peering at the dark flush across her face.

"Is there enough for earrings, Joe?"

"Sure," he said, touching her forehead.

"Then, one's for you," she insisted weakly. "You get one from me. The gold's half mine."

"Your head's real warm, Eva. Do you feel sick?"

She pushed his hand away with her own, and he could feel her trembling.

Joe looked down to where Pius and Fat Adam stood. "Uncle, I think she's sick or something."

"Joe," she whispered, "you wanna know what he said?"

"Who?"

"Drew Pearson. He said China will surely be defeated. But I couldn't tell Wah Gay." She sighed.

Fat Adam stood on the branch, looked at Eva, then motioned for Joe to help her down.

She let go her sleeping bag as Adam pushed it away, but warned him, "You can't eat my dog."

Fat Adam replied softly, "Naah. Dok too tough. Jus' like you."

"Joe," she said faintly, "tell Uncle Fatso what the radio said." She began shaking violently and was unconscious before she was still.

Pius was able to make the highway in the bright moonlit night and Yuba City in two hours even though the truck was heavily loaded. Joe awoke with a start as they pulled into a bright apron of light that bathed the entrance of the hospital. A young doctor assured Uncle Pius that Eva was a victim of sunstroke and seemed a bit dehydrated. He would keep her overnight to be sure, and they could pick her up in the afternoon. Joe reminded Uncle Pius that Eva liked to drink Ovaltine, and the doctor smiled benevolently and assured him that he would prescribe it.

Pius told Joe to wrap up in Eva's sleeping bag if he wanted to sleep. The night was warm and dry, the highway empty, so he made for the tannery at Tinkers Rest, where he could drop their load before they made their way back to camp. He bought the Sunday papers at a filling station, and Joe bought candy bars and two Dr. Peppers he would finish before their nocturnal loop was completed. Pius talked of the war in the Far East, confirmed by the headlines, in terms that only then was Joe beginning to understand. In less than two weeks, the Japanese army had attacked two cities, Shanghai, the second, and the civil war between the government and the Communist rebels was finally over.

"Would America fight for China or Japan?" Joe asked as they rolled through Knights Bridge, a single light bulb burning in the window of the bait-and-tackle shop.

"American ideas about democracy and science are very strong in China," he answered. "For China."

"Then China will win," Joe said.

"Oh, yes," Uncle Pius replied. "Eventually, China will win."

"Will Uncle Adam go back to China? He was a soldier, you said."

"I don't know. The young men want to."

"And what will we do, Uncle?" Joe asked tentatively.

"Us? We are *wah que,* the overseas Chinese. We send the money to help support the war just like during the revolution. *Gap min gee mo.* That's what they called us, Mother of the Revolution."

"That sounds funny," Joe said sleepily. "How can we be somebody's mother?"

"Well, it doesn't mean 'mother,' exactly," he laughed.

They saw the sun rise as the truck began to climb into the foothills just past the Sutter County dumps, and it was fully in their eyes as Uncle Pius turned east along the unpaved track that would lead them to camp. The hills surrounding them were pitted and spare, rising heaps of granite rubble mined, then quarried to bedrock. They reached the rim of the canyon, and Pius slipped gears to ease the descent. Only here, almost in sight of camp, a wisp of smoke visible above what seemed a garden of bay and juniper trees marking the river in a desert of broken rocks and the dried trash of dead scrub, came relief from the glare of the sun on this barren landscape, their refuge in this Sierra moraine. Now, Joe slept.

He woke up to a thunderclap sounding some distance away, the sky having become a torrent of swiftly moving clouds streaming west into the valley but too high for rain. Someone had carried him to rest beneath the oak tree, but he could see the flashes of summer lightning against the dark scudding clouds as a cool wind swirled through the trees and set the dry leaves rustling. He sat up and saw all the men, except Wah Gay and Mee Kee, seated around the truck. Uncle Pius straddled the driver's seat, his feet on the running board, translating the newspaper stories of China from the *Appeals Democrat*. The truck was loaded with all their equipment, and the fireplace was bare. Wisps of smoke and ash flew up in tiny whirlwinds as a sudden breeze whistled through the stones.

Joe walked to the stream to take a deep drink of water. Gathering some stones in both hands, he walked the bank, pitching them one by one into the underbrush where doves the color of the brown fields of the valley flared from their cover, a slight corona of white-tipped pinfeathers making his target. He hurled handfuls of river gravel in patterns across their flight path. The doves in their turn made for the safety of the scrub the other side of the river, and while he could see their movement among the barren bushes, he could not reach them with his arm. Uncle Pius called out to him, then. It was time to start home, again.

The men rode in the back of the truck all the way to Yuba City, leaving Joe to ride with Uncle Pius, who kept an irritable silence nearly the entire way. He had not slept, and he kept pushing his glasses up, rubbing his eyes and yawning.

"Just a little tired, boy," he said as he swerved, catching the shoulder.

"What did the men have to say about the news?" Joe attended the road, awakened now to the familiar details of the flat landscape.

"Oh, the same thing. Everybody wants to go back to fight. Wah Gay and Mee Kee left camp walking because they couldn't wait." He laughed sourly.

"They're gone? They left?"

"Mebbe. That's what Adam says anyway. Wouldn't be surprised, though, if they stopped to look for gold." Pius struck a match against the dashboard, lit a fresh cigar, then cranked his window down to relieve the smell of smoke. "At least this way I don't have to pay 'em. Heh, heh, that Adam's crazy."

"Does he want to go back too?"

"What? Oh, I asked him. None of my business, of course, but I asked him because I thought he wanted to be asked."

"What did he say?"

"He didn't say yes or no, if that's what you're asking. Said he couldn't decide. For him, China is a matter of the heart, not just a matter of the skin like it is for us." Pius glanced in the rearview mirror, then spit out the window.

"He doesn't like us, does he?"

"He just sounds that way. He likes Eva. Told me he always regretted not wanting a daughter." Pius snorted. "I know I don't have any regrets about my life. Stick to business, protect family, praise God. Only way to live, right boy?''

Joe agreed and would have said so, but there was Yuba City, where the crew would depart for other jobs in other places. He could only think of things he regretted that were really no fault of his own, but nothing from his past that would implicate him in the fate of others. Pius bumped across the bridge spanning the levees and took the shortcut through skid row, passing a line of people waiting for the midday meal at the Salvation Army, hurrying because Eva would be waiting for them.

In February of the following year, the twins' mother passed away and was buried in the Marysville cemetery, where Uncle Pius could tend her grave. The twins completed high school in 1941 and were called to war immediately, Joe enlisting in the navy, a pharmacist's mate serving on a destroyer that went down with all hands in November 1943, and Eva sent to nursing school, where she enlisted and completed her service in Honolulu, marrying a doctor at the end of the war. Uncle Pius made the trip to Honolulu to give the bride away, accompanied by his own wife, several years his junior, the eldest daughter of a business associate in Sacramento. At the ceremony, both wept for Joe in each other's arms as they had not been able to do during the war years and wished each other many children. And Pius recalled after the funeral of Eva's mother when Joe, wandering through the back room of the Suey Sin tong, had seen Fat Adam debating strategy with two strangers who held equal shares of second position at a *pai gow* table during the Bomb Day celebrations in Marysville.

David Wong Louie

(1954–   )

Included in every media story about the Asian American "model
minority" is a story about the bookish, quiet, and successful Asian
student studying too hard and ruining the grading curve of every
university science class in America. To make rubble of this myth
and to reinterpret the basic laws of nature comes David Wong
Louie's Antonio Ma, a bad driver with overactive hormones. Louie
is a graduate of Vassar and Iowa. His stories have appeared in *The
Iowa Review, Ploughshares, Chicago Review, Best American Short
Stories of 1989,* and other literary magazines. He is also a recipient
of a National Endowment for the Arts creative writing fellowship.
David Wong Louie was born in New York City and lives in Santa
Cruz, California.

————

In a World Small Enough

> I'm just an animal
> Looking for a home
> —Talking Heads

So it is; so it is. Antonio Ma is inside the urine house thinking.
Metabolism—apt metaphor for the turn in his life. Ha, ha. The
lemon yellow jet slows to a trickle. He doesn't hear the rusted
trough anymore. Lately things have been falling through his hands.
Escaping. He blames gravity. What remains of it. Just a look
around the urine house confirms his suspicions. Without the

uninterrupted presence of a gravitational field, who would dare
pee? Down the trough stands a boy about a third of Antonio
Ma's height, loaded with snack foods and souvenirs. For whatever
reasons he refuses to set his treasures down on the wet, concrete
floor. As a result he can't unzip his fly. He makes an awkward
attempt but the head of his pink cloud candy dips into the trough
and absorbs the last drops of Antonio Ma's contribution. The
boy regards his trough-mate, coarse and creased and disheveled,
his pants open and his partner out for an airing. The boy turns,
bewildered, and stares at a drawing, stenciled on the wall, of
gorillas mating, which city planners claim are genuine reproduc-
tions of artworks found in urine houses throughout the land,
reputedly executed by the common citizenry before the War. The
boy crosses his legs, chews his bottom lip. In a sense he is defying
gravity.

Around him, others pee and zip and even offer to help the boy in
a variety of ways, then go off to the rhino pit or the monkey house.
Antonio Ma pees and revises his thoughts. Not metaphor; too
serious for metaphor. Plain truth is he can't keep a hold on things.
It is not an exaggeration to say he didn't just excrete liquid waste
material, he's lost it.

**NEWTON'S FIRST LAW OF MOTION: Every body continues in
its state of uniform motion in a straight line, unless it is compelled
to change that state by forces impressed upon it.**
Antonio Ma is daydreaming and dangerous behind the wheel of
his gas guzzler. Out the corner of his eye he detects his dream-come-
true. A woman in black with legs in shimmery nylon, legs made
longer with skyscraper heels, a shrinking skirt, and a naughty tail
wind that toys with the hem. Antonio Ma Drives past, admiring her
laissez-faire approach to the exigencies of nature. His insensate foot
works the gas pedal propelling the auto forward. The dream now
resides in his rearview mirror. All at once he U-turns, hopping the
center divider, when he sees the woman wag her thumb at the
onrushing traffic. He hastens to curbside in front of the Dream Inn
Motel. Inorganic daydreams, he reminds himself, don't open car
doors.

**NEWTON'S THIRD LAW OF MOTION: To every action there is
an equal and opposite reaction.**
Where you headed?
Wherever you say.
Soon Antonio Ma attains cruising speed.

You don't mind if I have a look at your legs? He flicks the hem of
her skirt past where the nylons become panties.

Watch where you're going.

You have nice legs.

Hey, watch the fucking road.

You have a nice tongue too.

Antonio Ma lost his brother's deluxe ten-speed, lightweight, super-
hardened aluminum frame bicycle while he was busy in the urine
house. The bicycle had been secured to one of the zoo's Litter: Help
the Spread of Microbes signs with a theft-proof Kryptonite lock.
When he went to retrieve the bicycle a flock of pigeons was milling
in its space. If this incident had another man as its victim, we would
label this petty larceny. The authorities would be notified, a claim
filed with the insurance company, and a letter written excoriating
the lock's manufacturer. But in the case of Antonio Ma the perpe-
trator of the crime was also its victim.

Young Niels Bohr, twenty-six, standing beside a portmanteau at
the unloading dock in New York harbor, salutes his fellow physicist,
Enrico Fermi, who had arrived seven hours earlier on a different
steamer. From atop his portmanteau of genuine Italian leather,
Fermi waves to the Dane.

Enrico Fermi!

Niels Bohr!

During the voyage I experienced a recurring dream, says Bohr.
Allow me to demonstrate its central image. Bohr undoes his double-
breasted jacket. After a few practice swings he punches the top of
his portmanteau and the two halves of the chest fly open. Well? he
says. Fermi offers an interpretation of the dream: subconsciously,
Bohr wishes to challenge the American, Jack Dempsey, for the
heavyweight boxing crown.

No, no, no! says Bohr. Its greater significance escapes you.
Observe.

Fermi draws closer, dragging his portmanteau with great effort.
Once again Bohr demonstrates the central image of his dream; he
strikes his portmanteau and as before its wings fly open, only now
the left wing collides with the right flank of Fermi's portmanteau,
which spontaneously splits open as well.

Both geniuses eye each other, mouths agape. Simultaneously they
reach the same conclusion. They hail a taxicab. In the same breath
they command the driver: Take us to Albert!

LAVOISIER'S LAW OF CONSERVATION OF MATTER: Matter is neither created nor destroyed while undergoing chemical change.

Antonio Ma is headed nowhere. His passenger is going there too. They are making good time.

You live in this jalopy, don'tcha?

I like to keep still, he says. I feel safer that way.

What's so still about sixty miles an hour?

Do you see me moving?

Your paw hasn't stopped since I got in this car. In one quick motion she spins free of his offending hand and kneels with her back to the windshield. Look at all this junk, she says. We going to the waste disposal station?

That's my living room you're talking about. This junk, as you call it, is everything I own. He tells his sad story: The Endless Losses: First the insignificances (buttons, coins), then larger items (gloves, keys, combs), next the causes for concern (hair, molars). He lost his ladling job at Max Gross Chemicals. He missed payments on the rent and was forcibly removed from his apartment by the complex's security squad. As usually happens in cases of simultaneous dismissal and eviction, the Regional Control Board issues him a reconstituted Pre-War model auto.

I lost my body, too, he says, patting his flabby midsection. I lost my good looks.

Hey, if it's sympathy you want, I'm fresh out.

No, not me. Not sympathy. You're the best thing to come my way, he says, feeling up her leg, since I've been driving this car.

Yeah, I look pretty damn delicious now but doodle me once and you'll take back the poetry. Not that I'm not good. She flops back into a normal sitting posture. I've been around the track a few times. I know what's what. You look at me and I'm one thing; touch me and—WHAM—I've changed.

Nah, he says, and lifts his hand from her thigh long enough to brush away her remarks.

Then you'll change. I guarantee it. Touch my lovespot and you'll think your finger's gold till enough time's passed and you go hunting and find water and a bar of that antiradiation soap. The prettier you smell, the trashier I'll look. What's that on the side of the road? you'll say. Oh, that's what made my finger stink so bad.

Then we must marry, Antonio Ma says. There must be a machine around here. He scans the commercial establishments along the street for a marriage booth. I'll need to shave first for the photograph but you look good.

I don't know about marriage, she says, smiling sheepishly.

Oh now, now, look here. You're worried about the cuts in your benefits if you don't marry Anglo, aren't you? My family's been in this country so many generations, the Chinese so bred out of me, I've been reclassified.

My, my, my. I am impressed. She leans against the passenger-side door and regards the driver. I can almost see what you mean, she says. Now I've got a confession. If I don't tell it, the damned machine's fertility scan will. Your classification doesn't matter. I can't make babies anyway.

Neither can I!

My, my, my. O, barrenness! So what's your name?

Shhh! Listen!

She turns and sees one of the auto's hubcaps spinning down the road in the opposite direction. Stop, she says, go get it.

What, he says, and risk losing something else?

You're no loser, his wife-to-be says, as she mends her stockings with clear nail polish. They are camped in the giant parking lot of one of the new combination military-shopping mall complexes (mil-malls) the state has installed everywhere. She says, Look at me, hun. I'm not sore you can't doodle. I kinda like being with a guy without getting sweaty. Makes me feel like I have a personality.

A what?

Something from before the War. It's not important. She plants her foot in his lap. On the sole of the shoe the imprint says: All-Post-War-Materials. The daggerlike heel digs into his thigh. He'll be back, she says, nudging her nyloned foot against his groin. He'll be rearing to go as soon as we get married.

She can talk until all the fallout drops from the sky, but the woeful fact will remain—his erectile tissues had malfunctioned. No, I've lost it, he says, I've lost that too.

Don't go mourning the dead before they die, she says, as she starts to work on a run above her kneecap. I believe in reincarnation, she continues, infinite recycling. You follow me? There's nothing new in the world. Everything's been recycled from whatever was here on Day One. There aren't even any new ideas because the stuff that makes up the brains thinking them is as old as the oceans. Crazy, huh? For all I know, my brain could've been dinosaur turds. Same goes for that guy Einstein. It's all in the atoms.

The blotched, dried nail polish gives her stockings the look of scar tissue from burns. Think of yourself as a big-deal missile, she says. All the metal and plutonium and kilotons are you, this missile. You blow up over some city. The kaboom is you, the dying is you, she says blithely. The blindness. The messed-up water and vegetables, that's all you. A few years later down the road, a baby's born and she can't have babies. She's you, too, but in a slightly reorganized form.

Antonio Ma's erectile tissues stir beneath her foot, which lies inert like a malnourished crow on his crotch. Yeah, I feel it. I feel like I could explode, he says. You are a sweet-talking lady.

Ah, there! She points a finger at him. You see me differently already.

Antonio Ma wanders through the zoo. He goes to the Lost & Found but this proves fruitless. He considers phoning his brother, Bing, but this is prohibitively distasteful, and he decides to delay confessions. Bing, after all, had been his last resort.

Antonio Ma watches an elephant being put through its paces. By its pen a plaque acknowledges that this specimen, like so many others in the world, is the product of a process of artificial insemination that employed inexpensive irradiated sperm. Mark Bessie's thin ankles, barks the mustachioed trainer, mark her swollen eyes, her flaky tusks, and the sorry state of her memory. Unadulterated and synthetic sperm are so costly, the trainer says, please give generously to the Clean Genes Fund.

Later, Antonio Ma pays the extra fee and enters the Pre-War Bird exhibit. Immediately he is overwhelmed by its obvious chromosomal integrity. What an amazing variety of vegetation! he thinks. So many names to remember! What a confusing time that must've been! Banana trees, date palms, pomegranate, pistachio, algarroba, mandarin, simsim, gingely, and gutta-percha bushes. Ocatilla, oleander, bird-of-paradise in bloom. And the birds! Hummers, cockatoo, toucans, colibri, and a dozen subspecies of parrot. The music, such sublime melodies! How can he return to a world where the only genetically sound birds are those miserable pigeons?

Even here in this Eden he spots one. And the irony is too complete; this specimen is of mutant strain, a bloated ebon thing with thick wings and blue beak. The pigeon waddles up to Antonio Ma and cackles meaningfully, and then defying the laws of aerodynamics it rises up into the trees. Antonio Ma pursues the strange pigeon over footbridges, under canopies, through clots of vines.

The chase ends abruptly when he loses sight of his quarry and he stops to consider the significance of his latest loss. Then he hears the bird's lewd cackle and instantaneously, from above, a loose, pinguid substance strikes and ossifies on Antonio Ma's shoulder. Could the recycling process happen so quickly? Have her atoms already regrouped and found him again? Antonio Ma is standing on a rickety footbridge over dense foliage. When he pulls out a handkerchief, with which he intends to wipe up and save the moldering dollop on his shoulder, his wallet falls into the abyss below. But Antonio Ma isn't watching.

After the birds he heads for the zoo exit, passing the zebra enclosure along the way. What a rich life zebra lead: clumps of hay, aluminum trough, barn with roof, and banyan trees on acres of yellow dirt. He counts six zebra. Scrub brush manes, flicking tails, and oscillating stripes. Just as in picture books, Antonio Ma observes, must be something wrong with them; not making them that way anymore. He sidles along the fence, experiencing more of the same caliber of thought, when he sees under a banyan tree Bing's bicycle, its low-slung racing handlebars bent toward the ground in the precise angle zebra employ when grazing.

Quite simply, Einstein says, tapping his fingers on the portmanteau, your dream, Herr Bohr, illustrates one of the matters we have come together to discuss. Einstein buttons his cardigan. He shuts the doors of the portmanteaux and asks Bohr to repeat the demonstration, and the latter happily complies. Einstein says, Now imagine your fist is a neutron particle.

Yes, yes! ejaculates Bohr. And shall we say this portmanteau is a heavy atom?

Ah, so! says Fermi. Uranium, perhaps.

Correct, Einstein says, nuclear fission. He drags a third chest from a closet and positions it close to the open closet door. With the use of a straight edge, slide rule, and simple Euclidean geometry he calculates the optimum impact points and then painstakingly positions the other portmanteaux. (See Fig. 1 below.)

Preparations completed, Einstein says, Herr Bohr, please, you do the honors. Einstein marks an imaginary X on top of Bohr's portmanteau. The Dane strides forward and ferociously thumps the designated spot. One after another the doors of the portmanteaux fling open: boom, boom, boom, bang, the final explosion the result of the slamming closet door.

The chain reaction, Einstein says, folding his arms across his chest.

Yet another application of theoretical physics! says Bohr.

The macro world, Fermi says, again confirms our mathematical understanding of the micro.

Come, we have earned ourselves a treat. Einstein claps his hands. We have a delicatessen downstairs like you won't believe. Stuffed

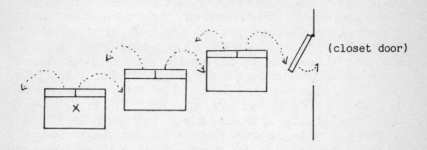

(closet door)

Fig. 1. An overhead view of the experiment. X marks the point of initial impact (or neutron penetration).

derma! All the sauerkraut you can eat! Now, there's a place to discuss that most perplexing of problems.

You don't mean to say the Unspeakable Device? Fermi says.

All in due time, says Einstein, opening the apartment door. First we must ponder the case of the Man-Who-Loses-Things.

Ah, Bohr sighs, a most tantalizing puzzle, best tackled over pastrami.

THE SECOND LAW OF THERMODYNAMICS: As formulated by Ludwig Blotzmann, it concerns Entropy, the measure of the disorder in the universe; for instance, a hot dog chewed cannot be unchewed, an atom split cannot be stuck back together.

A toaster, says the wife-to-be, rummaging through his belongings in the backseat.

That's a bread burner, Antonio Ma says. I understand that's how they got rid of stale bread before the War.

She is looking for a razor because he insists on shaving before they use the marriage machine in the mil-mall. When it takes their wedding picture he wants his good looks to show. They're still there somewhere, right on my face, he says.

The inevitable comes to pass and he goes to buy a new razor, leaving his wife-to-be behind in the auto while she does her face.

Midway through the crowded parking lot filled with Pre-War petroleum-powered vehicles and the new buzzmobiles and military vehicles—tanks, rocket launchers, jeeps—Antonio Ma looks back and realizes he has no idea where he left his auto.

He shows his I.D. card to the sentry at the mil-mall gate. Inside, he makes a special effort to pat each missile silo he passes. At a dry goods store he purchases a razor, a can of soap, and a liter of hot water. As he heads for the exit he sees a pair of BIMs (Bombed Irradiated Mutants) leaving a marriage machine. Police don't police these damned machines, he thinks, and the authorities wonder why the quality of the gene pool isn't improving. Then, in the generous cast of mind of a man in love, he admits, perhaps its best machines can't stop love. In this spirit Antonio Ma buys his bride-to-be a prenuptial dog-on-a-stick. He clears security and steps out to the giant parking lot.

He can't find his auto but he doesn't panic. He simply returns to the mil-mall and browses until the shoppers and the soldiers clear away their autos, buzzers, and tanks. At closing time he goes outside and the truth is obvious. The auto and his wife-to-be are gone from his life, and she didn't even know how to drive. What can he do but smash the dog-on-a-stick into a nearby rocket launcher?

Summary diagrams of Antonio Ma's predicament:

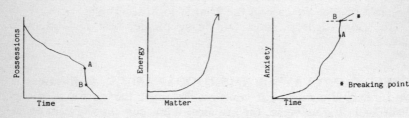

Fig. 1. Escalation of   Fig. 2. Conversation of   Fig. 3. Anxiety Index
Dissipation   Matter to (Nervous) Energy

Fig. 1. describes the Escalation of Dissipation in relationship to time elapsed. Note the precipitous drop between point A (loss of auto) and point B (loss of bicycle). Fig. 2. represents Einstein's Energy/Matter relationship, $E = mc^2$, here adapted and slightly modified, but the basic elements of the equation remain intact: each gram of matter (i.e., his possessions) lost is converted into measurable energy (i.e., nervous tension). Therefore, an extraordinary

amount of energy, albeit negative, is gained. Last, Fig. 3. illustrates
the Anxiety Index: as time passes, his feelings of anxiety increase in
inverse proportion to the quantity of things he has yet to lose.
Consider once more Fig. 1. specifically line AB.

Bohr passes Einstein the mustard, Fermi picks at the bowl of
pickled tomatoes and dills. On the table are latkes, tongue, sturgeon, and sides of sauerkraut and potato knishes.

Herr Z, Fermi says, is the personification and incarnation of
radioactivity.

His two colleagues move their chairs closer to the table.

Fermi swallows what is in his mouth and takes a drink from his
cream soda. Herr Z, he says, is no different than a radioactive
element such as radium. Both give off emanations. In the case of
radium these are particles and rays; for Herr Z they are his
possessions.

Fascinating, says Einstein. You believe then that Herr Z cannot
control what is happening to him. That is to say, it is not within his
power to prevent, as you call them, these emanations.

Bohr fishes a thick dill from the brine and slices it crosswise. He
clears a space on the table.

I think Niels has something for us, Fermi says. Have you
witnessed this, Alberto? It's wonderful, wonderful! He claps his
hands.

Say these pickles are electrons, Bohr begins. How do you suppose
they move? He spreads the green slices arbitrarily over the table.
Our friend Herr Z, how do the emanations leave him? Surely not
continuously; otherwise, at the current rate of his divestment, a
sustained outward flow would leave him with nothing. Putting it
bluntly, he would no longer be. Therefore, I say these emanations
act in a manner akin to electrons. They spontaneously and mysteriously leap from Herr Z, just as electrons leap from orbit to orbit
around the nuclear core. Bohr demonstrates his ideas by spastically
shifting the position of the pickle slices across the table.

Herr Bohr, says Einstein, this is utterly two-dimensional. Please
stop playing with your food.

**Evolutionary theorists, departing from orthodox Darwinism, have
recently postulated that Man adopted bipedalism long before his
brain realized it was a good idea to do so. With a brain the size of
Modern Ape's, Man assumed this more vulnerable verticality, and,
putting his liberated hands to work, he became a collector.**

Antonio Ma hops the metal fence that surrounds the zebra enclosure and runs zigzag over the lifeless ground to where Bing's bicycle stood. It is undamaged but someone has secured the frame to a pipe with the Kryptonite lock. He reaches for the key and discovers his pockets are empty; his wallet is gone, so is the soiled handkerchief. He takes a firm grasp of the bicycle and tries to tear it from its mooring. That's when he notices the peculiar label now stuck on the handlebars:

2 1154 84950 87129 9

Antonio Ma sinks to the ground. As he fears, he sees that his shoelaces are indeed untied.

Bing, trust me. Haven't I spared you up to now? Antonio Ma pleaded with his brother to loan him his bicycle. You're the last person I want to trouble. But I lost my auto and my woman was taken with it. I need the bike. Only BIMs don't go on wheels.

You're worried someone might mistake you for a BIM?

Bing, I'm worried about what this means the state can do to me next.

Maybe the state took the auto back.

Oh, Bing, don't even think such a thing.

Bing agreed to the loan of the bicycle. When he turned the bicycle over to Antonio Ma, he said, Have you seen a doctor?

Doctor! I need a detective. Antonio rode off. He meant to go to the police as he had promised Bing but he went to the zoo instead.

Bohr is explicating the theory of wave-particle duality of matter with wild manipulations of the pickle slides.

Herr Bohr, Einstein interrupts, picking up a pickle slice, you have said this is either a pickle or an electron, its reality determined by the observer. Tell me then, how do you explain this? He drops the pickle slice into his waiting mouth.

This is scandalous! says Bohr. Give me back my electron!

But it has taken your quantum leap, though it leapt unwisely. Now, now, Herr Bohr, what is it that disturbs you so? Is it the utter certainty of the electron's fate?

With a smirk on his face Bohr draws a sturgeon bone from between his teeth. His icy Scandinavian eyes focus in on Einstein's. I am certain you have ingested the pickle but like Herr Z's emanations, which vanish into the mysterious mouth of life, I can only assume with confidence the probability of the pickle's disappearance.

Alberto, Fermi says, I saw you eat it.

Of course you did, Bohr says. That's what you think you observed, but one's eyes can mislead. When you look at an atom through a microscope, isn't the device which achieves this gross magnification altering your experience of the atom? You do not see the atom, you see the microscope's interpretation of the atom. Leap with me. Can we say with absolute certainty that Herr Z loses things or does he misplace them or simply forgets he owns them? And the case of Professor Einstein. Was his an act of dining or an act of spite? My observation was distorted by the implicit hostility that motivated him. And because I am human, emotions colored my perception. So tell me, Einstein, how can I be absolutely certain of what just occurred?

They are drinking weak tea and eating a dessert of sponge cake. In order to circumvent further hostilities between them, discussion has switched to the topic of atomic weapons.

Let us merge what we have learned from the portmanteau demonstration and the case of Herr Z, Fermi says. Herr Z, we can surmise, is the victim of a chain reaction of dispossession. As the quantity of goods he owns diminishes, the rate at which he loses them seems to accelerate. This phenomenon is a product of Alberto's glorious mass-to-energy conversion formula. The more he loses, the more disoriented he feels; the more disoriented, the quicker he loses what remains. If this self-fueling chain reaction runs its course, Herr Z, like the autophagous sun, will soon also disappear. His atoms, those of his corporeal self and those of his accoutrements, will be dispersed throughout the universe. Like the closet door that slammed in Alberto's flat, Herr Z's chain reaction will come to an equally conclusive end.

You mean to say he will die, Bohr says.

Ha, ha, that depends on your point of view, Einstein says.

Gentlemen, Fermi admonishes the two scientists good-naturedly. Are we not at the threshold of the Unspeakable Device? All that is left for us to do is to apply the lesson of Herr Z to the principle of nuclear fission and—

Einstein stands abruptly and finishes his cup of tea. Signor Fermi, your insights—and I'm certain Herr Bohr is in complete agreement—are nothing short of breathtaking. But consider this possibility: Might we also interpret Herr Z as the product of such an instrument of destruction? Irradiated, his atoms shooting off in all directions into the cosmos? Don't we agree that one Herr Z is enough for this world? Come, you men of science, enough talk of weapons. There is much goodness on this planet. A new Greta Garbo show is playing in town.

Yes, Garbo!

Ah, the Madame Curie of the silver screen. What a place, America!

Antonio Ma doesn't bother to tie his laces. He knows only too well what the sign means. As he goes toward the ramshackle barn for assistance with the bicycle, he steps out of his shoes.

The instant he enters the barn he is greeted with high-pitched beeping sounds. From behind a dark curtain two BIMs in gray jumpsuits appear. They are speaking Cantonese.

Ma seen-saang, nay ho ma? Sik-jaw faan may? The BIMs attempt smiles; the presumptuousness of this gesture irritates Antonio Ma. Since when have they been allowed to smile? Nonetheless, he asks for help in reclaiming Bing's bicycle but doesn't have any luck.

Nay yau jai ge un i ver sal pro duct code. The BIMs brush back the hair that covers their foreheads and reveal labels similar to those on the handlebars. Nay yau in ter face toong ngaw-ge sys tem. From a vinyl binder they peel off a label and press it to their guest's forehead.

The BIMs lead him to the center of the barn where two poles stand linked by a shimmering thread of bright red light. Following the example of his hosts Antonio Ma sweeps his hair from the label so it makes clean contact with the red beam. They then go down a dusty flight of stairs that opens into a labyrinth of tunnels, lit with flambeaux positioned along the tamped earth walls. The place has the smell of old fur. For a brief instant he thinks he has entered the Paleolithic exhibit, but the items on display in the glass-enclosed shelves are of a slightly more recent vintage. The deeper he ventures into the tunnels the more items he recognizes. His wallet, his shoes, his toaster, each bearing a striped label. In one niche he encounters his former wife-to-be's runny stockings hanging from two hooks. He throws his hands through the glass. He experiences no pain. An alarm rings; immediately a pair of blond BIMs in orange jumpsuits arrive at the scene and Antonio Ma surrenders the hosiery without a tussle. Your belongings are safe, they tell him. You have nothing left to lose. We keep inventory here for you.

Antonio Ma rode tall in the saddle, ten forward speeds between his legs, off to the zoo. Wind crushed skin, teeth gnashed grit, face fierce as tigers snarled at the oncoming traffic. His thoughts then were hardly plentiful but those he did have centered on incidents of his childhood when bicycles were fun, before Bing was born.

Wing Tek Lum

(1946–   )

Wing Tek Lum was born and raised in Honolulu, Hawaii. He attended Brown University and the Union Theological Seminary. In 1970 his poetry won the Discovery Award of the Poetry Center in New York City. He spent four years working in Manhattan's Chinatown, followed by three years as a social worker in Hong Kong. His poems have appeared in numerous anthologies, newspapers, and magazines. At the 1988 Association of Asian American Studies conference in Pullman, Washington, Wing Tek Lum's poetry collection, *Expounding the Doubtful Points*, won the creative literature award. Instead of the usual gush of insincerity and insinuation, Lum accepted his award with the recital of an old Chinese American children's chant known as a *gum sahn paw*, or Gold Mountain Granny, about a woman grown old alone in China while her husband labors and jolly-times it in nineteenth-century California. He recited the *gum sahn paw* in the Cantonese that so many at the conference had long put behind them with the other embarrassments of childhood. His recital of the old immigrant Chinaman's imaginings of a young love-starved wife back in the village word-tripping crazy brought cheers from some and bewilderment to others.

Lum's poetry likewise is a dramatic expression of his Chinese American moral consciousness and conscience, a moral conscience inspired and informed by the fact, art, and artifacts of Chinese, particularly Cantonese and American pop history and culture.

Grateful Here

1

Emerging from the subway station,
then lost among the orange signs on Nedicks snackbars,
I could smell the thick rice soup and dumplings
I would order in that basement lunchroom
already beckoning me. I thought:
like a salmon returning to its spawning ground
—and, bemused, followed by Chinese nose.

2

Early one Sunday morning each spring,
our family would visit my grandparents' graves,
offering gifts of tea and suckling pig,
burning colored paper, incense, and loud firecrackers.
Later, my mother would take me to church.
I sang in the choir and would carry, that day,
fragile lilies to the altar of my risen Lord.

3

When walking with a Caucasian girl.
holding hands, I would pass by teenage hangouts,
overhearing insults. They would always pick on the girl,
as though she were a lesbian.
Separately, I guess, we would pretend
not to have noticed—avoiding embarrassment
for the other, tightening our grips.

4

Observing two gay Negroes, powdered gray,
and strutting regally on their high-heeled boots,
I followed them half-enviously with my eyes,
understanding, for the first time, that dark allure
of nighttime caresses. I was in rural Pennsylvania,
and found housewives at the grocer's brought their children
with small, craning necks to whisper about me.

5

After a sit-in at the Pentagon,
the arresting marshall misspelt my name.
Actually, though, I know I should feel grateful here.
In fact, just last week on the radio, I heard
that the Red Guards had broken the wrists
of a most promising young pianist. Among other things,
he had journeyed to the West to play Beethoven and Brahms.

Going Home

Ngoh m' sick gong tong hwa—
besides the usual menu words,
the only phrase I really know.
I say it loudly,
but he is not listening.
He keeps on talking with his smile,
staring, it would seem, past me
into the night without a moon.

He's lost, presumably.
But I don't know what he's saying.
He is an old man, wearing a hat,
and the kind of overcoat
my father wears:
the super-padded shoulders.
His nostrils trickle with wet drops,
which he does not care to wipe away.

Ngoh m' sick gong tong hwa—
I try again, to no avail.
I try in English: what street?
and think of taking out
some paper and a pen.

                         Just then,

two young fellows approach us
carrying a chair; one look
and I can tell
that *they* will oblige him.

I sigh, and point them out,
and hastily cross the street,
escaping. Once on the other side,
I glimpse around, and catch
their gestures from afar,
still able to hear those familiar,
yet no less incomprehensible sounds.

I head home, and visualize
this old man with his small beady eyes
and the two glistening lines
below them, vertical,
like makeup for some clown.
Out loud, I wonder:
but Chinamen aren't supposed to cry.

The Poet Imagines
His Grandfather's Thoughts
on the Day He Died

This is the first year
the Dragon Eyes tree has ever borne fruit:
let us see what this omen brings.
Atop one of its exposed roots
a small frog squats, not moving, not even blinking.
I remember when my children were young
and this whole front yard was a taro patch:
we would take them out at night with a lantern
blinding the frogs just long enough
to sneak a hook up under the belly.
In those days we grew taro
as far as the eye could see;
I even invented a new kind of trough
lined inside with a wire mesh
so we could peel the skins with ease.
The King bought our poi,
and gave me a pounder one day.
It is made of stone,

and looks like the clapper of a bell, smooth and heavy.
I keep it in my bedroom now—there—on the dresser.
The fish we call Big Eyes
lies on an oval plate beside it.
I have not been hungry today.
The full bowl of rice attracts a fly
buzzing in anticipation.
I hear the laughter of one of my grandchildren
from the next room: which one is it?
Maybe someday one of them will think of me
and see the rainbows that I have seen,
the opium den in Annam that frightened me so,
my mother's tears when I left home.

Dear ancestors, all this is still one in mind.

To My Father

In our store that day
they gathered together
my grandfather among them
each in his turn
to cut off their queues:
the end of subservience.
They could have returned
the Republic soon established
or, on the safe side,
waited a year
to grow back that braid.
No matter, they stayed.
Your father was young
and shrewd: the store flourished,
then the crops, the lands.

Out of your share
you sent us to the best schools;
we were to follow the dynasty
set by the Old Man.
But he had died

before I was born, his grave
all I could pay homage to.
I was freed from those old ways.
Today, unbraided,
my hair has grown long
because and in spite of those haircuts
you and he took.

Lawson Fusao Inada

(1938–   )

Lawson Inada is a Sansei, born in Fresno, California. During the war he was interned in Arkansas and Colorado. His book of poetry, *Before the War: Poems As They Happened* (William Morrow, 1971), was the first volume of poetry written by an Asian American and published by a major publishing company. His poetry has also been published in countless anthologies, magazines, and newspapers. In an essay on Inada, Ishmael Reed notes the Afro-American and jazz influence in his poetry as well as the influences of growing up on the west side of Fresno, a multicultural mixture of Chicano, black, Asian, and Armenian:

> Lawson uses it and uses it with care, but above all Lawson Inada is a Japanese American poet who is concerned with what has happened to Japanese Americans while here as well as what has happened to himself, his loves, his family.

The camps, jazz, blues, Fresno ride on the voice and words of Lawson Inada. He has read his poetry at festivals, community functions, colleges all over the country, and the White House. He has received two writing fellowships from the National Endowment for the Arts and been named one of America's "Heavy 100" by *Rolling Stone*. The Los Angeles Public Schools and Visual Communications produced a film based on Lawson Inada's life, called *I Told You So*. He lives with his wife, Janet, and his two sons, Miles and Lowell, in Ashland, Oregon, where he is a professor of English at Southern Oregon College.

———————

The Stand

"We like America in its buffaloness . . ."
—"Command," Chögyam Trungpa, Rinpoche

I am somewhere
where I have decided to stand.

There has been long
maneuvering,

having been staked to a land,
sowing in the heat,

moving huge tools
in an absurdity of moon.

Chanting, my own
tune in the machinery,

I find the chanting soothes.
That sweet voice is ruined.

I move now,
sifting pavements through my feet,

sweat in the eyes, a horizon.
Sun turns the wheat.

Braced to my spine,
I resume the chanting—

utterances in a sound
octaves older than my own.

The Discovery of Tradition

For Toshio Mori and John Okada

I can tell you about this, sure enough,
and I'll do the best job I can
out here in the perimeters,
but you've got to do it for your self.

And I had been told and told about it,
studied it, even, square in the face
and gone away wanting from home.
I had to feel it to really know.

What do you do in a case like that?
You don't even know what's missing
and the first thing you've got to do
is know what it is you need to know . . .

1. The Work in Progress

It was winter (gestures, wind, breathing),
things needed tending (men in a forest, armloads of wood)
and, of course, I needed tending too (a dropped log rolling down
                                                    the slope).

After all, was I to simply
see my self through again,
repeating what had been done
as its own accomplishment?

What would I see when I looked back,
emerging into spring and the echoes of children
calling to me their questions in the lower meadow?

After all, the descent to the valley
is deceptively easy, and therein lies the task:
to hold your own
is the most beautiful and natural thing—
a hand full of this, a hand full of that—
but the rest of the world comes
summoned at the asking,
implicit in the invitation of your just being here,
and before you know it.

children have arrived with visitors and leaves with the faces of
fish and before you know it,
High on the slopes, once more as usual, it starts to snow.

2. The Progress in Work

(Look: a car moving down a road
            banked with snow,
            the tires thick with traction
            grabbing and crunching.)

(Look: a classroom full of flowers,
            sunlight full of books
            and everyone laughing.)

Ah, yes. And still, though,
it had come easy
because I didn't know any better.

I want to know what I'm doing,
to emerge, to learn, to keep going.

How has it been with you?

3. The Observance of Rituals

Toppling, an eclipse off the top of my head now, up there
where the ranges run, the smooth things moving with the wind
    itself
as it counts, decked out in crevices that matter and laughing
with the whole thing in particular, part and parcel of the what
    what are
when the mind is full,

when the life is full,
when there is nothing missing in the eye and senses rocking
back and forth in the continuum
humming with stars, the light winding down and starting up
    again
to concern us all—
what crosses me crosses you with the force of shadows of sound
emerging and merging into where things quicken and everything
is enough—

rippling, the vision at the bottom of the self, here, down
here as we bob and walk in the moment of momentum and the
                                                    drop off coming
who knows where which is why we keep going into it with the
                                                    force of fortune
we know is there giving back and going forth rippling and toppling,

rippling and toppling as we go.

4. The Emergence of Topics

It starts to rain. It starts to snow.
Whatever "it" is, it's going through some heavy combinations
up there in the mountains, mind you,
whole lot of shaking going on
including some occasional sunlight, thank you,
and just the whole bunch of stuff in general
and on down the ranks to us in burrows
tucking heads under wings
the sweet way we like to think
wet women will always do and did.

I'm sitting here with Toshio and John,
talking over such momentous things:

*"Long ago, children, I lived in a country called Japan. Your
grandpa was already in California earning money for my boat
ticket. The village people rarely went out of Japan and were
shocked when they heard I was following your grandpa as soon
as the money came."*

                    Toshio Mori, Yokohama, California

*"Two weeks after his twenty-fifth birthday, Ichiro got off a bus
at Second and Main in Seattle. He had been gone four years, two
in camp and two in prison."*

                            John Okada, No-No Boy

The rain, the snow, the steady stream.
The observance of rituals.
The tribute of tributaries.
The rain, the snow, the steady stream.

This is how it began, for me.

5. The Tribute of Tributaries

The book comes out of the wrist,
with fingers.
It is a pool, an ocean, a delta:

the whorls of words for dreaming in the evening,
the lines of streams to follow on the palm, meandering,
spaces to see through, to get to and around,
pages, fingers, forests, frames;

and all of this for holding and waving,
for carrying around.

And this one is Toshio.
And this one is John.

Where had they been before?
Here, here, is the only answer.
Here, as ever more.

Those older ones, those I had always known
receding into the distance with women,
holding me at arm's length
like uncles from mountains.
gripping steering wheels and going by late
in trucks full of business,
sometimes handing me
tickets to a carnival, coins to a show.

Those older ones—
I had to claim them as my own.
I had to sit down with them
in a room ripe with rumor,
blatant with shadows
and claim them as my own.

And in the end, of course,
it was they who claimed me,
who bade me to be—
unafraid, unashamed—
who bade me to see,
clasping my face
with the faith of love.

"I am your mother's brother."
"I am your father's brother."

"Come."

6. The Coming and the Going

We were on the shore that would not be denied.
The ocean filled the eye with the wetness of memory
as we were witness to the journey we would know,
the long journey across the tatami of water
away from those who lay sleeping and would go on.

We were on the shore that would not be denied.
It was our own shore, the strength we had known.
We took this with us through the rage and the roar.
We came, we came, to Washington, to California, to Oregon.

7. The Going and the Coming

Toshio, being the oldest,
settled down.
He had had enough of travels and travail,
the hard times cropping up in rows,
and decided instead to learn the language
of plants and English.

The plants, naturally,
sprang from his hands
as a matter of course—
they did this all day long;
the English had to be pampered
under the tip of the tongue
but it, too, came furling from his fingers
firm and familiar in the rows of his own—
some nights, they surprised him with dawn.

So he worked hard, and the growing was glorious.
All around were horizons.
What he learned, he earned, and vice versa.
And this allowed John to go to college.

And John was the bright light
come the blackout.
And this allowed us all to go to war.

And it was a strange war of wire
coming at us from all sides.
But Toshio kept writing.

And when the war was over,
John was standing there
in a uniform and a novel.

Sometimes, we would sit watching the world
march by the living room, gesturing and threatening;
but Toshio pointed out the frost on the wisteria
barbed with beauty in the softness of the light;
and John showed how the eyes of the hysterical
froze at the lashes, barbed and blurred.

I learned there, the power of the word.

8. The Power of the Word

And so, in the middle of winter,
in the middle of mountains,
in the middle of night,

in the middle of a room,
in the middle of my hands,
I found my way again.

And so, in the middle of my life,
I found my way to you.

9. The Freedom of Tradition

Lest it seem too dramatic or mystical, allow me to assure you that
of what I speak is in reality very real—that is, it's a *feeling* I'm
talking about, which is very natural and how we really live, which
is very dramatic and mystical.

And what it's done for me is give me the feeling that I have so
much more to give.

Tradition is a place to start.

10. The Rhythm of Tradition

(water boiling) Well,
(voices outside) it's
(someone is launching a boat somewhere) about
(Just the other day, some of us folks
were making mochi in Henry's backyard, using the big
hollowed out hip and torso of an oak stump for a holder
and an ax handle stuck into half a baseball bat as the pounder)
that (and we, the hands, including Toshio and John,
looked up between the force of our strokes
and smiled, since mochi-making

brings your energy out into the rice and air
where it can be shared again) time
(and Henry, blowing thick mochi breath
into the thick mochi sky, said
"I wonder if we're the only ones in town doing this now.") again
(And I said "Maybe in the state, maybe in the nation,
maybe in the entire world because it's night over there and . . ."
And Henry said "So someone's making love."
And we all began to laugh
because mochi-making is also a continual process) to
(and is going on all the time:) say
(the rhythm of tradition.) good-bye.

Concentration Constellation

In this earthly configuration,
we have, not points of light,
but prominent barbs of dark.

It's all right there on the map.
It's all right there in the mind.
Find it. If you care to look.

Begin between the Golden State's
highest and lowest elevations
and name that location

Manzanar. Rattlesnake a line
southward to the zone
of Arizona, to the home
of natives on the reservation,
and call those *Gila, Poston.*

Then just take you time
winding your way across
the Southwest expanse, the Lone
Star State of Texas, gathering
up a mess of blues as you
meander around the banks
of the humid Mississippi; yes,
just make yourself at home

in the swamps of Arkansas,
for this is *Rohwer* and *Jerome*.

By now, you weary of the way.
It's a big country, you say.
It's a big history, hardly
halfway through—with *Amache*
looming in the Colorado desert,
Heart Mountain high in wide
Wyoming, *Minidoka* on the moon
of Idaho, then down to Utah's
jewel of *Topaz* before finding
yourself at northern California's
frozen shore of *Tule Lake* . . .

Now regard what sort of shape
this constellation takes.
It sits there like a jagged scar,
massive, on the massive landscape.
It lies there like the rusted wire
of a twisted and remembered fence.

Ainu Blues

"Ainu, you knew, I knew, you knew, too.
Ainu, you knew, I knew, you knew, too.
Ainu, you knew, you knew what I could do . . ."

1.

I arrive in the village
with only the clothes on my back.
The conditions of my situation,
more or less,
no different from the next person.

Have I been
driven here?
Am I fleeing?
Have I been
summoned?
Abandoned?

What does it matter?

The conditions of my situation
are circumstance
and act—
no more, no less,
no different from the next person.

I arrive in the village
with only the clothes on my back.

2.

The residents, of course,
regard me for what I am:

a man, one of them.

One of *those* men, perhaps,
but nevertheless
a man, obviously—
no more, no less.

Thus, they have no need
for suspicion,
for indifference,
for hostility,
certainly not envy,
and not necessarily
curiosity, either;

they know about me;
they've seen me before;
they've been there,
more or less,
in dreams, in prophecies,
through what comes
drifting back,
washed ashore
on the benevolent banks . . .

Therefore, on the path
to the meeting lodge,
they simply ask:

"Oi, Sensei—
what took you so long?"

3.

Things are in progress.

Things are always
in progress.
And, in a way,
I *have* been
here before:

I sense in the scent
some sense of myself:

sweat, smoke,
the blessings
of blood,
the dark depths
of lit interiors
recognized as ritual:

the charge, the pulse,
what I could
call upon
had I sense enough

in the common
elements, the trembling
moments of need . . .

Therefore, I am here.
Therefore, things are in progress.

Therefore, in the midst of things,
in the process of proceedings,
the residents pause;

the residents pause
and look at me—
one by one, the group,
individually;

and from far in the back,
through the smoke,
the shifting
shadows and light,
a little child laughs;

this spreads;
this builds, until

everyone laughs
in unison, until,
in a chanted
recitation, they say:

"Oi, Sensei—
man oh man
do you need a bath!"

4.

Ah, the secret
of secretions.

Here, in the suffocating
steam of this bathhouse,
in the all but boiling,
all but unbearable
heat of the water,

I am steeped,
I am stewing
in the broth of myself.

The pain, I can accept,
tolerate, even welcome—
suffering the punishment
for whatever this is
I have become.

I had this sense
that I had something,
was something
to overcome.

And the residents, of course,
had sensed, had *seen*
it in me: some pale, green,
luminous quality to my being

that would not simply
fade and diminish,
that would not wash . . .

Thus, the banishment
to the bathhouse:
thus, the scrubbing,
rinsing, soaking, steaming,
scrubbing, rinsing, soaking, steaming—

over and over,
for as long as it takes.

Thus, the fever
that accompanies it;
thus, the throb, the ache,
the delirious confusion
of my feverish state—

as my secrets
are secreted,
as they slowly
seep from my being.

Over and over and over—
I can not get
clean enough:

the poison, the secrets,
the substance stuck
deep and thick
to interior flesh,
holding onto my bones
with a vengeance.

Thus, exhausted,
numb, shuddering,
I slump into sleep;

thus, the old dreams
come flooding over me.

>the thick
>forbidden
>fears, the bulky
>tediousness
>accompanying
>this condition;
>these stick,
>these suffocate
>like glaze
>and will not
>be released . . .

5.

I awake. Shivering.
The steam. The dark.
The heat. The light.

This time, this time,
to see it through,
to do it right.

Scrubbing, scrubbing,
beyond the hurt,
beyond the raw.

Rinsing, rinsing,
until I can
rinse no more.

Then, with all
my life exposed,
I descend into
the steaming water.

And this time, this time,
it releases, it works.

I can *hear*
the secretions
seeping out of me;
I can *feel*
the secretions
flowing, flooding
out in the sound
of all the sounds
I have ever known—

whispers, screams, shouts, threats, moans,
cries of captivity, the prayers of industry . . .

And what flows out
floats like film—
oily and iridescent—
on the surface of water.

My eyes clear.
My fever breaks.
Crying, laughing,
I can find my fingers.
Crying, laughing,
I can raise my hands.
Crying, laughing,
I can take
this film, lift it to the light.

6.

Naked, I stand
In the sunlit clearing.
Naked, I stand,
glowing and steaming.

Naked, I cry:

"Here I am! Here I am! Here I am!"

Echoing. Echoing. Echoing.

7.

The residents gather
to receive my gift—
the silent ceremony
of burying my membrane
Under four stones
in the grassy graveyard.

I can hear the song
of stones,
the hum of earth.
I can hear the lyric
of warmth, of light.

Nothing has never
been this beautiful.

I can hear each
flame of fire
consume my clothes.

Then, as I am issued
my outfit,
the eldest elder
issues my directions:

> "See that mountain
> over there?"
>> "Yes."

> "Can you get there?"
>> "Yes."

> "See this sack?"
>> "Yes."

> "Can you carry it?"
>> "Yes."

"Then take this
over there,
get yourself settled,

and, after a while.
when you feel
exactly right,
you can go
here or there
or anyplace
else you like.

How does that sound?"
                                "Yes."

"How do you feel?"
                                "Yes."

"Any questions?"

                                "Yes. But
                                I will
                                answer it
                                    myself.

                                What do I
                                    owe you?
                                I owe you
                                    my self.

                                I shall re-
                                    pay you
                                by living
                                    my life."

At the edge of the clearing,
As I make my way
into the forest, I hear
a child's voice shout:

"Oi, Sensei—
be nice to the wolves!
And don't you dare
scare the bears!"

Everyone laughs.

Including my self.

8.

Far across the valley,
I see the smoke of the village.

The residents, going about their chores,
may pause, look up, and find the smoke from my fire.

Far up in the sky, the smokes mingle as one.

9.

From the being of me, this
receptacle I am.
I seek and reach
this particular pattern of clouds
clustered on the close horizon,
the ascension of sunlight on the mountains
and the procession therein,

become, then, in the sequence,
the presiding precedence of things
the ordered immediacies,
this graceful grove of trees
meditating
essence of forest
and the slow wind that stirs the sinews,
stimulating the accumulation

of small birds at their calling,
foraging for what abides with winter,
the stuff of what renews
me among grasses and leaves,
the ridges and hollows.

of the whole,
entire congregation of collective memory—

choruses, patterns in accordance
with density, intensity,
with destiny—

these sing, these glory, these bring
me pleasure and it spreads through the air
to where you are now,
likewise gifted with gratitude
gracing the brilliant
corners of enclaves

praising rain, this abiding rain
that brings us, takes us, keeps us
huddled in harmonies
now, as deserts, tundras, cities
signal dawn:

> charging, recharging;
>
> chanting, enchanting;
>
> sustenance, substance:
>
> *arise, arise, arise!*

10.

How long have I been here?

As long as it takes.

This way, that way—

establishing the paths.

The moon encounters me.

Stars hum at my back.

Perhaps we shall

encounter one another

on the path of society.

I am, after all,

one of you, more or less.

You are, after all,

one of me, more or less.

Here we are, before all,

with everything to bless.

"Ainu, you knew, I knew, you knew, too.
Ainu, you knew, I knew, you knew, too.
Ainu, you knew, I knew what you could do."

On Being Asian American

for Our Children

Of course, not everyone
can be an Asian American.
Distinctions are earned,
and deserve dedication.

Thus, from time of birth,
the journey awaits you
ventures through time,
the turns of the earth.

When you seem to arrive,
the journey continucs;
when you seem to arrive,
the journey continues.

Take me as I am, you cry.
I, I, am an individual.
Which certainly is true.
Which generates an echo.

Who are all your people
assembled in celebration,
with wisdom and strength,
to which you are entitled.

For you are at the head
of succeeding generations,
as the rest of the world
comes forward to greet you.

EXCITING CONTEMPORARY PLAYS

☐ **THE COLLECTED PLAYS OF NEIL SIMON, VOL 2, by Neil Simon.** From the most prolific and probably the most popular American playwright of our time come some of the best loved plays of today. Includes *Little Me; The Gingerbread Lady; The Prisoner of Second Avenue; The Sunshine Boys; The Good Doctor; God's Favorites; California Suite;* and *Chapter Two.* With a special Introduction by the author. (263581—$14.95)

☐ **PLENTY by David Hare.** This superbly crafted, razor-edged drama takes its remarkable heroine, a former French Resistance fighter, through twenty years of postwar changes. "David Hare is the most fascinating playwright since Harold Pinter. The play is unforgettable, an enigma wrapped in mystery with repressed and smoldering sexuality and high drama."—Liz Smith, *The New York Daily News.* (259568—$7.95)

☐ **FENCES: A Play by August Wilson.** The author of the 1984-85 Broadway season's best play, *Ma Rainey's Black Bottom,* returns with another powerful, stunning dramatic work. "Always absorbing . . . The work's protagonist—and greatest creation—is a Vesuvius of rage. . . . The play's finest moments perfectly capture that inky almost imperceptible agitated darkness just before the fences of racism, for a time, came crashing down."—Frank Rich, *The New York Times* (264014—$7.95)

☐ **THE HOUSE OF BLUE LEAVES AND TWO OTHER PLAYS by John Guare.** Artie Shaughnessy, a zoo-keeper and aspiring songwriter, is a man with a dream—which is put on a collision course with a devastating, wildly funny reality. THE HOUSE OF BLUE LEAVES, along with two other of Guare's fierce farces, form a trio of acerbic tragicomedies that painfully and hilariously reflect our world. "Mr. Guare . . . is in a class by himself."—*The New York Times* (264596—$9.95)

☐ **FOB AND OTHER PLAYS by David Henry Hwang.** From the Tony-award winning author of *M. Butterfly* comes a collection of six plays that capture the spirit, the struggles, and the secret language of the Chinese-American while exploring universal human issues. "Hwang is fast becoming the wunderkind of the American theater."—*San Francisco Chronicle* (263239—$8.95)

Prices slightly higher in Canada.

**Buy them at your local
bookstore or use this coupon
on next page for ordering.**

PL63Y